The Pioneers,

or the Sources of the Susquehanna

A Descriptive Tale

The Writings of
James Fenimore Cooper

The Pioneers,

or the Sources of the Susquehanna;

A Descriptive Tale

James Fenimore Cooper

Historical Introduction and Explanatory Notes
by James Franklin Beard
Text Established by Lance Schachterle
and Kenneth M. Andersen, Jr.

8800

"Extremes of habits, manners, time and space,

Brought close together, here stood face to face,

And gave at once a contrast to the view,

That other lands and ages never knew."

Paulding, *The Backwoodsman*, II, 571–4

State University of New York Press   Albany

The preparation of this volume was made possible (in part) by a grant from the Program for Editions of the National Endowment for the Humanities, an independent Federal agency.

CENTER FOR EDITIONS OF
AMERICAN AUTHORS

AN APPROVED TEXT

MODERN LANGUAGE
ASSOCIATION OF AMERICA

®

The Center emblem means that one of a panel of textual experts serving the Center has reviewed the text and textual apparatus of the printer's copy by thorough and scrupulous sampling, and has approved them for sound and consistent editorial principles employed and maximum accuracy attained. The accuracy of the text has been guarded by careful and repeated proofreading according to standards set by the Center.

Published by
State University of New York Press, Albany

© 1980 State University of New York

Printed in the United States of America

For information, address State University of New York
Press, State University Plaza, Albany, N.Y., 12246

Library of Congress Cataloging in Publication Data

Cooper, James Fenimore, 1789–1851.
　The pioneers.

　(Cooper editions)
　I. Beard, James Franklin, 1919–　II. Schachterle,
Lance. III. Andersen, Kenneth M. IV. Title.
V. Series: Cooper, James Fenimore, 1789–1851.
Selected works. 1979.
PZ3.C786Pio 1977 [PS1414]　813'.2　77-21795
ISBN 0-87395-359-2

Contents

Acknowledgments

The present edition of the Writings of James Fenimore Cooper was initiated in the late 1960s at a series of conferences of American Literature scholars arranged through the courtesy of Professor William M. Gibson, then Director of the Center for Editions of American Authors, at annual meetings of the Modern Language Association. At that time, four-fifths of Cooper's published works were out of print, and no book of his had ever been edited according to the standards of modern textual bibliography. Preliminary study of his literary manuscripts and printed texts had resulted in surprising discoveries; and the need for a new edition of his Writings, as complete as it was possible to make it, seemed obvious. Dr. Henry S. Fenimore Cooper and the late Paul Fenimore Cooper, great-grandsons of the novelist, responded to the proposal with generous encouragement and cooperation as did other members of the Cooper family, especially Dr. Paul Fenimore Cooper, Jr., and Henry S. Fenimore Cooper, Jr., the novelist's great-great-grandsons.

For institutional support, the editors wish to thank Presidents Frederick H. Jackson, Glenn W. Ferguson, and Mortimer H. Appley of Clark University; President George H. Hazzard of Worcester Polytechnic Institute and President Olin C. Robison of Middlebury College; and Marcus McCorison, Director and Librarian of the American Antiquarian Society. At a crucial stage of the work, presidents of three of the Worcester Consortium institutions—the Reverend John E. Brooks, S.J., President of the College of the Holy Cross, President George H. Hazzard of Worcester Polytechnic Institute, and President Mortimer H. Appley of Clark University—generously shared with the Cooper Edition part of a Mellon Foundation Grant to the institutions. The editors of the text were, early in their work, assisted by matching grants from the American Antiquarian Society and Worcester Polytechnic Institute. Timely assistance from the National Endowment for the Humanities ensured the completion of this and other volumes.

Among the many librarians and curators who helped in the preparation of this book, the editors wish especially to thank Frederick E. Bauer, Jr., Mary E. Brown, Nancy H. Burkett, Marion R. Snow, Carolyn A. Allen, Georgia B. Bumgardner, Sharon C. Davis, and Dorothy M. Gleason, American Antiquarian Society; Walter Muir Whitehill, Boston Athenaeum; Kamil Farid, Brooklyn Public Library; William H. Loos, Buffalo and Erie County Public Library; Tilton M. Barron, Marion Henderson, and Irene Walch, Goddard Library, Clark University; William H. Bond, Harvard University Libraries; Carey S. Bliss, Henry E. Huntington Library; William Matheson, Library of Congress; Henry M. Yaple, Michigan State University; Daniel P. Teisberg, Minneapolis Public Library; James T. Heslin, New York Historical Society; Lola Szladits, Berg Collection, New York Public Library; David S. Zeidberg, Syracuse University; Leslie S. Clark, University of California, Berkeley; Brook Whiting, University of California, Los Angeles; N. F. Nash, University of Illinois, Urbana-Champaign; Harriet C. Jameson, University of Michigan, Ann Arbor; Emmy Mills, University of North Carolina, Greensboro; Neda M. Westlake, University of Pennsylvania; David Farmer and John R. Paine, University of Texas, Austin; William H. Runge and Joan St. C. Crane, University of Virginia; Anita Danigelis, University of Wisconsin; Marleen B. Hansen, Washington and Lee University; Earle Connette, Washington State University; Eleanor L. Nicholes, Wellesley College; Albert Anderson, Diana Johnson, and Christina Yuan, Worcester Polytechnic Institute; and Donald C. Gallup, Beinecke Library, Yale University.

Institutions whose staffs supplied information anonymously include the Elmer Bobst Library, Boston Public Library, British Museum, Columbia University, Cornell University, Dartmouth College, Gettysburg College, Historical Society of Pennsylvania, Kansas State University, Lehigh University, McGill University, Newberry Library, New York Public Library, Northwestern University, Oxford University, Princeton University, Trinity College, Tufts University, University of Arkansas, University of Delaware, University of Minnesota, University of Notre Dame, University of Rochester, Washington University, Wesleyan University.

The editors of the text are grateful to the many students, graduate and undergraduate, who have aided them at various stages of the work, especially to Mark Antonio, Michael Dudas, John Goulet, Rosemary Haskell, David Horrocks, Robert Madison, Roland Moreau, Betty Murdock, Dennis Parker, Mark Richards, and Roger Yelle.

In addition, all those who have participated in the preparation of the volume wish to thank their colleagues Leonard Berry, Charles Brakeley, John Conron, Charles Heventhal, Edgar Heselbarth, John McCardell, Howard Munford, and David Nordloh. For lending their expertise to the solution of special problems, the editors are grateful to Counselor Richard W. Mirick, Rosemary L. Cullen, Special Collections Librarian, Harris Collection, John Hay Library, Brown University, and Arthur F. Schrader, Music Associate, Old Sturbridge Village, Sturbridge, Massachusetts.

The following persons, collections, or institutions have generously given permission for the use and publication of manuscript and illustrative materials: The Berg Collection, New York Public Library; Mr. Henry S. Fenimore Cooper, Jr.; Mr. Paul Fenimore Cooper, Jr.; The Brooklyn Museum; The Henry E. Huntington Library; Massachusetts Historical Society; The Metropolitan Museum of Art; The Museum of Fine Arts, Boston; The National Collection of Fine Arts, Smithsonian Institution; The New York State Historical Association, Cooperstown; and Mr. Robert C. Vose, Jr., Vose Galleries, Boston.

As any careful inspection of the Apparatus of this volume will reveal, the preparation of this edition required prolonged and extraordinary dedication on the part of the editors of the text; and the members of the Editorial Board wish to thank Professors Schachterle and Andersen for their extremely full and generous cooperation in what has proved to be an unexpectedly complex undertaking. The collection of contemporaneous reviews mentioned or quoted in the Historical Introduction resulted largely from the efforts of Professor Andersen. Professors Schachterle and Andersen wish, in turn, to recognize the invaluable assistance of their wives Melissa Schachterle and Ruth Andersen.

Miss Carol Garofoli, Miss Sheila Hones, and Mrs. Ella Conger prepared the typescripts; and Mr. Herbert Walden of the Worcester Art Museum a portion of the photographs.

Illustrations

According to the newspaper and periodical press in 1823, the publication of *The Pioneers* "excited a sensation among the artists, altogether unprecedented in the history of our domestic literature." Much of this art is, unfortunately, lost or unidentified. Two landscapes by Thomas Doughty, for example, one showing the hunting scene on the lake and the other the woods on fire, were exhibited at the Pennsylvania Academy of the Fine Arts in 1824; but no traces of these paintings, if they are extant, have been found. The paintings and engravings reproduced here, though not all strictly contemporaneous and certainly not all in the Hudson River School style which the book helped to form, do suggest to the modern reader how Cooper and his immediate readers viewed his scenes and characters. The series of engravings from *The Port Folio* of 1823 and 1824, together with the descriptive remarks quoted below, are reproduced from a separate entitled *Illustrations from* The Spy, The Pioneers, *and the Waverley Novels, with Explanatory and Critical Remarks*, published in Philadelphia at the *Port Folio* Office in 1826, from a copy owned by James F. Beard. The vignettes by Tony Johannot, reproduced from the original drawings by courtesy of the Henry E. Huntington Library, San Marino, California, appeared as frontispieces for Volumes XVI and XVII of the French translation of *The Pioneers* published by Charles Gosselin, Mame & Delaunay-Vallée in 1828. This set of translations was the first collected set of Cooper to be published anywhere and among the first Cooper volumes in any language to contain illustrations. The first illustrated American edition of Cooper, the Townsend-Darley, was not published until 1859–61.

all softened, though not subdued, by his conver-
sion to christianity, are depicted by Mr. Cooper
with a strong and vivid pencil."

PLATE XV.   The Departure of Leather-stocking. Drawn for
The Port Folio (January 1824) by Henry Inman,
engraved by Cephas Grier Childs (1793–1871)
and Gideon Fairman. *Description*: "This is the last
scene in the PIONEERS. It exhibits Leather-
stocking refusing the offer of a home among his
civilized friends, and about to depart for the west,
in order, as he expressed himself, 'to get a little
comfort in the close of his days, and to avoid losing himself in the clearings.' The ingenious author
probably derived this hint from the life of Daniel
Boon [sic], the great pioneer of the western wilds."

PLATE XVI.   Portrait of Elizabeth Fenimore Cooper (the novelist's mother) seated in Otsego Hall. *Watercolor*
(1816) by George Freeman (1789–1868). *Framed
size: 25 x 30 inches*. Courtesy of the New York State
Historical Association, Cooperstown. Freeman's
painting presumably shows the "enormous settee,
or sofa, covered with light chintz, stretched along
the walls" and the "Fahrenheit's thermometer, in
a mahogany case, and with a barometer annexed,"
referred to in Cooper's text on page 63.30–36.

Historical Introduction

The Pioneers was written during the most critical period of Cooper's adult life. When he began the book in November or December 1821, James Cooper* was, nominally at least, a man of substance—patrician, gentleman farmer, owner of a whaling ship, and (as the only surviving son of the late Judge William Cooper of Cooperstown) heir to numerous farms and some thousands of acres of undeveloped land in New York State. When *The Pioneers* was finally published in New York City by Charles Wiley on 1 February 1823, the author had been reduced to the status of mere novelist, stripped of his properties and responsible, as a man of honor, for thousands of dollars of debts accrued on behalf of his father's still unsettled estate, entirely dependent on his writing to support his wife and four small children. Whatever anguish this calamity inflicted, Cooper and his wife bore it in stoic silence. No whispers of complaint made then or later survive, despite the crushing severity of the loss. Though *The Pioneers* was not strictly or circumstantially autobiographical, as Cooper repeatedly warned in later years, it was evidently—in a manner he chose never publicly to explain—his effort to comprehend his own predicament, his private *"Tale of Possessors, Self-dispossessed."*† "[I]t was mine own humour that suggested this tale," he insisted, without elaboration, in his Preface to the first edition,

> but it is a humour that is deeply connected with feeling. Happier periods, more interesting events, and, possibly, more beautiful scenes, might have been selected, to exemplify my subject, but none of either that would be so dear to me (page 4).

*The "Fenimore" was added in 1826.
† Eugene O'Neill's descriptive title for his unfinished eleven-play cycle.

Much or most of *The Pioneers*, like *Precaution* (1820) and *The Spy* (1821), was composed on the fifty-seven acre farm the Coopers called Angevine at Scarsdale in Westchester County, New York. Little else is known of the actual writing except that it proceeded slowly, with many interruptions, in an atmosphere of loyal, even extravagant expectancy in the afterglow of *The Spy*, which was published with phenomenal success on 22 December 1821.

The earliest known references to *The Pioneers* are contained in two letters, both dated 7 January 1822, one from Charles Kitchell Gardner, an old friend from Cooper's navy years who edited Charles Wiley's new, patriotically inspired quarterly, *The Literary and Scientific Repository, and Critical Review*, the other from Wiley himself. Gardner remarked: "Wiley informs me of your letter to-day—and says you are engaged in a Chef d'oeuvre [*The Pioneers*]. Go on—and (you'll do it for yourself) prosper. Now and then write an article for the Repository and you'll be doing two good things."[1] Wiley jibed: "You speak of being engaged about 'The Pioneers.' Have you forgotten 'The American Tales,' which were commenced by a certain lady a long time ago?"[2]

Wiley's mention of *The American Tales* in the context of *The Pioneers* must have been a jolting reminder to Cooper of the altogether extraordinary exfoliation of his creative powers; for the earlier project had been a series of didactic stories imitating Mrs. Opie's moral tales, American only in setting and creative only by courtesy. Cooper had begun it during the writing of *The Spy*, probably when he despaired "of making American Manners and American scenes interesting to an American reader"[3] and, losing confidence temporarily, had ceased work on the romance, even though the first volume was in type. Eventually, he presented the first two stories of *The American Tales* to Wiley to publish for his own benefit as *Tales for Fifteen*, by Jane Morgan.[4] The title, one supposes, was an act of critical self-judgment.

Gardner's suggestion that the novelist write an article "[n]ow and then" for the *Repository* was more to Cooper's taste. He had joined Gardner's small unpaid staff in late 1820 or 1821 when the *Repository* seemed about to expire, and had promptly established himself as an accomplished and valued contributor.

His reviews of Catharine M. Sedgwick's *A New-England Tale* and Washington Irving's *Bracebridge Hall*,[5] published in the May issue for 1822 while *The Pioneers* was in full progress, are uniquely important in the Cooper canon; for he soon developed a strong distaste for critical pronouncements on fiction or for aesthetic theorizing of any kind; and these brief reviews contain his best exposition of his own theory and practice. They reveal a full comprehension of both, even at this early point in his literary career.

A novelist aspiring to write distinctively American fiction, he argued, should avoid such familiar topics as politics, education, and religion, and concentrate on "our domestic manners, the social and the moral influences, which operate in retirement, and in common intercourse, and the multitude of local peculiarities, which form our distinctive features upon the many peopled earth."[6] Such subjects, he noted, "have very seldom been happily exhibited in our literature." For all its inimitable charm, Irving's use of this material seemed to Cooper to "do little towards forming a history of the diversities of passion, sentiment, and behaviour, as they are manifest in any of our little communities, detached, as it were, from the great world."[7] *Bracebridge Hall* was British in both subject and point of view. Citing as examples of the kind of fiction he meant only an unidentified "story called Salem Witchcraft" and Royall Tyler's *Algerine Captive*, Cooper saluted their authors as

> early and authentic historians of a country. We say the historians—we do not mean to rank the writers of these tales, among the recorders of statutes, and battles, and party chronicles; but among those true historians . . . with whom Fielding classes himself, nearly in these words: "Those dignified authors who produce what are called true histories, are indeed writers of fictions, while I am a true historian, a describer of society as it exists, and of men as they are."[8]

Subscribing to Fielding's realism as the proper mode for representing American society, Cooper also dwelt insistently on that fidelity to universal human experience implied in the Aristotelian concept of plot. Indeed, for Cooper, it is through this fidelity to the general experience that the novelist avoids mere parochialism and presents human life in its perennial "modes of enjoyment and improvement, of suffering and degeneracy":

> [A]n interesting fiction . . . however paradoxical the assertion may appear . . . addresses our love of truth—not the mere love of facts expressed by true names and dates, but the love of that higher truth, the truth of nature and of principles, which is a primitive law of the human mind. . . . A good novel addresses itself very powerfully to our moral nature and conscience, and to those good feelings, and good principles, which Providence has planted within us, constantly to remind us that "we have, all of us, one human heart." [9]

Much of the fascination of serious art, as Cooper conceived it, inheres in the artist's skill at evoking in the participant a state of moral clarity. When the novelist as poet and painter of character brings

> before us the figure, passions, thoughts, expressions, and adventures of [his] ideal personages, our interests and prejudices disappear—then we give our homage to genius and virtue, and our pity to misfortune—we pour out our indignation upon crime, and plead for the tempted and the fallen, without a check from envy in ourselves, in the contemplation of greatness and goodness, and without a fear of censure from others, on account of our tenderness for infirmity, or our forgiveness of sin. We feel ourselves, as we look upon a touching picture, or as we read of a trying situation, to be just and generous, according to our emotions . . . and we applaud ourselves for them; and these are more or less lively, more or less efficacious in their practical operation on our habitual dispositions and conduct, according to the previous cultivation and ascendency of our moral sentiments and principles. [10]

The reader's moral faculties thus aroused and involved, Cooper posited, his participation in the imaginative experience would be continuous, critical, pleasurable and therapeutic:

> The writer of moral fiction always presumes upon the existence and susceptibility of these sentiments and principles,

when he distributes virtues and vices; and he directs his
train of retributions, not only in conformity to the obvious
system of Providence, but according to the demand of his
reader's probable judgment and moral sense; proving thus
his respect for the natural virtue of the common mind,
as well as his knowledge of the propriety of the individual
characters which he attempts to portray.[11]

Beyond this "gratification of the moral sense" Cooper recog-
nized an aesthetic dimension in "fine fiction" inherent, his own
formulations suggest, in its formal qualities, particularly in its
capacity to sustain sensory patterns (for him primarily visual)
and other kinds of internal designs:

The delight of pure imagination, the transportation of
ourselves beyond our own bounded vision and existence to
the past and the distant, into scenes of splendor, into conditions which fancy has devised, and fancy only could sustain or enjoy, are among the rarest pleasures that the
reader of fiction tastes.[12]

This power of fiction at once to dramatize "society as it exists"
and to induce states of mind transcending selfish concerns,
prejudices and parochial experience seemed to Cooper to establish a crucial role for literature, especially for popular fiction, in a republican society whose institutions were also committed to the ends of disinterested human justice. Recognizing
a distinction between popular forms of art and forms that "can
be experienced in their strongest power only by the most cultivated and exalted minds,"[13] Cooper clearly aspired to be the
popular, the democratic, artist

who enters into the concerns and sufferings of the humble,
whose genius condescends to men of low estate, and who
allies himself to the Father of mercies, when he teaches
the callous and the cruel, how deep are the wounds they
inflict, and how terrible the retribution they may provoke.
We admire the inventive talent which employs itself in the
province of daily life, which delineates what we have all felt
and observed, which detects the vices that poison domestic
peace, and corrupt social virtue, or which displays the
opinions and passions that dignify and sweeten, or debase

and embitter our earthly existence just as they are disciplined and directed by education and self-government.[14]

Cooper saw no absolute conflict, apparently, between breadth
of appeal and intrinsic literary quality and, in fact, regarded
the persistent popularity of certain of his own works as the best
evidence of their worth. To "sustain his reputation," Cooper
asserted, "a living author" must either "cultivate a new field,
or produce a richer harvest from the old."[15] In *The Pioneers*,
he reached out self-consciously in both directions, hoping, his
first Preface indicated, to carry as many readers with him as
possible. That undisguised prefatory wooing of readers, which
some thought inappropriate or in need of explanation, was, he
implied at its close, less than a Preface. What he did not tell
readers, surely could not have brought himself to tell them, was
the extent to which his future as a literary man depended on
their favorable response.

II

Whether or not the early chapters of *The Pioneers* were inspired
by the sequence of Christmas vignettes in Irving's *Sketch Book*,
as Thomas Philbrick has plausibly suggested,[16] they were
American counterparts, with the important distinction that
they were dramatically connected and invested with a full range
of painterly values. The interest and wonder Geoffrey Crayon,
a self-styled "grown-up child,"[17] attached to holiday customs
and rural games of old England *could* and *should*, Cooper
seemed to say in his review of *Bracebridge Hall*, be infused into
American scenes by a writer who felt them with sufficient in-
tensity. Cooper considered himself such a writer. "[B]rought an
infant into this valley" of Otsego where "all his first impressions
were . . . obtained" (page 8), he assigned the book's action to
the year 1793–94, when he was four or five, though the wealth
of impressions that inform its carefully composed descriptions
and landscapes derived almost necessarily from rich overlays
of sensory experience stored up from an entire childhood and
youth, assignable to no specific year. This reservoir of images,
extraordinary for their clarity of detail as well as their profu-

sion, was the storehouse from which the solid-seeming world
of the book is furnished.

Though he called his book *A Descriptive Tale* and though
some readers still insist that his description is literal, Cooper
wrote not as historiographer or mythologist, but as novelist.
His chief concern, as the *Repository* reviews affirm, was with
human relationships; and his interest in defining the characteristics of American frontier life by graphic illustration was,
he understood, secondary to his purpose as storyteller. As a
novelist with the conscience of an historian, however, he con-
fessed to a "constant temptation to delineate that which he had
known rather than that which he might have imagined" (page
6), and his early comments on the book stressed his pleasure
in this fidelity. "If there be any value in truth," he wrote John
Murray, his British publisher, on 29 November 1822, "the pictures are very faithful, and I can safely challenge a scrutiny
in this particular."[18] Many years later, when hostile and even
friendly readers who had never known Cooper's father or his
sister Hannah began to identify them with characters in the
novel,[19] Cooper attempted, in a sharp disclaimer to the editor
of *Brother Jonathan*, to distinguish meticulously between the
literal and the general truth:

> Although the country around Cooperstown is described
> in the scene of the Pioneers, *the village is not*. Some few
> objects that did exist in Cooperstown *are* described, it is
> true; but more that *never existed there*. . . . If the court-house
> and tavern are excepted, I do not remember a single *build-
> ing* in the account of the Templeton of the Pioneers, that
> ever had its original in Cooperstown. . . . Not an incident
> of the Pioneers, that I can recall, ever occurred. Deer have
> been taken on the lake; trees have fallen; panthers prowled
> through the woods, and men have been put in the stocks,
> certainly, but no scenes, or events strictly like those of the
> Pioneers ever had a real existence to my knowledge. The
> same is generally true as to the characters, though, tempted
> by his recollections, the author has thrown in a few *touches*,
> here and there, which have induced many to think more
> was intended, than was the case.
>   . . . . The family and personal histories of Marmaduke

Temple are not in the least—in a *distinctive sense*—like those of my father. It is true the parties filled similar stations in a new country; this was *generally characteristic*, and as applicable to fifty other landed proprietors in New York, half a century since, as it was to Judge Cooper. . . . Beyond this the resemblance ceased; although a few personal *touches* were occasionally thrown in, but with a very tender hand. The dissertations on the preservation of the trees, are instances of what I mean.

. . . Elizabeth Temple . . . is described as having *raven* locks, a *full rounded form*, a nose approaching to Roman, with a high color, &c. My unfortunate sister was as little like this as possible. Her . . . cheeks were usually colorless, her hair was almost *flaxen*, and her form was the extreme of lightness and delicacy. . . . [T]here never were in my father's household such persons as Remarkable Pettibone, or Ben Pump; or, in the village of Cooperstown such a clergyman as Mr. Grant or any one to correspond to his daughter. In *some* of the other characters, there are *touches* from life, though in *most*, there are not. The resemblances were *general*, and not *personal.* . . .

No house like that described in the Pioneers, *ever existed in Cooperstown!* In the general description, I . . . followed principally a house *out* of Cooperstown. Happening to recollect that the pediment of the entrance to the paternal door upheld the columns, instead of the columns upholding the pediment, I introduced that fact in the book as characteristic of frontier architecture, and this first gave me the idea of saying anything about the house of my father. I then described *one room*, the hall, which is accurately given, even to the urn which was supposed to contain the ashes of Queen Dido.[20]

Cooper's posture here was transparently defensive: enough unspecified correspondences between Cooperstown and Templeton may remain to justify his fear (page 6) of a too "rigid adhesion to truth." Elsewhere, he had reported (page 9) that "the Academy, and Court house, and gaol, and inn, and most similar things are tolerably exact." In *Chronicles of Cooperstown* (1838), he described an actual M. Le Quoy, befriended by

Judge Cooper,[21] and a Richard Smith, appointed sheriff, who considered himself "altogether superior to . . . the lower duties of the office," and who, as amateur artist, painted the sign for the old Red Lion inn.[22] An old hunter named Shipman is there identified as "the 'Leatherstocking' of the region."[23] And Cooper's daughter Susan stated that the "original" of Dr. Elnathan Todd was "a half-fledged medical genius, from New England" whose empirical practice amused Midshipman Cooper when stationed at Oswego, New York, during 1808–1809.[24] And, despite two paragraphs interpolated in the 1850 revision (page 11) of the 1832 Introduction disclaiming once more a connection between Elizabeth Temple and his sister Hannah, Cooper neglected to cancel a footnote (page 233) confessing that Elizabeth's equestrian enthusiasm owed something to his memory of Hannah's death in a fall from a horse. If, as tradition has it, he once inscribed "on the fly leaf" of *The Pioneers* "the names of the principal characters and their originals,"[25] the action would not be uncharacteristic. Further knowledge of early Cooperstown and of Cooper's experience there and elsewhere would undoubtedly yield a plethora of yet unsuspected correspondences.

Yet if *every* individual detail could be documented, the feat would still not invalidate Cooper's contention that *The Pioneers* is fiction and not history or autobiography. The control with which he dissociated particulars from their matrices, whether in the real world or printed sources, and redeployed them in the structured world of his fiction was an automatic reflex of his art. Writers of fiction, he asserted,

> frequently blend traits chosen from different persons in one individual, make their beauties, as the Grecian statue of Venus is said to have been designed, and otherwise take such liberties with facts, as may happen to suit their purposes. Even known *historical events* are allowed to be perverted, to aid them in rendering their works more interesting.[26]

Once assimilated to the specifications of an imagined world, the detail, whatever its origin, whether it relates to character or to setting, has its proper reference only within that created

cosmos and the experience of the reader it informs. If, as
Cooper wrote of the Leather-stocking, "different individuals
known to the writer in early life . . . presented themselves as
models,"[27] knowledge that two old woodsmen named Shipman,
Nathaniel and Daniel, lived in or near Cooperstown during
Cooper's youth and that Natty has some attributes of each indicates only that he is a composite.[28] The probable circumstance that Natty's personal appearance and one of his most
pronounced mannerisms, his peculiar silent laugh, were borrowed from Captain David Hand, whom Cooper knew in Sag
Harbor,[29] only illustrates the extreme dexterity with which
authentic detail was transmuted and transposed to serve imaginative ends. And Cooper apparently did not permit personal
considerations to constrain his artistic freedom. The involuted
speech of the frontier lawyer, Dirck Van der School, appropri-
ates a feature of the style of Judge Cooper's worst enemy,
Judge Jedediah Peck, who "put his parentheses into one another, like spare pill-boxes."[30] The detail enhances the authen-
ticity of the portrait without introducing irrelevant associations.

III

While these composite effects contribute brilliantly to Cooper's
exhibition of the surfaces of frontier life and to the realistic tex-
ture of the fiction, they contribute only indirectly to the significant action, which, as usual in Cooper, adapts conventional plot
elements without losing itself in them. To the extent that he
intended to evolve that action from the "general characteristics,
usages, and the state of a new country,"[31] or "the sort of life
that belongs to a 'new country,' forming a link in the great
social chain of the American community,"[32] Cooper would
seem to have committed himself to illustrating a phase of the
historical process itself; and he did, in fact, draw the contours
of his tale from that dynamic, hypostatic moment Frederick
Jackson Turner was to call the "distinguishing feature of American life,"[33] the inescapably painful rite of passage from "savagery" to "civilization"[34] to be enacted and re-enacted along
the indeterminate, moving line of the American frontier as
long as there were new lands to settle. With uncanny exactness,

he responded also, and simultaneously, to the epic moment of "challenge and response" which Arnold Toynbee would identify as the mythological center of the civilizing process, the obstinate human resolution of an apparently insoluble logical problem.[35] For those who must make it, consciously or not, the choice between the values of "savagery" or "wildness" and "civilization" involves a voluntary assumption of difficult and irretrievable risks.

In an 1842 letter to *Brother Jonathan*, Cooper revealed that his source for the personal history of Judge Temple, and a major source for the significant action in *The Pioneers*, was a footnote in Robert Proud's *The History of Pennsylvania in North America, from the Original Institution and Settlement of that Province, under the First Proprietor and Governor William Penn in 1681, till after the Year 1742* . . . (Philadelphia, 1797):

> *Note*, Many who came servants, and were industrious, succeeded better, than some who brought estates, or fortunes, &c. [T]he former, being more generally better suited to encounter the hardships and difficulties of a new country, often acquired considerable possessions; while the latter, being accustomed to live, and depend, on their fortunes, and what they brought with them, had the disadvantage; and sometimes spent all they had, and were reduced to indigence, in a country, where servants were difficult to be had or kept; and the lower class of people naturally became more independant, than in old countries, &c.[36]

The reference in Proud explains precisely the motif of upward and downward mobility so central to the Effingham-Temple plot; but if Cooper used the passage as he indicated and remembered doing for twenty years, one must infer that he had been forcibly struck by its pertinence to his own situation, particularly since he paraphrased the source in the text of *The Pioneers* in a manner that makes it more directly applicable than Proud to his own predicament and that of his four deceased brothers:

> Accustomed to ease, and unequal to the struggles incident to an infant society, the affluent emigrant was barely enabled to maintain his own rank, by the weight of his per-

sonal superiority and acquirements; but the moment that
his head was laid in the grave, his indolent, and comparatively uneducated offspring, were compelled to yield
precedency to the more active energies of a class, whose
energies had been stimulated by necessity. This is a very
common course of things, even in the present state of the
Union (pages 30–31).

In the paragraph that follows, Cooper may even have been al-
luding guardedly to the motivation for his own experiments as
writer:

> The posterity of Marmaduke did not escape the common
> lot of those, who depend rather on their hereditary posses-
> sions than on their own powers; and in the third genera-
> tion, they had descended to a point, below which, in this
> happy country, it is barely possible for honesty, intellect,
> and sobriety to fall. The same pride of family, that had, by
> its self-satisfied indolence, conduced to aid their fall, now
> became a principle to stimulate them to endeavor to rise
> again (page 31).

But lest the reader of *The Pioneers* in 1842 confuse the personal history of Judge Temple's family with "the personal history of the *emigrant* of my family [William Cooper, the emigrant, mentioned by name in Proud, I, 150 ff.],," Cooper in his
Brother Jonathan letter excerpted a passage from Thomas F.
Gordon's *A Gazetteer of the State of New Jersey* . . . (Trenton, 1834)
attesting to the uninterrupted fortune and prosperity of the
descendants of the earliest William Cooper, at least in New
Jersey.

Without misstating the facts, Cooper appears here to have
been somewhat disingenuous. Though a New Jersey descendant
of the emigrant remained, as he asserted, "owner of *one* of the
largest hereditary landed estates in New Jersey,"[37] and though
Judge Cooper died—as Cooper did not say—one of the wealthiest land owners in New York State, *his* descendants, including
the novelist, *were* in 1821–1823 in the circumstances attributed
to the "posterity of Marmaduke." Moreover, Judge Cooper acquired his patent to the Cooperstown lands at a mortgage sale
in which the ownership was complicated by the Tory interests

of Governor William Franklin and the claims of heirs of George Croghan, the original patentee, thus creating an oblique parallel to the Effingham situation in *The Pioneers* potentially embarrassing to the novelist.[38] The Croghan heirs, like Oliver Effingham in the novel, distrusted the Judge's business methods and had, Cooper knew, attempted to bring suit. The novelist's distress at efforts to connect the two Judges is understandable. Accepting their identity, even without countenancing the Croghan claims, might have seemed a gratuitous questioning of his father's integrity. In truth, Judge Cooper, like Judge Temple, appears to have been exceedingly scrupulous; and the relationship between the Effinghams and Judge Temple in the novel is so different from any conceivable actual relationship between the Croghans and Judge Cooper that one must assume Cooper introduced the Effingham-Temple plot for its pertinence as an historical link and for its usefulness in clarifying and magnifying the force of the actual dispossessions of the Leatherstocking and Indian John. Their plight engaged Cooper's imagination more fully, perhaps because it more nearly resembled his own.

When Judge Cooper died in 1809, victim of a blow on the head by a political assailant, his will awarded each of his six surviving children $50,000 in cash from an estate estimated at about $750,000, most of it in land. The cash bequests represented liquid assets which the prudent Judge, knowing the vicissitudes of land speculation, had kept ready for unexpected needs or opportunities. His heirs, preoccupied with their families and personal lives and accustomed to consider their means abundant, proceeded to build fine residences and otherwise expend these cash inheritances. In the depression following the War of 1812, the flow of specie was drastically reduced; and land, which formed the residue of the Judge's estate, became unsalable. Cooper's brothers, more involved than he in the management of the estate, allowed debts to accumulate—debts small in proportion to the full value of the estate, but still too large to be easily discharged. Pressures from creditors accumulated gradually; and, eventually, creditors or speculators who had obtained claims descended with writs of *fieri facias*, acquiring the whole of Judge Cooper's real property at an absurdly small part of its estimated value.[39] Thus it can hardly have been accident that the economically helpless novelist turned in 1822–1823, the period of the forced sales, to an imaginative repossession of his heritage. It was no accident either that his attention was arrested by the passage in Proud's *History*, a book he apparently found useful in various ways.

Like *The Pioneers*, Proud's encyclopedic compilation of early accounts of the settlement of Pennsylvania aimed to be "descriptive of the progress of society."[40] For Cooper it was surely an absorbing book, for it identified his first American forebear and established the Cooper family among the colleagues and co-religionists of Penn, the Great Proprietor.[41] His intention, wrote Proud, was to furnish "a general information" "more particularly for . . . the descendants of the first and early settlers . . . but also . . . to all others . . . that by beholding the means, by which small things become great, and what formerly made the country happy, it might excite a similar conduct in posterity."[42] Proud's scope was self-consciously epic; and his philosophic tone, especially in the "Preface dedicatory" and "Conclusion," was sustained by copious quotation from Homer, Virgil, Milton, and Pope. In Proud's telling, the founding and development of Pennsylvania replicated the glories of the classical "golden age" as well as the Christian myth of Adam and Eve. "Pennsylvania," he wrote euphorically, has long been

> . . . justly famed . . . [as] a state . . . resembling that of those *saturnian* times, in *Italy*, which, we are told formerly produced the *golden age*, and so far actually realizing ancient fable, that to its inhabitants, perhaps, . . . might particularly, and with great propriety, have been applied the exclamation of the poet Virgil,
> "Felices nimium sua si bona norint, Agricolee!" as well as that of Milton . . .
> ——— "and, O! yet happiest, if ye seek
> No happier state, and know to know no more."[43]

Burlington, New Jersey—Cooper's birthplace—had been "a brave country indeed," suggested the unidentified author of a letter quoted by Proud and dated 1680:

> I have seen orchards laden with fruit to admiration; their very limbs torn to pieces with the weight, and most deli-

cious to the taste, and lovely to behold. I have seen an apple-tree, from a pippin-kernel, yield a barrel of curious cyder; and peaches in such plenty, that some people took their carts a peach-gathering. . . . We have . . . great store of very good wild fruits; as, strawberries, cranberries and hurtleberries. . . . It is my judgment . . . that fruit trees, in this country, destroy themselves by the very weight of their fruit.[44]

The letter continues with its catalogue of edenic plenitude:

As for venison and fowls, . . . we have brought home to our houses, by the *Indians*, seven or eight fat bucks in a day; and sometimes put by as many, . . . and fish, in their season very plenteous.[45]

Like the settlers in *The Pioneers*, these early inhabitants of Burlington found means of ensnaring fish in the "thousands":

. . . and then we began to hawl them on shore, as fast as three or four of us could, by two or three at a time; and, after this manner, in half an hour, we could have filled a three bushel sack of as good large herrings as ever I saw.[46]

The paradisiacal tone of this letter, with its equipoise between delight in the beauty and bounty of Nature and a spontaneous urge to aggrandize, corresponds exactly to the tension Cooper sought in *The Pioneers*. He shared Proud's belief in Man's heritage from the Fall; and he also shared Proud's commitment to the Platonic and Ciceronian faith, quite at odds with the Christian plan of supernatural redemption, that prudent leadership and salubrious civil laws were the best hope for human amelioration. Proud's *History*, however, incongruously combines Christian skepticism towards Man qua Man with an anachronistic projection of the "golden age." It suggests that Pennsylvania was one of the "special examples" placed "before the eyes of the human race" to show "the absolute possibility of a still superior bliss, and more exalted felicity, than is commonly experienced in the world, not only in an individual, but also in a collective, or national, and more universal capacity"[47]—all the while warning of an inevitable doomsday.

Whether because he sought a more satisfying dramatic reso-

lution to this dilemma or because his memory of the legendary
confiscation of Virgil's ancestral estate induced a feeling of kin-
ship, Cooper turned also to the *Eclogues*. He quoted the Latin
text of the first two verses of the first *Eclogue*—probably from
memory—in the text of *The Pioneers* (page 102), and we know
that his boyhood schoolmaster in Albany, the Reverend Thomas Ellison, was a formidable Latinist who required his students
to scan and memorize long passages from the *Eclogues*, passages Cooper and his roommate William Jay recited to each
other.[48]

The subject of the first *Eclogue* is the unqualified grief and
sense of injustice experienced by Meliboeus, who is expelled
from his ancestral lands and exiled by Octavian (later Augus-
tus) through a policy of land division and reallocation that has,
simultaneously and seemingly without reason, rewarded Tityrus, an elderly manumitted slave. As William Empson and
others have shown, the fascination of the sophisticated pastoral,
in the *Eclogues* and elsewhere, is its facility for "putting the complex into the simple," or apparently simple.[49] Virgil trans-
formed the pastoral from a mode for gratifying the human
longing for a simplified, Arcadian existence to a medium for
exploring the inconsistencies and dissatisfactions implicit in
that longing, a stage for dramatizing the most complex states
of mind and the most baffling contradictions. Employing such
devices as multiple plots, ironic juxtapositions, symbolic elaboration of character, contests, and complicated forms of word-
play, Virgil and his successors evolved conventions adaptable to
any genre and susceptible of exquisitely refined statement.

IV

The Pioneers adapts all these devices of the sophisticated pastoral to frontier materials in an action that at once epitomizes
the dialectic of frontier settlement and expresses, seemingly,
Cooper's resignation to the harsh reality of his dispossession,
resolving presumably the complexities of his feelings. The result is a philosophic tale belonging, according to Northrop
Frye's classification of fictional types, to the hybrid form called
"romance-anatomy,"[50] along with such works as *Tristram Shandy*

and *Moby-Dick*. Cooper wrote without reference to critical categories, no doubt; but in affirming his father's vision of a civilizing conquest of the wilderness in the immediate context of his own dispossession, he was compelled to grapple with one of the great themes of world literature. His feelings were deeply and genuinely divided. Himself dispossessed, he knew now, if he had not known before, the anguish of those earlier claimants to the land his father's enterprise had irresistibly pushed aside; but his imaging their predicament in an almost autobiographical context was less an admission of self-pity than of guilt. For the cruelties that life inflicts are relentlessly envisaged as the penalty of man's moral imperfection. It is not Man or Nature that is or can be moral, but the universal processes encompassing them both.

Nature, society, and man, as the novel projects them in lavish, nostalgic particularity, are creatures of time and circumstance, imponderably enmeshed in cycles and epicycles of change. The limitation of man's reason, the Reverend Mr. Grant urges, should inspire humility and charity; but, by an irony implicit in the cosmic scheme, the uncertainty, insecurity, and impermanence of life breed self-deceptions and aggressions. The moral ordering of experience—which underlies the significant action—is evoked panoramically in a pattern of ironic contrasts and conflicts between the crude, unformed society ruled by Judge Marmaduke Temple, his "prime minister," his "nobles," and his favored retainers, and a trio this society has supposedly dispossessed. John Mohegan (Chingachgook), an old degraded Indian whose race once owned the Judge's acres, must now weave baskets for his shirts; Natty Bumppo (the Leather-stocking), an aged hunter who preceded the Judge on the lands, finds his immemorial hunting privileges curtailed by a new game law; and Oliver Effingham, a mysterious young stranger, erroneously believes the Judge has cheated his family of its fortune. Individually and collectively, both groups convict themselves of the cardinal sin of pride. The settlers, luxuriating in their new freedom and power, are snobbish or arrogant; and the dispossessed, bitterly resenting their displacement, are self-righteously indignant or contemptuous. These refractory attitudes, humanly understandable but not philosophically justifiable, are doomed by a social dynamic as

inexorable as the progression of the seasons which interpene-
trates the action; and the passing of the frontier, thus divinely
ordained, is celebrated as a physical and moral necessity in a
complex image of mutability.

Two deer-killing episodes, one at the beginning of the book
and another near the middle, define the thematic development.
In the first, the Judge accidentally wounds Oliver (whom he
has already unintentionally injured) while shooting at a deer
which the young man kills. The Judge insists on buying the
carcass, against the owner's wish, to claim public credit for the
kill. To the rarified ethical consciousness of the Leather-stocking, this insensitive conduct epitomizes all the heartless, coer-
cive, wasteful ways of the settlement he detests. "Might often
makes right here, as well as in the old country, for what I can
see,"[51] he stoutly protests. In the vignette-like scenes that follow, Natty and his friends are set off against a variegated frontier society in characteristic postures. Individualism is rampant.
The settlers burn sugar maples as firewood, massacre pigeons
by the thousands with a small cannon, and net the delicious
Otsego bass in outrageous numbers. On Christmas Eve, they
listen attentively to Mr. Grant's sermon on humility and ad-
journ forthwith to the nearby tavern to vent their several vanities and thirsts. Their almost childish irresponsibility, delightful
as spectacle, requires—as Judge Temple increasingly urges—
social and legal forms to avert chaos or self-destruction. Natty's
vehement opposition to these forms, exposing his inability to
accept the implications of his own perception, is an assertion of
intellectual pride, a resistance to the inevitable, in its full context a protest against divine justice.

In the second crucial episode (pages 295–301), the Leather-
stocking kills a deer impulsively and unseasonably by cutting
its throat, after his hounds have been released by a meddling
deputy of the law, and then resists a search warrant brought
by the deputy who is seeking silver ore. Natty's disrespect for
the law has brought him into active conflict with it; and the
Judge, who owes his daughter's life to the hunter, reluctantly
inflicts a human wrong to sustain a legal right. Arrested, tried,
and humiliated in the stocks, the indignant Natty—now increasingly given to nostalgic boasting about his youthful exploits—can no longer endure the "wasty ways" of a society as

careless of its human as of its natural resources. What goodness is in him is not lost, for it is absorbed into the consciousness of the more sensitive members of the society that has rejected him. But Natty is trapped, as surely by his own attitudes as by the greed and cunning of the Yankee deputy. The Judge easily solves the Effingham problem by proving his innocence of any intent to defraud and by giving his daughter and half his fortune to Oliver, but he cannot assist Indian John and Natty. They are the two eagles (pages 242–43) which settle themselves, contemptuous of other birds, in undisputed possession of the ice on Otsego Lake. When, after a week, the ice melts, they must take flight. The Indian dies a wished-for death; and the Leather-stocking escapes the Judge's belated liberality by fleeing westward, "the foremost of that band of Pioneers, who are opening the way for the march of the nation across the continent," thus again becoming an instrument of the progress he deplores.

This impingement of moral and cultural reality on pastoral appearance is woven thoroughly into the setting and the minor characters as well as the main action. The landscape is invested with enchantment, but it is also stump-scarred, and (in Templeton) profaned with a rude, pretentious architecture. The characters, idiosyncratic in thought, speech, and manners, form a gallery of frontier grotesques, who are nevertheless the agents of civilization. As the heroine exclaims, "Every thing in this magical country seems to border on the marvellous. . . . The actors are as unique as the scenery" (page 214). Yet the idyl is mocked by pervasive ironies. Winter does not yield to spring without a struggle. When a sleigh teeters on the brink of a precipice, a canoe glides too swiftly, a giant pine topples, a panther springs, or a forest fire rages, man's apparent mastery of Nature is exposed as precarious adaptation. The closely observed portraits of the Yankees, the Irishwoman, the Frenchman, the Dutchman, the sheriff, the sailor, the Negroes, the lawyers, the woodchopper, and the clergymen complicate and reinforce the theme in innumerable ways by suggesting how Man's human nature betrays him into self-contradiction when his own interests are touched. Despite themselves, according to Cooper's myth, men serve transcendent purposes that only time and circumstance reveal; and Man's seeming injustice may prove to be the involuted expression of a higher order of justice. In a sense beyond the Leather-stocking's grasp, "*might does make right.*"

V

If Cooper at first saw himself making a quartet of his trio of the dispossessed, he quickly dispelled self-pity and welcomed his new profession and his growing celebrity among writers, artists and *littérateurs* who frequented the small back room ("The Den," as he called it) of Charles Wiley's bookshop. Though his own means were limited, Wiley prided himself on publishing "original American books," cultivated newspaper editors who would review them favorably, and was—in a small way—an entrepreneur promoting Knickerbocker and American letters.[52] His favorite projects, it seems, were his quarterly journal, the *Repository*, and the advancement of Cooper's literary career. By mid-1822, it had become obvious that the *Repository* would have to be discontinued and that even Cooper was a doubtful risk. Having found it expedient to reduce the publisher's role from principal to agent, to publish "solely" at his own "risque" and for his own benefit, the novelist was unwilling, in his desperate need of funds, to make concessions to publishers. Though the contract with Wiley and Halsted for *The Pioneers* is apparently not extant, its terms can be reliably inferred from exactly contemporaneous contracts for the second and third editions of *The Spy*, dated 14 February and 2[6?] April 1822.[53] The retail price was $2 a copy; and Wiley, as primary distributor, was authorized to give a maximum discount of 33⅓ percent, 25 percent for quantities under twenty-four. For itself, the Wiley firm was permitted to retain only 5 percent of the net sales, except in New York where Wiley was also a retailer and where the total discount allowable was 33⅓ percent. When the leading American wholesaler, Carey and Lea in Philadelphia, protested so small a discount for *The Pioneers*, Wiley replied that the novelist

> thinks ⅓ discount a liberal allowance for a Copyright Book. Besides he is so confident that the whole edition will sell without delay, and that another will be called for in less

than sixty days, that he can see no inducement to offer more favourable terms.[54]

Henry Carey, the economist, retorted:

> We can sell we think 2000 Pioneers if it possess equal merit with the Spy but we can make 750 answer our purposes & we supply many places to w[hic]h not a single copy will go unless through us. If Mr. C. give the matter proper consideration we think he will see the advantage of having us engaged on his side.[55]

Cooper did consent to a 40 percent discount on 300 additional copies of *The Spy*;[56] but Carey, who had stocked hundreds of copies at the smaller discount, preferred to let economic laws argue for him.

These laws had cost Cooper heavily in loss of profit from British sales. Without international copyright, *Precaution* and *The Spy* had been pirated while he and Wiley fumbled uncertainly to obtain British contracts; but the effort to publish *The Pioneers* advantageously in England is one of the happiest displays of cooperation in the history of Knickerbocker letters. After preliminary inquiries, Cooper entrusted the London negotiations to his mercantile friend Benjamin U. Coles, who was on the scene and could interview publishers and act in concert with Washington Irving. "Cooper has been quite successful in *the Spy* here—" wrote Coles from London to Henry D. Sedgwick on 26 June 1822,

> W. Irving tells me he hears it spoken of in all societies among the nobility & literary gentry frequent enquiries being made of him about the author &c—
> The booksellers are anxious to obtain his next work the Pioneers and publish it dividing the profits with him—
> Murray proposed this to Irving who spoke with him at my suggestion and I am to call & see Murray with Irving when he comes to town which will be in a day or two—[57]

Murray was out when Coles and Irving called, but sent his regrets in a note of 10 July, requesting Coles to

> inform Mr Cooper that I am disposed to publish his novel at my own expense & risque & to give him half of the

profits . . . but as the most profitable sale of the work will I presume be in this country—Mr Cooper should take care that it is first published here—13 cop[ie]s of the Work & an entry at Stationers Hall secures the Copyright in England —& this I will attend to—[58]

Assuming incorrectly that the laws were identical in both countries, Coles objected that Murray's method might imperil Cooper's American right and proposed alternative "terms to which I think Mr C. will accede—":

That the copy right be secured to the author in America . . . that the work should be exposed for sale there a day or two before it is offered for sale in England—

That it be published by you at your own risk and expense dividing with the author the profits—you charging no commission—[59]

The anxious Murray accepted "immediately."[60] Ten days later, on 21 July, Fitz-Greene Halleck, "the admirable Croaker," arrived at Liverpool with "the first hundred pages of the work in print."[61] The next copy delivered, "matter enough" for two English volumes, was brought in person on 7 January 1823 by Cooper's friend Charles Wilkes.[62] Wilkes explained that he was unable to see Murray until 13 January, when by accident he encountered Thomas Malthus at Murray's door and "made" Malthus introduce him. Previously, complained Wilkes, Murray

had made me wait rather longer in his shop before I was admitted to his august presence than appeared to me necessary between any gentleman & a bookseller however exalted. He spoke of the success of the Spy & of his expectation from the present work which he said would excite great attention, he thought.[63]

The long delay in the printing, Cooper wrote Murray on 29 November, proceeded from the yellow fever epidemic that depopulated lower Manhattan in August and September and drove business and residents uptown.[64] Wiley and Halsted, at 3 Wall Street, were in the infected district. A notice in the *Commercial Advertiser* of 11 September reported:

The Pioneers.—We regret to learn that in consequence of
the fever, and the consequent breaking up of business, the
appearance of this Novel will be delayed for several weeks
—probably until the middle of December. We are pleased
to state, that Mr. Murray, the celebrated London publisher, who at the instigation of Gifford, the Editor of the
Quarterly Review, refused to republish *The Spy*, has bought
the copy right of the anticipated work for England, and
will publish it nearly at the same time that it will appear
here.

The postponement in publication, however, and Cooper's admitted carelessness in proofreading, must have been affected
by a multiplicity of other distractions: the return of the novelist's whaling ship on 22 June with a cargo of 16,532 gallons
of oil and the necessity if disposing of ship and cargo, and also
a series of family crises and an endless maze of debts, suits,
decrees, and foreclosures. The Coopers, still at Angevine but
planning to move to the City, waited in the country, presumably, until the Board of Health discontinued its daily reports
of the fever near the end of October.

Once Cooper obtained proofs, the progressive discovery of
hundreds of errors, some by printers, some his own, cannot
have contributed to his peace of mind. His letter to Murray
on 29 November advised that "the remainder of the work"
would be sent by 20 December and publication follow by 20
January,[65] but even this schedule could not be kept. Before the
formes of the first edition were completely broken up, Cooper
and Wiley decided that the printing was too small to satisfy
the probable demand and contracted with Jonathan Seymour
for a corrected second edition approximating a line-by-line re-
print of the first. The second or Wiley-Seymour-Clayton edition retained only six formes from the last seven signatures of
the second volume. Though the evidence available establishes
the size of neither edition, a statement in the *Commercial Advertiser* (16 January) that "the edition is large, and the trade requires the whole of it, and more too" suggests that the com-
bined editions were in excess of 5,000 copies. "A complete set"
of sheets "tolerably corrected" was forwarded to Murray on 15
January by "the 'Criterion' which ship sail[ed] direct to Lon-

don."[66] Murray's edition of 1,000 copies appeared in three volumes on 26 February 1823.[67]

VI

The distribution of 3,500 copies of *The Pioneers* in New York City by noon on 1 February 1823[68]—only hours after publication—was "indeed 'something new' in the United States," as *Niles' Weekly Register* remarked on 8 February. Though *The North American Review* and the great British quarterlies ignored its existence, no previous American book, not even *The Spy*, had been so auspiciously greeted. Booksellers quoted the early sales figure to stimulate further sales; and newspaper notices of the arrival of shipments—Philadelphia on February third, Baltimore on the fifth, Washington on the seventh—testified to a lively interest and a demand at times outrunning supply. Copies were "hourly expected" in Boston on February seventh, and a new shipment replenished the short supply on the seventeenth.[69] Much of this excitement was attributable to the continuing success of *The Spy*. Jacob Sutherland, to whom Cooper dedicated *The Pioneers*, had assured him on 15 March 1822: "You have . . . so thoroughly ingratiated yourself with the public, that you can take your own time for your next publication without incurring the risque of being forgotten."[70] And on 12 November, as the time for publication approached, Ralph Waldo Emerson, a recent Harvard graduate, had written his classmate John Boynton Hill:

> Since Scott has failed to equal himself in his last two works our young novelist has grown the greater; I suppose you know that the Spy, translated into French, is popular at Paris; but of the "Sources of the Susquehannah," his second birth, I have heard nothing. What is the reason? Have you never yet sanctioned it with a "bon!"[71]

Responses in reviews and private letters confirmed Emerson's expectations.[72] An early reader in Charleston, South Carolina, who identified himself only as "A lover of every *nail* in the temple of American fame," wrote Wiley on 20 February: "My eyes are scarcely yet sufficiently dry to enable me to write you, requesting that you will convey to the author of the Pioneers my heartiest thanks for the pleasure he has given me. The book is certainly the greatest literary honour yet conferred on the country."[73] The patriotism was endemic. An editor for the Washington *National Intelligencer* (21 February), confessing he had not yet read the book, rejoiced "to find any American Novel, descriptive of our own scenery, history, and character, excite such a sensation among us as this has done, both before and after its appearance. It proves that National Feeling is not dead, but sleepeth." *The Pioneers* was an emphatic rebuttal to Sydney Smith, declared *Niles' Register* (22 March), and would "be read by tens of thousands even in Great Britain." The London *Examiner* (16 March), in a review reprinted in the United States, invoked the inevitable comparison with Sir Walter Scott in Cooper's favor—as was customary at first, merely postponing its readiness to place

> this writer on a par with Sir Walter; we must behold something like an approach to similar fertility, before that can be done; but we are decidedly of opinion, that an American has caught the style of his free and easy pencil, better than any British emulator we have yet seen, which if no great deal to the purpose, is at least sufficient to make Mr. Gifford overflow with bile for a whole article.

Most sensitive American readers responded with naive but intense delight, especially to the book's descriptive passages. Cooper's graphic representations—like the utterances of Emerson's Poet-to-be—apparently signified the things themselves and thus defined the reality. "The descriptions of scenery are perfect," wrote Eliza Cabot of Boston to her friend Catharine M. Sedgwick:

> the fishing the little boat coming across the Lake—the killing the deer in it—the panther scene—the trial, & many more scenes . . . are very fine I think—[74]

Miss Cabot added that Professor Andrews Norton, Dexter Professor of Biblical Literature at Harvard, was "extravagant in praise" of the novel, but was—she implied—too occupied with his own book to write the all-important *North American* review Cooper would have welcomed. Other critics, less busy or less

cautious, cited or excerpted these "[v]ivid pictures" and "animated sketches"[75] to demonstrate the special power of the
work: the turkey shoot, the visit to Billy Kirby, the spear fishing after dark, the killing of the deer in the lake, the prospect
view from Pine Orchard in the Catskills, the attack of the
panther, the conflagration on the mountain, and many other
scenes.

Curiously, almost the only negative responses in New York
seem to have been inspired by encomiums from the pro-Cooper
press. Perhaps encouraged by Wiley, William Leete Stone,
former resident of Cooperstown and editor of the *New York
Commercial Advertiser*, and Nathaniel Hazeltine Carter, editor of
the *New York Statesman*, had acted unofficially as Cooper's press
agents, inserting notices at frequent intervals. Stone was the
more assiduous. By "repeated solicitation," he even obtained
corrected excerpts from the novel for prepublication viewing
(see pages 189–99 and 290–99); and he did not immediately
discontinue these "viewings" after publication.[76] Some thought
this attention claquish. George Houston, editor of *The Minerva*,
published a withering review on 8 February objecting to what
he termed "puffs" and advising Cooper, "should he write again,
to have less puffing in advance; to let his work stand or fall
by itself; and not to rely on newspaper paragraphs for gaining
a reputation."[77] Stone, the self-confessed culprit, immediately
absolved Cooper of any complicity.[78] *The United States Magazine*, a short-lived successor to Wiley's *Repository*, had already—
probably on Cooper's insistence—stated it would not review
The Spy and *The Pioneers* because "the author of The Spy is
known to be a frequent contributor to our pages."[79] Cooper,
Wiley, Gardner, Stone and nearly a hundred other prominent
New Yorkers were attacked shortly afterward in a vicious and
libelous verse satire called *Gotham and The Gothamites* (1823).
The author, an embittered editor and playwright, S. B. H.
Judah, was sued, convicted, fined and jailed for his effort.
James Gates Percival, a frustrated poet the novelist had tried
to assist, was "glad" Judah had "rubbed up Cooper"[80] and in-
furiated at the success of *The Pioneers*:

> It might do well enough to amuse the select society of a
> barber's shop or a porter-house. But to have the author

step forward on such stilts and claim to be the lion of our national literature, and fall to roaring himself and set all his jackals howling (S[tone], C[arter], & Co.) to put better folks out of countenance,—why, it is pitiful, 't is wondrous pitiful, at least for the country that not only suffers it, but encourages it.[81]

Percival's rage was consuming and uncompromising:

I ask nothing of a people who will lavish their patronage on such a vulgar book as the Pioneers. They and I are well quit. They neglect me, and I despise them.[82]

Though *The Pioneers* was received with few "discordant notes," as one reviewer said,[83] it was still far from being the unqualified popular success Percival imagined, its initial sale augured, and Cooper had hoped for. Taking account of his successes and failures in 1844 at Rufus W. Griswold's request, Cooper wrote, somewhat surprisingly, that the novel was "only moderately successful, its present popularity being ⟨slightly⟩ in a great degree factitious. It never was a *loyal* success, though criticism has rather favored it."[84] In fact, as Cooper had feared and as astute reviewers noted, he had not been sufficiently cognizant of opportunities for "action and strong excitement"[85] and "moonlight rambles by the margin of the sequestered Lake."[86] Female readers disagreed emphatically with the critic who applauded by quoting: "Happy's the wooing / That's not long a doing."[87] If some critics preferred *The Pioneers* to *The Spy* as "a more finished composition and of a higher order,"[88] the reading public was not immediately persuaded. Whereas *The Spy* went through three American and two British printings after its first appearance and before 1825, demand for *The Pioneers* in the two countries was satisfied during the same period by copies in print on the day of publication. When James De Peyster Ogden visited John Murray to obtain an accounting in early September 1823, he discovered that only 800 of the 1,000 copies printed had been sold (Cooper's share was £110.15.9); and, he reported:

Mr Murray spoke flatteringly of the "Pioneers," but more so of the "Spy"—He said there was not much interest felt

in the description of the local scenery of the former, there
was an impression he said that the description of some of
the games &c in the Pioneers was taken from Walter Scott,
altho he said very can[didly?] he had no doubt they were
original—but he said there was no one here, who possessed
the requisite knowledge of the scenery &c therein described, to review the work, as it should be done—[89]

When Cooper visited John Miller in July 1826, after Miller had
taken over Murray's stock of *The Pioneers*, there were apparently six copies still unsold.[90] Ogden was surely correct when he
wrote: "It is certain Colonel that the Spy is by far the most popular of the two works."[91]

If, thus, Cooper could not consider *The Pioneers* the "Chef
d'oeuvre" he set out somewhat prematurely to write, he could
take satisfaction in having written a *success d'estime*. According
to the press, the book "excited a sensation among the artists,
altogether unprecedented in the history of our domestic literature."[92] In New York, William Dunlap was reported to have
on his easel "a painting from the work, in oil, five or six feet
square,"[93] and a competitor was reputed to be at work on another of similar size. The *New York Statesman* singled out "two
beautiful Illustrations of the Pioneers," exhibited in New York
by a young artist of great "genius and taste," one a pencil sketch
of the Leather-stocking and the other a drawing of the death of
Mohegan.[94] Thomas Doughty of Philadelphia, whose summer
painting expeditions into the Catskills were influential in forming the style of the Hudson River Valley School, exhibited two
landscapes from *The Pioneers* at the Pennsylvania Academy of
the Fine Arts in 1824, one of the hunting scene on the lake, and
another of the woods on fire.[95] Thomas Cole, admiring and
studying Doughty's work in Philadelphia, would begin his own
painting expeditions in 1825. Mrs. Sarah Hall, an influential
New York critic to whom Cooper presented "one of a few" copies of *The Spy* "printed in a superior style, with his name on the
title page," informed her son John E. Hall, editor of the Philadelphia *Port Folio*, that the "artists, both at New York and Philadelphia, are at work on illustrations, both of the Spy and Pioneers. The latter is a work of more ability than the former."[96]
Whether or not as a result of this communication, Hall con-

tracted with Henry Inman and Gideon Fairman for a series of drawings and engravings, mainly from *The Pioneers*, as "embellishments" (frontispieces) in monthly issues of his journal.[97] Since relatively few of the other art works have survived or been identified, the effect of *The Pioneers* on the emergence of the Hudson River Valley School is difficult to assess precisely, but its impact would seem to have been direct and decided.

About the impact of the Leather-stocking as a new, distinctive, triumphant, American creation, testimony is unanimous and enthusiastic. Natty "comes upon our . . . imaginations like an ungracious anomaly," wrote one reviewer, "and departs, like a dream, towards the setting sun, leaving the reader his friend for ever."[98] His lineaments already existed, it was noted, in the "effigies of old Daniel Boone" and his fellows; but the significance of his withdrawal "as the path of civilization *invaded* his wild domains"[99] was still an enigma. Perplexed by the genus, Timothy Dwight had concluded in his *Travels* (1821) that the isolated "forester" and "pioneer" were persons whose business

> is no other than to . . . prepare the way for those who come
> after them. These men cannot live in regular society. They
> are too idle, too talkative, too passionate, too prodigal,
> and too shiftless to acquire either property or character.
> They are impatient of the restraints of law, religion, and
> morality. . . . At the same time, they are usually possessed
> in their own view of uncommon wisdom.[100]

Such men had been more "lout" than "hero," as J. A. Leo Lemay reminds us. Though the transformation, Lemay persuasively argues,[101] may be described as the culmination of developments in the history of ideas in which Crevecoeur's *Letters from an American Farmer* was crucial, the creation of the Leather-stocking marks the exact point of the metamorphosis in the popular estimate.

Whether reflecting or effecting it, Cooper was careful—as he suggested to three young admirers in 1847, discussing his selection of Natty's name—to preserve the uncouthness of the reality;[102] but, as he wrote still later, "in a moral sense this man of

the forest is purely a creation."[103] Transcending realistic possibility, his "uncommon wisdom" embodies an ideal of toler-
ance, fairness, and human justice far more sensitive than any
to be found in statutory codes or social accommodations in
Templeton or elsewhere and reaches towards those principles
of "higher or Natural Law" once held to undergird American
institutions. Unassailable proof of his basic humanity, his pride,
his ungainly exterior, and his ignorance of civilized amenities
domesticate and make acceptable the incongruous sublimity of
his moral vision, giving his portrait a tragic tinge. Paradoxi-
cally and ironically, he cannot comprehend the need for civilization because he personifies its highest aspirations, as perhaps
only a pastoral character could. "[T]his is no abstract creation
of the author," said one reviewer; "he has compressed the
whole tribe into an individual . . . and rendered him . . . an object of infinite interest and progressive admiration."[104] Contemporaneous readers, who tended to overlook the cantanker-
ous manner and stubborn pride, responded more often to the
pathos than to the finer, tragic note. Overcoming his natural
shyness, Richard H. Dana, Sr., one of the more perceptive
and articulate readers, wrote Cooper from Cambridge on 2
April 1823 to express his appreciation of Natty and the book:

> Grand & elevated as he is, making him so is no departure
> from truth. He read in a book filled with inspiration, look
> on it where we [will]. But, alas, too few feel the inspiration
> there—or scarcely in that [other] Book which God has
> given us. Natty's uneducated mind [shown?] us in his pro-
> nunciation & use of words belonging to low life, mingled
> with his inborn eloquence—his solitary life, his old age,
> his simplicity, & delicate feelings, create a grateful & very
> peculiar emotion made up of admiration & pity & concern.
> So highly is his character wrought that I was fearful lest
> he would not hold out to the end. But he does grow upon
> us to the very close of the last scene, which is, perhaps,
> the finest, certainly the most touching in the book.—A
> friend of mine said at Natty's departure, "I longed to go
> with him."[105]

Dana's friend spoke for many; but if the author intended to
gratify their wish—as he would in the four subsequent volumes

of the Leather-stocking Tales—he did not say so in his reply
to Dana's letter on 14 April 1823.

In that reply, Cooper modestly attributed much or most of his
"success to the desire that is now so prevalent in the Country to
see our manners exhibited on paper" and spoke of his desire
"to create an excitement that may rouse the sleeping talents of
the nation."[106] Later, he admitted to R. W. Griswold that the
"character of Natty Bumppo . . . took very well, and did much
for the book";[107] but his attitude towards its reception remained one of suppressed disappointment. Except for the few,
like Dana or Emerson, who recalled an "old debt . . . of happy
days, on the first appearance of the Pioneers" and "the unanim-
ity with which that national novel was greeted,"[108] American
criticism was not equipped to deal appropriately with a work
so complex as *The Pioneers*. And Dana and Emerson did not
review it. When W. H. Gardiner finally undertook to discuss it
(along with *The Last of the Mohicans*) in the prestigious *North
American* three years after its publication, he explained half-
apologetically that Mr. Cooper "has the almost singular merit
of writing American novels which everybody reads, and which
we are of course bound to review now and then." In this forty-
seven-page article, of which about five were devoted to *The
Pioneers*, Gardiner observed that he had concerned himself
"chiefly to notice our author's faults, because Mr. Cooper is
already too far advanced to stand in need of our praise."[109]

As if to make amends after Cooper's death in 1851, the *North
American* published two extended essays on collections of Cooper's works: a review of G. P. Putnam's Author's Edition (1849–
1851) by Francis Parkman in 1852 and a review of the early
volumes of the Townsend-Darley Edition by Henry T. Tuckerman in 1859. Both critics admired Cooper and both placed
The Pioneers at or near the head of his writings—and for much
the same reasons. "Of all Cooper's works, The Pioneers" seemed
to Parkman "most likely to hold a permanent place in literature" because "it preserves a vivid reflection of scenes and characters which will soon have passed away";[110] and Tuckerman,
another historian, valued the book because its "minute details
. . . conserve scenery, habits, costume, phrases, which progress
has long ago modified or made obsolete. The rural life of
America, in its normal traits, there first found a 'local habita-

tion and a name.'"[111] These are not, of course, small accomplishments; but such praise takes no account whatever of Cooper's primary intention as a literary man to address the reader's "love of truth—not the mere love of facts expressed by true names and dates, but the love of that higher truth, the truth of nature and of principles, which is the primitive law of the human mind."[112] In *The Pioneers*, as in few other works in American literature, literary and historical values are indissolubly wedded; and if, as Cooper remarked in the Preface, its "one battle . . . is not of the most Homeric kind," the book remains our closest early approach to prose epic.

NOTES

1. Charles K. Gardner to JFC, 7 January 1822; MS: Cooper Family Papers.
2. Charles Wiley to JFC, 7 January 1822; MS: Cooper Family Papers.
3. *The Letters and Journals of James Fenimore Cooper*, ed., James Franklin Beard (Cambridge, Mass.: Belknap Press of Harvard University Press, 1960–1968), I, 44 (cited hereafter as *Letters and Journals*).
4. For a discussion of the writing of *Tales for Fifteen*, see Introduction by James Franklin Beard to *Tales for Fifteen (1823) by James Fenimore Cooper*, a Facsimile Reproduction (Delmar, New York: Scholars' Facsimiles & Reprints, 1977 [1959]).
5. Reproduced in facsimile with Introduction and Headnotes by James Franklin Beard in *Early Critical Essays (1820–1822) by James Fenimore Cooper* (Delmar, New York: Scholars' Facsimiles & Reprints, 1977 [1955]) (hereafter cited as *Early Critical Essays*).
6. *Early Critical Essays*, p. 97.
7. Ibid., p. 97.
8. Ibid., pp. 97–98.
9. Ibid., pp. 98–99.
10. Ibid., p. 99.
11. Ibid., pp. 99–100.
12. Ibid., p. 100.
13. Ibid.
14. Ibid., pp. 100–01.
15. Ibid., p. 134.

16. Thomas Philbrick, "Cooper's *The Pioneers*: Origins and Structure," *PMLA*, 79 (1964), 583.

17. Washington Irving, *Bracebridge Hall or The Humourists*, ed., Herbert F. Smith (Boston, 1977), p. 5.

18. *Letters and Journals*, I, 85.

19. Significantly, reviewers and friends who had known Judge William Cooper and the novelist's sister Hannah apparently did not identify the real with the fictitious characters. These identifications became current in the 1830s. In the *Brother Jonathan* letter (*Letters and Journals*, IV, 252–61), Cooper specifically refuted a statement to this effect by his friend Charles A. Murray, the British actor, in his *Travels in North America During the Years 1834, 1835, & 1836* . . . (New York, 1839), II, 235.

20. *Letters and Journals*, IV, 254–58.

21. *The Chronicles of Cooperstown* (Cooperstown, 1838), pp. 35–38.

22. Ibid., pp. 26–28, 30, 76.

23. Ibid., p. 26.

24. Susan Fenimore Cooper, Introduction to the Household Edition of *The Pathfinder* (New York and Cambridge, 1876), pp. xxxi-xxxii. See also Cooper's *Lives of Distinguished American Naval Officers* (Philadelphia, 1846), II, 126–27.

25. "The Real 'Natty' an Elder Brother," *Proceedings of the New York State Historical Association*, 16 (1917), 191.

26. *Letters and Journals*, IV, 74.

27. Cooper's Preface to the Leather-stocking Tales, *The Deerslayer* (New York, 1850), p. vii.

28. Since Natty Bumppo belonged to a familiar type of frontiersman that included Daniel Boone, and since his moral endowments were Cooper's contribution, identification of specific frontiersmen known to Cooper in his youth is of mainly antiquarian interest. For a summary of the respective claims of Nathaniel Shipman of Hoosick Falls, New York, and David shipman of Fly Creek, near Cooperstown, see articles by Edith Beaumont in *The Valley Sampler* (Bennington, Vt., 24, 31 July 1969). A German prototype is nominated by Carl Suesser (*Westermanns Monatshefte*, May 1934, pp. 245–49).

29. Anna Mulford, *A Sketch of Dr. John Smith Sage, of Sag-Harbor, N.Y.* (Sag Harbor, 1897), pp. 34–35.

30. In *A Letter to His Countrymen* (New York, 1834), p. 108, Cooper recalled "at Cooperstown, some thirty or forty years ago, a political writer who put his parentheses into one another, like spare pill-boxes. . . ." Like Dirck Van der School in *The Pioneers,* Judge Jedediah Peck followed this practice in *The Political*

Wars of Otsego County (Cooperstown, 1796). The Explanatory
Notes in this edition provide further instances of authentic
detail employed in a similarly felicitous manner.

31. *Letters and Journals*, IV, 253.
32. Ibid., IV, 73.
33. Frederick Jackson Turner, "The Significance of the Frontier in
American History," *Annual Report of the American Historical Association for the Year 1893* (Washington, D.C., 1894), p. 199.
34. Ibid., p. 200.
35. See Arnold J. Toynbee, *A Study of History* (London, 1934), I,
271–93.
36. *Letters and Journals*, IV, 255. Cooper's quotation from Robert
Proud, *The History of Pennsylvania* (Philadelphia, 1797), I, 149,
in the *Brother Jonathan* letter altered Proud's punctuation and
omitted the final clause, both of which are here supplied.
37. *Letters and Journals*, IV, 256. Cooper believed unequivocally, but
mistakenly, that he was descended in the sixth generation from
William Cooper, the emigrant. *Letters and Journals*, V, 304.
38. In an address to the New York State Historical Association on
22 September 1922 ["George Croghan and the Development
of Central New York, 1763–1800," *New York State Historical
Association Proceedings*, 21 (1923), pp. 21–40] and later in his
book *George Croghan and the Westward Movement, 1741–1782*
(Cleveland, 1926), pp. 252–54, 326–35, Albert T. Volwiler
questioned the legality of the proceedings by which William
Cooper and his partner Andrew Craig acquired title to their
20,000 acres from the original "Croghan Patent." The late
James Fenimore Cooper, great-grandson of Judge Cooper, replied ["William Cooper and Andrew Craig's Purchase of
Croghan Land," *New York State Historical Association Journal*,
12 (1931), 390–96], citing documents in his possession to refute Volwiler's claims, which were apparently based on mere
statements of the Croghan heirs. Ignoring the 1931 article,
Andrew Nelson published an article ["James Cooper and
George Croghan," *Philological Quarterly*, 20 (January 1941),
69–73], drawing on Volwiler's findings to suggest that the Effingham plot of *The Pioneers* originated in Cooper's knowledge
of his father's transactions with the Croghan estate. Though
the parallels are extremely inexact, Nelson's suggestion should
not be completely ignored. Croghan and his chief mortgagor,
Governor William Franklin, and Augustin Prevost, Croghan's
son-in-law, *were* all Tory or suspected of being Tory. However,

William Cooper, who purchased the Croghan land at a mortgage sale initiated by Governor Franklin, is not known to have
protected Tory interests. He was, he maintained at the time,
willing for the Croghan heirs or creditors to redeem their
property by paying the principal and interest of the mortgage;
and he personally guaranteed titles to the land he sold to
settlers, making himself and his heirs liable for any legitimate
claims. This voluntary assumption of responsibility, which his
heirs *did* assume, is perhaps the best evidence of his integrity.

39. The story of the loss of Judge Cooper's estate and the impoverish-
ment of at least a part of his family is part of a critical biog-
raphy of Cooper—in progress—by the writer of the present
Introduction.
40. *Letters and Journals*, IV, 255.
41. Proud, *History of Pennsylvania*, I, 150, 156, 159, 160. A copy of
Proud containing genealogical notes by Cooper has been
passed down in the Fenimore Cooper family.
42. Ibid., I, 3.
43. Ibid., II, 235.
44. Ibid., I, 153.
45. Ibid.
46. Ibid., I, 154.
47. Ibid., II, 236.
48. *Letters and Journals*, I, 4–5.
49. William Empson, *Some Versions of Pastoral* (London, 1935), p. 23.
50. Northrop Frye, *Anatomy of Criticism* (Princeton, N.J., 1957), pp.
312–14.
51. Cooper here begins to erect what Empson calls "a staircase on
a contradiction," that is, to achieve the "ideal simplicity" of
pastoral "by resolving contradictions." In fact, Empson uses
the epigram "Might makes right" as an illustration in *Some
Versions of Pastoral*, pp. 143–44.
52. Charles Wiley to Richard H. Dana, Sr., 17 March 1822; MS:
Massachusetts Historical Society.
53. MS: Cooper Family Papers.
54. Quoted by David Kaser, *Messrs. Carey & Lea of Philadelphia* (Philadelphia, 1957), pp. 77–78.
55. Quoted by David Kaser, ibid., p. 78.
56. Ibid.
57. Benjamin U. Coles to Henry D. Sedgwick, 26 June 1822; MS:
Sedgwick Papers, Massachusetts Historical Society.
58. John Murray to Benjamin U. Coles, Wednesday [10 July 1822];

the holograph is in the Collection of American Literature, Beinecke Rare Book and Manuscript Library, Yale University (cited hereafter as YCAL).

59. Benjamin U. Coles to JFC, London, 13 July 1822; MS: YCAL. The text of Coles' letter includes a copy of his letter to Murray, dated 11 July 1822. See Professor Robert E. Spiller's pioneering essay describing the state of American and British copyright law during the period of Cooper's authorship in Spiller and Blackburn, *A Descriptive Bibliography of the Writings of James Fenimore Cooper* (New York, 1934), pp. 1–12.

60. Benjamin U. Coles to JFC, London, 17 July 1822; MS: YCAL. In this letter, Coles included a copy of Murray's acceptance of the terms proposed in his letter of 13 July. Murray stated: "I will very willingly accede to the terms which you have very judiciously proposed for the publication of your friends novel in this Country—"

61. *Letters and Journals*, I, 75; Nelson F. Adkins, *Fitz-Greene Halleck: An Early Knickerbocker Wit and Poet* (New Haven, 1930), p. 134.

62. Charles Wilkes to JFC, 13 January 1823; MS: YCAL.

63. Ibid.

64. *Letters and Journals*, I, 85; see also *New York Commercial Advertiser*, 29 August 1822.

65. *Letters and Journals*, I, 86.

66. Ibid., I, 92.

67. Spiller and Blackburn, *Descriptive Bibliography*, p. 27.

68. The *New York Commercial Advertiser* triumphantly proclaimed on 1 February 1823:

> "*The Pioneers* was announced in the papers of yesterday to be published this morning, and at 12 o'clock, Mr. Wiley, the publisher, had delivered THIRTY-FIVE HUNDRED COPIES!"

Newspapers in other cities across the country reprinted the gist of this notice, as did many booksellers in their advertisements.

69. Contemporaneous newspapers consulted include: *Albany Argus*, *Baltimore American*, *Baltimore Patriot*, *Boston Daily Advertiser*, *Boston Evening Gazette*, *New York American*, *New York Commercial Advertiser*, *New York Statesman*, *Philadelphia Gazette and Daily Advertiser*, Philadelphia *National Gazette and Literary Register*, *Washington* [D.C.] *Republican*.

70. Jacob Sutherland to JFC, New York, 15 March 1822; MS: YCAL.

71. *The Letters of Ralph Waldo Emerson*, ed., Ralph L. Rusk (New York, 1939), I, 124–25.

72. The following citations locate American reviews or contempora-

neous references to *The Pioneers*: *The Albion* (N.Y.C.), 23 November 1850, p. 561; *The American Quarterly Review*, 17 (June 1835), 413–14; *Baltimore American & Commercial Daily Advertiser*, 4 March 1823, p. 2; *Baltimore Patriot and Mercantile Advertiser*, 5 February 1823, p. 2; *Daily National Intelligencer* (Washington, D.C.), 21 February 1823, p. 3; *The Literary World* (N.Y.C.), 7 (7 December 1850), 456; *The Minerva* (N.Y.C.), 1 (8 February 1823), 348–49; *National Gazette and Literary Register*, 3 #708 (12 February 1823), 1–2; 3 #709 (13 February 1823), 2 (Reprinted in Cooperstown *Freeman's Journal*, 10 March 1823); Paulding, James K., *Köningsmark, the Long Finne* (New York, 1823), Volume II, Book Sixth, Chapter I, pp. 67–74; *New-York Commercial Advertiser*, 18, 25 January 1823; *The New-York Mirror*, 9 August 1823, pp. 12–13; 16 August 1823, pp. 20–21; 4 August 1827, p. 31; *New York Statesman*, 4, 5 February 1823; *Niles' Weekly Register*, 8 June 1822, p. 225; 8 February 1823, p. 354; 22 March 1823, p. 34; 24 May 1823, p. 178; 3 December 1825, p. 217; *The North American Review*, 23 (July 1826), 150–97; 74 (January 1852), 147–61; 89 (October 1859), 289–316; *The Port Folio*, 15 (March 1823), 230–48; 15 (June 1823), 520; *The United States Magazine and Democratic Review*, 28 (January 1851), 92. British reviews or notices include: *The Album*, 3 (May 1823), 155–78; *The Athenaeum*, 7 April 1832, p. 225; *British Critic*, s. 3, 2 (July 1826), 427–29, 436–39; *Blackwood's Edinburgh Magazine*, 16 (October 1824), p. 427–28; *Colburn's New Monthly Magazine* (July 1827), p. 80; *Examiner*, no. 790 (16 March 1823), 185–86; *Kaleidoscope, or Literary and Scientific Mirror and Retrospective Review*, 9 Pt. 2 (1824), 326; *Lady's Magazine*, n.s. 4 (1823), 193–98; *Literary Gazette*, no. 352 (18 October 1823), 661–63; *Literary Museum and Register*, no. 45–46 (1823), 134–36, 150–52; *Literary Register*, no. 39 (29 March 1823), 197–98; *Monthly Literary Register*, 3 (March 1823), 218–20; *Monthly Magazine or British Register*, n.s. 4 (July 1827), 84–85; *Newcastle Magazine*, n.s. 3 (1824), 35–37; *Repository of Modern Literature*, 1 (1823), 177–92.

73. Anonymous letter to Charles Wiley, Charleston, South Carolina, 20 February 1823; MS: Cooper Family Papers.

74. Eliza Cabot to Catharine M. Sedgwick, Boston, 27 March 1823; MS: Sedgwick Papers, Massachusetts Historical Society.

75. *London Literary Gazette*, no. 352 (18 October 1823), p. 661.

76. Stone published excerpts from *The Pioneers* in his *Commercial Advertiser* on 18, 25 January and 3, 5, 7 February. These excerpts, which included much of the text of the book, were rou-

tinely reprinted in his bi-weekly paper the *New-York Spectator* and also by other newspapers. Stone apparently intended one final excerpt on 8 February, but substituted a summary and a half-apology, probably after interdiction by Cooper or Wiley.

77. *The Minerva*, 1 (8 February 1823), 349.

78. *New York Commercial Advertiser*, 11 February 1823. See also p. 472.

79. *The United States Magazine, and Literary and Political Repository*, 1 (January 1823), 92.

80. Julius H. Ward, *The Life and Letters of James Gates Percival* (Boston, 1866), p. 170.

81. Ibid., p. 171.

82. Ibid., p. 155.

83. *United States Gazette*, as quoted in *The Port Folio*, 15 (June 1823), 520.

84. *Letters and Journals*, IV, 342.

85. Ibid., I, 85.

86. *The Port Folio*, 15 (March 1823), 236.

87. *The British Critic*, Series 3, Vol. 2 (July 1826), 428.

88. *The Port Folio*, 15 (March 1823), 248.

89. James De Peyster Ogden to JFC, London, 6 September 1823; MS: Cooper Family Papers.

90. Account sheet with John Miller, apparently July 1826, crediting Cooper with £3.12 for 6 copies of "'Pioneers'/on hand" (MS: Cooper Family Papers).

91. James De Peyster Ogden to JFC, London, 6 September 1823; MS: Cooper Family Papers.

92. *United States Gazette*, as quoted in *The Port Folio*, 15 (June 1823), 520.

93. Ibid.

94. *New York Statesman*, 28 February 1823.

95. *Thirteenth Annual Exhibition of the Pennsylvania Academy of the Fine Arts* (Philadelphia, 1824), pp. 7–8.

96. *Selections from the Writings of Mrs. Sarah Hall . . . with a Memoir of Her Life* (Philadelphia, 1833), p. xxiii.

97. See the descriptions of these engravings (pp. xiii–xvii) and the engravings themselves reproduced in the present volume.

98. London *Retrospective Review, and Historical and Antiquarian Magazine*, 9, Pt. 2 (1824), 326.

99. *The Port Folio*, 15 (March 1823), 232.

100. Timothy Dwight, *Travels in New England and New York*, ed. Barbara Miller Solomon, assisted by Patricia M. King (Cambridge, Mass., 1969), II, 321.

101. J. A. Leo Lemay, "The Frontiersman from Lout to Hero,"

Proceedings of the American Antiquarian Society, 88, Pt. 2 (1978), 187–223.

102. *Letters and Journals*, V, 183–84.
103. JFC's Preface to the Leather-stocking Tales, *The Deerslayer* (New York, 1850), p. vii.
104. *National Gazette and Literary Register* (13 February 1823), p. 2.
105. Richard H. Dana, Sr. to JFC, Cambridge, Mass., 2 April 1823. Words conjecturally supplied to the damaged manuscript are placed in square brackets. (MS: Cooper Family Papers.) Published with variants in *Correspondence of James Fenimore-Cooper*, ed., James Fenimore Cooper (New Haven, 1922), I, 93–94.
106. *Letters and Journals*, I, 94.
107. Ibid., IV, 460.
108. R. W. Emerson to Rufus W. Griswold, Concord, Mass., [n.d.], *Memorial of James Fenimore Cooper* (New York, 1852), p. 33.
109. *The North American Review*, 23 (July 1826), 150, 197.
110. Ibid., 74 (January 1852), 157.
111. Ibid., 89 (October 1859), 310.
112. *Early Critical Essays*, p. 99.

TO

Jacob Sutherland,

OF BLENHEIM, SCHOHARIE,

ESQUIRE.

The length of our friendship would be a
sufficient reason for prefixing your name to
these pages; but your residence so near the scene
of the tale, and your familiarity with much of the
character and kind of life that I have attempted
to describe, render it more peculiarly proper.
You, at least, dear Sutherland, will not receive
this dedication as a cold compliment, but as an
evidence of the feeling that makes me,

Warmly and truly,

Your friend,

———— ————.

Preface.
[1823]

TO MR. CHARLES WILEY, *Bookseller*.

Every man is, more or less, the sport of accident; nor do I know that authors are at all exempted from this humiliating influence. This is the third of my novels, and it depends on two very uncertain contingencies, whether it will not be the last;— the one being the public opinion, and the other mine own humour. The first book was written, because I was told that I could not write a grave tale; so, to prove that the world did not know me, I wrote one that was so grave nobody would read it; wherein I think that I had much the best of the argument. The second was written to see if I could not overcome this neglect of the reading world. How far I have succeeded, Mr. Charles Wiley, must ever remain a secret between ourselves. The third has been written, exclusively, to please myself; so it would be no wonder if it displeased every body else; for what two ever thought alike, on a subject of the imagination!

I should think criticism to be the perfection of human acquirements, did there not exist this discrepancy in taste. Just as I have made up my mind to adopt the very sagacious hints of one learned Reviewer, a pamphlet is put into my hands, containing the remarks of another, who condemns all that his rival praises, and praises all that his rival condemns. There I am, left like an ass between two locks of hay; so that I have determined to relinquish my animate nature, and remain stationary, like a lock of hay between two asses.

It is now a long time, say the wise ones, since the world has been told all that is new and novel. But the Reviewers (the cunning wights!) have adopted an ingenious expedient, to give a freshness to the most trite idea. They clothe it in a language so obscure and metaphysical, that the reader is not about to comprehend their pages without some labour. This is called a great "range of thought;" and not improperly, as I can testify; for, in my own case, I have frequently ranged the universe of ideas, and come back again in as perfect ignorance of their meaning as when I set out. It is delightful, to see the literati of a circulating library get hold of one of these difficult periods! Their praise of the performance is exactly commensurate with its obscurity. Every body knows that to seem wise is the first requisite in a great man.

A common word in the mouths of all Reviewers, readers of magazines, and young ladies, when speaking of novels, is "*keeping;*" and yet there are but few who attach the same meaning to it. I belong, myself, to the old school, in this particular, and think that it applies more to the subject in hand, than to any use of terms, or of cant expressions. As a man might just as well be out of the world as out of "keeping," I have endeavoured to confine myself, in this tale, strictly to its observance. This is a formidable curb to the imagination, as, doubtless, the reader will very soon discover; but under its influence I have come to the conclusion, that the writer of a tale, who takes the earth for the scene of his story, is in some degree bound to respect human nature. Therefore I would advise any one, who may take up this book, with the expectation of meeting gods and goddesses, spooks or witches, or of feeling that strong excitement that is produced by battles and murders, to throw it aside at once, for no such interest will be found in any of its pages.

I have already said, that it was mine own humour that suggested this tale; but it is a humour that is deeply connected with feeling. Happier periods, more interesting events, and, possibly, more beautiful scenes, might have been selected, to exemplify my subject; but none of either that would be so dear to me. I wish, therefore, to be judged more by what I have done, than by my sins of omission. I have introduced one battle, but it is not of the most Homeric kind. As for murders, the population of a new country will not admit of such a waste of human life. There might possibly have been one or two hangings, to the manifest advantage of the "settlement;" but then it would have been out of "keeping" with the humane laws of this compassionate country.

The "Pioneers" is now before the world, Mr. Wiley, and I shall look to you for the only true account of its reception. The critics may write as obscurely as they please, and look much wiser than they are; the papers may puff or abuse, as their changeful humours dictate; but if you meet me with a smiling face, I shall at once know that all is essentially well.

If you should ever have occasion for a preface, I beg you will let me hear from you, in reply.

Yours, truly,

THE AUTHOR.

New-York, January 1st, 1823.

Introduction.
[1832]

As this work professes, in its title page, to be a descriptive tale, they who will take the trouble to read it, may be glad to know how much of its contents is literal fact, and how much is intended to represent a general picture. The author is very sensible, that had he confined himself to the latter, always the most effective, as it is the most valuable mode of conveying knowledge of this nature, he would have made a far better book. But, in commencing to describe scenes, and perhaps he may add characters, that were so familiar to his own youth, there was a constant temptation to delineate that which he had known rather than that which he might have imagined. This rigid adhesion to truth, an indispensable requisite in history and travels, destroys the charm of fiction, for all that is necessary to be conveyed to the mind by the latter had better be done by delineations of principles and of characters in their classes, than by a too fastidious attention to originals.

New-York having but one county of Otsego, and the Susquehannah but one proper source, there can be no mistake as to the site of the Tale. The history of this district of Country, so far as it is connected with civilized man, is soon told.

Otsego, in common with most of the interior of the Province of New-York, was included in the county of Albany, previously to the war of the separation. It then became, in a subsequent division of territory, a part of Montgomery; and, finally, having obtained a sufficient population of its own, it was set apart as a county by itself, shortly after the peace of 1783. It lies among those low spurs of the Alleganies which cover the midland counties of New-York, and it is a little east of a meridional line drawn through the centre of the state. As the waters of New-York either flow southerly into the Atlantic, or northerly into Ontario and its outlet, Otsego Lake, being the source of the Susquehannah, is, of necessity, among its highest lands. The face of the country, the climate as it was found by the whites, and the manners of the settlers, are described with a minute-

ness for which the author has no other apology than the force
of his own recollections.

Otsego is said to be a word compounded of Ot, a place of
meeting, and Sego, or Sago, the ordinary term of salutation,
used by the Indians of this region. There is a tradition which
says, that the neighbouring tribes were accustomed to meet on
the banks of the lake, to make their treaties, and otherwise to
strengthen their alliances, and which refers the name to this
practice. As the Indian Agent of New-York had a log dwelling
at the foot of the lake, however, it is not impossible that the
appellation grew out of the meetings that were held at his
"Council Fires." The war drove off the agent, in common with
the other officers of the crown, and his rude dwelling was soon
abandoned. The author remembers it, a few years later, reduced to the humble office of a smoke-house.

In 1779, an expedition was sent against the hostile Indians
who dwelt, about a hundred miles west of Otsego, on the banks
of the Cayuga. The whole country was then a wilderness, and it
was necessary to transport the baggage of the troops, by means
of the rivers, a devious but practicable route. One brigade ascended the Mohawk, until it reached the point nearest to the
sources of the Susquehannah, whence it cut a lane through the
forest to the head of the Otsego. The boats and baggage were
carried over this 'portage,' and the troops proceeded to the
other extremity of the lake, where they disembarked and en-
camped. The Susquehannah, a narrow though rapid stream at
its source, was much filled with "flood wood," or fallen trees,
and the troops adopted a novel expedient to facilitate their passage. The Otsego is about nine miles in length, varying in
breadth, from half a mile to a mile and a half. The water is of
great depth, limpid, and supplied from a thousand springs. At
its foot, the banks are rather less than thirty feet high, the remainder of its margin being in mountains, intervals, and points.
The outlet, or the Susquehannah, flows through a gorge, in the
low banks just mentioned, which may have a width of two hundred feet. This gorge was dammed, and the waters of the lake
collected. The Susquehannah was converted into a rill. When
all was ready, the troops embarked, the dam was knocked away,
the Otsego poured out its torrent, and the boats went merrily
down with the current.

Gen. James Clinton, the brother of George Clinton, then Governor of New-York, and the father of De Witt Clinton, who died Governor of the same state in 1827, commanded the brigade employed on this duty. During the stay of the troops at the foot of the Otsego, a soldier was shot for desertion. The grave of this unfortunate man was the first place of human interment that the author ever beheld, as the smoke-house was the first ruin! The swivel, alluded to in this work, was buried, and abandoned by the troops, on this occasion, and it was subsequently found in digging the cellars of the author's paternal residence.

Soon after the close of the war, Washington, accompanied by many distinguished men, visited the scene of this tale, it is said with a view to examine the facilities for opening a communication by water, with other points of the Country. He staid but a few hours.

In 1785, the author's father, who had an interest in extensive tracts of land in this wilderness, arrived with a party of Surveyors. The manner in which the scene met his eye is described by Judge Temple. At the commencement of the following year, the settlement began, and from that time to this, the county has continued to flourish. It is a singular feature in American life, that, at the beginning of this century, when the proprietor of the estate, had occasion for settlers, on a new settlement and in a remote county, he was enabled to draw them from among the increase of the former colony.

Although the settlement of this part of Otsego a little preceded the birth of the author, it was not sufficiently advanced to render it desirable that an event, so important to himself, should take place in the wilderness. Perhaps his mother had a reasonable distrust of the practice of Dr. Todd, who must then have been in the noviciate of his experimental acquirements. Be that as it may, the author was brought an infant into this valley and all his first impressions were here obtained. He has inhabited it, ever since, at intervals, and he thinks he can answer for the faithfulness of the picture he has drawn.

Otsego has now become one of the most populous districts of New-York. It sends forth its emigrants like any other old region, and it is pregnant with industry and enterprise. Its manufactures are prosperous, and, it is worthy of remark, that one of the most ingenious machines known in European art, is derived from the keen ingenuity which is exercised in this remote region.

In order to prevent mistake, it may be well to say that the incidents of this tale are purely a fiction. The literal facts are chiefly connected with the natural and artificial objects, and the customs of the inhabitants. Thus the Academy, and Court house, and gaol, and inn, and most similar things are tolerably exact. They have all, long since, given place to other buildings of a more pretending character. There is also some liberty taken with the truth in the description of the principal dwelling: the real building had no "firstly" and "lastly." It was of bricks and not of stones, and its roof exhibited none of the peculiar beauties of the "composite order." It was erected in an age too primitive for that ambitious school of architecture. But the author indulged his recollections freely, when he had fairly entered the door. Here all is literal, even to the severed arm of Wolfe and the urn which held the ashes of Queen Dido.*

The author has elsewhere said that the character of the Leather Stocking is a creation, rendered probable by such auxiliaries as were necessary to produce that effect. Had he drawn still more upon fancy, the lovers of fiction would not have so much cause for their objections to his work. Still the picture would not have been in the least true, without some substitutes for most of the other personages. The great Proprietor resident on his lands, and giving his name to instead of receiving it from his estates, as in Europe, is common over the whole of New York. The physician, with his theory rather obtained than corrected by experiments on the human constitution, the pious, self-denying, laborious, and ill paid missionary, the half-educated, litigious, envious and disreputable lawyer with his counterpoise, a brother of the profession of better origin and of better character, the shiftless, bargaining, discontented seller of his "betterments," the plausible carpenter, and most of the

---

* Though forests still crown the mountains of Otsego, the bear, the wolf and the panther are nearly strangers to them. Even the innocent deer is rarely seen bounding beneath their arches, for the rifle and the activity of the settlers have driven them to other haunts. To this change, which in some particulars is melancholy to one who knew the country in its infancy, it may be added that the Otsego is beginning to be a niggard of its treasures.

others are more familiar to all who have ever dwelt in a new Country.

From circumstances, which, after this introduction, will be obvious to all, the author has had more pleasure in writing The Pioneers, than the book will probably ever give any of its readers. He is quite aware of its numerous faults, some of which he has endeavoured to repair in this edition, but as he has, in intention at least, done his full share in amusing the world, he trusts to its good nature for overlooking this attempt to please himself.

Paris, March, 1832.

Introduction.
[1851]

The following paragraphs were interpolated in the 1832 Introduction, immediately preceding the last paragraph when it was reprinted in the 1851 Putnam edition.

It may be well to say here, a little more explicitly, that there was no intention to describe with particular accuracy any real characters in this book. It has been often said, and in published statements, that the heroine of this book was drawn after a sister of the writer, who was killed by a fall from a horse now near half a century since. So ingenious is conjecture, that a personal resemblance has been discovered between the fictitious character and the deceased relative! It is scarcely possible to describe two females of the same class in life, who would be less alike, personally, than Elizabeth Temple and the sister of the author who met with the deplorable fate mentioned. In a word, they were as unlike in this respect, as in history, character, and fortunes.

Circumstances rendered this sister singularly dear to the author. After a lapse of half a century, he is writing this paragraph with a pain that would induce him to cancel it, were it not still more painful to have it believed that one whom he regarded with a reverence that surpassed the love of a brother, was converted by him into the heroine of a work of fiction.

The Pioneers;

or The Sources of The Susquehanna.

Chapter I.

"See, Winter comes, to rule the varied year,
Sullen and sad, with all his rising train;
Vapours, and clouds, and storms—"
                    Thomson, *The Seasons*, "Winter," 1–3.

Near the centre of the State of New-York lies an extensive district of country, whose surface is a succession of hills and dales, or, to speak with greater deference to geographical definitions, of mountains and valleys. It is among these hills that the Delaware takes its rise; and flowing from the limpid lakes and thousand springs of this region, the numerous sources of the Susquehanna meander through the valleys, until, uniting their streams, they form one of the proudest rivers of the United States. The mountains are generally arable to the tops, although instances are not wanting, where the sides are jutted with rocks, that aid greatly in giving to the country that romantic and picturesque character which it so eminently possesses. The vales are narrow, rich, and cultivated; with a stream uniformly winding through each. Beautiful and thriving villages are found interspersed along the margins of the small lakes, or situated at those points of the streams which are favourable to manufacturing; and neat and comfortable farms, with every indication of wealth about them, are scattered profusely through the vales, and even to the mountain tops. Roads diverge in every direction, from the even and graceful bottoms of the valleys, to the most rugged and intricate passes of the hills. Academies, and minor edifices of learning, meet the eye of the stranger, at every few miles, as he winds his way through this uneven territory; and places for the worship of God, abound with that frequency which characterises a moral and reflecting people, and with that variety of exterior and canonical government which flows from unfettered liberty of conscience. In short, the whole district is hourly exhibiting how much can be done, in even a rugged country, and with a severe climate, under the dominion of mild laws, and where every man feels a direct interest in the prosperity of a commonwealth, of which he knows himself to form a part. The expedients of the pioneers who first broke ground in the settlement of this country, are succeeded by the permanent improvements of the yeoman, who intends to leave his remains to moulder under the sod which he tills, or, perhaps, of the son, who, born in the land, piously wishes to linger around the grave of his father.——Only forty years* have passed since this territory was a wilderness.

Very soon after the establishment of the independence of the States by the peace of 1783, the enterprise of their citizens was directed to a development of the natural advantages of their widely extended dominions. Before the war of the revolution, the inhabited parts of the colony of New-York were limited to less than a tenth of its possessions. A narrow belt of country, extending for a short distance on either side of the Hudson, with a similar occupation of fifty miles on the banks of the Mohawk, together with the islands of Nassau and Staten, and a few insulated settlements on chosen land along the margins of streams, composed the country, which was then inhabited by less than two hundred thousand souls. Within the short period we have mentioned, the population has spread itself over five degrees of latitude and seven of longitude, and has swelled to a million and a half of inhabitants†, who are maintained in abundance, and can look forward to ages before the evil day must arrive, when their possessions shall become unequal to their wants.

Our tale begins in 1793, about seven years after the commencement of one of the earliest of those settlements, which have conduced to effect that magical change in the power and condition of the state, to which we have alluded.

It was near the setting of the sun, on a clear, cold day in December, when a sleigh was moving slowly up one of the mountains in the district we have described. The day had been fine for the season, and but two or three large clouds, whose colour seemed brightened by the light reflected from the mass of snow that covered the earth, floated in a sky of the purest blue. The road wound along the brow of a precipice, and on

* The book was written in 1821–22. [1832]

† The population of New York is now (1831) quite 2,000,000. [1832]

one side was upheld by a foundation of logs, piled one upon the other, while a narrow excavation in the mountain, in the opposite direction, had made a passage of sufficient width for the ordinary travelling of that day. But logs, excavation, and every thing that did not reach several feet above the earth, lay alike buried beneath the snow. A single track, barely wide enough to receive the sleigh*, denoted the route of the highway, and this was sunk nearly two feet below the surrounding surface. In the vale, which lay at a distance of several hundred feet lower, there was what in the language of the country was called a *clearing*, and all the usual improvements of a new settlement: these even extended up the hill to the point where the road turned short and ran across the level land, which lay on the summit of the mountain; but the summit itself remained in forest. There was a glittering in the atmosphere, as if it were filled with innumerable shining particles, and the noble bay horses that drew the sleigh were covered, in many parts, with a coat of hoar frost. The vapour from their nostrils was seen to issue like smoke; and every object in the view, as well as every arrangement of the travellers, denoted the depth of a winter in the mountains. The harness, which was of a deep dull black, differing from the glossy varnishing of the present day, was ornamented with enormous plates and buckles of brass, that shone like gold in those transient beams of the sun, which found their way obliquely through the tops of the trees. Huge saddles, studded with nails, and fitted with cloths that served as blankets to the shoulders of the animals, supported four high, square-topped turrets, through which the stout reins led from the mouths of the horses to the hands of the driver, who was a negro, of apparently twenty years of age. His face, which nature had coloured with a glistening black, was now mottled with the cold,

---

* Sleigh is the word used in every part of the United States to denote a traineau. It is of local use in the west of England, whence it is most probably derived by the Americans. The latter draw a distinction between a sled, or sledge, and a sleigh; the sleigh being shod with metal. Sleighs are also subdivided into two-horse and one-horse sleighs. Of the latter, there are the cutter, with thills so arranged as to permit the horse to travel in the side track; the "pung," or "tow-pung," which is driven with a pole, and the "jumper," a rude construction used for temporary purposes, in the new countries.

Many of the American sleighs are elegant, though the use of this mode of conveyance is much lessened with the melioration of the climate, consequent on the clearing of the forests. [1832]

and his large shining eyes filled with tears; a tribute to its
power, that the keen frosts of those regions always extracted
from one of his African origin. Still there was a smiling expression of good humour in his happy countenance, that was
created by the thoughts of home, and a Christmas fire-side,
with its Christmas frolics. The sleigh was one of those large,
comfortable, old-fashioned conveyances, which would admit a
whole family within its bosom, but which now contained only
two passengers besides the driver. The colour of its outside was
of a modest green, and that of its inside a fiery red. The latter
was intended to convey the idea of heat in that cold climate.
Large buffalo skins, trimmed around the edges with red cloth,
cut into festoons, covered the back of the sleigh, and were
spread over its bottom, and drawn up around the feet of the
travellers—one of whom was a man of middle age, and the
other a female, just entering upon womanhood. The former
was of a large stature; but the precautions he had taken to
guard against the cold, left but little of his person exposed to
view. A great-coat, that was abundantly ornamented by a profusion of furs, enveloped the whole of his figure, excepting the
head, which was covered with a cap of marten skins, lined with
morocco, the sides of which were made to fall, if necessary, and
were now drawn close over the ears, and fastened beneath his
chin with a black ribbon. The top of the cap was surmounted
with the tail of the animal whose skin had furnished the rest of
the materials, which fell back, not ungracefully, a few inches
behind the head. From beneath this masque were to be seen
part of a fine manly face, and particularly a pair of expressive,
large blue eyes, that promised extraordinary intellect, covert
humour, and great benevolence. The form of his companion
was literally hid beneath the garments she wore. There were
furs and silks peeping from under a large camblet cloak, with a
thick flannel lining, that, by its cut and size, was evidently intended for a masculine wearer. A huge hood of black silk, that
was quilted with down, concealed the whole of her head, except
at a small opening in front for breath, through which occasionally sparkled a pair of animated jet-black eyes.

Both the father and daughter (for such was the connexion
between the two travellers) were too much occupied with their
reflections to break a stillness, that received little or no interrup-

tion from the easy gliding of the sleigh, by the sound of their voices. The former was thinking of the wife that had held this their only child to her bosom, when, four years before, she had reluctantly consented to relinquish the society of her daughter, in order that the latter might enjoy the advantages of an education, which the city of New York could only offer at that period. A few months afterwards death had deprived him of the remaining companion of his solitude; but still he had enough of real regard for his child, not to bring her into the comparative wilderness in which he dwelt, until the full period had expired, to which he had limited her juvenile labours. The reflections of the daughter were less melancholy, and mingled with a pleased astonishment at the novel scenery she met at every turn in the road.

The mountain on which they were journeying was covered with pines, that rose without a branch some seventy or eighty feet, and which frequently doubled that height, by the addition of the tops. Through the innumerable vistas that opened beneath the lofty trees the eye could penetrate, until it was met by a distant inequality in the ground, or was stopped by a view of the summit of the mountain which lay on the opposite side of the valley to which they were hastening. The dark trunks of the trees, rose from the pure white of the snow, in regularly formed shafts, until, at a great height, their branches shot forth horizontal limbs, that were covered with the meager foliage of an evergreen, affording a melancholy contrast to the torpor of nature below. To the travellers there seemed to be no wind; but these pines waved majestically at their topmost boughs, sending forth a dull, plaintive sound, that was quite in consonance with the rest of the melancholy scene.

The sleigh had glided for some distance along the even surface, and the gaze of the female was bent in inquisitive, and, perhaps, timid glances, into the recesses of the forest, when a loud and continued howling was heard, pealing under the long arches of the woods, like the cry of a numerous pack of hounds. The instant the sound reached the ears of the gentleman, he cried aloud to the black—

"Hold up, Aggy; there is old Hector; I should know his bay among ten thousand. The Leather-stocking has put his hounds into the hills this clear day, and they have started their game.

There is a deer-track a few rods ahead;—and now, Bess, if thou canst muster courage enough to stand fire, I will give thee a saddle for thy Christmas dinner."

The black drew up, with a cheerful grin upon his chilled features, and began thrashing his arms together, in order to restore the circulation to his fingers, while the speaker stood erect, and, throwing aside his outer covering, stept from the sleigh upon a bank of snow, which sustained his weight without yielding.

In a few moments the speaker succeeded in extricating a double-barrelled fowling piece from amongst a multitude of trunks and bandboxes. After throwing aside the thick mittens which had encased his hands, that now appeared in a pair of leather gloves tipped with fur, he examined his priming, and was about to move forward, when the light bounding noise of an animal plunging through the woods was heard, and a fine buck darted into the path, a short distance ahead of him. The appearance of the animal was sudden, and his flight inconceivably rapid; but the traveller appeared to be too keen a sportsman to be disconcerted by either. As it came first into view he raised the fowling piece to his shoulder, and, with a practised eye and steady hand, drew a trigger. The deer dashed forward undaunted, and apparently unhurt. Without lowering his piece, the traveller turned its muzzle towards his victim, and fired again. Neither discharge, however, seemed to have taken effect.

The whole scene had passed with a rapidity that confused the female, who was unconsciously rejoicing in the escape of the buck, as he rather darted like a meteor, than ran across the road, when a sharp, quick sound struck her ear, quite different from the full, round reports of her father's gun, but still sufficiently distinct to be known as the concussion produced by fire-arms. At the same instant that she heard this unexpected report, the buck sprang from the snow, to a great height in the air, and directly a second discharge, similar in sound to the first, followed, when the animal came to the earth, falling headlong, and rolling over on the crust with its own velocity. A loud shout was given by the unseen marksman, and a couple of men instantly appeared from behind the trunks of two of the pines, where they had evidently placed themselves in expectation of the passage of the deer.

"Ha! Natty, had I known you were in ambush, I should not have fired," cried the traveller, moving towards the spot where the deer lay—near to which he was followed by the delighted black, with his sleigh; "but the sound of old Hector was too exhilarating to be quiet; though I hardly think I struck him either."

"No—no—Judge," returned the hunter, with an inward chuckle, and with that look of exultation, that indicates a consciousness of superior skill; "you burnt your powder, only to warm your nose this cold evening. Did ye think to stop a full grown buck, with Hector and the slut open upon him, within sound, with that pop-gun in your hand? There's plenty of pheasants amongst the swamps; and the snow birds are flying round your own door, where you may feed them with crumbs, and shoot them at pleasure, any day; but if you're for a buck, or a little bear's meat, Judge, you'll have to take the long rifle, with a greased wadding, or you'll waste more powder than you'll fill stomachs, I'm thinking."

As the speaker concluded he drew his bare hand across the bottom of his nose, and again opened his enormous mouth with a kind of inward laugh.

"The gun scatters well, Natty, and it has killed a deer before now," said the traveller, smiling good humouredly. "One barrel was charged with buck shot; but the other was loaded for birds only.—Here are two hurts; one through the neck, and the other directly through the heart. It is by no means certain, Natty, but I gave him one of the two."

"Let who will kill him," said the hunter, rather surlily, "I suppose the cretur is to be eaten." So saying, he drew a large knife from a leathern sheath, which was stuck through his girdle or sash, and cut the throat of the animal. "If there is two balls through the deer, I would ask if there wasn't two rifles fired—besides, who ever saw sich a ragged hole from a smooth-bore, as this through the neck?—and you will own yourself, Judge, that the buck fell at the last shot, which was sent from a truer and a younger hand, than your'n or mine 'ither; but for my part, although I am a poor man, I can live without the venison, but I don't love to give up my lawful dues in a free country.—

Though, for the matter of that, might often makes right here, as well as in the old country, for what I can see."

An air of sullen dissatisfaction pervaded the manner of the hunter during the whole of this speech; yet he thought it prudent to utter the close of the sentence in such an under tone, as to leave nothing audible but the grumbling sounds of his voice.

"Nay, Natty," rejoined the traveller, with undisturbed good humour, "it is for the honour that I contend. A few dollars will pay for the venison; but what will requite me for the lost honour of a buck's tail in my cap? Think, Natty, how I should triumph over that quizzing dog, Dick Jones, who has failed seven times already this season, and has only brought in one wood-chuck and a few grey squirrels."

"Ah! the game is becoming hard to find, indeed, Judge, with your clearings and betterments," said the old hunter, with a kind of compelled resignation. "The time has been, when I have shot thirteen deer, without counting the fa'ns, standing in the door of my own hut;—and for bear's meat, if one wanted a ham or so, he had only to watch a-nights, and he could shoot one by moonlight, through the cracks of the logs; no fear of his over-sleeping himself, n'ither, for the howling of the wolves was sartin to keep his eyes open. There's old Hector,"—patting with affection a tall hound, of black and yellow spots, with white belly and legs, that just then came in on the scent, accompanied by the slut he had mentioned; "see where the wolves bit his throat, the night I druve them from the venison that was smoking on the chimbly top—that dog is more to be trusted than many a Christian man; for he never forgets a friend, and loves the hand that gives him bread."

There was a peculiarity in the manner of the hunter, that attracted the notice of the young female, who had been a close and interested observer of his appearance and equipments, from the moment he came into view. He was tall, and so meager as to make him seem above even the six feet that he actually stood in his stockings. On his head, which was thinly covered with lank, sandy hair, he wore a cap made of fox-skin, resembling in shape the one we have already described, although much inferior in finish and ornaments. His face was skinny, and thin almost to emaciation; but yet it bore no signs of disease;—on the contrary, it had every indication of the most robust and enduring health. The cold and the exposure had, together, given it a colour of uniform red; his grey eyes were glancing under a pair of shaggy brows, that overhung them in long hairs of grey mingled with their natural hue; his scraggy neck was bare, and burnt to the same tint with his face; though a small part of a shirt collar, made of the country check, was to be seen above the over-dress he wore. A kind of coat, made of dressed deer-skin, with the hair on, was belted close to his lank body, by a girdle of coloured worsted. On his feet were deer-skin moccasins, ornamented with porcupines' quills, after the manner of the Indians, and his limbs were guarded with long leggings of the same material as the moccasins, which, gartering over the knees of his tarnished buck-skin breeches, had obtained for him, among the settlers, the nick name of Leatherstocking. Over his left shoulder was slung a belt of deer-skin, from which depended an enormous ox horn, so thinly scraped, as to discover the powder it contained. The larger end was fitted ingeniously and securely with a wooden bottom, and the other was stopped tight by a little plug. A leathern pouch hung before him, from which, as he concluded his last speech, he took a small measure, and, filling it accurately with powder, he commenced re-loading the rifle, which, as its butt rested on the snow before him, reached nearly to the top of his fox-skin cap.

The traveller had been closely examining the wounds during these movements, and now, without heeding the ill humour of the hunter's manner, he exclaimed—

"I would fain establish a right, Natty, to the honour of this death; and surely if the hit in the neck be mine, it is enough; for the shot in the heart was unnecessary—what we call an act of supererogation, Leather-stocking."

"You may call it by what larned name you please, Judge," said the hunter, throwing his rifle across his left arm, and knocking up a brass lid in the breech, from which he took a small piece of greased leather, and wrapping a ball in it, forced them down by main strength on the powder, where he continued to pound them while speaking. "It's far easier to call names, than to shoot a buck on the spring; but the cretur come by his end from a younger hand than 'ither your'n or mine, as I said before."

"What say you, my friend," cried the traveller, turning pleasantly to Natty's companion; "shall we toss up this dollar for the honour, and you keep the silver if you lose—what say you, friend?"

"That I killed the deer," answered the young man, with a little haughtiness, as he leaned on another long rifle, similar to that of Natty's.

"Here are two to one, indeed," replied the Judge, with a smile; "I am out-voted—over-ruled, as we say on the bench. There is Aggy, he can't vote, being a slave; and Bess is a minor—so I must even make the best of it. But you'll sell me the venison; and the deuce is in it, but I make a good story about its death."

"The meat is none of mine to sell," said Leather-stocking, adopting a little of his companion's hauteur; "for my part, I have known animals travel days with shots in the neck, and I'm none of them who'll rob a man of his rightful dues."

"You are tenacious of your rights, this cold evening, Natty," returned the Judge, with unconquerable good nature; "but what say you, young man, will three dollars pay you for the buck?"

"First let us determine the question of right to the satisfaction of us both," said the youth, firmly but respectfully, and with a pronunciation and language vastly superior to his appearance; "with how many shot did you load your gun?"

"With five, sir," said the Judge, a little struck with the other's manner; "are they not enough to slay a buck like this?"

"One would do it; but," moving to the tree from behind which he had appeared, "you know, sir, you fired in this direction—here are four of the bullets in the tree."

The Judge examined the fresh marks in the bark of the pine, and, shaking his head, said, with a laugh—

"You are making out the case against yourself, my young advocate—where is the fifth?"

"Here," said the youth, throwing aside the rough over-coat that he wore, and exhibiting a hole in his under garment, through which large drops of blood were oozing.

"Good God!" exclaimed the Judge, with horror; "have I been trifling here about an empty distinction, and a fellow creature suffering from my hands without a murmur? But hasten—quick—get into my sleigh—it is but a mile to the village, where surgical aid can be obtained;—all shall be done at my expence, and thou shalt live with me until thy wound is healed—aye, and for ever afterwards."

"I thank you for your good intention, but I must decline your offer. I have a friend who would be uneasy were he to hear that I am hurt and away from him. The injury is but slight, and the bullet has missed the bones; but I believe, sir, you will now admit my title to the venison."

"Admit it!" repeated the agitated Judge; "I here give thee a right to shoot deer, or bears, or any thing thou pleasest in my woods, forever. Leather-stocking is the only other man that I have granted the same privilege to; and the time is coming when it will be of value. But I buy your deer—here, this bill will pay thee, both for thy shot and my own."

The old hunter gathered his tall person up into an air of pride, during this dialogue, but he waited until the other had done speaking.

"There's them living who say, that Nathaniel Bumppo's right to shoot on these hills, is of older date than Marmaduke Temple's right to forbid him," he said. "But if there's a law about it at all, though who ever heard of a law, that a man should'nt kill deer where he pleased!—but if there is a law at all, it should be to keep people from the use of smooth-bores. A body never knows where his lead will fly, when he pulls the trigger of one of them uncertain fire-arms."

Without attending to the soliloquy of Natty, the youth bowed his head silently to the offer of the bank note, and replied—

"Excuse me; I have need of the venison."

"But this will buy you many deer," said the Judge; "take it I entreat you," and lowering his voice to a whisper, he added—"it is for a hundred dollars."

For an instant only, the youth seemed to hesitate, and then, blushing even through the high colour that the cold had given to his cheeks, as if with inward shame at his own weakness, he again declined the offer.

During this scene the female arose, and, regardless of the cold air, she threw back the hood which concealed her features, and now spoke, with great earnestness——

"Surely, surely—young man—sir—you would not pain my

father so much, as to have him think that he leaves a fellow creature in this wilderness, whom his own hand has injured. I entreat you will go with us, and receive medical aid."

Whether his wound became more painful, or there was something irresistible in the voice and manner of the fair pleader for her father's feelings, we know not, but the distance of the young man's manner was sensibly softened by this appeal, and he stood, in apparent doubt, as if reluctant to comply with, and yet unwilling to refuse her request. The Judge, for such being his office, must, in future, be his title, watched, with no little interest, the display of this singular contention in the feelings of the youth, and advancing, kindly took his hand, and, as he pulled him gently towards the sleigh, urged him to enter it.

"There is no human aid nearer than Templeton," he said, "and the hut of Natty is full three miles from this;—come—come, my young friend, go with us, and let the new doctor look to this shoulder of thine. Here is Natty will take the tidings of thy welfare to thy friend; and should'st thou require it, thou shalt return home in the morning."

The young man succeeded in extricating his hand from the warm grasp of the Judge, but he continued to gaze on the face of the female, who, regardless of the cold, was still standing with her fine features exposed, which expressed feelings that eloquently seconded the request of her father. Leatherstocking stood, in the mean time, leaning upon his long rifle, with his head turned a little to one side, as if engaged in sagacious musing; when, having apparently satisfied his doubts, by revolving the subject in his mind, he broke silence——

"It may be best to go, lad, after all; for if the shot hangs under the skin, my hand is getting too old to be cutting into human flesh, as I once used to could. Though some thirty years agone, in the old war, when I was out under Sir William, I travelled seventy miles alone in the howling wilderness, with a rifle bullet in my thigh, and then cut it out with my own jack-knife. Old Indian John knows the time well. I met him with a party of the Delawares, on the trail of the Iroquois, who had been down and taken five scalps on the Schoharie. But I made a mark on the red-skin that I'll warrant he carried to his grave. I took him on his posterum, saving the lady's presence, as he got up from the amboosh, and rattled three buck shot into his naked hide, so close, that you might have laid a broad joe upon them all—" here Natty stretched out his long neck, and straightened his body, as he opened his mouth, which exposed a single tusk of yellow bone, while his eyes, his face, even his whole frame, seemed to laugh, although no sound was emitted, except a kind of thick hissing, as he inhaled his breath in quavers. "I had lost my bullet mould in crossing the Oneida outlet, and had to make shift with the buck shot; but the rifle was true, and did'nt scatter like your two legged thing there, Judge, which don't do, I find, to hunt in company with."

Natty's apology to the delicacy of the young lady was unnecessary, for, while he was speaking, she was too much employed in helping her father to remove certain articles of baggage to hear him. Unable to resist the kind urgency of the travellers any longer, the youth, though still with an unaccountable reluctance, suffered himself to be persuaded to enter the sleigh. The black with the aid of his master threw the buck across the baggage, and entering the vehicle themselves, the Judge invited the hunter to do so likewise.

"No—no—" said the old man, shaking his head; "I have work to do at home this Christmas eve—drive on with the boy, and let your doctor look to the shoulder; though if he will only cut out the shot, I have yarbs that will heal the wound quicker than all his foreign 'intments." He turned and was about to move off, when, suddenly recollecting himself, he again faced the party, and added—"If you see any thing of Indian John about the foot of the lake, you had better take him with you, and let him lend the doctor a hand; for, old as he is, he is curous at cuts and bruises, and it's likelier than not he'll be in with brooms to sweep your Christmas ha'arths."

"Stop—stop," cried the youth, catching the arm of the black as he prepared to urge his horses forward; "Natty—you need say nothing of the shot, nor of where I am going—remember, Natty, as you love me."

"Trust old Leather-stocking," returned the hunter, significantly; "he has'nt lived fifty years in the wilderness, and not larnt from the savages how to hold his tongue—trust to me, lad; and remember old Indian John."

"And, Natty," said the youth, eagerly, still holding the black by the arm, "I will just get the shot extracted, and bring you up, to-night, a quarter of the buck, for the Christmas dinner."

He was interrupted by the hunter, who held up his finger with an expressive gesture for silence. He then moved softly along the margin of the road, keeping his eyes steadfastly fixed on the branches of a pine. When he had obtained such a position as he wished, he stopped, and cocking his rifle, threw one leg far behind him, and stretching his left arm to its utmost extent along the barrel of his piece, he began slowly to raise its muzzle in a line with the straight trunk of the tree. The eyes of the group in the sleigh naturally preceded the movement of the rifle, and they soon discovered the object of Natty's aim. On a small dead branch of the pine, which, at the distance of seventy feet from the ground, shot out horizontally, immediately beneath the living members of the tree, sat a bird, that in the vulgar language of the country, was indiscriminately called a pheasant or a partridge. In size, it was but little smaller than a common barn-yard fowl. The baying of the dogs, and the conversation that had passed near the root of the tree on which it was perched, had alarmed the bird, which was now drawn up near the body of the pine, with a head and neck so erect, as to form nearly a straight line with its legs. As soon as the rifle bore on the victim, Natty drew his trigger, and the partridge fell from its height with a force that buried it in the snow.

"Lie down, you old villain," exclaimed Leather-stocking, shaking his ramrod at Hector as he bounded towards the foot of the tree, "lie down, I say." The dog obeyed, and Natty proceeded with great rapidity, though with the nicest accuracy, to reload his piece. When this was ended, he took up his game, and showing it to the party without a head, he cried—"Here is a tit bit for an old man's Christmas—never mind the venison, boy, and remember Indian John; his yarbs are better than all the foreign 'intments. Here, Judge," holding up the bird again, "do you think a smooth-bore would pick game off their roost, and not ruffle a feather?" The old man gave another of his remarkable laughs, which partook so largely of exultation, mirth, and irony, and shaking his head, he turned, with his rifle at a trail, and moved into the forest with steps that were between a walk and a trot. At each movement he made, his body lowered several inches, his knees yielding with an inclination inward; but as the sleigh turned at a bend in the road, the youth cast his eyes in quest of his old companion, and he saw that he was already nearly concealed by the trunks of the trees, while his dogs were following quietly in his footsteps, occasionally scenting the deer track, that they seemed to know instinctively was now of no farther use to them. Another jerk was given to the sleigh, and Leather-stocking was hid from view.

Chapter II.

"All places that the eye of Heaven visits,
Are to a wise man ports and happy havens:—
Think not the king did banish thee;
But thou the king.—"

Richard II, I.iii.275–76, 279–80.

AN ancestor of Marmaduke Temple had, about one hundred and twenty years before the commencement of our tale, come to the colony of Pennsylvania, a friend and co-religionist of its great patron. Old Marmaduke, for this formidable prenomen was a kind of appellative to the race, brought with him to that asylum of the persecuted, an abundance of the good things of this life. He became the master of many thousands of acres of uninhabited territory, and the supporter of many a score of dependents. He lived greatly respected for his piety, and not a little distinguished as a sectary; was entrusted by his associates with many important political stations; and died, just in time to escape the knowledge of his own poverty. It was his lot to share the fortune of most of those, who brought wealth with them into the new settlements of the middle colonies.

The consequence of an emigrant into these provinces was generally to be ascertained by the number of his white servants or dependents, and the nature of the public situations that he held. Taking this rule as a guide, the ancestor of our Judge must have been a man of no little note.

It is, however, a subject of curious inquiry at the present day, to look into the brief records of that early period, and observe how regular, and with few exceptions how inevitable, were the gradations, on the one hand, of the masters to poverty, and on the other, of their servants to wealth. Accustomed to ease, and unequal to the struggles incident to an infant society, the affluent emigrant was barely enabled to maintain his own rank, by the weight of his personal superiority and acquirements; but the moment that his head was laid in the grave, his indolent, and comparatively uneducated offspring, were compelled to yield precedency to the more active energies of a class, whose exertions had been stimulated by necessity. This is a very common course of things, even in the present state of the Union; but it was peculiarly the fortunes of the two extremes of society, in the peaceful and unenterprising colonies of Pennsylvania and New-Jersey.

The posterity of Marmaduke did not escape the common lot of those, who depend rather on their hereditary possessions than on their own powers; and in the third generation, they had descended to a point, below which, in this happy country, it is barely possible for honesty, intellect, and sobriety, to fall. The same pride of family, that had, by its self-satisfied indolence, conduced to aid their fall, now became a principle to stimulate them to endeavour to rise again. The feeling, from being morbid, was changed to a healthful and active desire to emulate the character, the condition, and, peradventure, the wealth, of their ancestors also. It was the father of our new acquaintance, the Judge, who first began to re-ascend in the scale of society; and in this undertaking he was not a little assisted by a marriage, which aided in furnishing the means of educating his only son, in a rather better manner than the low state of the common schools in Pennsylvania could promise; or than had been the practice in the family, for the two or three preceding generations.

At the school where the reviving prosperity of his father was enabled to maintain him, young Marmaduke formed an intimacy with a youth, whose years were about equal to his own. This was a fortunate connexion for our Judge, and paved the way to most of his future elevation in life.

There was not only great wealth, but high court interest, amongst the connexions of Edward Effingham. They were one of the few families, then resident in the colonies, who thought it a degradation to its members, to descend to the pursuits of commerce; and who never emerged from the privacy of domestic life, unless to preside in the councils of the colony, or to bear arms in her defence. The latter had, from youth, been the only employment of Edward's father. Military rank, under the crown of Great Britain, was attained with much longer probation, and by much more toilsome services, sixty years ago, than at the present time. Years were passed, without murmuring, in the subordinate grades of the service; and those soldiers who were stationed in the colonies, felt, when they obtained the command of a company, that they were entitled to receive the greatest deference from the peaceful occupants of the soil. Any one of our readers, who has occasion to cross the Niagara, may easily observe, not only the self-importance, but the real estimation enjoyed by the humblest representative of the Crown, even in that polar region of royal sunshine. Such, and at no very distant period, was the respect paid to the military in these States, where now, happily, no symbol of war is ever seen, unless at the free and fearless voice of their people. When therefore, the father of Marmaduke's friend, after forty years' service, retired with the rank of Major, maintaining in his domestic establishment a comparative splendour, he became a man of the first consideration in his native colony—which was that of New-York. He had served with fidelity and courage, and, having been, according to the custom of the provinces, entrusted with commands much superior to those to which he was entitled by rank, with reputation also. When Major Effingham yielded to the claims of age, he retired with dignity, refusing his half-pay or any other compensation for services, that he felt he could no longer perform. The ministry proffered various civil offices, which yielded not only honour but profit; but he declined them all, with the chivalrous independence and loyalty, that had marked his character through life. The veteran soon caused this act of patriotic disinterestedness, to be followed by another of private munificence, that, however little it accorded with prudence, was in perfect conformity with the simple integrity of his own views. The friend of Marmaduke was his only child; and to this son, on his marriage with a lady to whom the father was particularly partial, the Major gave a complete conveyance of his whole estate, consisting of moneys in the funds, a town and country residence, sundry valuable farms in the old parts of the colony, and large tracts of wild land in the new;—in this manner throwing himself upon the filial piety of his child for his own future maintenance. Major Effingham, in declining the liberal offers of the British ministry, had subjected himself to the suspicion of having attained his dotage, by all those who throng the avenues to court patronage, even in the remotest corners of that vast empire; but, when he thus voluntarily stript himself of his great personal wealth, the remainder of the community seemed instinctively to adopt the conclusion also, that he had reached a second childhood. This may explain the fact of his importance rapidly declining; and, if privacy was his object, the veteran had soon a free indulgence of his wishes. Whatever views the world might entertain of this act of the Major, to himself and to his child, it seemed no more than a natural gift by a father, of those immunities which he could no longer enjoy or improve, to a son, who was formed, both by nature and education, to do both. The younger Effingham did not object to the amount of the donation; for he felt, that while his parent reserved a moral controul over his actions, he was relieving himself from a fatiguing burthen; such, indeed, was the confidence existing between them, that to neither did it seem any thing more, than removing money from one pocket to another.

One of the first acts of the young man, on coming into possession of his wealth, was to seek his early friend, with a view to offer any assistance, that it was now in his power to bestow.

The death of Marmaduke's father, and the consequent division of his small estate, rendered such an offer extremely acceptable to the young Pennsylvanian: he felt his own powers, and saw, not only the excellencies, but the foibles, in the character of his friend. Effingham was by nature indolent, confiding, and at times impetuous and indiscreet; but Marmaduke was uniformly equable, penetrating, and full of activity and enterprise. To the latter, therefore, the assistance, or rather connexion, that was proffered to him, seemed to produce a mutual advantage. It was cheerfully accepted, and the arrangement of its conditions was easily completed. A mercantile house was established in the metropolis of Pennsylvania, with the avails of Mr. Effingham's personal property; all, or nearly all, of which was put into the possession of Temple, who was the only ostensible proprietor in the concern, while in secret, the other was entitled to an equal participation in the profits. This connexion was thus kept private for two reasons; one of which, in the freedom of their intercourse, was frankly avowed to Marmaduke, while the other continued profoundly hid in the bosom of his friend. The last was nothing more than pride. To the descendant of a line of soldiers, commerce, even in that indirect manner, seemed a degrading pursuit;—but an insuperable obstacle to the disclosure existed in the prejudices of his father.

We have already said that Major Effingham had served as a soldier, with reputation. On one occasion, while in command on the western frontier of Pennsylvania, against a league of the French and Indians, not only his glory, but the safety of himself and his troops were jeoparded, by the peaceful policy of that colony. To the soldier, this was an unpardonable offence. He was fighting in their defence—he knew that the mild principles of this little nation of practical christians, would be disregarded by their subtle and malignant enemies; and he felt the injury the more deeply, because he saw that the avowed object of the colonists, in withholding their succours, would only have a tendency to expose his command, without preserving the peace. The soldier succeeded, after a desperate conflict, in extricating himself with a handful of his men, from their murderous enemy; but he never forgave the people who had exposed him to a danger, which they left him to combat alone. It was in vain to tell him, that they had no agency in his being placed on their frontier at all; it was evidently for their benefit that he had been so placed, and it was their "religious duty," so the Major always expressed it, "it was their religious duty to have supported him."

At no time was the old soldier an admirer of the peaceful disciples of Fox. Their disciplined habits, both of mind and body, had endowed them with great physical perfection, and the eye of the veteran was apt to scan the fair proportions and athletic frames of the colonists, with a look that seemed to utter volumes of contempt for their moral imbecility. He was also a little addicted to the expression of a belief, that, where there was so great an observance of the externals of religion, there could not be much of the substance.—It is not our task to explain what is, or what ought to be, the substance of christianity, but merely to record in this place the opinions of Major Effingham.

Knowing the sentiments of the father, in relation to this people, it was no wonder that the son hesitated to avow his connexion with, nay, even his dependence on the integrity of, a quaker.

It has been said that Marmaduke deduced his origin from the

cotemporaries and friends of Penn. His father had married without the pale of the church to which he belonged, and had, in this manner, forfeited some of the privileges which would have descended to his offspring. Still, as young Marmaduke was educated in a colony and society, where even the ordinary intercourse between friends, was tinctured with the aspect of this mild religion, his habits and language were somewhat marked by its peculiarities. His own marriage at a future day with a lady without, not only the pale, but the influence of this sect of religionists, had a tendency, it is true, to weaken his early impressions; still he retained them, in some degree, to the hour of his death, and was observed uniformly, when much interested or agitated, to speak in the language of his youth——But this is anticipating our tale.

When Marmaduke first became the partner of young Effingham, he was quite the quaker in externals; and it was too dangerous an experiment for the son to think of encountering the prejudices of the father on this subject. The connexion, therefore, remained a profound secret to all but those who were interested in it.

For a few years, Marmaduke directed the commercial operations of his house with a prudence and sagacity, that afforded rich returns. He married the lady we have mentioned, who was the mother of Elizabeth, and the visits of his friend were becoming more frequent. There was a speedy prospect of removing the veil from their intercourse, as its advantages became each hour more apparent to Mr. Effingham, when the troubles that preceded the war of the revolution, extended themselves to an alarming degree.

Educated in the most dependent loyalty, Mr. Effingham had, from the commencement of the disputes between the colonists and the crown, warmly maintained, what he believed to be, the just prerogatives of his prince; while, on the other hand, the clear head and independent mind of Temple had induced him to espouse the cause of the people. Both might have been influenced by early impressions; for, if the son of the loyal and gallant soldier bowed in implicit obedience to the will of his sovereign, the descendant of the persecuted follower of Penn, looked back, with a little bitterness, to the unmerited wrongs that had been heaped upon his ancestors.

This difference in opinion had long been a subject of amicable dispute between them, but, latterly, the contest was getting to be too important to admit of trivial discussions on the part of Marmaduke, whose acute discernment was already catching faint glimmerings of the important events that were in embryo. The sparks of dissension soon kindled into a blaze; and the colonies, or, rather, as they quickly declared themselves, THE STATES, became a scene of strife and bloodshed for years.

A short time before the battle of Lexington, Mr. Effingham, already a widower, transmitted to Marmaduke for safe keeping, all his valuable effects and papers; and left the colony without his father. The war had, however, scarcely commenced in earnest, when he re-appeared in New-York, wearing the livery of his king, and in a short time, he took the field at the head of a provincial corps. In the mean time, Marmaduke had completely committed himself in the cause, as it was then called, of the rebellion: of course all intercourse between the friends ceased—on the part of Col. Effingham, it was unsought, and on that of Marmaduke, there was a cautious reserve. It soon became necessary for the latter to abandon the capital of Philadelphia; but he had taken the precaution to remove the whole of his effects, beyond the reach of the royal forces, including the papers of his friend also. There he continued serving his country during the struggle, in various civil capacities, and always with dignity and usefulness. While, however, he discharged his functions with credit and fidelity, Marmaduke never seemed to lose sight of his own interests; for, when the estates of the adherents of the crown fell under the hammer, by the acts of confiscation, he appeared in New-York, and became the purchaser of extensive possessions, at, comparatively, low prices.

It is true that Marmaduke, by thus purchasing estates that had been wrested by violence from others, rendered himself obnoxious to the censures of that sect, which, at the same time that it discards its children from a full participation in the family union, seems ever unwilling to abandon them entirely to the world. But either his success, or the frequency of the transgression in others, soon wiped off this slight stain from his character; and although there were a few, who, dissatisfied with their own fortunes, or conscious of their own demerits, would

make dark hints concerning the sudden prosperity of the un-
portioned quaker, yet his services, and possibly his wealth, soon
drove the recollection of these vague conjectures from men's
minds.

When the war ended, and the independence of the states was
acknowledged, Mr. Temple turned his attention from the pursuit of commerce, which was then fluctuating and uncertain, to
the settlement of those tracts of land which he had purchased.
Aided by a good deal of money, and directed by the suggestions
of a strong and practical reason, his enterprise throve to a degree, that the climate and rugged face of the country which he
selected, would seem to forbid. His property increased in a ten-
fold ratio, and he was already ranked among the most wealthy
and important of his countrymen. To inherit this wealth he had
but one child—the daughter whom we have introduced to the
reader, and whom he was now conveying from school, to preside over a household that had too long wanted a mistress.

When the district in which his estates lay, had become
sufficiently populous to be set off as a county, Mr. Temple had,
according to the custom of the new settlements, been selected to
fill its highest judicial station. This might make a Templar
smile, but in addition to the apology of necessity, there is ever a
dignity in talents and experience, that is commonly sufficient, in
any station, for the protection of its possessor; and Marmaduke, more fortunate in his native clearness of mind, than
the judge of king Charles, not only decided right, but was generally able to give a very good reason for it. At all events, such
was the universal practice of the country and the times; and
Judge Temple, so far from ranking among the lowest of his
judicial cotemporaries in the courts of the new counties, felt
himself, and was unanimously acknowledged to be, among the
first.

We shall here close this brief explanation of the history and
character of some of our personages, leaving them in future to
speak and act for themselves.

Chapter III.

"All that thou see'st, is nature's handy work:
Those rocks, that upward throw their mossy brows,
Like castled pinnacles of elder times!
These venerable stems, that slowly rock
Their tow'ring branches in the wintry gale!
That field of frost, which glitters in the sun,
Mocking the whiteness of a marble breast!—
Yet man can mar such works with his rude taste,
Like some sad spoiler of a virgin's fame." *Duo.*

SOME little time elapsed ere Marmaduke Temple was sufficiently recovered from his agitation, to scan the person of his new companion. He now observed, that he was a youth of some two or three and twenty years of age; and rather above the middle height. Further observation was prevented by the rough over-coat, which was belted close to his form by a worsted sash, much like the one worn by the old hunter. The eyes of the Judge, after resting a moment on the figure of the stranger, were raised to a scrutiny of his countenance. There had been a look of care, visible in the features of the youth, when he first entered the sleigh, that had not only attracted the notice of Elizabeth, but which she had been much puzzled to interpret. His anxiety seemed the strongest when he was enjoining his old companion to secrecy; and even when he had decided, and was, rather passively, suffering himself to be conveyed to the village, the expression of his eyes by no means indicated any great degree of self-satisfaction at the step. But the lines of an uncommonly prepossessing countenance were gradually becoming composed; and he now sat silent, and apparently musing. The Judge gazed at him for some time with earnestness, and then smiling, as if at his own forgetfulness, he said—

"I believe, my young friend, that terror has driven you from my recollection—your face is very familiar, and yet for the honour of a score of bucks'-tails in my cap, I could not tell your name."

"I came into the county but three weeks since," returned the youth coldly, "and, I understand you have been absent twice that time."

"It will be five to-morrow. Yet your face is one that I have seen; though it would not be strange, such has been my affright, should I see thee in thy winding-sheet, walking by my bedside, to-night. What say'st thou, Bess? Am I compos mentis or not?—Fit to charge a grand jury, or, what is just now of more pressing necessity, able to do the honours of a Christmas-eve, in the hall of Templeton?"

"More able to do either, my dear father," said a playful voice from under the ample enclosures of the hood, "than to kill deer with a smooth-bore." A short pause followed; and the same voice, but in a different accent continued—"We shall have good reasons for our thanksgiving to-night, on more accounts than one."

The horses soon reached a point, where they seemed to know by instinct that the journey was nearly ended, and, bearing on the bits, as they tossed their heads, they rapidly drew the sleigh over the level land, which lay on the top of the mountain, and soon came to the point where the road descended suddenly, but circuitously, into the valley.

The Judge was roused from his reflections, when he saw the four columns of smoke, which floated above his own chimneys. As house, village, and valley burst on his sight, he exclaimed cheerfully to his daughter—

"See, Bess, there is thy resting-place for life! And thine too, young man, if thou wilt consent to dwell with us."

The eyes of his auditors involuntarily met; and if the colour, that gathered over the face of Elizabeth, was contradicted by the cold expression of her eye, the ambiguous smile that again played about the lips of the stranger, seemed equally to deny the probability of his consenting to form one of this family group. The scene was one, however, which might easily warm a heart less given to philanthropy than that of Marmaduke Temple.

The side of the mountain, on which our travellers were journeying, though not absolutely perpendicular, was so steep as to render great care necessary in descending the rude and narrow path, which, in that early day, wound along the precipices. The Negro reined in his impatient steeds, and time was given

Elizabeth to dwell on a scene which was so rapidly altering under the hands of man, that it only resembled, in its outlines, the picture she had so often studied, with delight, in childhood. Immediately beneath them lay a seeming plain, glittering, without inequality, and buried in mountains. The latter were precipitous, especially on the side of the plain, and chiefly in forest. Here and there the hills fell away in long, low points, and broke the sameness of the outline; or setting to the long and wide field of snow, which, without house, tree, fence, or any other fixture, resembled so much spotless cloud settled to the earth. A few dark and moving spots were, however, visible on the even surface, which the eye of Elizabeth knew to be so many sleighs going their several ways, to or from the village. On the western border of the plain, the mountains, though equally high, were less precipitous, and as they receded, opened into irregular valleys and glens, or were formed into terraces and hollows that admitted of cultivation. Although the evergreens still held dominion over many of the hills that rose on this side of the valley, yet the undulating outlines of the distant mountains, covered with forests of beech and maple, gave a relief to the eye, and the promise of a kinder soil. Occasionally, spots of white were discoverable amidst the forests of the opposite hills, which announced, by the smoke that curled over the tops of the trees, the habitations of man, and the commencement of agriculture. These spots were, sometimes, by the aid of united labour, enlarged into what were called settlements; but more frequently were small and insulated; though so rapid were the changes, and so persevering the labors of those who had cast their fortunes on the success of the enterprise, that it was not difficult for the imagination of Elizabeth to conceive they were enlarging under her eye, while she was gazing, in mute wonder, at the alterations that a few short years had made in the aspect of the country. The points on the western side of this remarkable plain, on which no plant had taken root, were both larger and more numerous than those on its eastern, and one in particular thrust itself forward in such a manner, as to form beautifully curved bays of snow on either side. On its extreme end an oak stretched forward, as if to overshadow, with its branches, a spot which its roots were forbidden to enter. It had released itself from the thraldom, that a growth of centuries had imposed on the branches of the surrounding forest trees, and threw its gnarled and fantastic arms abroad, in the wildness of liberty. A dark spot of a few acres in extent at the southern extremity of this beautiful flat, and immediately under the feet of our travellers, alone showed, by its rippling surface, and the vapors which exhaled from it, that what at first might seem a plain, was one of the mountain lakes, locked in the frosts of winter. A narrow current rushed impetuously from its bosom at the open place we have mentioned, and was to be traced, for miles, as it wound its way towards the south through the real valley, by its borders of hemlock and pine, and by the vapour which arose from its warmer surface into the chill atmosphere of the hills. The banks of this lovely basin, at its outlet, or southern end, were steep but not high, and in that direction the land continued, far as the eye could reach, a narrow but graceful valley, along which the settlers had scattered their humble habitations, with a profusion that bespoke the quality of the soil, and the comparative facilities of intercourse. Immediately on the bank of the lake and at its foot, stood the village of Templeton. It consisted of some fifty buildings, including those of every description, chiefly built of wood, and which, in their architecture, bore no great marks of taste, but which also, by the unfinished appearance of most of the dwellings, indicated the hasty manner of their construction. To the eye, they presented a variety of colours. A few were white in both front and rear, but more bore that expensive color on their fronts only, while their economical but ambitious owners had covered the remaining sides of the edifices, with a dingy red. One or two were slowly assuming the russet of age; while the uncovered beams that were to be seen through the broken windows of their second stories, showed, that either the taste, or the vanity of their proprietors, had led them to undertake a task, which they were unable to accomplish. The whole were grouped in a manner that aped the streets of a city, and were evidently so arranged, by the directions of one, who looked to the wants of posterity, rather than to the convenience of the present incumbents. Some three or four of the better sort of buildings, in addition to the uniformity of their colour, were fitted with green blinds, which, at that season at least, were rather strangely contrasted to the chill aspect of the lake, the mountains, the forests, and the wide fields of snow. Before the doors of these pretending dwellings, were placed a few saplings either without branches, or possessing only the feeble shoots of one or two summers' growth, that looked not unlike tall grenadiers on post, near the threshold of princes. In truth, the occupants of these favoured habitations were the nobles of Templeton, as Marmaduke was its king. They were the dwellings of two young men who were cunning in the law; an equal number of that class who chaffered to the wants of the community, under the title of storekeepers; and a disciple of Æsculapius, who, for a novelty, brought more subjects into the world than he sent out of it. In the midst of this incongruous group of dwellings, rose the mansion of the Judge, towering above all its neighbours. It stood in the centre of an enclosure of several acres, which were covered with fruit-trees. Some of the latter had been left by the Indians, and began already to assume the moss and inclination of age, therein forming a very marked contrast to the infant plantations that peer'd over most of the picketed fences of the village. In addition to this show of cultivation, were two rows of young Lombardy poplars, a tree but lately introduced into America, formally lining either side of a path-way, which led from a gate, that opened on the principal street, to the front door of the building. The house itself had been built entirely under the superintendence of a certain Mr. Richard Jones, whom we have already mentioned, and who, from his cleverness in small matters, and an entire willingness to exert his talents, added to the circumstance of their being sisters' children, ordinarily superintended all the minor concerns of Marmaduke Temple. Richard was fond of saying, that this child of his invention, consisted of nothing more nor less, than what should form the ground work of every clergyman's discourse; viz. a firstly, and a lastly. He had commenced his labours in the first year of their residence, by erecting a tall, gaunt edifice of wood, with its gable towards the highway. In this shelter, for it was little more, the family resided three years. By the end of that period, Richard had completed his design. He had availed himself, in this heavy undertaking, of the experience of a certain wandering, eastern mechanic, who, by exhibiting a few soiled plates of English architecture, and talking learnedly of friezes, entablatures, and particularly of the composite order, had obtained a very undue influence over Richard's taste, in every thing that pertained to that branch of the fine arts. Not that Mr. Jones did not affect to consider Hiram Doolittle a perfect empyric in his profession; being in the constant habit of listening to his treatises on architecture, with a kind of indulgent smile, yet, either from an inability to oppose them by any thing plausible from his own stores of learning, or from secret admiration, Richard generally submitted to the arguments of his co-adjutor. Together, they had not only erected a dwelling for Marmaduke, but they had given a fashion to the architecture of the whole county. The composite order, Mr. Doolittle would contend, was an order composed of many others, and was intended to be the most useful of all, for it admitted into its construction such alterations, as convenience or circumstances might require. To this proposition, Richard usually assented; and when rival geniuses, who monopolise not only all the reputation, but most of the money of a neighbourhood, are of a mind, it is not uncommon to see them lead the fashion, even in graver matters. In the present instance, as we have already hinted, the castle, as Judge Temple's dwelling was termed in common parlance, came to be the model, in some one or other of its numerous excellencies, for every aspiring edifice within twenty miles of it.

The house itself, or the lastly, was of stone; large, square, and far from uncomfortable. These were four requisites, on which Marmaduke had insisted with a little more than his ordinary pertinacity. But every thing else was peaceably assigned to Richard and his associate. These worthies found the material a little too solid for the tools of their workmen, which, in general, were employed on a substance no harder than the white pine of the adjacent mountains, a wood so proverbially soft, that it is commonly chosen by the hunters for pillows. But for this awkward dilemma, it is probable that the ambitious tastes of our two architects would have left us much more to do in the way of description. Driven from the faces of the house by the obduracy of the material, they took refuge in the porch and on the roof. The former, it was decided, should be severely classical, and the latter a rare specimen of the merits of the composite order.

A roof, Richard contended, was a part of the edifice that the ancients always endeavoured to conceal, it being an excrescence in architecture that was only to be tolerated on account of its usefulness. Besides, as he wittily added, a chief merit in a dwelling was to present a front, on whichever side it might happen to be seen; for as it was exposed to all eyes in all weathers, there should be no weak flank, for envy or unneighbourly criticism to assail. It was, therefore, decided, that the roof should be flat, and with four faces. To this arrangement, Marmaduke objected the heavy snows that lay for months, frequently covering the earth to a depth of three or four feet. Happily, the facilities of the composite order presented themselves to effect a compromise, and the rafters were lengthened, so as to give a descent that should carry off the frozen element. But unluckily, some mistake was made in the admeasurement of these material parts of the fabric, and as one of the greatest recommendations of Hiram, was his ability to work by the "square rule," no opportunity was found of discovering the effect, until the massive timbers were raised, on the four walls of the building. Then, indeed, it was soon seen, that, in defiance of all rule, the roof was by far the most conspicuous part of the whole edifice. Richard and his associate consoled themselves with the belief, that the covering would aid in concealing this unnatural elevation; but every shingle that was laid only multiplied objects to look at. Richard essayed to remedy the evil with paint, and four different colours were laid on by his own hands. The first, was a sky-blue, in the vain expectation that the eye might be cheated into the belief, it was the heavens themselves that hung so imposingly over Marmaduke's dwelling: the second was, what he called, a cloud-colour, being nothing more nor less than an imitation of smoke: the third was what Richard termed an invisible green, an experiment that did not succeed against a back-ground of sky. Abandoning the attempt to conceal, our architects drew upon their invention for means to ornament the offensive shingles. After much deliberation, and two or three essays by moonlight, Richard ended the affair by boldly covering the whole beneath a colour that he christened "sunshine," a cheap way, as he assured his cousin, the Judge, of always keeping fair weather over his head. The platform, as well as the eaves of the house, were surmounted by gaudily painted railings, and the genius of Hiram was exerted in the fabrication of divers urns and mouldings, that were scattered profusely around this part of their labours. Richard had originally a cunning expedient, by which the chimneys were intended to be so low, and so situated, as to resemble ornaments on the balustrades; but comfort required that the chimneys should rise with the roof, in order that the smoke might be carried off, and they thus became four extremely conspicuous objects in the view.

As this roof was much the most important architectural undertaking in which Mr. Jones was ever engaged, his failure produced a correspondent degree of mortification. At first, he whispered among his acquaintances, that it proceeded from ignorance of the square rule on the part of Hiram, but as his eye became gradually accustomed to the object, he grew better satisfied with his labours, and instead of apologizing for the defects, he commenced praising the beauties of the mansion house. He soon found hearers; and, as wealth and comfort are at all times attractive, it was, as has been said, made a model for imitation on a small scale. In less than two years from its erection, he had the pleasure of standing on the elevated platform, and of looking down on three humble imitators of its beauty. —Thus it is ever with fashion, which even renders the faults of the great, subjects of admiration.

Marmaduke bore this deformity in his dwelling with great good nature, and soon contrived, by his own improvements, to give an air of respectability and comfort to his place of residence; still there was much of incongruity, even immediately about the mansion-house. Although poplars had been brought from Europe to ornament the grounds, and willows and other trees were gradually springing up nigh the dwelling, yet many a pile of snow betrayed the presence of the stump of a pine; and even, in one or two instances, unsightly remnants of trees that had been partly destroyed by fire, were seen rearing their black, glistening columns twenty or thirty feet above the pure white of the snow. These, which in the language of the country are termed stubbs, abounded in the open fields adjacent to the village, and were accompanied, occasionally, by the ruin of a pine or a hemlock that had been stripped of its bark, and which waved in melancholy grandeur its naked limbs to the blast, a skeleton of its former glory. But these and many other unpleasant additions to the view were unseen by the delighted Elizabeth, who, as the horses moved down the side of the mountain, saw only in gross, the cluster of houses that lay like a map at her feet; the fifty smokes that were curling from the valley to the clouds; the frozen lake, as it lay embedded in mountains of evergreen, with the long shadows of the pines on its white surface, lengthening in the setting sun; the dark ribband of water, that gushed from the outlet, and was winding its way towards the distant Chesapeake—the altered, though still remembered, scenes of her childhood.

Five years had wrought greater changes, than a century would produce in countries, where time and labour have given permanency to the works of man. To the young hunter and the Judge the scene had less novelty; though none ever emerge from the dark forests of that mountain, and witness the glorious scenery of that beauteous valley, as it bursts unexpectedly upon them, without a feeling of delight. The former cast one admiring glance from north to south, and sunk his face, again, beneath the folds of his coat; while the latter contemplated, with philanthropic pleasure, the prospect of affluence and comfort, that was expanding around him; the result of his own enterprise, and, much of it, the fruits of his own industry.

The cheerful sound of sleigh bells, however, attracted the attention of the whole party, as they came jingling up the sides of the mountain, at a rate that announced a powerful team and a hard driver. The bushes which lined the highway interrupted the view, and the two sleighs were close upon each other before either was seen.

Chapter IV.

"How now? whose mare's dead? what's the matter?"

2 Henry IV, II.i.43–44.

ALARGE lumber-sleigh, drawn by four horses, was soon seen dashing through the leafless bushes, which fringed the road. The leaders were of gray, and the pole-horses of a jet black. Bells, innumerable, were suspended from every part of the harness, where one of the tinkling balls could be placed, while the rapid movement of the equipage, in defiance of the steep ascent, announced the desire of the driver to ring them to the utmost. The first glance at this singular arrangement acquainted the Judge with the character of those in the sleigh. It contained four male figures. On one of those stools that are used at writing desks, lashed firmly to the sides of the vehicle, was seated a little man, enveloped in a great coat fringed with fur, in such a manner that no part of him was visible excepting a face, of an unvarying red colour. There was an habitual upward look about the head of this gentleman, as if dissatisfied with its natural proximity to the earth, and the expression of his countenance was that of busy care. He was the charioteer, and he guided the mettled animals along the precipice, with a fearless eye, and a steady hand. Immediately behind him, with his face toward the other two, was a tall figure, to whose appearance not even the duplicate over-coats which he wore, aided by the corner of a horse blanket, could give the appearance of strength. His face was protruding from beneath a woollen night-cap, and when he turned to the vehicle of Marmaduke as the sleighs approached each other, it seemed formed by nature to cut the atmosphere with the least possible resistance. The eyes alone appeared to create an obstacle, for from either side of his forehead their light, blue, glassy balls projected. The sallow of his countenance was too permanent to be affected even by the intense cold of the evening. Opposite to this personage, sat a solid, short, and square figure. No part of his form was to be

discovered, through his over dress, but a face that was illuminated by a pair of black eyes, that gave the lie to every demure
feature in his countenance.—— A fair, jolly wig furnished a
neat and rounded outline to his visage, and he, as well as the
other two, wore marten-skin caps. The fourth, was a meek-
looking, long-visaged man, without any other protection from
the cold than that which was furnished by a black surtout, made
with some little formality, but which was rather thread bare and
rusty. He wore a hat of extremely decent proportions, though
frequent brushing had quite destroyed its nap. His face was
pale, and withal a little melancholy, or what might be termed of
a studious complexion. The air had given it, just now, a slight
and somewhat feverish flush. The character of his whole appearance, especially contrasted to the air of humour in his next
companion, was that of habitual mental care. No sooner had
the two sleighs approached within speaking distance, than the
driver of this fantastic equipage shouted aloud—

"Draw up in the quarry—draw up, thou king of the Greeks;
draw into the quarry, Agamemnon, or I shall never be able to
pass you. Welcome home, cousin 'duke—welcome, welcome,
black-eyed Bess. Thou seest, Marmaduke, that I have taken the
field with an assorted cargo, to do thee honour. Monsieur Le
Quoi has come out with only one cap; Old Fritz would not stay
to finish the bottle; and Mr. Grant has got to put the lastly to his
sermon, yet. Even all the horses would come—by-the-by, Judge,
I must sell the blacks for you, immediately; they interfere, and
the nigh one is a bad goer in double harness. I can get rid of
them to——"

"Sell what thou wilt, Dickon," interrupted the cheerful voice
of the Judge, "so that thou leavest me my daughter and my
lands. Ah! Fritz, my old friend, this is a kind compliment, indeed, for seventy to pay to five and forty. Monsieur Le Quoi, I
am your servant. Mr. Grant," lifting his cap, "I feel indebted to
your attention. Gentlemen, I make you acquainted with my
child. Yours are names with which she is very familiar."

"Velcome, velcome, Tchooge," said the elder of the party,
with a strong German accent. "Miss Petsy vilt owe me a kiss."

"And cheerfully will I pay it, my good sir," cried the soft voice
of Elizabeth; which sounded in the clear air of the hills, like
tones of silver, amid the loud cries of Richard. "I have always a
kiss for my old friend, Major Hartmann."

By this time the gentleman in the front seat, who had been addressed as Monsieur Le Quoi, had arisen with some difficulty, owing to the impediment of his over coats, and steadying himself by placing one hand on the stool of the charioteer, with the other, he removed his cap, and bowing politely to the Judge, and profoundly to Elizabeth, he paid his compliments.

"Cover thy poll, Gaul, cover thy poll," cried the driver, who was Mr. Richard Jones; "cover thy poll, or the frost will pluck out the remnant of thy locks. Had the hairs on the head of Absalom been as scarce as thine, he might have been living to this day." The jokes of Richard never failed of exciting risibility, for he uniformly did honor to his own wit; and he enjoyed a hearty laugh on the present occasion, while Mr. Le Quoi resumed his seat with a polite reciprocation in his mirth. The clergyman, for such was the office of Mr. Grant, modestly, though quite affectionately, exchanged his greetings with the travellers also, when Richard prepared to turn the heads of his horses homewards.

It was in the quarry alone that he could effect this object, without ascending to the summit of the mountain. A very considerable excavation had been made in the side of the hill, at the point where Richard had succeeded in stopping the sleighs, from which the stones used for building in the village, were ordinarily quarried, and in which he now attempted to turn his team. Passing itself, was a task of difficulty, and frequently of danger, in that narrow road; but Richard had to meet the additional risk of turning his four-in-hand. The black civilly volunteered his services to take off the leaders, and the Judge very earnestly seconded the measure, with his advice. Richard treated both proposals with great disdain—

"Why, and wherefore, cousin 'duke," he exclaimed a little angrily; "the horses are gentle as lambs. You know that I broke the leaders myself, and the pole-horses are too near my whip to be restive. Here is Mr. Le Quoi, now, who must know something about driving, because he has rode out so often with me; I will leave it to Mr. Le Quoi whether there is any danger."

It was not in the nature of the Frenchman to disappoint expectations so confidently formed; although he sat looking down the precipice which fronted him, as Richard turned his leaders into the quarry, with a pair of eyes that stood out like those of lobsters. The German's muscles were unmoved, but his quick sight scanned each movement. Mr. Grant placed his hands on the side of the sleigh, in preparation for a spring, but moral timidity deterred him from taking the leap, that bodily apprehension strongly urged him to attempt.

Richard, by a sudden application of the whip, succeeded in forcing the leaders into the snow bank that covered the quarry; but the instant that the impatient animals suffered by the crust, through which they broke at each step, they positively refused to move an inch further in that direction. On the contrary, finding that the cries and blows of their driver, were redoubled at this juncture, the leaders backed upon the pole-horses, who, in their turn, backed the sleigh. Only a single log lay above the pile which upheld the road, on the side toward the valley, and this was now buried in the snow. The sleigh was easily forced across so slight an impediment, and before Richard became conscious of his danger, one half of the vehicle was projected over a precipice, which fell, perpendicularly, more than a hundred feet. The Frenchman, who, by his position, had a full view of their threatened flight, instinctively threw his body as far forward as possible, and cried, "Ah! Mon cher monsieur Deeck! mon Dieu! que faites vous!"

"Donner and blitzen, Richart," exclaimed the veteran German, looking over the side of the sleigh with unusual emotion, "put you will preak ter sleigh and kilt ter horses."

"Good Mr. Jones," said the clergyman, "be prudent, good sir—be careful."

"Get up, obstinate devils," cried Richard, catching a bird's-eye view of his situation, and, in his eagerness to move forward, kicking the stool on which he sat,—"Get up, I say—Cousin 'duke, I shall have to sell the grays too; they are the worst broken horses—Mr. Le Quaw!" Richard was too much agitated to regard his pronunciation, of which he was commonly a little vain, "Monsieur Le Quaw, pray get off my leg; you hold my leg so tight that it's no wonder the horses back."

"Merciful Providence!" exclaimed the Judge, "they will be all killed!"

Elizabeth gave a piercing shriek, and the black of Agamemnon's face changed to a muddy white.

At this critical moment, the young hunter, who, during the salutations of the parties, had sat in rather sullen silence,

sprang from the sleigh of Marmaduke to the heads of the refractory leaders. The horses, who were yet suffering under the
injudicious and somewhat random blows of Richard, were
dancing up and down with that ominous movement, that
threatens a sudden and uncontrollable start, still pressing
backward. The youth gave the leaders a powerful jerk, and they
plunged aside, and re-entered the road in the position in which
they were first halted. The sleigh was whirled from its dangerous position, and upset with the runners outwards. The German and the divine, were thrown rather unceremoniously into
the highway, but without danger to their bones. Richard appeared in the air, describing the segment of a circle, of which
the reins were the radii, and landed at the distance of some
fifteen feet, in that snow bank which the horses had dreaded,
right end uppermost. Here, as he instinctively grasped the
reins, as drowning men seize at straws, he admirably served the
purpose of an anchor. The Frenchman, who was on his legs in
the act of springing from the sleigh, took an aerial flight also,
much in the attitude which boys assume when they play leap-
frog, and flying off in a tangent to the curvature of his course,
came into the snow bank head foremost, where he remained,
exhibiting two lathy legs on high, like scare-crows waving in a
corn field. Major Hartmann, whose self-possession had been
admirably preserved during the whole evolution, was the first
of the party that gained his feet and his voice.

"Ter deyvel, Richart," he exclaimed, in a voice half serious,
half comical, "Put you unloat your sleigh very hantily."

It may be doubtful, whether the attitude in which Mr. Grant
continued for an instant after his overthrow, was the one into
which he had been thrown, or was assumed, in humbling himself before the power that he reverenced, in thanksgiving at his
escape. When he rose from his knees, he began to gaze about
him, with anxious looks, after the welfare of his companions,
while every joint in his body trembled with nervous agitation.
There was some confusion in the faculties of Mr. Jones, also;
but as the mist gradually cleared from before his eyes, he saw
that all was safe, and with an air of great self-satisfaction, he
cried, "well—that was neatly saved, any how——It was a lucky
thought in me to hold on the reins, or the fiery devils would
have been over the mountain by this time. How well I recovered

myself, 'duke; another moment would have been too late—
But I knew just the spot where to touch the off-leader; that
blow under his right flank, and the sudden jerk I gave the rein,
brought them round quite in rule, I must own myself."

The spectators, from immemorial usage, have a right to laugh
at the casualties of a sleigh-ride; and the Judge was no sooner
certain that no harm was done, than he made full use of the privilege.

"Thou jerk! thou recover thyself, Dickon!" he said; "but for that
brave lad yonder, thou and thy horses, or rather mine, would
have been dashed to pieces—But where is Monsieur Le Quoi?"

"Oh! mon cher Juge! Mon ami!" cried a smothered voice,
"praise be God I live; vill-a you, Mister Agamemnon, be pleas
come down ici, and help-a me on my leg?"

The divine and the negro seized the incarcerated Gaul by his
legs, and extricated him from a snow-bank of three feet in
depth, whence his voice had sounded as from the tombs. The
thoughts of Mr. Le Quoi, immediately on his liberation, were
not extremely collected; and when he reached the light, he
threw his eyes upwards, in order to examine the distance he
had fallen. His good humour returned however, with a knowledge of his safety, though it was some little time before he clearly comprehended the case.

"What, monsieur," said Richard, who was busily assisting the
black in taking off the leaders; "are you there? I thought I saw
you flying towards the top of the mountain just now."

"Praise be God, I no fly down into de lake," returned the
Frenchman, with a visage that was divided between pain, occasioned by a few large scratches that he had received in forcing
his head through the crust, and the look of complaisance that
seemed natural to his pliable features; "ah! mon cher Mister
Deeck, vat you shall do next?—dere be noting you no try."

"The next thing, I trust, will be to learn to drive," said the
Judge, who had busied himself in throwing the buck, together
with several other articles of baggage, from his own sleigh into
the snow; "here are seats for you all, gentlemen; the evening
grows piercingly cold, and the hour approaches for the service
of Mr. Grant: we will leave friend Jones to repair the damages,
with the assistance of Agamemnon, and hasten to a warm fire.
Here, Dickon, are a few articles of Bess's trumpery, that you

can throw into your sleigh when ready, and there is also a deer of my taking, that I will thank you to bring—Aggy! remember there will be a visit from Santaclaus* to-night."

The black grinned, conscious of the bribe that was offered him for silence on the subject of the deer, while Richard, without, in the least, waiting for the termination of his cousin's speech, began his reply—

"Learn to drive, sayest thou, cousin 'duke? Is there a man in the county who knows more of horse-flesh than myself? Who broke in the filly, that no one else dare mount; though your coachman did pretend that he had tamed her before I took her in hand, but any body could see that he lied—he was a great liar, that John—what's that, a buck?"—Richard abandoned the horses, and ran to the spot where Marmaduke had thrown the deer; "It is a buck! I am amazed! Yes, here are two holes in him; he has fired both barrels, and hit him each time. Ecod! how Marmaduke will brag! he is a prodigious bragger about any small matter like this now; well, to think that 'duke has killed a buck before christmas! There will be no such thing as living with him—they are both bad shots though, mere chance—mere chance;—now, I never fired twice at a cloven hoof in my life;— it is hit or miss with me—dead or runaway:—had it been a bear, or a wild-cat, a man might have wanted both barrels. Here! you Aggy! how far off was the Judge when this buck was shot?"

"Eh! Massa Richard, may be a ten rod," cried the black, bending under one of the horses, with the pretence of fastening a buckle, but in reality to conceal the grin that opened a mouth from ear to ear.

"Ten rod!" echoed the other; "why, Aggy, the deer I killed last winter was at twenty—yes! if any thing it was nearer thirty than twenty. I wouldn't shoot at a deer at ten rod: besides, you may remember, Aggy, I only fired once."

"Yes, Massa Richard, I 'member 'em! Natty Bumppo fire t'oder gun. You know, sir, all 'e folk say, Natty kill 'em."

"The folks lie, you black devil!" exclaimed Richard in great heat. "I have not shot even a gray squirrel these four years, to

---

* The periodical visits of St. Nicholas, or Santaclaus as he is termed, were never forgotten among the inhabitants of New York, until the emigration from New England brought in the opinions and usages of the puritans. Like the "bon homme de Noël," he arrives at each Christmas. [1832]

which that old rascal has not laid claim, or some one else for him. This is a damn'd envious world that we live in—people are always for dividing the credit of a thing, in order to bring down merit to their own level. Now they have a story about the Patent*, that Hiram Doolittle helped to plan the steeple to St. Paul's; when Hiram knows that it is entirely mine; a little taken from a print of its namesake in London, I own; but essentially, as to all points of genius, my own."

"I don't know where he come from," said the black, losing every mark of humour in an expression of admiration, "but eb'ry body say, he wonnerful hansome."

"And well they may say so, Aggy," cried Richard, leaving the buck, and walking up to the negro with the air of a man who has new interest awakened within him. "I think I may say, without bragging, that it is the handsomest and the most scientific country church in America. I know that the Connecticut settlers talk about their Wethersfield meeting-house: but I never believe more than half what they say, they are such unconscionable braggers. Just as you have got a thing done, if they see it likely to be successful they are always for interfering, and then it is ten to one but they lay claim to half, or even all of the credit. You may remember, Aggy, when I painted the sign of the bold dragoon for Capt. Hollister, there was that fellow, who was about town laying brick dust on the houses, came one day and offered to mix what I call the streaky black, for the tail and mane, and then, because it looks like horse hair, he tells every body that the sign was painted by himself and Squire Jones. If Marmaduke don't send that fellow off the Patent, he may ornament his village with his own hands, for me." Here Richard paused a moment, and cleared his throat by a loud hem, while the negro, who was all this time busily engaged in preparing the sleigh, proceeded with his work in respectful silence. Owing to the religious scruples of the Judge, Aggy was the servant of

* The grants of land, made either by the crown or the state, were by letters patent under the great seal, and the term "patent" is usually applied to any district of extent, thus conceded. Though under the crown, manorial rights being often granted with the soil, in the older counties, the word "manor" is frequently used. There are many "manors" in New York, though all political and judicial rights have ceased. [1832]

Richard, who had his services for a *time**, and who, of course, commanded a legal claim to the respect of the young negro. But when any dispute between his lawful and his real master occurred, the black felt too much deference for both to express any opinion. In the mean while, Richard continued watching the negro as he fastened buckle after buckle, until, stealing a look of consciousness toward the other, he continued, "Now, if that young man, who was in your sleigh, is a real Connecticut settler, he will be telling every body how he saved my horses, when, if he had let them alone for half-a-minute longer, I would have brought them in much better, without upsetting, with the whip and rein—it spoils a horse to give him his head. I should not wonder if I had to sell the whole team, just for that one jerk he gave them." Richard paused, and hemmed, for his conscience smote him a little, for censuring a man who had just saved his life—"who is the lad, Aggy—I don't remember to have seen him before?"

The black recollected the hint about Santaclaus, and while he briefly explained how they had taken up the person in question on the top of the mountain, he forbore to add any thing concerning the accident of the wound, only saying, that he believed the youth was a stranger. It was so usual for men of the first rank to take into their sleighs any one they found toiling through the snow, that Richard was perfectly satisfied with this explanation. He heard Aggy, with great attention, and then remarked, "Well, if the lad has not been spoiled by the people in Templeton, he may be a modest young man, and as he certainly meant well, I shall take some notice of him,—perhaps he is land-hunting—I say, Aggy—may be he is out hunting?"

"Eh! yes, massa Richard," said the black, a little confused; for

* The manumission of the slaves in New York has been gradual. When public opinion became strong in their favour, then grew up a custom of buying the services of a slave, for six or eight years, with a condition to liberate him at the end of the period. Then the law provided that all born after a certain day should be free, the males at twenty-eight, and the females at twenty-five. After this the owner was obliged to cause his servants to be taught to read and write before they reached the age of eighteen, and, finally, the few that remained were all unconditionally liberated in 1826, or after the publication of this tale. It was quite usual for men more or less connected with the quakers, who never held slaves, to adopt the first expedient. [1832]

as Richard did all the flogging, he stood in great terror of his master, in the main—"yes, sir, I b'lieve he be."

"Had he a pack and an ax?"

"No, sir, only he rifle."

"Rifle!" exclaimed Richard, observing the confusion of the negro, which now amounted to terror. "By Jove! he kill'd the deer—I knew that Marmaduke couldn't kill a buck on the jump—How was it, Aggy; tell me all about it, and I'll roast 'duke quicker than he can roast his saddle—How was it, Aggy? the lad shot the buck, and the Judge bought it, ha! and he is taking the youth down to get the pay?"

The pleasure of this discovery had put Richard in such a good humour, that the negro's fears in some measure vanished, and he remembered the stocking of Santaclaus. After a gulp or two he made out to reply.

"You forgit a two shot, Sir."

"Don't lie, you black rascal," cried Richard, stepping on the snow bank to measure the distance from his lash to the negro's back; "speak truth, or I trounce you." While speaking, the stock was slowly rising in Richard's right hand, and the lash drawing through his left, in the scientific manner with which drummers apply the cat, and Agamemnon, after turning each side of himself towards his master, and finding both equally unwilling to remain there, fairly gave in. In a very few words he made his master acquainted with the truth, at the same time earnestly conjuring Richard to protect him from the displeasure of the Judge.

"I'll do it, boy, I'll do it," cried the other, rubbing his hands with delight; "say nothing, but leave me to manage 'duke—I have a great mind to leave the deer on the hill, and to make the fellow send for his own carcass: but no, I will let Marmaduke tell a few bouncers about it before I come out upon him— Come, hurry in, Aggy, I must help to dress the lad's wound; this Yankee* Doctor knows nothing of surgery—I had to hold

* In America the term Yankee is of local meaning. It is thought to be derived from the manner in which the Indians of New England pronounced the word "English" or "Yengeese." New York being originally a Dutch province, the term of course was not known there, and further south different dialects among the natives, themselves, probably produced a different pronunciation. Marmaduke and his cousin being Pennsylvanians by birth were not Yankees in the American sense of the word. [1832]

old Milligan's leg for him, while he cut it off." Richard was now seated on the stool again, and the black taking the hind seat, the steeds were put in motion towards home. As they dashed down the hill, on a fast trot, the driver occasionally turned his face to Aggy, and continued speaking; for, notwithstanding their recent rupture, the most perfect cordiality was again existing between them. "This goes to prove that I turned the horses with the reins, for no man who is shot in the right shoulder, can have strength enough to bring round such obstinate devils—I knew I did it from the first; but I did not want to multiply words with Marmaduke about it—Will you bite? you villain!—hip, boys, hip—Old Natty too, that is the best of it—Well, well—'duke will say no more about my deer—and the Judge fired both barrels, and hit nothing but a poor lad, who was behind a pine tree—I must help that quack to take out the buck shot for the poor fellow." In this manner Richard descended the mountain; the bells ringing and his tongue going, until they entered the village, when the whole attention of the driver was devoted to a display of his horsemanship, to the admiration of all the gaping women and children, who thronged the windows, to witness the arrival of their landlord and his daughter.

Chapter V.

"Nathaniel's coat, sir, was not fully made,
And Gabriel's pumps were all unfinish'd i' th' heel;
There was no link to colour Peter's hat,
And Walter's dagger was not come from sheathing:
There were none fine, but Adam, Ralph and Gregory."
The Taming of the Shrew, IV.i.132–36.

AFTER winding along the side of the mountain, the road, on reaching the gentle declivity which lay at the base of the hill, turned at a right angle to its former course, and shot down an inclined plane, directly into the village of Templeton. The rapid little stream that we have already mentioned, was crossed by a bridge of hewn timber, which manifested, by its rude construction, and the unnecessary size of its frame-work, both the value of labour, and the abundance of materials. This little torrent, whose dark waters gushed over the limestones that lined its bottom, was nothing less than one of the many sources of the Susquehanna; a river, to which the Atlantic herself, has extended an arm in welcome. It was at this point, that the powerful team of Mr. Jones, brought him up to the more sober steeds of our travellers. A small hill was risen, and Elizabeth found herself, at once, amid the incongruous dwellings of the village. The street was of the ordinary width, notwithstanding the eye might embrace in one view, thousands, and tens of thousands, of acres, that were yet tenanted only by the beasts of the forest. But such had been the will of her father, and such had also met the wishes of his followers. To them, the road, that made the most rapid approaches to the condition of the old, or, as they expressed it, the *down* countries, was the most pleasant; and surely nothing could look more like civilization, than a city, even if it lay in a wilderness! The width of the street, for so it was called, might have been one hundred feet; but the track for the sleighs was much more limited. On either side of the highway, were piled huge heaps of logs that were daily increasing rather than diminishing in size, notwithstanding the enormous fires that might be seen through every window.

The last object at which Elizabeth gazed when they renewed their journey, after the rencontre with Richard, was the sun, as it expanded in the refraction of the horizon, and over whose disk, the dark umbrage of a pine was stealing, while it slowly sunk behind the western hills. But its setting rays darted along the openings of the mountain she was on, and lighted the shining covering of the birches, until their smooth and glossy coats, nearly rivalled the mountain-sides in colour. The outline of each dark pine was delineated far in the depths of the forest; and the rocks, too smooth and too perpendicular to retain the snow that had fallen, brightened, as if smiling at the leavetaking of the luminary. But at each step, as they descended, Elizabeth observed that they were leaving the day behind them. Even the heartless, but bright rays of a December sun, were missed, as they glided into the cold gloom of the valley. Along the summits of the mountains in the eastern range, it is true, the light still lingered, receding step by step from the earth into the clouds that were gathering, with the evening mist, about the limited horizon; but the frozen lake lay without a shadow on its bosom; the dwellings were becoming already gloomy and indistinct; and the wood-cutters were shouldering their axes, and preparing to enjoy, throughout the long evening before them, the comforts of those exhilarating fires that their labour had been supplying with fuel. They paused only to gaze at the passing sleighs, to lift their caps to Marmaduke, to exchange familiar nods with Richard, and each disappeared in his dwelling. The paper curtains dropped behind our travellers in every window, shutting from the air even the fire-light of the cheerful apartments; and when the horses of her father turned, with a rapid whirl, into the open gate of the mansion-house, and nothing stood before her but the cold, dreary stone-walls of the building, as she approached them through an avenue of young and leafless poplars, Elizabeth felt as if all the loveliness of the mountain-view had vanished like the fancies of a dream. Marmaduke had retained so much of his early habits as to reject the use of bells, but the equipage of Mr. Jones came dashing through the gate after them, sending its jingling sounds through every cranny of the building, and in a moment the dwelling was in an uproar.

On a stone platform, of rather small proportions, considering the size of the building, Richard and Hiram had, conjointly, reared four little columns of wood, which in their turn supported the shingled roofs of the portico—this was the name that Mr. Jones had thought proper to give to a very plain, covered, entrance. The ascent to the platform was by five or six stone steps, somewhat hastily laid together, and which the frost had already begun to move from their symmetrical positions. But the evils of a cold climate, and a superficial construction, did not end here. As the steps lowered, the platform necessarily fell also, and the foundations actually left the superstructure suspended in the air, leaving an open space of a foot between the base of the pillars and the stones on which they had originally been placed. It was lucky for the whole fabric, that the carpenter, who did the manual part of the labour, had fastened the canopy of this classic entrance so firmly to the side of the house, that, when the base deserted the superstructure in the manner we have described, and the pillars, for the want of a foundation, were no longer of service to support the roof, the roof was able to uphold the pillars. Here was indeed an unfortunate gap left in the ornamental part of Richard's column; but, like the window in Aladdin's palace, it seemed only left in order to prove the fertility of its master's resources. The composite order again offered its advantages, and a second edition of the base was given, as the booksellers say, with additions and improvements. It was necessarily larger, and it was properly ornamented with mouldings; still the steps continued to yield, and, at the moment when Elizabeth returned to her father's door, a few rough wedges were driven under the pillars to keep them steady, and to prevent their weight from separating them from the pediment which they ought to have supported.

From the great door, which opened into the porch, emerged two or three female domestics, and one male. The latter was bare-headed, but evidently more dressed than usual, and on the whole, was of so singular a formation and attire, as to deserve a more minute description. He was about five feet in height, of a square and athletic frame, with a pair of shoulders that would have fitted a grenadier. His low stature was ren-

dered the more striking by a bend forward that he was in the
habit of assuming, for no apparent reason, unless it might be to
give greater freedom to his arms, in a particularly sweeping
swing, that they constantly practised when their master was in
motion. His face was long, of a fair complexion, burnt to a fiery
red; with a snub nose, cocked into an inveterate pug; a mouth
of enormous dimensions, filled with fine teeth; and a pair of
blue eyes, that seemed to look about them, on surrounding objects, with habitual contempt. His head composed full one
fourth of his whole length, and the queue that depended from
its rear occupied another. He wore a coat of very light drab
cloth, with buttons as large as dollars, bearing the impression of
a foul anchor. The skirts were extremely long, reaching quite to
the calf, and were broad in proportion. Beneath, there were a
vest and breeches of red plush, somewhat worn and soiled. He
had shoes with large buckles, and stockings of blue and white
stripes.

This odd-looking figure reported himself to be a native of the
county of Cornwall, in the island of Great Britain. His boyhood
had passed in the neighbourhood of the tin mines, and his
youth, as the cabin-boy of a smuggler, between Falmouth and
Guernsey. From this trade he had been impressed into the service of his king, and, for the want of a better, had been taken into
the cabin, first as a servant, and finally as steward to the captain.
Here he acquired the art of making chowder, lobskous, and one
or two other sea-dishes, and, as he was fond of saying, had an
opportunity of seeing the world. With the exception of one or
two out-ports in France, and an occasional visit to Portsmouth,
Plymouth, and Deal, he had in reality seen no more of man-
kind, however, than if he had been riding a donkey in one of
his native mines. But, being discharged from the navy at the
peace of '83, he declared, that, as he had seen all the civilized
parts of the earth, he was inclined to make a trip to the wilds of
America. We will not trace him in his brief wanderings, under
the influence of that spirit of emigration, that sometimes in-
duces a dapper Cockney to quit his home, and lands him, before the sound of Bow-bells is out of his ears, within the roar of
the cataract of Niagara, but shall only add, that, at a very early
day, even before Elizabeth had been sent to school, he had
found his way into the family of Marmaduke Temple, where,

owing to a combination of qualities that will be developed in the course of the tale, he held, under Mr. Jones, the office of major-domo. The name of this worthy was Benjamin Penguillan, according to his own pronunciation; but, owing to a marvellous tale that he was in the habit of relating, concerning the length of time he had to labour to keep his ship from sinking after Rodney's victory, he had universally acquired the nickname of Ben Pump.

By the side of Benjamin, and pressing forward as if a little jealous of her station, stood a middle-aged woman, dressed in calico, rather violently contrasted in colour, with a tall, meager, shapeless figure, sharp features, and a somewhat acute expression of her physiognomy. Her teeth were mostly gone, and what did remain were of a light yellow. The skin of her nose was drawn tightly over the member, to hang in large wrinkles in her cheeks and about her mouth. She took snuff in such quantities, as to create the impression, that she owed the saffron of her lips and the adjacent parts, to this circumstance; but it was the unvarying colour of her whole face. She presided over the female part of the domestic arrangements, in the capacity of housekeeper, was a spinster, and bore the name of Remarkable Pettibone. To Elizabeth she was an entire stranger, having been introduced into the family since the death of her mother.

In addition to these, were three or four subordinate menials, mostly black, some appearing at the principal door, and some running from the end of the building, where stood the entrance to the cellar-kitchen.

Besides these, there was a general rush from Richard's kennel, accompanied with every canine tone, from the howl of the wolf-dog to the petulant bark of the terrier. The master received their boisterous salutations with a variety of imitations from his own throat, when the dogs, probably from shame at being outdone, ceased their outcry. One stately, powerful mastiff, who wore around his neck a brass collar, with "M. T." engraved in large letters on the rim, alone was silent. He walked majestically, amid the confusion, to the side of the Judge, where, receiving a kind pat or two, he turned to Elizabeth, who even stooped to kiss him, as she called him kindly by the name of "Old Brave." The animal seemed to know her, as she ascended the steps, supported by Monsieur Le Quoi and her father, in order to protect her from falling on the ice, with which they were covered. He looked wistfully after her figure, and when the door closed on the whole party, he laid himself in a kennel that was placed nigh by, as if conscious that the house contained something of additional value to guard.

Elizabeth followed her father, who paused a moment to whisper a message to one of his domestics, into a large hall, that was dimly lighted by two candles, placed in high, old-fashioned, brass candlesticks. The door closed, and the party were at once removed from an atmosphere that was nearly at zero, to one of sixty degrees above. In the centre of the hall stood an enormous stove, the sides of which appeared to be quivering with heat; from which a large, straight pipe, leading through the ceiling above, carried off the smoke. An iron basin, containing water, was placed on this furnace, for such only it could be called, in order to preserve a proper humidity in the apartment. The room was carpeted, and furnished with convenient, substantial furniture; some of which was brought from the city, and the remainder having been manufactured by the mechanics of Templeton. There was a sideboard of mahogany, inlaid with ivory, and bearing enormous handles of glittering brass, and groaning under the piles of silver plate. Near it stood a set of prodigious tables, made of the wild cherry, to imitate the imported wood of the sideboard, but plain, and without ornament of any kind. Opposite to these stood a smaller table, formed from a lighter coloured wood, through the grains of which the wavy lines of the curled-maple of the mountains were beautifully undulating. Near to this, in a corner, stood a heavy, old-fashioned, brass-faced clock, encased in a high box, of the dark hue of the black-walnut from the seashore. An enormous settee, or sofa, covered with light chintz, stretched along the walls for near twenty feet on one side of the hall, and chairs of wood, painted a light yellow, with black lines that were drawn by no very steady hand, were ranged opposite, and in the intervals between the other pieces of furniture. A Fahrenheit's thermometer, in a mahogany case, and with a barometer annexed, was hung against the wall, at some little distance from the stove, which Benjamin consulted, every half-hour, with prodigious exactitude. Two small glass chandeliers were suspended at equal distances between the stove and the outer doors, one of which opened at each end of the hall, and gilt lustres were affixed to the frame-work of the numerous side doors, that led from the apartment. Some little display in architecture had been made in constructing these frames and casings, which were surmounted with pediments, that bore each a little pedestal in its centre. On these pedestals were small busts in blacked plaster of Paris. The style of the pedestals, as well as the selection of the busts, were all due to the taste of Mr. Jones. On one stood Homer, a most striking likeness, Richard affirmed, "as any one might see, for it was blind." Another bore the image of a smooth visaged gentleman, with a pointed beard, whom he called Shakspeare. A third ornament, was an urn, which, from its shape, Richard was accustomed to say, intended to represent itself as holding the ashes of Dido. A fourth was certainly old Franklin, in his cap and spectacles. A fifth as surely bore the dignified composure of the face of Washington. A sixth was a non-descript, representing "a man with a shirt-collar open," to use the language of Richard, "with a laurel on his head;—it was Julius Cæsar or Dr. Faustus; there were good reasons for believing either."

The walls were hung with a dark, lead-coloured English paper, that represented Britannia weeping over the tomb of Wolfe. The hero himself stood at a little distance from the mourning goddess, and at the edge of the paper. Each width contained the figure, with the slight exception of one arm of the General, which ran over on to the next piece, so that when Richard essayed, with his own hands, to put together this delicate outline, some difficulties occurred, that prevented a nice conjunction, and Britannia had reason to lament, in addition to the loss of her favourite's life, numberless cruel amputations of his right arm.

The luckless cause of these unnatural divisions now announced his presence in the hall by a loud crack of his whip.

"Why, Benjamin! you Ben Pump! is this the manner in which you receive the heiress?" he cried. "Excuse him, cousin Elizabeth. The arrangements were too intricate to be trusted to every one; but now I am here, things will go on better. Come, light up, Mr. Penguillan, light up, light up, and let us see one another's faces. Well, 'duke, I have brought home your deer; what is to be done with it, ha?"

"By the Lord, Squire," commenced Benjamin in reply, first giving his mouth a wipe with the back of his hand, "if this here thing had been ordered sum'at earlier in the day, it might have been got up, d'ye see, to your liking. I had mustered all hands, and was exercising candles, when you hove in sight; but when the women heard your bells, they started an end, as if they were riding the boatswain's colt; and, if-so-be there is that man in the house, who can bring up a parcel of women when they have got headway on them, until they've run out the end of their rope, his name is not Benjamin Pump. But Miss Betsy here, must have altered more than a privateer in disguise, since she has got on her woman's duds, if she will take offence with an old fellow, for the small matter of lighting a few candles."

Elizabeth and her father continued silent, for both experienced the same sensation on entering the hall. The former had resided one year in the building before she left home for school, and the figure of its lamented mistress was missed by both husband and child.

But candles had been placed in the chandeliers and lustres, and the attendants were so far recovered from surprise as to recollect their use: the oversight was immediately remedied, and in a minute the apartment was in a blaze of light.

The slight melancholy of our heroine and her father was banished by this brilliant interruption, and the whole party began to lay aside the numberless garments they had worn in the air.

During this operation, Richard kept up a desultory dialogue with the different domestics, occasionally throwing out a remark to the Judge concerning the deer; but as his conversation at such moments was much like an accompaniment on a piano, a thing that is heard without being attended to, we will not undertake the task of recording his diffuse discourse.

The instant that Remarkable Pettibone had executed her portion of the labour in illuminating, she returned to a position near Elizabeth, with the apparent motive of receiving the clothes that the other threw aside, but in reality to examine, with an air of curiosity—not unmixed with jealousy,—the appearance of the lady who was to supplant her in the administration of their domestic economy. The housekeeper felt a little appalled, when, after cloaks, coats, shawls and socks had been taken off in succession, the large black hood was removed, and the dark ringlets, shining like the raven's wing, fell from her head, and left the sweet but commanding features of the young lady exposed to view. Nothing could be fairer and more spotless than the forehead of Elizabeth, and preserve the appearance of life and health. Her nose would have been called Grecian, but for a softly rounded swell, that gave in character to the feature what it lost in beauty. Her mouth, at first sight, seemed only made for love, but the instant that its muscles moved, every expression that womanly dignity could utter, played around it, with the flexibility of female grace. It spoke not only to the ear, but to the eye. So much, added to a form of exquisite proportions, rather full and rounded for her years, and of the tallest medium height, she inherited from her mother. Even the colour of her eye, the arched brows, and the long silken lashes, came from the same source; but its expression was her father's. Inert and composed, it was soft, benevolent, and attractive; but it could be roused, and that without much difficulty. At such moments it was still beautiful, though it was a little severe. As the last shawl fell aside, and she stood, dressed in a rich blue riding-habit, that fitted her form with the nicest exactness; her cheeks burning with roses, that bloomed the richer for the heat of the hall, and her eyes slightly suffused with moisture, that rendered their ordinary beauty more dazzling, and with every feature of her speaking countenance illuminated by the lights that flared around her, Remarkable felt that her own power had ended.

The business of unrobing had been simultaneous. Marmaduke appeared in a suit of plain neat black; Monsieur Le Quoi, in a coat of snuff-colour, covering a vest of embroidery, with breeches, and silk stockings, and buckles—that were commonly thought to be of paste. Major Hartmann wore a coat of sky-blue, with large brass buttons, a club wig, and boots; and Mr. Richard Jones had set off his dapper little form in a frock of bottle-green, with bullet buttons; by one of which the sides were united over his well-rounded waist, opening above, so as to show a jacket of red cloth, with an under vest of flannel, faced with green velvet, and below, so as to exhibit a pair of buckskin breeches, with long, soiled, white-top boots, and spurs; one of the latter a little bent, from its recent attacks on the stool.

When the young lady had extricated herself from her garments, she was at liberty to gaze about her, and to examine not only the household over which she was to preside, but also the air and manner in which their domestic arrangements were conducted. Although there was much incongruity in the furniture and appearance of the hall, there was nothing mean. The floor was carpeted, even in its remotest corners. The brass candlesticks, the gilt lustres, and the glass chandeliers, whatever might be their *keeping* as to propriety and taste, were admirably kept as to all the purposes of use and comfort. They were clean, and glittering in the strong light of the apartment. Compared with the chill aspect of the December night without, the warmth and brilliancy of the apartment produced an effect that was not unlike enchantment. Her eye had not time to detect in detail the little errors, which, in truth, existed, but was glancing around her in delight, when an object arrested her view, that was in strong contrast to the smiling faces and neatly attired personages who had thus assembled to do honour to the heiress of Templeton.

In a corner of the hall, near the grand entrance, stood the young hunter, unnoticed, and for the moment apparently forgotten. But even the forgetfulness of the Judge, which, under the influence of strong emotion, had banished the recollection of the wound of this stranger, seemed surpassed by the absence of mind in the youth himself. On entering the apartment he had mechanically lifted his cap, and exposed a head, covered with hair that rivalled in colour and gloss the locks of Elizabeth. Nothing could have wrought a greater transformation, than the single act of removing the rough fox-skin cap. If there was much that was prepossessing in the countenance of the young hunter, there was something even noble in the rounded outlines of his head and brow. The very air and manner with which the member haughtily maintained itself over the coarse, and even wild attire, in which the rest of his frame was clad, bespoke not only familiarity with a splendour that in those new settlements was thought to be unequalled, but something very like contempt also.

The hand that held the cap, rested lightly on the little ivory-mounted piano of Elizabeth, with neither rustic restraint, nor obtrusive vulgarity. A single finger touched the instrument, as if accustomed to dwell on such places. His other arm was extended to its utmost length, and the hand grasped the barrel of his long rifle, with something like convulsive energy. The act and the attitude were both involuntary, and evidently proceeded from a feeling much deeper than that of vulgar surprise. His appearance, connected as it was with the rough exterior of his dress, rendered him entirely distinct from the busy group that were moving across the other end of the long hall, occupied in receiving the travellers, and exchanging their welcomes; and Elizabeth continued to gaze at him in wonder. The contraction of the stranger's brows increased, as his eyes moved slowly from one object to another. For moments the expression of his countenance was fierce, and then again it seemed to pass away in some painful emotion. The arm, that was extended, bent, and brought the hand nigh to his face, when his head dropped upon it, and concealed the wonderfully speaking lineaments.

"We forget, dear sir, the strange gentleman," (for her life Elizabeth could not call him otherwise,) "whom we have brought here for assistance, and to whom we owe every attention."

All eyes were instantly turned in the direction of those of the speaker, and the youth, rather proudly, elevated his head again, while he answered—

"My wound is trifling, and I believe that Judge Temple sent for a physician the moment we arrived."

"Certainly," said Marmaduke; "I have not forgotten the object of thy visit, young man, nor the nature of my debt."

"Oh!" exclaimed Richard, with something of a waggish leer, "thou owest the lad for the venison, I suppose, that thou killed, cousin 'duke! Marmaduke! Marmaduke! That was a marvellous tale of thine about the buck! Here, young man, are two dollars for the deer, and Judge Temple can do no less than pay the Doctor. I shall charge you nothing for my services, but you shall not fare the worse for that. Come, come, 'duke, don't be down-hearted about it; if you missed the buck, you contrived to shoot this poor fellow through a pine tree. Now I own that you have beat me; I never did such a thing in all my life."

"And I hope never will," returned the Judge, "if you are to experience the uneasiness that I have suffered. But be of good cheer, my young friend, the injury must be small, as thou movest thy arm with apparent freedom."

"Don't make the matter worse, 'duke, by pretending to talk about surgery," interrupted Mr. Jones, with a contemptuous wave of the hand; "it is a science that can only be learnt by practice. You know that my grandfather was a doctor, but you haven't got a drop of medical blood in your veins; these kind of things run in families. All my family by the father's side had a knack at physic. There was my uncle that was killed at Brandywine, he died as easy again as any other man in the regiment, just from knowing how to hold his breath naturally. Few men know how to breathe, naturally."

"I doubt not, Dickon," returned the Judge, meeting the bright smile, which, in spite of himself, stole over the stranger's features, "that thy family thoroughly understood the art of letting life slip through their fingers."

Richard heard him quite coolly, and, putting a hand in either pocket of his surtout, so as to press forward the skirts, began to whistle a tune; but the desire to reply overcame his philosophy, and with great heat he exclaimed—

"You may affect to smile, Judge Temple, at hereditary virtues, if you please; but there is not a man on your Patent who don't know better.—Here, even this young man, who has never seen any thing but bears, and deer, and wood-chucks, knows better, than to believe virtues are not transmitted in families. Don't you, friend?"

"I believe that vice is not," said the stranger abruptly, his eye glancing from the father to the daughter.

"The Squire is right, Judge," observed Benjamin, with a knowing nod of his head towards Richard, that bespoke the cordiality between them. "Now, in the old-country, the King's Majesty touches for the evil, and that is a disorder that the greatest doctor in the fleet, or, for the matter of that, Admiral either, can't cure; only the King's Majesty, or a man that's been hanged. Yes, the Squire is right, for if-so-be that he wasn't, how is it that the seventh son always is a doctor, whether he ships for the cock-pit or not? Now when we fell in with the mounsheers, under De Grasse, d'ye see, we had aboard of us a doctor"——

"Very well, Benjamin," interrupted Elizabeth, glancing her eyes from the hunter to Monsieur Le Quoi, who was most politely attending to what fell from each individual in succession, "you shall tell me of that, and all your entertaining adventures together; just now, a room must be prepared, in which the arm of this gentleman can be dressed."

"I will attend to that myself, cousin Elizabeth," observed Richard, somewhat haughtily.—"The young man shall not suffer, because Marmaduke chooses to be a little obstinate. Follow me, my friend, and I will examine the hurt myself."

"It will be well to wait for the physician," said the hunter coldly; "he cannot be distant."

Richard paused, and looked at the speaker, a little astonished at the language, and a good deal appalled at the refusal. He construed the latter into an act of hostility, and, placing his hands in the pockets again, he walked up to Mr. Grant, and putting his face close to the countenance of the divine, said in an under tone—

"Now mark my words: there will be a story among the settlers, that all our necks would have been broken, but for that fellow—as if I did not know how to drive. Why you might have turned the horses yourself, sir; nothing was easier; it was only pulling hard on the nigh rein, and touching the off flank of the leader. I hope, my dear sir, you are not at all hurt by the upset the lad gave us?"

The reply was interrupted by the entrance of the village physician.

Chapter VI.

"———And about his shelves,
A beggarly account of empty boxes,
Green earthen pots, bladders, and musty seeds,
Remnants of pack-thread, and old cakes of roses,
Were thinly scattered to make up a show."

Romeo and Juliet, V.i.44–48.

DOCTOR Elnathan Todd, for such was the name of the man of physic, was commonly thought to be, among the settlers, a gentleman of great mental endowments; and he was assuredly of rare personal proportions. In height he measured, without his shoes, exactly six feet and four inches. His hands, feet, and knees, corresponded in every respect with this formidable stature; but every other part of his frame appeared to have been intended for a man several sizes smaller, if we except the length of the limbs. His shoulders were square, in one sense at least, being in a right line from one side to the other; but they were so narrow, that the long, dangling arms they supported, seemed to issue out of his back. His neck possessed, in an eminent degree, the property of length to which we have alluded, and it was topped by a small bullet-head, that exhibited, on one side, a bush of bristling brown hair, and on the other, a short, twinkling visage, that appeared to maintain a constant struggle with itself in order to look wise. He was the youngest son of a farmer in the western part of Massachusetts, who, being in somewhat easy circumstances, had allowed this boy to shoot up to the height we have mentioned, without the ordinary interruptions of field-labour, wood-chopping, and such other toils as were imposed on his brothers. Elnathan was indebted for this exemption from labour, in some measure, to his extraordinary growth, which, leaving him pale, inanimate, and listless, induced his tender mother to pronounce him "a sickly boy, and one that was not equal to work, but who might arn a living, comfortably enough, by taking to pleading law, or turning minister, or doctoring, or some sitch-like easy calling." Still there was great uncertainty which of these vocations the youth was best endowed to fill; but, having no other employment, the stripling was constantly lounging about the "homestead," munching green apples, and hunting for sorrel; when the same sagacious eye, that had brought to light his latent talents, seized upon this circumstance, as a clue to his future path through the turmoils of the world. "Elnathan was cut out for a doctor," she knew, "for he was for ever digging for yarbs, and tasting all kinds of things that grow'd about the lots. Then again he had a naateral love for doctor-stuff, for when she had left the bilious pills out for her man, all nicely covered with maple sugar, just ready to take, Nathan had come in, and swallowed them, for all the world as if they were nothing, while Ichabod (her husband) could never get one down without making sitch desperate faces, that it was awful to look on."

This discovery decided the matter. Elnathan, then about fifteen, was, much like a wild colt, caught and trimmed, by clipping his bushy locks; dressed in a suit of homespun, died in the butternut bark; furnished with a "New Testament," and a "Webster's Spelling-Book," and sent to school. As the boy was by nature quite shrewd enough, and had previously, at odd times, laid the foundations of reading, writing, and arithmetic, he was soon conspicuous in the school for his learning. The delighted mother had the gratification of hearing, from the lips of the master, that her son was a "prodigious boy, and far above all his class." He also thought that "the youth had a natural love for doctoring, as he had known him frequently advise the smaller children against eating too much, and once or twice, when the ignorant little things had persevered in opposition to Elnathan's advice, he had known her son empty the school-baskets with his own mouth, to prevent the consequences."

Soon after this comfortable declaration from his schoolmaster, the lad was removed to the house of the village doctor, a gentleman whose early career had not been unlike that of our hero, where he was to be seen, sometimes watering a horse, at others watering medicines, blue, yellow and red; then again he might be noticed, lolling under an apple tree, with Ruddiman's Latin Grammar in his hand, and a corner of Denman's Midwifery sticking out of a pocket;—for his instructor held it absurd to teach his pupil how to despatch a patient regularly from this world, before he knew how to bring him into it.

This kind of life continued for a twelvemonth, when he suddenly appeared at meeting in a long coat (and well did it deserve the name) of black homespun, with little bootees, bound with uncoloured calf-skin, for the want of red morocco.

Soon after, he was seen shaving with a dull razor. Three or four months had scarce elapsed before several elderly ladies were observed hastening towards the house of a poor woman in the village, while others were running to and fro in great apparent distress. One or two boys were mounted, bareback, on horses, and sent off at speed in various directions. Several indirect questions were put, concerning the place where the physician was last seen; but all would not do; and at length Elnathan was seen issuing from his door, with a very grave air, preceded by a little white-headed boy, out of breath, trotting before him. The following day the youth appeared in the street, as the highway was called, and the neighbourhood was much edified by the additional gravity of his air. The same week he bought a new razor; and the succeeding Sunday he entered the meeting-house with a red silk handkerchief in his hand, and with an extremely demure countenance. In the evening he called upon a young woman of his own class in life, for there were no others to be found, and, when he was left alone with the fair, he was called, for the first time in his life, Doctor Todd, by her prudent mother. The ice once broken in this manner, Elnathan was greeted from every mouth with his official appellation.

Another year passed under the superintendence of the same master, during which the young physician had the credit of "riding with the old doctor," although they were generally observed to travel different roads. At the end of that period, Dr. Todd attained his legal majority. He then took a jaunt to Boston, to purchase medicines, and, as some intimated, to walk the hospital; we know not how the latter might have been, but if true, he soon walked through it, for he returned within a fortnight, bringing with him a suspicious-looking box, that smelt powerfully of brimstone.

The next Sunday he was married; and the following morning he entered a one-horse sleigh with his bride, having before him the box we have mentioned, with another filled with home-made household linen, a paper-covered trunk, with a red umbrella lashed to it, a pair of quite new saddle-bags, and a bandbox. The next intelligence that his friends received of the bride and bridegroom was, that the latter was "settled in the new-countries, and well to do as a doctor, in Templetown, in York state."

If a templar would smile at the qualifications of Marmaduke to fill the judicial seat he occupied, we are certain that a graduate of Leyden or Edinburgh would be extremely amused with this true narration of the servitude of Elnathan in the temple of Æsculapius. But the same consolation was afforded to both the jurist and the leech; for Dr. Todd was quite as much on a level with his compeers of the profession, in that country, as was Marmaduke with his brethren on the bench.

Time and practice did wonders for the physician. He was naturally humane, but possessed of no small share of moral courage; or, in other words, he was chary of the lives of his patients, and never tried uncertain experiments on such members of society as were considered useful; but once or twice, when a luckless vagrant had come under his care, he was a little addicted to trying the effects of every vial in his saddle-bags on the stranger's constitution. Happily their number was small, and in most cases their natures innocent. By these means Elnathan had acquired a certain degree of knowledge in fevers and agues, and could talk with much judgment concerning intermittents, remittents, tertians, quotidians, &c.—In certain cutaneous disorders, very prevalent in new settlements, he was considered to be infallible; and there was no woman on the Patent, but would as soon think of becoming a mother without a husband, as without the assistance of Dr. Todd. In short, he was rearing, on this foundation of sand, a superstructure, cemented by practice, though composed of somewhat brittle materials. He, however, occasionally renewed his elementary studies, and, with the observation of a shrewd mind, was comfortably applying his practice to his theory.

In surgery, having the least experience, and it being a business that spoke directly to the senses, he was most apt to distrust his own powers; but he had applied oils to several burns, cut round the roots of sundry defective teeth, and sewed up the wounds of numberless wood-choppers, with considerable eclat, when an unfortunate jobber* suffered a fracture of his leg, by

*People who clear land by the acre or job, are thus called. [1832]

the tree that he had been felling. It was on this occasion that our hero encountered the greatest trial his nerves and moral feeling had ever sustained. In the hour of need, however, he was not found wanting. Most of the amputations in the new settlements, and they were quite frequent, were performed by some one practitioner, who, possessing originally a reputation, was enabled by this circumstance to acquire an experience that rendered him deserving of it; and Elnathan had been present at one or two of these operations. But on the present occasion the man of practice was not to be obtained, and the duty fell, as a matter of course, to the share of Mr. Todd. He went to work with a kind of blind desperation, observing, at the same time, all the externals of decent gravity and great skill. The sufferer's name was Milligan, and it was to this event that Richard alluded, when he spoke of assisting the Doctor, at an amputation—by holding the leg! The limb was certainly cut off, and the patient survived the operation. It was, however, two years before poor Milligan ceased to complain that they had buried the leg in so narrow a box, that it was straitened for room; he could feel the pain shooting up from the inhumed fragment into the living members. Marmaduke suggested that the fault might lie in the arteries and nerves, but Richard, considering the amputation as part of his own handy-work, strongly repelled the insinuation, at the same time declaring, that he had often heard of men who could tell when it was about to rain, by the toes of amputated limbs. After two or three years, notwithstanding Milligan's complaints gradually diminished, the leg was dug up, and a larger box furnished, and from that hour no one had heard the sufferer utter another complaint on the subject. This gave the public great confidence in Doctor Todd, whose reputation was hourly increasing, and, luckily for his patients, his information also.

Notwithstanding Mr. Todd's practice, and his success with the leg, he was not a little appalled, on entering the hall of the mansion-house. It was glaring with the light of day; it looked so splendid and imposing, compared with the hastily built and scantily furnished apartments which he frequented in his ordinary practice, and contained so many well-dressed persons, and anxious faces, that his usually firm nerves were a good deal discomposed. He had heard from the messenger who summoned him, that it was a gun-shot wound, and had come from his own home, wading through the snow, with his saddle-bags thrown over his arm, while separated arteries, penetrated lungs, and injured vitals, were whirling through his brain, as if he were stalking over a field of battle, instead of Judge Temple's peaceable enclosure.

The first object that met his eye, as he moved into the room, was Elizabeth, in her riding-habit, richly laced with gold cord, her fine form bending towards him, and her face expressing deep anxiety in every one of its beautiful features. The enormous bony knees of the physician struck each other with a noise that was audible, for in the absent state of his mind, he mistook her for a general officer, perforated with bullets, hastening from the field of battle to implore assistance. The delusion, however, was but momentary, and his eye glanced rapidly from the daughter to the earnest dignity of the father's countenance; thence to the busy strut of Richard, who was cooling his impatience at the hunter's indifference to his assistance, by pacing the hall and cracking his whip; from him to the Frenchman, who had stood for several minutes unheeded with a chair for the lady; thence to Major Hartmann, who was very coolly lighting a pipe three feet long by a candle in one of the chandeliers; thence to Mr. Grant, who was turning over a manuscript with much earnestness at one of the lustres; thence to Remarkable, who stood, with her arms demurely folded before her, surveying with a look of admiration and envy the dress and beauty of the young lady; and from her to Benjamin, who, with his feet standing wide apart, and his arms a-kimbo, was balancing his square little body, with the indifference of one who is accustomed to wounds and bloodshed. All of these seemed to be unhurt, and the operator began to breathe more freely; but before he had time to take a second look, the Judge, advancing, shook him kindly by the hand, and spoke.

"Thou art welcome, my good sir, quite welcome, indeed; here is a youth, whom I have unfortunately wounded in shooting a deer this evening, and who requires some of thy assistance."

"Shooting at a deer, 'duke," interrupted Richard,—"Shooting at a deer. Who do you think can prescribe, unless he knows the truth of the case? It is always so, with some people; they think a doctor can be deceived, with the same impunity as another man."

"Shooting at a deer truly," returned the Judge, smiling, "although it is by no means certain that I did not aid in destroying the buck; but the youth is injured by my hand, be that as it may; and it is thy skill, that must cure him, and my pocket shall amply reward thee for it."

"Two ver good tings to depend on," observed Monsieur Le Quoi, bowing politely, with a sweep of his head, to the Judge and the practitioner.

"I thank you, Monsieur," returned the Judge; "but we keep the young man in pain. Remarkable, thou wilt please to provide linen, for lint and bandages."

This remark caused a cessation of the compliments, and induced the physician to turn an inquiring eye in the direction of his patient. During the dialogue, the young hunter had thrown aside his over coat, and now stood clad in a plain suit of the common, light-coloured homespun of the country, that was evidently but recently made. His hand was on the lapels of his coat, in the attitude of removing the garment, when he suddenly suspended the movement, and looked towards the commiserating Elizabeth, who was standing in an unchanged posture, too much absorbed with her anxious feelings to heed his actions. A slight colour appeared on the brow of the youth.

"Possibly the sight of blood may alarm the lady; I will retire to another room, while the wound is dressing."

"By no means," said Doctor Todd, who, having discovered that his patient was far from being a man of importance, felt much emboldened to perform the duty.—"The strong light of these candles is favourable to the operation, and it is seldom that we hard students enjoy good eyesight."

While speaking, Elnathan placed a pair of large, iron-rimmed spectacles on his face, where they dropped, as it were by long practice, to the extremity of his slim, pug nose; and if they were of no service as assistants to his eyes, neither were they any impediment to his vision; for his little, gray organs were twinkling above them, like two stars emerging from the envious cover of a cloud. The action was unheeded by all but Remarkable, who observed to Benjamin—

"Doctor Todd is a comely man to look on, and disp'ut pretty.

How well he seems in spectacles. I declare, they give a grand look to a body's face. I have quite a great mind to try them myself."

The speech of the stranger recalled the recollection of Miss Temple, who started, as if from deep abstraction, and, colouring excessively, she motioned to a young woman, who served in the capacity of maid, and retired, with an air of womanly reserve.

The field was now left to the physician and his patient, while the different personages who remained, gathered around the latter, with faces expressing the various degrees of interest, that each one felt in his condition. Major Hartmann alone retained his seat, where he continued to throw out vast quantities of smoke, now rolling his eyes up to the ceiling, as if musing on the uncertainty of life, and now bending them on the wounded man, with an expression, that bespoke some consciousness of his situation.

In the mean time, Elnathan, to whom the sight of a gun-shot wound was a perfect novelty, commenced his preparations, with a solemnity and care that were worthy of the occasion. An old shirt was procured by Benjamin, and placed in the hands of the other, who tore divers bandages from it, with an exactitude, that marked both his own skill, and the importance of the operation.

When this preparatory measure was taken, Dr. Todd selected a piece of the shirt with great care, and, handing it to Mr. Jones, without moving a muscle, said—

"Here, Squire Jones, you are well acquainted with these things; will you please to scrape the lint? It should be fine, and soft, you know, my dear sir; and be cautious that no cotton gets in, or it may p'ison the wownd. The shirt has been made with cotton thread, but you can easily pick it out."

Richard assumed the office, with a nod at his cousin, that said, quite plainly, "you see, this fellow can't get along without me;" and began to scrape the linen on his knee, with great diligence.

A table was now spread, with vials, boxes of salve, and divers surgical instruments. As the latter appeared, in succession, from a case of red morocco, their owner held up each implement, to the strong light of the chandelier, near to which he stood, and examined it, with the nicest care. A red silk handkerchief was frequently applied to the glittering steel, as if to remove from the polished surfaces, the least impediment, which might exist, to the most delicate operation. After the rather scantily furnished pocket-case, which contained these instruments, was exhausted, the physician turned to his saddle-bags, and produced various vials, filled with liquids, of the most radiant colours. These were arranged, in due order, by the side of the murderous saws, knives, and scissors, when Elnathan stretched his long body to its utmost elevation, placing his hand on the small of his back, as if for support, and looked about him, to discover what effect this display of professional skill, was likely to produce on the spectators.

"Upon my wort, toctor," observed Major Hartmann, with a roguish roll of his little black eyes, but with every other feature of his face in a state of perfect rest, "put you have a very pretty pocket-pook of tools tere, and your toctor-stuff glitters, as if it was petter for ter eyes as for ter pelly."

Elnathan gave a hem,—one that might have been equally taken, for that kind of noise, which cowards are said to make, in order to awaken their dormant courage, or for a natural effort, to clear the throat: if for the latter, it was successful; for, turning his face to the veteran German, he said—

"Very true, Major Hartmann, very true, sir; a prudent man will always strive to make his remedies agreeable to the eyes, though they may not altogether suit the stomach. It is no small part of our art, sir," and he now spoke with the confidence of a man who understood his subject, "to reconcile the patient to what is for his own good, though, at the same time, it may be unpalatable."

"Sartain! Doctor Todd is right," said Remarkable, "and has scripter for what he says. The Bible tells us, how things mought be sweet to the mouth, and bitter to the inwards."

"True, true," interrupted the Judge, a little impatiently; "but here is a youth who needs no deception to lure him to his own benefit. I see, by his eye, that he fears nothing more than delay."

The stranger had, without assistance, bared his own shoulder, when the slight perforation, produced by the passage of the buck-shot, was plainly visible. The intense cold of the evening, had stopped the bleeding, and Dr. Todd, casting a furtive glance at the wound, thought it by no means so formidable an affair as he had anticipated. Thus encouraged, he approached his patient, and made some indication of an intention to trace the route that had been taken by the lead.

Remarkable often found occasions, in after days, to recount the minutiæ of that celebrated operation; and when she arrived at this point, she commonly proceeded as follows:—"And then the Doctor tuck out of the pocket-book a long thing, like a knitting-needle, with a button fastened to the end on't; and then he pushed it into the wownd; and then the young man looked awful; and then I thought I should have swan'd away—I felt in sitch a disp'ut taking; and then the Doctor had run it right through his shoulder, and shoved the bullet out on t'other side; and so Doctor Todd cured the young man—of a ball that the Judge had shot into him, for all the world, as easy as I could pick out a splinter, with my darning-needle."

Such were the impressions of Remarkable on the subject; and such, doubtless, were the opinions of most of those, who felt it necessary to entertain a species of religious veneration for the skill of Elnathan; but such was far from the truth.

When the physician attempted to introduce the instrument, described by Remarkable, he was repulsed by the stranger, with a good deal of decision, and some little contempt, in his manner.

"I believe, sir," he said, "that a probe is not necessary; the shot has missed the bone, and has passed directly through the arm, to the opposite side, where it remains, but skin-deep, and whence, I should think, it might be easily extracted."

"The gentleman knows best," said Dr. Todd, laying down the probe, with the air of a man who had assumed it merely in compliance with forms; and, turning to Richard, he fingered the lint, with the appearance of great care and foresight. "Admirably well scraped, Squire Jones! it is about the best lint I have ever seen. I want your assistance, my good sir, to hold the patient's arm, while I make an incision for the ball. Now, I rather guess, there is not another gentleman present, who could scrape the lint so well as Squire Jones."

"Such things run in families," observed Richard, rising with alacrity, to render the desired assistance; "my father, and my grandfather before him, were both celebrated for their knowledge of surgery; they were not, like Marmaduke here, puffed up with an accidental thing, such as the time when he drew in the hip-joint of the man, who was thrown from his horse; that was the fall before you came into the settlement, Doctor; but they were men who were taught the thing regularly, spending half their lives in learning those little niceties; though, for the matter of that, my grandfather was a college-bred physician, and the best in the colony, too—that is, in his neighbourhood."

"So it goes with the world, Squire," cried Benjamin; "if-so-be a man want to walk the quarter-deck with credit, d'ye see, and with regular-built swabs on his shoulders, he mus'nt think to do it, by getting in at the cabin-windows. There are two ways to get into a top, besides the lubber-holes. The true way to walk aft, is to begin forrard; tho'f it be only in a humble way, like myself, d'ye see, which was, from being only a hander of top-gallant-sails, and a stower of the flying-jib, to keeping the key of the Captain's locker."

"Benjamin speaks quite to the purpose," continued Richard. "I dare say, that he has often seen shot extracted, in the different ships in which he has served; suppose we get him to hold the basin; he must be used to the sight of blood."

"That he is, Squire, that he is," interrupted the ci-devant steward; "many's the good shot, round, double-headed, and grape, that I've seen the doctors at work on. For the matter of that, I was in a boat, alongside the ship, when they cut out the twelve-pound shot from the thigh of the Captain of the Foody-rong, one of Mounsheer Ler Quaw's countrymen!"*

"A twelve-pound ball, from the thigh of a human being!" exclaimed Mr. Grant, with great simplicity, dropping the sermon he was again reading, and raising his spectacles to the top of his forehead.

"A twelve-pounder!" echoed Benjamin, staring around him, with much confidence; "a twelve-pounder! ay! a twenty-four pound shot can easily be taken from a man's body, if-so-be a

* It is possible that, the reader may start at this declaration of Benjamin, but those who have lived in the new settlements of America, are too much accustomed to hear of these European exploits, to doubt it. [1832]

doctor only knows how. There's Squire Jones, now, ask him, sir; he reads all the books; ask him, if he never fell in with a page, that keeps the reckoning of such things."

"Certainly, more important operations than that have been performed," observed Richard; "the Encyclopædia mentions much more incredible circumstances than that, as, I dare say, you know, Doctor Todd."

"Certainly, there are incredible tales told in the Encyclopædias," returned Elnathan, "though I cannot say, that I have ever seen, myself, any thing larger than a musket bullet extracted."

During this discourse, an incision had been made, through the skin of the young hunter's shoulder, and the lead was laid bare. Elnathan took a pair of glittering forceps, and was in the act of applying them to the wound, when a sudden motion of the patient, caused the shot to fall out of itself. The long arm and broad hand of the operator were now of singular service; for the latter expanded itself, and caught the lead, while at the same time, an extremely ambiguous motion was made, by its brother, so as to leave it doubtful to the spectators, how great was its agency in releasing the shot. Richard, however, put the matter at rest, by exclaiming—

"Very neatly done, Doctor! I have never seen a shot more neatly extracted; and, I dare say, Benjamin will say the same."

"Why, considering," returned Benjamin, "I must say, that it was ship-shape, and Brister-fashion.—Now all that the Doctor has to do, is to clap a couple of plugs in the holes, and the lad will float in any gale, that blows in these here hills."

"I thank you, sir, for what you have done," said the youth, with a little distance: "But here is a man, who will take me under his care, and spare you all, gentlemen, any further trouble on my account."

The whole group turned their heads, in surprise, and beheld, standing at one of the distant doors of the hall, the person of Indian John.

Chapter VII.

"From Susquehanna's utmost springs,
Where savage tribes pursue their game,
His blanket tied with yellow strings,
The shepherd of the forest came."
                              Freneau, "The Indian Student," ll. 1–4.

BEFORE the Europeans, or, to use a more significant term, the Christians, dispossessed the original owners of the soil, all that section of country, which contains the New-England States, and those of the Middle which lie east of the mountains, was occupied by two great nations of Indians, from whom had descended numberless tribes. But, as the original distinctions between these nations, were marked by a difference in language, as well as by repeated and bloody wars, they never were known to amalgamate, until after the power and inroads of the whites had reduced some of the tribes to a state of dependence, that rendered not only their political, but, considering the wants and habits of a savage, their animal existence also, extremely precarious.

These two great divisions consisted, on the one side, of the Five, or, as they were afterwards called, the Six Nations, and their allies; and, on the other, of the Lenni Lenape, or Delawares, with the numerous and powerful tribes, that owned that nation as their Grandfather. The former were generally called, by the Anglo-Americans, Iroquois, or the Six Nations, and sometimes Mingoes. Their appellation, among their rivals, seems generally to have been the Mengwe, or Maqua. They consisted of the tribes, or, as their allies were fond of asserting, in order to raise their consequence, of the several nations, of the Mohawks, the Oneidas, the Onondagas, Cayugas, and Senecas; who ranked, in the confederation, in the order in which they are named. The Tuscaroras were admitted to this union, near a century after its formation, and thus completed the number to six.

Of the Lenni Lenape, or, as they were called by the whites,

from the circumstance of their holding their great council-fire on the banks of that river, the Delaware nation, the principal tribes, besides that which bore the generic name, were, the Mahicanni, Mohicans, or Mohegans, and the Nanticokes, or Néntigoes. Of these, the latter held the country along the waters of the Chesapeake, and the seashore; while the Mohegans occupied the district between the Hudson and the ocean, including much of New-England: of course, these two tribes were the first who were dispossessed of their lands by the Europeans.

The wars of a portion of the latter, are celebrated among us, as the wars of King Philip; but the peaceful policy of William Penn, or Miquon, as he was termed by the natives, effected its object, with less difficulty, though not with less certainty. As the natives gradually disappeared from the country of the Mohegans, some scattering families sought a refuge around the council-fire of the mother tribe, or the Delawares.

This people had been induced to suffer themselves to be called *women*, by their old enemies, the Mingoes, or Iroquois, after the latter, having in vain tried the effects of hostility, had recourse to artifice, in order to prevail over their rivals.— According to this declaration, the Delawares were to cultivate the arts of peace, and to intrust their defence, entirely, to the *men*, or warlike tribes of the Six nations.

This state of things continued until the war of the revolution, when the Lenni Lenape formally asserted their independence, and fearlessly declared, that they were again men. But, in a government, so peculiarly republican as the Indian polity, it was not, at all times, an easy task, to restrain its members within the rules of the nation. Several fierce and renowned warriors, of the Mohegans, finding the conflict with the whites to be in vain, sought a refuge with their Grandfather, and brought with them the feelings and principles, that had so long distinguished them in their own tribe. These chieftains kept alive, in some measure, the martial spirit of the Delawares; and would, at times, lead small parties against their ancient enemies, or such other foes as incurred their resentment.

Among these warriors, was one race, particularly famous for their prowess, and for those qualities that render an Indian hero celebrated. But war, time, disease, and want, had conspired to thin their number; and the sole representative of this once renowned family, now stood in the hall of Marmaduke

Temple. He had, for a long time, been an associate of the white-men, particularly in their wars; and, having been, at a season when his services were of importance, much noticed and flattered, he had turned Christian, and was baptized by the name of John. He had suffered severely, in his family, during the recent war, having had every soul to whom he was allied, cut off by an inroad of the enemy; and when the last, lingering remnant of his nation, extinguished their fires, amongst the hills of the Delaware, he alone had remained, with a determination of laying his bones in that country, where his fathers had so long lived and governed.

It was only, however, within a few months, that he had appeared among the mountains that surrounded Templeton. To the hut of the old hunter, he seemed peculiarly welcome; and, as the habits of the "Leather-stocking," were so nearly assimilated to those of the savages, the conjunction of their interests excited no surprise. They resided in the same cabin, ate of the same food, and were chiefly occupied in the same pursuits.

We have already mentioned the baptismal name of this ancient chief; but in his conversation with Natty, held in the language of the Delawares, he was heard uniformly to call himself Chingachgook, which, interpreted, means the "Great Snake." This name he had acquired in youth, by his skill and prowess in war; but when his brows began to wrinkle with time, and he stood alone, the last of his family, and his particular tribe, the few Delawares, who yet continued about the head-waters of their river, gave him the mournful appellation of Mohegan. Perhaps there was something of deep feeling, excited in the bosom of this inhabitant of the forest, by the sound of a name, that recalled the idea of his nation in ruins, for he seldom used it himself—never, indeed, excepting on the most solemn occasions; but the settlers had united, according to the Christian custom, his baptismal with his national name, and to them, he was generally known as John Mohegan, or, more familiarly, as Indian John.

From his long association with the white-men, the habits of Mohegan, were a mixture of the civilized and savage states, though there was certainly a strong preponderance in favour of the latter. In common with all his people, who dwelt within the influence of the Anglo-Americans, he had acquired new wants, and his dress was a mixture of his native and European fashions. Notwithstanding the intense cold without, his head was uncovered; but a profusion of long, black, coarse hair, concealed his forehead, his crown, and even hung about his cheeks, so as to convey the idea, to one who knew his present and former conditions, that he encouraged its abundance, as a willing veil, to hide the shame of a noble soul, mourning for glory once known. His forehead, when it could be seen, appeared lofty, broad, and noble. His nose was high, and of the kind called Roman, with nostrils, that expanded, in his seventieth year, with the freedom that had distinguished them in youth. His mouth was large, but compressed, and possessing a great share of expression and character, and, when opened, it discovered a perfect set of short, strong, and regular teeth. His chin was full, though not prominent; and his face bore the infallible mark of his people, in its square, high cheek-bones. The eyes were not large, but their black orbs glittered in the rays of the candles, as he gazed intently down the hall, like two balls of fire.

The instant that Mohegan observed himself to be noticed by the group, around the young stranger, he dropped the blanket, which covered the upper part of his frame, from his shoulders, suffering it to fall over his leggins, of untanned deer-skin, where it was retained by a belt of bark, that confined it to his waist.

As he walked slowly down the long hall, the dignified and deliberate tread of the Indian, surprised the spectators. His shoulders, and body, to his waist, were entirely bare, with the exception of a silver medallion of Washington, that was suspended from his neck by a thong of buck-skin, and rested on his high chest, amidst many scars. His shoulders were rather broad and full; but the arms, though straight and graceful, wanted the muscular appearance, that labour gives to a race of men. The medallion was the only ornament he wore, although enormous slits, in the rim of either ear, which suffered the cartilages to fall two inches below the members, had evidently been used for the purposes of decoration, in other days. In his hand, he held a small basket, of the ash-wood slips, coloured in divers fantastical conceits, with red and black paints mingled with the white of the wood.

As this child of the forest approached them, the whole party stood aside, and allowed him to confront the object of his visit.

He did not speak, however, but stood, fixing his glowing eyes on the shoulder of the young hunter, and then turning them intently on the countenance of the Judge. The latter was a good deal astonished, at this unusual departure from the ordinarily subdued and quiet manner of the Indian; but he extended his hand, and said—

"Thou art welcome, John. This youth entertains a high opinion of thy skill, it seems, for he prefers thee, to dress his wound, even to our good friend Dr. Todd."

Mohegan now spoke, in tolerable English, but in a low, monotonous, guttural tone:—

"The children of Miquon do not love the sight of blood; and yet, the Young Eagle has been struck, by the hand that should do no evil!"

"Mohegan! old John!" exclaimed the Judge, "thinkest thou, that my hand has ever drawn human blood willingly? For shame! for shame, old John! thy religion should have taught thee better."

"The evil spirit sometimes lives in the best heart," returned John, "but my brother speaks the truth; his hand has never taken life, when awake; no! not even when the children of the great English Father, were making the waters red with the blood of his people."

"Surely, John," said Mr. Grant, with much earnestness, "you remember the divine command of our Saviour, 'judge not, lest ye be judged.' What motive could Judge Temple have, for injuring a youth like this; one to whom he is unknown, and from whom he can receive neither injury nor favour?"

John listened respectfully to the divine, and when he had concluded, he stretched out his arm, and said with energy—

"He is innocent—my brother has not done this."

Marmaduke received the offered hand of the other, with a smile, that showed, however he might be astonished at his suspicion, he had ceased to resent it; while the wounded youth stood, gazing from his red friend to his host, with interest powerfully delineated in his countenance. No sooner was this act of pacification exchanged, than John proceeded to discharge the duty, on which he had come. Dr. Todd was far from manifesting any displeasure at this invasion of his rights, but made way for the new leech, with an air that expressed a willingness to gratify the humours of his patient, now that the all-important part of the business was so successfully performed, and nothing remained to be done, but what any child might effect. Indeed, he whispered as much to Monsieur Le Quoi, when he said—

"It was fortunate that the ball was extracted before this Indian came in; but any old woman can dress the wound. The young man, I hear, lives with John and Natty Bumppo, and it's always best to humour a patient, when it can be done discreetly—I say, discreetly, Mounsheer."

"Certainement," returned the Frenchman; "you seem ver happy, Mister Toad, in your practeece. I tink de elder lady might ver well finish, vat you so skeelfully begin."

But Richard had, at the bottom, a great deal of veneration for the knowledge of Mohegan, especially in external wounds; and retaining all his desire for a participation in glory, he advanced nigh the Indian, and said—

"Sago, sago, Mohegan! sago, my good fellow! I am glad you have come; give me a regular physician, like Doctor Todd, to cut into flesh, and a native to heal the wound. Do you remember, John, the time when I and you set the bone of Natty Bumppo's little finger, after he broke it, by falling from the rock, when he was trying to get the partridge that fell on the cliffs. I never could tell yet, whether it was I or Natty, who killed that bird: he fired first, and the bird stooped, but then it was rising again as I pulled trigger. I should have claimed it, for a certainty, but Natty said the hole was too big for shot, and he fired a single ball from his rifle; but the piece I carried then, didn't scatter, and I have known it to bore a hole through a board, when I've been shooting at a mark, very much like rifle-bullets. Shall I help you, John? You know I have a knack at these things."

Mohegan heard this disquisition quite patiently, and when Richard concluded, he held out the basket, which contained his specifics, indicating, by a gesture, that he might hold it. Mr. Jones was quite satisfied with this commission; and, ever after, in speaking of the event, was used to say, that "Doctor Todd and I cut out the bullet, and I and Indian John dressed the wound."

The patient was much more deserving of that epithet, while under the hands of Mohegan, than while suffering under the practice of the physician. Indeed, the Indian gave him but little opportunity for the exercise of a forbearing temper, as he had come prepared for the occasion. His dressings were soon applied, and consisted only of some pounded bark, moistened with a fluid, that he had expressed from some of the simples of the woods.

Among the native tribes of the forest, there were always two kinds of leeches to be met with. The one placed its whole dependence on the exercise of a supernatural power, and was held in greater veneration than their practice could at all justify; but the other was really endowed with great skill, in the ordinary complaints of the human body, and was, more particularly, as Natty had intimated, "curous in cuts and bruises."

While John and Richard were placing the dressings on the wound, Elnathan was acutely eyeing the contents of Mohegan's basket, which Mr. Jones, in his physical ardour, had transferred to the Doctor, in order to hold, himself, one end of the bandages. Here he was soon enabled to detect sundry fragments of wood and bark, of which he, quite coolly, took possession, very possibly without any intention of speaking at all upon the subject; but when he beheld the full, blue eye of Marmaduke, watching his movements, he whispered to the Judge—

"It is not to be denied, Judge Temple, but what the savages are knowing, in small matters of physic. They hand these things down in their traditions. Now, in cancers, and hydrophoby, they are quite ingenous. I will just take this bark home, and analyze it; for, though it can't be worth sixpence to the young man's shoulder, it may be good for the tooth-ache, or rhoomatis, or some of them complaints. A man should never be above larning, even if it be from an Indian."

It was fortunate for Dr. Todd, that his principles were so liberal, as, coupled with his practice, they were the means by which he acquired all his knowledge, and by which he was gradually qualifying himself for the duties of his profession. The process to which he subjected the specific, differed, however, greatly from the ordinary rules of chemistry; for, instead of separating, he afterwards united the component parts of Mohegan's remedy, and thus was able to discover the tree, whence the Indian had taken it.

Some ten years after this event, when civilization and its

refinements had crept, or rather rushed, into the settlements among these wild hills, an affair of honour occurred, and Elnathan was seen to apply a salve to the wound received by one of the parties, which had the flavour that was peculiar to the tree, or root, that Mohegan had used. Ten years later still, when England and the United States were again engaged in war, and the hordes of the western parts of the state of New-York, were rushing to the field, Elnathan, presuming on the reputation obtained by these two operations, followed in the rear of a brigade of militia, as its surgeon!

When Mohegan had applied the bark, he freely relinquished to Richard the needle and thread, that were used in sewing the bandages, for these were implements of which the native but little understood the use; and, stepping back, with decent gravity, awaited the completion of the business by the other.

"Reach me the scissors," said Mr. Jones, when he had finished, and finished for the second time, after tying the linen in every shape and form that it could be placed; "reach me the scissors, for here is a thread that must be cut off, or it might get under the dressings, and inflame the wound. See, John, I have put the lint I scraped, between two layers of the linen; for though the bark is certainly best for the flesh, yet the lint will serve to keep the cold air from the wound. If any lint will do it good, it is this lint; I scraped it myself, and I will not turn my back, at scraping lint, to any man on the Patent. I ought to know how, if any body ought, for my grandfather was a doctor, and my father had a natural turn that way."

"Here, Squire, is the scissors," said Remarkable, producing from beneath her petticoat of green moreen, a pair of dull-looking shears; "well, upon my say so, you *have* sewed on the rags, as well as a woman."

"As well as a woman!" echoed Richard, with indignation; "what do women know of such matters? and you are proof of the truth of what I say. Who ever saw such a pair of shears used about a wound? Dr. Todd, I will thank you for the scissors from the case. Now, young man, I think you'll do. The shot has been very neatly taken out, although, perhaps, seeing I had a hand in it, I ought not to say so; and the wound is admirably dressed. You will soon be well again; though the jerk you gave my leaders, must have a tendency to inflame the shoulder, yet, you will do, you will do. You were rather flurried, I suppose, and not used to horses; but I forgive the accident, for the motive;—no doubt, you had the best of motives;—yes, now you will do."

"Then, gentlemen," said the wounded stranger, rising, and resuming his clothes, "it will be unnecessary for me to trespass longer on your time and patience. There remains but one thing more to be settled, and that is, our respective rights to the deer, Judge Temple."

"I acknowledge it to be thine," said Marmaduke; "and much more deeply am I indebted to thee, than for this piece of venison. But in the morning, thou wilt call here, and we can adjust this, as well as more important matters. Elizabeth,"—for the young lady, being apprized that the wound was dressed, had re-entered the hall,—"thou wilt order a repast, for this youth, before we proceed to the church; and Aggy will have a sleigh prepared, to convey him to his friend."

"But, sir, I cannot go, without a part of the deer," returned the youth, seemingly struggling with his own feelings: "I have already told you, that I needed the venison for myself."

"Oh! we will not be particular," exclaimed Richard; "the Judge will pay you, in the morning, for the whole deer; and, Remarkable, give the lad all the animal excepting the saddle: so, on the whole, I think, you may consider yourself as a very lucky young man;—you have been shot, without being disabled; have had the wound dressed in the best possible manner, here in the woods, as well as it would have been done in the Philadelphia hospital, if not better; have sold your deer at a high price, and yet can keep most of the carcass, with the skin in the bargain. 'Marky, tell Tom to give him the skin too; and in the morning, bring the skin to me, and I will give you half-a-dollar for it, or at least, three-and-sixpence. I want just such a skin, to cover the pillion that I am making for cousin Bess."

"I thank you, sir, for your liberality, and, I trust, am also thankful for my escape," returned the stranger; "but you reserve the very part of the animal that I wish for my own use. I must have the saddle myself."

"Must!" echoed Richard; "must is harder to be swallowed than the horns of the buck."

"Yes, must," repeated the youth; when, turning his head proudly around him, as if to see who would dare to controvert

his rights, he met the astonished gaze of Elizabeth, and proceeded more mildly—"that is, if a man is allowed the possession
of that which his hand hath killed, and the law will protect him
in the enjoyment of his own."

"The law will do so," said Judge Temple, with an air of mortification, mingled with surprise. "Benjamin, see that the whole
deer is placed in the sleigh; and have this youth conveyed to the
hut of Leather-stocking. But, young man, thou hast a name,
and I shall see you again, in order to compensate thee for the
wrong I have done thee?"

"I am called Edwards," returned the hunter, "Oliver Edwards. I am easily to be seen, sir, for I live nigh by, and am not
afraid to show my face, having never injured any man."

"It is we, who have injured you, sir," said Elizabeth; "and the
knowledge, that you decline our assistance, would give my father great pain. He would gladly see you in the morning."

The young hunter gazed at the fair speaker, until his earnest
look brought the blood to her temples; when, recollecting himself, he bent his head, dropping his eyes to the carpet, and replied—

"In the morning, then, will I return, and see Judge Temple;
and I will accept his offer of the sleigh, in token of amity."

"Amity!" repeated Marmaduke; "there was no malice in the
act that injured thee, young man; there should be none in the
feelings which it may engender."

"Forgive us our trespasses, as we forgive those who trespass
against us," observed Mr. Grant, "is the language used by our
Divine Master himself, and it should be the golden rule of us,
his humble followers."

The stranger stood a moment, lost in thought, and then,
glancing his dark eyes, rather wildly, around the hall, he bowed
low to the divine, and moved from the apartment, with an air
that would not admit of detention.

"'Tis strange, that one so young should harbour such feelings
of resentment," said Marmaduke, when the door closed behind
the stranger; "but while the pain is recent, and the sense of the
injury so fresh, he must feel more strongly than in cooler moments. I doubt not, we shall see him, in the morning, more
tractable."

Elizabetn, to whom this speech was addressed, did not reply, but moved slowly up the hall, by herself, fixing her eyes on the little figure of the English ingrained carpet, that covered the floor; while, on the other hand, Richard gave a loud crack with his whip, as the stranger disappeared, and cried—

"Well, 'duke, you are your own master, but I would have tried law for the saddle, before I would have given it to the fellow. Do you not own the mountains, as well as the valleys? are not the woods your own? what right has this chap, or the Leather-stocking, to shoot in your woods, without your permission? Now, I have known a farmer, in Pennsylvania, order a sportsman off his farm, with as little ceremony as I would order Benjamin to put a log in the stove. By-the-by, Benjamin, see how the thermometer stands. Now, if a man has a right to do this, on a farm of a hundred acres, what power must a landlord have, who owns sixty thousand—ay! for the matter of that, including the late purchases, a hundred thousand? There is Mohegan, to-be-sure, he may have some right, being a native; but it's little the poor fellow can do now with his rifle. How is this managed in France, Monsieur Le Quoi? do you let every body run over your land, in that country, helter-skelter, as they do here, shooting the game, so that a gentleman has but little or no chance with his gun?"

"Bah! diable, no, Meester Deeck," replied the Frenchman; "we give, in France, no liberty, except to de ladi."

"Yes, yes, to the women, I know," said Richard; "that is your Sallick law. I read, sir, all kinds of books; of France, as well as England; of Greece, as well as Rome. But if I were in 'duke's place, I would stick up advertisements, to-morrow morning, forbidding all persons to shoot, or trespass, in any manner, on my woods. I could write such an advertisement myself, in an hour, as would put a stop to the thing at once."

"Richart," said Major Hartmann, very coolly knocking the ashes from his pipe into the spitting-box by his side, "now listen: I have livet seventy-five years on ter Mohawk, and in ter woots.—You hat petter mettle as mit ter deyvel, as mit ter hunters. Tey live mit ter gun, and a rifle is petter as ter law."

"A'nt Marmaduke a Judge?" said Richard, indignantly; "where is the use of being a Judge or having a Judge, if there is no law? Damn the fellow, I have a great mind to sue him in the morning myself, before Squire Doolittle, for meddling with my leaders. I am not afraid of his rifle. I can shoot too. I have hit a dollar, many a time, at fifty rods."

"Thou hast missed more dollars than ever thou hast hit, Dickon," exclaimed the cheerful voice of the Judge.—"But we will now take our evening's repast, which, I perceive by Remarkable's physiognomy, is ready. Monsieur Le Quoi, Miss Temple has a hand at your service. Will you lead the way, my child?"

"Ah! ma chère Mam'selle, comme je suis enchanté!" said the Frenchman. "Il ne manque que les dames de faire un paradis de Templeton."

Mr. Grant and Mohegan, continued in the hall, while the remainder of the party withdrew to an eating parlour, if we except Benjamin, who civilly remained, to close the rear after the clergyman, and to open the front door, for the exit of the Indian.

"John," said the divine, when the figure of Judge Temple disappeared, the last of the group, "to-morrow is the festival of the nativity of our blessed Redeemer, when the church has appointed prayers and thanksgivings, to be offered up by her children, and when all are invited to partake of the mystical elements. As you have taken up the cross, and become a follower of good, and an eschewer of evil, I trust I shall see you before the altar, with a contrite heart, and a meek spirit."

"John will come," said the Indian, betraying no surprise, though he did not understand all the terms used by the other.

"Yes," continued Mr. Grant, laying his hand gently on the tawny shoulder of the aged chief, "but it is not enough to be there in the body; you must come in the spirit, and in truth. The Redeemer died for all, for the poor Indian, as well as for the white man. Heaven knows no difference in colour; nor must earth witness a separation of the church. It is good and profitable, John, to freshen the understanding, and support the wavering, by the observance of our holy festivals; but all form is but stench, in the nostrils of the Holy One, unless it be accompanied by a devout and humble spirit."

The Indian stepped back a little, and, raising his body to its utmost powers of erection, he stretched his right arm on high, and dropped his fore-finger downward, as if pointing from the heavens, then striking his other hand on his naked breast, he said, with energy—

1. *Vignette Title Page, for* The Port Folio *(September 1823), by Gideon Fairman.*

Inman Del.   F. Kearny Sc.

11. *Edwards Showing His Wound to Judge Temple, for* The Port Folio *(August 1823), by Henry Inman.*

III. *Conversation between Mr. Grant & Mohegan, for* The Port Folio *(November 1823), by Henry Inman.*

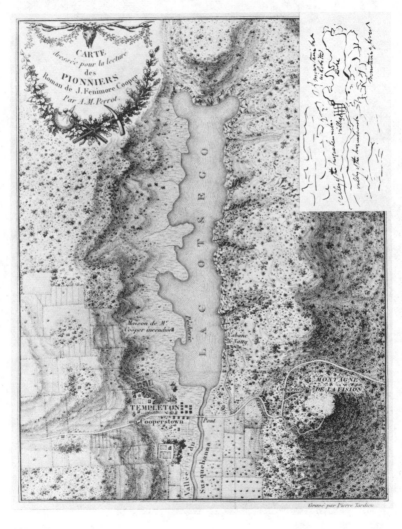

Maison de M.
Cooper incendiée

Cabane
de Natty

L   A   C   O   T   S   E   G   O

MONTAGNE
DE LA VISION

TEMPLETON
ou Cooperstown   Pont

Vallée du Susquehanna

Gravé par Pierre Tardieu.

IV. *Map Showing the Setting for* The Pioneers, *by A. M. Perrot for Volume XVIII,
Gosselin's edition of Cooper's Œuvres Complètes. The inset is Cooper's sketch
correcting an earlier version of the map.*

"The eye of the Great Spirit can see from the clouds;—the bosom of Mohegan is bare."

"It is well, John, and I hope you will receive profit and consolation, from the performance of this duty. The Great Spirit overlooks none of his children; and the man of the woods, is as much an object of his care, as he who dwells in a palace. I wish you a good night, and pray God to bless you."

The Indian bent his head, and they separated—the one to seek his hut, and the other to join the party at the supper-table. While Benjamin was opening the door, for the passage of the chief, he cried, in a tone that was meant to be encouraging—

"The parson says the word that is true, John. If-so-be, that they took count of the colour of the skin in heaven, why, they might refuse to muster on their books, a christian-born, like myself, just for the matter of a little tan, from cruising in warm latitudes; though, for the matter of that, this damned norwester is enough to whiten the skin of a blackamoor. Let the reef out of your blanket, man, or your red hide will hardly weather the night, without a touch from the frost."

Chapter VIII.

"For here the exile met from every clime,
And spoke, in friendship, every distant tongue."
Campbell, *Gertrude of Wyoming*, I.iv.3–4.

WE have made our readers acquainted with some variety in character and nations, in introducing the most important personages of this legend to their notice: but in order to establish the fidelity of our narrative, we shall briefly attempt to explain the reason why we have been obliged to present so motley a dramatis personæ.

Europe, at the period of our tale, was in the commencement of that commotion, which afterwards shook her political institutions to the centre. Louis the Sixteenth had been beheaded, and a nation, once esteemed the most refined amongst the civilized people of the world, was changing its character, and substituting cruelty for mercy, and subtlety and ferocity for magnanimity and courage. Thousands of Frenchmen were compelled to seek protection in distant lands. Among the crowds who fled from France and her islands, to the United States of America, was the gentleman whom we have already mentioned as Monsieur Le Quoi. He had been recommended to the favour of Judge Temple, by the head of an eminent mercantile house in New-York, with whom Marmaduke was in habits of intimacy, and accustomed to exchange good offices. At his first interview with the Frenchman, our Judge had discovered him to be a man of breeding, and one who had seen much more prosperous days, in his own country. From certain hints that had escaped him, Monsieur Le Quoi was suspected of having been a West-India planter, great numbers of whom had fled from St. Domingo and the other islands, and were now living in the Union, in a state of comparative poverty, and some in absolute want. The latter was not, however, the lot of Monsieur Le Quoi. He had but little, he acknowledged, but that little was enough to furnish, in the language of the country, an "assortment for a store."

The knowledge of Marmaduke was eminently practical, and there was no part of a *settler's* life with which he was not familiar. Under his direction, Monsieur Le Quoi made some purchases, consisting of a few cloths; some groceries, with a good deal of gunpowder and tobacco; a quantity of iron-ware, among which was a large proportion of Barlow's jack-knives, potash-kettles, and spiders; a very formidable collection of crockery, of the coarsest quality, and most uncouth forms; together with every other common article, that the art of man has devised for his wants, not forgetting the luxuries of looking-glasses and Jew's-harps. With this collection of valuables, Monsieur Le Quoi had stepped behind a counter, and, with a wonderful pliability of temper, had dropped into his assumed character, as gracefully as he had ever moved in any other. The gentleness and suavity of his manners, rendered him extremely popular; besides this, the women soon discovered that he had a taste; his calicoes were the finest, or, in other words, the most showy, of any that were brought into the country; and it was impossible to look at the prices, asked for his goods, by "so pretty a spoken man." Through these conjoint means, the affairs of Monsieur Le Quoi were again in a prosperous condition, and he was looked up to by the settlers as the second best man on the "Patent."

This term, "Patent," which we have already used, and for which we may have further occasion, meant the district of country that had been originally granted to old Major Effingham, by the "King's letters patent," and which had now become, by purchase under the act of confiscation, the property of Marmaduke Temple. It was a term in common use, throughout the *new* parts of the state, and was usually annexed to the landlord's name, as, "Temple's, or Effingham's Patent."

Major Hartmann was the descendant of a man, who, in company with a number of his countrymen, had emigrated, with their families, from the banks of the Rhine, to those of the Mohawk. This migration had occurred as far back as the reign of Queen Anne; and their descendants were now living, in great peace and plenty, on the fertile borders of that beautiful stream.

The Germans, or "High Dutchers," as they were called, to distinguish them from the original, or Low Dutch colonists, were a very peculiar people. They possessed all the gravity of the latter, without any of their phlegm; and, like them, the "High Dutchers" were industrious, honest, and economical.

Fritz, or Frederick Hartmann, was an epitome of all the vices and virtues, foibles and excellencies, of his race. He was passionate, though silent, obstinate, and a good deal suspicious of strangers; of immoveable courage, inflexible honesty, and undeviating in his friendships. Indeed, there was no change about him, unless it were from grave to gay. He was serious by months, and jolly by weeks. He had, early in their acquaintance, formed an attachment for Marmaduke Temple, who was the only man, that could not speak High Dutch, that ever gained his entire confidence. Four times in each year, at periods equidistant, he left his low stone dwelling, on the banks of the Mohawk, and travelled thirty miles, through the hills, to the door of the mansion-house in Templeton. Here he generally staid a week, and was reputed to spend much of that time in riotous living, greatly countenanced by Mr. Richard Jones. But every one loved him, even to Remarkable Pettibone, to whom he occasioned some additional trouble, he was so frank, so sincere, and, at times, so mirthful. He was now on his regular Christmas visit, and had not been in the village an hour, when Richard summoned him to fill a seat in the sleigh, to meet the landlord and his daughter.

Before explaining the character and situation of Mr. Grant, it will be necessary to recur to times, far back in the brief history of the settlement.

There seems to be a tendency in human nature, to endeavour to provide for the wants of this world, before our attention is turned to the business of the other. Religion was a quality but little cultivated, amid the stumps of Temple's Patent, for the first few years of its settlement; but as most of its inhabitants were from the moral states of Connecticut and Massachusetts, when the wants of nature were satisfied, they began seriously to turn their attention to the introduction of those customs and observances, which had been the principal care of their forefathers. There was certainly a great variety of opinions, on the subject of grace and free-will, amongst the tenantry of Marmaduke; and, when we take into consideration the variety of religious instruction which they received, it can easily be seen, that it could not well be otherwise.

Soon after the village had been formally laid out, into the streets and *blocks* that resembled a city, a meeting of its inhabitants had been convened, to take into consideration the propriety of establishing an Academy. This measure originated with Richard, who, in truth, was much disposed to have the institution designated a University, or at least a College. Meeting after meeting was held, for this purpose, year after year. The *resolutions* of these assemblages, appeared in the most conspicuous columns of a little, blue-looking newspaper, that was already issued weekly from the garret of a dwelling-house in the village, and which the traveller might as often see, stuck into the fissure of a stake, erected at the point where the footpath from the log cabin of some settler entered the highway, as a post-office for an individual. Sometimes the stake supported a small box, and a whole neighbourhood received a weekly supply, for their literary wants, at this point, where the man who "rides post," regularly deposited a bundle of the precious commodity. To these flourishing resolutions, which briefly recounted the general utility of education, the political and geographical rights of the village of Templeton, to a participation in the favours of the regents of the university, the salubrity of the air, and wholesomeness of the water, together with the cheapness of food, and the superior state of morals in the neighbourhood, were uniformly annexed, in large Roman capitals, the names of Marmaduke Temple, as chairman, and Richard Jones, as secretary.

Happily for the success of this undertaking, the regents were not accustomed to resist these appeals to their generosity, whenever there was the smallest prospect of a donation to second the request. Eventually, Judge Temple concluded to bestow the necessary land, and to erect the required edifice at his own expense. The skill of Mr., or, as he was now called, from the circumstance of having received the commission of a justice of the peace, Squire Doolittle, was again put in requisition, and the science of Mr. Jones was once more resorted to.

We shall not recount the different devices of the architects on the occasion; nor would it be decorous so to do, seeing that there was a convocation of the society of the ancient and honourable fraternity "of the free and accepted masons," at the head of whom was Richard, in the capacity of master, doubtless to approve or reject such of the plans as, in their wisdom, they deemed to be for the best. The knotty point was, however, soon decided; and, on the appointed day, the brotherhood marched, in great state, displaying sundry banners and mysterious symbols, each man with a little mimic apron before him, from a most cunningly contrived apartment in the garret of the "Bold Dragoon," an inn, kept by one Captain Hollister, to the site of the intended edifice. Here Richard laid the corner-stone, with suitable gravity, amidst an assemblage of more than half the men, and all the women, within ten miles of Templeton.

In the course of the succeeding week, there was another meeting of the people, not omitting swarms of the gentler sex, when the abilities of Hiram, at the "square rule," were put to the test of experiment. The frame fitted well; and the skeleton of the fabric was reared without a single accident, if we except a few falls from horses, while the labourers were returning home in the evening. From this time, the work advanced with great rapidity, and in the course of the season, the labour was completed; the edifice standing, in all its beauty and proportions, the boast of the village, the study of young aspirants for architectural fame, and the admiration of every settler on the Patent.

It was a long, narrow house, of wood, painted white, and more than half windows; and when the observer stood at the western side of the building, the edifice offered but a small obstacle to a full view of the rising sun. It was, in truth, but a very comfortless, open place, through which the daylight shone with natural facility. On its front were divers ornaments, in wood, designed by Richard, and executed by Hiram; but a window in the centre of the second story, immediately over the door, or grand entrance, and the "steeple," were the pride of the building. The former was, we believe, of the composite order, for it included in its composition a multitude of ornaments, and a great variety of proportions. It consisted of an arched compartment in the centre, with a square and small division on either side, the whole encased in heavy frames, deeply and laboriously moulded in pine wood, and lighted with a vast number of blurred and green-looking glass, of those dimensions which are commonly called "eight by ten." Blinds, that were intended to be painted green, kept the window in a state of preservation, and probably might have contributed to the effect of the whole, had not the failure in the public funds, which seems always to be incidental to any undertaking of this kind, left them in the sombre coat of lead-colour with which they had been originally clothed. The "steeple" was a little cupola, reared on the very centre of the roof, on four tall pillars of pine, that were fluted with a gouge, and loaded with mouldings. On the tops of the columns was reared a dome, or cupola, resembling in shape an inverted tea-cup without its bottom, from the centre of which projected a spire, or shaft of wood, transfixed with two iron rods, that bore on their ends the letters N.S.E. and W., in the same metal. The whole was surmounted by an imitation of one of the finny tribe, carved in wood, by the hands of Richard, and painted, what he called, a "scale-colour." This animal Mr. Jones affirmed to be an admirable resemblance of a great favourite of the epicures in that country, which bore the title of "lake-fish;" and doubtless the assertion was true; for, although intended to answer the purposes of a weather-cock, the fish was observed invariably to look, with a longing eye, in the direction of the beautiful sheet of water that lay imbedded in the mountains of Templeton.

For a short time after the charter of the regents was received, the trustees of this institution employed a graduate of one of the eastern colleges, to instruct such youth as aspired to knowledge, within the walls of the edifice which we have described. The upper part of the building was in one apartment, and was intended for gala-days and exhibitions; and the lower contained two rooms, that were intended for the great divisions of education, viz. the Latin and the English scholars. The former were never very numerous; though the sounds of "nominative, *pennaa;* genitive, *penny*," were soon heard to issue from the windows of the room, to the great delight and manifest edification of the passengers.

Only one labourer in this temple of Minerva, however, was known to get so far as to attempt a translation of Virgil. He, indeed, appeared at the annual exhibition, to the prodigious exultation of all his relatives, a farmer's family in the vicinity, and repeated the whole of the first eclogue from memory, observing the intonations of the dialogue with much judgment and effect. The sounds, as they proceeded from his mouth, of

"Titty-ree too patty-lee ree-coo-bans sub teg-mi-nee faa-gy
Syl-ves-trem ten-oo-i moo-sam med-i-taa-ris aa-ve-ny"—

were the last that had been heard in that building, as probably they were the first that had ever been heard, in the same language, there or any where else. By this time, the trustees discovered, that they had anticipated the age, and the *instructor*, or *principal*, was superseded by a *master*, who went on to teach the more humble lesson, of "the more haste the worse speed," in good, plain English.

From this time until the date of our incidents, the Academy was a common country school; and the great room of the building was sometimes used as a court-room, on extraordinary trials; sometimes for conferences of the religious, and the morally disposed, in the evening; at others for a ball in the afternoon, given under the auspices of Richard; and on Sundays, invariably, as a place of public worship.

When an itinerant priest, of the persuasion of the Methodists, Baptists, Universalists, or of the more numerous sect of the Presbyterians, was accidentally in the neighbourhood, he was ordinarily invited to officiate, and was commonly rewarded for his services by a collection in a hat, before the congregation separated. When no such regular minister offered, a kind of colloquial prayer or two was made, by some of the more gifted members, and a sermon was usually read, from Sterne, by Mr. Richard Jones.

The consequence of this desultory kind of priesthood was, as we have already intimated, a great diversity of opinion, on the more abstruse points of faith. Each sect had its adherents, though neither was regularly organized and disciplined. Of the religious education of Marmaduke, we have already written, nor was the doubtful character of his faith completely removed by his marriage. The mother of Elizabeth was an Episcopalian, as, indeed, was the mother of the Judge himself; and the good taste of Marmaduke revolted at the familiar colloquies which the leaders of the conferences held with the Deity, in their nightly meetings. In form, he was certainly an Episcopalian, though not a sectary of that denomination. On the other hand, Richard was as rigid in the observance of the canons of his church, as he was inflexible in his opinions. Indeed, he had once or twice essayed to introduce the Episcopal form of service, on the Sundays that the pulpit was vacant; but Richard was a good deal addicted to carrying things to an excess, and then there was something so papal in his air, that the greater part of his hearers deserted him on the second Sabbath—on the third, his only auditor was Ben Pump, who had all the obstinate and enlightened orthodoxy of a high-churchman.

Before the war of the revolution, the English church was supported, in the colonies, with much interest, by some of its adherents in the mother country, and a few of the congregations were very amply endowed. But, for a season, after the independence of the states was established, this sect of Christians languished, for the want of the highest order of its priesthood. Pious and suitable divines were at length selected, and sent to the mother country, to receive that authority, which, it is understood, can only be transmitted directly from one to the other, and thus obtain, in order to preserve, that unity in their churches, which properly belonged to a people of the same nation. But unexpected difficulties presented themselves, in the oaths with which the policy of England had fettered their establishment, and much time was spent, before a conscientious sense of duty would permit the prelates of Britain to delegate the authority so earnestly sought. Time, patience, and zeal, however, removed every impediment, and the venerable men, who had been set apart by the American churches, at length returned to their expecting dioceses, endowed with the most elevated functions of their earthly church. Priests and Deacons were ordained; and missionaries provided, to keep alive the expiring flame of devotion, in such members as were deprived of the ordinary administrations, by dwelling in new and unorganized districts.

Of this number was Mr. Grant. He had been sent into the county of which Templeton was the capital, and had been kindly invited by Marmaduke, and officiously pressed by Richard, to take up his abode in the village. A small and humble dwelling was prepared for his family, and the divine had made his appearance in the place, but a few days before the time of his introduction to the reader. As his forms were entirely new to most of the inhabitants, and a clergyman of another denomination had previously occupied the field, by engaging the academy, the first Sunday after his arrival was suffered to pass in silence; but now that his rival had passed on, like a meteor, filling the air with the light of his wisdom, Richard was empowered to give notice, that "Public worship, after the forms of the Protestant Episcopal Church, would be held, on the night before Christmas, in the long-room of the academy in Templeton, by the Rev. Mr. Grant."

This annunciation excited great commotion among the different sectaries. Some wondered as to the nature of the exhibition; others sneered; but a far greater part, recollecting the essays of Richard in that way, and mindful of the liberality, or rather laxity, of Marmaduke's notions on the subject of sectarianism, thought it most prudent to be silent.

The expected evening was, however, the wonder of the hour; nor was the curiosity at all diminished, when Richard and Benjamin, on the morning of the eventful day, were seen to issue from the woods in the neighbourhood of the village, each bearing on his shoulders a large bunch of evergreens. This worthy pair was observed to enter the academy, and carefully to fasten the door, after which their proceedings remained a profound secret to the rest of the village; Mr. Jones, before he commenced this mysterious business, having informed the schoolmaster, to the great delight of the white-headed flock he governed, that there could be no school that day. Marmaduke was apprized of all these preparations, by letter, and it was especially arranged, that he and Elizabeth should arrive in season, to participate in the solemnities of the evening.

After this digression, we shall return to our narrative.

Chapter IX.

"Now all admire, in each high-flavour'd dish,
The capabilities of flesh—fowl—fish;
In order due each guest assumes his station,
Throbs high his breast with fond anticipation,
And prelibates the joys of mastication." *Heliogabaliad.*

THE apartment to which Monsieur Le Quoi handed Elizabeth, communicated with the hall, through the door that led under the urn which was supposed to contain the ashes of Dido. The room was spacious, and of very just proportions; but in its ornaments and furniture, the same diversity of taste, and imperfection of execution, were to be observed, as existed in the hall. Of furniture, there were a dozen green, wooden arm-chairs, with cushions of moreen, taken from the same piece as the petticoat of Remarkable. The tables were spread, and their materials and workmanship could not be seen; but they were heavy, and of great size. An enormous mirror, in a gilt frame, hung against the wall, and a cheerful fire, of the hard or sugar-maple, was burning on the hearth. The latter was the first object that struck the attention of the Judge, who, on beholding it, exclaimed, rather angrily, to Richard—

"How often have I forbidden the use of the sugar-maple, in my dwelling. The sight of that sap, as it exudes with the heat, is painful to me, Richard. Really, it behooves the owner of woods so extensive as mine, to be cautious what example he sets his people, who are already felling the forests, as if no end could be found to their treasures, nor any limits to their extent. If we go on in this way, twenty years hence, we shall want fuel."

"Fuel in these hills, cousin 'duke!" exclaimed Richard, in derision—"fuel! why, you might as well predict, that the fish will die, for the want of water in the lake, because I intend, when the frost gets out of the ground, to lead one or two of the springs, through logs, into the village. But you are always a little wild on such subjects, Marmaduke."

"Is it wildness," returned the Judge, earnestly, "to condemn a practice, which devotes these jewels of the forest, these precious gifts of nature, these mines of comfort and wealth, to the common uses of a fire-place? But I must, and will, the instant the snow is off the earth, send out a party into the mountains, to explore for coal."

"Coal!" echoed Richard; "who the devil do you think will dig for coal, when in hunting for a bushel, he would have to rip up more roots of trees, than would keep him in fuel for a twelvemonth? Poh! poh! Marmaduke, you should leave the management of these things to me, who have a natural turn that way. It was I that ordered this fire, and a noble one it is, to warm the blood of my pretty cousin Bess."

"The motive, then, must be your apology, Dickon," said the Judge.—"But, gentlemen, we are waiting. Elizabeth, my child, take the head of the table; Richard, I see, means to spare me the trouble of carving, by sitting opposite to you."

"To be sure I do," cried Richard; "here is a turkey to carve, and I flatter myself that I understand carving a turkey, or, for that matter, a goose, as well as any man alive. Mr. Grant! where's Mr. Grant? will you please to say grace, sir? Every thing is getting cold. Take a thing from the fire, this cold weather, and it will freeze in five minutes. Mr. Grant! we want you to say grace. 'For what we are about to receive, the Lord make us thankful.' Come, sit down, sit down. Do you eat wing or breast, cousin Bess?"

But Elizabeth had not taken her seat, nor was she in readiness to receive either the wing or breast. Her laughing eyes were glancing at the arrangements of the table, and the quality and selection of the food. The eyes of the father soon met the wondering looks of his daughter, and he said, with a smile—

"You perceive, my child, how much we are indebted to Remarkable, for her skill in housewifery; she has indeed provided a noble repast; such as well might stop the cravings of hunger."

"Law!" said Remarkable, "I'm glad if the Judge is pleased; but I'm notional that you'll find the sa'ce overdone. I thought, as Elizabeth was coming home, that a body could do no less than make things agreeable."

"My daughter has now grown to woman's estate, and is from this moment mistress of my house," said the Judge; "it is proper, that all, who live with me, address her as Miss Temple."

"*Do* tell!" exclaimed Remarkable, a little aghast; "well who

ever heerd of a young woman's being called Miss? If the Judge
had a wife now, I shouldn't think of calling her any thing but
Miss Temple; but—"

"Having nothing but a daughter, you will observe that style to
her, if you please, in future," interrupted Marmaduke.

As the Judge look'd seriously displeased, and, at such moments, carried a particularly commanding air with him, the
wary housekeeper made no reply; and, Mr. Grant entering the
room, the whole party were soon seated at the table. As the
arrangements of this repast were much in the prevailing taste
of that period and country, we shall endeavour to give a short
description of the appearance of the banquet.

The table-linen was of the most beautiful damask, and the
plates and dishes of real china, an article of great luxury at this
early period in American commerce. The knives and forks
were of exquisitely polished steel, and were set in unclouded
ivory. So much being furnished by the wealth of Marmaduke,
was not only comfortable, but even elegant. The contents of the
several dishes, and their positions, however, were the result of
the sole judgment of Remarkable. Before Elizabeth, was placed
an enormous roasted turkey, and before Richard, one boiled.
In the centre of the table, stood a pair of heavy silver castors,
surrounded by four dishes; one a fricassee, that consisted of
gray squirrels; another of fish fried; a third of fish boiled; the
last was a venison steak. Between these dishes and the turkeys,
stood, on the one side, a prodigious chine of roasted bear's
meat, and on the other a boiled leg of delicious mutton. Interspersed among this load of meats, was every species of veg-
etables that the season and country afforded. The four corners
were garnished with plates of cake. On one was piled certain
curiously twisted and complicated figures, called "nut-cakes."
On another were heaps of a black-looking substance, which, receiving its hue from molasses, was properly termed "sweet-
cake;" a wonderful favourite in the coterie of Remarkable. A
third was filled, to use the language of the housekeeper, with
"caards of gingerbread;" and the last held a "plum-cake," so
called from the number of large raisins that were showing their
black heads, in a substance of a suspiciously similar colour. At
each corner of the table, stood saucers, filled with a thick fluid,
of somewhat equivocal colour and consistence, variegated with

small dark lumps of a substance that resembled nothing but itself, which Remarkable termed her "sweet-meats." At the side of each plate, which was placed bottom upwards, with its knife and fork most accurately crossed above it, stood another, of smaller size, containing a motley-looking pie, composed of triangular slices of apple, mince, pumpkin, craneberry, and *custard*, so arranged as to form an entire whole. Decanters of brandy, rum, gin, and wine, with sundry pitchers of cider, beer, and one hissing vessel of "flip," were put wherever an opening would admit of their introduction. Notwithstanding the size of the tables, there was scarcely a spot where the rich damask could be seen, so crowded were the dishes, with their associated bottles, plates and saucers. The object seemed to be profusion, and it was obtained entirely at the expense of order and elegance.

All the guests, as well as the Judge himself, seemed perfectly familiar with this description of fare, for each one commenced eating, with an appetite that promised to do great honour to Remarkable's taste and skill. What rendered this attention to the repast a little surprising, was the fact, that both the German and Richard had been summoned from another table, to meet the Judge; but Major Hartmann both ate and drank without any rule, when on his excursions; and Mr. Jones invariably made it a point, to participate in the business in hand, let it be what it would. The host seemed to think some apology necessary, for the warmth he had betrayed on the subject of the fire-wood, and when the party were comfortably seated, and engaged with their knives and forks, he observed—

"The wastefulness of the settlers, with the noble trees of this country, is shocking, Monsieur Le Quoi, as doubtless you have noticed. I have seen a man fell a pine, when he has been in want of fencing-stuff, and roll his first cuts into the gap, where he left it to rot, though its top would have made rails enough to answer his purpose, and its butt would have sold in the Philadelphia market for twenty dollars."

"And how the devil—I beg your pardon, Mr. Grant," interrupted Richard; "but how is the poor devil to get his logs to the Philadelphia market, pray? put them in his pocket, ha! as you would a handful of chestnuts, or a bunch of chicker-berries? I should like to see you walking up High-street, with a pine log in

each pocket.—Poh! poh! cousin 'duke, there are trees enough for us all, and some to spare. Why I can hardly tell which way the wind blows, when I'm out in the clearings, they are so thick, and so tall;—I couldn't at all, if it wasn't for the clouds, and I happen to know all the points of the compass, as it were, by heart."

"Ay! ay! Squire," cried Benjamin, who had now entered, and taken his place behind the Judge's chair, a little aside withal, in order to be ready for any observation like the present; "look aloft, sir, look aloft. The old seamen say, 'that the devil wouldn't make a sailor, unless he look'd aloft.' As for the compass, why, there is no such thing as steering without one. I'm sure I never lose sight of the main-top, as I call the Squire's look-out on the roof, but I set my compass, d'ye see, and take the bearings and distance of things, in order to work out my course, if-so-be that it should cloud up, or the tops of the trees should shut out the light of heaven. The steeple of St. Paul's, now that we have got it on end, is a great help to the navigation of the woods, for, by the Lord Harry, as I was"—

"It is well, Benjamin," interrupted Marmaduke, observing that his daughter manifested displeasure at the major-domo's familiarity; "but you forget there is a lady in company, and the women love to do most of the talking themselves."

"The Judge says the true word," cried Benjamin, with one of his discordant laughs: "now here is Mistress Remarkable Prettybones; just take the stopper off her tongue, and you'll hear a gabbling, worse like than if you should happen to fall to leeward, in crossing a French privateer, or some such thing, mayhap, as a dozen monkeys stowed in one bag."

It were impossible to say, how perfect an illustration of the truth of Benjamin's assertion the housekeeper would have furnished, if she had dared; but the Judge looked sternly at her, and, unwilling to incur his resentment, yet unable to contain her anger, she threw herself out of the room, with a toss of the body, that nearly separated her frail form in the centre.

"Richard," said Marmaduke, observing that his displeasure had produced the desired effect, "can you inform me of any thing concerning the youth, whom I so unfortunately wounded? I found him on the mountain, hunting in company with the Leather-stocking, as if they were of the same family; but there is a manifest difference in their manners. The youth delivers himself in chosen language; such as is seldom heard in these hills, and such as occasions great surprise to me, how one so meanly clad, and following so lowly a pursuit, could attain. Mohegan also knew him. Doubtless he is a tenant of Natty's hut. Did you remark the language of the lad, Monsieur Le Quoi?"

"Certainement, Monsieur Templ'," returned the Frenchman, "he deed, conevairse in de excellent Anglaise."

"The boy is no miracle," exclaimed Richard; "I've known children that were sent to school early, talk much better, before they were twelve years old. There was Zared Coe, old Nehemiah's son, who first settled on the beaver-dam meadow, he could write almost as good a hand as myself, when he was fourteen; though it's true, I helped to teach him a little, in the evenings. But this shooting gentleman ought to be put in the stocks, if he ever takes a rein in his hand again. He is the most awkward fellow about a horse I ever met with. I dare say, he never drove any thing but oxen in his life."

"There I think, Dickon, you do the lad injustice," said the Judge; "he uses much discretion in critical moments.—Dost thou not think so, Bess?"

There was nothing in this question particularly to excite blushes, but Elizabeth started from the reverie into which she had fallen, and coloured to her forehead, as she answered—

"To me, dear sir, he appeared extremely skillful, and prompt, and courageous; but perhaps cousin Richard will say, I am as ignorant as the gentleman himself."

"Gentleman!" echoed Richard; "do you call such chaps gentlemen, at school, Elizabeth?"

"Every man is a gentleman, who knows how to treat a woman with respect and consideration," returned the young lady, promptly, and a little smartly.

"So much for hesitating to appear before the heiress in his shirt sleeves," cried Richard, winking at Monsieur Le Quoi, who returned the wink with one eye, while he rolled the other, with an expression of sympathy, towards the young lady.—"Well, well, to me he seemed any thing but a gentleman. I must say, however, for the lad, that he draws a good trigger, and has a true aim. He's good at shooting a buck, ha! Marmaduke?"

"Richart," said Major Hartmann, turning his grave countenance towards the gentleman he addressed, with much earnestness, "ter poy is goot. He savet your life, and my life, and ter life of Tominie Grant, and ter life of ter Frenchman; and, Richart, he shall never vant a pet to sleep in, vile olt Fritz Hartmann hast a shingle to cover his het mit."

"Well, well, as you please, old gentleman," returned Mr. Jones, endeavouring to look indifferent; "put him into your own stone house, if you will, Major. I dare say, the lad never slept in any thing better than a bark shanty in his life, unless it was some such hut as the cabin of Leather-stocking. I prophesy, you will soon spoil him; any one could see how proud he grew, in a short time, just because he stood by my horses' heads, while I turned them into the highway."

"No, no, my old friend," cried Marmaduke, "it shall be my task, to provide in some manner for the youth: I owe him a debt of my own, besides the service he has done me, through my friends. And yet I anticipate some little trouble, in inducing him to accept of my services. He showed a marked dislike, I thought, Bess, to my offer of a residence within these walls for life."

"Really, dear sir," said Elizabeth, projecting her beautiful under-lip, "I have not studied the gentleman so closely, as to read his feelings in his countenance. I thought he might very naturally feel pain from his wound, and therefore pitied him; but"—and as she spoke, she glanced her eye, with suppressed curiosity, towards the major-domo—"I dare say, sir, that Benjamin can tell you something about him. He cannot have been in the village, and Benjamin not have seen him often."

"Ay! I have seen the boy before," said Benjamin, who wanted little encouragement to speak: "he has been backing and filling in the wake of Natty Bumppo, through the mountains, after deer, like a Dutch long-boat in tow of an Albany sloop. He carries a good rifle too. The Leather-stocking said, in my hearing, before Betty Hollister's bar-room fire, no later than the Tuesday night, that the younker was certain death to the wild beasts. If-so-be he can kill the wild cat, that has been heard moaning on the lake-side, since the hard frosts and deep snows have driven the deer to herd, he will be doing the thing that is good. Your wild cat is a bad shipmate, and should be made to cruize out of the track of christian-men."

"Lives he in the hut of Bumppo?" asked Marmaduke, with some interest.

"Cheek by jowl: the Wednesday will be three weeks since he first hove in sight, in company with Leather-stocking. They had captured a wolf between them, and had brought in his scalp for the bounty. That Mister Bump-ho has a handy turn with him, in taking off a scalp; and there's them, in this here village, who say he larnt the trade by working on christian-men. If-so-be that there is truth in the saying, and I commanded along shore here, as your honour does, why d'ye see, I'd bring him to the gangway for it, yet. There's a very pretty post rigged alongside of the stocks, and for the matter of a cat, I can fit one with my own hands; ay! and use it too, for the want of a better."

"You are not to credit the idle tales you hear of Natty: he has a kind of natural right to gain a livelihood in these mountains; and if the idlers in the village take it into their heads to annoy him, as they sometimes do reputed rogues, they shall find him protected by the strong arm of the law."

"Ter rifle is petter as ter law," said the Major, sententiously.

"That for his rifle!" exclaimed Richard, snapping his fingers; "Ben is right, and I"—He was stopped by the sounds of a common ship-bell, that had been elevated to the belfry of the academy, which now announced, by its incessant ringing, that the hour for the appointed service had arrived. "'For this, and every other instance of his goodness'—I beg pardon, Mr. Grant; will you please to return thanks, sir? it is time we should be moving, as we are the only Episcopalians in the neighbourhood; that is, I, and Benjamin, and Elizabeth; for I count half-breeds, like Marmaduke, as bad as heretics."

The divine arose, and performed the office, meekly and fervently, and the whole party instantly prepared themselves for the church—or rather academy.

Chapter X.

"And calling sinful man to pray,
Loud, long, and deep the bell had toll'd."
        Bürger, "The Wild Huntsman," ll.11–12 (tr. Scott).

WHILE Richard and Monsieur Le Quoi, attended by Benjamin, proceeded to the academy, by a foot-path through the snow, the Judge, his daughter, the Divine, and the Major, took a more circuitous route to the same place by the streets of the village.

The moon had risen, and its orb was shedding a flood of light over the dark outline of pines, which crowned the eastern mountain. In many climates, the sky would have been thought clear and lucid for a noontide. The stars twinkled in the heavens, like the last glimmerings of distant fire, so much were they obscured by the overwhelming radiance of the atmosphere; the rays from the moon striking upon the smooth white surfaces of the lake and fields, reflecting upwards a light that was brightened by the spotless colour of the immense bodies of snow.

Elizabeth employed herself with reading the signs, one of which appeared over almost every door, while the sleigh moved, steadily and at an easy gait, along the principal street. Not only new occupations, but names that were strangers to her ears, met her gaze at every step they proceeded. The very houses seemed changed. This had been altered by an addition; that had been painted; another had been erected on the site of an old acquaintance, which had been banished from the earth, almost as soon as it made its appearance on it. All were, however, pouring forth their inmates, who uniformly held their way towards the point where the expected exhibition, of the conjoint taste of Richard and Benjamin, was to be made.

After viewing the buildings, which really appeared to some advantage, under the bright but mellow light of the moon, our heroine turned her eyes to a scrutiny of the different figures that they passed, in search of any form that she knew. But all seemed alike, as, muffled in cloaks, hoods, coats, or tippets, they glided along the narrow passages in the snow, which led under the houses, half hid by the bank that had been thrown up in excavating the deep path in which they trod. Once or twice she thought there was a stature, or a gait, that she recollected, but the person who owned it instantly disappeared behind one of those enormous piles of wood, that lay before most of the doors. It was only as they turned from the main street into another that intersected it at right angles, and which led directly to the place of meeting, that she recognised a face and building that she knew.

The house stood at one of the principal corners in the village, and, by its well-trodden doorway, as well as the sign, that was swinging, with a kind of doleful sound, in the blasts that occasionally swept down the lake, was clearly one of the most frequented inns in the place. The building was only of one story, but the dormer windows in the roof, the paint, the window-shutters, and the cheerful fire that shone through the open door, gave it an air of comfort, that was not possessed by many of its neighbours. The sign was suspended from a common ale-house post, and represented the figure of a horseman, armed with sabre and pistols, and surmounted by a bear-skin cap, with the fiery animal that he bestrode "rampant." All these particulars were easily to be seen, by the aid of the moon, together with a row of somewhat illegible writing, in black paint, but in which Elizabeth, to whom the whole was familiar, read with facility, "The Bold Dragoon."

A man and a woman were issuing from the door of this habitation, as the sleigh was passing. The former moved with a stiff, military step, that was a good deal heightened by a limp in one leg; but the woman advanced with a measure and an air, that seemed not particularly regardful of what she might encounter. The light of the moon fell directly upon her full, broad, and red visage; exhibiting her masculine countenance, under the mockery of a ruffled cap, that was intended to soften the lineaments of features that were by no means squeamish. A small bonnet, of black silk, and of a slightly formal cut, was placed on the back of her head, but not so as to shade her visage in the least. Her face, as it encountered the rays of the moon from the east, seemed not unlike a sun rising in the west. She advanced, with masculine strides, to intercept the sleigh, and the Judge, directing the namesake of the Grecian king, who held the lines, to check his horses, the parties were soon near to each other.

"Good luck to ye, and a wilcome home, Jooge," cried the female, with a strong Irish accent; "and I'm sure it's to me that ye'r always wilcome. Sure! and there's Miss 'Lizzy, and a fine young woman is she grown. What a heart-ach would she be giving the young men now, if there was sich a thing as a rigiment in the town. Och! but it's idle to talk of sich vanities, while the bell is calling us to mating, jist as we shall be call'd away unexpictedly, some day, when we are the laist calkilating. Good even, Major; will I make the bowl of gin-toddy the night?—or it's likely ye'll stay at the big house, the Christmas eve, and the very night of ye'r getting there."

"I am glad to see you, Mrs. Hollister," returned Elizabeth. "I've been trying to find a face that I knew, since we left the door of the mansion-house, but none have I seen except your own. Your house, too, is unaltered, while all the others are so changed, that, but for the places where they stand, they would be utter strangers. I observe you also keep the dear sign, that I saw cousin Richard paint, and even the name at the bottom, about which, you may remember, you had the disagreement."

"Is it the bould dragoon ye mane? and what name would he have, who niver was known by any other, as my husband here, the Captain, can tistify. He was a pleasure to wait upon, and was iver the foremost in need. Och! but he had a sudden ind! But it's to be hoped, that he was justified by the cause. And it's not Parson Grant there, who'll gainsay that same.—Yes, yes—the Squire would paint, and so I thought that we might have *his* face up there, who had so often shared good and evil wid us. The eyes is no so large nor so fiery as the Captain's own, but the whiskers and the cap is as like as two paas. Well, well——I'll not keep ye in the cowld, talking, but will drop in, the morrow, after sarvice, and ask ye how ye do. It's our bounden duty to make the most of this present, and to go to the house which is open to all: so God bless ye, and keep ye from evil.—Will I make the gin-twist the night, or no, Major?"

To this question the German replied, very sententiously, in the affirmative; and, after a few words had passed between the husband of this fiery-faced hostess and the Judge, the sleigh moved on. It soon reached the door of the academy, where the party alighted and entered the building.

In the mean time, Mr. Jones and his two companions, having a much shorter distance to journey, had arrived before the appointed place several minutes sooner than the party in the sleigh. Instead of hastening into the room, in order to enjoy the astonishment of the settlers, Richard placed a hand in either pocket of his surtout, and affected to walk about, in front of the academy, like one to whom the ceremonies were familiar.

The villagers proceeded uniformly into the building, with a decorum and gravity that nothing could move, on such occasions; but with a haste, that was probably a little heightened by curiosity. Those who came in from the adjacent country, spent some little time in placing certain blue and white blankets over their horses, before they proceeded to indulge their desire to view the interior of the house. Most of these men Richard approached, and inquired after the health and condition of their families. The readiness with which he mentioned the names of even the children, showed how very familiarly acquainted he was with their circumstances; and the nature of the answers he received, proved that he was a general favourite.

At length one of the pedestrians from the village stopped also, and fixed an earnest gaze at a new brick edifice, that was throwing a long shadow across the fields of snow, as it rose, with a beautiful gradation of light and shade, under the rays of a full moon. In front of the academy was a vacant piece of ground, that was intended for a public square. On the side opposite to Mr. Jones, the new, and as yet unfinished, church of St. Paul's was erected. This edifice had been reared, during the preceding summer, by the aid of what was called a subscription; though all, or nearly all, of the money, came from the pocket of the landlord. It had been built under a strong conviction of the necessity of a more seemly place of worship than "the long-room of the academy," and under an implied agreement, that, after its completion, the question should be fairly put to the people, that they might decide to what denomination it should belong. Of course, this expectation kept alive a strong excitement, in some few of the sectaries who were interested in its decision; though but little was said openly on the subject. Had Judge Temple espoused the cause of any particular sect, the question would have been immediately put at rest, for his influence was too powerful to be opposed; but he declined interference in the matter, positively refusing to lend even the weight of his name on the side of Richard, who had secretly given an assurance to his Diocesan, that both the building and the congregation would cheerfully come within the pale of the Protestant Episcopal Church. But when the neutrality of the Judge was clearly ascertained, Mr. Jones discovered that he had to contend with a stiff-necked people. His first measure was to go among them, and commence a course of reasoning, in order to bring them round to his own way of thinking. They all heard him patiently, and not a man uttered a word in reply, in the way of argument: and Richard thought, by the time that he had gone through the settlement, the point was conclusively decided in his favour. Willing to strike while the iron was hot, he called a meeting, through the newspaper, with a view to decide the question, by a vote, at once. Not a soul attended, and one of the most anxious afternoons that he had ever known, was spent by Richard in a vain discussion with Mrs. Hollister, who strongly contended that the Methodist (her own) church was the best entitled to, and most deserving of, the possession of the new tabernacle. Richard now perceived that he had been too sanguine, and had fallen into the error of all those who, ignorantly, deal with that wary and sagacious people. He assumed a disguise himself, that is, as well as he knew how, and proceeded step by step to advance his purpose.

The task of erecting the building had been unanimously transferred to Mr. Jones and Hiram Doolittle. Together they had built the mansion-house, the academy, and the jail; and they alone knew how to plan and rear such a structure as was now required. Early in the day, these architects had made an equitable division of their duties. To the former was assigned the duty of making all the plans, and to the latter, the labour of superintending the execution.

Availing himself of this advantage, Richard silently determined that the windows should have the Roman arch; the first positive step in effecting his wishes. As the building was made of bricks, he was enabled to conceal his design, until the moment arrived for placing the frames: then, indeed, it became necessary to act. He communicated his wishes to Hiram, with great caution; and without in the least adverting to the spiritual part of his project, he pressed the point a little warmly, on the score of architectural beauty. Hiram heard him patiently, and without contradiction; but still Richard was unable to discover the views of his coadjutor, on this interesting subject. As the right to plan was duly delegated to Mr. Jones, no direct objection was made in words, but numberless unexpected difficulties arose in the execution. At first, there was a scarcity in the right kind of material necessary to form the frames; but this objection was instantly silenced, by Richard running his pencil through two feet of their length at one stroke. Then the expense was mentioned; but Richard reminded Hiram that his cousin paid, and that *he* was his treasurer. This last intimation had great weight, and, after a silent and protracted, but fruitless opposition, the work was suffered to proceed on the original plan.

The next difficulty occurred in the steeple, which Richard had modelled after one of the smaller of those spires that adorn the great London Cathedral. The imitation was somewhat lame, it is true, the proportions being but indifferently observed; but, after much difficulty, Mr. Jones had the satisfaction of seeing an object reared, that bore, in its outlines, a striking resemblance to a vinegar-cruet. There was less opposition to this model than to the windows, for the settlers were fond of novelty, and their steeple was without a precedent.

Here the labour ceased for the season, and the difficult question of the interior remained for further deliberation. Richard well knew, that when he came to propose a reading-desk and a chancel, he must unmask; for these were arrangements, known to no church in the country, but his own. Presuming, however, on the advantages he had already obtained, he boldly styled the building St. Paul's, and Hiram prudently acquiesced in this appellation, making, however, the slight addition of calling it "*New* St. Paul's," feeling less aversion to a name taken from the English Cathedral, than from the saint.

The pedestrian, whom we have already mentioned, as pausing to contemplate this edifice, was no other than the gentleman so frequently named as Mr., or Squire Doolittle. He was of a tall, gaunt formation, with rather sharp features, and a face that expressed formal propriety, mingled with low cunning.

Richard approached him, followed by Monsieur Le Quoi and the Major-Domo.

"Good evening, Squire," said Richard, bobbing his head, but without moving his hands from his pockets.

"Good evening, Squire," echoed Hiram, turning his body, in order to turn his head also.

"A cold night, Mr. Doolittle, a cold night, sir."

"Coolish; a tedious spell on't."

"What, looking at our church, ha! it looks well by moonlight; how the tin of the cupola glistens. I warrant you, the dome of the other St. Paul's never shines so in the smoke of London."

"It is a pretty meeting-house to look on," returned Hiram, "and I believe that Monshure Ler Quow and Mr. Penguilliam will allow it."

"Sairtainlee!" exclaimed the complaisant Frenchman, "it ees ver fine."

"I thought the Monshure would say so. The last molasses that we had was excellent good. It isn't likely that you have any more of it on hand?"

"Ah! oui; ees, sair," returned Monsieur Le Quoi, with a slight shrug of his shoulder, and a trifling grimace, "dere is more. I feel ver happi dat you love eet. I hope dat Madame Dooleet' is in good 'ealth."

"Why, so as to be stirring," said Hiram.—"The Squire hasn't finished the plans for the inside of the meeting-house yet?"

"No—no—no," returned Richard, speaking quickly, but making a significant pause between each negative—"it requires reflection. There is a great deal of room to fill up, and I am afraid we shall not know how to dispose of it to advantage. There will be a large vacant spot around the pulpit, which I do not mean to place against the wall, like a sentry-box stuck up on the side of a fort."

"It is ruleable to put the deacons' box under the pulpit," said Hiram; and then, as if he had ventured too much, he added, "but there's different fashions in different countries."

"That there is," cried Benjamin; "now, in running down the coast of Spain and Portingal, you may see a nunnery stuck out on every head-land, with more steeples and outriggers, such as dog-vanes and weather-cocks, than you'll find aboard of a three-masted schooner. If-so-be that a well-built church is wanting, Old England, after all, is the country to go to, after your models and fashion-pieces. As to Paul's, thof I've never seen it, being that it's a long way up town from Radcliffe-highway and the docks, yet every body knows that it's the grandest place in the world. Now, I've no opinion but this here church over there, is as like one end of it, as a grampus is to a whale; and that's only a small difference in bulk. Mounsheer Ler Quaw here, has been in foreign parts, and thof that is not the same as having been at home, yet he must have seen churches in France too, and can form a small idee of what a church should be: now, I ask the Mounsheer to his face, if it is not a clever little thing, taking it by and large?"

"It ees ver apropos of saircumstonce," said the Frenchman—"ver judgement—but it is in de Catholique country dat dey build de—vat you call—ah-a-ah-ha—la grande cathédrale—de big church. St. Paul Londre, is ver fine; ver bootiful; ver grand—vat you call beeg; but, Monsieur Ben, pardonnez moi, it is no vort so much as Notre Dame"—

"Ha! Mounsheer, what is that you say?" cried Benjamin—"St. Paul's Church not worth so much as a damn! mayhap you may be thinking, too, that the Royal Billy isn't so good a ship as the Billy de Paris; but she would have lick'd two of her, any day, and in all weathers."

As Benjamin had assumed a very threatening kind of attitude, flourishing an arm, with a bunch at the end of it, that was half as big as Monsieur Le Quoi's head, Richard thought it time to interpose his authority.

"Hush, Benjamin, hush," he said; "you both misunderstand Monsieur Le Quoi, and forget yourself.—But here comes Mr. Grant, and the service will commence. Let us go in."

The Frenchman, who received Benjamin's reply with a well-bred good humour, that would not admit of any feeling but pity for the other's ignorance, bowed in acquiescence, and followed his companion.

Hiram and the Major-Domo brought up the rear, the latter grumbling, as he entered the building—

"If-so-be that the King of France had so much as a house to live in, that would lay alongside of Paul's, one might put up with their jaw. It's more than flesh and blood can bear, to hear a

Frenchman run down an English church in this manner. Why, Squire Doolittle, I've been at the whipping of two of them in one day—clean built, snug frigates, with standing-royals and them new-fashioned cannonades on their quarters—such as, if they had only Englishmen aboard of them, would have fout the devil."

With this ominous word in his mouth, Benjamin entered the church!

Chapter XI.

"And fools, who came to scoff, remain'd to pray."
                    Goldsmith, "The Deserted Village," l. 179.

NOTWITHSTANDING the united labours of Richard and Benjamin, the "long-room" was but an extremely inartificial temple. Benches, made in the coarsest manner, and entirely with a view to usefulness, were arranged in rows, for the reception of the congregation, while a rough, unpainted box, was placed against the wall, in the centre of the length of the apartment, as an apology for a pulpit. Something like a reading-desk was in front of this rostrum, and a small mahogany table, from the mansion-house, covered with a spotless damask cloth, stood a little on one side, by the way of an altar. Branches of pines and hemlocks were stuck in each of the fissures that offered, in the unseasoned, and hastily completed wood-work, of both the building and its furniture; while festoons and hieroglyphics met the eye, in vast profusion, along the brown sides of the scratch-coated walls. As the room was only lighted by some ten or fifteen miserable candles, and the windows were without shutters, it would have been but a dreary, cheerless place for the solemnities of a Christmas-eve, had not the large fire, that was crackling at each end of the apartment, given an air of cheerfulness to the scene, by throwing an occasional glare of light through the vistas of bushes and faces.

The two sexes were separated by an area in the centre of the room, immediately before the pulpit, and a few benches lined this space, that were occupied by the principal personages of the village and its vicinity. This distinction was rather a gratuitous concession, made by the poorer and less polished part of the population, than a right claimed by the favoured few. One bench was occupied by the party of Judge Temple, including his daughter; and, with the exception of Dr. Todd, no one else appeared willing to incur the imputation of pride, by taking a seat in what was, literally, the high place of the tabernacle.

Richard filled the chair, that was placed behind another table, in the capacity of clerk; while Benjamin, after heaping sundry logs on the fires, posted himself nigh by, in reserve for any movement that might require co-operation.

It would greatly exceed our limits, to attempt a description of the congregation, for the dresses were as various as the individuals. Some one article of more than usual finery, and perhaps the relic of other days, was to be seen about most of the females, in connexion with the coarse attire of the woods. This, wore a faded silk, that had gone through at least three generations, over coarse, woollen, black stockings; that, a shawl, whose dies were as numerous as those of the rainbow, over an awkwardly-fitting gown, of rough, brown "woman's-wear." In short, each one exhibited some favourite article, and all appeared in their best, both men and women; while the ground-works in dress, in either sex, were the coarse fabrics manufactured within their own dwellings. One man appeared in the dress of a volunteer company of artillery, of which he had been a member, in the "down-countries," precisely for no other reason, than because it was the best suit he had. Several, particularly of the younger men, displayed pantaloons of blue, edged with red cloth down the seams, part of the equipments of the "Templeton Light Infantry," from a little vanity to be seen in "boughten clothes." There was also one man in a "rifle frock," with its fringes and folds of spotless white, striking a chill to the heart with the idea of its coolness; although the thick coat of brown "home-made," that was concealed beneath, preserved a proper degree of warmth.

There was a marked uniformity of expression in countenance, especially in that half of the congregation, who did not enjoy the advantages of the polish of the village. A sallow skin, that indicated nothing but exposure, was common to all, as was an air of great decency and attention, mingled, generally, with an expression of shrewdness, and, in the present instance, of active curiosity. Now and then a face and dress were to be seen, among the congregation, that differed entirely from this description. If pock-marked, and florid, with gaitered legs, and a coat that snugly fitted the person of the wearer, it was surely an English emigrant, who had bent his steps to this retired quarter of the globe. If hard-featured, and without colour, with high cheek-bones, it was a native of Scotland, in similar circumstances. The short, black-eyed man, with a cast of the swarthy Spaniard in his face, who rose repeatedly, to make room for the belles of the village, as they entered, was a son of Erin, who had lately left off his pack, and become a stationary trader in Templeton. In short, half the nations in the north of Europe had their representatives in this assembly, though all had closely assimilated themselves to the Americans, in dress and appearance, except the Englishman. He, indeed, not only adhered to his native customs, in attire and living, but usually drove his plough, among the stumps, in the same manner as he had before done, on the plains of Norfolk, until dear-bought experience taught him the useful lesson, that a sagacious people knew what was suited to their circumstances, better than a casual observer; or a sojourner, who was, perhaps, too much prejudiced to compare, and, peradventure, too conceited to learn.

Elizabeth soon discovered that she divided the attention of the congregation with Mr. Grant. Timidity, therefore, confined her observation of the appearances which we have described, to stolen glances; but, as the stamping of feet was now becoming less frequent, and even the coughing, and other little preliminaries of a congregation settling themselves down into reverential attention, were ceasing, she felt emboldened to look around her. Gradually all noises diminished, until the suppressed cough denoted, that it was necessary to avoid singularity, and the most profound stillness pervaded the apartment. The snapping of the fires, as they threw a powerful heat into the room, was alone heard, and each face, and every eye, were turned on the divine.

At this moment, a heavy stamping of feet was heard in the passage below, as if a new comer was releasing his limbs from the snow, that was necessarily clinging to the legs of a pedestrian. It was succeeded by no audible tread; but directly Mohegan, followed by the Leather-stocking and the young hunter, made his appearance. Their footsteps would not have been heard, as they trod the apartment in their moccasins, but for the silence which prevailed.

The Indian moved with great gravity, across the floor, and, observing a vacant seat next to the Judge, he took it, in a manner that manifested his sense of his own dignity. Here, drawing his blanket closely around him, so as partly to conceal his countenance, he remained during the service, immoveable, but deeply attentive. Natty passed the place, that was so freely taken by his red companion, and seated himself on one end of a log, that was lying near the fire, where he continued, with his rifle standing between his legs, absorbed in reflections, seemingly, of no very pleasing nature. The youth found a seat, among the congregation, and another silence prevailed.

Mr. Grant now arose, and commenced his service, with the sublime declaration of the Hebrew prophet—"The Lord is in his holy temple; let all the earth keep silence before him." The example of Mr. Jones was unnecessary, to teach the congregation to rise: the solemnity of the divine, effected this as by magic. After a short pause, Mr. Grant proceeded with the solemn and winning exhortation of his service. Nothing was heard but the deep, though affectionate, tones of the reader, as he slowly went through this exordium; until, something unfortunately striking the mind of Richard as incomplete, he left his place, and walked on tip-toe from the room.

When the clergyman bent his knees in prayer and confession, the congregation so far imitated his example, as to resume their seats; whence no succeeding effort of the divine, during the evening, was able to remove them in a body. Some rose, at times, but by far the larger part continued unbending; observant, it is true, but it was the kind of observation that regarded the ceremony as a spectacle, rather than a worship in which they were to participate. Thus deserted by his clerk, Mr. Grant continued to read; but no response was audible. The short and solemn pause, that succeeded each petition, was made; still no voice repeated the eloquent language of the prayer.

The lips of Elizabeth moved, but they moved in vain; and, accustomed, as she was, to the service in the churches of the metropolis, she was beginning to feel the awkwardness of the circumstance most painfully, when a soft, low, female voice repeated after the priest, "We have left undone those things which we ought to have done." Startled, at finding one of her own sex in that place, who could rise superior to natural timidity, Miss Temple turned her eyes in the direction of the penitent. She observed a young female, on her knees, but a short distance from her, with her meek face humbly bent over her book. The appearance of this stranger, for such she was, entirely, to Elizabeth, was light and fragile. Her dress was neat and becoming; and her countenance, though pale, and slightly agitated, excited deep interest, by its sweet, and melancholy expression. A second and third response were made by this juvenile assistant, when the manly sounds of a male voice, proceeded from the opposite part of the room. Miss Temple knew the tones of the young hunter instantly, and, struggling to overcome her own diffidence, she added her low voice to the number.

All this time, Benjamin stood thumbing the leaves of a prayer-book with great industry, but some unexpected difficulties prevented his finding the place. Before the divine reached the close of the confession, however, Richard re-appeared at the door, and, as he moved lightly across the room, he took up the response, in a voice that betrayed no other concern than that of not being heard. In his hand he carried a small open box, with the figures of "8 by 10" written, in black paint, on one of its sides; which having placed in the pulpit, apparently as a footstool for the divine, he returned to his station, in time to say, sonorously, "amen." The eyes of the congregation, very naturally, were turned to the windows, as Mr. Jones entered with this singular load, and then, as if accustomed to his "general agency," were again bent on the priest, in close, and curious attention.

The long experience of Mr. Grant admirably qualified him to perform his present duty. He well understood the character of his listeners, who were mostly a primitive people in their habits; and who, being a good deal addicted to subtleties and nice distinctions in their religious opinions, viewed the introduction of any such temporal assistance as form, into their spiritual worship, not only with jealousy, but frequently with disgust. He had acquired much of his knowledge, from studying the great book of human nature, as it lay open in the world; and, knowing how dangerous it was to contend with ignorance, uniformly endeavoured to avoid dictating, where his better reason taught him it was the most prudent to attempt to lead. His orthodoxy had no dependence on his cassock; he could pray, with fervour and with faith, if circumstances required it, without the assistance of his clerk; and he had even been known to preach a most

evangelical sermon, in the winning manner of native eloquence, without the aid of a cambric handkerchief!

In the present instance he yielded, in many places, to the
prejudices of his congregation; and when he had ended, there
was not one of his new hearers, who did not think the ceremonies less papal and offensive, and more conformant to his or
her own notions of devout worship, than they had been led to
expect from a service of forms. Richard found in the divine,
during the evening, a most powerful co-operator in his religious schemes. In preaching, Mr. Grant endeavoured to steer a
middle course, between the mystical doctrines of those subli-
mated creeds, which daily involve their professors in the most
absurd contradictions, and those fluent rules of moral government, which would reduce the Saviour to a level with the
teacher of a school of ethics. Doctrine it was necessary to
preach, for nothing less would have satisfied the disputatious
people who were his listeners, and who would have interpreted
silence on his part, into a tacit acknowledgment of the superficial nature of his creed. We have already said that, amongst
the endless variety of religious instructors, the settlers were accustomed to hear every denomination urge its own distinctive
precepts; and to have found one indifferent to this interesting
subject, would have been destructive to his influence. But Mr.
Grant so happily blended the universally received opinions of
the Christian faith, with the dogmas of his own church, that,
although none were entirely exempt from the influence of his
reasons, very few took any alarm at the innovation.

"When we consider the great diversity of the human character, influenced as it is by education, by opportunity, and by the
physical and moral conditions of the creature, my dear hearers," he earnestly concluded, "it can excite no surprise, that
creeds, so very different in their tendencies, should grow out of
a religion, revealed, it is true, but whose revelations are
obscured by the lapse of ages, and whose doctrines were, after
the fashion of the countries in which they were first promul-
gated, frequently delivered in parables, and in a language
abounding in metaphors and loaded with figures. On points
where the learned have, in purity of heart, been compelled to
differ, the unlettered will necessarily be at variance. But, hap-

pily for us, my brethren, the fountain of divine love flows from a source, too pure to admit of pollution in its course; it extends, to those who drink of its vivifying waters, the peace of the righteous, and life everlasting; it endures through all time, and it pervades creation. If there be mystery in its workings, it is the mystery of a Divinity. With a clear knowledge of the nature, the might, and majesty of God, there might be conviction, but there could be no faith. If we are required to believe in doctrines, that seem not in conformity with the deductions of human wisdom, let us never forget, that such is the mandate of a wisdom that is infinite. It is sufficient for us, that enough is developed to point our path aright, and to direct our wandering steps to that portal, which shall open on the light of an eternal day. Then, indeed, it may be humbly hoped, that the film, which has been spread by the subtleties of earthly arguments, will be dissipated, by the spiritual light of heaven; and that our hour of probation, by the aid of divine grace, being once passed in triumph, will be followed by an eternity of intelligence, and endless ages of fruition. All that is now obscure, shall become plain to our expanded faculties; and what, to our present senses, may seem irreconcilable to our limited notions of mercy, of justice, and of love, shall stand, irradiated by the light of truth, confessedly the suggestions of Omniscience, and the acts of an All-powerful Benevolence.

"What a lesson of humility, my brethren, might not each of us obtain, from a review of his infant hours, and the recollection of his juvenile passions. How differently do the same acts of parental rigour appear, in the eyes of the suffering child, and of the chastened man. When the sophist would supplant, with the wild theories of his worldy wisdom, the positive mandates of inspiration, let him remember the expansion of his own feeble intellects, and pause—let him feel the wisdom of God, in what is partially concealed, as well as in that which is revealed;—in short, let him substitute humility for pride of reason—let him have faith, and live!

"The consideration of this subject is full of consolation, my hearers, and does not fail to bring with it lessons of humility and of profit, that, duly improved, would both chasten the heart, and strengthen the feeble-minded man in his course. It is a blessed consolation, to be able to lay the misdoubtings of our arrogant nature at the threshold of the dwelling-place of the Deity, from whence they shall be swept away, at the great opening of the portal, like the mists of the morning before the rising sun. It teaches us a lesson of humility, by impressing us with the imperfection of human powers, and by warning us of the many weak points, where we are open to the attacks of the great enemy of our race; it proves to us, that we are in danger of being weak, when our vanity would fain soothe us into the belief that we are most strong; it forcibly points out to us the vain-glory of intellect, and shows us the vast difference between a saving faith, and the corollaries of a philosophical theology; and it teaches us to reduce our self-examination to the test of good works. By good works must be understood, the fruits of repentance, the chiefest of which is charity. Not that charity only, which causes us to help the needy and comfort the suffering, but that feeling of universal philanthropy, which, by teaching us to love, causes us to judge with lenity, all men; striking at the root of self-righteousness, and warning us to be sparing of our condemnation of others, while our own salvation is not yet secure.

"The lesson of expediency, my brethren, which I would gather from the consideration of this subject, is most strongly inculcated by humility. On the leading and essential points of our faith, there is but little difference, amongst those classes of Christians, who acknowledge the attributes of the Saviour, and depend on his mediation. But heresies have polluted every church, and schisms are the fruits of disputation. In order to arrest these dangers, and to insure the union of his followers, it would seem, that Christ had established his visible church, and delegated the ministry. Wise and holy men, the fathers of our religion, have expended their labours, in clearing what was revealed from the obscurities of language; and the results of their experience and researches have been embodied in the form of evangelical discipline. That this discipline must be salutary, is evident, from the view of the weakness of human nature, that we have already taken: and that it may be profitable to us, and all who listen to its precepts and its liturgy, may God, in his infinite wisdom, grant.—And now to," &c.

With this ingenious reference to his own forms and ministry, Mr. Grant concluded the discourse. The most profound attention had been paid to the sermon during the whole of its delivery, although the prayers had not been received with so perfect a demonstration of respect. This was by no means an intended slight of that liturgy, to which the divine alluded, but was the habit of a people, who owed their very existence, as a distinct nation, to the doctrinal character of their ancestors. Sundry looks of private dissatisfaction were exchanged between Hiram and one or two of the leading members of the *conference*, but the feeling went no farther at that time; and the congregation, after receiving the blessing of Mr. Grant, dispersed in silence, and with great decorum.

Chapter XII.

"Your creeds, and dogmas of a learned church,
May build a fabric, fair with moral beauty;
But it would seem, that the strong hand of God
Can, only, 'rase the devil from the heart." *Duo.*

WHILE the congregation was separating, Mr. Grant approached the place where Elizabeth and her father were seated, leading the youthful female, whom we have mentioned in the preceding chapter, and presented her as his daughter. Her reception was as cordial and frank, as the manners of the country, and the value of good society, could render it; the two young women feeling, instantly, that they were necessary to the comfort of each other. The Judge, to whom the clergyman's daughter was also a stranger, was pleased to find one, who, from habits, sex, and years, could probably contribute largely to the pleasures of his own child, during her first privations, on her removal from the associations of a city to the solitude of Templeton; while Elizabeth, who had been forcibly struck with the sweetness and devotion of the youthful suppliant, removed the slight embarrassment of the timid stranger, by the ease of her own manners. They were at once acquainted, and, during the ten minutes while the "academy" was clearing, engagements were made between the young people, not only for the succeeding day, but they would probably have embraced in their arrangements half of the winter, had not the divine interrupted them, by saying—

"Gently, gently, my dear Miss Temple, or you will make my girl too dissipated. You forget that she is my housekeeper, and that my domestic affairs must remain unattended to, should Louisa accept of half the kind offers you are so good as to make her."

"And why should they not be neglected entirely, sir?" interrupted Elizabeth. "There are but two of you, and certain I am that my father's house will not only contain you both, but will open its doors spontaneously, to receive such guests. Society is a good, not to be rejected on account of cold forms, in this wilderness, sir; and I have often heard my father say, that hospitality is not a virtue in a new country, the favour being conferred by the guest."

"The manner in which Judge Temple exercises its rites, would confirm this opinion; but we must not trespass too freely. Doubt not that you will see us often, my child particularly, during the frequent visits, that I shall be compelled to make, to the distant parts of the county. But to obtain an influence with such a people," he continued, glancing his eyes towards the few, who were still lingering, curious observers of the interview, "a clergyman must not awaken envy or distrust, by dwelling under so splendid a roof as that of Judge Temple."

"You like the roof, then, Mr. Grant," cried Richard, who had been directing the extinguishment of the fires, and other little necessary duties, and who approached, in time, to hear the close of the divine's speech—"I am glad to find one man of taste at last. Here's 'duke now, pretends to call it by every abusive name he can invent; but though 'duke is a very tolerable judge, he is a very poor carpenter, let me tell him.—Well, sir, well, I think we may say, without boasting, that the service was as well performed this evening as you often see; I think, quite as well as I ever knew it to be done in old Trinity—that is, if we except the organ. But there is the schoolmaster, leads the psalm with a very good air. I used to lead myself, but latterly I have sung nothing but bass. There is a good deal of science to be shown in the bass, and it affords a fine opportunity to show off a full, deep voice. Benjamin, too, sings a good bass, though he is often out in the words. Did you ever hear Benjamin sing the 'Bay of Biscay, O?' "

"I believe he gave us part of it this evening," said Marmaduke, laughing.—"There was, now and then, a fearful quaver in his voice, and it seems that Mr. Penguillian, like most others who do one thing particularly well, knows nothing else. He has, certainly, a wonderful partiality to one tune, and he has a prodigious self-confidence in that one, for he delivers himself like a north-wester sweeping across the lake.——But come, gentlemen, our way is clear, and the sleigh waits.—Good evening, Mr. Grant. Good night, young lady. Remember that you dine beneath the Corinthian roof to-morrow, with Elizabeth."

The parties separated, Richard holding a close dissertation

with Mr. Le Quoi, as they descended the stairs, on the subject of psalmody, which he closed by a violent eulogium on the air of the "Bay of Biscay, O," as particularly connected with his friend Benjamin's execution.

During the preceding dialogue, Mohegan retained his seat, with his head shrouded in his blanket, as seemingly inattentive to surrounding objects, as the departing congregation was, itself, to the presence of the aged chief. Natty, also, continued on the log, where he had first placed himself, with his head resting on one of his hands, while the other held the rifle, which was thrown carelessly across his lap. His countenance expressed uneasiness, and the occasional unquiet glances, that he had thrown around him, during the service, plainly indicated some unusual causes for unhappiness. His continuing seated was, however, out of respect to the Indian chief, to whom he paid the utmost deference, on all occasions, although it was mingled with the rough manner of a hunter.

The young companion of these two ancient inhabitants of the forest, remained, also, standing before the extinguished brands, probably from an unwillingness to depart without his comrades. The room was now deserted by all but this group, the divine and his daughter. As the party from the Mansion-House disappeared, John arose, and dropping the blanket from his head, he shook back the mass of black hair from his face, and approaching Mr. Grant, he extended his hand, and said, solemnly—

"Father, I thank you. The words that have been said, since the rising moon, have gone upward, and the Great Spirit is glad. What you have told your children, they will remember, and be good." He paused a moment, and then elevating himself with the grandeur of an Indian chief, he added—"If Chingachgook lives to travel towards the setting sun, after his tribe, and the Great Spirit carries him over the lakes and mountains, with the breath in his body, he will tell his people the good talk he has heard; and they will believe him, for who can say that Mohegan has ever lied?"

"Let him place his dependence on the goodness of Divine mercy," said Mr. Grant, to whom the proud consciousness of the Indian sounded a little heterodox, "and it never will desert him. When the heart is filled with love to God, there is no room for sin.—But, young man, to you I owe not only an obligation, in common with those you saved this evening, on the mountain, but my thanks, for your respectful and pious manner, in assisting in the service, at a most embarrassing moment. I should be happy to see you sometimes, at my dwelling, when, perhaps, my conversation may strengthen you in the path which you appear to have chosen. It is so unusual to find one of your age and appearance, in these woods, at all acquainted with our holy liturgy, that it lessens at once the distance between us, and I feel we are no longer strangers. You seem quite at home in the service: I did not perceive that you had even a book, although good Mr. Jones had laid several in different parts of the room."

"It would be strange, if I were ignorant of the service of our church, sir," returned the youth, modestly, "for I was baptized in its communion, and I have never yet attended public worship, elsewhere. For me, to use the forms of any other denomination, would be as singular as our own have proved, to the people here this evening."

"You give me great pleasure, my dear sir," cried the divine, seizing the other by the hand, and shaking it cordially.—"You will go home with me now—indeed you must—my child has yet to thank you for saving my life. I will listen to no apologies. This worthy Indian, and your friend there, will accompany us.— Bless me! to think, that he has arrived at manhood, in this country, without entering a dissenting* meeting-house!"

"No, no," interrupted the Leather-stocking, "I must away to the wigwam: there's work there, that mus'nt be forgotten, for all your churchings and merry-makings. Let the lad go with you in welcome; he is used to keeping company with ministers, and talking of such matters; so is old John, who was christianized by the Moravians, about the time of the old war. But I am a plain, unlarned man, that has sarved both the king and his country, in his day, ag'in the French and savages, but never so much as looked into a book, or larnt a letter of scholarship, in my born days. I've never seen the use of sich in-door work, though I've lived to be partly bald, and in my time, have killed two hundred beaver in a season, and that without counting the other game.

* The divines of the Protestant Episcopal Church of the United States, commonly call other denominations *Dissenters*, though there never was an established church in their own country! [1832]

If you mistrust what I'm telling you, you can ask Chingachgook there, for I did it in the heart of the Delaware country, and the old man is knowing to the truth of every word I say."

"I doubt not, my friend, that you have been both a valiant soldier and skilful hunter, in your day," said the divine; "but more is wanting, to prepare you for that end which approaches. —You may have heard the maxim, that 'young men *may* die, but that old men *must*.'"

"I'm sure I never was so great a fool as to expect to live for ever," said Natty, giving one of his silent laughs: "no man need do that, who trails the savages through the woods, as I have done, and lives, for the hot months, on the lake-streams. I've a strong constitution, I must say that for myself, as is plain to be seen, for I've drunk the Onondaga water a hundred times, while I've been watching the deer-licks, when the fever-an-agy seeds was to be seen in it, as plain and as plenty as you can see the rattle-snakes on old Crumhorn. But then, I never expected to hold out for ever; though there's them living, who have seen the Garman Flats a wilderness, ay! and them that's larned, and acquainted with religion too; though you might look a week now, and not find even the stump of a pine on them; and that's a wood, that lasts in the ground the better part of a hundred years after the tree is dead."

"This is but time, my good friend," returned Mr. Grant, who began to take an interest in the welfare of his new acquaintance, "but I would have you prepare for eternity. It is incumbent on you to attend places of public worship, as I am pleased to see that you have done this evening. Would it not be heedless in you to start on a day's toil of hard hunting, and leave your ram-rod and flint behind?"

"It must be a young hand in the woods," interrupted Natty, with another laugh, "that didn't know how to dress a rod out of an ash sapling, or find a fire-stone in the mountains. No, no, I never expected to live for ever; but I see, times be altering in these mountains from what they was thirty years ago, or for that matter, ten years. But might makes right, and the law is stronger than an old man, whether he is one that has much larning, or only one like me, that is better now at standing at the passes than in following the hounds, as I once used to could. —Heigh-ho! I never know'd preaching come into a settlement, but it made game scearce, and raised the price of gun-powder; and that's a thing that's not as easily made as a ramrod, or an Indian flint."

The divine, perceiving that he had given his opponent an argument, by his own unfortunate selection of a comparison, very prudently relinquished the controversy; although he was fully determined to resume it, at a more happy moment. Repeating his request to the young hunter, with great earnestness, the youth and Indian consented to accompany him and his daughter to the dwelling, that the care of Mr. Jones had provided for their temporary residence. Leather-stocking persevered in his intention of returning to the hut, and at the door of the building they separated.

After following the course of one of the streets of the village a short distance, Mr. Grant, who led the way, turned into a field, through a pair of open bars, and entered a foot-path, of but sufficient width to admit one person to walk in it, at a time. The moon had gained a height, that enabled her to throw her rays perpendicularly on the valley; and the distinct shadows of the party flitted along on the banks of the silvery snow, like the presence of aerial figures, gliding to their appointed place of meeting. The night still continued intensely cold, although not a breath of wind was felt. The path was beaten so hard, that the gentle female, who made one of the party, moved with ease along its windings; though the frost emitted a low creaking, at the impression of even her light footsteps.

The clergyman, in his dark dress of broadcloth, with his mild, benevolent countenance occasionally turned towards his companions, expressing that look of subdued care, which was its characteristic, presented the first object in this singular group. Next to him moved the Indian, his hair falling about his face, his head uncovered, and the rest of his form concealed beneath his blanket. As his swarthy visage, with its muscles fixed in rigid composure, was seen under the light of the moon, which struck his face obliquely, he seemed a picture of resigned old age, on whom the storms of winter had beaten in vain, for the greater part of a century; but when, in turning his head, the rays fell directly on his dark, fiery eyes, they told a tale of passions unrestrained, and of thoughts free as air. The slight person of Miss

Grant, which followed next, and which was but too thinly clad for the severity of the season, formed a marked contrast to the wild attire, and uneasy glances of the Delaware chief; and more than once, during their walk, the young hunter, himself no insignificant figure in the group, was led to consider the difference in the human form, as the face of Mohegan, and the gentle countenance of Miss Grant, with eyes that rivalled the soft hue of the sky, met his view, at the instant that each turned, to throw a glance at the splendid orb which lighted their path. Their way, which led through fields, that lay at some distance in the rear of the houses, was cheered by a conversation, that flagged or became animated with the subject. The first to speak was the divine.

"Really," he said, "it is so singular a circumstance, to meet with one of your age, that has not been induced, by idle curiosity, to visit any other church than the one in which he has been educated, that I feel a strong curiosity to know the history of a life so fortunately regulated.—Your education must have been excellent; as indeed is evident from your manners and language. Of which of the states are you a native, Mr. Edwards? for such, I believe, was the name that you gave Judge Temple."

"Of this——"

"Of this! I was at a loss to conjecture, from your dialect, which does not partake, particularly, of the peculiarities of any country with which I am acquainted. You have, then, resided much in the cities, for no other part of this country is so fortunate, as to possess the constant enjoyment of our excellent liturgy."

The young hunter smiled, as he listened to the divine, while he so clearly betrayed from what part of the country he had come himself; but, for reasons, probably, connected with his present situation, he made no answer.

"I am delighted to meet with you, my young friend, for I think an ingenuous mind, such as I doubt not yours must be, will exhibit all the advantages of a settled doctrine and devout liturgy. You perceive how I was compelled to bend to the humours of my hearers this evening. Good Mr. Jones wished me to read the communion, and, in fact, all the morning service; but, happily, the canons do not require this of an evening.

It would have wearied a new congregation; but to-morrow I propose administering the sacrament——do you commune, my young friend?"

"I believe not, sir," returned the youth, with a little embarrassment, that was not at all diminished by Miss Grant's pausing involuntarily, and turning her eyes on him in surprise—"I fear that I am not qualified; I have never yet approached the altar; neither would I wish to do it, while I find so much of the world clinging to my heart."

"Each must judge for himself," said Mr. Grant; "though I should think, that a youth who had never been blown about by the wind of false doctrines, and who has enjoyed the advantages of our liturgy for so many years, in its purity, might safely come. Yet, sir, it is a solemn festival, which none should celebrate, until there is reason to hope it is not mockery. I observed, this evening, in your manner to Judge Temple, a resentment, that bordered on one of the worst of human passions.—We will cross this brook on the ice: it must bear us all, I think, in safety.—Be careful not to slip, my child." While speaking, he descended a little bank, by the path, and crossed one of the small streams that poured their waters into the lake; and, turning to see his daughter pass, observed that the youth had advanced, and was kindly directing her footsteps. When all were safely over, he moved up the opposite bank, and continued his discourse:—"It was wrong, my dear sir, very wrong, to suffer such feelings to rise, under any circumstances, and especially in the present, where the evil was not intended."

"There is good in the talk of my father," said Mohegan, stopping short, and causing those who were behind him to pause also; "It is the talk of Miquon. The white man may do as his fathers have told him; but the 'Young Eagle' has the blood of a Delaware chief in his veins: it is red, and the stain it makes, can only be washed out with the blood of a Mingo."*

Mr. Grant was surprised by the interruption of the Indian, and, stopping, faced the speaker. His mild features were confronted to the fierce and determined looks of the chief, and expressed the horror he felt, at hearing such sentiments, from

* His enemy.

one who professed the religion of his Saviour. Raising his hands to a level with his head, he exclaimed—

"John, John! is this the religion that you have learned from the Moravians? But no—I will not be so uncharitable as to suppose it. They are a pious, a gentle, and a mild people, and could never tolerate these passions. Listen to the language of the Redeemer—'But I say unto you, love your enemies, bless them that curse you; do good to them that hate you; pray for them that despitefully use you and persecute you.'—This is the command of God, John, and without striving to cultivate such feelings, no man can see him."

The Indian heard the divine with attention; the unusual fire of his eye gradually softened, and his muscles relaxed into their ordinary composure; but, slightly shaking his head, he motioned with dignity for Mr. Grant to resume his walk, and followed himself in silence. The agitation of the divine caused him to move with unusual rapidity along the deep path, and the Indian, without any apparent exertion, kept an equal pace; but the young hunter observed the female to linger in her steps, until a trifling distance intervened between the two former and the latter. Struck by the circumstance, and not perceiving any new impediment to retard her footsteps, the youth made a tender of his assistance.

"You are fatigued, Miss Grant," he said: "the snow yields to the foot, and you are unequal to the strides of us men. Step on the crust, I entreat you, and take the help of my arm. Yonder light is, I believe, the house of your father; but it seems yet at some distance."

"I am quite equal to the walk," returned a low, tremulous voice, "but I am startled by the manner of that Indian. Oh! his eye was horrid, as he turned to the moon, in speaking to my father.—But I forget, sir; he is your friend, and, by his language, may be your relative; and yet, of you I do not feel afraid."

The young man stepped on the bank of snow, which firmly sustained his weight, and by a gentle effort, induced his companion to follow. Drawing her arm through his own, he lifted his cap from his head, allowing the dark locks to flow in rich curls over his open brow, and walked by her side, with an air of conscious pride, as if inviting an examination of his inmost thoughts. Louisa took but a furtive glance at his person, and moved quietly along, at a rate that was greatly quickened by the aid of his arm.

"You are but little acquainted with this peculiar people, Miss Grant," he said, "or you would know that revenge is a virtue with an Indian. They are taught, from infancy upward, to believe it a duty, never to allow an injury to pass unrevenged; and nothing but the stronger claims of hospitality, can guard one against their resentments, where they have power."

"Surely, sir," said Miss Grant, involuntarily withdrawing her arm from his, "you have not been educated with such unholy sentiments."

"It might be a sufficient answer, to your excellent father, to say that I was educated in the church," he returned; "but to you I will add, that I have been taught deep and practical lessons of forgiveness. I believe that, on this subject, I have but little cause to reproach myself; it shall be my endeavour, that there yet be less."

While speaking, he stopped, and stood with his arm again proffered to her assistance. As he ended, she quietly accepted his offer, and they resumed their walk.

Mr. Grant and Mohegan had reached the door of the former's residence, and stood waiting near its threshold, for the arrival of their young companions. The former was earnestly occupied, in endeavouring to correct, by his precepts, the evil propensities, that he had discovered in the Indian, during their conversation; to which the latter listened in profound, but respectful attention. On the arrival of the young hunter and the lady, they entered the building.

The house stood at some distance from the village, in the centre of a field, surrounded by stumps, that were peering above the snow, bearing caps of pure white, nearly two feet in thickness. Not a tree nor a shrub was nigh it; but the house, externally, exhibited that cheerless, unfinished aspect, which is so common to the hastily-erected dwellings of a new country. The uninviting character of its outside was, however, happily relieved by the exquisite neatness, and comfortable warmth, within.

They entered an apartment, that was fitted as a parlour,

though the large fire-place, with its culinary arrangements, betrayed the domestic uses to which it was occasionally applied. The bright blaze from the hearth, rendered the light that proceeded from the candle Louisa produced, unnecessary; for the scanty furniture of the room was easily seen and examined, by the former. The floor was covered, in the centre, by a carpet made of rags, a species of manufacture that was, then, and yet continues to be, much in use, in the interior; while its edges, that were exposed to view, were of unspotted cleanliness. There was a trifling air of better life, in a tea-table and work-stand, as well as in an old-fashioned mahogany book-case; but the chairs, the dining-table, and the rest of the furniture, were of the plainest and cheapest construction. Against the walls were hung a few specimens of needle-work and drawing, the former executed with great neatness, though of somewhat equivocal merit in their designs, while the latter were strikingly deficient in both.

One of the former represented a tomb, with a youthful female weeping over it, exhibiting a church with arched windows, in the back-ground. On the tomb were the names, with the dates of the births and deaths, of several individuals, all of whom bore the name of Grant. An extremely cursory glance at this record, was sufficient to discover to the young hunter the domestic state of the divine. He there read, that he was a widower, and that the innocent and timid maiden, who had been his companion, was the only survivor of six children. The knowledge of the dependence, which each of these meek christians had on the other, for happiness, threw an additional charm around the gentle, but kind attentions, which the daughter paid to the father.

These observations occurred while the party were seating themselves before the cheerful fire, during which time, there was a suspension of discourse. But when each was comfortably arranged, and Louisa, after laying aside a thin coat of faded silk, and a Gipsy hat, that was more becoming to her modest, ingenuous countenance, than appropriate to the season, had taken a chair between her father and the youth, the former resumed the conversation.

"I trust, my young friend," he said, "that the education you have received, has eradicated most of those revengeful principles, which you may have inherited by descent; for I understand, from the expressions of John, that you have some of the blood of the Delaware tribe. Do not mistake me, I beg, for it is not colour, nor lineage, that constitutes merit; and I know not, that he, who claims affinity to the proper owners of this soil, has not the right to tread these hills with the lightest conscience."

Mohegan turned solemnly to the speaker, and, with the peculiarly significant gestures of an Indian, he spoke:—

"Father, you are not yet past the summer of life; your limbs are young. Go to the highest hill, and look around you. All that you see, from the rising to the setting sun, from the head-waters of the great spring, to where the 'crooked river'* is hid by the hills, is his. He has Delaware blood, and his right is strong. But the brother of Miquon is just: he will cut the country in two parts, as the river cuts the low-lands, and will say to the 'Young Eagle,' Child of the Delawares! take it—keep it—and be a chief in the land of your fathers."

"Never!" exclaimed the young hunter, with a vehemence that destroyed the rapt attention with which the divine and his daughter were listening to the Indian—"The wolf of the forest is not more rapacious for his prey, than that man is greedy of gold; and yet his glidings into wealth are subtle as the movements of a serpent."

"Forbear, forbear, my son, forbear," interrupted Mr. Grant.—"These angry passions must be subdued. The accidental injury you have received from Judge Temple, has heightened the sense of your hereditary wrongs. But remember, that the one was unintentional, and that the other is the effect of political changes, which have, in their course, greatly lowered the pride of kings, and swept mighty nations from the face of the earth. Where now are the Philistines, who so often held the children of Israel in bondage! or that city of Babylon, which rioted in luxury and vice, and who styled herself the Queen of Nations, in the drunkenness of her pride? Remember the prayer of our holy litany, where we implore the Divine power —'That it may please thee to forgive our enemies, persecutors, and slanderers, and to turn their hearts.' The sin of the wrongs

* The Susquehannah means crooked river, "hannah," or hannock, meant "river," in many of the native dialects. Thus we find Rappehannock, as far south as Virginia. [1832]

which have been done to the natives, are to be alleged against Judge Temple, only, in common with a whole people, and your arm will speedily be restored to its strength."

"This arm!" repeated the youth, pacing the floor in violent agitation; "think you, sir, that I believe the man a murderer?— oh, no! he is too wily, too cowardly, for such a crime. But, let him and his daughter riot in their wealth—a day of retribution will come. No, no, no," he continued, as he trod the floor more calmly—"it is for Mohegan to suspect him of an intent to injure me; but the trifle is not worth a second thought."

He seated himself, and hid his face between his hands, as they rested on his knees.

"It is the hereditary violence of a native's passion, my child," said Mr. Grant, in a low tone, to his affrighted daughter, who was clinging, in terror, to his arm. "He is mixed with the blood of the Indians, you have heard; and neither the refinements of education, nor the advantages of our excellent liturgy, have been able entirely to eradicate the evil. But care and time will do much for him yet."

Although the divine spoke in a low tone, yet what he uttered was heard by the youth, who raised his head, with a smile of indefinite expression, and spoke more calmly:—

"Be not alarmed, Miss Grant, at either the wildness of my manner, or that of my dress. I have been carried away by passions, that I should struggle to repress. I must attribute it, with your father, to the blood in my veins, although I would not impeach my lineage willingly; for it is all that is left me to boast of. Yes! I am proud of my descent from a Delaware chief, who was a warrior that ennobled human nature. Old Mohegan, was his friend, and will vouch for his virtues."

Mr. Grant here took up the discourse, and, finding the young man more calm, and the aged chief attentive, he entered into a full and theological discussion of the duty of forgiveness. The conversation lasted for more than an hour, when the visiters arose, and, after exchanging good wishes with their entertainers, they departed. At the door they separated, Mohegan taking the direct route to the village, while the youth moved towards the lake. The divine stood at the entrance of his dwelling, regarding the figure of the aged chief, as it glided, at an astonishing gait, for his years, along the deep path; his black, straight hair, just visible over the bundle formed by his blanket, which was sometimes blended with the snow under the silvery light of the moon. From the rear of the house was a window, that overlooked the lake; and here Louisa was found by her father, when he entered, gazing, intently on some object, in the direction of the eastern mountain. He approached the spot, and saw the figure of the young hunter, at the distance of half a mile, walking with prodigious steps, across the wide fields of frozen snow, that covered the ice, towards the point, where he knew the hut inhabited by the Leather-stocking was situated, on the margin of the lake, under a rock, that was crowned by pines and hemlocks. At the next instant, the wildly looking form entered the shadow, cast from the overhanging trees, and was lost to view.

"It is marvellous, how long the propensities of the savage continue, in that remarkable race," said the good divine; "but if he persevere, as he has commenced, his triumph shall yet be complete. Put me in mind, Louisa, to lend him the homily 'against peril of idolatry,' at his next visit."

"Surely, father, you do not think him in danger of relapsing into the worship of his ancestors!"

"No, my child," returned the clergyman, laying his hand affectionately on her flaxen locks, and smiling, "his white blood would prevent it; but there is such a thing as the idolatry of our passions."

Chapter XIII.

"And I'll drink out of the quart pot,
Here's a health to the barley mow."

Anon., "The Barley-Mow."

ON one of the corners, where the two principal streets of Templeton intersected each other, stood, as we have already mentioned, the inn called the "Bold Dragoon." In the original plan, it was ordained that the village should stretch along the little stream, that rushed down the valley, and the street which led from the lake to the academy, was intended to be its western boundary. But convenience frequently frustrates the best regulated plans. The house of Mr., or as, in consequence of commanding the militia of that vicinity, he was called, Captain Hollister, had, at an early day, been erected directly facing the main street, and ostensibly interposed a barrier to its further progress. Horsemen, and subsequently teamsters, however, availed themselves of an opening, at the end of the building, to shorten their passage westward, until, in time, the regular highway was laid out along this course, and houses were gradually built, on either side, so as effectually to prevent any subsequent correction of the evil.

Two material consequences followed this change in the regular plans of Marmaduke. The main street, after running about half its length, was suddenly reduced to precisely that difference in its width; and the "Bold Dragoon" became, next to the Mansion-house, by far the most conspicuous edifice in the place.

This conspicuousness, aided by the characters of the host and hostess, gave the tavern an advantage over all its future competitors, that no circumstances could conquer. An effort was, however, made to do so; and, at the corner diagonally opposite, stood a new building, that was intended, by its occupants, to look down all opposition. It was a house of wood, ornamented in the prevailing style of architecture, and about the roof and balustrades, was one of the three imitators of the Mansion-House. The upper windows were filled with rough boards, secured by nails, to keep out the cold air; for the edifice was far from finished, although glass was to be seen in the lower apartments, and the light of the powerful fires, within, denoted that it was already inhabited. The exterior was painted white, on the front, and on the end which was exposed to the street; but in the rear, and on the side which was intended to join the neighbouring house, it was coarsely smeared with Spanish brown. Before the door stood two lofty posts, connected at the top by a beam, from which was suspended an enormous sign, ornamented around its edges, with certain curious carvings, in pine boards, and on its faces, loaded with masonic emblems. Over these mysterious figures, was written, in large letters, "The Templetown Coffee-House, and Traveller's Hotel," and beneath them, "By Habakkuk Foote and Joshua Knapp." This was a fearful rival to the "Bold Dragoon," as our readers will the more readily perceive, when we add, that the same sonorous names were to be seen over the door of a newly-erected store in the village, a hatter's shop, and the gates of a tan-yard. But, either because too much was attempted to be executed well, or that the "Bold Dragoon" had established a reputation which could not be easily shaken, not only Judge Temple and his friends, but most of the villagers also, who were not in debt to the powerful firm we have named, frequented the inn of Captain Hollister, on all occasions where such a house was necessary.

On the present evening, the limping veteran, and his consort, were hardly housed, after their return from the academy, when the sounds of stamping feet at their threshold announced the approach of visiters, who were probably assembling, with a view to compare opinions, on the subject of the ceremonies they had witnessed.

The public, or, as it was called, the "bar-room," of the "Bold Dragoon," was a spacious apartment, lined on three sides with benches, and on the fourth by fire-places. Of the latter, there were two, of such size as to occupy, with their enormous jambs, the whole of that side of the apartment where they were placed, excepting room enough for a door or two, and a little apartment in one corner, which was protected by miniature pallisadoes, and profusely garnished with bottles and glasses. In the entrance to this sanctuary, Mrs. Hollister was seated, with great gravity in her air, while her husband occupied himself with stirring the fires; moving the logs with a large stake, burnt to a point at one end.

"There, Sargeant dear," said the landlady, after she thought the veteran had got the logs arranged in the most judicious manner, "give over poking, for it's no good yee'll be doing, now that they burn so convaniently. There's the glasses on the table there, and the mug that the Doctor was taking his cider and ginger in, before the fire here,—jist put them in the bar, will ye? for we'll be having the Joodge, and the Major, and Mr. Jones, down the night, widout reckoning Benjamin Poomp, and the Lawyers: so yee'll be fixing the room tidy; and put both flip-irons in the coals; and tell Jude, the lazy, black baste, that if she's no be claning up the kitchen, I'll turn her out of the house, and she may live wid the jontlemen that kape the 'Coffee-house,' good luck to 'em. Och! Sargeant, sure it's a great privilege to go to a mateing, where a body can sit asy, widout joomping up and down so often, as this Mr. Grant is doing that same."

"It's a privilege at all times, Mistress Hollister, whether we stand or be seated; or, as good Mr. Whitefield used to do, after he had made a wearisome day's march, get on our knees and pray, like Moses of old, with a flanker to the right and left, to lift his hands to heaven," returned her husband, who composedly performed what she had directed to be done. "It was a very pretty fight, Betty, that the Israelites had, on that day, with the Amalekites. It seems that they fout on a plain, for Moses is men-tioned, as having gone on to the heights, to overlook the battle, and wrestle in prayer; and if I should judge, with my little larn-ing, the Israelites depended mainly on their horse, for it is writ-ten, that Joshua cut up the enemy with the edge of the *sword:* from which I infar, not only that they were horse, but well dis-ciplyn'd troops. Indeed, it says as much, as that they were cho-sen men; quite likely volunteers; for raw dragoons seldom strike with the *edge* of their swords, particularly if the weapon be any way crooked."

"Pshaw! why do ye bodder yourself wid taxts, man, about so small a matter," interrupted the landlady; "sure it was the Lord who was wid 'em; for he always sided wid the Jews, before they fell away; and it's but little matter what kind of men Joshua commanded, so that he was doing the right bidding. Aven them cursed millishy, the Lord forgi'e me for swearing, that was the death of him, wid their cowardice, would have carried the day in old times. There's no rason to be thinking that the soldiers was used to the drill."

"I must say, Mrs. Hollister, that I have not often seen raw troops fight better than the left flank of the militia, at the time you mention. They rallied handsomely, and that without beat of drum, which is no easy thing to do under fire, and were very steady till he fell. But the scriptures contain no unnecessary words; and I will maintain, that horse, who know how to strike with the *edge* of the sword, must be well disciplyn'd. Many a good sarmon has been preached about smaller matters than that one word. If the text was not meant to be particular, why wasn't it written, with the sword, and not with the edge? Now, a back-handed stroke, on the edge, takes long practice. Goodness! what an argument would Mr. Whitefield make of that word edge!—As to the Captain, if he had only called up the guard of dragoons, when he rallied the foot, they would have shown the inimy what the edge of a sword was; for, although there was no commissioned officer with them, yet I think I may say,"—the veteran continued, stiffening his cravat about the throat, and raising himself up, with the air of a drill-sergeant,—"they were led by a man, who know'd how to bring them on, in spite of the ravine."

"Is it lade on ye would?" cried the landlady, "when ye know yourself, Mr. Hollister, that the baste he rode was but little able to joomp from one rock to another, and the animal was as spry as a squirrel? Och! but it's useless to talk, for he's gone this many a year. I would that he had lived to see the true light; but there's mercy for a brave sowl, that died in the saddle, fighting for the liberty. It's a poor tomb-stone they have given him, any way, and many a good one that died like himself: but the sign is very like, and I will be kapeing it up, while the blacksmith can make a hook for it to swing on, for all the 'coffee-houses' be-twane this and Albany."

There is no saying where this desultory conversation would have led the worthy couple, had not the men who were stamping the snow off their feet, on the little platform before the door, suddenly ceased their occupation, and entered the bar-room.

For ten or fifteen minutes, the different individuals, who intended either to bestow or receive edification, before the fires of the "Bold Dragoon," on that evening, were collecting, until the benches were nearly filled with men of different occupations. Dr. Todd, and a slovenly-looking, shabby genteel young man, who took tobacco profusely, wore a coat of imported cloth, cut with something like a fashionable air, frequently exhibited a large, French, silver watch, with a chain of woven hair and a silver key, and who, altogether, seemed as much above the artisans around him, as he was himself inferior to the real gentlemen, occupied a high-back, wooden settee, in the most comfortable corner in the apartment.

Sundry brown mugs, containing cider or beer, were placed between the heavy andirons, and little groups were formed among the guests, as subjects arose, or the liquor was passed from one to the other. No man was seen to drink by himself, nor in any instance was more than one vessel considered necessary, for the same beverage; but the glass, or the mug, was passed from hand to hand, until a chasm in the line, or a regard to the rights of ownership, would regularly restore the dregs of the potation to him who defrayed the cost.

Toasts were uniformly drunk; and occasionally, some one, who conceived himself peculiarly endowed by nature to shine in the way of wit, would attempt some such sentiment as "hoping that he" who treated "might make a better man than his father;" or "live till all his friends wished him dead;" while the more humble pot-companion contented himself by saying, with a most imposing gravity in his air, "come, here's luck," or by expressing some other equally comprehensive wish. In every instance, the veteran landlord was requested to imitate the custom of the cup-bearers to kings, and taste the liquor he presented, by the invitation of "after you is manners;" with which request he ordinarily complied, by wetting his lips, first expressing the wish of "here's hoping," leaving it to the imagination of the hearers to fill the vacuum by whatever good each thought most desirable. During these movements, the landlady was busily occupied with mixing the various compounds required by her customers, with her own hands, and occasionally exchanging greetings and inquiries concerning the conditions of their respective families, with such of the villagers as approached "the bar."

At length, the common thirst being in some measure assuaged, conversation of a more general nature became the order of the hour. The physician, and his companion, who was one of the two lawyers of the village, being considered the best qualified to maintain a public discourse with credit, were the principal speakers, though a remark was hazarded, now and then, by Mr. Doolittle, who was thought to be their inferior, only in the enviable point of education. A general silence was produced on all but the two speakers, by the following observation from the practitioner of the law:—

"So, Doctor Todd, I understand that you have been performing an important operation, this evening, by cutting a charge of buck-shot from the shoulder of the son of Leather-stocking?"

"Yes, sir," returned the other, elevating his little head, with an air of importance. "I had a small job, up at the Judge's, in that way: it was, however, but a trifle to what it might have been, had it gone through the body. The shoulder is not a very vital part; and I think the young man will soon be well. But I did not know that the patient was a son of Leather-stocking: it is news to me, to hear that Natty had a wife."

"It is by no means a necessary consequence," returned the other, winking, with a shrewd look around the bar-room; "there is such a thing, I suppose you know, in law, as a 'filius nullius.' "

"Spake it out, man," exclaimed the landlady, "spake it out in king's English; what for should ye be talking Indian, in a room full of Christian folks, though it is about a poor hunter, who is but a little better in his ways than the wild savages themselves? Och! it's to be hoped that the missionaries will, in his own time, make a convarsion of the poor divils; and then it will matter little of what colour is the skin, or wedder there be wool or hair on the head."

"Oh! it is Latin, not Indian, Miss Hollister," returned the lawyer, repeating his winks and shrewd looks; "and Dr. Todd understands Latin, or how would he read the labels on his gallipots and drawers? No, no, Miss Hollister, the Doctor understands me; don't you, Doctor?"

"Hem—why I guess I am not far out of the way," returned Elnathan, endeavouring to imitate the expression of the other's countenance, by looking jocular; "Latin is a queer language, gentlemen;—now, I rather guess there is no one in the room, except Squire Lippet, who can believe that 'Far. Av.' means oatmeal, in English."

The lawyer, in his turn, was a good deal embarrassed by this display of learning; for although he actually had taken his first degree at one of the eastern universities, he was somewhat puzzled with the terms used by his companion. It was dangerous, however, to appear to be outdone in learning in a public bar-room, and before so many of his clients; he therefore put the best face on the matter, and laughed knowingly, as if there were a good joke concealed under it, that was understood only by the physician and himself. All this was attentively observed by the listeners, who exchanged looks of approbation; and the expressions of "tonguey man," and "I guess Squire Lippet knows, if any body doos," were heard in different parts of the room, as vouchers for the admiration of his auditors. Thus encouraged, the lawyer rose from his chair, and, turning his back to the fire, and facing the company, he continued—

"The son of Natty, or the son of nobody, I hope the young man is not going to let the matter drop. This is a country of laws; and I should like to see it fairly tried, whether a man who owns, or says he owns, a hundred thousand acres of land, has any more right to shoot a body, than another. What do you think of it, Dr. Todd?"

"Oh! sir, I am of opinion that the gentleman will soon be well, as I said before; the wownd isn't in a vital part, and as the ball was extracted so soon, and the shoulder was what I call well attended to, I do not think there is as much danger as there might have been."

"I say, Squire Doolittle," continued the attorney, raising his voice, "you are a magistrate, and know what is law, and what is not law. I ask you, sir, if shooting a man is a thing that is to be settled so very easily? Suppose, sir, that the young man had a wife and family; and suppose that he was a mechanic, like yourself, sir; and suppose that his family depended on him for bread; and suppose that the ball, instead of merely going through the flesh, had broken the shoulder-blade, and crippled him for ever;—I ask you all, gentlemen, supposing this to be the case, whether a jury wouldn't give what I call handsome damages?"

As the close of this supposititious case was addressed to the company, generally, Hiram did not, at first, consider himself called on for a reply; but finding the eyes of the listeners bent on him in expectation, he remembered his character for judicial discrimination, and spoke, observing a due degree of deliberation and dignity.

"Why, if a man should shoot another," he said, "and if he should do it on purpose, and if the law took notice on't, and if a jury should find him guilty, it would be likely to turn out a state-prison matter."

"It would so, sir," returned the attorney.—"The law, gentlemen, is no respecter of persons, in a free country. It is one of the great blessings that has been handed down to us from our ancestors, that all men are equal in the eye of the law, as they are by nater. Though some may get property, no one knows how, yet they are not privileged to trangress the laws, any more than the poorest citizen in the state. This is my notion, gentlemen; and I think that if a man had a mind to bring this matter up, something might be made out of it, that would help pay for the salve—ha! Doctor?"

"Why, sir," returned the physician, who appeared a little uneasy at the turn the conversation was taking, "I have the promise of Judge Temple, before men—not but what I would take his word as soon as his note of hand—but it was before men. Let me see—there was Mounshier Ler Quow, and Squire Jones, and Major Hartmann, and Miss Pettibone, and one or two of the blacks by, when he said that his pocket would amply reward me for what I did."

"Was the promise made before or after the service was performed?" asked the attorney.

"It might have been both," returned the discreet physician, "though I'm certain he said so, before I undertook the dressing."

"But it seems that he said his pocket should reward you, Doctor," observed Hiram; "now I don't know that the law will hold a man to such a promise: he might give you his pocket with sixpence in't, and tell you to take your pay out on't."

"That would not be a reward in the eye of the law," interrupted the attorney—"not what is called a 'quid pro quo;' nor is the pocket to be considered as an agent, but as part of a man's own person, that is, in this particular. I am of opinion that an action would lie on that promise, and I will undertake to bear him out, free of costs, if he don't recover."

To this proposition the physician made no reply, but he was observed to cast his eyes around him, as if to enumerate the witnesses, in order to substantiate this promise also, at a future day, should it prove necessary. A subject so momentous, as that of suing Judge Temple, was not very palatable to the present company, in so public a place; and a short silence ensued, that was only interrupted by the opening of the door, and the entrance of Natty himself.

The old hunter carried in his hand his never-failing companion, the rifle; and, although all of the company were uncovered, excepting the lawyer, who wore his hat on one side, with a certain dam'me air, Natty moved to the front of one of the fires, without in the least altering any part of his dress or appearance. Several questions were addressed to him, on the subject of the game he had killed, which he answered readily, and with some little interest; and the landlord, between whom and Natty there existed much cordiality, on account of their both having been soldiers in youth, offered him a glass of a liquid, which, if we might judge from its reception, was no unwelcome guest. When the forester had gotten his potation also, he quietly took his seat on the end of one of the logs, that lay nigh the fires, and the slight interruption, produced by his entrance, seemed to be forgotten.

"The testimony of the blacks could not be taken, sir," continued the lawyer, "for they are all the property of Mr. Jones, who owns their time. But there is a way by which Judge Temple, or any other man, might be made to pay for shooting another, and for the cure in the bargain.—There is a way, I say, and that without going into the 'court of errors' too."

"And a mighty big error ye would make of it, Mister Todd," cried the landlady, "should ye be putting the matter into the law at all, with Joodge Temple, who has a purse as long as one of them pines on the hill, and who is an asy man to dale wid, if yees but mind the humour of him. He's a good man is Joodge Temple, and a kind one, and one who will be no the likelier to do the pratty thing, bekaase ye would wish to tarrify him wid the law. I know of but one objaction to the same, which is an over care-lessness about his sowl. It's nather a Methodie, nor a Papish, nor a Prasbetyrian, that he is, but jist nothing at all; and it's hard to think that he 'who will not fight the good fight, under the banners of a rig'lar church, in this world, will be mustered among the chosen in heaven,' as my husband, the Captain there, as ye call him, says—though there is but one captain that I know, who desaarves the name. I hopes, Lather-stocking, ye'll no be foolish, and putting the boy up to try the law in the mat-ter; for 'twill be an evil day to ye both, when ye first turn the skin of so paceable an animal as a sheep into a bone of conten-tion. The lad is wilcome to his drink for nothing, until his shouther will bear the rifle ag'in."

"Well, that's gin'rous," was heard from several mouths at once, for this was a company in which a liberal offer was not thrown away; while the hunter, instead of expressing any of that indignation which he might be supposed to feel, at hearing the hurt of his young companion alluded to, opened his mouth, with the silent laugh for which he was so remarkable; and after he had indulged his humour, made this reply—

"I know'd the Judge would do nothing with his smooth-bore, when he got out of his sleigh. I never see'd but one smooth-bore, that would carry at all, and that was a French ducking-piece, upon the big lakes: it had a barrel half as long ag'in as my rifle, and would throw fine shot into a goose, at a hundred yards; but it made dreadful work with the game, and you wanted a boat to carry it about in. When I went with Sir William ag'in the French, at Fort Niagara, all the rangers used the rifle; and a dreadful weepon it is, in the hands of one who knows how to charge it, and keeps a steady aim. The Captain knows, for he says he was a soldier in Shirley's, and though they were nothing but baggonet-men, he must know how we cut up the French and Iroquois in the skrimmages, in that war. Chingachgook, which means 'Big Sarpent' in English, old John Mohegan, who lives up at the hut with me, was a great warrior then, and was out with us; he can tell all about it, too; though he was overhand for the tomahawk, never firing more than once or twice, before he was running in for the scalps. Ah! times is dreadfully altered since then. Why, Doctor, there was nothing but a foot-path, or at the most a track for pack-horses, along the Mohawk, from the Garman Flats up to the forts. Now, they say, they talk of running one of them wide roads with gates on't, along the river; first making a road, and then fencing it up! I hunted one season back of the Kaatskills, nigh-hand to the settlements, and the dogs often lost the scent, when they com'd to them highways, there was so much travel on them; though I can't say that the brutes was of a very good breed.—Old Hector will wind a deer in the fall of the year, across the broadest place in the Otsego, and that is a mile and a half, for I paced it myself on the ice, when the tract was first surveyed under the Indian grant."

"It sames to me, Natty, but a sorry compliment, to call your cumrad after the evil one," said the landlady; "and it's no much like a snake that old John is looking now. Nimrood would be a more besaming name for the lad, and a more Christian too, seeing that it comes from the Bible. The Sargeant read me the chapter about him, the night before my christening, and a mighty asement it was, to listen to any thing from the book."

"Old John and Chingachgook were very different men to look on," returned the hunter, shaking his head at his melancholy recollections.—"In the 'fifty-eight war,' he was in the middle of manhood, and taller than now by three inches. If you had seen him, as I did, the morning we beat Dieskau, from behind our log walls, you would have called him as comely a red-skin as ye ever set eyes on. He was naked, all to his breech-cloth and leggens; and you never seed a creater so handsomely painted. One side of his face was red, and the other black. His head was shaved clean, all to a few hairs on the crown, where he wore a tuft of eagle's feathers, as bright as if they had come from a peacock's tail. He had coloured his sides, so that they looked like an atomy, ribs and all; for Chingachgook had a great taste in such things: so that, what with his bold, fiery countenance, his knife and his tomahawk, I have never seed a fiercer warrior on the ground. He played his part, too, like a man; for I seen him next day, with thirteen scalps on his pole. And I will say this for the 'Big Snake,' that he always dealt fair, and never scalped any that he didn't kill with his own hands."

"Well, well," cried the landlady, "fighting is fighting, any way, and there's different fashions in the thing; though I can't say that I relish mangling a body after the breath is out of it; neither do I think it can be uphild by doctrine. I hopes, Sargeant, ye niver was helping in sich evil worrek."

"It was my duty to keep my ranks, and to stand or fall by the baggonet or lead," returned the veteran. "I was then in the fort, and seldom leaving my place, saw but little of the savages, who kept on the flanks, or in front, skrimmaging. I remember, howsomever, to have heard mention made of the 'Great Snake,' as he was called, for he was a chief of renown; but little did I ever expect to see him enlisted in the cause of Christianity, and civilized, like old John."

"Oh! he was christianized by the Moravians, who was always over intimate with the Delawares," said Leather-stocking. "It's my opinion, that had they been left to themselves, there would be no such doings now, about the head-waters of the two rivers, and that these hills mought have been kept as good hunting-ground, by their right owner, who is not too old to carry a rifle, and whose sight is as true as a fish-hawk, hovering—"

He was interrupted by more stamping at the door, and presently the party from the Mansion-house entered, followed by the Indian himself.

Chapter XIV.

"There's quart pot, pint pot, half-pint,
Gill pot, half-gill, nipperkin,
    And the brown bowl.—
Here's a health to the barley mow,
    My brave boys,
Here's a health to the barley mow." Anon., "The Barley-Mow."

SOME little commotion was produced by the appearance of the new guests, during which the lawyer slunk from the room. Most of the men approached Marmaduke, and shook his offered hand, hoping "that the Judge was well;" while Major Hartmann, having laid aside his hat and wig, and substituted for the latter a warm, peaked, woollen night-cap, took his seat very quietly, on one end of the settee which was relinquished by its former occupants. His tobacco-box was next produced, and a clean pipe was handed him by the landlord. When he had succeeded in raising a smoke, the Major gave a long whiff, and turning his head towards the bar, he said—

"Petty, pring in ter toddy."

In the mean time, the Judge had exchanged his salutations with most of the company, and taken a place by the side of the Major, and Richard had bustled himself into the most comfortable seat in the room. Mr. Le Quoi was the last seated, nor did he venture to place his chair finally, until, by frequent removals, he had ascertained that he could not possibly intercept a ray of heat from any individual present. Mohegan found a place on an end of one of the benches, and somewhat approximated to the bar. When these movements had subsided, the Judge remarked, pleasantly—

"Well, Betty, I find you retain your popularity, through all weathers, against all rivals, and amongst all religions.—How liked you the sermon?"

"Is it the sarmon?" exclaimed the landlady. "I can't say but it was rasonable; but the prayers is mighty unasy. It's no so small a matter for a body, in their fifty-nint' year, to be moving so much

in church. Mr. Grant sames a godly man, any way, and his gar-
rel is a hoomble one, and a devout.—Here, John, is a mug of
cider lac'd with whisky. An Indian will drink cider, though he
niver be athirst."

"I must say," observed Hiram, with due deliberation, "that it
was a tonguey thing; and I rather guess that it gave considerable satisfaction. There was one part, though, which might have
been left out, or something else put in; but then, I s'pose that, as
it was a written discourse, it is not so easily altered, as where a
minister preaches without notes."

"Ay! there's the rub, Joodge," cried the landlady; "how can a
man stand up and be praching his word, when all that he is
saying is written down, and he is as much tied to it as iver a
thaving dragoon was to the pickets?"

"Well, well," cried Marmaduke, waving his hand for silence,
"there is enough said; as Mr. Grant told us, there are different
sentiments on such subjects, and in my opinion he spoke most
sensibly.—So, Jotham, I am told you have sold your betterments to a new settler, and have moved into the village and
opened a school. Was it cash or dicker?"

The man who was thus addressed, occupied a seat immediately behind Marmaduke; and one who was ignorant of the
extent of the Judge's observation, might have thought he would
have escaped notice. He was of a thin, shapeless figure, with a
discontented expression of countenance, and with something
extremely shiftless in his whole air. Thus spoken to, after turning and twisting a little, by way of preparation, he made a reply.

"Why, part cash, and part dicker. I sold out to a Pumfret-
man, who was so'thin forehanded. He was to give me ten dollars an acre for the clearin, and one dollar an acre over the first
cost, on the wood-land: and we agreed to leave the buildins to
men. So I tuck Asa Mountagu, and he tuck Absalom Bement,
and they two tuck old Squire Naphtali Green. And so they had
a meetin, and made out a vardict of eighty dollars for the buildins. There was twelve acres of clearin, at ten dollars, and
eighty-eight at one, and the whull came to two hundred and
eighty-six dollars and a half, after paying the men."

"Hum," said Marmaduke; "what did you give for the place?"

"Why, besides what's comin to the Judge, I gi'n my brother
Tim, a hundred dollars for his bargain; but then there's a new

house on't, that cost me sixty more, and I paid Moses a hundred dollars, for choppin, and loggin, and sowin; so that the whull stood me in about two hundred and sixty dollars. But then I had a great crop off on't, and as I got twenty-six dollars and a half more than it cost, I conclude I made a pretty good trade on't."

"Yes, but you forgot that the crop was yours without the trade, and you have turned yourself out of doors for twenty-six dollars."

"Oh! the Judge is clean out," said the man, with a look of sagacious calculation; "he turned out a span of horses, that is wuth a hundred and fifty dollars of any man's money, with a bran new wagon; fifty dollars in cash; and a good note for eighty more; and a side-saddle, that was valood at seven and a half—so there was jist twelve shillings betwixt us. I wanted him to turn out a set of harness, and take the cow and the sap-troughs. He wouldn't—but I saw through it; he thought I should have to buy the tacklin afore I could use the wagon and horses; but I know'd a thing or two myself: I should like to know of what use is the tacklin to him! I offered him to trade back ag'in, for one hundred and fifty-five. But my woman said she wanted a churn, so I tuck a churn for the change."

"And what do you mean to do with your time, this winter? you must remember that time is money."

"Why, as the master is gone down country, to see his mother, who, they say, is going to make a die on't, I agreed to take the school in hand, till he comes back. If times doosn't get wuss in the spring, I've some notion of going into trade, or maybe I may move off to the Genessee; they say they are carryin on a great stroke of business that-a-way. If the wust comes to the wust, I can but work at my trade, for I was brought up in a shoe manufactory."

It would seem, that Marmaduke did not think his society of sufficient value, to attempt inducing him to remain where he was; for he addressed no further discourse to the man, but turned his attention to other subjects.—After a short pause, Hiram ventured a question:—

"What news doos the Judge bring us from the legislater? it's not likely that congress has done much this session; or maybe the French haven't fit any more battles lately?"

"The French, since they have beheaded their king, have done nothing but fight," returned the Judge. "The character of the nation seems changed. I knew many French gentlemen, during our war, and they all appeared to me to be men of great humanity and goodness of heart; but these Jacobins are as bloodthirsty as bull-dogs."

"There was one Roshambow wid us, down at Yorrek-town," cried the landlady; "a mighty pratty man he was too; and their horse was the very same. It was there that the Sargeant got the hurt in the leg, from the English batteries, bad luck to 'em."

"Ah! mon pauvre Roi!" murmured Monsieur Le Quoi.

"The legislature have been passing laws," continued Marmaduke, "that the country much required. Among others, there is an act, prohibiting the drawing of seines, at any other than proper seasons, in certain of our streams and small lakes; and another, to prohibit the killing of deer in the teeming months. These are laws that were loudly called for, by judicious men; nor do I despair of getting an act, to make the unlawful felling of timber a criminal offence."

The hunter listened to this detail with breathless attention, and when the Judge had ended, he laughed in open derision.

"You may make your laws, Judge," he cried, "but who will you find to watch the mountains through the long summer days, or the lakes at night? Game is game, and he who finds may kill; that has been the law in these mountains for forty years, to my sartain knowledge; and I think one old law is worth two new ones. None but a green-one would wish to kill a doe with a fa'n by its side, unless his moccasins was gettin old, or his leggins ragged, for the flesh is lean and coarse. But a rifle rings amongst them rocks along the lake shore, sometimes, as if fifty pieces was fired at once; it would be hard to tell where the man stood who pulled the trigger."

"Armed with the dignity of the law, Mr. Bumppo," returned the Judge, gravely, "a vigilant magistrate can prevent much of the evil that has hitherto prevailed, and which is already rendering the game scarce. I hope to live to see the day, when a man's rights in his game shall be as much respected as his title to his farm."

"Your titles and your farms are all new together," cried Natty; "but laws should be equal, and not more for one than another. I shot a deer, last Wednesday was a fortnight, and it floundered through the snow-banks till it got over a brush fence; I catch'd the lock of my rifle in the twigs, in following, and was kept back, until finally the creater got off. Now I want to know who is to pay me for that deer; and a fine buck it was. If there hadn't been a fence, I should have gotten another shot into it; and I never draw'd upon any thing that hadn't wings, three times running, in my born days.—No, no, Judge, it's the farmers that makes the game scearce, and not the hunters."

"Ter teer is not so plenty as in ter olt war, Pumppo," said the Major, who had been an attentive listener, amidst clouds of smoke; "put ter lant is not mate, as for ter teer to live on, put for Christians."

"Why, Major, I believe you're a friend to justice and the right, though you go so often to the grand house; but it's a hard case to a man, to have his honest calling for a livelihood stopt by laws, and that too when, if right was done, he mought hunt or fish on any day in the week, or on the best flat in the Patent, if he was so minded."

"I unterstant you, Letter-stockint," returned the Major, fixing his black eyes, with a look of peculiar meaning, on the hunter; "put you tidn't use to pe so prutent, as to look ahet mit so much care."

"Maybe there wasn't so much 'casion," said the hunter, a little sulkily; when he sunk into a silence, from which he was not roused for some time.

"The Judge was saying so'thin about the French," Hiram observed, when the pause in the conversation had continued a decent time.

"Yes, sir," returned Marmaduke, "the Jacobins of France seem rushing from one act of licentiousness to another. They continue those murders, which are dignified by the name of executions. You have heard, that they have added the death of their Queen to the long list of their crimes."

"Les monstres!" again murmured Monsieur Le Quoi, turning himself suddenly in his chair, with a convulsive start.

"The province of La Vendée is laid waste by the troops of the republic, and hundreds of its inhabitants, who are royalists in their sentiments, are shot at a time.—La Vendée is a district in the south-west of France, that continues yet much attached to the family of the Bourbons: doubtless Monsieur Le Quoi is acquainted with it, and can describe it more faithfully."

"Non, non, non, mon cher ami," returned the Frenchman, in a suppressed voice, but speaking rapidly, and gesticulating with his right hand, as if for mercy, while with his left he concealed his eyes.

"There have been many battles fought lately," continued Marmaduke, "and the infuriated republicans are too often victorious. I cannot say, however, that I am sorry they have captured Toulon from the English, for it is a place to which they have a just right."

"Ah—ha!" exclaimed Monsieur Le Quoi, springing on his feet, and flourishing both arms with great animation; "ces Anglais!"

The Frenchman continued to move about the room with great alacrity for a few minutes, repeating his exclamations to himself; when, overcome by the contradictory nature of his emotions, he suddenly burst out of the house, and was seen wading through the snow towards his little shop, waving his arms on high, as if to pluck down honour from the moon. His departure excited but little surprise, for the villagers were used to his manner; but Major Hartmann laughed outright, for the first time during his visit, as he lifted the mug, and observed—

"Ter Frenchman is mat—put he is goot as for notting to trink; he is trunk mit joy."

"The French are good soldiers," said Captain Hollister; "they stood us in hand a good turn, down at York-town; nor do I think, although I am an ignorant man about the great movements of the army, that his Excellency would have been able to march against Cornwallis, without their reinforcements."

"Ye spake the trut', Sargeant," interrupted his wife, "and I would iver have ye be doing the same. It's varry pratty men is the French; and jist when I stopt the cart, the time when ye was pushing on in front it was, to kape the rig'lars in, a rigiment of the jontlemen marched by, and so I dealt them out to their liking. Was it pay I got? sure did I, and in good, solid crowns; the divil a bit of continental could they muster among them all, for love nor money. Och! the Lord forgive me for swearing and spakeing of sich vanities; but this I will say for the French, that they paid in good silver; and one glass would go a great way wid 'em, for they gin'rally handed it back wid a drop in the cup; and that's a brisk trade, Joodge, where the pay is good, and the men not over partic'lar."

"A thriving trade, Mrs. Hollister," said Marmaduke. "But what has become of Richard? he jumped up as soon as seated, and has been absent so long that I am fearful he has frozen."

"No fear of that, cousin 'duke," cried the gentleman himself; "business will sometimes keep a man warm, the coldest night that ever snapt in the mountains. Betty, your husband told me, as we came out of church, that your hogs were getting mangy, so I have been out to take a look at them, and found it true. I stepped across, Doctor, and got your boy to weigh me out a pound of salts, and have been mixing it with their swill. I'll bet a saddle of venison against a gray squirrel, that they are better in a week. And now, Mrs. Hollister, I'm ready for a hissing mug of flip."

"Sure, I know'd yee'd be wanting that same," said the land-lady; "it's mixt and ready to the boiling. Sargeant dear, be handing up the iron, will ye?—no the one in the far fire, it's black, ye will see.—Ah! you've the thing now; look if it's not as red as a cherry."

The beverage was heated, and Richard took that kind of draught which men are apt to indulge in, who think that they have just executed a clever thing, especially when they like the liquor.

"Oh! you have a hand, Betty, that was formed to mix flip," cried Richard, when he paused for breath. "The very iron has a flavour in it. Here, John; drink, man, drink. I and you and Dr. Todd, have done a good thing with the shoulder of that lad, this very night. 'Duke, I made a song while you were gone; one day when I had nothing to do; so I'll sing you a verse or two, though I haven't really determined on the tune yet.

> What is life but a scene of care,
>> Where each one must toil in his way?
> Then let us be jolly, and prove that we are
> A set of good fellows, who seem very rare,
>> And can laugh and sing all the day.
>>> Then let us be jolly,
>>> And cast away folly,
>> For grief turns a black head to gray.

There, 'duke, what do you think of that? There is another verse of it, all but the last line; I haven't got a rhyme for the last line yet.—Well, old John, what do you think of the music? as good as one of your war-songs, ha!"

"Good," said Mohegan, who had been sharing deeply in the potations of the landlady, besides paying a proper respect to the passing mugs of the Major and Marmaduke.

"Pravo! pravo! Richart," cried the Major, whose black eyes were beginning to swim in moisture; "pravissimo! it is a goot song; put Natty Pumppo hast a petter. Letter-stockint, vilt sing? say, olt poy, vilt sing ter song, as apout ter woots?"

"No, no, Major," returned the hunter, with a melancholy shake of the head, "I have lived to see what I thought eyes could never behold in these hills, and I have no heart left for singing. If he, that has a right to be master and ruler here, is forced to squinch his thirst, when a-dry, with snow-water, it ill becomes them that have lived by his bounty to be making merry, as if there was nothing in the world but sunshine and summer."

When he had spoken, Leather-stocking again dropped his head on his knees, and concealed his hard and wrinkled features with his hands. The change from the excessive cold without to the heat of the bar-room, coupled with the depth and frequency of Richard's draughts, had already levelled whatever inequality there might have existed between him and the other guests, on the score of spirits; and he now held out a pair of swimming mugs of foaming flip towards the hunter, as he cried—

"Merry! ay! merry Christmas to you, old boy! Sunshine and summer! no! you are blind, Leather-stocking, 'tis moonshine and winter;—take these spectacles, and open your eyes.

> So let us be jolly,
> And cast away folly,
> For grief turns a black head to gray.

Hear how old John turns his quavers. What damned dull music an Indian song is, after all, Major. I wonder if they ever sing by note?"

While Richard was singing and talking, Mohegan was uttering dull, monotonous tones, keeping time by a gentle motion of his head and body. He made use of but few words, and such as he did utter were in his native language, and consequently, only understood by himself and Natty. Without heeding Richard, he continued to sing a kind of wild, melancholy air, that rose, at times, in sudden and quite elevated notes, and then fell again into the low, quavering sounds, that seemed to compose the character of his music.

The attention of the company was now much divided, the men in the rear having formed themselves into little groups, where they were discussing various matters, among the principal of which were, the treatment of mangy hogs, and Parson Grant's preaching; while Dr. Todd was endeavouring to explain to Marmaduke the nature of the hurt received by the young hunter. Mohegan continued to sing, while his countenance was becoming vacant, though, coupled with his thick bushy hair, it was assuming an expression very much like brutal ferocity. His notes were gradually growing louder, and soon rose to a height that caused a general cessation in the discourse. The hunter now raised his head again, and addressed the old warrior, warmly, in the Delaware language, which, for the benefit of our readers, we shall render freely into English.

"Why do you sing of your battles, Chingachgook, and of the warriors you have slain, when the worst enemy of all is near you, and keeps the Young Eagle from his rights? I have fought in as many battles as any warrior in your tribe, but cannot boast of my deeds at such a time as this."

"Hawk-eye," said the Indian, tottering with a doubtful step from his place, "I am the Great Snake of the Delawares; I can track the Mingoes, like an adder that is stealing on the whip-poor-will's eggs, and strike them, like the rattle-snake, dead at a blow. The white man made the tomahawk of Chingachgook bright as the waters of Otsego, when the last sun is shining; but it is red with the blood of the Maquas."

"And why have you slain the Mingo warriors? was it not to keep these hunting-grounds and lakes to your father's children? and were they not given in solemn council to the Fire-eater? and does not the blood of a warrior run in the veins of a young chief, who should speak aloud, where his voice is now too low to be heard?"

The appeal of the hunter seemed, in some measure, to recall the confused faculties of the Indian, who turned his face towards the listeners, and gazed intently on the Judge. He shook his head, throwing his hair back from his countenance, and exposed eyes, that were glaring with an expression of wild resentment. But the man was not himself. His hand seemed to make a fruitless effort to release his tomahawk, which was confined by its handle to his belt, while his eyes gradually became vacant. Richard at that instant thrusting a mug before him, his features changed to the grin of idiocy, and seizing the vessel with both hands, he sunk backward on the bench, and drunk until satiated, when he made an effort to lay aside the mug, with the helplessness of total inebriety.

"Shed not blood!" exclaimed the hunter, as he watched the countenance of the Indian in its moment of ferocity—"but he is drunk, and can do no harm. This is the way with all the savages; give them liquor, and they make dogs of themselves. Well, well—the time will come when right will be done, and we must have patience."

Natty still spoke in the Delaware language, and of course was not understood. He had hardly concluded, before Richard cried—

"Well, old John is soon sowed up. Give him a berth, Captain, in the barn, and I will pay for it. I am rich to-night, ten times richer than 'duke, with all his lands, and military lots, and funded debts, and bonds, and mortgages.

> Come let us be jolly,
> And cast away folly,
> For grief—

Drink, King Hiram—drink, Mr. Doo-nothing—drink, sir, I say. This is a Christmas eve, which comes, you know, but once a year."

"He! he! he! the Squire is quite moosical to-night," said Hiram, whose visage began to give marvellous signs of relaxation. "I rather guess we shall make a church on't yet, Squire?"

"A church, Mr. Doolittle! we will make a cathedral of it! bishops, priests, deacons, wardens, vestry and choir; organ, organist and bellows! By the Lord Harry, as Benjamin says, we will clap a steeple on the other end of it, and make two churches of it. What say you, 'duke, will you pay? ha! my cousin Judge, wilt pay?"

"Thou makest such a noise, Dickon," returned Marmaduke, "it is impossible that I can hear what Dr. Todd is saying. I think thou observed, it is probable the wound will fester, so as to occasion danger to the limb, in this cold weather?"

"Out of nater, sir, quite out of nater;" said Elnathan, attempting to expectorate, but succeeding only in throwing a light, frothy substance, like a flake of snow, into the fire—"quite out of nater, that a wownd so well dressed, and with the ball in my pocket, should fester. I s'pose, as the Judge talks of taking the young man into his house, it will be most convenient if I make but one charge on't."

"I should think one would do," returned Marmaduke, with that arch smile that so often beamed on his face; leaving the beholder in doubt whether he most enjoyed the character of his companion, or his own covert humour.

The landlord had succeeded in placing the Indian on some straw, in one of his out-buildings, where, covered with his own blanket, John continued for the remainder of the night.

In the mean time, Major Hartmann began to grow noisy and jocular; glass succeeded glass, and mug after mug was introduced, until the carousal had run deep into the night, or rather morning; when the veteran German expressed an inclination to return to the Mansion-house. Most of the party had already retired, but Marmaduke knew the habits of his friend too well to suggest an earlier adjournment. So soon, however, as the proposal was made, the Judge eagerly availed himself of it, and the trio prepared to depart. Mrs. Hollister attended them to the door in person, cautioning her guests as to the safest manner of leaving her premises.

"Lane on Mister Jones, Major," said she, "he's young, and will be a support to ye. Well, it's a charming sight to see ye, any way, at the Bould Dragoon; and sure it's no harm to be kaping a Christmas-eve wid a light heart, for it's no telling when we may have sorrow come upon us. So good night Joodge, and a merry Christmas to ye all, to-morrow morning."

The gentlemen made their adieus as well as they could, and taking the middle of the road, which was a fine, wide, and well-beaten path, they did tolerably well until they reached the gate of the Mansion-house; but on entering the Judge's domains, they encountered some slight difficulties. We shall not stop to relate them, but will just mention that, in the morning, sundry diverging paths were to be seen in the snow; and that once during their progress to the door, Marmaduke, missing his companions, was enabled to trace them by one of these paths to a spot, where he discovered them with nothing visible but their heads; Richard singing in a most vivacious strain,

> "Come let us be jolly,
> And cast away folly,
> For grief turns a black head to gray."

Chapter XV.

"As she lay, on that day, in the Bay of Biscay, O!"
                    Anon., "The Bay of Biscay, O." ll. 15–16

PREVIOUSLY to the occurrence of the scene at the "Bold Dragoon," Elizabeth had been safely reconducted to the Mansion-house, where she was left, as its mistress, either to amuse or employ herself during the evening, as best suited her own inclinations. Most of the lights were extinguished; but as Benjamin adjusted, with great care and regularity, four large candles, in as many massive candlesticks of brass, in a row on the sideboard, the hall possessed a peculiar air of comfort and warmth, contrasted with the cheerless aspect of the room she had left, in the academy.

Remarkable had been one of the listeners to Mr. Grant, and returned with her resentment, which had been not a little excited by the language of the Judge, somewhat softened by reflection and the worship. She recollected the youth of Elizabeth, and thought it no difficult task, under present appearances, to exercise that power indirectly, which hitherto she had enjoyed undisputed. The idea of being governed, or of being compelled to pay the deference of servitude, was absolutely intolerable; and she had already determined within herself, some half-dozen times, to make an effort, that should at once bring to an issue the delicate point of her domestic condition. But as often as she met the dark, proud eye of Elizabeth, who was walking up and down the apartment, musing on the scenes of her youth, and the change in her condition, and perhaps the events of the day, the housekeeper experienced an awe, that she would not own to herself could be excited by any thing mortal. It, however, checked her advances, and for some time held her tongue-tied. At length she determined to commence the discourse, by entering on a subject that was apt to level all human distinctions, and in which she might display her own abilities.

"It was quite a wordy sarmont that Parson Grant give us to-night," said Remarkable.—"Them church ministers be commonly smart sarmonizers; but they write down their idees, which is a great privilege. I don't think that by nater they are as tonguey speakers for an off-hand discourse, as the standing-order ministers."

"And what denomination do you distinguish as the standing-order?" inquired Miss Temple, with some surprise.

"Why, the Presbyterans, and Congregationals, and Baptists too, for-ti-'now, and all sich as don't go on their knees to prayer."

"By that rule, then, you would call those who belong to the persuasion of my father, the sitting-order," observed Elizabeth.

"I'm sure I've never heer'n 'em spoken of by any other name than Quakers, so called," returned Remarkable, betraying a slight uneasiness. "I should be the last to call them otherwise, for I never in my life used a disparaging tarm of the Judge, or any of his family. I've always set store by the Quakers, they are so pretty-spoken, clever people; and it's a wonderment to me, how your father come to marry into a church family, for they are as contrary in religion as can be. One sits still, and for the most part, says nothing, while the church folks practyse all kinds of ways, so that I sometimes think it quite moosical to see them; for I went to a church-meeting once before, down country."

"You have found an excellence in the church liturgy, that has hitherto escaped me. I will thank you to inquire whether the fire in my room burns; I feel fatigued with my journey, and will retire."

Remarkable felt a wonderful inclination to tell the young mistress of the mansion, that by opening a door she might see for herself; but prudence got the better of resentment, and after pausing some little time, as a salve to her dignity, she did as desired. The report was favourable, and the young lady, wishing Benjamin, who was filling the stove with wood, and the housekeeper, each a good night, withdrew.

The instant the door closed on Miss Temple, Remarkable commenced a sort of mysterious, ambiguous discourse, that was neither abusive nor commendatory of the qualities of the absent personage; but which seemed to be drawing nigh, by regular degrees, to a most dissatisfied description. The Major-domo made no reply, but continued his occupation with great indus-

try, which being happily completed, he took a look at the thermometer, and then, opening a drawer of the sideboard, he
produced a supply of stimulants, that would have served to
keep the warmth in his system, without the aid of the enormous
fire he had been building. A small stand was drawn up near the
stove, and the bottles and the glasses necessary for convenience,
were quietly arranged. Two chairs were placed by the side of
this comfortable situation, when Benjamin, for the first time,
appeared to observe his companion.

"Come," he cried, "come, Mistress Remarkable, bring yourself to an anchor in this chair. It's a peeler without, I can tell
you, good woman; but what cares I, blow high or blow low, d'ye
see, it's all the same thing to Ben. The niggers are snug stowed
below, before a fire that would roast an ox whole. The thermometer stands now at fifty-five, but if there's any vartue in
good maple wood, I'll weather upon it, before one glass, as
much as ten points more, so that the Squire, when he comes
home from Betty Hollister's warm room, will feel as hot as a
hand that has given the rigging a lick with bad tar. Come, Mistress, bring up in this here chair, and tell me how you like our
new heiress."

"Why, to my notion, Mr. Penguillum—"

"Pump——Pump," interrupted Benjamin, "it's Christmas-
eve, Mistress Remarkable, and so d'ye see, you had better call
me Pump. It's a shorter name, and as I mean to pump this here
decanter till it sucks, why you may as well call me Pump."

"Did you ever!" cried Remarkable, with a laugh that seemed
to unhinge every joint in her body; "You're a moosical creater,
Benjamin, when the notion takes you. But as I was saying, I
rather guess that times will be altered now in this house."

"Altered!" exclaimed the Major-domo, eyeing the bottle, that
was assuming the clear aspect of cut glass with astonishing
rapidity; "it don't matter much, Mistress Remarkable, so long as
I keep the keys of the lockers in my pocket."

"I can't say," continued the housekeeper, "but there's good
eatables and drinkables enough in the house for a body's
content—a little more sugar, Benjamin, in the glass—for Squire
Jones is an excellent provider. But new lords, new laws; and I
shouldn't wonder if you and I had an unsartin time on't in
footer."

"Life is as unsartin as the wind that blows," said Benjamin

with a moralizing air; "and nothing is more varible than the wind, Mistress Remarkable, unless you happen to fall in with the trades, d'ye see, and then you may run for the matter of a month at a time, with studding-sails on both sides, alow and aloft, and with the cabin-boy at the wheel."

"I know that life is disp'ut unsartain," said Remarkable, compressing her features to the humour of her companion; "but I expect there will be great changes made in the house to rights; and that you will find a young man put over your head, as there is one that wants to be over mine; and after having been settled as long as you have, Benjamin, I should judge that to be hard."

"Promotion should go according to length of sarvice," said the Major-domo, "and if-so-be that they ship a hand for my berth, or place a new steward aft, I shall throw up my commission in less time than you can put a pilot-boat in stays. Thof Squire Dickens"—this was a common misnomer with Benjamin—"is a nice gentleman, and as good a man to sail with as heart could wish, yet I shall tell the Squire, d'ye see, in plain English, and that's my native tongue, that if-so-be he is thinking of putting any Johnny-raw over my head, why I shall resign. I began forrard, Mistress Pretty-bones, and worked my way aft, like a man. I was six months aboard a Garnsey lugger, hauling in the slack of the lee-sheet, and coiling up rigging. From that I went a few trips in a fore-and-after, in the same trade, which after all, was but a blind kind of sailing in the dark, where a man larns but little, excepting how to steer by the stars. Well! then d'ye see, I larnt how a topmast should be slushed, and how a top-gallant-sail was to be becketted; and then I did small jobs in the cabin, sich as mixing the skipper's grog. 'Twas there I got my taste, which you must have often seen, is excellent.—Well, here's better acquaintance to us."

Remarkable nodded a return to the compliment, and took a sip of the beverage before her; for, provided it was well sweetened, she had no objection to a small potation now and then. After this observance of courtesy between the worthy couple, the dialogue proceeded.

"You have had great experunces in life, Benjamin; for, as the scripter says, 'they that go down to the sea in ships see the works of the Lord.'"

"Ay! for that matter, they in brigs and schooners too; and it mought say the works of the devil. The sea, Mistress Remark-able, is a great advantage to a man, in the way of knowledge, for he sees the fashions of nations, and the shape of a country. Now, I suppose, for myself here, who is but an unlarned man to some that follows the seas, I suppose that, taking the coast from Cape Ler-Hogue as low down as Cape Finish-there, there isn't so much as a head-land, or an island, that I don't know either the name of it, or something more or less about it. Take enough, woman, to colour the water. Here's sugar. It's a sweet tooth, that fellow that you hold on upon yet, Mistress Pretty-bones. But as I was saying, take the whole coast along, I know it as well as the way from here to the Bold Dragoon; and a devil of an acquaintance is that Bay of Biscay. Whew! I wish you could but hear the wind blow there. It sometimes takes two to hold one man's hair on his head. Scudding through the Bay is pretty much the same thing as travelling the roads in this country, up one side of a mountain, and down the other."

"Do tell!" exclaimed Remarkable, "and doos the sea run as high as mountains, Benjamin?"

"Well I will tell; but first let's taste the grog.—Hem! it's the right kind of stuff, I must say, that you keeps in this country; but then you're so close aboard the West Indees, you make but a small run of it. By the Lord Harry, woman, if Garnsey only lay somewhere between Cape Hatteras and the Bite of Logann, but you'd see rum cheap. As to the seas, they runs more in lippers in the Bay of Biscay, unless it may be in a sow-wester, when they tumble about quite handsomely; thof it's not in the narrow sea that you are to look for a swell; just go off the Western Islands, in a westerly blow, keeping the land on your larboard hand, with the ship's head to the south'ard, and bring to, under a close-reef'd topsail; or mayhap a reef'd foresail, with a fore-topmast staysail; and mizzen staysail, to keep her up to the sea, if she will bear it; and lay there for the matter of two watches, if you want to see mountains. Why, good woman, I've been off there in the Boadishey frigate, when you could see nothing but some such matter as a piece of sky, mayhap, as big as the main-sail; and then again, there was a hole under your lee-quarter, big enough to hold the whole British navy."

"Oh! for massy's sake! and wa'nt you afeard, Benjamin? and how did you get off?"

"Afeard! who the devil do you think was to be frightened at a little salt water tumbling about his head? As for getting off, when we had enough of it, and had washed our decks down pretty well, we called all hands, for d'ye see, the watch below was in their hammocks, all the same as if they were in one of your best bed-rooms; and so we watched for a smooth time; clapt her helm hard a-weather, let fall the foresail, and got the tack aboard; and so, when we got her afore it, I ask you, Mistress Pretty-bones, if she didn't walk? didn't she! I'm no liar, good woman, when I say that I saw that ship jump from the top of one sea to another, just like one of these squirrels, that can fly, jumps from tree to tree."

"What, clean out of the water!" exclaimed Remarkable, lifting her two lank arms, with their bony hands spread in astonishment.

"It was no such easy matter to get out of the water, good woman, for the spray flew so that you couldn't tell which was sea and which was cloud. So there we kept her afore it, for the matter of two glasses. The First Lieutenant he cun'd the ship himself, and there was four quarter-masters at the wheel, besides the master, with six forecastle men in the gun-room, at the relieving tackles. But then she behaved herself so well! Oh! she was a sweet ship, mistress! That one frigate was well worth more, to live in, than the best house in the island. If I was King of England, I'd have her hauled up above Lon'on bridge, and fit her up for a palace; because why? If any body can afford to live comfortably, his majesty can."

"Well! but Benjamin," cried the listener, who was in an ecstasy of astonishment, at this relation of the steward's dangers, "what *did* you do?"

"Do! why we did our duty, like hearty fellows. Now, if the countrymen of Mounsheer Ler Quaw had been aboard of her, they would have just struck her ashore on some of them small islands; but we run along the land until we found her dead to leeward off the mountains of Pico, and dam'me if I know to this day how we got there, whether we jumped over the island, or hauled round it: but there we was, and there we lay, under easy sail, fore-reaching, first upon one tack and then upon t'other, so as to poke her nose out now and then, and take a look to wind'ard, till the gale blow'd its pipe out."

"I wonder now!" exclaimed Remarkable, to whom most of the terms used by Benjamin were perfectly unintelligible, but who had got a confused idea of a raging tempest; "it must be an awful life, that going to sea! and I don't feel astonishment that you're so affronted with the thoughts of being forced to quit a comfortable home like this. Not that a body cares much for't, as there's more housen than one to live in. Why, when the Judge agreed with me to come and live with him, I'd no more notion of stopping any time, than any thing. I happened in, just to see how the family did, about a week after Miss Temple died, thinking to be back home agin night; but the family was in sich a distressed way, that I couldn't but stop awhile and help 'em on. I thought the sitooation a good one, seeing that I was an unmarried body, and they was so much in want of help; so I tarried."

"And a long time have you left your anchors down in the same place, mistress; I think you must find that the ship rides easy."

"How you talk, Benjamin! there's no believing a word you say. I must say that the Judge and Squire Jones have both acted quite clever, so long; but I see that now we shall have a spicimin to the contrary. I heer'n say that the Judge was gone a great 'broad, and that he meant to bring his darter hum, but I didn't calcoolate on sich carrins on. To my notion, Benjamin, she's likely to turn out a disp'ut ugly gall."

"Ugly!" echoed the Major-domo, opening eyes, that were beginning to close in a very suspicious sleepiness, in wide amazement; "by the Lord Harry, woman, I should as soon think of calling the Boadishey a clumsy frigate. What the devil would you have? arn't her eyes as bright as the morning and evening stars! and isn't her hair as black and glistening as rigging that has just had a lick of tar! doesn't she move as stately as a first-rate in smooth water, on a bow line! Why, woman, the figure-head of the Boadishey was a fool to her, and that, as I've often heard the captain say, was an image of a great Queen; and arn't Queens always comely, woman? for who do you think would be a King, and not choose a handsome bed-fellow?"

"Talk decent, Benjamin," said the housekeeper, "or I won't keep your company. I don't gainsay her being comely to look on, but I will maintain that she's likely to show poor conduct.

She seems to think herself too good to talk to a body. From what Squire Jones had tell'd me, I some expected to be quite captivated by her company. Now, to my reckoning, Lowizy Grant is much more pritty behaved than Betsy Temple. She wouldn't so much as hold discourse with me, when I wanted to ask her how she felt, on coming home and missing her mammy."

"Perhaps she didn't understand you, woman; you are none of the best linguister, and then Miss Lizzy has been exercising the King's English under a great Lon'on lady, and, for that matter, can talk the language almost as well as myself, or any native born British subject. You've forgot your schooling, and the young mistress is a great scollard."

"Mistress!" cried Remarkable; "don't make one out to be a nigger, Benjamin. She's no mistress of mine, and never will be. And as to speech, I hold myself as second to nobody out of New-England. I was born and raised in Essex county, and I've always heer'n say, that the Bay State was provarbal for pronounsation."

"I've often heard of that Bay of State," said Benjamin, "but can't say that I've ever been in it, nor do I know exactly where away it is that it lays; but I suppose there's good anchorage in it, and that it's no bad place for the taking of ling; but for size, it can't be so much as a yawl to a sloop of war, compared with the Bay of Biscay, or mayhap, Tor-bay. And as for language, if you want to hear dictionary overhauled, like a log-line in a blow, you must go to Wapping, and listen to the Lon'oners, as they deal out their lingo. Howsomever, I see no such mighty matter that Miss Lizzy has been doing to you, good woman, so take another drop of your brew, and forgive and forget, like an honest soul."

"No, indeed! and I shan't do sich a thing, Benjamin. This treatment is a newity to me, and what I won't put up with. I have a hundred and fifty dollars at use, besides a bed and twenty sheep, to good; and I don't crave to live in a house where a body musn't call a young woman by her given name to her face. I *will* call her Betsy as much as I please; it's a free country, and no one can stop me. I did intend to stop while summer, but I shall quit to-morrow morning; and I will talk just as I please."

"For that matter, Mistress Remarkable," said Benjamin, "there's none here who will contradict you, for I'm of opinion that it would be as easy to stop a hurricane with a Barcelony hankerchy, as to bring up your tongue, when the stopper is off. I say, good woman, do they grow many monkeys along the shores of that Bay of State?"

"You're a monkey yourself, Mr. Penguillum," cried the enraged housekeeper, "or a bear! a black, beastly bear! and an't fit for a decent woman to stay with. I'll never keep your company agin, sir, if I should live thirty years with the Judge. Sitch talk is more befitting the kitchen than the keeping-room of a house of one who is well to do in the world."

"Look you, Mistress Pitty—Patty—Pretty-bones, mayhap I'm some such matter as a bear, as they will find who come to grapple with me; but dam'me if I'm a monkey—a thing that chatters without knowing a word of what it says—a parrot, that will hold dialogue, for what an honest man knows, in a dozen languages; mayhap in the Bay of State lingo; mayhap in Greek or High Dutch. But dost it know what it means itself? canst answer me that, good woman? Your Midshipman can sing out, and pass the word, when the Captain gives the order, but just set him adrift by himself, and let him work the ship of his own head, and, stop my grog, if you don't find all the Johnny-raws laughing at him."

"Stop your grog indeed!" said Remarkable, rising with great indignation, and seizing a candle; "you're groggy now, Benjamin, and I'll quit the room before I hear any misbecoming words from you."

The housekeeper retired, with a manner but little less dignified, as she thought, than the air of the heiress, muttering, as she drew the door after her, with a noise like the report of a musket, the opprobrious terms of "drunkard," "sot," and "beast."

"Who's that you say is drunk?" cried Benjamin, fiercely, rising and making a movement towards Remarkable. "You talk of mustering yourself with a lady! you're just fit to grumble and find fault. Where the devil should you larn behaviour and dictionary? in your damn'd Bay of State, ha!"

Benjamin here fell back in his chair, and soon gave vent to certain ominous sounds, which resembled, not a little, the growling of his favourite animal, the bear itself. Before, however, he was quite locked, to use the language that would suit the Della-cruscan humour of certain refined minds of the present day, "in the arms of Morpheus," he spoke aloud, observing due pauses between his epithets, the impressive terms of "monkey," "parrot," "pic-nic," "tar-pot," and "linguisters."

We shall not attempt to explain his meaning, nor connect his sentences, and our readers must be satisfied with our informing them, that they were expressed with all that coolness of contempt that a man might well be supposed to feel for a monkey.

Nearly two hours passed in this sleep, before the Major-domo was awakened by the noisy entrance of Richard, Major Hartmann, and the master of the mansion. Benjamin so far rallied his confused faculties, as to shape the course of the two former to their respective apartments, when he disappeared himself, leaving the task of securing the house to him who was most interested in its safety. Locks and bars were but little attended to, in the early day of that settlement; and so soon as Marmaduke had given an eye to the enormous fires of his dwelling, he retired. With this act of prudence closes the first night of our tale.

Chapter XVI.

"*Watch.(aside.)* Some treason, masters—
Yet stand close." *Much Ado about Nothing, III.iii.* 106–7.

IT was fortunate for more than one of the bacchanalians, who left the "Bold Dragoon" late in the evening, that the severe cold of the season was becoming, rapidly, less dangerous, as they threaded the different mazes, through the snow-banks, that led to their respective dwellings. Thin, driving clouds began, towards morning, to flit across the heavens, and the moon set behind a volume of vapour, that was impelled furiously towards the north, carrying with it the softer atmosphere from the distant ocean. The rising sun was obscured by denser and increasing columns of clouds, while the southerly wind that rushed up the valley, brought the never-failing symptoms of a thaw.

It was quite late in the morning, before Elizabeth, observing the faint glow which appeared on the eastern mountain, long after the light of the sun had struck the opposite hills, ventured from the house, with a view to gratify her curiosity with a glance by daylight at the surrounding objects, before the tardy revellers of the Christmas-eve should make their appearance at the breakfast-table. While she was drawing the folds of her pelisse more closely around her form, to guard against a cold that was yet great, though rapidly yielding, in the small enclosure that opened in the rear of the house on a little thicket of low pines, that were springing up where trees of a mightier growth had lately stood, she was surprised at the voice of Mr. Jones.

"Merry Christmas, merry Christmas to you, cousin Bess," he shouted. "Ah, ha! an early riser, I see; but I knew I should steal a march on you. I never was in a house yet, where I didn't get the first Christmas greeting on every soul in it, man, woman and child; great and small; black, white and yellow. But stop a minute, till I can just slip on my coat; you are about to look at the improvements, I see, which no one can explain so well as I, who planned them all. It will be an hour before 'duke and the

Major can sleep off Mrs. Hollister's confounded distillations, and so I'll come down and go with you."

Elizabeth turned, and observed her cousin in his night-cap, with his head out of his bed-room window, where his zeal for pre-eminence, in defiance of the weather, had impelled him to thrust it. She laughed, and promising to wait for his company, re-entered the house, making her appearance again, holding in her hand a packet that was secured by several large and important seals, just in time to meet the gentleman.

"Come, Bessy, come," he cried, drawing one of her arms through his own; "the snow begins to give, but it will bear us yet. Don't you snuff old Pennsylvania in the very air? This is a vile climate, girl; now at sunset last evening it was cold enough to freeze a man's zeal, and that, I can tell you, takes a thermometer near zero for me; then about nine or ten it began to moderate; at twelve it was quite mild, and here all the rest of the night I have been so hot as not to bear a blanket on the bed.— Holla! Aggy!—merry Christmas, Aggy—I say, do you hear me, you black dog! there's a dollar for you; and if the gentlemen get up before I come back, do you come out and let me know. I wouldn't have 'duke get the start of me for the worth of your head."

The black caught the money from the snow, and promising a due degree of watchfulness, he gave the dollar a whirl of twenty feet in the air, and catching it as it fell, in the palm of his hand, he withdrew to the kitchen, to exhibit his present, with a heart as light as his face was happy in its expression.

"Oh, rest easy, my dear coz," said the young lady; "I took a look in at my father, who is likely to sleep an hour; and by using due vigilance you will secure all the honours of the season."

"Why, 'duke is your father, Elizabeth, but 'duke is a man who likes to be foremost, even in trifles. Now, as for myself, I care for no such things, except in the way of competition; for a thing which is of no moment in itself, may be made of importance in the way of competition. So it is with your father, he loves to be first; but I only struggle with him as a competitor."

"It's all very clear, sir," said Elizabeth; "you would not care a fig for distinction, if there were no one in the world but yourself; but as there happen to be a great many others, why you must struggle with them all—in the way of competition."

"Exactly so; I see you are a clever girl, Bess, and one who does credit to her masters. It was my plan to send you to that school; for when your father first mentioned the thing, I wrote a private letter for advice to a judicious friend in the city, who recommended the very school you went to. 'Duke was a little obstinate at first, as usual, but when he heard the truth, he was obliged to send you."

"Well, a truce to 'duke's foibles, sir; he is my father; and if you knew what he has been doing for you while we were in Albany, you would deal more tenderly with his character."

"For me!" cried Richard, pausing a moment in his walk to reflect. "Oh! he got the plans of the new Dutch meeting-house for me, I suppose; but I care very little about it, for a man, of a certain kind of talent, is seldom aided by any foreign suggestions; his own brain is the best architect."

"No such thing," said Elizabeth, looking provokingly knowing.

"No! let me see—perhaps he had my name put in the bill for the new turnpike, as a director?"

"He might possibly; but it is not to such an appointment that I allude."

"Such an appointment!" repeated Mr. Jones, who began to fidget with curiosity; "then it is an appointment. If it is in the militia, I won't take it."

"No, no, it is not in the militia," cried Elizabeth, showing the packet in her hand, and then drawing it back, with a coquettish air; "it is an office of both honour and emolument."

"Honour and emolument!" echoed Richard, in painful suspense; "show me the paper, girl. Say, is it an office where there is any thing to *do?*"

"You have hit it, cousin Dickon; it is the executive office of the county; at least so said my father, when he gave me this packet to offer you as a Christmas box—'Surely, if any thing will please Dickon,' he said, 'it will be to fill the executive chair of the county.'"

"Executive chair! what nonsense!" cried the impatient gentleman, snatching the packet from her hand; "there is no such office in the county. Eh! what! it is, I declare, a commission, appointing Richard Jones, Esquire, Sheriff of the county. Well, this is kind in 'duke, positively. I must say 'duke has a warm heart, and never forgets his friends. Sheriff! High Sheriff of —! It sounds well, Bess, but it shall execute better. 'Duke is a judicious man, after all, and knows human nature thoroughly. I'm sure I'm much obliged to him," continued Richard, using the skirt of his coat, unconsciously, to wipe his eyes; "though I would do as much for him any day, as he shall see, if I can have an opportunity to perform any of the duties of my office on him. It shall be well done, cousin Bess—it shall be well done I say.—How this cursed south wind makes one's eyes water."

"Now, Richard," said the laughing maiden, "now I think you will find something to do. I have often heard you complain of old, that there was nothing to do in this new country, while to my eyes, it seemed as if every thing remained to be done."

"Do!" echoed Richard, who blew his nose, raised his little form to its greatest elevation, and looked serious. "Every thing depends on system, girl. I shall sit down this afternoon, and systematize the county. I must have deputies, you know. I will divide the county into districts, over which I will place my deputies; and I will have one for the village, which I will call my home department. Let me see—oh! Benjamin! yes, Benjamin will make a good deputy; he has been naturalized, and would answer admirably, if he could only ride on horseback."

"Yes, Mr. Sheriff," said his companion, "and as he understands ropes so well, he would be very expert, should occasion happen for his services, in another way."

"No," interrupted the other, "I flatter myself that no man could hang a man better than—that is—ha—oh! yes, Benjamin would do extremely well, in such an unfortunate dilemma, if he could be persuaded to attempt it. But I should despair of the thing. I never could induce him to hang, or teach him to ride on horseback. I must seek another deputy."

"Well, sir, as you have abundant leisure for all these important affairs, I beg that you will forget that you are High Sheriff, and devote some little of your time to gallantry. Where are the beauties and improvements which you were to show me?"

"Where! why every where. Here I have laid out some new streets; and when they are opened, and the trees felled, and they are all built up, will they not make a fine town? Well, 'duke is a liberal-hearted fellow, with all his stubbornness.—Yes, yes, I must have at least four deputies, besides a jailer."

"I see no streets in the direction of our walk," said Elizabeth, "unless you call the short avenues through these pine bushes by that name. Surely you do not contemplate building houses, very soon, in that forest before us, and in those swamps."

"We must run our streets by the compass, coz, and disregard trees, hills, ponds, stumps, or, in fact, any thing but posterity. Such is the will of your father, and your father, you know—"

"Had you made Sheriff, Mr. Jones," interrupted the lady, with a tone that said very plainly to the gentleman, that he was touching a forbidden subject.

"I know it, I know it," cried Richard; "and if it were in my power, I'd make 'duke a king. He is a noble-hearted fellow, and would make an excellent king; that is, if he had a good prime minister.—But who have we here? voices in the bushes;—a combination about mischief, I'll wager my commission. Let us draw near, and examine a little into the matter."

During this dialogue, as the parties had kept in motion, Richard and his cousin advanced some distance from the house, into the open space in the rear of the village, where, as may be gathered from the conversation, streets were planned and future dwellings contemplated; but where, in truth, the only mark of improvement that was to be seen, was a neglected clearing along the skirt of a dark forest of mighty pines, over which the bushes or sprouts of the same tree had sprung up, to a height that interspersed the fields of snow with little thickets of evergreen. The rushing of the wind, as it whistled through the tops of these mimic trees, prevented the footsteps of the pair from being heard, while the branches concealed their persons. Thus aided, the listeners drew nigh to a spot where the young hunter, Leather-stocking and the Indian chief were collected in an earnest consultation. The former was urgent in his manner, and seemed to think the subject of deep importance, while Natty appeared to listen with more than his usual attention, to what the other was saying. Mohegan stood a little on one side, with his head sunken on his chest, his hair falling forward, so as to conceal most of his features, and his whole attitude expressive of deep dejection, if not of shame.

"Let us withdraw," whispered Elizabeth; "we are intruders,

and can have no right to listen to the secrets of these men."

"No right!" returned Richard, a little impatiently, in the same tone, and drawing her arm so forcibly through his own as to prevent her retreat; "you forget, cousin, that it is my duty to preserve the peace of the county, and see the laws executed. These wanderers frequently commit depredations; though I do not think John would do any thing secretly. Poor fellow! he was quite boozy last night, and hardly seems to be over it yet. Let us draw nigher, and hear what they say."

Notwithstanding the lady's reluctance, Richard, stimulated doubtless by his nice sense of duty, prevailed; and they were soon so near as distinctly to hear sounds.

"The bird must be had," said Natty, "by fair means or foul. Heigho! I've known the time, lad, when the wild turkeys wasn't over scarce in the country; though you must go into the Virginy gaps, if you want them now. To be sure, there is a different taste to a partridge, and a well-fatted turkey; though, to my eating, beaver's tail and bear's hams makes the best of food. But then every one has his own appetite. I gave the last farthing, all to that shilling, to the French trader, this very morning, as I come through the town, for powder; so, as you have nothing, we can have but one shot for it. I know that Billy Kirby is out, and means to have a pull of the trigger at that very turkey. John has a true eye for a single fire, and somehow, my hand shakes so, whenever I have to do any thing extrawnary, that I often lose my aim. Now when I killed the she-bear this fall, with her cubs, though they were so mighty ravenous, I knocked them over one at a shot, and loaded while I dodged the trees in the bargain; but this is a very different thing, Mr. Oliver."

"This," cried the young man, with an accent that sounded as if he took a bitter pleasure in his poverty, while he held a shilling up before his eyes—"this is all the treasure that I possess—this and my rifle! Now, indeed, I have become a man of the woods, and must place my sole dependence on the fruits of the chase. Come, Natty, let us stake the last penny for the bird; with your aim, it cannot fail to be successful."

"I would rather it should be John, lad; my heart jumps into my mouth, because you set your mind so much on't; and I'm sartain that I shall miss the bird. Them Indians can shoot one time as well as another; nothing ever troubles them. I say, John, here's a shilling; take my rifle, and get a shot at the big turkey they've put up at the stump. Mr. Oliver is over anxious for the creater, and I'm sure to do nothing when I have over anxiety about it."

The Indian turned his head gloomily, and after looking keenly for a moment, in profound silence, at his companions, he replied—

"When John was young, eyesight was not straighter than his bullet. The Mingo squaws cried out at the sound of his rifle. The Mingo warriors were made squaws. When did he ever shoot twice! The eagle went above the clouds, when he passed the wigwam of Chingachgook; his feathers were plenty with the women.—But see," he said, raising his voice from the low, mournful tones in which he had spoken, to a pitch of keen excitement, and stretching forth both hands—"they shake like a deer at the wolf's howl. Is John old? When was a Mohican a squaw, with seventy winters! No! the white man brings old age with him—rum is his tomahawk!"

"Why then do you use it, old man?" exclaimed the young hunter; "why will one so noble by nature, aid the devices of the devil, by making himself a beast!"

"Beast! is John a beast?" replied the Indian, slowly; "yes; you say no lie, child of the Fire-eater! John is a beast. The smokes were once few in these hills. The deer would lick the hand of a white man, and the birds rest on his head. They were strangers to him. My fathers came from the shores of the salt lake. They fled before rum. They came to their grandfather, and they lived in peace; or when they did raise the hatchet, it was to strike it into the brain of a Mingo. They gathered around the council-fire, and what they said was done. Then John was the man. But warriors and traders with light eyes followed them. One brought the long knife, and one brought rum. They were more than the pines on the mountains; and they broke up the councils, and took the lands. The evil spirit was in their jugs, and they let him loose.—Yes, yes—you say no lie, Young Eagle, John is a Christian beast."

"Forgive me, old warrior," cried the youth, grasping his hand; "I should be the last to reproach you. The curses of

Heaven light on the cupidity that has destroyed such a race. Remember, John, that I am of your family, and it is now my greatest pride."

The muscles of Mohegan relaxed a little, and he said more mildly—

"You are a Delaware, my son; your words are not heard.— John cannot shoot."

"I thought that lad had Indian blood in him," whispered Richard, "by the awkward way he handled my horses, last night. You see, coz, they never use harness. But the poor fellow shall have two shots at the turkey, if he wants it, for I'll give him another shilling myself; though, perhaps, I had better offer to shoot for him. They have got up their Christmas sports, I find, in the bushes yonder, where you hear the laughter;—though it is a queer taste this chap has for turkey; not but what it is good eating too."

"Hold, cousin Richard," exclaimed Elizabeth, clinging to his arm, "would it be delicate to offer a shilling to that gentleman?"

"Gentleman again! do you think a half-breed, like him, will refuse money? No, no, girl; he will take the shilling; ay! and even rum too, notwithstanding he moralizes so much about it.—But I'll give the lad a chance for his turkey, for that Billy Kirby is one of the best marksmen in the country; that is, if we except the—the gentleman."

"Then," said Elizabeth, who found her strength unequal to her will, "then, sir, I will speak."—She advanced, with an air of determination, in front of her cousin, and entered the little circle of bushes that surrounded the trio of hunters. Her appearance startled the youth, who at first made an unequivocal motion towards retiring, but, recollecting himself, bowed, by lifting his cap, and resumed his attitude of leaning on his rifle. Neither Natty nor Mohegan betrayed any emotion, though the appearance of Elizabeth was so entirely unexpected.

"I find," she said, "that the old Christmas sport of shooting the turkey is yet in use among you. I feel inclined to try my chance for a bird. Which of you will take this money, and, after paying my fee, give me the aid of his rifle?"

"Is this a sport for a lady!" exclaimed the young hunter, with an emphasis that could not well be mistaken, and with a rapidity that showed he spoke without consulting any thing but feeling.

"Why not, sir? If it be inhuman, the sin is not confined to one sex only. But I have my humour as well as others. I ask not your assistance; but"—turning to Natty, and dropping a dollar in his hand—"this old veteran of the forest will not be so ungallant, as to refuse one fire for a lady."

Leather-stocking dropped the money into his pouch, and throwing up the end of his rifle, he freshened his priming; and, first laughing in his usual manner, he threw the piece over his shoulder, and said—

"If Billy Kirby don't get the bird before me, and the Frenchman's powder don't hang fire this damp morning, you'll see as fine a turkey dead, in a few minutes, as ever was eaten in the Judge's shanty. I have know'd the Dutch women on the Mohawk and Scoharie count greatly on coming to the merry-makings; and so, lad, you shouldn't be short with the lady. Come, let us go forward, for if we wait, the finest bird will be gone."

"But I have a right before you, Natty, and shall try my own luck first. You will excuse me, Miss Temple; I have much reason to wish that bird, and may seem ungallant, but I must claim my privileges."

"Claim any thing that is justly your own, sir," returned the lady; "we are both adventurers, and this is my knight. I trust my fortune to his hand and eye. Lead on, Sir Leather-stocking, and we will follow."

Natty, who seemed pleased with the frank address of the young and beauteous Elizabeth, who had so singularly intrusted him with such a commission, returned the bright smile with which she had addressed him, by his own peculiar mark of mirth, and moved across the snow, towards the spot whence the sounds of boisterous mirth proceeded, with the long strides of a hunter. His companions followed in silence, the youth casting frequent and uneasy glances towards Elizabeth, who was detained by a motion from Richard.

"I should think, Miss Temple," he said, so soon as the others were out of hearing, "that if you really wished a turkey, you would not have taken a stranger for the office, and such a one as Leather-stocking. But I can hardly believe that you are serious, for I have fifty at this moment shut up in the coops, in every stage of fat, so that you might choose any quality you pleased. There are six that I am trying an experiment on, by giving them brick-bats with—"

"Enough, cousin Dickon," interrupted the lady; "I do wish the bird, and it is because I so wish, that I commissioned this Mr. Leather-stocking."

"Did you ever hear of the great shot that I made at the wolf, cousin Elizabeth, who was carrying off your father's sheep?" said Richard, drawing himself up into an air of displeasure.— "He had the sheep on his back; and had the head of the wolf been on the other side, I should have killed him dead; as it was—"

"You killed the sheep,—I know it all, dear coz. But would it have been decorous, for the High Sheriff of ———— to mingle in such sports as these?"

"Surely you did not think I intended actually to fire with my own hands?" said Mr. Jones.—"But let us follow, and see the shooting. There is no fear of any thing unpleasant occurring to a female, in this new country, especially to your father's daughter, and in my presence."

"My father's daughter fears nothing, sir, more especially, when escorted by the highest executive officer in the county."

She took his arm, and he led her through the mazes of the bushes, to the spot where most of the young men of the village were collected for the sports of shooting a Christmas match, and whither Natty and his companions had already preceded them.

Chapter XVII.

"I guess, by all this quaint array,
The burghers hold their sports to-day."
                    Scott, *The Lady of the Lake*, V.xx.31–32.

THE ancient amusement of shooting the Christmas turkey, is one of the few sports that the settlers of a new country
seldom or never neglect to observe. It was connected with the
daily practices of a people, who often laid aside the axe or the
sithe, to seize the rifle, as the deer glided through the forests
they were felling, or the bear entered their rough meadows, to
scent the air of a clearing, and to scan, with a look of sagacity,
the progress of the invader.

On the present occasion, the usual amusement of the day had
been a little hastened, in order to allow a fair opportunity to
Mr. Grant, whose exhibition was not less a treat to the young
sportsmen, than the one which engaged their present attention.
The owner of the birds was a free black, who had prepared for
the occasion a collection of game, that was admirably qualified
to inflame the appetite of an epicure, and was well adapted to
the means and skill of the different competitors, who were of all
ages. He had offered to the younger and more humble
marksmen divers birds of an inferior quality, and some shooting had already taken place, much to the pecuniary advantage
of the sable owner of the game. The order of the sports was
extremely simple, and well understood. The bird was fastened
by a string to the stump of a large pine, the side of which, towards the point where the marksmen were placed, had been
flattened with an axe, in order to serve the purpose of a target,
by which the merit of each individual might be ascertained. The
distance between the stump and shooting-stand was one hundred measured yards; a foot more or a foot less being thought
an invasion of the rights of one of the parties. The negro
affixed his own price to every bird, and the terms of the chance;
but when these were once established, he was obliged, by the
strict principles of public justice that prevailed in the country,
to admit any adventurer who chose to offer.

The throng consisted of some twenty or thirty young men, most of whom had rifles, and a collection of all the boys in the village. The little urchins, clad in coarse but warm garments, stood gathered around the more distinguished marksmen, with their hands stuck under their waistbands, listening eagerly to the boastful stories of skill that had been exhibited on former occasions, and were already emulating in their hearts these wonderful deeds in gunnery.

The chief speaker was the man who had been mentioned by Natty, as Billy Kirby. This fellow, whose occupation, when he did labour, was that of clearing lands, or chopping jobs, was of great stature, and carried, in his very air, the index of his character. He was a noisy, boisterous, reckless lad, whose good-natured eye contradicted the bluntness and bullying tenor of his speech. For weeks he would lounge around the taverns of the county, in a state of perfect idleness, or doing small jobs for his liquor and his meals, and cavilling with applicants about the prices of his labour; frequently preferring idleness to an abatement of a tittle of his independence, or a cent in his wages. But when these embarrassing points were satisfactorily arranged, he would shoulder his axe and his rifle, slip his arms through the straps of his pack, and enter the woods with the tread of a Hercules. His first object was to learn his limits, round which he paced, occasionally freshening, with a blow of his axe, the marks on the boundary trees. Then he would proceed, with an air of great deliberation, to the centre of his premises, and throwing aside his superfluous garments, measure, with a knowing eye, one or two of the nearest trees, that were towering apparently into the very clouds, as he gazed upward. Commonly selecting one of the most noble, for the first trial of his power, he approached it with a listless air, whistling a low tune; and wielding his axe, with a certain flourish not unlike the salutes of a fencing-master, he would strike a light blow into the bark, and measure his distance. A pause of a moment was ominous of the fall of the forest, which had flourished there for centuries. The heavy and brisk blows that he struck, were soon succeeded by the thundering report of the tree, as it came, first cracking and threatening, with the separation of its own last ligaments, then threshing and tearing with its branches the tops of its surrounding brethren, and finally meeting the ground, with a shock but little inferior to an earthquake. From that moment, the sounds of the axe were ceaseless, while the falling of the trees was like a distant cannonading; and the daylight broke into the depths of the woods, with the suddenness of a morning in winter.

For days, weeks, nay, months, Billy Kirby would toil, with an ardour that evinced his native spirit, and with an effect that seemed magical; until, his chopping being ended, his stentorian lungs could be heard, emitting sounds, as he called to his patient oxen, which rung through the hills like the cries of an alarm. He had been often heard, on a mild summer's evening, a long mile across the vale of Templeton; the echoes from the mountains taking up his cries, until they died away in feeble sounds, from the distant rocks that overhung the lake. His piles, or, to use the language of the country, his logging, ended, with a despatch that could only accompany his dexterity and Herculean strength, the jobber would collect together his implements of labour, light the heaps of timber, and march away, under the blaze of the prostrate forest, like the conqueror of some city, who, having first prevailed over his adversary, applies the torch as the finishing blow to his conquest. For a long time Billy Kirby would then be seen, sauntering around the taverns, the rider of scrub-races, the bully of cock-fights, and, not unfrequently, the hero of such sports as the one in hand.

Between him and the Leather-stocking there had long existed a jealous rivalry, on the point of skill with the rifle. Notwithstanding the long practice of Natty, it was commonly supposed that the steady nerves and quick eye of the wood-chopper, rendered him his equal. The competition had, however, been confined, hitherto, to boastings, and comparisons made from their success in various hunting excursions; but the present occasion was the first time that they had ever come in open collision. A good deal of higgling, about the price of a shot at the choicest bird, had taken place between Billy Kirby and its owner, before Natty and his companions rejoined the sportsmen. It had, however, been settled at one shilling* a shot,

---

* Before the revolution each province had its own money of account, though neither coined any but copper pieces. In New York the Spanish dollar was divided into eight shillings, each of the value of a fraction more than sixpence sterling. At present the Union has provided a decimal system, and coins to represent it. [1832]

which was the highest sum ever exacted, the black taking care to protect himself from losses, as much as possible, by the conditions of the sport. The turkey was already fastened at the "mark," its body being entirely hid by the surrounding snow, nothing being visible but its red, swelling head, and long neck. If the bird was injured by any bullet that struck beneath the snow, it was to continue the property of its present owner; but if a feather was touched in a visible part, the animal became the prize of the successful adventurer.

These terms were loudly proclaimed by the negro, who was seated in the snow, in a somewhat hazardous vicinity to his favourite bird, when Elizabeth, and her cousin approached the noisy sportsmen. The sounds of mirth and contention sensibly lowered at this unexpected visit, but after a moment's pause, the curious interest exhibited in the face of the young lady, together with her smiling air, restored the freedom of the morning; though it was somewhat chastened, both in language and vehemence, by the presence of such a spectator.

"Stand out of the way there, boys," cried the wood-chopper, who was placing himself at the shooting-point—"stand out of the way, you little rascals, or I will shoot through you. Now, Brom, take leave of your turkey."

"Stop!" cried the young hunter; "I am a candidate for a chance. Here is my shilling, Brom; I wish a shot too."

"You may wish it in welcome," cried Kirby; "but if I ruffle the gobbler's feathers, how are you to get it? is money so plenty in your deer-skin pocket, that you pay for a chance you may never have?"

"How know you, sir, how plenty money is in my pocket?" said the youth, fiercely. "Here is my shilling, Brom, and I claim a right to shoot."

"Don't be crabbed, my boy," said the other, who was very coolly fixing his flint. "They say you have a hole in your left shoulder, yourself; so I think Brom may give you a fire for half-price. It will take a keen one to hit that bird, I can tell you, my lad, even if I give you a chance, which is what I have no mind to do."

"Don't be boasting, Billy Kirby," said Natty, throwing the breech of his rifle into the snow, and leaning on its barrel; "you'll get but one shot at the creater, for if the lad misses his aim, which wouldn't be a wonder if he did, with his arm so stiff and sore, you'll find a good piece and an old eye comin a'ter you. Maybe it's true, that I can't shoot as I used to could, but a hundred yards is a short distance for a long rifle."

"What, old Leather-stocking, are you out this morning?" cried his reckless opponent. "Well, fair play's a jewel. I've the lead of you, old fellow; so here goes, for a dry throat or a good dinner."

The countenance of the negro evinced not only all the interest which his pecuniary adventure might occasion, but also the keen excitement that the sport produced in the others, though certainly with a very different wish as to the result. While the wood-chopper was slowly and steadily raising his rifle, he bawled—

"Fair play, Billy Kirby—stand back—make 'em stand back, boys—gib a nigger fair play—poss up, gobbler; shake a head, fool; don't a see 'em taking aim?"

These cries, which were intended as much to distract the attention of the marksman, as for any thing else, were fruitless. The nerves of the wood-chopper were not so easily shaken, and he took his aim with the utmost deliberation. Stillness prevailed for a moment, and he fired. The head of the turkey was seen to dash on one side, and its wings were spread in momentary fluttering; but it settled itself down, calmly, into its bed of snow, and glanced its eyes uneasily around. For a time long enough to draw a deep breath, not a sound was heard. The silence was then broken, by the noise of the negro, who laughed, and shook his body, with all kinds of antics, rolling over in the snow in the excess of delight.

"Well done a gobbler," he cried, jumping up, and affecting to embrace his bird; "I tell 'em to poss up, and you see 'em dodge. Gib anoder shillin, Billy, and hab anoder shot."

"No—the shot is mine," said the young hunter; "you have my money already. Leave the mark, and let me try my luck."

"Ah! it's but money thrown away, lad," said Leather-stocking. "A turkey's head and neck is but a small mark for a new hand and a lame shoulder. You'd best let me take the fire, and maybe we can make some sittlement with the lady about the bird."

"The chance is mine," said the young hunter. "Clear the ground, that I may take it."

The discussions and disputes concerning the last shot were now abating, it having been determined, that if the turkey's head had been any where but just where it was at the moment, the bird must certainly have been killed. There was not much excitement produced by the preparations of the youth, who proceeded in a hurried manner to take his aim, and was in the act of pulling the trigger, when he was stopped by Natty.

"Your hand shakes, lad," he said, "and you seem over eager. Bullet wownds are apt to weaken flesh, and, to my judgment, you'll not shoot so well as in common. If you will fire, you should shoot quick, before there is time to shake off the aim."

"Fair play," again shouted the negro; "fair play—gib a nigger fair play. What right a Natty Bumppo advise a young man? Let 'em shoot—clear a ground."

The youth fired with great rapidity; but no motion was made by the turkey; and when the examiners for the ball returned from the "mark," they declared that he had missed the stump.

Elizabeth observed the change in his countenance, and could not help feeling surprise, that one evidently so superior to his companions, should feel a trifling loss so sensibly. But her own champion was now preparing to enter the lists.

The mirth of Brom, which had been again excited, though in a much smaller degree than before, by the failure of the second adventurer, vanished, the instant Natty took his stand. His skin became mottled with large brown spots, that fearfully sullied the lustre of his native ebony, while his enormous lips gradually compressed around two rows of ivory, that had hitherto been shining in his visage, like pearls set in jet. His nostrils, at all times the most conspicuous features of his face, dilated, until they covered the greater part of the diameter of his countenance; while his brown and bony hands unconsciously grasped the snow-crust near him, the excitement of the moment completely overcoming his native dread of cold.

While these indications of apprehension were exhibited in the sable owner of the turkey, the man who gave rise to this extraordinary emotion was as calm and collected, as if there was not to be a single spectator of his skill.

"I was down in the Dutch settlements on the Scoharie," said Natty, carefully removing the leathern guard from the lock of his rifle, "jist before the breaking out of the last war, and there

v. *The Tavern Scene (left) and the Turkey Shoot (right), designed and engraved by Tony Johannot.*

VI. *The Turkey Shoot* (c. *1850*) *by William W. Walcutt.*

VII. *Turkey Shoot (c. 1857) by Tompkins H. Matteson.*

VIII. *Leatherstocking Meets the Law* (1832) by John Quidor.

was a shooting-match amongst the boys; so I took a hand. I think I opened a good many Dutch eyes that day, for I won the powder-horn, three pounds of lead, and a pound of as good powder as ever flashed in pan. Lord! how they did swear in Garman! They did tell of one drunken Dutchman, who said he'd have the life of me, before I got back to the lake ag'in. But if he had put his rifle to his shoulder, with evil intent, God would have punished him for it; and even if the Lord didn't, and he had missed his aim, I know one that would have given him as good as he sent, and better too, if good shooting could come into the 'count."

By this time the old hunter was ready for his business, and, throwing his right leg far behind him, and stretching his left arm along the barrel of his piece, he raised it towards the bird. Every eye glanced rapidly from the marksman to the mark; but at the moment when each ear was expecting the report of the rifle, they were disappointed by the ticking sound of the flint.

"A snap—a snap," shouted the negro, springing from his crouching posture, like a madman, before his bird. "A snap good as fire—Natty Bumppo gun he snap—Natty Bumppo miss a turkey."

"Natty Bumppo hit a nigger," said the indignant old hunter, "if you don't get out of the way, Brom. It's contrary to the reason of the thing, boy, that a snap should count for a fire, when one is nothing more than a fire-stone striking a steel pan, and the other is sudden death; so get out my way, boy, and let me show Billy Kirby how to shoot a Christmas turkey."

"Gib a nigger fair play," cried the black, who continued resolutely to maintain his post, and making that appeal to the justice of his auditors, which the degraded condition of his caste so naturally suggested. "Ebbery body know dat snap as good as fire. Leab it to Massa Jone—leab it to young lady."

"Sartain," said the wood-chopper; "it's the law of the game in this part of the country, Leather-stocking. If you fire ag'in, you must pay up the other shilling. I b'lieve I'll try luck once more myself; so, Brom, here's my money, and I take the next fire."

"It's likely you know the laws of the woods better than I do, Billy Kirby!" returned Natty. "You come in with the settlers, with an ox goad in your hand, and I come in with moccasins on my feet, and with a good rifle on my shoulders, so long back as afore the old war; which is likely to know best! I say, no man need tell me that snapping is as good as firing, when I pull the trigger."

"Leab it to Massa Jone," said the alarmed negro; "he know ebbery ting."

This appeal to the knowledge of Richard was too flattering to be unheeded. He therefore advanced a little from the spot whither the delicacy of Elizabeth had induced her to withdraw, and gave the following opinion, with the gravity that the subject and his own rank demanded:—

"There seems to be a difference in opinion," he said, "on the subject of Nathaniel Bumppo's right to shoot at Abraham Freeborn's turkey, without the said Nathaniel paying one shilling for the privilege." This fact was too evident to be denied, and after pausing a moment, that the audience might digest his premises, Richard proceeded:—"It seems proper that I should decide this question, as I am bound to preserve the peace of the county; and men with deadly weapons in their hands, should not be heedlessly left to contention, and their own malignant passions. It appears that there was no agreement, either in writing or in words, on the disputed point; therefore we must reason from analogy, which is, as it were, comparing one thing with another. Now, in duels, where both parties shoot, it is generally the rule that a snap is a fire; and if such is the rule, where the party has a right to fire back again, it seems to me unreasonable, to say that a man may stand snapping at a defenceless turkey all day. I therefore am of opinion, that Nathaniel Bumppo has lost his chance, and must pay another shilling before he renews his right."

As this opinion came from so high a quarter, and was delivered with effect, it silenced all murmurs, for the whole of the spectators had begun to take sides with great warmth, except from the Leather-stocking himself.

"I think Miss Elizabeth's thoughts should be taken," said Natty. "I've known the squaws give very good counsel, when the Indians have been dumb-foundered. If she says that I ought to lose, I agree to give it up."

"Then I adjudge you to be a loser, for this time," said Miss Temple; "but pay your money, and renew your chance; unless

Brom will sell me the bird for a dollar. I will give him the money to save the life of the poor victim."

This proposition was evidently but little relished by any of the listeners, even the negro feeling the evil excitement of the chances. In the mean while, as Billy Kirby was preparing himself for another shot, Natty left the stand, with an extremely dissatisfied manner, muttering—

"There hasn't been such a thing as a good flint sold at the foot of the lake, sin' the Indian traders used to come into the country;—and if a body should go into the flats or along the streams in the hills, to hunt for such a thing, it's ten to one but they be all covered up with the plough. Heigho! it seems to me, that just as the game grows scarce, and a body wants the best of ammunition, to get a livelihood, every thing that's bad falls on him, like a judgment. But I'll change the stone, for Billy Kirby hasn't the eye for such a mark, I know."

The wood-chopper seemed now entirely sensible that his reputation depended on his care; nor did he neglect any means to insure success. He drew up his rifle, and renewed his aim, again and again, still appearing reluctant to fire. No sound was heard from even Brom, during these portentous movements, until Kirby discharged his piece, with the same want of success as before. Then, indeed, the shouts of the negro rung through the bushes, and sounded among the trees of the neighbouring forest, like the outcries of a tribe of Indians. He laughed, rolling his head, first on one side, then on the other, until nature seemed exhausted with mirth. He danced, until his legs were wearied with motion, in the snow; and, in short, he exhibited all that violence of joy that characterizes the mirth of a thoughtless negro.

The wood-chopper had exerted all his art, and felt a proportionate degree of disappointment at the failure. He first examined the bird with the utmost attention, and more than once suggested that he had touched its feathers; but the voice of the multitude was against him, for it felt disposed to listen to the often repeated cries of the black, to "gib a nigger fair play."

Finding it impossible to make out a title to the bird, Kirby turned fiercely to the black, and said—

"Shut your oven, you crow. Where is the man that can hit a

turkey's head at a hundred yards? I was a fool for trying. You needn't make an uproar, like a falling pine tree, about it. Show me the man who can do it."

"Look this a-way, Billy Kirby," said Leather-stocking, "and let them clear the mark, and I'll show you a man who's made better shots afore now, and that when he's been hard pressed by the savages and wild beasts."

"Perhaps there is one whose right comes before ours, Leather-stocking," said Miss Temple; "if so, we will waive our privilege."

"If it be me that you have reference to," said the young hunter, "I shall decline another chance. My shoulder is yet weak, I find."

Elizabeth regarded his manner, and thought that she could discern a tinge on his cheek, that spoke the shame of conscious poverty. She said no more, but suffered her own champion to make a trial.

Although Natty Bumppo had certainly made hundreds of more momentous shots, at his enemies or his game, yet he never exerted himself more to excel. He raised his piece three several times; once to get his range; once to calculate his distance; and once because the bird, alarmed by the death-like stillness, turned its head quickly, to examine its foes. But the fourth time he fired. The smoke, the report, and the momentary shock, prevented most of the spectators from instantly knowing the result; but Elizabeth, when she saw her champion drop the end of his rifle in the snow, and open his mouth in one of its silent laughs, and then proceed, very coolly, to re-load his piece, knew that he had been successful. The boys rushed to the mark, and lifted the turkey on high, lifeless, and with nothing but the remnant of a head.

"Bring in the creater," said Leather-stocking, "and put it at the feet of the lady. I was her deputy in the matter, and the bird is her property."

"And a good deputy you have proved yourself," returned Elizabeth—"so good, cousin Richard, that I would advise you to remember his qualities." She paused, and the gayety that beamed on her face gave place to a more serious earnestness. She even blushed a little, as she turned to the young hunter, and, with the charm of a woman's manner, added—"But it was only to see an exhibition of the far-famed skill of Leather-stocking, that I tried my fortunes. Will you, sir, accept the bird, as a small peace-offering, for the hurt that prevented your own success?"

The expression with which the youth received this present was indescribable. He appeared to yield to the blandishment of her air, in opposition to a strong inward impulse to the contrary. He bowed, and raised the victim silently from her feet, but continued silent.

Elizabeth handed the black a piece of silver, as a remuneration for his loss, which had some effect in again unbending his muscles, and then expressed to her companion her readiness to return homeward.

"Wait a minute, cousin Bess," cried Richard; "there is an uncertainty about the rules of this sport, that it is proper I should remove.—If you will appoint a committee, gentlemen, to wait on me this morning, I will draw up, in writing, a set of regulations——" He stopped, with some indignation, for at that instant a hand was laid familiarly on the shoulder of the High Sheriff of ——.

"A merry Christmas to you, cousin Dickon," said Judge Temple, who had approached the party unperceived: "I must have a vigilant eye to my daughter, sir, if you are to be seized daily with these gallant fits. I admire the taste, which would introduce a lady to such scenes!"

"It is her own perversity, 'duke," cried the disappointed Sheriff, who felt the loss of the first salutation as grievously as many a man would a much greater misfortune; "and I must say that she comes honestly by it. I led her out to show her the improvements, but away she scampered, through the snow, at the first sound of fire-arms, the same as if she had been brought up in a camp, instead of a first-rate boarding-school. I do think, Judge Temple, that such dangerous amusements should be suppressed by statute; nay, I doubt whether they are not already indictable at common law."

"Well, sir, as you are Sheriff of the county, it becomes your duty to examine into the matter," returned the smiling Marmaduke. "I perceive that Bess has executed her commission, and I hope it met with a favourable reception."

Richard glanced his eye at the packet, which he held in his

hand, and the slight anger produced by disappointment vanished instantly.

"Ah! 'duke, my dear cousin," he said, "step a little on one side; I have something I would say to you." Marmaduke complied, and the Sheriff led him to a little distance in the bushes, and continued—"First, 'duke, let me thank you for your friendly interest with the Council and the Governor, without which, I am confident that the greatest merit would avail but little. But we are sisters' children—we are sisters' children; and you may use me like one of your horses; ride me or drive me, 'duke, I am wholly yours.—But in my humble opinion, this young companion of Leather-stocking requires looking after. He has a very dangerous propensity for turkey."

"Leave him to my management, Dickon," said the Judge, "and I will cure his appetite by indulgence. It is with him that I would speak. Let us rejoin the sportsmen."

Chapter XVIII.

"Poor wretch! the mother that him bare,
If she had been in presence there,
    In his wan face, and sun-burn'd hair,
She had not known her child."

Scott, Marmion, I.xxviii.13–16.

IT diminished, in no degree, the effect produced by the conversation which passed between Judge Temple and the young hunter, that the former took the arm of his daughter, and drew it through his own, when he advanced from the spot whither Richard had led him, to that where the youth was standing, leaning on his rifle, and contemplating the dead bird at his feet. The presence of Marmaduke did not interrupt the sports, which were resumed, by loud and clamorous disputes concerning the conditions of a chance, that involved the life of a bird of much inferior quality to the last. Leather-stocking and Mohegan had alone drawn aside to their youthful companion; and, although in the immediate vicinity of such a throng, the following conversation was heard only by those who were interested in it.

"I have greatly injured you, Mr. Edwards," said the Judge; but the sudden and inexplicable start with which the person spoken to received this unexpected address, caused him to pause a moment. As no answer was given, and the strong emotion exhibited in the countenance of the youth gradually passed away, he continued—"But, fortunately, it is in some measure in my power to compensate you for what I have done. My kinsman, Richard Jones, has received an appointment that will, in future, deprive me of his assistance, and leaves me, just now, destitute of one who might greatly aid me with his pen. Your manner, notwithstanding appearances, is a sufficient proof of your education, nor will thy shoulder suffer thee to labour, for some time to come." (Marmaduke insensibly relapsed into the language of the Friends as he grew warm.) "My doors are open to thee, my young friend, for in this infant country, we harbour no suspicions; little offering to tempt the cupidity of the evil disposed. Become my assistant, for at least a season, and receive such compensation as thy services will deserve."

There was nothing in the manner or the offer of the Judge, to justify the reluctance, amounting nearly to loathing, with which the youth listened to his speech; but, after a powerful effort, for self-command, he replied—

"I would serve you, sir, or any other man, for an honest support, for I do not affect to conceal that my necessities are very great, even beyond what appearances would indicate; but I am fearful that such new duties would interfere too much with more important business; so that I must decline your offer, and depend on my rifle, as before, for subsistence."

Richard here took occasion to whisper to the young lady, who had shrunk a little from the foreground of the picture—

"This, you see, cousin Bess, is the natural reluctance of a half-breed to leave the savage state. Their attachment to a wandering life is, I verily believe, unconquerable."

"It is a precarious life," observed Marmaduke, without hearing the Sheriff's observation, "and one that brings more evils with it than present suffering. Trust me, young friend, my experience is greater than thine, when I tell thee, that the unsettled life of these hunters is of vast disadvantage for temporal purposes, and it totally removes one from the influence of more sacred things."

"No, no, Judge," interrupted the Leather-stocking; who was hitherto unseen, or disregarded; "take him into your shanty in welcome, but tell him truth. I have lived in the woods for forty long years, and have spent five at a time without seeing the light of a clearing, bigger than a wind-row in the trees, and I should like to know where you'll find a man, in his sixty-eighth year, who can get an easier living, for all your betterments, and your deer-laws; and, as for honesty, or doing what's right between man and man, I'll not turn my back to the longest winded deacon on your Patent."

"Thou art an exception, Leather-stocking," returned the Judge, nodding good-naturedly at the hunter; "for thou hast a temperance unusual in thy class, and a hardihood exceeding thy years. But this youth is made of materials too precious to be wasted in the forest. I entreat thee to join my family, if it be but till thy arm be healed. My daughter here, who is mistress of my dwelling, will tell thee that thou art welcome."

"Certainly," said Elizabeth, whose earnestness was a little checked by female reserve. "The unfortunate would be welcome at any time, but doubly so, when we feel that we have occasioned the evil ourselves."

"Yes," said Richard, "and if you relish turkey, young man, there are plenty in the coops, and of the best kind, I can assure you."

Finding himself thus ably seconded, Marmaduke pushed his advantage to the utmost. He entered into a detail of the duties that would attend the situation, and circumstantially mentioned the reward, and all those points which are deemed of importance among men of business. The youth listened in extreme agitation. There was an evident contest in his feelings; at times he appeared to wish eagerly for the change, and then again, the incomprehensible expression of disgust would cross his features, like a dark cloud obscuring a noon-day sun.

The Indian, in whose manner the depression of self-abasement was most powerfully exhibited, listened to the offers of the Judge, with an interest that increased with each syllable. Gradually he drew nigher to the group, and when, with his keen glance, he detected the most marked evidence of yielding in the countenance of his young companion, he changed at once from his attitude and look of shame, to the front of an Indian warrior, and moving, with great dignity, closer to the parties, he spoke—

"Listen to your Father," he said; "his words are old. Let the Young Eagle and the Great Land Chief eat together; let them sleep, without fear, near each other. The children of Miquon love not blood; they are just, and will do right. The sun must rise and set often, before men can make one family: it is not the work of a day, but of many winters. The Mingoes and the Delawares are born enemies; their blood can never mix in the wigwam; it never will run in the same stream in the battle. What makes the brother of Miquon and the Young Eagle foes! they are of the same tribe; their fathers and mothers are one. Learn to wait, my son: you are a Delaware, and an Indian warrior knows how to be patient."

This figurative address seemed to have great weight with the young man, who gradually yielded to the representations of Marmaduke, and eventually consented to his proposal. It was, however, to be an experiment only; and if either of the parties thought fit to rescind the engagement, it was left at his option so to do. The remarkable and ill-concealed reluctance of the youth, to accept of an offer, which most men in his situation would consider as an unhoped for elevation, occasioned no little surprise in those to whom he was a stranger; and it left a slight impression to his disadvantage. When the parties separated, they very naturally made the subject the topic of a conversation, which we shall relate; first commencing with the Judge, his daughter, and Richard, who were slowly pursuing the way back to the Mansion-house.

"I have surely endeavoured to remember the holy mandates of our Redeemer, when he bids us 'love them who despitefully use you,' in my intercourse with this incomprehensible boy," said Marmaduke. "I know not what there is in my dwelling, to frighten a lad of his years, unless it may be thy presence and visage, Bess."

"No, no," said Richard, with great simplicity; "it is not cousin Bess. But when did you ever know a half-breed, 'duke, who could bear civilization? for that matter, they are worse than the savages themselves. Did you notice how knock-kneed he stood, Elizabeth, and what a wild look he had in his eyes?"

"I heeded not his eyes, nor his knees, which would be all the better for a little humbling. Really, my dear sir, I think you did exercise the Christian virtue of patience to the utmost. I was disgusted with his airs, long before he consented to make one of our family. Truly, we are much honoured by the association. In what apartment is he to be placed, sir, and at what table is he to receive his nectar and ambrosia?"

"With Benjamin and Remarkable," interrupted Mr. Jones; "you surely would not make the youth eat with the blacks! He is part Indian, it is true, but the natives hold the negroes in great contempt. No, no—he would starve before he would break a crust with the negroes."

"I am but too happy, Dickon, to tempt him to eat with ourselves," said Marmaduke, "to think of offering even the indignity you propose."

"Then, sir," said Elizabeth, with an air that was slightly affected, as if submitting to her father's orders in opposition to her own will, "it is your pleasure that he be a gentleman."

"Certainly; he is to fill the station of one; let him receive the treatment that is due to his place, until we find him unworthy of it."

"Well, well, 'duke," cried the Sheriff, "you will find it no easy matter to make a gentleman of him. The old proverb says, 'that it takes three generations to make a gentleman.' There was my father, whom every body knew; my grandfather was an M.D.; and his father a D.D.; and his father came from England. I never could come at the truth of his origin, but he was either a great merchant, in London, or a great country lawyer, or the youngest son of a bishop."

"Here is a true American genealogy for you," said Marmaduke, laughing. "It does very well, till you get across the water, where, as every thing is obscure, it is certain to deal in the superlative. You are sure that your English progenitor was great, Dickon, whatever his profession might have been?"

"To be sure I am," returned the other; "I have heard my old aunt talk of him by the month. We are of a good family, Judge Temple, and have never filled any but honourable stations in life."

"I marvel that you should be satisfied with so scanty a provision of gentility, in the olden time, Dickon. Most of the American genealogists commence their traditions, like the stories for children, with three brothers, taking especial care that one of the triumvirate shall be the progenitor of any of the same name who may happen to be better furnished with worldly gear than themselves. But, here, all are equal who know how to conduct themselves with propriety; and Oliver Edwards comes into my family, on a footing with both the High Sheriff and the Judge."

"Well, 'duke, I call this democracy, not republicanism; but I say nothing; only let him keep within the law, or I shall show him, that the freedom of even this country is under wholesome restraint."

"Surely, Dickon, you will not execute till I condemn! But what says Bess to the new inmate. We must pay a deference to the ladies, in this matter, after all."

"Oh! sir," returned Elizabeth, "I believe I am much like a

certain Judge Temple, in this particular; not easily to be turned from my opinion. But, to be serious, although I must think the introduction of a demi-savage into the family a somewhat startling event, whomsoever you think proper to countenance, may be sure of my respect."

The Judge drew her arm more closely in his own, and smiled, while Richard led the way through the gate of the little court-yard in the rear of the dwelling, dealing out his ambiguous warnings, with his accustomed loquacity.

On the other hand, the foresters, for the three hunters, notwithstanding their difference in character, well deserved this common name, pursued their course along the skirts of the village in silence. It was not until they had reached the lake, and were moving over its frozen surface, towards the foot of the mountain, where the hut stood, that the youth exclaimed—

"Who could have foreseen this, a month since! I have consented to serve Marmaduke Temple! to be an inmate in the dwelling of the greatest enemy of my race! yet what better could I do? The servitude cannot be long, and when the motive for submitting to it ceases to exist, I will shake it off, like the dust from my feet."

"Is he a Mingo, that you will call him enemy?" said Mohegan. "The Delaware warrior sits still, and waits the time of the Great Spirit. He is no woman, to cry out like a child."

"Well, I'm mistrustful, John," said Leather-stocking, in whose air there had been, during the whole business, a strong expression of doubt and uncertainty. "They say that there's new laws in the land, and I am sartain that there's new ways in the mountains. They alter the country so much, one hardly knows the lakes and streams. I must say I'm mistrustful of such smooth speakers, for I've known the whites talk fair, when they wanted the Indian lands most. This I will say, though I'm white myself, and was born nigh York, and of honest parents too."

"I will submit," said the youth; "I will forget who I am. Cease to remember, old Mohegan, that I am the descendant of a Delaware chief, who once was master of these noble hills, these beautiful vales, and of this water, over which we tread. Yes, yes——I will become his bondsman—his slave! Is it not an honourable servitude, old man?"

"Old man!" repeated the Indian, solemnly, and pausing in his walk, as usual when much excited—"yes; John is old. Son of my brother! if Mohegan was young, when would his rifle be still? where would the deer hide, and he not find him? But John is old; his hand is the hand of a squaw; his tomahawk is a hatchet; brooms and baskets are his enemies—he strikes no other. Hunger and old age come together.—See, Hawk-eye! when young, he would go days, and eat nothing; but should he not put the brush on the fire now, the blaze would go out. Take the son of Miquon by the hand, and he will help you."

"I'm not the man I was, I'll own, Chingachgook," returned the Leather-stocking; "but I can go without a meal now, on occasion. When we tracked the Iroquois through the 'Beech-woods,' they druv the game afore them, for I hadn't a morsel to eat from Monday morning, come Wednesday sundown; and then I shot as fat a buck, on the Pennsylvany line, as ever mortal laid eyes on. It would have done your heart good to have seen the Delaware eat,—for I was out scouting and scrimmaging with their tribe, at the time. Lord! the Indians, lad, lay still, and just waited till Providence should send them their game; but I foraged about, and put a deer up, and put him down too, 'fore he had made a dozen jumps. I was too weak, and too ravenous to stop for his flesh; so I took a good drink of his blood, and the Indians eat of his meat raw. John was there, and John knows. But then starvation would be apt to be too much for me now, I will own, though I'm no great eater at any time."

"Enough is said, my friends," cried the youth; "I feel that everywhere the sacrifice is required at my hands, and it shall be made; but say no more, I entreat you; I cannot bear this subject now."

His companions were silent, and they soon reached the hut, which they entered, after removing certain complicated and ingenious fastenings, that were put there, apparently, to guard a property of but very little value. Immense piles of snow lay against the log walls of this secluded habitation, on one side, while fragments of small trees, and branches of oak and chestnut, that had been torn from their parent stems by the winds, were thrown into a pile, on the other. A small column of smoke rose through a chimney of sticks, cemented with clay, along the side of the rock; and had marked the snow above with its dark tinges, in a wavy line, from the point of emission to another where the hill receded from the brow of a precipice, and held a soil that nourished trees of a gigantic growth, that overhung the little bottom beneath.

The remainder of the day passed off as such days are commonly spent, in a new country.—The settlers thronged to the academy again, to witness the second effort of Mr. Grant; and Mohegan was one of his hearers. But, notwithstanding the divine fixed his eyes intently on the Indian, when he invited his congregation to advance to the table, the shame of last night's abasement was yet too keen in the old chief to suffer him to move.

When the people were dispersing, the clouds, that had been gathering all the morning, were dense and dirty; and before half of the curious congregation had reached their different cabins, that were placed in every glen and hollow of the mountains, or perched on the summits of the hills themselves, the rain was falling in torrents. The dark edges of the stumps began to exhibit themselves, as the snow settled rapidly; the fences of logs and brush, which before had been only traced by long lines of white mounds, that ran across the valley and up the mountains, peeped out from their covering; and the black stubs were momentarily becoming more distinct, as large masses of snow and ice fell from their sides, under the influence of the thaw.

Sheltered in the warm hall of her father's comfortable mansion, Elizabeth, accompanied by Louisa Grant, looked abroad with admiration at the ever varying face of things without. Even the village, which had just before been glittering with the colour of the frozen element, reluctantly dropped its mask, and the houses exposed their dark roofs and smoked chimneys. The pines shook off the covering of snow, and every thing seemed to be assuming its proper hue, with a transition that bordered on the supernatural.

Chapter XIX.

"And yet, poor Edwin was no vulgar boy."

Beattie, *The Minstrel*, I.xvi.1.

THE close of Christmas day, A.D. 1793, was tempestuous, but comparatively warm. When darkness had again hid the objects in the village from the gaze of Elizabeth, she turned from the window, where she had remained while the least vestige of light lingered over the tops of the dark pines, with a curiosity that was rather excited than appeased by the passing glimpses of woodland scenery that she had caught during the day.

With her arm locked in that of Miss Grant, the young mistress of the mansion walked slowly up and down the hall, musing on scenes that were rapidly recurring to her memory, and possibly dwelling, at times, in the sanctuary of her thoughts, on the strange occurrences that had led to the introduction to her father's family of one, whose manners so singularly contradicted the inferences to be drawn from his situation. The expiring heat of the apartment, for its great size required a day to reduce its temperature, had given to her cheeks a bloom that exceeded their natural colour, while the mild and melancholy features of Louisa were brightened with a faint tinge, that, like the hectic of disease, gave a painful interest to her beauty.

The eyes of the gentlemen, who were yet seated around the rich wines of Judge Temple, frequently wandered from the table, that was placed at one end of the hall, to the forms that were silently moving over its length. Much mirth, and that, at times, of a boisterous kind, proceeded from the mouth of Richard; but Major Hartmann was not yet excited to his pitch of merriment, and Marmaduke respected the presence of his clerical guest too much, to indulge in even the innocent humour that formed no small ingredient in his character.

Such were, and such continued to be, the pursuits of the party, for half an hour after the shutters were closed, and candles were placed in various parts of the hall, as substitutes for the departing daylight. The appearance of Benjamin, staggering under the burthen of an armful of wood, was the first interruption to the scene.

"How now, Master Pump!" roared the newly appointed Sheriff; "is there not warmth enough in 'duke's best Madeira, to keep up the animal heat through this thaw? Remember, old boy, that the Judge is particular with his beech and maple, beginning to dread, already, a scarcity of the precious articles. Ha! ha! ha! 'duke, you are a good, warm-hearted relation, I will own, as in duty bound, but you have some queer notions about you, after all. 'Come let us be jolly, and cast away folly.' "—

The notes gradually sunk into a hum, while the Major-domo threw down his load, and turning to his interrogator with an air of earnestness, replied—

"Why, look you, Squire Dickens, mayhap there's a warm latitude round about the table there, thof it's not the stuff to raise the heat in my body neither; the raal Jamaiky being the only thing to do that, beside good wood, or some such matter as Newcastle coal. But if I know any thing of weather, d'ye see, it's time to be getting all snug, and for putting the ports in, and stirring the fires abit. Mayhap I've not followed the seas twenty-seven years, and lived another seven in these here woods, for nothing, gemmen."

"Why, does it bid fair for a change in the weather, Benjamin?" inquired the master of the house.

"There's a shift of wind, your honour," returned the steward; "and when there's a shift of wind, you may look for a change, in this here climate. I was aboard of one of Rodney's fleet, d'ye see, about the time we licked De Grasse, Mounsheer Ler Quaw's countryman, there; and the wind was here at the south'ard and east'ard; and I was below, mixing a toothful of hot-stuff for the Captain of marines, who dined, d'ye see, in the cabin, that there very same day; and I suppose he wanted to put out the Captain's fire with a gun-room ingyne: and so, just as I got it to my own liking, after tasting pretty often, for the soldier was difficult to please, slap come the foresail ag'inst the mast, and whiz went the ship round on her heel, like a whirlygig. And a lucky thing was it that our helm was down; for as she gathered starnway she payed off, which was more than every ship in the fleet did, or could do. But she strained herself in the trough of the sea, and she shipped a deal of water over her quarter. I never swallowed so much clear water at a time, in my life, as I did then, for I was looking up the after-hatch at the instant."

"I wonder, Benjamin, that you did not die with a dropsy!" said Marmaduke.

"I mought, Judge," said the old tar, with a broad grin; "but there was no need of the med'cine chest for a cure; for, as I thought the brew was spoilt for the marine's taste, and there was no telling when another sea might come and spoil it for mine, I finished the mug on the spot. So then all hands was called to the pumps, and there we began to ply the pumps—"

"Well, but the weather?" interrupted Marmaduke; "what of the weather without doors?"

"Why, here the wind has been all day at the south, and now there's a lull, as if the last blast was out of the bellows; and there's a streak along the mountains, to the north'ard, that, just now, wasn't wider than the bigness of your hand; and then the clouds drive afore it as you'd brail a mainsail, and the stars are heaving in sight, like so many lights and beacons, put there to warn us to pile on the wood; and, if-so-be that I'm a judge of weather, it's getting to be time to build on a fire; or you'll have half of them there porter-bottles, and them dimmy-johns of wine, in the locker here, breaking with the frost, afore the morning watch is called."

"Thou art a prudent sentinel," said the Judge. "Act thy pleasure with the forests, for this night at least."

Benjamin did as he was ordered; nor had two hours elapsed, before the prudence of his precautions became very visible. The south wind had, indeed, blown itself out, and it was succeeded by the calmness that usually gave warning of a serious change in the weather. Long before the family retired to rest, the cold had become cuttingly severe; and when Monsieur Le Quoi sallied forth, under a bright moon, to seek his own abode, he was compelled to beg a blanket, in which he might envelope his form, in addition to the numerous garments that his sagacity had provided for the occasion. The divine and his daughter remained, as inmates of the Mansion-house, during the night, and the excess of last night's merriment induced the gentlemen to make an early retreat to their several apartments. Long before midnight, the whole family were invisible.

Elizabeth and her friend had not yet lost their senses in sleep, when the howlings of the northwest wind were heard around the buildings, and brought with them that exquisite sense of comfort, that is ever excited under such circumstances, in an apartment where the fire has not yet ceased to glimmer, and curtains, and shutters, and feathers, unite to preserve the desired temperature. Once, just as her eyes had opened, apparently in the last stage of drowsiness, the roaring winds brought with them a long and plaintive howl, that seemed too wild for a dog, and yet resembled the cries of that faithful animal, when night awakens his vigilance, and gives sweetness and solemnity to his alarms. The form of Louisa Grant instinctively pressed nearer to that of the young heiress, who, finding her companion was yet awake, said, in a low tone, as if afraid to break a charm with her voice—

"Those distant cries are plaintive, and even beautiful. Can they be the hounds from the hut of Leather-stocking?"

"They are wolves, who have ventured from the mountain, on the lake," whispered Louisa, "and who are only kept from the village by the lights. One night, since we have been here, hunger drove them to our very door. Oh! what a dreadful night it was! But the riches of Judge Temple have given him too many safeguards, to leave room for fear in this house."

"The enterprise of Judge Temple is taming the very forests!" exclaimed Elizabeth, throwing off the covering, and partly rising in the bed. "How rapidly is civilization treading on the footsteps of nature!" she continued, as her eye glanced over not only the comforts, but the luxuries of her apartment, and her ear again listened to the distant, but often repeated howls from the lake. Finding, however, that the timidity of her companion rendered the sounds painful to her, Elizabeth resumed her place, and soon forgot the changes in the country, with those in her own condition, in a deep sleep.

The following morning, the noise of the female servant, who entered the apartment to light the fire, awoke the females. They arose, and finished the slight preparations of their toilettes in a clear, cold atmosphere, that penetrated through all the defences of even Miss Temple's warm room. When Elizabeth was attired, she approached a window and drew its curtain, and, throwing open its shutters, she endeavoured to look abroad on the village and the lake. But a thick covering of frost, on the glass, while it admitted the light, shut out the view. She

raised the sash, and then, indeed, a glorious scene met her delighted eye.

The lake had exchanged its covering of unspotted snow, for a
face of dark ice, that reflected the rays of the rising sun, like a
polished mirror. The houses were clothed in a dress of the
same description, but which, owing to its position, shone like
bright steel; while the enormous icicles that were pendent from
every roof, caught the brilliant light, apparently throwing it
from one to the other, as each glittered, on the side next the
luminary, with a golden lustre, that melted away, on its opposite, into the dusky shades of a back-ground. But it was the appearance, of the boundless forests, that covered the hills, as
they rose, in the distance, one over the other, that most attracted the gaze of Miss Temple. The huge branches of the
pines and hemlocks bent with the weight of the ice they supported, while their summits rose above the swelling tops of the
oaks, beeches, and maples, like spires of burnished silver issuing from domes of the same material. The limits of the view, in
the west, were marked by an undulating outline of bright light,
as if, reversing the order of nature, numberless suns might
momentarily be expected to heave above the horizon. In the
foreground of the picture, along the shores of the lake, and
near to the village, each tree seemed studded with diamonds.
Even the sides of the mountains, where the rays of the sun
could not yet fall, were decorated with a glassy coat, that presented every gradation of brilliancy, from the first touch of the
luminary to the dark foliage of the hemlock, glistening through
its coat of crystal. In short, the whole view was one scene of
quivering radiancy, as lake, mountains, village, and woods, each
emitted a portion of light, tinged with its peculiar hue, and varied by its position and its magnitude.

"See!" cried Elizabeth—"see, Louisa; hasten to the window,
and observe the miraculous change."

Miss Grant complied; and, after bending for a moment in
silence from the opening, she observed, in a low tone, as if
afraid to trust the sound of her voice—

"The change is indeed wonderful! I am surprised that he
should be able to effect it so soon."

Elizabeth turned in amazement, to hear so sceptical a sentiment from one educated like her companion; but was surprised to find that, instead of looking at the view, the mild, blue eyes of Miss Grant were dwelling on the form of a well-dressed young man, who was standing before the door of the building, in earnest conversation with her father. A second look was necessary, before she was able to recognise the person of the young hunter, in a plain, but, assuredly, the ordinary garb of a gentleman.

"Every thing in this magical country seems to border on the marvellous," said Elizabeth; "and among all the changes, this is certainly not the least wonderful. The actors are as unique as the scenery."

Miss Grant coloured, and drew in her head.

"I am a simple country girl, Miss Temple, and I am afraid you will find me but a poor companion," she said. "I—I am not sure that I understand all you say. But I really thought that you wished me to notice the alteration in Mr. Edwards. Is it not more wonderful, when we recollect his origin? They say he is part Indian."

"He is a genteel savage; but let us go down, and give the Sachem his tea;—for I suppose he is a descendant of King Philip, if not a grandson of Pocahontas."

The ladies were met in the hall by Judge Temple, who took his daughter aside, to apprize her of that alteration in the appearance of their new inmate, with which she was already acquainted.

"He appears reluctant to converse on his former situation," continued Marmaduke; "but I gather from his discourse, as is apparent from his manner, that he has seen better days; and I really am inclining to the opinion of Richard, as to his origin; for it was no unusual thing for the Indian Agents to rear their children in a very laudable manner, and——"

"Very well, my dear sir," interrupted his daughter, laughing, and averting her eyes; "it is all well enough, I dare say; but as I do not understand a word of the Mohawk language, he must be content to speak English; and as for his behaviour, I trust to your discernment to control it."

"Ay! but, Bess," said the Judge, detaining her gently, with his hand, "nothing must be said to him of his past life. This he has begged particularly of me, as a favour. He is, perhaps, a little soured, just now, with his wounded arm; the injury seems very light, and another time he may be more communicative."

"Oh! I am not much troubled, sir, with that laudable thirst after knowledge, that is called curiosity. I shall believe him to be the child of Corn-stalk, or Corn-planter, or some other renowned chieftain; possibly of the Big Snake himself; and shall treat him as such, until he sees fit to shave his good-looking head, borrow some half-dozen pair of my best ear-rings, shoulder his rifle again, and disappear as suddenly as he made his entrance. So come, my dear sir, and let us not forget the rites of hospitality, for the short time he is to remain with us."

Judge Temple smiled, at the playfulness of his child, and taking her arm, they entered the breakfast parlour, where the young hunter was seated, with an air that showed his determination to domesticate himself in the family, with as little parade as possible.

Such were the incidents that led to this extraordinary increase in the family of Judge Temple, where, having once established the youth, the subject of our tale requires us to leave him, for a time, to pursue with diligence and intelligence the employments that were assigned him by Marmaduke.

Major Hartmann made his customary visit, and took his leave of the party, for the next three months. Mr. Grant was compelled to be absent much of his time, in remote parts of the country, and his daughter became almost a constant visiter at the Mansion-house. Richard entered, with his constitutional eagerness, on the duties of his new office; and, as Marmaduke was much employed, with the constant applications of adventurers, for farms, the winter passed swiftly away. The lake was a principal scene for the amusements of the young people; where the ladies, in their one-horse cutter, driven by Richard, and attended, when the snow would admit of it, by young Edwards, on his skates, spent many hours, taking the benefit of exercise in the clear air of the hills. The reserve of the youth gradually gave way to time and his situation, though it was still evident, to a close observer, that he had frequent moments of bitter and intense feeling.

Elizabeth saw many large openings appear in the sides of the mountains, during the three succeeding months, where different settlers had, in the language of the country, "made their pitch;" while the numberless sleighs that passed through the village, loaded with wheat and barrels of pot-ashes, afforded a clear demonstration that all these labours were not undertaken in vain. In short, the whole country was exhibiting the bustle of a thriving settlement, where the highways were thronged with sleighs, bearing piles of rough household furniture, studded, here and there, with the smiling faces of women and children, happy in the excitement of novelty; or with loads of produce, hastening to the common market at Albany, that served as so many snares, to induce the emigrants to enter into those wild mountains in search of competence and happiness.

The village was alive with business, the artisans increasing in wealth with the prosperity of the country, and each day witnessing some nearer approach to the manners and usages of an old-settled town. The man who carried the mail, or "the post," as he was called, talked much of running a stage, and once or twice, during the winter, he was seen taking a single passenger in his cutter, through the snow-banks towards the Mohawk, along which a regular vehicle glided, semi-weekly, with the velocity of lightning, and under the direction of a knowing whip from the "down countries." Towards spring, divers families, who had been into the "old states," to see their relatives, returned, in time to save the snow, frequently bringing with them whole neighbourhoods, who were tempted by their representations to leave the farms of Connecticut and Massachusetts, to make a trial of fortune in the woods.

During all this time, Oliver Edwards, whose sudden elevation excited no surprise in that changeful country, was earnestly engaged in the service of Marmaduke, during the days; but his nights were often spent in the hut of Leather-stocking. The intercourse between the three hunters was maintained with a certain air of mystery, it is true, but with much zeal and apparent interest to all the parties. Even Mohegan seldom came to the Mansion-house, and Natty, never; but Edwards sought every leisure moment to visit his former abode, from which he would often return in the gloomy hours of night, through the snow, or, if detained beyond the time at which the family retired to rest, with the morning sun. These visits certainly excited much speculation in those to whom they were known, but no comments were made, excepting occasionally in whispers from Richard, who would say—

"It is not at all remarkable;—a half-breed can never be weaned from the savage ways—and for one of his lineage, the boy is much nearer civilisation than could, in reason, be expected."

Chapter XX.

"Away! nor let me loiter in my song,
For we have many a mountain path to tread."
                    Byron, *Childe Harold's Pilgrimage*, II.xxxv.1–2.

As the spring gradually approached, the immense piles of snow, that, by alternate thaws and frosts, and repeated storms, had obtained a firmness which threatened a tiresome durability, begun to yield to the influence of milder breezes and a warmer sun. The gates of Heaven, at times, seemed to open, and a bland air diffused itself over the earth, when animate and inanimate nature would awaken, and, for a few hours, the gayety of spring shone in every eye, and smiled on every field. But the shivering blasts from the north would carry their chill influence over the scene again, and the dark and gloomy clouds that intercepted the rays of the sun, were not more cold and dreary, than the re-action. These struggles between the seasons became, daily, more frequent, while the earth, like a victim to contention, slowly lost the animated brilliancy of winter, without obtaining the aspect of spring.

Several weeks were consumed, in this cheerless manner, during which the inhabitants of the country gradually changed their pursuits from the social and bustling movements of the time of snow, to the laborious and domestic engagements of the coming season. The village was no longer thronged with visiters; the trade, that had enlivened the shops for several months, begun to disappear; the highways lost their shining coats of beaten snow in impassable sloughs, and were deserted by the gay and noisy travellers who, in sleighs, had, during the winter, glided along their windings; and, in short, every thing seemed indicative of a mighty change, not only in the earth, but in those who derived their sources of comfort and happiness from its bosom.

The younger members of the family in the Mansion-house, of which Louisa Grant was now habitually one, were by no means indifferent observers of these fluctuating and tardy changes. While the snow rendered the roads passable, they had partaken largely in the amusements of the winter, which included not only daily rides over the mountains, and through every valley within twenty miles of them, but divers ingenious and varied sources of pleasure, on the bosom of their frozen lake. There had been excursions in the equipage of Richard, when, with his four horses, he had outstripped the winds, as it flew over the glassy ice which invariably succeeded a thaw. Then the exciting and dangerous "whirligig" would be suffered to possess its moment of notice. Cutters, drawn by a single horse, and hand-sleds, impelled by the gentlemen, on skates, would each in turn be used; and, in short, every source of relief against the tediousness of a winter in the mountains, was resorted to by the family. Elizabeth was willing to acknowledge to her father, that the season, with the aid of his library, was much less irksome than she had anticipated.

As exercise in the open air was, in some degree necessary to the habits of the family, when the constant recurrence of frosts and thaws rendered the roads, which were dangerous, at the most favourable times, utterly impassable for wheels, saddle-horses were used as substitutes for other conveyances. Mounted on small and sure-footed beasts, the ladies would again attempt the passages of the mountains, and penetrate into every retired glen, where the enterprise of a settler had induced him to establish himself. In these excursions they were attended by some one or all of the gentlemen of the family, as their different pursuits admitted. Young Edwards was hourly becoming more familiarized to his situation, and not unfrequently mingled in the parties, with an unconcern and gayety, that, for a short time, would expel all unpleasant recollections from his mind. Habit, and the buoyancy of youth, seemed to be getting the ascendency over the secret causes of his uneasiness; though there were moments, when the same remarkable expression of disgust, would cross his intercourse with Marmaduke, that had distinguished their conversations in the first days of their acquaintance.

It was at the close of the month of March, that the Sheriff succeeded in persuading his cousin and her young friend to accompany him in a ride to a hill, that was said to overhang the lake, in a manner peculiar to itself.

"Besides, cousin Bess," continued the indefatigable Richard, "we will stop and see the 'sugar bush' of Billy Kirby: he is on the east end of the Ransom lot, making sugar for Jared Ransom. There is not a better hand over a kettle in the county, than that same Kirby. You remember, 'duke, that I had him his first season, in our own camp; and it is not a wonder that he knows something of his trade."

"He's a good chopper, is Billy," observed Benjamin, who held the bridle of the horse while the Sheriff mounted; "and he handles an axe, much the same as a forecastle-man does his marling-spike, or a tailor his goose. They say he'll lift a potash kettle off the arch alone, thof I can't say that I've ever seen him do it with my own eyes; but that is the say. And I've seen sugar of his making, which, maybe, wasn't as white as an old top-gallantsail, but which my friend Mistress Pretty-bones, within there, said, had the true molasses smack to it; and you are not the one, Squire Dickens, to be told that Mistress Remarkable has a remarkable tooth for sweet things in her nut-grinder."

The loud laugh that succeeded the wit of Benjamin, and in which he participated, with no very harmonious sounds, himself, very fully illustrated the congenial temper which existed between the pair. Most of its point was, however, lost on the rest of the party, who were either mounting their horses, or assisting the ladies at the moment. When all were safely in their saddles, they moved through the village in great order. They paused for a moment, before the door of Monsieur Le Quoi, until he could bestride his steed, and then, issuing from the little cluster of houses, they took one of the principal of those highways, that centered in the village.

As each night brought with it a severe frost, which the heat of the succeeding day served to dissipate, the equestrians were compelled to proceed singly, along the margin of the road, where the turf, and firmness of the ground, gave the horses a secure footing. Very trifling indications of vegetation were to be seen, the surface of the earth presenting a cold, wet, and cheerless aspect, that chilled the blood. The snow yet lay scattered over most of those distant clearings that were visible in different parts of the mountains; though here and there an opening might be seen, where, as the white covering yielded to the season, the bright and lively green of the wheat served to enkindle the hopes of the husbandman. Nothing could be more marked, than the contrast between the earth and the heavens; for, while the former presented the dreary view that we have described, a warm and invigorating sun was dispensing his heats, from a sky that contained but a solitary cloud, and through an atmosphere, that softened the colours of the sensible horizon, until it shone like a sea of blue.

Richard led the way, on this, as on all other occasions, that did not require the exercise of unusual abilities; and as he moved along, he essayed to enliven the party with the sounds of his experienced voice.

"This is your true sugar weather, 'duke," he cried; "a frosty night, and a sunshiny day. I warrant me that the sap runs like a mill-tail up the maples, this warm morning. It is a pity, Judge, that you do not introduce a little more science into the manufacture of sugar, among your tenants. It might be done, sir, without knowing as much as Dr. Franklin—it might be done, Judge Temple."

"The first object of my solicitude, friend Jones," returned Marmaduke, "is to protect the sources of this great mine of comfort and wealth, from the extravagance of the people themselves. When this important point shall be achieved, it will be in season to turn our attention to an improvement in the manufacture of the article. But thou knowest, Richard, that I have already subjected our sugar to the process of the refiner, and that the result has produced loaves as white as the snow on yon fields, and possessing the saccharine quality in its utmost purity."

"Saccharine, or turpentine, or any other -ine, Judge Temple, you have never made a loaf larger than a good sized sugar-plum," returned the Sheriff. "Now, sir, I assert, that no experiment is fairly tried, until it be reduced to practical purposes. If, sir, I owned a hundred, or, for that matter, two hundred thousand acres of land, as you do, I would build a sugar-house in the village; I would invite learned men to an investigation of the subject,—and such are easily to be found, sir; yes, sir, they are not difficult to find,—men who unite theory with practice; and I would select a wood of young and thrifty trees; and, instead of making loaves of the size of a lump of candy, dam'me, 'duke, but I'd have them as big as a hay-cock."

"And purchase the cargo of one of those ships that, they say, are going to China," cried Elizabeth; "turn your potash-kettles into tea-cups, the scows on the lake into saucers; bake your cake in yonder lime-kiln, and invite the county to a tea-party. How wonderful are the projects of genius! Really, sir, the world is of opinion that Judge Temple has tried the experiment fairly, though he did not cause his loaves to be cast in moulds of the magnitude that would suit your magnificent conceptions."

"You may laugh, cousin Elizabeth—you may laugh, madam," retorted Richard, turning himself so much in his saddle as to face the party, and making dignified gestures with his whip; "but I appeal to common sense, good sense, or, what is of more importance than either, to the sense of taste, which is one of the five natural senses, whether a big loaf of sugar is not likely to contain a better illustration of a proposition, than such a lump as one of your Dutch women puts under her tongue when she drinks her tea. There are two ways of doing every thing; the right way, and the wrong way. You make sugar now, I will admit, and you may, possibly, make loaf-sugar; but I take the question to be, whether you make the best possible sugar, and in the best possible loaves."

"Thou art very right, Richard," observed Marmaduke, with a gravity in his air, that proved how much he was interested in the subject. "It is very true that we manufacture sugar, and the inquiry is quite useful, how much? and in what manner? I hope to live to see the day, when farms and plantations shall be devoted to this branch of business. Little is known concerning the properties of the tree itself, the source of all this wealth; how much it may be improved by cultivation, by the use of the hoe and plough."

"Hoe and plough!" roared the Sheriff;—"would you set a man hoeing round the root of a maple like this,"—pointing to one of the noble trees, that occur so frequently in that part of the country.—"Hoeing trees! are you mad, 'duke? This is next to hunting for coal! Poh! poh! my dear cousin, hear reason, and leave the management of the sugar-bush to me. Here is Mr. Le Quoi, he has been in the West-Indies, and has seen sugar made. Let him give an account of how it is made there, and you will hear the philosophy of the thing.—Well, Monsieur, how is it that you make sugar in the West-Indies; any thing in Judge Temple's fashion?"

The gentleman to whom this query was put, was mounted on

a small horse, of no very fiery temperament, and was riding with his stirrups so short, as to bring his knees, while the animal rose a small ascent in the wood-path they were now travelling, into a somewhat hazardous vicinity to his chin. There was no room for gesticulation or grace in the delivery of his reply, for the mountain was steep and slippery; and although the Frenchman had an eye of uncommon magnitude on either side of his face, they did not seem to be half competent to forewarn him of the impediments of bushes, twigs, and fallen trees, that were momentarily crossing his path. With one hand employed in averting these dangers, and the other grasping his bridle, to check an untoward speed that his horse was assuming, the native of France responded as follows:—

"Sucre! dey do make sucre in Martinique: mais—mais ce n'est pas, one tree;—ah—ah—vat you call—Je voudrois que ces chemins fussent au diable—vat you call—steeck pour le promenade."

"Cane," said Elizabeth, smiling at the imprecation which the wary Frenchman supposed was understood only by himself.

"Oui, Mam'selle, cane."

"Yes, yes," cried Richard, "cane is the vulgar name for it, but the real term is saccharum officinarum: and what we call the sugar, or hard maple, is acer saccharinum. These are the learned names, Monsieur, and are such as, doubtless, you well understand."

"Is this Greek or Latin, Mr. Edwards?" whispered Elizabeth to the youth, who was opening a passage for herself and her companions through the bushes—"or perhaps it is a still more learned language, for an interpretation of which we must look to you."

The dark eye of the young man glanced towards the speaker, but its resentful expression changed, in a moment.

"I shall remember your doubts, Miss Temple, when next I visit my old friend Mohegan, and either his skill, or that of Leather-stocking, shall solve them."

"And are you, then, really ignorant of their language?"

"Not absolutely; but the deep learning of Mr. Jones is more familiar to me, or even the polite masquerade of Monsieur Le Quoi."

"Do you speak French?" said the lady, with quickness.

"It is a common language with the Iroquois, and through the Canadas," he answered, smiling.

"Ah! but they are Mingoes, and your enemies."

"It will be well for me, if I have no worse," said the youth, dashing ahead with his horse, and putting an end to the evasive dialogue.

The discourse, however, was maintained with great vigour by Richard, until they reached an open wood on the summit of the mountain, where the hemlocks and pines totally disappeared, and a grove of the very trees that formed the subject of debate, covered the earth with their tall, straight trunks and spreading branches, in stately pride. The underwood had been entirely removed from this grove, or bush, as, in conjunction, with the simple arrangements for boiling, it was called, and a wide space of many acres was cleared, which might be likened to the dome of a mighty temple, to which the maples formed the columns, their tops composing the capitals, and the heavens the arch. A deep and careless incision had been made into each tree, near its root, into which little spouts, formed of the bark of the alder, or of the sumach, were fastened; and a trough, roughly dug out of the linden, or bass-wood, was lying at the root of each tree, to catch the sap that flowed from this extremely wasteful and inartificial arrangement.

The party paused a moment, on gaining the flat, to breathe their horses, and, as the scene was entirely new to several of their number, to view the manner of collecting the fluid. A fine, powerful voice aroused them from their momentary silence, as it rung under the branches of the trees, singing the following words of that inimitable doggrel, whose verses, if extended, would reach from the waters of the Connecticut to the shores of Ontario. The tune was, of course, that familiar air, which, although it is said to have been first applied to his nation in derision, circumstances have since rendered so glorious, that no American ever hears its jingling cadence, without feeling a thrill at his heart.

> "The Eastern States be full of men,
>   The Western full of woods, sir;
> The hills be like a cattle pen,
>   The roads be full of goods, sir,

> Then flow away, my sweety sap,
>   And I will make you boily;
> Nor catch a woodman's hasty nap,
>   For fear you should get roily.

"The maple tree's a precious one,
  'Tis fuel, food, and timber;
And when your stiff day's work is done,
  Its juice will make you limber.
      Then flow away, &c.

"And what's a man without his glass,
  His wife without her tea, sir?
But neither cup nor mug would pass,
  Without this honey-bee, sir.
      Then flow away," &c.

During the execution of this sonorous doggrel, Richard kept time with his whip on the mane of his charger, accompanying the gestures with a corresponding movement of his head and body. Towards the close of the song, he was overheard humming the chorus, and at its last repetition, to strike in at "sweety sap," and carry a second through, with a prodigious addition to the "effect" of the noise, if not to that of the harmony.

"Well done us!" roared the Sheriff, on the same key with the tune; "a very good song, Billy Kirby, and very well sung. Where got you the words, lad? is there more of it, and can you furnish me with a copy?"

The sugar-boiler, who was busy in his "camp," at a short distance from the equestrians, turned his head with great indifference, and surveyed the party, as they approached, with admirable coolness. To each individual, as he or she rode close by him, he gave a nod, that was extremely good-natured and affable, but which partook largely of the virtue of equality, for not even to the ladies did he in the least vary his mode of salutation, by touching the apology for a hat that he wore, or by any other motion than the one we have mentioned.

"How goes it, how goes it, Sheriff?" said the wood-chopper; "what's the good word in the village?"

"Why, much as usual, Billy," returned Richard. "But how is this! where are your four kettles, and your troughs, and your iron coolers? Do you make sugar in this slovenly way! I thought you were one of the best sugar-boilers in the county."

"I'm all that, Squire Jones," said Kirby, who continued his occupation; "I'll turn my back to no man in the Otsego hills, for chopping and logging; for boiling down the maple sap; for tending brick-kiln; splitting out rails; making potash, and parling too; or hoeing corn. Though I keep myself, pretty much, to the first business, seeing that the axe comes most nateral to me."

"You be von Jack All-trade, Mister Beel," said Monsieur Le Quoi.

"How?" said Kirby, looking up, with a simplicity which, coupled with his gigantic frame and manly face, was a little ridiculous—"if you be for trade, Mounsher, here is some as good sugar as you'll find the season through. It's as clear from dirt as the Jarman Flats is free from stumps, and it has the raal maple flavour. Such stuff would sell in York for candy."

The Frenchman approached the place where Kirby had deposited his cakes of sugar, under the cover of a bark roof, and commenced the examination of the article, with the eye of one who well understood its value. Marmaduke had dismounted, and was viewing the works and the trees very closely, and not without frequent expressions of dissatisfaction, at the careless manner in which the manufacture was conducted.

"You have much experience in these things, Kirby," he said; "what course do you pursue in making your sugar? I see you have but two kettles."

"Two is as good as two thousand, Judge; I'm none of your polite sugar-makers, that boils for the great folks; but if the raal sweet maple is wanted, I can answer your turn. First, I choose, and then I tap my trees; say along about the last of February, or, in these mountains, maybe not afore the middle of March; but any way, just as the sap begins to cleverly run——"

"Well, in this choice," interrupted Marmaduke, "are you governed by any outward signs, that prove the quality of the tree?"

"Why, there's judgment in all things," said Kirby, stirring the liquor in his kettles briskly. "There's something in knowing when and how much to stir the pot. It's a thing that must be larnt. Rome wasn't built in a day, nor, for that matter, Templetown 'ither, though it may be said to be a quick-growing place. I never put my axe into a stunty tree, or one that hasn't a good, fresh-looking bark; for trees have disorders like creaturs; and where's the policy of taking a tree that's sickly, any more than you'd choose a foundered horse to ride post, or an overheated ox to do your logging——"

"All this is true; but what are the signs of illness? how do you distinguish a tree that is well from one that is diseased?"

"How does the doctor tell who has fever, and who colds?" interrupted Richard—"by examining the skin, and feeling the pulse, to be sure."

"Sartain," continued Billy; "the Squire a'nt far out of the way. It's by the look of the thing, sure enough.—Well, when the sap begins to get a free run, I hang over the kettles, and set up the bush. My first boiling I push pretty smart, till I get the vartoo of the sap; but when it begins to grow of a molasses nater, like this in the kettle, one musn't drive the fires too hard, or you'll burn the sugar; and burny sugar is bad to the taste, let it be never so sweet. So you ladle out from one kettle into the other, till it gets so, when you put the stirring-stick into it, that it will draw into a thread; when it takes a kerful hand to manage it. There is a way to drain it off, after it has grained, by putting clay into the pans; but it isn't always practysed: some doos, and some doosn't. ——Well, Mounsher, be we likely to make a trade?"

"I vill give you, Mister Beel, for von pound——dix sous."

"No; I expect cash for't; I never dicker my sugar. But, seeing that it's you, Mounsher," said Billy, with a coaxing smile, "I'll agree to receive a gallon of rum, and cloth enough for two shirts, if you will take the molasses in the bargain. It's raal good. I wouldn't deceive you or any man; and to my drinking, it's about the best molasses that come out of a sugar-bush."

"Mr. Le Quoi has offered you ten pence," said young Edwards.

The manufacturer stared at the speaker, with an air of great freedom, but made no reply.

"Oui," said the Frenchman, "ten penny. Je vous remercie, Monsieur; ah! mon Anglois! je l'oublie toujours."

The wood-chopper looked from one to the other, with some displeasure; and evidently imbibed the opinion that they were amusing themselves at his expense. He seized the enormous ladle, which was lying in one of his kettles, and began to stir the boiling liquid with great diligence. After a moment, passed in dipping the ladle full, and then raising it on high, as the thick, rich fluid fell back into the kettle, he suddenly gave it a whirl, as if to cool what yet remained, and offered the bowl to Mr. Le Quoi, saying—

"Taste that, Mounsher, and you will say it is worth more than you offer. The molasses itself would fetch the money."

The complaisant Frenchman, after several timid efforts to trust his lips in contact with the bowl of the ladle, got a good swallow of the scalding liquid. He clapped his hand on his breast, and looked most piteously at the ladies, for a single instant, and then, to use the language of Billy, when he afterwards recounted the tale, "no drum-sticks ever went faster on the skin of a sheep, than the Frenchman's legs, for a round or two: and then, such swearing and spitting, in French, you never seen. But it's a knowing one, from the old countries, that thinks to get his jokes smoothly over a wood-chopper."

The air of innocence with which Kirby resumed the occupation of stirring the contents of his kettle, would have completely deceived the spectators, as to his agency in the temporary suffering of Mr. Le Quoi, had not the reckless fellow thrust his tongue into his cheek, and cast his eyes over the party, with a simplicity of expression that was too exquisite to be natural. Mr. Le Quoi soon recovered his presence of mind, and his decorum; he briefly apologized to the ladies for one or two very intemperate expressions, that had escaped him in a moment of extraordinary excitement, and remounting his horse, he continued in the back-ground during the reminder of the visit, the wit of Kirby putting a violent termination, at once, to all negotiations on the subject of trade. During all this time, Marmaduke had been wandering about the grove, making observations on his favourite trees, and the wasteful manner in which the wood-chopper conducted his manufacture.

"It grieves me to witness the extravagance that pervades this country," said the Judge, "where the settlers trifle with the blessings they might enjoy, with the prodigality of successful adventurers. You are not exempt from the censure yourself, Kirby, for you make dreadful wounds in these trees, where a small incision would effect the same object. I earnestly beg you will remember, that they are the growth of centuries, and when once gone, none living will see their loss remedied."

"Why, I don't know, Judge," returned the man he addressed: "It seems to me, if there's a plenty of any thing in this moun- taynous country, it's the trees. If there's any sin in chopping them, I've a pretty heavy account to settle; for I've chopped over the best half of a thousand acres, with my own hands, counting both Varmount and York states; and I hope to live to finish the whull, before I lay up my axe. Chopping comes quite nateral to me, and I wish no other emplyment; but Jared Ran- som said that he thought the sugar was likely to be scurce this season, seeing that so many folks was coming into the settle- ment, and so I concluded to take the 'bush' on sheares, for this one spring. What's the best news, Judge, concarning ashes? do pots hold so that a man can live by them still? I s'pose they will if they keep on fighting across the water."

"Thou reasonest with judgment, William," returned Mar- maduke. "So long as the old world is to be convulsed with wars, so long will the harvest of America continue."

"Well, it's an ill wind, Judge, that blows nobody any good. I'm sure the country is in a thriving way; and, though I know you kalkilate greatly on the trees, setting as much store by them as some men would by their children, yet, to my eyes, they are a sore sight at any time, unless I'm privileged to work my will on them; in which case, I can't say but they are more to my liking. I have heern the settlers from the old countries say, that their rich men keep great oaks and elms, that would make a barrel of pots to the tree, standing round their doors and humsteads, and scattered over their farms, just to look at. Now, I call no country much improved, that is pretty well covered with trees. Stumps are a different thing, for they don't shade the land; and besides, if you dig them, they make a fence that will turn any thing bigger than a hog, being grand for breachy cattle."

"Opinions on such subjects vary much, in different coun- tries," said Marmaduke; "but it is not as ornaments that I value the noble trees of this country; it is for their usefulness. We are stripping the forests, as if a single year would replace what we destroy. But the hour approaches, when the laws will take notice of not only the woods, but the game they contain also."

With this consoling reflection, Marmaduke remounted, and the equestrians passed the sugar-camp, on their way to the promised landscape of Richard. The wood-chopper was left alone, in the bosom of the forest, to pursue his labours. Elizabeth turned her head, when they reached the point where they were to descend the mountain, and thought that the slow fires, that were glimmering under his enormous kettles, his little brush shelter, covered with pieces of hemlock bark, his gigantic size, as he wielded his ladle with a steady and knowing air, aided by the back-ground of stately trees, with their spouts and troughs, formed, altogether, no unreal picture of human life in its first stages of civilization. Perhaps whatever the scene possessed of a romantic character was not injured by the powerful tones of Kirby's voice, ringing through the woods, as he again awoke his strains to another tune, which was but little more scientific than the former. All that she understood of the words, were—

"And when the proud forest is falling,
To my oxen cheerfully calling,
From morn until night I am bawling,
    Woe, back there, and hoy and gee;
Till our labour is mutually ended,
By my strength and cattle befriended,
And against the musquitoes defended,
    By the bark of the walnut tree.—

"Away! then, you lads who would buy land,
Choose the oak that grows on the high land,
Or the silvery pine on the dry land,
    It matters but little to me."

Chapter XXI.

"Speed! Malise, speed! such cause of haste
Thine active sinews never brac'd."
                    Scott, *The Lady of the Lake*, III.xiii.3–4.

T HE roads of Otsego, if we except the principal highways, were, at the early day of our tale, but little better than wood-paths. The high trees that were growing on the very verge of the wheel-tracks, excluded the sun's rays, unless at meridian, and the slowness of the evaporation, united with the rich mould of vegetable decomposition, that covered the whole country, to the depth of several inches, occasioned but an indifferent foundation for the footing of travellers. Added to these were the inequalities of a natural surface, and the constant recurrence of enormous and slippery roots, that were laid bare by the removal of the light soil, together with stumps of trees, to make a passage not only difficult, but dangerous. Yet the riders, among these numerous obstructions, which were such as would terrify an unpractised eye, gave no demonstrations of uneasiness, as their horses toiled through the sloughs, or trotted with uncertain paces along the dark route. In many places, the marks on the trees were the only indications of a road, with, perhaps, an occasional remnant of a pine, that, by being cut close to the earth, so as to leave nothing visible but its base of roots, spreading for twenty feet in every direction, was apparently placed there as a beacon, to warn the traveller that it was the centre of a highway.

Into one of these roads the active Sheriff led the way, first striking out of the footpath, by which they had descended from the sugar-bush, across a little bridge, formed of round logs laid loosely on sleepers of pine, in which large openings, of a formidable width, were frequent. The nag of Richard, when it reached one of these gaps, laid its nose along the logs, and stepped across the difficult passage with the sagacity of a man; but the blooded filly which Miss Temple rode disdained so humble a movement. She made a step or two with an unusual caution, and then, on reaching the broadest opening, obedient to the curb and whip of her fearless mistress, she bounded across the dangerous pass, with the activity of a squirrel.

"Gently, gently, my child," said Marmaduke, who was following in the manner of Richard——"this is not a country for equestrian feats. Much prudence is requisite, to journey through our rough paths with safety. Thou mayst practise thy skill in horsemanship on the plains of New-Jersey, with safety, but in the hills of Otsego, they must be suspended for a time."

"I may as well, then, relinquish my saddle at once, dear sir," returned his daughter; "for if it is to be laid aside until this wild country be improved, old age will overtake me, and put an end to what you term my equestrian feats."

"Say not so, my child," returned her father; "but if thou venturest again, as in crossing this bridge, old age will never overtake thee, but I shall be left to mourn thee, cut off in thy pride, my Elizabeth. If thou hadst seen this district of country, as I did, when it lay in the sleep of nature, and had witnessed its rapid changes, as it awoke to supply the wants of man, thou wouldst curb thy impatience for a little time, though thou shouldst not check thy steed."

"I recollect hearing you speak of your first visit to these woods, but the impression is faint, and blended with the confused images of childhood. Wild and unsettled as it may yet seem, it must have been a thousand times more dreary then. Will you repeat, dear sir, what you then thought of your enterprise, and what you felt?"

During this speech of Elizabeth, which was uttered with the fervour of affection, young Edwards rode more closely to the side of the Judge, and bent his dark eyes on his countenance, with an expression that seemed to read his thoughts.

"Thou wast then young, my child, but must remember when I left thee and thy mother, to take my first survey of these uninhabited mountains," said Marmaduke. "But thou dost not feel all the secret motives that can urge a man to endure privations in order to accumulate wealth. In my case they have not been trifling, and God has been pleased to smile on my efforts. If I have encountered pain, famine, and disease, in accomplishing the settlement of this rough territory, I have not the misery of failure to add to the grievances."

"Famine!" echoed Elizabeth; "I thought this was the land of abundance! had you famine to contend with?"

"Even so, my child," said her father. "Those who look around them now, and see the loads of produce that issue out of every wild path in these mountains, during the season of travelling, will hardly credit that no more than five years have elapsed, since the tenants of these woods were compelled to eat the scanty fruits of the forest to sustain life, and, with their unpractised skill, to hunt the beasts as food for their starving families."

"Ay!" cried Richard, who happened to overhear the last of this speech, between the notes of the wood-chopper's song, which he was endeavouring to breathe aloud; "that was the starving-time*, cousin Bess. I grew as lank as a weasel that fall, and my face was as pale as one of your fever-and-ague visages. Monsieur Le Quoi, there, fell away like a pumpkin in drying; nor do I think you have got fairly over it yet, Monsieur. Benjamin, I thought, bore it with a worse grace than any of the family, for he swore it was harder to endure than a short allowance in the calm latitudes. Benjamin is a sad fellow to swear, if you starve him ever so little. I had half a mind to quit you then, 'duke, and to go into Pennsylvania to fatten; but, damn it, thinks I, we are sisters' children, and I will live or die with him, after all."

"I do not forget thy kindness," said Marmaduke, "nor that we are of one blood."

"But, my dear father," cried the wondering Elizabeth, "was there actual suffering? where were the beautiful and fertile vales of the Mohawk? could they not furnish food for your wants?"

---

* The author has no better apology for interrupting the interest of a work of fiction by these desultory dialogues, than that they have reference to facts. In reviewing his work, after so many years, he is compelled to confess it is injured by too many allusions to incidents that are not at all suited to satisfy the just expectations of the general reader. One of these events is slightly touched on, in the commencement of this chapter.

More than thirty years since, a very near and dear relative of the writer, an elder sister and a second mother, was killed by a fall from a horse, in a ride among the very mountains mentioned in this tale. Few of her sex and years were more extensively known, or more universally beloved, than the admirable woman who thus fell a victim to the chances of the wilderness. [1832]

"It was a season of scarcity; the necessities of life commanded a high price in Europe, and were greedily sought after by the speculators. The emigrants, from the east to the west, invariably passed along the valley of the Mohawk, and swept away the means of subsistence, like a swarm of locusts. Nor were the people on the Flats in a much better condition. They were in want themselves, but they spared the little excess of provisions, that nature did not absolutely require, with the justice of the German character. There was no grinding of the poor. The word speculator was then unknown to them. I have seen many a stout man, bending under the load of the bag of meal, which he was carrying from the mills of the Mohawk, through the rugged passes of these mountains, to feed his half-famished children, with a heart so light, as he approached his hut, that the thirty miles he had passed seemed nothing. Remember, my child, it was in our very infancy: we had neither mills, nor grain, nor roads, nor often clearings;——we had nothing of increase, but the mouths that were to be fed; for, even at that inauspicious moment, the restless spirit of emigration was not idle; nay, the general scarcity, which extended to the east, tended to increase the number of adventurers."

"And how, dearest father, didst thou encounter this dreadful evil?" said Elizabeth, unconsciously adopting the dialect of her parent, in the warmth of her sympathy. "Upon thee must have fallen the responsibility, if not the suffering."

"It did, Elizabeth," returned the Judge, pausing for a single moment, as if musing on his former feelings. "I had hundreds, at that dreadful time, daily looking up to me for bread. The sufferings of their families, and the gloomy prospect before them, had paralysed the enterprise and efforts of my settlers; hunger drove them to the woods for food, but despair sent them, at night, enfeebled and wan, to a sleepless pillow. It was not a moment for inaction. I purchased cargoes of wheat from the granaries of Pennsylvania; they were landed at Albany, and brought up the Mohawk in boats; from thence it was transported on pack-horses into the wilderness, and distributed amongst my people. Seines were made, and the lakes and rivers were dragged for fish. Something like a miracle was wrought in our favour, for enormous shoals of herrings were discovered to have wandered five hundred miles, through the windings of the impetuous Susquehanna, and the lake was alive with their numbers. These were at length caught, and dealt out to the people, with proper portions of salt; and from that moment, we again began to prosper."*

"Yes," cried Richard, "and I was the man who served out the fish and the salt. When the poor devils came to receive their rations, Benjamin, who was my deputy, was obliged to keep them off by stretching ropes around me, for they smelt so of garlic, from eating nothing but the wild onion, that the fumes put me out, often, in my measurement. You were a child then, Bess, and knew nothing of the matter, for great care was observed to keep both you and your mother from suffering. That year put me back, dreadfully, both in the breed of my hogs, and of my turkeys."

"No, Bess," cried the Judge, in a more cheerful tone, disregarding the interruption of his cousin, "he who hears of the settlement of a country, knows but little of the toil and suffering by which it is accomplished. Unimproved and wild as this district now seems to your eyes, what was it when I first entered the hills! I left my party, the morning of my arrival, near the farms of the Cherry Valley, and, following a deer-path, rode to the summit of the mountain, that I have since called Mount Vision; for the sight that there met my eyes seemed to me as the deceptions of a dream. The fire had run over the pinnacle, and, in a great measure, laid open the view. The leaves were fallen, and I mounted a tree, and sat for an hour looking on the silent wilderness. Not an opening was to be seen in the boundless forest, except where the lake lay, like a mirror of glass. The water was covered by myriads of the wild-fowl that migrate with the changes in the season; and, while in my situation on the branch of the beech, I saw a bear, with her cubs, descend to the shore to drink. I had met many deer, gliding through the woods, in my journey; but not the vestige of a man could I trace, during my progress, nor from my elevated observatory. No clearing, no hut, none of the winding roads that are now to be seen, were there; nothing but mountains rising behind mountains, and the valley, with its surface of branches, enlivened here and there with the faded foliage of some tree, that parted from its leaves with more than ordinary reluctance.

* All this was literally true. [1832]

Even the Susquehanna was then hid, by the height and density of the forest."

"And were you alone?" asked Elizabeth;——"passed you the night in that solitary state?"

"Not so, my child," returned her father. "After musing on the scene for an hour, with a mingled feeling of pleasure and desolation, I left my perch, and descended the mountain. My horse was left to browse on the twigs that grew within his reach, while I explored the shores of the lake, and the spot where Templeton stands. A pine of more than ordinary growth stood where my dwelling is now placed; a wind-row had been opened through the trees from thence to the lake, and my view was but little impeded. Under the branches of that tree I made my solitary dinner; I had just finished my repast as I saw a smoke curling from under the mountain, near the eastern bank of the lake. It was the only indication of the vicinity of man that I had then seen. After much toil, I made my way to the spot, and found a rough cabin of logs, built against the foot of a rock, and bearing the marks of a tenant, though I found no one within it.—"

"It was the hut of Leather-stocking," said Edwards, quickly.

"It was; though I, at first, supposed it to be a habitation of the Indians. But while I was lingering around the spot, Natty made his appearance, staggering under the carcass of a buck that he had slain. Our acquaintance commenced at that time; before, I had never heard that such a being tenanted the woods. He launched his bark canoe, and set me across the foot of the lake, to the place where I had fastened my horse, and pointed out a spot where he might get a scanty browsing until the morning; when I returned and passed the night in the cabin of the hunter."

Miss Temple was so much struck by the deep attention of young Edwards, during this speech, that she forgot to resume her interrogatories; but the youth himself continued the discourse, by asking—

"And how did the Leather-stocking discharge the duties of a host, sir?"

"Why, simply but kindly, until late in the evening, when he discovered my name and object, and the cordiality of his manner very sensibly diminished, or, I might better say, disappeared. He considered the introduction of the settlers as an innovation on his rights, I believe; for he expressed much dissatisfaction at the measure, though it was in his confused and ambiguous manner. I hardly understood his objections myself, but supposed they referred chiefly to an interruption of the hunting."

"Had you then purchased the estate, or were you examining it with an intent to buy?" asked Edwards, a little abruptly.

"It had been mine for several years. It was with a view to people the land that I visited the lake. Natty treated me hospitably, but coldly, I thought, after he learnt the nature of my journey. I slept on his own bear-skin, however, and in the morning joined my surveyors again."

"Said he nothing of the Indian rights, sir? The Leather-stocking is much given to impeach the justice of the tenure by which the whites hold the country."

"I remember that he spoke of them, but I did not clearly comprehend him, and may have forgotten what he said; for the Indian title was extinguished so far back as the close of the old war; and if it had not been at all, I hold under the patents of the Royal Governors, confirmed by an act of our own State Legislature, and no court in the country can affect my title."

"Doubtless, sir, your title is both legal and equitable," returned the youth, coldly, reining his horse back, and remaining silent till the subject was changed.

It was seldom Mr. Jones suffered any conversation to continue, for a great length of time, without his participation. It seems that he was of the party that Judge Temple had designated as his surveyors; and he embraced the opportunity of the pause that succeeded the retreat of young Edwards, to take up the discourse, and with it a narration of their further proceedings, after his own manner. As it wanted, however, the interest that had accompanied the description of the Judge, we must decline the task of committing his sentences to paper.

They soon reached the point where the promised view was to be seen. It was one of those picturesque and peculiar scenes, that belong to the Otsego, but which required the absence of the ice, and the softness of a summer's landscape, to be enjoyed in all its beauty. Marmaduke had early forewarned his daughter of the season, and of its effect on the prospect, and after casting a cursory glance at its capabilities, the party returned homeward, perfectly satisfied that its beauties would repay them for the toil of a second ride, at a more propitious season.

"The spring is the gloomy time of the American year," said the Judge; "and it is more peculiarly the case in these mountains. The winter seems to retreat to the fastnesses of the hills, as to the citadel of its dominion, and is only expelled, after a tedious siege, in which either party, at times, would seem to be gaining the victory."

"A very just and apposite figure, Judge Temple," observed the Sheriff; "and the garrison under the command of Jack Frost make formidable sorties—you understand what I mean by sorties, Monsieur; sallies, in English—and sometimes drive General Spring and his troops back again into the low countries."

"Yes, sair," returned the Frenchman, whose prominent eyes were watching the precarious footsteps of the beast he rode, as it picked its dangerous way among the roots of trees, holes, log-bridges, and sloughs, that formed the aggregate of the highway. "Je vous entend; de low countrie is freeze up for half de year."

The error of Mr. Le Quoi was not observed by the Sheriff; and the rest of the party were yielding to the influence of the changeful season, which was already teaching the equestrians that a continuance of its mildness was not to be expected for any length of time. Silence and thoughtfulness succeeded the gayety and conversation that had prevailed during the commencement of the ride, as clouds began to gather about the heavens, apparently collecting from every quarter, in quick motion, without the agency of a breath of air.

While riding over one of the cleared eminences that occurred in their route, the watchful eye of Judge Temple pointed out to his daughter the approach of a tempest. Flurries of snow already obscured the mountain that formed the northern boundary of the lake, and the genial sensation which had quickened the blood through their veins, was already succeeded by the deadening influence of an approaching *northwester*.

All of the party were now busily engaged in making the best of their way to the village, though the badness of the roads frequently compelled them to check the impatience of their horses, which often carried them over places that would not admit of any gait faster than a walk.

Richard continued in advance, followed by Mr. Le Quoi; next to whom rode Elizabeth, who seemed to have imbibed the distance which pervaded the manner of young Edwards, since the termination of the discourse between the latter and her father. Marmaduke followed his daughter, giving her frequent and tender warnings as to the management of her horse. It was, possibly, the evident dependence that Louisa Grant placed on his assistance, which induced the youth to continue by her side, as they pursued their way through a dreary and dark wood, where the rays of the sun could but rarely penetrate, and where even the daylight was obscured and rendered gloomy by the deep forests that surrounded them. No wind had yet reached the spot where the equestrians were in motion, but that dead stillness that often precedes a storm, contributed to render their situation more irksome than if they were already subjected to the fury of the tempest. Suddenly the voice of young Edwards was heard shouting, in those appalling tones that carry alarm to the very soul, and which curdle the blood of those that hear them—

"A tree! a tree! whip—spur for your lives! a tree! a tree!"

"A tree! a tree!" echoed Richard, giving his horse a blow, that caused the alarmed beast to jump nearly a rod, throwing the mud and water into the air, like a hurricane.

"Von tree! von tree!" shouted the Frenchman, bending his body on the neck of his charger, shutting his eyes, and playing on the ribs of his beast with his heels, at a rate that caused him to be conveyed, on the crupper of the Sheriff, with a marvellous speed.

Elizabeth checked her filly, and looked up, with an unconscious but alarmed air, at the very cause of their danger, while she listened to the crackling sounds that awoke the stillness of the forest; but, at the next instant, her bridle was seized by her father, who cried—

"God protect my child!" and she felt herself hurried onward, impelled by the vigour of his nervous arm.

Each one of the party bowed to his saddle-bows, as the tearing of branches was succeeded by a sound like the rushing of the winds, which was followed by a thundering report, and a shock that caused the very earth to tremble, as one of the noblest ruins of the forest fell directly across their path.

One glance was enough to assure Judge Temple that his daughter, and those in front of him, were safe, and he turned his eyes, in dreadful anxiety, to learn the fate of the others. Young Edwards was on the opposite side of the tree, his form thrown back in his saddle to its utmost distance, his left hand drawing up his bridle with its greatest force, while the right grasped that of Miss Grant, so as to draw the head of her horse under its body. Both the animals stood shaking in every joint with terror, and snorting fearfully. Louisa herself had relinquished her reins, and with her hands pressed on her face, sat bending forward in her saddle, in an attitude of despair mingled strangely with resignation.

"Are you safe?" cried the Judge, first breaking the awful silence of the moment.

"By God's blessing," returned the youth; "but if there had been branches to the tree we must have been lost—"

He was interrupted by the figure of Louisa, slowly yielding in her saddle; and but for his arm, she would have sunken to the earth. Terror, however, was the only injury that the clergyman's daughter had sustained, and, with the aid of Elizabeth, she was soon restored to her senses. After some little time was lost in recovering her strength, the young lady was replaced in her saddle, and, supported on either side, by Judge Temple and Mr. Edwards, she was enabled to follow the party in their slow progress.

"The sudden falling of the trees," said Marmaduke, "are the most dangerous accidents in the forest, for they are not to be foreseen, being impelled by no winds, nor any extraneous or visible cause, against which we can guard."

"The reason of their falling, Judge Temple, is very obvious," said the Sheriff. "The tree is old and decayed, and it is gradually weakened by the frosts, until a line drawn from the centre of gravity falls without its base, and then the tree comes of a certainty; and I should like to know, what greater compulsion there can be for any thing, than a mathematical certainty. I studied mathe——"

"Very true, Richard," interrupted Marmaduke; "thy reasoning is true, and, if my memory be not over treacherous, was furnished by myself, on a former occasion. But how is one to guard against the danger? canst thou go through the forests, measuring the bases, and calculating the centres of the oaks? answer me that, friend Jones, and I will say thou wilt do the country a service."

"Answer thee that, friend Temple!" returned Richard; "a well-educated man can answer thee any thing, sir. Do any trees fall in this manner, but such as are decayed? Take care not to approach the roots of a rotten tree, and you will be safe enough."

"That would be excluding us entirely from the forests," said Marmaduke. "But, happily, the winds usually force down most of these dangerous ruins, as their currents are admitted into the woods by the surrounding clearings, and such a fall as this has been is very rare."

Louisa, by this time, had recovered so much strength, as to allow the party to proceed at a quicker pace; but long before they were safely housed, they were overtaken by the storm; and when they dismounted at the door of the Mansion-house, the black plumes of Miss Temple's hat were drooping with the weight of a load of damp snow, and the coats of the gentlemen were powdered with the same material.

While Edwards was assisting Louisa from her horse, the warm-hearted girl caught his hand with fervour, and whispered—

"Now, Mr. Edwards, both father and daughter owe their lives to you."

A driving, north-westerly storm succeeded; and before the sun was set, every vestige of spring had vanished; the lake, the mountains, the village, and the fields, being again hid under one dazzling coat of snow.

Chapter XXII.

"Men, boys, and girls,
Desert th' unpeopled village; and wild crowds
Spread o'er the plain, by the sweet frenzy driven."
Somerville, *The Chace*, II.197–99.

FROM this time to the close of April, the weather continued to be a succession of great and rapid changes. One day, the soft airs of spring seemed to be stealing along the valley, and, in unison with an invigorating sun, attempting, covertly, to rouse the dormant powers of the vegetable world; while on the next, the surly blasts from the north would sweep across the lake, and erase every impression left by their gentle adversaries. The snow, however, finally disappeared, and the green wheat fields were seen in every direction, spotted with the dark and charred stumps that had, the preceding season, supported some of the proudest trees of the forest. Ploughs were in motion, wherever those useful implements could be used, and the smokes of the sugar-camps were no longer seen issuing from the woods of maple. The lake had lost the beauty of a field of ice, but still a dark and gloomy covering concealed its waters, for the absence of currents left them yet hid under a porous crust, which, saturated with the fluid, barely retained enough strength to preserve the contiguity of its parts. Large flocks of wild geese were seen passing over the country, which hovered, for a time, around the hidden sheet of water, apparently searching for a resting-place; and then, on finding themselves excluded by the chill covering, would soar away to the north, filling the air with discordant screams, as if venting their complaints at the tardy operations of nature.

For a week, the dark covering of the Otsego was left to the undisturbed possession of two eagles, who alighted on the centre of its field, and sat eyeing their undisputed territory. During the presence of these monarchs of the air, the flocks of migrating birds avoided crossing the plain of ice, by turning into the hills, apparently seeking the protection of the forests, while the white and bald heads of the tenants of the lake were turned upward, with a look of contempt. But the time had come, when even these kings of birds were to be dispossessed. An opening had been gradually increasing, at the lower extremity of the lake, and around the dark spot where the current of the river prevented the formation of ice, during even the coldest weather; and the fresh southerly winds, that now breathed freely upon the valley, made an impression on the waters. Mimic waves begun to curl over the margin of the frozen field, which exhibited an outline of crystallizations, that slowly receded towards the north. At each step the power of the winds and the waves increased, until, after a struggle of a few hours, the turbulent little billows succeeded in setting the whole field in motion, when it was driven beyond the reach of the eye, with a rapidity, that was as magical as the change produced in the scene by this expulsion of the lingering remnant of winter. Just as the last sheet of agitated ice was disappearing in the distance, the eagles rose, and soared with a wide sweep above the clouds, while the waves tossed their little caps of snow into the air, as if rioting in their release from a thraldom of five months' duration.

The following morning Elizabeth was awakened by the exhilarating sounds of the martins, who were quarreling and chattering around the little boxes suspended above her windows, and the cries of Richard, who was calling, in tones animating as the signs of the season itself—

"Awake! awake! my fair lady! the gulls are hovering over the lake already, and the heavens are alive with pigeons. You may look an hour before you can find a hole, through which, to get a peep at the sun. Awake! awake! lazy ones! Benjamin is overhauling the ammunition, and we only wait for our breakfasts, and away for the mountains and pigeon-shooting."

There was no resisting this animated appeal, and in a few minutes Miss Temple and her friend descended to the parlour. The doors of the hall were thrown open, and the mild, balmy air of a clear spring morning was ventilating the apartment, where the vigilance of the ex-steward had been so long maintaining an artificial heat, with such unremitted diligence. The gentlemen were impatiently waiting for their morning's repast, each equipt in the garb of a sportsman. Mr. Jones made many visits to the southern door, and would cry—

"See, cousin Bess! see, 'duke! the pigeon-roosts of the south have broken up! They are growing more thick every instant. Here is a flock that the eye cannot see the end of. There is food enough in it to keep the army of Xerxes for a month, and feathers enough to make beds for the whole country. Xerxes, Mr. Edwards, was a Grecian king, who—no, he was a Turk, or a Persian, who wanted to conquer Greece, just the same as these rascals will overrun our wheat-fields, when they come back in the fall.——Away! away! Bess; I long to pepper them."

In this wish both Marmaduke and young Edwards seemed equally to participate, for the sight was exhilarating to a sportsman; and the ladies soon dismissed the party, after a hasty breakfast.

If the heavens were alive with pigeons, the whole village seemed equally in motion, with men, women, and children. Every species of fire-arms, from the French ducking-gun, with a barrel near six feet in length, to the common horseman's pistol, was to be seen in the hands of the men and boys; while bows and arrows, some made of the simple stick of a walnut sapling, and others in a rude imitation of the ancient cross-bows, were carried by many of the latter.

The houses, and the signs of life apparent in the village, drove the alarmed birds from the direct line of their flight, towards the mountains, along the sides and near the bases of which they were glancing in dense masses, equally wonderful by the rapidity of their motion, and their incredible numbers.

We have already said, that across the inclined plane which fell from the steep ascent of the mountain to the banks of the Susquehanna, ran the highway, on either side of which a clearing of many acres had been made, at a very early day. Over those clearings, and up the eastern mountain, and along the dangerous path that was cut into its side, the different individuals posted themselves, and in a few moments the attack commenced.

Amongst the sportsmen was the tall, gaunt form of Leatherstocking, walking over the field, with his rifle hanging on his arm, his dogs at his heels; the latter now scenting the dead or wounded birds, that were beginning to tumble from the flocks, and then crouching under the legs of their master, as if they

participated in his feelings, at this wasteful and unsportsman-
like execution.

The reports of the fire-arms became rapid, whole volleys rising from the plain, as flocks of more than ordinary numbers
darted over the opening, shadowing the field, like a cloud; and
then the light smoke of a single piece would issue from among
the leafless bushes on the mountain, as death was hurled on the
retreat of the affrighted birds, who were rising from a volley, in
a vain effort to escape. Arrows, and missiles of every kind, were
in the midst of the flocks; and so numerous were the birds, and
so low did they take their flight, that even long poles, in the
hands of those on the sides of the mountain, were used to strike
them to the earth.

During all this time, Mr. Jones, who disdained the humble
and ordinary means of destruction used by his companions, was
busily occupied, aided by Benjamin, in making arrangements
for an assault of a more than ordinarily fatal character. Among
the relics of the old military excursions, that occasionally are
discovered throughout the different districts of the western
part of New-York, there had been found in Templeton, at its
settlement, a small swivel, which would carry a ball of a pound
weight. It was thought to have been deserted by a war-party of
the whites, in one of their inroads into the Indian settlements,
when, perhaps, convenience or their necessity induced them to
leave such an encumbrance behind them in the woods. This
miniature cannon had been released from the rust, and being
mounted on little wheels, was now in a state for actual service.
For several years, it was the sole organ for extraordinary rejoicings used in those mountains. On the mornings of the Fourths
of July, it would be heard ringing among the hills, and even
Captain Hollister, who was the highest authority in that part of
the country on all such occasions, affirmed that, considering its
dimensions, it was no despicable gun for a salute. It was somewhat the worse for the service it had performed, it is true, there
being but a trifling difference in size between the touch-hole
and the muzzle. Still, the grand conceptions of Richard had
suggested the importance of such an instrument, in hurling
death at his nimble enemies. The swivel was dragged by a horse
into a part of the open space, that the Sheriff thought most

eligible for planting a battery of the kind, and Mr. Pump proceeded to load it. Several handfuls of duck-shot were placed on top of the powder, and the Major-domo announced that his piece was ready for service.

The sight of such an implement collected all the idle spectators to the spot, who, being mostly boys, filled the air with cries of exultation and delight. The gun was pointed high, and Richard, holding a coal of fire in a pair of tongs, patiently took his seat on a stump, awaiting the appearance of a flock worthy of his notice.

So prodigious was the number of the birds, that the scattering fire of the guns, with the hurling of missiles, and the cries of the boys, had no other effect than to break off small flocks from the immense masses that continued to dart along the valley, as if the whole of the feathered tribe were pouring through that one pass. None pretended to collect the game, which lay scattered over the fields in such profusion, as to cover the very ground with the fluttering victims.

Leather-stocking was a silent, but uneasy spectator of all these proceedings, but was able to keep his sentiments to himself until he saw the introduction of the swivel into the sports.

"This comes of settling a country!" he said—"here have I known the pigeons to fly for forty long years, and, till you made your clearings, there was nobody to skear or to hurt them. I loved to see them come into the woods, for they were company to a body; hurting nothing; being, as it was, as harmless as a garter-snake. But now it gives me sore thoughts when I hear the frighty things whizzing through the air, for I know it's only a motion to bring out all the brats in the village. Well! the Lord won't see the waste of his creaters for nothing, and right will be done to the pigeons, as well as others, by-and-by.——There's Mr. Oliver, as bad as the rest of them, firing into the flocks as if he was shooting down nothing but Mingo warriors."

Among the sportsmen was Billy Kirby, who, armed with an old musket, was loading, and, without even looking into the air, was firing, and shouting as his victims fell even on his own person. He heard the speech of Natty, and took upon himself to reply—

"What! old Leather-stocking," he cried, "grumbling at the loss of a few pigeons! If you had to sow your wheat twice, and three times, as I have done, you wouldn't be so massyfully feeling'd to'ards the divils.—Hurrah, boys! scatter the feathers. This is better than shooting at a turkey's head and neck, old fellow."

"It's better for you, maybe, Billy Kirby," replied the indignant old hunter, "and all them that don't know how to put a ball down a rifle-barrel, or how to bring it up ag'in with a true aim; but it's wicked to be shooting into flocks in this wastey manner; and none do it, who know how to knock over a single bird. If a body has a craving for pigeon's flesh, why! it's made the same as all other creater's, for man's eating, but not to kill twenty and eat one. When I want such a thing, I go into the woods till I find one to my liking, and then I shoot him off the branches without touching a feather of another, though there might be a hundred on the same tree. You couldn't do such a thing, Billy Kirby—you couldn't do it if you tried."

"What's that, old corn-stalk! you sapless stub!" cried the wood-chopper. "You've grown wordy, since the affair of the turkey; but if you're for a single shot, here goes at that bird which comes on by himself."

The fire from the distant part of the field had driven a single pigeon below the flock to which it belonged, and, frightened with the constant reports of the muskets, it was approaching the spot where the disputants stood, darting first from one side, and then to the other, cutting the air with the swiftness of lightning, and making a noise with its wings, not unlike the rushing of a bullet. Unfortunately for the wood-chopper, notwithstanding his vaunt, he did not see this bird until it was too late to fire as it approached, and he pulled his trigger at the unlucky moment when it was darting immediately over his head. The bird continued its course with the usual velocity.

Natty lowered the rifle from his arm, when the challenge was made, and, waiting a moment, until the terrified victim had got in a line with his eye, and had dropped near the bank of the lake, he raised it again with uncommon rapidity, and fired. It might have been chance, or it might have been skill, that produced the result; it was probably a union of both; but the pigeon whirled over in the air, and fell into the lake, with a broken wing. At the sound of his rifle, both his dogs started from his feet, and in a few minutes the "slut" brought out the bird, still alive.

The wonderful exploit of Leather-stocking was noised through the field with great rapidity, and the sportsmen gathered in to learn the truth of the report.

"What," said young Edwards, "have you really killed a pigeon on the wing, Natty, with a single ball?"

"Haven't I killed loons before now, lad, that dive at the flash?" returned the hunter. "It's much better to kill only such as you want, without wasting your powder and lead, than to be firing into God's creaters in this wicked manner. But I come out for a bird, and you know the reason why I like small game, Mr. Oliver, and now I have got one I will go home, for I don't relish to see these wasty ways that you are all practysing, as if the least thing was not made for use, and not to destroy."

"Thou sayest well, Leather-stocking," cried Marmaduke, "and I begin to think it time to put an end to this work of destruction."

"Put an ind, Judge, to your clearings. An't the woods his work as well as the pigeons? Use, but don't waste. Wasn't the woods made for the beasts and birds to harbour in? and when man wanted their flesh, their skins, or their feathers, there's the place to seek them. But I'll go to the hut with my own game, for I wouldn't touch one of the harmless things that kiver the ground here, looking up with their eyes on me, as if they only wanted tongues to say their thoughts."

With this sentiment in his mouth, Leather-stocking threw his rifle over his arm, and, followed by his dogs, stepped across the clearing with great caution, taking care not to tread on one of the wounded birds in his path. He soon entered the bushes on the margin of the lake, and was hid from view.

Whatever impression the morality of Natty made on the Judge, it was utterly lost on Richard. He availed himself of the gathering of the sportsmen, to lay a plan for one "fell swoop" of destruction. The musketmen were drawn up in battle array, in a line extending on each side of his artillery, with orders to await the signal of firing from himself.

"Stand by, my lads," said Benjamin, who acted as an aide-de-camp, on this occasion, "stand by, my hearties, and when Squire Dickens heaves out the signal to begin the firing, d'ye see, you may open upon them in a broadside. Take care and fire low, boys, and you'll be sure to hull the flock."

"Fire low!" shouted Kirby—"hear the old fool! If we fire low, we may hit the stumps, but not ruffle a pigeon."

"How should you know, you lubber?" cried Benjamin, with a very unbecoming heat, for an officer on the eve of battle—"how should you know, you grampus? Havn't I sailed aboard of the Boadishy for five years? and wasn't it a standing order to fire low, and to hull your enemy? Keep silence at your guns, boys, and mind the order that is passed."

The loud laughs of the musketmen were silenced by the more authoritative voice of Richard, who called for attention and obedience to his signals.

Some millions of pigeons were supposed to have already passed, that morning, over the valley of Templeton; but nothing like the flock that was now approaching had been seen before. It extended from mountain to mountain in one solid blue mass, and the eye looked in vain over the southern hills to find its termination. The front of this living column was distinctly marked by a line, but very slightly indented, so regular and even was the flight. Even Marmaduke forgot the morality of Leather-stocking as it approached, and, in common with the rest, brought his musket to a poise.

"Fire!" cried the Sheriff, clapping a coal to the priming of the cannon. As half of Benjamin's charge escaped through the touch-hole, the whole volley of the musketry preceded the report of the swivel. On receiving this united discharge of small-arms, the front of the flock darted upward, while, at the same instant, myriads of those in the rear rushed with amazing rapidity into their places, so that when the column of white smoke gushed from the mouth of the little cannon, an accumulated mass of objects was gliding over its point of direction. The roar of the gun echoed along the mountains, and died away to the north, like distant thunder, while the whole flock of alarmed birds seemed, for a moment, thrown into one disorderly and agitated mass. The air was filled with their irregular flight, layer rising above layer, far above the tops of the highest pines, none daring to advance beyond the dangerous pass; when, suddenly, some of the leaders of the feathered tribe shot across the valley, taking their flight directly over the village, and hundreds of thousands in their rear followed the example, deserting the eastern side of the plain to their persecutors and the slain.

"Victory!" shouted Richard, "victory! we have driven the enemy from the field."

"Not so, Dickon," said Marmaduke; "the field is covered with them; and, like the Leather-stocking, I see nothing but eyes, in every direction, as the innocent sufferers turn their heads in terror. Full one half of those that have fallen are yet alive: and I think it is time to end the sport; if sport it be."

"Sport!" cried the Sheriff; "it is princely sport. There are some thousands of the blue-coated boys on the ground, so that every old woman in the village may have a pot-pie for the asking."

"Well, we have happily frightened the birds from this side of the valley," said Marmaduke, "and the carnage must of necessity end, for the present.——Boys, I will give thee sixpence a hundred for the pigeons' heads only; so go to work, and bring them into the village."

This expedient produced the desired effect, for every urchin on the ground went industriously to work to wring the necks of the wounded birds. Judge Temple retired towards his dwelling with that kind of feeling, that many a man has experienced before him, who discovers, after the excitement of the moment has passed, that he has purchased pleasure at the price of misery to others. Horses were loaded with the dead; and, after this first burst of sporting, the shooting of pigeons became a business, with a few idlers, for the remainder of the season. Richard, however, boasted for many a year, of his shot with the "cricket;" and Benjamin gravely asserted, that he thought they killed nearly as many pigeons on that day, as there were Frenchmen destroyed on the memorable occasion of Rodney's victory.

Chapter XXIII.

"Help, masters, help; here's a fish hangs in the net, like a poor man's right in the law." *Pericles*, II.i.116–17.

THE advance of the season now became as rapid, as its first approach had been tedious and lingering. The days were uniformly mild, while the nights, though cool, were no longer chilled by frosts. The whip-poor-will was heard whistling his melancholy notes along the margin of the lake, and the ponds and meadows were sending forth the music of their thousand tenants. The leaf of the native poplar was seen quivering in the woods; the sides of the mountains began to lose their hue of brown, as the lively green of the different members of the forest blended their shades with the permanent colours of the pine and hemlock; and even the buds of the tardy oak were swelling with the promise of the coming summer. The gay and fluttering blue-bird, the social robin, and the industrious little wren, were all to be seen, enlivening the fields with their presence and their songs; while the soaring fish-hawk was already hovering over the waters of the Otsego, watching, with native voracity, for the appearance of his prey.

The tenants of the lake were far-famed for both their quantities and their quality, and the ice had hardly disappeared, before numberless little boats were launched from the shores, and the lines of the fishermen were dropped into the inmost recesses of its deepest caverns, tempting the unwary animals with every variety of bait, that the ingenuity or the art of man had invented. But the slow, though certain adventures with hook and line were ill-suited to the profusion and impatience of the settlers. More destructive means were resorted to; and, as the season had now arrived when the bass-fisheries were allowed by the provisions of the law, that Judge Temple had procured, the Sheriff declared his intention by availing himself of the first dark night, to enjoy the sport in person—

"And you shall be present, cousin Bess," he added, when he announced this design, "and Miss Grant, and Mr. Edwards; and

I will show you what I call fishing—not nibble, nibble, nibble, as 'duke does, when he goes after the salmon-trout. There he will sit, for hours, in a broiling sun, or, perhaps, over a hole in the ice, in the coldest days in winter, under the lee of a few bushes, and not a fish will he catch, after all this mortification of the flesh. No, no—give me a good seine, that's fifty or sixty fathoms in length, with a jolly parcel of boatmen to crack their jokes, the while, with Benjamin to steer, and let us haul them in by thousands; I call that fishing."

"Ah! Dickon," cried Marmaduke, "thou knowest but little of the pleasure there is in playing with the hook and line, or thou wouldst be more saving of the game. I have known thee to leave fragments enough behind thee, when thou hast headed a night-party on the lake, to feed a dozen famishing families."

"I shall not dispute the matter, Judge Temple: this night will I go; and I invite the company to attend, and then let them decide between us."

Richard was busy, during most of the afternoon, making his preparations for the important occasion. Just as the light of the setting sun had disappeared, and a new moon had begun to throw its shadows on the earth, the fishermen took their departure in a boat, for a point that was situated on the western shore of the lake, at the distance of rather more than half a mile from the village. The ground had become settled, and the walking was good and dry. Marmaduke, with his daughter, her friend, and young Edwards, continued on the high, grassy banks, at the outlet of the placid sheet of water, watching the dark object that was moving across the lake, until it entered the shade of the western hills, and was lost to the eye. The distance round by land, to the point of destination, was a mile, and he observed—

"It is time for us to be moving; the moon will be down ere we reach the point, and then the miraculous hauls of Dickon will commence."

The evening was warm, and, after the long and dreary winter from which they had just escaped, delightfully invigorating. Inspirited by the scene, and their anticipated amusement, the youthful companions of the Judge followed his steps, as he led them along the shores of the Otsego, and through the skirts of the village.

"See!" said young Edwards; "they are building their fire already; it glimmers for a moment, and dies again, like the light of a fire-fly."

"Now it blazes," cried Elizabeth; "you can perceive figures moving around the light. Oh! I would bet my jewels against the gold beads of Remarkable, that my impatient cousin Dickon had an agency in raising that bright flame;—and see; it fades again, like most of his brilliant schemes."

"Thou hast guessed the truth, Bess," said her father; "he has thrown an armful of brush on the pile, which has burnt out as soon as lighted. But it has enabled them to find a better fuel, for their fire begins to blaze with a more steady flame. It is the true fisherman's beacon now; observe how beautifully it throws its little circle of light on the water."

The appearance of the fire urged the pedestrians on, for even the ladies had become eager to witness the miraculous draught. By the time they reached the bank which rose above the low point, where the fishermen had landed, the moon had sunk behind the tops of the western pines, and, as most of the stars were obscured by clouds, there was but little other light than that which proceeded from the fire. At the suggestion of Marmaduke, his companions paused to listen to the conversation of those below them, and examine the party, for a moment, before they descended to the shore.

The whole group were seated around the fire, with the exception of Richard and Benjamin; the former of whom occupied the root of a decayed stump, that had been drawn to the spot as part of their fuel, and the latter was standing, with his arms a-kimbo, so near to the flame, that the smoke occasionally obscured his solemn visage, as it waved around the pile, in obedience to the night-airs, that swept gently over the water.

"Why, look you, Squire," said the Major-domo, "you may call a lake-fish that will weigh twenty or thirty pounds a serious matter; but to a man who has hauled in a shovel-nosed shirk, d'ye see, it's but a poor kind of fishing, after all."

"I don't know, Benjamin," returned the Sheriff; "a haul of one thousand Otsego bass, without counting pike, pickerel, perch, bull-pouts, salmon-trouts, and suckers, is no bad fishing, let me tell you. There may be sport in sticking a shark, but what is he good for after you have got him? Now any one of the fish that I have named is fit to set before a king."

"Well, Squire," returned Benjamin, "just listen to the philosophy of the thing. Would it stand to reason, that such fish should live and be catched in this here little pond of water, where it's hardly deep enough to drown a man, as you'll find in the wide ocean, where, as every body knows, that is, every body that has followed the seas, whales and grampuses are to be seen, that are as long as one of them pine trees on yonder mountain?"

"Softly, softly, Benjamin," said the Sheriff, as if he wished to save the credit of his favourite; "why some of the pines will measure two hundred feet, and even more."

"Two hundred or two thousand, it's all the same thing," cried Benjamin, with an air which manifested that he was not easily to be bullied out of his opinion, on a subject like the present—"Haven't I been there, and haven't I seen? I have said that you fall in with whales as long as one of them there pines; and what I have once said I'll stand to!"

During this dialogue, which was evidently but the close of a much longer discussion, the huge frame of Billy Kirby was seen extended on one side of the fire, where he was picking his teeth with splinters of the chips near him, and occasionally shaking his head, with distrust of Benjamin's assertions.

"I've a notion," said the wood-chopper, "that there's water in this lake to swim the biggest whale that ever was invented; and, as to the pines, I think I ought to know so'thing consarning them; I have chopped many a one that was sixty times the length of my helve, without counting the eye; and I b'lieve, Benny, that if the old pine that stands in the hollow of the Vision Mountain, just over the village,—you may see the tree itself by looking up, for the moon is on its top yet;—well, now I b'lieve, if that same tree was planted out in the deepest part of the lake, there would be water enough for the biggest ship that ever was built to float over it, without touching its upper branches, I do."

"Did'ee ever see a ship, Master Kirby?" roared the steward—"did'ee ever see a ship, man? or any craft bigger than a lime-scow, or a wood-boat, on this here small bit of fresh water?"

"Yes, I have," said the wood-chopper, stoutly; "I can say that I have, and tell no lie."

"Did'ee ever see a British ship, Master Kirby? an English

line-of-battle ship, boy? Where away did'ee ever fall in with a regular-built vessel, with starn-post and cutwater, garboard streak and plank-shear, gangways and hatchways, and water-ways, quarter-deck and forecastle, ay, and flush-deck?—tell me that, man, if you can; where away did'ee ever fall in with a full-rigged, regular-built, decked vessel?"

The whole company were a good deal astounded with this overwhelming question, and even Richard afterwards re-marked, that it "was a thousand pities that Benjamin could not read, or he must have made a valuable officer to the British marine. It is no wonder that they overcome the French so easily on the water, when even the lowest sailor so well understood the different parts of a vessel." But Billy Kirby was a fearless wight, and had great jealousy of foreign dictation; he had aris-en on his feet, and turned his back to the fire, during the volu-ble delivery of this interrogatory, and when the steward ended, contrary to all expectation, he gave the following spirited re-ply:—

"Where! why on the North River, and maybe on Champlain. There's sloops on the river, boy, that would give a hard time on't to the stoutest vessel King George owns. They carry masts of ninety feet in the clear, of good, solid pine, for I've been at the chopping of many a one in Varmount state. I wish I was captain in one of them, and you was in that Board-dish that you talk so much about, and we'd soon see what good Yankee stuff is made on, and whether a Varmounter's hide an't as thick as an Englishman's."

The echoes from the opposite hills, which were more than half a mile from the fishing point, sent back the discordant laugh that Benjamin gave forth at this challenge; and the woods that covered their sides, seemed, by the noise that issued from their shades, to be full of mocking demons.

"Let us descend to the shore," whispered Marmaduke, "or there will soon be ill blood between them. Benjamin is a fearless boaster, and Kirby, though good-natured, is a careless son of the forest, who thinks one American more than a match for six Englishmen. I marvel that Dickon is silent, where there is such a trial of skill in the superlative!"

The appearance of Judge Temple and the ladies produced, if not a pacification, at least a cessation of hostilities. Obedient to the directions of Mr. Jones, the fishermen prepared to launch their boat, which had been seen in the back-ground of the view, with the net carefully disposed on a little platform in its stern, ready for service. Richard gave vent to his reproaches at the tardiness of the pedestrians, when all the turbulent passions of the party were succeeded by a calm, as mild and as placid as that which prevailed over the beautiful sheet of water, that they were about to rifle of its best treasures.

The night had now become so dark as to render objects, without the reach of the light of the fire, not only indistinct, but, in most cases, invisible. For a little distance the water was discernible, glistening, as the glare from the fire danced over its surface, touching it, here and there, with red, quivering streaks; but at a hundred feet from the shore, there lay a boundary of impenetrable gloom. One or two stars were shining through the openings of the clouds, and the lights were seen in the village, glimmering faintly, as if at an immeasurable distance. At times, as the fire lowered, or as the horizon cleared, the outline of the mountain, on the other side of the lake, might be traced, by its undulations; but its shadow was cast, wide and dense, on the bosom of the water, rendering the darkness, in that direction, trebly deep.

Benjamin Pump was invariably the cockswain and net-caster of Richard's boat, unless the Sheriff saw fit to preside in person; and, on the present occasion, Billy Kirby, and a youth of about half his strength, were assigned to the oars. The remainder of the assistants were stationed at the drag ropes. The arrangements were speedily made, and Richard gave the signal to "shove off."

Elizabeth watched the motion of the batteau, as it pulled from the shore, letting loose its rope as it went, but it very soon disappeared in the darkness, when the ear was her only guide to its evolutions. There was great affectation of stillness, during all these manœuvres, in order, as Richard assured them, "not to frighten the bass, who were running into the shoal waters, and who would approach the light, if not disturbed by the sounds from the fishermen."

The hoarse voice of Benjamin was alone heard, issuing out of the gloom, as he uttered, in authoritative tones, "pull larboard oar," "pull starboard," "give way together, boys," and such other dictative mandates as were necessary for the right disposition of his seine. A long time was passed in this necessary part of the process, for Benjamin prided himself greatly on his skill in throwing the net, and, in fact, most of the success of the sport depended on its being done with judgment. At length a loud splash in the water, as he threw away the "staff," or "stretcher," with a hoarse call from the steward, of "clear," announced that the boat was returning; when Richard seized a brand from the fire, and ran to a point, as far above the centre of the fishing ground, as the one from which the batteau had started was below it.

"Stick her in dead for the Squire, boys," said the steward, "and we'll have a look at what grows in this here pond."

In place of the falling net, were now to be heard the quick strokes of the oars, and the noise of the rope, running out of the boat. Presently the batteau shot into the circle of light, and in an instant she was pulled to shore. Several eager hands were extended, to receive the line, and, both ropes being equally well manned, the fishermen commenced hauling in, with slow and steady drags, Richard standing in the centre, giving orders, first to one party and then to the other, to increase or slacken their efforts, as occasion required. The visiters were posted near him, and enjoyed a fair view of the whole operation, which was slowly advancing to an end.

Opinions, as to the result of their adventure, were now freely hazarded by all the men, some declaring that the net came in as light as a feather, and others affirming that it seemed to be full of logs. As the ropes were many hundred feet in length, these opposing sentiments were thought to be of little moment by the Sheriff, who would go first to one line and then to the other, giving each a small pull, in order to enable him to form an opinion for himself.

"Why, Benjamin," he cried, as he made his first effort in this way, "you did not throw the net clear. I can move it with my little finger. The rope slackens in my hand."

"Did you ever see a whale, Squire?" responded the steward: "I say that if that there net is foul, the devil is in the lake in the shape of a fish, for I cast it as fair as ever rigging was rove over the quarter-deck of a flag-ship."

But Richard discovered his mistake, when he saw Billy Kirby

before him, standing with his feet in the water, at an angle of forty-five degrees, inclining shorewards, and expending his gigantic strength in sustaining himself in that posture. He ceased his remonstrances, and proceeded to the party at the other line.

"I see the 'staffs,' " shouted Mr. Jones;—"gather in, boys, and away with it; to shore with her—to shore with her."

At this cheerful sound, Elizabeth strained her eyes, and saw the ends of the two sticks on the seine, emerging from the darkness, while the men closed near to each other, and formed a deep bag of their net. The exertions of the fishermen sensibly increased, and the voice of Richard was heard, encouraging them to make their greatest efforts, at the present moment.

"Now's the time, my lads," he cried; "let us get the ends to land, and all we have will be our own—away with her!"

"Away with her it is," echoed Benjamin—"hurrah! ho-a-hoy, ho-a-hoy, ho-a!"

"In with her," shouted Kirby, exerting himself in a manner that left nothing for those in his rear to do, but to gather up the slack of the rope which passed through his hands.

"Staff, ho!" shouted the steward.

"Staff, ho!" echoed Kirby, from the other rope.

The men rushed to the water's edge, some seizing the upper rope, and some the lower, or lead-rope, and began to haul with great activity and zeal. A deep semicircular sweep, of the little balls that supported the seine in its perpendicular position, was plainly visible to the spectators, and, as it rapidly lessened in size, the bag of the net appeared, while an occasional flutter on the water, announced the uneasiness of the prisoners it contained.

"Haul in, my lads," shouted Richard—"I can see the dogs kicking to get free. Haul in, and here's a cast that will pay for the labour."

Fishes of various sorts were now to be seen, entangled in the meshes of the net, as it was passed through the hands of the labourers, and the water, at a little distance from the shore, was alive with the movements of the alarmed victims. Hundreds of white sides were glancing up to the surface of the water, and glistening in the fire-light, when, frightened at the uproar and the change, the fish would again dart to the bottom, in fruitless efforts for freedom.

"Hurrah!" shouted Richard; "one or two more heavy drags, boys, and we are safe."

"Cheerily, boys, cheerily!" cried Benjamin; "I see a salmon-trout that is big enough for a chowder."

"Away with you, you varmint!" said Billy Kirby, plucking a bull-pout from the meshes, and casting the animal back into the lake with contempt. "Pull, boys, pull; here's all kinds, and the Lord condemn me for a liar, if there an't a thousand bass!"

Inflamed beyond the bounds of discretion at the sight, and forgetful of the season, the wood-chopper rushed to his middle into the water, and begun to drive the reluctant animals before him from their native element.

"Pull heartily, boys," cried Marmaduke, yielding to the excitement of the moment, and laying his hands to the net, with no trifling addition to the force. Edwards had preceded him, for the sight of the immense piles of fish, that were slowly rolling over on the gravelly beach, had impelled him also to leave the ladies, and join the fishermen.

Great care was observed in bringing the net to land, and, after much toil, the whole shoal of victims was safely deposited in a hollow of the bank, where they were left to flutter away their brief existence, in the new and fatal element.

Even Elizabeth and Louisa were greatly excited and highly gratified, by seeing two thousand captives thus drawn from the bosom of the lake, and laid as prisoners at their feet. But when the feelings of the moment were passing away, Marmaduke took in his hands a bass, that might have weighed two pounds, and, after viewing it a moment, in melancholy musing, he turned to his daughter, and observed—

"This is a fearful expenditure of the choicest gifts of Providence. These fish, Bess, which thou seest lying in such piles before thee, and which, by to-morrow evening, will be rejected food on the meanest table in Templeton, are of a quality and flavour that, in other countries, would make them esteemed a luxury on the tables of princes or epicures. The world has no better fish than the bass of Otsego: it unites the richness of the shad* to the firmness of the salmon."

"But surely, dear sir," cried Elizabeth, "they must prove a

* Of all the fish the writer has ever tasted, he thinks the one in question the best. [1832]

great blessing to the country, and a powerful friend to the poor."

"The poor are always prodigal, my child, where there is plenty, and seldom think of a provision against the morrow. But if there can be any excuse for destroying animals in this manner, it is in taking the bass. During the winter, you know, they are entirely protected from our assaults by the ice, for they refuse the hook; and during the hot months, they are not seen. It is supposed they retreat to the deep and cool waters of the lake, at that season; and it is only in the spring and autumn, that, for a few days, they are to be found, around the points where they are within the reach of a seine. But, like all the other treasures of the wilderness, they already begin to disappear, before the wasteful extravagance of man."

"Disappear, 'duke! disappear!" exclaimed the Sheriff; "if you don't call this appearing, I know not what you will. Here are a good thousand of the shiners, some hundreds of suckers, and a powerful quantity of other fry. But this is always the way with you, Marmaduke; first it's the trees, then it's the deer, after that it's the maple sugar, and so on to the end of the chapter. One day, you talk of canals, through a country where there's a river or a lake every half-mile, just because the water won't run the way you wish it to go; and the next, you say something about mines of coal, though any man who has good eyes, like myself —I say with good eyes—can see more wood than would keep the city of London in fuel for fifty years;—wouldn't it, Benjamin?"

"Why, for that, Squire," said the steward, "Lon'on is no small place. If it was stretched an end, all the same as a town on one side of a river, it would cover some such matter as this here lake. Thof I dar'st to say, that the wood in sight might sarve them a good turn, seeing that the Lon'oners mainly burn coal."

"Now we are on the subject of coal, Judge Temple," interrupted the Sheriff, "I have a thing of much importance to communicate to you; but I will defer it until to-morrow. I know that you intend riding into the eastern part of the Patent, and I will accompany you, and conduct you to a spot, where some of your projects may be realized. We will say no more now, for there are listeners; but a secret has this evening been revealed to me, 'duke, that is of more consequence to your welfare, than all your estate united."

Marmaduke laughed at the important intelligence, to which in a variety of shapes he was accustomed, and the Sheriff, with an air of great dignity, as if pitying his want of faith, proceeded in the business more immediately before them. As the labour of drawing the net had been very great, he directed one party of his men to commence throwing the fish into piles, preparatory to the usual division, while another, under the superintendence of Benjamin, prepared the seine for a second haul.

Chapter XXIV.

"While from its margin, terrible to tell!
Three sailors with their gallant boatswain fell."
Falconer, *The Shipwreck*, II.354–55.

WHILE the fishermen were employed in making the preparations for an equitable division of the spoil, Elizabeth and her friend strolled a short distance from the group, along the shore of the lake. After reaching a point, to which even the brightest of the occasional gleams of the fire did not extend, they turned, and paused a moment, in contemplation of the busy and lively party they had left, and of the obscurity, which, like the gloom of oblivion, seemed to envelope the rest of the creation.

"This is indeed a subject for the pencil," exclaimed Elizabeth. "Observe the countenance of that wood-chopper, while he exults in presenting a larger fish than common to my cousin Sheriff; and see, Louisa, how handsome and considerate my dear father looks, by the light of that fire, where he stands viewing the havoc of the game. He seems melancholy, as if he actually thought that a day of retribution was to follow this hour of abundance and prodigality! Would they not make a picture, Louisa?"

"You know that I am ignorant of all such accomplishments, Miss Temple."

"Call me by my christian name," interrupted Elizabeth; "this is not a place, neither is this a scene, for forms."

"Well, then, if I may venture an opinion," said Louisa, timidly, "I should think it might indeed make a picture. The selfish earnestness of that Kirby over his fish, would contrast finely with the—the—expression of Mr. Edwards' face. I hardly know what to call it; but it is—a—is—you know what I would say, dear Elizabeth."

"You do me too much credit, Miss Grant," said the heiress; "I am no diviner of thoughts, or interpreter of expressions."

There was certainly nothing harsh, or even cold, in the manner of the speaker, but still it repressed the conversation, and they continued to stroll still further from the party, retaining each other's arm, but observing a profound silence. Elizabeth, perhaps conscious of the improper phraseology of her last speech, or perhaps excited by the new object that met her gaze, was the first to break the awkward cessation in the discourse, by exclaiming—

"Look, Louisa! we are not alone; there are fishermen lighting a fire on the other side of the lake, immediately opposite to us: it must be in front of the cabin of Leather-stocking!"

Through the obscurity, which prevailed most, immediately under the eastern mountain, a small and uncertain light was plainly to be seen, though, as it was occasionally lost to the eye, it seemed struggling for existence. They observed it to move, and sensibly to lower, as if carried down the descent of the bank to the shore. Here, in a very short time, its flame gradually expanded, and grew brighter, until it became of the size of a man's head, when it continued to shine, a steady ball of fire.

Such an object, lighted as it were by magic, under the brow of the mountain, and in that retired and unfrequented place, gave double interest to the beauty and singularity of its appearance. It did not at all resemble the large and unsteady light of their own fire, being much more clear and bright, and retaining its size and shape with perfect uniformity.

There are moments when the best regulated minds are, more or less, subjected to the injurious impressions, which few have escaped in infancy, and Elizabeth smiled at her own weakness, while she remembered the idle tales, which were circulated through the village, at the expense of the Leather-stocking. The same ideas seized her companion, and at the same instant, for Louisa pressed nearer to her friend, as she said, in a low voice, stealing a timid glance towards the bushes and trees that overhung the bank near them—

"Did you ever hear the singular ways of this Natty spoken of, Miss Temple? They say that, in his youth, he was an Indian warrior, or, what is the same thing, a white man leagued with the savages; and it is thought he has been concerned in many of their inroads, in the old wars."

"The thing is not at all improbable," returned Elizabeth: "he is not alone in that particular."

"No, surely; but is it not strange, that he is so cautious with his hut? He never leaves it, without fastening it in a remarkable manner; and, in several instances, when the children, or even the men of the village have wished to seek a shelter there from the storms, he has been known to drive them from his door, with rudeness and threats. That surely is singular in this country."

"It is certainly not very hospitable; but we must remember his aversion to the customs of civilized life. You heard my father say, a few days since, how kindly he was treated by him, on his first visit to this place." Elizabeth paused, and smiled, with an expression of peculiar archness, though the darkness hid its meaning from her companion, as she continued:—"Besides, he certainly admits the visits of Mr. Edwards, whom we both know to be far from a savage."

To this speech Louisa made no reply, but continued gazing on the object which had elicited her remarks. In addition to the bright and circular flame, was now to be seen a fainter, though a vivid light, of an equal diameter to the other at the upper end, but which, after extending, downward, for many feet, gradually tapered to a point at its lower extremity. A dark space was plainly visible between the two, and the new illumination was placed beneath the other, the whole forming an appearance not unlike an inverted note of admiration. It was soon evident that the latter was nothing but the reflection from the water of the former, and that the object, whatever it might be, was advancing across, or rather over the lake, for it seemed to be several feet above its surface, in a direct line with themselves. Its motion was amazingly rapid, the ladies having hardly discovered that it was moving at all, before the waving light of a flame was discerned, losing its regular shape, while it increased in size, as it approached.

"It appears to be supernatural!" whispered Louisa, beginning to retrace her steps towards the party.

"It is beautiful!" exclaimed Elizabeth.

A brilliant, though waving flame was now plainly visible, gracefully gliding over the lake, and throwing its light on the water, in such a manner as to tinge it slightly; though, in the air, so strong was the contrast, the darkness seemed to have the distinctness of material substances, as if the fire were embedded in a setting of ebony. This appearance, however, gradually wore off, and the rays from the torch struck out, and enlightened the atmosphere in front of it, leaving the background in a darkness that was more impenetrable than ever.

"Ho! Natty, is that you?" shouted the Sheriff—"paddle in, old boy, and I'll give you a mess of fish that is fit to place before the Governor."

The light suddenly changed its direction, and a long and slightly-built boat hove up out of the gloom, while the red glare fell on the weather-beaten features of the Leather-stocking, whose tall person was seen erect in the frail vessel, wielding, with the grace of an experienced boatman, a long fishing-spear, which he held by its centre, first dropping one end and then the other into the water, to aid in propelling the little canoe of bark, we will not say through, but over the water. At the farther end of the vessel, a form was faintly seen, guiding its motions, and using a paddle with the ease of one who felt there was no necessity for exertion. The Leather-stocking struck his spear lightly against the short staff which upheld, on a rude grating framed of old hoops of iron, the knots of pine that composed the fuel; and the light, which glared high, for an instant fell on the swarthy features, and dark, glancing eyes of Mohegan.

The boat glided along the shore until it arrived opposite the fishing-ground, when it again changed its direction, and moved on to the land, with a motion so graceful, and yet so rapid, that it seemed to possess the power of regulating its own progress. The water, in front of the canoe, was hardly ruffled by its passage, and no sound betrayed the collision, when the light fabric shot on the gravelly beach, for nearly half its length, Natty receding a step or two from its bow, in order to facilitate the landing.

"Approach, Mohegan," said Marmaduke; "approach, Leather-stocking, and load your canoe with the bass. It would be a shame to assail the animals with the spear, when such multitudes of victims lie here, that will be lost as food, for the want of mouths to consume them."

"No, no, Judge," returned Natty, his tall figure stalking over the narrow beach, and ascending to the little grassy bottom where the fish were laid in piles; "I eat of no man's wasty ways. I strike my spear into the eels, or the trout, when I crave the creaters, but I wouldn't be helping to such a sinful kind of fishing, for the best rifle that was ever brought out from the old countries. If they had fur, like a beaver, or you could tan their hides, like a buck, something might be said in favour of taking them by the thousands with your nets; but as God made them for man's food, and for no other disarnable reason, I call it sinful and wasty to catch more than can be eat."

"Your reasoning is mine: for once, old hunter, we agree in opinion; and I heartily wish we could make a convert of the Sheriff. A net of half the size of this would supply the whole village with fish, for a week, at one haul."

The Leather-stocking did not relish this alliance in sentiment, and he shook his head doubtingly, as he answered—

"No, no; we are not much of one mind, Judge, or you'd never turn good hunting grounds into stumpy pastures. And you fish and hunt out of rule; but to me, the flesh is sweeter, where the creater has some chance for its life; for that reason, I always use a single ball, even if it be at a bird or a squirrel; besides, it saves lead, for, when a body knows how to shoot, one piece of lead is enough for all, except hard-lived animals."

The Sheriff heard these opinions with great indignation, and when he completed the last arrangement for the division, by carrying, with his own hands, a trout of a large size, and placing it on four different piles in succession, as his vacillating ideas of justice required, he gave vent to his spleen.

"A very pretty confederacy, indeed! Judge Temple, the land-lord and owner of a township, with Nathaniel Bumppo, a law-less squatter, and professed deer-killer, in order to preserve the game of the county! But, 'duke, when I fish, I fish; so, away, boys, for another haul, and we'll send out wagons and carts, in the morning, to bring in our prizes!"

Marmaduke appeared to understand that all opposition to the will of the Sheriff would be useless, and he strolled from the fire, to the place where the canoe of the hunters lay, whither the ladies and Oliver Edwards had already preceded him.

Curiosity induced the females to approach this spot, but it was a different motive that led the youth thither. Elizabeth examined the light ashen timbers and thin bark covering of the canoe, in admiration of its neat but simple execution, and with wonder, that any human being could be so daring as to trust his life in so frail a vessel. But the youth explained to her the buoyant properties of the boat, and its perfect safety, when under proper management, adding, in such glowing terms, a description of the manner in which the fish were struck with the spear, that she changed, suddenly, from an apprehension of the danger of the excursion, to a desire to participate in its pleasures. She even ventured a proposition to that effect to her father, laughing, at the same time, at her own wish, and accusing herself of acting under a woman's caprice.

"Say not so, Bess," returned the Judge; "I would have you above the idle fears of a silly girl. These canoes are the safest kind of boats, to those who have skill and steady nerves. I have crossed the broadest part of the Oneida in one much smaller than this."

"And I the Ontary," interrupted the Leather-stocking; "and that with squaws in the canoe, too. But the Delaware women are used to the paddle, and are good hands in a boat of this nater. If the young lady would like to see an old man strike a trout for his breakfast, she is welcome to a seat. John will say the same, seeing that he built the canoe, which was only launched yesterday; for I'm not over curous at such small work as brooms, and basket-making, and other like Indian trades."

Natty gave Elizabeth one of his significant laughs, with a kind nod of the head, when he concluded his invitation; but Mohegan, with the native grace of an Indian, approached, and taking her soft, white hand into his own swarthy and wrinkled palm, said—

"Come, grand-daughter of Miquon, and John will be glad. Trust the Indian: his head is old, though his hand is not steady. The Young Eagle will go, and see that no harm hurts his sister."

"Mr. Edwards," said Elizabeth, blushing slightly, "your friend Mohegan has given a promise for you. Do you redeem the pledge?"

"With my life, if necessary, Miss Temple," cried the youth, with fervour. "The sight is worth some little apprehension, for of real danger there is none. I will go with you and Miss Grant, however, to save appearances."

"With me!" exclaimed Louisa; "no, not with me, Mr. Edwards; nor surely do you mean to trust yourself in that slight canoe."

"But I shall, for I have no apprehensions any longer," said Elizabeth, stepping into the boat, and taking a seat where the

Indian directed. "Mr. Edwards, you may remain, as three do seem to be enough for such an egg-shell."

"It shall hold a fourth," cried the young man, springing to her side, with a violence that nearly shook the weak fabric of the vessel asunder;—"pardon me, Miss Temple, that I do not permit these venerable Charons to take you to the shades, unattended by your genius."

"Is it a good or evil spirit?" asked Elizabeth.

"Good to you."

"And mine," added the maiden, with an air that strangely blended pique with satisfaction. But the motion of the canoe gave rise to new ideas, and fortunately afforded a good excuse to the young man to change the discourse.

It appeared to Elizabeth, that they glided over the water by magic, so easy and graceful was the manner in which Mohegan guided his little bark. A slight gesture with his spear, indicated the way in which the Leather-stocking wished to go, and a profound silence was preserved by the whole party, as a precaution necessary to the success of their fishery. At that point of the lake, the water shoaled regularly, differing, in this particular, altogether, from those parts, where the mountains rose, nearly in perpendicular precipices, from the beach. There, the largest vessels could have lain, with their yards interlocked with the pines; while here, a scanty growth of rushes lifted their tops above the lake, gently curling the waters, as their bending heads waved with the passing breath of the night air. It was at the shallow points, only, that the bass could be found, or the net cast with success.

Elizabeth saw thousands of these fish, swimming in shoals along the shallow and warm waters of the shore; for the flaring light of their torch laid bare the mysteries of the lake, as plainly as if the limpid sheet of the Otsego was but another atmosphere. Every instant she expected to see the impending spear of Leather-stocking darting into the thronging hosts that were rushing beneath her, where it would seem that a blow could not go amiss; and where, as her father had already said, the prize that would be obtained was worthy any epicure. But Natty had his peculiar habits; and, it would seem, his peculiar tastes also. His tall stature, and his erect posture, enabled him to see much further than those who were seated in the bottom of the canoe;

and he turned his head warily, in every direction, frequently bending his body forward, and straining his vision, as if desirous of penetrating the water, that surrounded their boundary of light. At length his anxious scrutiny was rewarded with success, and, waving his spear from the shore, he said, in a cautious tone—

"Send her outside the bass, John; I see a laker there, that has run out of the school. It's sildom one finds such a creater in shallow water, where a spear can touch it."

Mohegan gave a wave of assent with his hand, and in the next instant the canoe was without the "run of the bass," and in water nearly twenty feet in depth. A few additional knots were laid on the grating, and the light penetrated to the bottom. Elizabeth then saw a fish of unusual size, floating above small pieces of logs and sticks. The animal was only distinguishable, at that distance, by a slight, but almost imperceptible motion of its fins and tail. The curiosity excited by this unusual exposure of the secrets of the lake, seemed to be mutual between the heiress of the land and the lord of these waters, for the "salmon-trout" soon announced his interest, by raising his head and body, for a few degrees above a horizontal line, and then dropping them again into a horizontal position.

"Whist, whist," said Natty, in a low voice, on hearing a slight sound made by Elizabeth, in bending over the side of the canoe, in curiosity; " 'tis a sceary animal, and it's a far stroke for a spear. My handle is but fourteen foot, and the creater lies a good eighteen from the top of the water; but I'll try him, for he's a ten-pounder."

While speaking, the Leather-stocking was poising and directing his weapon. Elizabeth saw the bright, polished tines, as they slowly and silently entered the water, where the refraction pointed them many degrees from the true direction of the fish; and she thought that the intended victim saw them also, as he seemed to increase the play of his tail and fins, though without moving his station. At the next instant, the tall body of Natty bent to the water's edge, and the handle of his spear disappeared in the lake. The long, dark streak of the gliding weapon, and the little bubbling vortex, which followed its rapid flight, were easily to be seen; but it was not until the handle shot again into the air, by its own re-action, and its master, catching it in his hand, threw its tines uppermost, that Elizabeth was acquainted with the success of the blow. A fish of great size was transfixed by the barbed steel, and was very soon shaken from its impaled situation into the bottom of the canoe.

"That will do, John," said Natty, raising his prize by one of his fingers, and exhibiting it before the torch; "I shall not strike another blow to-night."

The Indian again waved his hand, and replied with the simple and energetic monosyllable of—

"Good."

Elizabeth was awakened from the trance, created by this scene, and by gazing in that unusual manner at the bottom of the lake, by the hoarse sounds of Benjamin's voice, and the dashing of oars, as the heavier boat of the seine-drawers approached the spot where the canoe lay, dragging after it the folds of the net.

"Haul off, haul off, Master Bumppo," cried Benjamin; "your top-light frightens the fish, who see the net, and sheer off soundings. A fish knows as much as a horse, or, for that matter, more, seeing that it's brought up on the water. Haul off, Master Bumppo, haul off, I say, and give a wide berth to the seine."

Mohegan guided their little canoe to a point where the movements of the fishermen could be observed, without interruption to the business, and then suffered it to lie quietly on the water, looking like an imaginary vessel floating in air. There appeared to be much ill-humour among the party in the batteau, for the directions of Benjamin were not only frequent, but issued in a voice that partook largely of dissatisfaction.

"Pull larboard oar, will ye, Master Kirby," cried the old seaman; "pull larboard, best. It would puzzle the oldest admiral in the British fleet to cast this here net fair, with a wake like a corkscrew. Pull starboard, boy, pull starboard oar, with a will."

"Harkee, Mister Pump," said Kirby, ceasing to row, and speaking with some spirit; "I'm a man that likes civil language and decent treatment; such as is right 'twixt man and man. If you want us to go hoy, say so, and hoy I'll go, for the benefit of the company; but I'm not used to being ordered about like dumb cattle."

"Who's dumb cattle!" echoed Benjamin, fiercely, turning his

forbidding face to the glare of light from the canoe, and exhibiting every feature teeming with the expression of disgust. "If you want to come aft and cun the boat round, come and be damned, and pretty steerage you'll make of it. There's but another heave of the net in the stern-sheets, and we're clear of the thing. Give way, will ye? and shoot her ahead for a fathom or two, and if you catch me afloat again with such a horse-marine as yourself, why rate me a ship's jackass, that's all."

Probably encouraged by the prospect of a speedy termination to his labour, the wood-chopper resumed his oar, and, under strong excitement, gave a stroke, that not only cleared the boat of the net, but of the steward, at the same instant. Benjamin had stood on the little platform that held the seine, in the stern of the boat, and the violent whirl, occasioned by the vigour of the wood-chopper's arm, completely destroyed his balance. The position of the lights rendered objects in the batteau distinguishable, both from the canoe and the shore; and the heavy fall on the water drew all eyes to the steward, as he lay struggling, for a moment, in sight.

A loud burst of merriment, to which the lungs of Kirby contributed no small part, broke out like a chorus of laughter, and rung along the eastern mountain, in echoes, until it died away in distant, mocking mirth, among the rocks and woods. The body of the steward was seen slowly to disappear, as was expected; but when the light waves, which had been raised by his fall, begun to sink in calmness, and the water finally closed over his head, unbroken and still, a very different feeling pervaded the spectators.

"How fare you, Benjamin?" shouted Richard from the shore.

"The dumb devil can't swim a stroke!" exclaimed Kirby, rising, and beginning to throw aside his clothes.

"Paddle up, Mohegan," cried young Edwards, "the light will show us where he lies, and I will dive for the body."

"Oh! save him! for God's sake, save him!" exclaimed Elizabeth, bowing her head on the side of the canoe in horror.

A powerful and dexterous sweep of Mohegan's paddle sent the canoe directly over the spot, where the steward had fallen, and a loud shout from the Leather-stocking announced that he saw the body.

"Steady the boat while I dive," again cried Edwards.

"Gently, lad, gently," said Natty; "I'll spear the creater up in half the time, and no risk to any body."

The form of Benjamin was lying, about half way to the bottom, grasping with both hands some broken rushes. The blood of Elizabeth curdled to her heart, as she saw the figure of a fellow-creature thus extended under an immense sheet of water, apparently in motion, by the undulations of the dying waves, with its face and hands, viewed by that light, and through the medium of the fluid, already coloured with hues like death.

At the same instant, she saw the shining tines of Natty's spear approaching the head of the sufferer, and entwining themselves, rapidly and dexterously, in the hairs of his queue and the cape of his coat. The body was now raised slowly, looking ghastly and grim, as its features turned upward to the light, and approached the surface. The arrival of the nostrils of Benjamin into their own atmosphere, was announced by a breathing, that would have done credit to a porpoise. For a moment, Natty held the steward suspended, with his head just above the water, while his eyes slowly opened, and stared about him, as if he thought that he had reached a new and unexplored country.

As all the parties acted and spoke together, much less time was consumed in the occurrence of these events, than in their narration. To bring the batteau to the end of the spear, and to raise the form of Benjamin into the boat, and for the whole party to gain the shore, required but a minute. Kirby, aided by Richard, whose anxiety induced him to run into the water to meet his favourite assistant, carried the motionless steward up the bank, and seated him before the fire, while the Sheriff proceeded to order the most approved measures then in use, for the resuscitation of the drowned.

"Run, Billy," he cried, "to the village, and bring up the rum-hogshead that lies before the door, in which I am making vinegar, and be quick, boy, don't stay to empty the vinegar; and stop at Mr. Le Quoi's, and buy a paper of tobacco and half-a-dozen pipes; and ask Remarkable for some salt, and one of her flannel petticoats; and ask Dr. Todd to send his lancet, and to come himself; and——ha! 'duke, what are you about? would you strangle a man, who is full of water, by giving him rum! Help me to open his hand, that I may pat it."

All this time Benjamin sat, with his muscles fixed, his mouth shut, and his hands clenching the rushes, which he had seized in the confusion of the moment, and which, as he held fast, like a true seaman, had been the means of preventing his body from rising again to the surface. His eyes, however, were open, and stared wildly on the group about the fire, while his lungs were playing like a blacksmith's bellows, as if to compensate themselves for the minute of inaction to which they had been subjected. As he kept his lips compressed, with a most inveterate determination, the air was compelled to pass through his nostrils, and he rather snorted than breathed, and in such a manner, that nothing, but the excessive agitation of the Sheriff, could at all justify his precipitous orders.

The bottle, applied to the steward's lips by Marmaduke, acted like a charm. His mouth opened instinctively; his hands dropped the rushes, and seized the glass; his eyes raised from their horizontal stare, to the heavens; and the whole man was lost, for a moment, in a new sensation. Unhappily for the propensity of the steward, breath was as necessary after one of these draughts, as after his submersion, and the time at length arrived when he was compelled to let go the bottle.

"Why, Benjamin!" roared the Sheriff; "you amaze me! for a man of your experience in drownings to act so foolishly! just now, you were half full of water, and now you are"—

"Full of grog," interrupted the steward, his features settling down, with amazing flexibility, into their natural economy. "But, d'ye see, Squire, I kept my hatches close, and it is but little water that ever gets into my scuttle-butt.——Harkee, Master Kirby! I've follow'd the salt water for the better part of a man's life, and have seen some navigation on the fresh; but this here matter I will say in your favour, and that is, that you're the awk-'ardest green'un that ever straddled a boat's thwart. Them that likes you for a shipmate, may sail with you, and no thanks; but dam'me if I even walk on the lake shore in your company. For why? you'd as lief drown a man as one of them there fish; not to throw a christian creature so much as a rope's end, when he was adrift, and no life-buoy in sight!—Natty Bumppo, give us your fist. There's them that says you're an Indian, and a scalper, but you've sarved me a good turn, and you may set me down for a friend; thof it would have been more ship-shape to lower the bight of a rope, or running bow-line, below me, than to seize an old seaman by his head-lanyard; but I suppose you are used to taking men by the hair, and seeing you did me good instead of harm thereby, why, it's the same thing, d'ye see."

Marmaduke prevented any reply, and assuming the direction of matters, with a dignity and discretion that at once silenced all opposition from his cousin, Benjamin was despatched to the village by land, and the net was hauled to shore, in such a manner that the fish, for once, escaped its meshes with impunity.

The division of the spoils was made in the ordinary manner, by placing one of the party with his back to the game, who named the owner of each pile. Billy Kirby stretched his large frame on the grass, by the side of the fire, as sentinel until morning, over net and fish; and the remainder of the party embarked in the batteau, to return to the village.

The wood-chopper was seen broiling his supper on the coals, as they lost sight of the fire; and when the boat approached the shore, the torch of Mohegan's canoe was shining again under the gloom of the eastern mountain. Its motion ceased suddenly; a scattering of brands was in the air, and then all remained dark as the conjunction of night, forest, and mountain, could render the scene.

The thoughts of Elizabeth wandered from the youth, who was holding a canopy of shawls over herself and Louisa, to the hunter and the Indian warrior; and she felt an awakening curiosity to visit a hut, where men of such different habits and temperament were drawn together, as by common impulse.

Chapter XXV.

"Cease all this parlance about hills and dales:
None listen to thy scenes of boyish frolic,
Fond dotard! with such tickled ears as thou dost;
Come! to thy tale." *Duo.*

M R. JONES arose, on the following morning, with the
sun, and, ordering his own and Marmaduke's steeds to be sad-
dled, he proceeded, with a countenance big with some business
of unusual moment, to the apartment of the Judge. The door
was unfastened, and Richard entered, with the freedom that
characterized, not only the intercourse between the cousins, but
the ordinary manners of the Sheriff.

"Well, 'duke, to horse," he cried, "and I will explain to you
my meaning in the allusions I made last night. David says, in the
Psalms—no, it was Solomon, but it was all in the family—
Solomon said, there was a time for all things; and, in my humble opinion, a fishing party is not the moment for discussing
important subjects—Ha! why what the devil ails you, Marmaduke? an't you well? let me feel your pulse; my grandfather,
you know"—

"Quite well in the body, Richard," interrupted the Judge, re-
pulsing his cousin, who was about to assume the functions that
properly belonged to Dr. Todd; "but ill at heart. I received letters by the post of last night, after we returned from the point,
and this among the number."

The Sheriff took the letter, but without turning his eyes on
the writing, for he was examining the appearance of the other
with astonishment. From the face of his cousin, the gaze of
Richard wandered to the table, which was covered with letters,
packets, and newspapers; then to the apartment, and all that it
contained. On the bed there was the impression that had been
made by a human form, but the coverings were unmoved, and
every thing indicated that the occupant of the room had passed
a sleepless night. The candles were burnt to the sockets, and
had evidently extinguished themselves in their own fragments.
Marmaduke had drawn his curtains, and opened both the shut-

ters and the sashes, to admit the balmy air of a spring morning; but his pale cheek, his quivering lip, and his sunken eye, presented, altogether, so very different an appearance from the usual calm, manly, and cheerful aspect of the Judge, that the Sheriff grew each moment more and more bewildered with astonishment. At length Richard found time to cast his eyes on the direction of the letter, which he still held unopened, crumbling it in his hand.

"What! a ship letter!" he exclaimed; "and from England! ha! 'duke, there must be news of importance indeed!"

"Read it," said Marmaduke, pacing the floor in excessive agitation.

Richard, who commonly thought aloud, was unable to read a letter, without suffering part of its contents to escape him in audible sounds. So much of the epistle as was divulged in that manner, we shall lay before the reader, accompanied by the passing remarks of the Sheriff:—

" 'London, February 12th, 1793.' What a devil of a passage she had! but the wind has been northwest, for six weeks, until within the last fortnight. 'Sir, your favours, of August 10th, September 23d, and of December 1st, were received in due season, and the first answered by return of packet. Since the receipt of the last, I' "—Here a long passage was rendered indistinct, by a kind of humming noise, made by the Sheriff. " 'I grieve to say, that'—hum, hum, bad enough, to be sure—'but trust that a merciful Providence has seen fit'—hum, hum, hum; seems to be a good, pious sort of a man, 'duke; belongs to the established church, I dare say; hum, hum—'vessel sailed from Falmouth on or about the 1st September of last year, and'—hum, hum, hum. 'If any thing should transpire, on this afflicting subject, shall not fail'—hum, hum; really a good-hearted man, for a lawyer—'but can communicate nothing further at present.'—Hum, hum. 'The national convention'—hum, hum —'unfortunate Louis'—hum, hum—'example of your Washington'—a very sensible man, I declare, and none of your crazy democrats. Hum, hum—'our gallant navy'—hum, hum—'under our most excellent monarch'—ay, a good man enough, that King George, but bad advisers; hum, hum—'I beg to conclude with assurances of my perfect respect,'—hum, hum—'ANDREW HOLT.'—Andrew Holt—a very sensible, feeling man, this Mr.

Andrew Holt, but the writer of evil tidings. What will you do next, cousin Marmaduke?"

"What can I do, Richard, but trust to time, and the will of Heaven? Here is another letter, from Connecticut, but it only repeats the substance of the last. There is but one consoling reflection to be gathered from the English news, which is, that my last letter was received by him, before the ship sailed."

"This is bad enough indeed! 'duke, bad enough indeed! and away go all my plans of putting the wings to the house, to the devil. I had made arrangements for a ride, to introduce you to something of a very important nature. You know how much you think of mines"—

"Talk not of mines," interrupted the Judge; "there is a sacred duty to be performed, and that without delay. I must devote this day to writing; and thou must be my assistant, Richard; it will not do to employ Oliver in a matter of such secrecy and interest."

"No, no, 'duke," cried the Sheriff, squeezing his hand, "I am your man, just now; we are sisters' children, and blood, after all, is the best cement to make friendship stick together. Well, well, there is no hurry about the silver mine, just now; another time will do as well. We shall want Dirky Van, I suppose?"

Marmaduke assented to this indirect question, and the Sheriff relinquished all his intentions, on the subject of the ride, and, repairing to the breakfast parlour, he despatched a messenger to require the immediate presence of Dirck Van der School.

The village of Templeton, at that time, supported but two lawyers, one of whom was introduced to our readers in the bar-room of the "Bold Dragoon," and the other was the gentleman of whom Richard spoke, by the friendly, but familiar appellation of Dirck or Dirky Van. Great good nature, a very tolerable share of skill in his profession, and, considering the circumstances, no contemptible degree of honesty, were the principal ingredients in the character of this man; who was known to the settlers as Squire Van der School, and sometimes by the flattering, though anomalous title of "the Dutch," or "honest lawyer." We would not wish to mislead our readers in their conceptions of any of our characters, and we therefore feel it necessary to add, that the adjective, in the preceding agnomen of Mr. Van der School, was used in direct reference to its substantive. Our orthodox friends need not be told that all merit in this world is comparative; and, once for all, we desire to say, that where any thing which involves qualities or character is asserted, we must be understood to mean, "under the circumstances."

During the remainder of the day, the Judge was closeted with his cousin and his lawyer; and no one else was admitted to his apartment, excepting his daughter. The deep distress, that so evidently afflicted Marmaduke, was, in some measure, communicated to Elizabeth also; for a look of dejection shaded her intelligent features, and the buoyancy of her animated spirits was sensibly softened. Once, on that day, young Edwards, who was a wondering and observant spectator of the sudden alteration produced in the heads of the family, detected a tear stealing over the cheek of Elizabeth, and suffusing her bright eyes, with a softness that did not always belong to their expression.

"Have any evil tidings been received, Miss Temple?" he inquired, with an interest and voice that caused Louisa Grant to raise her head from her needle-work, with a quickness, at which she instantly blushed herself. "I would offer my services to your father, if, as I suspect, he needs an agent in some distant place, and I thought it would give you relief."

"We have certainly heard bad news," returned Elizabeth, "and it may be necessary that my father should leave home, for a short period; unless I can persuade him to trust my cousin Richard with the business, whose absence from the county, just at this time, too, might be inexpedient."

The youth paused a moment, and the blood gathered slowly to his temples, as he continued—

"If it be of a nature that I could execute"—

"It is such as can only be confided to one we know—one of ourselves."

"Surely, you know me, Miss Temple!" he added, with a warmth that he seldom exhibited, but which did sometimes escape him, in the moments of their frank communications—"Have I lived five months under your roof to be a stranger!"

Elizabeth was engaged with her needle, also; and she bent her head to one side, affecting to arrange her muslin; but her hand shook, her colour heightened, and her eyes lost their moisture, in an expression of ungovernable interest, as she said—

"How much do we know of you, Mr. Edwards?"

"How much!" echoed the youth, gazing from the speaker to the mild countenance of Louisa, that was also illuminated with curiosity; "how much! have I been so long an inmate with you, and not known?"

The head of Elizabeth slowly turned from its affected position, and the look of confusion that had blended so strongly with an expression of interest, changed to a smile.

"We know you, sir, indeed: you are called Mr. Oliver Edwards. I understand that you have informed my friend, Miss Grant, that you are a native"—

"Elizabeth!" exclaimed Louisa, blushing to the eyes, and trembling like an aspen; "you misunderstood me, dear Miss Temple; I—I—it was only conjecture. Besides, if Mr. Edwards is related to the natives, why should we reproach him! in what are we better? at least I, who am the child of a poor and unsettled clergyman?"

Elizabeth shook her head, doubtingly, and even laughed, but made no reply, until, observing the melancholy which pervaded the countenance of her companion, who was thinking of the poverty and labours of her father, she continued—

"Nay, Louisa, humility carries you too far. The daughter of a minister of the church can have no superiors. Neither I nor Mr. Edwards is quite your equal, unless," she added, again smiling, "he is in secret a king."

"A faithful servant of the King of kings, Miss Temple, is inferior to none on earth," said Louisa; "but his honours are his own; I am only the child of a poor and friendless man, and can claim no other distinction. Why, then, should I feel myself elevated above Mr. Edwards, because—because—perhaps, he is only very, very distantly related to John Mohegan?"

Glances of a very comprehensive meaning were exchanged between the heiress and the young man, as Louisa betrayed, while vindicating his lineage, the reluctance with which she admitted his alliance to the old warrior; but not even a smile at the simplicity of their companion was indulged by either.

"On reflection, I must acknowledge that my situation here is somewhat equivocal," said Edwards, "though I may be said to have purchased it with my blood."

"The blood, too, of one of the native lords of the soil!" cried Elizabeth, who evidently put little faith in his aboriginal descent.

"Do I bear the marks of my lineage so very plainly impressed on my appearance? I am dark, but not very red—not more so than common?"

"Rather more so, just now."

"I am sure, Miss Temple," cried Louisa, "you cannot have taken much notice of Mr. Edwards. His eyes are not so black as Mohegan's, or even your own, nor is his hair!"

"Very possibly, then, I can lay claim to the same descent. It would be a great relief to my mind to think so, for I own that I grieve when I see old Mohegan walking about these lands, like the ghost of one of their ancient possessors, and feel how small is my own right to possess them."

"Do you!" cried the youth, with a vehemence that startled the ladies.

"I do, indeed," returned Elizabeth, after suffering a moment to pass in surprise; "but what can I do? what can my father do? Should we offer the old man a home and a maintenance, his habits would compel him to refuse us. Neither, were we so silly as to wish such a thing, could we convert these clearings and farms, again, into hunting-grounds, as the Leather-stocking would wish to see them."

"You speak the truth, Miss Temple," said Edwards. "What can you do, indeed! But there is one thing that I am certain you can and will do, when you become the mistress of these beautiful valleys—use your wealth with indulgence to the poor and charity to the needy;—indeed, you can do no more."

"And that will be doing a good deal," said Louisa, smiling in her turn. "But there will, doubtless, be one to take the direction of such things from her hands."

"I am not about to disclaim matrimony, like a silly girl, who dreams of nothing else from morning till night; but I am a nun, here, without the vow of celibacy. Where shall I find a husband, in these forests?"

"There is none, Miss Temple," said Edwards, quickly, "there

is none who has a right to aspire to you, and I know that you will wait to be sought by your equal; or die, as you live, loved, respected, and admired, by all who know you."

The young man seemed to think that he had said all that was required by gallantry, for he arose, and taking his hat, hurried from the apartment. Perhaps Louisa thought that he had said more than was necessary, for she sighed, with an aspiration so low that it was scarcely audible to herself, and bent her head over her work again. And it is possible that Miss Temple wished to hear more, for her eyes continued fixed, for a minute, on the door through which the young man had passed, then glanced quickly towards her companion, when the long silence that succeeded manifested how much zest may be given to the conversation of two maidens under eighteen, by the presence of a youth of three and twenty.

The first person encountered by Mr. Edwards, as he rather rushed than walked from the house, was the little, square-built lawyer, with a large bundle of papers under his arm, a pair of green spectacles on his nose, with glasses at the sides, as if to multiply his power of detecting frauds, by additional organs of vision.

Mr. Van der School was a well-educated man, but of slow comprehension, who had imbibed a wariness in his speeches and actions, from having suffered by his collisions with his more mercurial and apt brethren who had laid the foundations of their practice in the eastern courts, and who had sucked in shrewdness with their mothers' milk. The caution of this gentleman was exhibited in his actions, by the utmost method and punctuality, tinctured with a good deal of timidity; and in his speeches, by a parenthetical style, that frequently left to his auditors a long search after his meaning.

"A good morning to you, Mr. Van der School," said Edwards; "it seems to be a busy day with us, at the Mansion-house."

"Good morning, Mr. Edwards, (if that is your name, (for, being a stranger, we have no other evidence of the fact than your own testimony,) as I understand you have given it to Judge Temple,) good morning, sir. It is, apparently, a busy day, (but a man of your discretion need not be told, (having, doubtless, discovered it of your own accord,) that appearances are often deceitful,) up at the Mansion-house."

"Have you papers of consequence, that will require copying? can I be of assistance in any way?"

"There are papers (as, doubtless, you see (for your eyes are young) by the outsides) that require copying."

"Well, then I will accompany you to your office, and receive such as are most needed, and by night I shall have them done, if there be much haste."

"I shall be always glad to see you, sir, at my office, (as in duty bound, (not that it is obligatory to receive any man within your dwelling, (unless so inclined,) which is a castle,) according to the forms of politeness,) or at any other place; but the papers are most strictly confidential, (and, as such, cannot be read by any one, (unless so directed,) by Judge Temple's solemn injunctions,) and are invisible to all eyes; excepting those whose duties (I mean assumed duties) require it of them."

"Well, sir, as I perceive that I can be of no service, I wish you another good morning; but beg you will remember that I am quite idle, just now, and I wish you would intimate as much to Judge Temple, and make him a tender of my services, in any part of the world; unless—unless—it be far from Templeton."

"I will make the communication, sir, in your name, (with your own qualifications,) as your agent. Good morning, sir.—But stay proceedings, Mr. Edwards, (so called,) for a moment. Do you wish me to state the offer of travelling, as a final contract, (for which consideration has been received, at former dates, (by sums advanced,) which would be binding,) or as a tender of services, for which compensation is to be paid (according to future agreement between the parties) on performance of the conditions?"

"Any way——any way," said Edwards—"he seems in distress, and I would assist him."

"The motive is good, sir, (according to appearances, (which are often deceitful,) on first impressions,) and does you honour. I will mention your wish, young gentleman, (as you now seem,) and will not fail to communicate the answer, by five o'clock, P.M. of this present day, (God willing,) if you give me an opportunity so to do."

The ambiguous nature of the situation and character of Mr. Edwards, had rendered him an object of peculiar suspicion to the lawyer, and the youth was consequently too much accustomed to similar equivocal and guarded speeches, to feel any unusual disgust at the present dialogue. He saw, at once, that it was the intention of the practitioner to conceal the nature of his business, even from the private secretary of Judge Temple; and he knew too well the difficulty of comprehending the meaning of Mr. Van der School, when the gentleman most wished to be luminous in his discourse, not to abandon all thoughts of a discovery, when he perceived that the attorney was endeavouring to avoid any thing like an approach to a cross-examination. They parted at the gate, the lawyer walking, with an important and hurried air, towards his office, keeping his right hand firmly clenched on the bundle of papers.

It must have been obvious to all our readers, that the youth entertained an unusual and deeply-seated prejudice against the character of the Judge; but, owing to some counteracting cause, his sensations were now those of powerful interest in the state of his patron's present feelings, and in the causes of his secret uneasiness.

He remained gazing after the lawyer, until the door closed on both the bearer and the mysterious packet, when he returned slowly to the dwelling, and endeavoured to forget his curiosity, in the usual avocations of his office.

When the Judge made his re-appearance in the circle of his family, his cheerfulness was tempered by a shade of melancholy, that lingered for many days around his manly brow; but the magical progression of the season aroused him from his temporary apathy, and his smiles returned with the summer.

The heats of the days, and the frequent occurrence of balmy showers, had completed, in an incredibly short period, the growth of plants, which the lingering spring had so long retarded in the germ; and the woods presented every shade of green that the American forests know. The stumps in the cleared fields were already hid beneath the wheat, that was waving with every breath of the summer air, shining, and changing its hues, like velvet.

During the continuance of his cousin's dejection, Mr. Jones forbore, with much consideration, to press on his attention a business that each hour was drawing nearer to the heart of the Sheriff, and which, if any opinion could be formed by his frequent private conferences with the man, who was introduced in

these pages, by the name of Jotham, at the bar-room of the
Bold Dragoon, was becoming also of great importance.

At length the Sheriff ventured to allude again to the subject,
and one evening, in the beginning of July, Marmaduke made
him a promise of devoting the following day to the desired excursion.

Chapter XXVI.

> "Speak on, my dearest father!
> Thy words are like the breezes of the west."
> Milman, *Belshazzar*, III.73–74.

IT was a mild and soft morning, when Marmaduke and Richard mounted their horses, to proceed on the expedition that had so long been uppermost in the thoughts of the latter; and Elizabeth and Louisa appeared at the same instant in the hall, attired for an excursion on foot.

The head of Miss Grant was covered by a neat, little hat of green silk, and her modest eyes peered from under its shade, with the soft languor that characterized her whole appearance; but Miss Temple trod her father's wide apartments, with the step of their mistress, holding in her hand, dangling by one of its ribands, the gipsy that was to conceal the glossy locks that curled around her polished forehead, in rich profusion.

"What, are you for a walk, Bess!" cried the Judge, suspending his movements for a moment, to smile, with a father's fondness, at the display of womanly grace and beauty that his child presented. "Remember the heats of July, my daughter; nor venture further than thou canst retrace before the meridian. Where is thy parasol, girl? thou wilt lose the polish of that brow, under this sun and southern breeze, unless thou guard it with unusual care."

"I shall then do more honour to my connexions," returned the smiling daughter. "Cousin Richard has a bloom that any lady might envy. At present, the resemblance between us is so trifling, that no stranger would know us to be 'sisters' children.'"

"Grand-children, you mean, cousin Bess," said the Sheriff. "But on, Judge Temple; time and tide wait for no man; and if you take my counsel, sir, in twelve months from this day, you may make an umbrella for your daughter of her camel's-hair shawl, and have its frame of solid silver. I ask nothing for myself, 'duke; you have been a good friend to me already; besides, all that I have will go to Bess, there, one of these melancholy days, so it's as long as it's short, whether I or you leave it. But we have a day's ride before us, sir; so move forward, or dismount, and say you won't go, at once."

"Patience, patience, Dickon," returned the Judge, checking his horse, and turning again to his daughter. "If thou art for the mountains, love, stray not too deep into the forest, I entreat thee; for, though it is done often with impunity, there is sometimes danger."

"Not at this season, I believe, sir," said Elizabeth; "for, I will confess, it is the intention of Louisa and myself to stroll among the hills."

"Less at this season than in the winter, dear; but still there may be danger in venturing too far. But though thou art resolute, Elizabeth, thou art too much like thy mother not to be prudent."

The eyes of the parent turned reluctantly from his child, and the Judge and Sheriff rode slowly through the gateway, and disappeared among the buildings of the village.

During this short dialogue, young Edwards stood, an attentive listener, holding in his hand a fishing-rod, the day and the season having tempted him also to desert the house, for the pleasure of exercise in the air. As the equestrians turned through the gate, he approached the young females, who were already moving towards the street, and was about to address them, as Louisa paused, and said quickly—

"Mr. Edwards would speak to us, Elizabeth."

The other stopped also, and turned to the youth, politely, but with a slight coldness in her air, that sensibly checked the freedom with which he had approached them.

"Your father is not pleased that you should walk unattended in the hills, Miss Temple. If I might offer myself as a protector"—

"Does my father select Mr. Oliver Edwards as the organ of his displeasure?" interrupted the lady.

"Good Heaven! you misunderstand my meaning; I should have said uneasy, for not pleased. I am his servant, madam, and in consequence yours. I repeat that, with your consent, I will change my rod for a fowling-piece, and keep nigh you on the mountain."

"I thank you, Mr. Edwards; but where there is no danger, no

protection is required. We are not yet reduced to wandering among these free hills accompanied by a body-guard. If such a one is necessary, there he is, however.—Here, Brave,—Brave —my noble Brave!"

The huge mastiff that has been already mentioned, appeared from his kennel, gaping and stretching himself, with pampered laziness; but as his mistress again called—"Come, dear Brave; once have you served your master well; let us see how you can do your duty by his daughter"—the dog wagged his tail, as if he understood her language, walked with a stately gait to her side, where he seated himself, and looked up at her face, with an intelligence but little inferior to that which beamed in her own lovely countenance.

She resumed her walk, but again paused, after a few steps, and added, in tones of conciliation—

"You can be serving us, equally, and, I presume, more agreeably to yourself, Mr. Edwards, by bringing us a string of your favourite perch, for the dinner-table."

When they again begun to walk, Miss Temple did not look back, to see how the youth bore this repulse; but the head of Louisa was turned several times, before they reached the gate, on that considerate errand.

"I am afraid, Elizabeth," she said, "that we have mortified Oliver. He is still standing where we left him, leaning on his rod. Perhaps he thinks us proud."

"He thinks justly," exclaimed Miss Temple, as if awaking from a deep musing; "he thinks justly, then. We are too proud to admit of such particular attentions from a young man whose situation is so equivocal. What! make him the companion of our most private walks! It is pride, Louisa, but it is the pride of our sex."

It was several minutes before Oliver aroused himself from the contemplative posture in which he was standing when Louisa last saw him; but when he did, he muttered something, rapidly and incoherently, and throwing his rod over his shoulder, he strode down the walk, through the gate, and along one of the streets of the village, until he reached the lake-shore, with the air of an emperor. At this spot boats were kept, for the use of Judge Temple and his family. The young man threw himself into a light skiff, and seizing the oars, he sent it across the lake, towards the hut of Leather-stocking, with a pair of vigorous arms. By the time he had rowed a quarter of a mile, his reflections were less bitter; and when he saw the bushes that lined the shore in front of Natty's habitation gliding by him, as if they possessed the motion which proceeded from his own efforts, he was quite cooled in mind, though somewhat heated in body. It is quite possible, that the very same reason which guided the conduct of Miss Temple, suggested itself to a man of the breeding and education of the youth; and it is very certain, that if such were the case, Elizabeth rose instead of falling in the estimation of Mr. Edwards.

The oars were now raised from the water, and the boat shot close into the land, where it lay gently agitated by waves of its own creating, while the young man, first casting a cautious and searching glance around him in every direction, put a small whistle to his mouth, and blew a long, shrill note, that rung among the echoing rocks behind the hut. At this alarm, the hounds of Natty rushed out of their bark kennel, and commenced their long, piteous howls, leaping about as if half frantic, though restrained by the leashes of buck-skin, by which they were fastened.

"Quiet, Hector, quiet," said Oliver, again applying his whistle to his mouth, and drawing out notes still more shrill than before. No reply was made, the dogs having returned to their kennel at the sounds of his voice.

Edwards pulled the bows of the boat on the shore, and landing, ascended the beach and approached the door of the cabin. The fastenings were soon undone, and he entered, closing the door after him, when all was as silent, in that retired spot, as if the foot of man had never trod the wilderness. The sounds of the hammers, that were in incessant motion in the village, were faintly heard across the water; but the dogs had crouched into their lairs, satisfied that none but the privileged had approached the forbidden ground.

A quarter of an hour elapsed before the youth re-appeared, when he fastened the door again and spoke kindly to the hounds. The dogs came out at the well-known tones, and the slut jumped upon his person, whining and barking, as if entreating Oliver to release her from prison. But Old Hector raised his nose to the light current of air, and opened a long howl, that might have been heard for a mile.

"Ha! what do you scent, old veteran of the woods?" cried Edwards. "If a beast, it is a bold one; and if a man, an impudent."

He sprung through the top of a pine, that had fallen near the side of the hut, and ascended a small hillock, that sheltered the cabin to the south, where he caught a glimpse of the formal figure of Hiram Doolittle, as it vanished, with unusual rapidity for the architect, amid the bushes.

"What can that fellow be wanting here?" muttered Oliver. "He has no business in this quarter, unless it be curiosity, which is an endemic in these woods. But against that I will effectually guard, though the dogs should take a liking to his ugly visage, and let him pass." The youth returned to the door, while giving vent to this soliloquy, and completed the fastenings, by placing a small chain through a staple, and securing it there by a padlock. "He is a pettifogger, and surely must know that there is such a thing as feloniously breaking into a man's house."

Apparently well satisfied with this arrangement, the youth again spoke to the hounds; and, descending to the shore, he launched his boat, and taking up his oars, pulled off into the lake.

There were several places in the Otsego that were celebrated fishing-ground for perch. One was nearly opposite to the cabin, and another, still more famous, was near a point, at the distance of a mile and a half above it, under the brow of the mountain, and on the same side of the lake with the hut. Oliver Edwards pulled his little skiff to the first, and sat, for a minute, undecided whether to continue there, with his eyes on the door of the cabin, or to change his ground, with a view to get superior game. While gazing about him, he saw the light-coloured bark canoe of his old companions, riding on the water, at the point we have mentioned, and containing two figures, that he at once knew to be Mohegan and the Leather-stocking. This decided the matter, and the youth pulled, in a very few minutes, to the place where his friends were fishing, and fastened his boat to the light vessel of the Indian.

The old men received Oliver with welcoming nods, but

neither drew his line from the water, nor, in the least, varied his occupation. When Edwards had secured his own boat, he baited his hook and threw it into the lake, without speaking.

"Did you stop at the wigwam, lad, as you rowed past?" asked Natty.

"Yes, and I found all safe; but that carpenter and justice of the peace, Mr., or, as they call him, Squire Doolittle, was prowling through the woods. I made sure of the door, before I left the hut, and I think he is too great a coward to approach the hounds."

"There's little to be said in favour of that man," said Natty, while he drew in a perch and baited his hook. "He craves dreadfully to come into the cabin, and has as good as asked me as much to my face; but I put him off with unsartain answers, so that he is no wiser than Solomon. This comes of having so many laws that such a man may be called on to intarpret them."

"I fear he is more knave than fool," cried Edwards: "he makes a tool of that simple man, the Sheriff, and I dread that his impertinent curiosity may yet give us much trouble."

"If he harbours too much about the cabin, lad, I'll shoot the creater," said the Leather-stocking, quite simply.

"No, no, Natty, you must remember the law," said Edwards, "or we shall have you in trouble; and that, old man, would be an evil day, and sore tidings to us all."

"Would it, boy!" exclaimed the hunter, raising his eyes with a look of friendly interest towards the youth. "You have the true blood in your veins, Mr. Oliver, and I'll support it, to the face of Judge Temple, or in any court in the country. How is it, John? do I speak the true word? is the lad stanch, and of the right blood?"

"He is a Delaware," said Mohegan, "and my brother. The Young Eagle is brave, and he will be a chief. No harm can come."

"Well, well," cried the youth, impatiently; "say no more about it, my good friends; if I am not all that your partiality would make me, I am yours through life—in prosperity as in poverty. We will talk of other matters."

The old hunters yielded to his wish, which seemed to be their law. For a short time a profound silence prevailed, during which each man was very busy with his hook and line; but Edwards, probably feeling that it remained with him to renew the discourse, soon observed, with the air of one who knew not what he said—

"How beautifully tranquil and glassy the lake is. Saw you it ever more calm and even than at this moment, Natty?"

"I have known the Otsego water for five-and-forty year," said Leather-stocking, "and I will say that for it, which is, that a cleaner spring or better fishing is not to be found in the land. Yes, yes—I had the place to myself once; and a cheerful time I had of it. The game was plenty as heart could wish, and there was none to meddle with the ground, unless there might have been a hunting party of the Delawares crossing the hills, or, maybe, a rifling scout of them thieves, the Iroquois. There was one or two Frenchmen that squatted in the flats, further west, and married squaws; and some of the Scotch-Irishers, from the Cherry Valley, would come on to the lake, and borrow my canoe, to take a mess of parch, or drop a line for salmon-trout; but, in the main, it was a cheerful place, and I had but little to disturb me in it. John would come, and John knows."

Mohegan turned his dark face, at this appeal, and, moving his hand forward with a graceful motion of assent, he spoke, using the Delaware language—

"The land was owned by my people: we gave it to my brother, in council—to the Fire-Eater; and what the Delawares give, lasts as long as the waters run. Hawk-eye smoked at that council, for we loved him."

"No, no, John," said Natty, "I was no chief, seeing that I know'd nothing of scholarship, and had a white skin. But it was a comfortable hunting-ground then, lad, and would have been so to this day, but for the money of Marmaduke Temple, and the twisty ways of the law."

"It must have been a sight of melancholy pleasure, indeed," said Edwards, while his eye roved along the shores and over the hills, where the clearings, groaning with the golden corn, were cheering the forests with the signs of life, "to have roamed over these mountains, and along this sheet of beautiful water, without a living soul to speak to, or to thwart your humour."

"Haven't I said it was cheerful!" said Leather-stocking. "Yes, yes——when the trees begun to be kivered with leaves, and the ice was out of the lake, it was a second paradise. I have travelled

the woods for fifty-three year, and have made them my home
for more than forty, and I can say that I have met but one place
that was more to my liking; and that was only to eyesight, and
not for hunting or fishing."

"And where was that?" asked Edwards.

"Where! why up on the Cattskills. I used often to go up into
the mountains after wolves' skins, and bears; once they paid me
to get them a stuffed painter; and so I often went. There's a
place in them hills that I used to climb to, when I wanted to see
the carryings on of the world, that would well pay any man for a
barked shin or a torn moccasin. You know the Cattskills, lad,
for you must have seen them on your left, as you followed the
river up from York, looking as blue as a piece of clear sky, and
holding the clouds on their tops, as the smoke curls over the
head of an Indian chief at the council fire. Well, there's the
High-peak and the Round-top, which lay back, like a father and
mother among their children, seeing they are far above all the
other hills. But the place I mean is next to the river, where one
of the ridges juts out a little from the rest, and where the rocks
fall for the best part of a thousand feet, so much up and down,
that a man standing on their edges is fool enough to think he
can jump from top to bottom."

"What see you when you get there?" asked Edwards.

"Creation!" said Natty, dropping the end of his rod into the
water, and sweeping one hand around him in a circle——"all
creation, lad. I was on that hill when Vaughan burnt 'Sopus, in
the last war, and I seen the vessels come out of the highlands as
plain as I can see that lime-scow rowing into the Susquehanna,
though one was twenty times further from me than the other.
The river was in sight for seventy miles, looking like a curled
shaving, under my feet, though it was eight long miles to its
banks. I saw the hills in the Hampshire grants, the high lands of
the river, and all that God had done or man could do, far as eye
could reach—you know that the Indians named me for my
sight, lad——and from the flat on the top of that mountain, I
have often found the place where Albany stands; and as for
'Sopus! the day the royal troops burnt the town, the smoke
seemed so nigh, that I thought I could hear the screeches of the
women."

"It must have been worth the toil, to meet with such a glorious view!"

"If being the best part of a mile in the air, and having men's farms and housen at your feet, with rivers looking like ribands, and mountains bigger than the 'Vision,' seeming to be haystacks of green grass under you, gives any satisfaction to a man, I can recommend the spot. When I first come into the woods to live, I used to have weak spells, when I felt lonesome; and then I would go into the Cattskills and spend a few days on that hill, to look at the ways of man; but it's now many a year since I felt any such longings, and I'm getting too old for rugged rocks. But there's a place, a short two miles back of that very hill, that in late times I relished better than the mountains; for it was kivered with the trees, and nateral."

"And where was that?" inquired Edwards, whose curiosity was strongly excited by the simple description of the hunter.

"Why, there's a fall in the hills, where the water of two little ponds that lie near each other breaks out of their bounds, and runs over the rocks into the valley. The stream is, maybe, such a one as would turn a mill, if so useless a thing was wanted in the wilderness. But the hand that made that 'Leap' never made a mill! There the water comes crooking and winding among the rocks, first so slow that a trout could swim in it, and then starting and running like a creater that wanted to make a far spring, till it gets to where the mountain divides, like the cleft hoof of a deer, leaving a deep hollow for the brook to tumble into. The first pitch is nigh two hundred feet, and the water looks like flakes of driven snow, afore it touches the bottom; and there the stream gathers together again for a new start, and maybe flutters over fifty feet of flat-rock, before it falls for another hundred, when it jumps about from shelf to shelf, first turning this-away and then turning that-away, striving to get out of the hollow, till it finally comes to the plain."

"I have never heard of this spot before: it is not mentioned in the books."

"I never read a book in my life," said Leather-stocking; "and how should a man who has lived in towns and schools know any thing about the wonders of the woods! No, no, lad; there has that little stream of water been playing among them hills, since

He made the world, and not a dozen white men have ever laid eyes on it. The rock sweeps like mason-work, in a half-round, on both sides of the fall, and shelves over the bottom for fifty feet; so that when I've been sitting at the foot of the first pitch, and my hounds have run into the caverns behind the sheet of water, they've looked no bigger than so many rabbits. To my judgment, lad, it's the best piece of work that I've met with in the woods; and none know how often the hand of God is seen in the wilderness, but them that rove it for a man's life."

"What becomes of the water? in which direction does it run? is it a tributary of the Delaware?"

"Anan!" said Natty.

"Does the water run into the Delaware?"

"No, no, it's a drop for the old Hudson; and a merry time it has till it gets down off the mountain. I've sat on the shelving rock many a long hour, boy, and watched the bubbles as they shot by me, and thought how long it would be before that very water, which seemed made for the wilderness, would be under the bottom of a vessel, and tossing in the salt sea. It is a spot to make a man solemnize. You can see right down into the valley that lies to the east of the High-Peak, where, in the fall of the year, thousands of acres of woods are afore your eyes, in the deep hollow, and along the side of the mountain, painted like ten thousand rainbows, by no hand of man, though not without the ordering of God's providence."

"You are eloquent, Leather-stocking!" exclaimed the youth.

"Anan!" repeated Natty.

"The recollection of the sight has warmed your blood, old man. How many years is it since you saw the place?"

The hunter made no reply; but, bending his ear near the water, he sat holding his breath, and listening attentively, as if to some distant sound. At length he raised his head, and said—

"If I hadn't fastened the hounds with my own hands, with a fresh leash of green buck-skin, I'd take a bible oath that I heard old Hector ringing his cry on the mountain."

"It is impossible," said Edwards; "it is not an hour since I saw him in his kennel."

By this time the attention of Mohegan was attracted to the sounds; but, notwithstanding the youth was both silent and attentive, he could hear nothing but the lowing of some cattle from the western hills. He looked at the old men, Natty sitting with his hand to his ear, like a trumpet, and Mohegan bending forward, with an arm raised to a level with his face, holding the fore finger elevated as a signal for attention, and laughed aloud at what he deemed to be their imaginary sounds.

"Laugh if you will, boy," said Leather-stocking; "the hounds be out, and be hunting a deer. No man can deceive me in such a matter. I wouldn't have had the thing happen for a beaver's skin. Not that I care for the law! but the venison is lean now, and the dumb things run the flesh off their own bones for no good. Now do you hear the hounds?"

Edwards started, as a full cry broke on his ear, changing from the distant sounds that were caused by some intervening hill, to confused echoes that rung among the rocks that the dogs were passing, and then directly to a deep and hollow baying that pealed under the forest on the lake shore. These variations in the tones of the hounds passed with amazing rapidity, and while his eyes were glancing along the margin of the water, a tearing of the branches of the alder and dog-wood caught his attention, at a spot near them, and, at the next moment, a noble buck sprung on the shore, and buried himself in the lake. A full-mouthed cry followed, when Hector and the slut shot through the opening in the bushes, and darted into the lake also, bearing their breasts gallantly against the water.

Chapter XXVII.

"Oft in the full-descending flood he tries
To lose the scent, and lave his burning sides."
                    Thomson, *The Seasons*, "Autumn," 445–46.

"I know'd it—I know'd it!" cried Natty, when both deer and hounds were in full view;—"the buck has gone by them with the wind, and it has been too much for the poor rogues; but I must break them of these tricks, or they'll give me a deal of trouble. He-ere, he-ere—shore with you, rascals—shore with you—will ye?—Oh! off with you, old Hector, or I'll hatchel your hide with my ramrod when I get ye."

The dogs knew their master's voice, and, after swimming in a circle, as if reluctant to give over the chase, and yet afraid to persevere, they finally obeyed, and returned to the land, where they filled the air with their cries.

In the mean time, the deer, urged by his fears, had swam over half the distance between the shore and the boats, before his terror permitted him to see the new danger. But at the sounds of Natty's voice he turned short in his course, and, for a few moments, seemed about to rush back again, and brave the dogs. His retreat in this direction was, however, effectually cut off, and, turning a second time, he urged his course obliquely for the centre of the lake, with an intention of landing on the western shore. As the buck swam by the fishermen, raising his nose high into the air, curling the water before his slim neck like the beak of a galley, the Leather-stocking began to sit very uneasy in his canoe.

" 'Tis a noble creater!" he exclaimed; "what a pair of horns! a man might hang up all his garments on the branches. Lets me see—July is the last month, and the flesh must be getting good." While he was talking, Natty had instinctively employed himself in fastening the inner end of the bark rope, that served him for a cable, to a paddle, and, rising suddenly on his legs, he cast this buoy away, and cried—"Strike out, John! let her go. The creater's a fool, to tempt a man in this way."

Mohegan threw the fastening of the youth's boat from the canoe, and with one stroke of his paddle, sent the light bark over the water like a meteor.

"Hold!" exclaimed Edwards. "Remember the law, my old friends. You are in plain sight of the village, and I know that Judge Temple is determined to prosecute all, indiscriminately, who kill deer out of season."

The remonstrance came too late; the canoe was already far from the skiff, and the two hunters were too much engaged in the pursuit to listen to his voice.

The buck was now within fifty yards of his pursuers, cutting the water gallantly, and snorting at each breath with terror and his exertions, while the canoe seemed to dance over the waves, as it rose and fell with the undulations made by its own motion. Leather-stocking raised his rifle and freshened the priming, but stood in suspense whether to slay his victim or not.

"Shall I, John, or no?" he said. "It seems but a poor advantage to take of the dumb thing, too. I won't; it has taken to the water on its own nater, which is the reason that God has given to a deer, and I'll give it the lake play; so, John, lay out your arm, and mind the turn of the buck; it's easy to catch them, but they'll turn like a snake."

The Indian laughed at the conceit of his friend, but continued to send the canoe forward, with a velocity that proceeded much more from his skill than his strength. Both of the old men now used the language of the Delawares when they spoke.

"Hooh!" exclaimed Mohegan; "the deer turns his head. Hawk-eye, lift your spear."

Natty never moved abroad without taking with him every implement that might, by possibility, be of service in his pursuits. From his rifle he never parted; and, although intending to fish with the line, the canoe was invariably furnished with all its utensils, even to its grate. This precaution grew out of the habits of the hunter, who was often led, by his necessities or his sports, far beyond the limits of his original destination. A few years earlier than the date of our tale, the Leather-stocking had left his hut on the shores of the Otsego, with his rifle and his hounds, for a few days' hunting in the hills; but before he returned, he had seen the waters of Ontario. One, two, or even three hundred miles, had once been nothing to his sinews, which were now a little stiffened by age. The hunter did as Mohegan advised, and prepared to strike a blow with the barbed weapon into the neck of the buck.

"Lay her more to the left, John," he cried, "lay her more to the left; another stroke of the paddle, and I have him."

While speaking, he raised the spear, and darted it from him like an arrow. At that instant the buck turned. The long pole glanced by him, the iron striking against his horn, and buried itself, harmlessly, in the lake.

"Back water," cried Natty, as the canoe glided over the place where the spear had fallen, "hold water, John."

The pole soon re-appeared, shooting upward from the lake, and as the hunter seized it in his hand, the Indian whirled the light canoe round, and renewed the chase. But this evolution gave the buck a great advantage; and it also allowed time for Edwards to approach the scene of action.

"Hold your hand, Natty," cried the youth, "hold your hand; remember it is out of season."

This remonstrance was made as the batteau arrived close to the place where the deer was struggling with the water, his back now rising to the surface, now sinking beneath it, as the waves curled from his neck, the animal still sustaining itself nobly against the odds.

"Hurrah!" shouted Edwards, inflamed beyond prudence at the sight; "mind him as he doubles—mind him as he doubles; sheer more to the right, Mohegan, more to the right, and I'll have him by the horns; I'll throw the rope over his antlers."

The dark eye of the old warrior was dancing in his head, with a wild animation, and the sluggish repose in which his aged frame had been resting in the canoe, was now changed to all the rapid inflections of practised agility. The canoe whirled, with each cunning evolution of the chase, like a bubble floating in a whirlpool; and when the direction of the pursuit admitted of a straight course, the little bark skimmed the lake with a velocity, that urged the deer to seek its safety in some new turn. The frequency of these circuitous movements, by confining the action to so small a compass, enabled the youth to keep near his companions. More than twenty times both the pursued and the pursuers glided by him, just without the reach of his oars, until he thought the best way to view the sport was to remain stationary, and, by watching a favourable opportunity, assist as much as he could in taking the victim.

He was not required to wait long, for no sooner had he adopted this resolution, and risen in the boat, than he saw the deer coming bravely towards him, with an apparent intention of pushing for a point of land at some distance from the hounds, which were still barking and howling on the shore. Edwards caught the painter of his skiff, and, making a noose, cast it from him with all his force, and luckily succeeded in drawing its knot close around one of the antlers of the buck.

For one instant, the skiff was drawn through the water, but in the next, the canoe glided before it, and Natty, bending low, passed his knife across the throat of the animal, whose blood followed the wound, dying the waters. The short time that was passed in the last struggles of the animal, was spent by the hunters in bringing their boats together, and securing them in that position; when Leather-stocking drew the deer from the water, and laid its lifeless form in the bottom of the canoe. He placed his hands on the ribs, and on different parts of the body of his prize, and then, raising his head, he laughed in his peculiar manner—

"So much for Marmaduke Temple's law!" he said. "This warms a body's blood, old John; I haven't killed a buck in the lake afore this, sin' many a year. I call that good venison, lad; and I know them that will relish the creater's steaks, for all the betterments in the land."

The Indian had long been drooping with his years, and perhaps under the calamities of his race, but this invigorating and exciting sport caused a gleam of sunshine to cross his swarthy face, that had long been absent from his features. It was evident the old man enjoyed the chase more as a memorial of his youthful sports and deeds, than with any expectation of profiting by the success. He felt the deer, however, lightly, his hand already trembling with the re-action of his unusual exertions, and smiled with a nod of approbation, as he said, in the emphatic and sententious manner of his people—

"Good."

"I am afraid, Natty," said Edwards, when the heat of the moment had passed, and his blood began to cool, "that we have all been equally transgressors of the law. But keep your own counsel, and there are none here to betray us. Yet, how came those dogs at large? I left them securely fastened, I know, for I felt the thongs, and examined the knots, when I was at the hut."

"It has been too much for the poor things," said Natty, "to have such a buck take the wind of them. See, lad, the pieces of the buck-skin are hanging from their necks yet. Let us paddle up, John, and I will call them in, and look a little into the matter."

When the old hunter landed, and examined the thongs that were yet fast to the hounds, his countenance sensibly changed, and he shook his head doubtingly.

"Here has been a knife at work," he said—"this skin was never torn, nor is this the mark of a hound's tooth. No, no—Hector is not in fault, as I feared."

"Has the leather been cut?" cried Edwards.

"No, no—I didn't say it had been cut, lad; but this is a mark that was never made by a jump or a bite."

"Could that rascally carpenter have dared!"

"Ay! he durst to do any thing when there is no danger," said Natty; "he is a curous body, and loves to be helping other people on with their concarns. But he had best not harbour so much near the wigwam."

In the mean time, Mohegan had been examining, with an Indian's sagacity, the place where the leather thong had been separated. After scrutinizing it closely, he said, in Delaware—

"It was cut with a knife—a sharp blade and a long handle—the man was afraid of the dogs."

"How is this, Mohegan!" exclaimed Edwards; "You saw it not! how can you know these facts?"

"Listen, son," said the warrior. "The knife was sharp, for the cut is smooth;—the handle was long, for a man's arm would not reach from this gash to the cut that did not go through the skin;—he was a coward, or he would have cut the thongs around the necks of the hounds."

"On my life," cried Natty, "John is on the scent! It was the carpenter; and he has got on the rock back of the kennel, and let the dogs loose by fastening his knife to a stick. It would be an easy matter to do it, where a man is so minded."

"And why should he do so?" asked Edwards; "who has done him wrong, that he should trouble two old men like you?"

"It's a hard matter, lad, to know men's ways, I find, since the settlers have brought in their new fashions. But is there nothing to be found out in the place? and maybe he is troubled with his longings after other people's business, as he often is."

"Your suspicions are just. Give me the canoe: I am young and strong, and will get down there yet, perhaps, in time to interrupt his plans. Heaven forbid, that we should be at the mercy of such a man!"

His proposal was accepted, the deer being placed in the skiff in order to lighten the canoe, and in less than five minutes the little vessel of bark was gliding over the glassy lake, and was soon hid by the points of land, as it shot close along the shore.

Mohegan followed slowly with the skiff, while Natty called his hounds to him, bade them keep close, and, shouldering his rifle, he ascended the mountain, with an intention of going to the hut by land.

Chapter XXVIII.

"Ask me not what the maiden feels,
    Left in that dreadful hour alone;
Perchance, her reason stoops, or reels;
    Perchance, a courage not her own,
    Braces her mind to desperate tone."
                    Scott, *Marmion*, VI.xxix.1–5.

WHILE the chase was occurring on the lake, Miss Temple and her companion pursued their walk on the mountain. Male attendants, on such excursions, were thought to be altogether unnecessary, for none were ever known to offer an insult to a female who respected herself. After the embarrassment, created by the parting discourse with Edwards, had dissipated, the girls maintained a conversation that was as innocent and cheerful as themselves.

The path they took led them but a short distance above the hut of Leather-stocking, and there was a point in the road which commanded a bird's-eye view of the sequestered spot.

From a feeling, that might have been natural, and must have been powerful, neither of the friends, in their frequent and confidential dialogues, had ever trusted herself to utter one syllable concerning the equivocal situation in which the young man, who was now so intimately associated with them, had been found. If Judge Temple had deemed it prudent to make any inquiries on the subject, he had also thought it proper to keep the answers to himself; though it was so common an occurrence to find the well-educated youth of the eastern states, in every stage of their career to wealth, that the simple circumstance of his intelligence, connected with his poverty, would not, at that day, and in that country, have excited any very powerful curiosity. With his breeding it might have been different; but the youth himself had so effectually guarded against surprise on this subject, by his cold, and even, in some cases, rude deportment, that when his manners seemed to soften by time, the Judge, if he thought about it at all, would have been most likely to imagine that the improvement was the result of his late association. But women are always more alive to such subjects than men; and what the abstraction of the father had overlooked, the observation of the daughter had easily detected. In the thousand little courtesies of polished life, she had early discovered that Edwards was not wanting, though his gentleness was so often crossed by marks of what she conceived to be fierce and uncontrollable passions. It may, perhaps, be unnecessary to tell the reader that Louisa Grant never reasoned so much after the fashions of the world. The gentle girl, however, had her own thoughts on the subject, and, like others, she drew her own conclusions.

"I would give all my other secrets, Louisa," exclaimed Miss Temple, laughing, and shaking back her dark locks, with a look of childish simplicity that her intelligent face seldom expressed, "to be mistress of all that those rude logs have heard and witnessed."

They were both looking at the secluded hut, at the instant, and Miss Grant raised her mild eyes, as she answered—

"I am sure they would tell nothing to the disadvantage of Mr. Edwards."

"Perhaps not; but they might, at least, tell who he is."

"Why, dear Miss Temple, we know all that already. I have heard it all very rationally explained by your cousin"—

"The executive chief! he can explain any thing. His ingenuity will one day discover the philosopher's stone. But what did he say?"

"Say!" echoed Louisa, with a look of surprise; "why every thing that seemed to me to be satisfactory; and I have believed it to be true. He said that Natty Bumppo had lived most of his life in the woods, and among the Indians, by which means he had formed an acquaintance with old John, the Delaware chief."

"Indeed! that was quite a matter of fact tale for cousin Dickon. What came next?"

"I believe he accounted for their close intimacy, by some story about the Leather-stocking saving the life of John in a battle."

"Nothing more likely," said Elizabeth, a little impatiently; "but what is all this to the purpose?"

"Nay, Elizabeth, you must bear with my ignorance, and I will repeat all that I remember to have overheard; for the dialogue was between my father and the Sheriff, so lately as the last time they met. He then added, that the kings of England used to keep gentlemen as agents among the different tribes of Indians, and sometimes officers in the army, who frequently passed half their lives on the edge of the wilderness."

"Told with wonderful historical accuracy! And did he end there?"

"Oh! no—then he said that these agents seldom married; and—and—they must have been wicked men, Elizabeth! but I assure you he said so."

"Never mind," said Miss Temple, blushing and smiling, though so slightly that both were unheeded by her companion—"skip all that."

"Well, then he said that they often took great pride in the education of their children, whom they frequently sent to England, and even to the colleges; and this is the way that he accounts for the liberal manner in which Mr. Edwards has been taught; for he acknowledges that he knows almost as much as your father—or mine—or even himself!"

"Quite a climax in learning! And so he made Mohegan the grand-uncle or grandfather of Oliver Edwards."

"You have heard him yourself, then?" said Louisa.

"Often; but not on this subject. Mr. Richard Jones, you know, dear, has a theory for every thing; but has he one which will explain the reason why that hut is the only habitation within fifty miles of us, whose door is not open to every person who may choose to lift its latch?"

"I have never heard him say any thing on this subject," returned the clergyman's daughter; "but I suppose that, as they are poor, they very naturally are anxious to keep the little that they honestly own. It is sometimes dangerous to be rich, Miss Temple; but you cannot know how hard it is to be very, very poor."

"Nor you, I trust, Louisa; at least I should hope, that in this land of abundance, no minister of the church could be left to absolute suffering."

"There cannot be actual misery," returned the other, in a low and humble tone, "where there is a dependence on our Maker;

but there may be such suffering as will cause the heart to ache."

"But not you—not you," said the impetuous Elizabeth—"not you, dear girl; you have never known the misery that is connected with poverty."

"Ah! Miss Temple, you little understand the troubles of this life, I believe. My father has spent many years as a missionary, in the new countries, where his people were poor, and frequently we have been without bread; unable to buy, and ashamed to beg, because we would not disgrace his sacred calling. But how often have I seen him leave his home, where the sick and the hungry felt, when he left them, that they had lost their only earthly friend, to ride on a duty which could not be neglected for domestic evils. Oh! how hard it must be, to preach consolation to others, when your own heart is bursting with anguish!"

"But it is all over now! your father's income must now be equal to his wants—it must be—it shall be"—

"It is," replied Louisa, dropping her head on her bosom to conceal the tears which flowed in spite of her gentle Christianity, "for there are none left to be supplied but me."

The turn the conversation had taken drove from the minds of the young maidens all other thoughts but those of holy charity, and Elizabeth folded her friend in her arms, when the latter gave vent to her momentary grief in audible sobs. When this burst of emotion had subsided, Louisa raised her mild countenance, and they continued their walk in silence.

By this time they had gained the summit of the mountain, where they left the highway, and pursued their course, under the shade of the stately trees that crowned the eminence. The day was becoming warm, and the girls plunged more deeply into the forest, as they found its invigorating coolness agreeably contrasted to the excessive heat they had experienced in the ascent. The conversation, as if by mutual consent, was entirely changed to the little incidents and scenes of their walk, and every tall pine, and every shrub or flower, called forth some simple expression of admiration.

In this manner they proceeded along the margin of the precipice, catching occasional glimpses of the placid Otsego, or pausing to listen to the rattling of wheels and the sounds of hammers, that rose from the valley, to mingle the signs of men with the scenes of nature, when Elizabeth suddenly started, and exclaimed—

"Listen! there are the cries of a child on this mountain! is there a clearing near us? or can some little one have strayed from its parents?"

"Such things frequently happen," returned Louisa. "Let us follow the sounds; it may be a wanderer, starving on the hill."

Urged by this consideration, the females pursued the low, mournful sounds, that proceeded from the forest, with quick and impatient steps. More than once, the ardent Elizabeth was on the point of announcing that she saw the sufferer, when Louisa caught her by the arm, and pointing behind them, cried—

"Look at the dog!"

Brave had been their companion, from the time the voice of his young mistress lured him from his kennel, to the present moment. His advanced age had long before deprived him of his activity; and when his companions stopped to view the scenery, or to add to their bouquets, the mastiff would lay his huge frame on the ground, and await their movements, with his eyes closed, and a listlessness in his air that ill accorded with the character of a protector. But when, aroused by this cry from Louisa, Miss Temple turned, she saw the dog with his eyes keenly set on some distant object, his head bent near the ground, and his hair actually rising on his body, through fright or anger. It was most probably the latter, for he was growling in a low key, and occasionally showing his teeth, in a manner that would have terrified his mistress, had she not so well known his good qualities.

"Brave!" she said, "be quiet, Brave! what do you see, fellow?"

At the sounds of her voice, the rage of the mastiff, instead of being at all diminished, was very sensibly increased. He stalked in front of the ladies, and seated himself at the feet of his mistress, growling louder than before, and occasionally giving vent to his ire by a short, surly barking.

"What does he see?" said Elizabeth; "there must be some animal in sight."

Hearing no answer from her companion, Miss Temple turned her head, and beheld Louisa, standing with her face whitened to the colour of death, and her finger pointing upward, with a sort of flickering, convulsed motion. The quick eye of Elizabeth glanced in the direction indicated by her friend, where she saw the fierce front and glaring eyes of a female panther, fixed on them in horrid malignity, and threatening to leap.

"Let us fly!" exclaimed Elizabeth, grasping the arm of Louisa, whose form yielded like melting snow.

There was not a single feeling in the temperament of Elizabeth Temple, that could prompt her to desert a companion in such an extremity. She fell on her knees, by the side of the inanimate Louisa, tearing from the person of her friend, with instinctive readiness, such parts of her dress as might obstruct her respiration, and encouraging their only safeguard, the dog, at the same time, by the sounds of her voice.

"Courage, Brave," she cried, her own tones beginning to tremble, "courage, courage, good Brave."

A quarter-grown cub, that had hitherto been unseen, now appeared, dropping from the branches of a sapling, that grew under the shade of the beech which held its dam. This ignorant, but vitious creature, approached the dog, imitating the actions and sounds of its parent, but exhibiting a strange mixture of the playfulness of a kitten with the ferocity of its race.——Standing on its hind legs, it would rend the bark of a tree with its fore paws, and play the antics of a cat; and then, by lashing itself with its tail, growling, and scratching the earth, it would attempt the manifestations of anger that rendered its parent so terrific.

All this time Brave stood firm and undaunted, his short tail erect, his body drawn backward on its haunches, and his eyes following the movements of both dam and cub. At every gambol played by the latter, it approached nigher to the dog, the growling of the three becoming more horrid at each moment, until the younger beast overleaping its intended bound, fell directly before the mastiff. There was a moment of fearful cries and struggles, but they ended almost as soon as commenced, by the cub appearing in the air, hurled from the jaws of Brave, with a violence that sent it against a tree so forcibly, as to render it completely senseless.

Elizabeth witnessed the short struggle, and her blood was

warming with the triumph of the dog, when she saw the form of the old panther in the air, springing twenty feet from the branch of the beech to the back of the mastiff. No words of ours can describe the fury of the conflict that followed. It was a confused struggle on the dried leaves, accompanied by loud and terrific cries. Miss Temple continued on her knees, bending over the form of Louisa, her eyes fixed on the animals, with an interest so horrid, and yet so intense, that she almost forgot her own stake in the result. So rapid and vigorous were the bounds of the inhabitant of the forest, that its active frame seemed constantly in the air, while the dog nobly faced his foe, at each successive leap. When the panther lighted on the shoulders of the mastiff, which was its constant aim, old Brave, though torn with her talons, and stained with his own blood, that already flowed from a dozen wounds, would shake off his furious foe, like a feather, and rearing on his hind legs, rush to the fray again, with jaws distended, and a dauntless eye. But age, and his pampered life, greatly disqualified the noble mastiff for such a struggle. In every thing but courage, he was only the vestige of what he had once been. A higher bound than ever, raised the wary and furious beast far beyond the reach of the dog, who was making a desperate, but fruitless dash at her, from which she alighted in a favourable position, on the back of her aged foe. For a single moment, only, could the panther remain there, the great strength of the dog returning with a convulsive effort. But Elizabeth saw, as Brave fastened his teeth in the side of his enemy, that the collar of brass around his neck, which had been glittering throughout the fray, was of the colour of blood, and directly, that his frame was sinking to the earth, where it soon lay prostrate and helpless. Several mighty efforts of the wild-cat to extricate herself from the jaws of the dog, followed, but they were fruitless, until the mastiff turned on his back, his lips collapsed, and his teeth loosened; when the short convulsions and stillness that succeeded, announced the death of poor Brave.

Elizabeth now lay wholly at the mercy of the beast. There is said to be something in the front of the image of the Maker, that daunts the hearts of the inferior beings of his creation; and it would seem that some such power, in the present instance, suspended the threatened blow. The eyes of the monster and

IX. *The Panther Scene (c. 1832) by Robert Farrier.*

x. *Leatherstocking's Rescue (1832) by John Quidor.*

XI. *Leatherstocking Kills the Panther* (1834) *by George Loring Brown.*

XII. *The Panther Scene (1826–1833?) by Alexis François Girard.*

the kneeling maiden met, for an instant, when the former stooped to examine her fallen foe; next to scent her luckless cub. From the latter examination it turned, however, with its eyes apparently emitting flashes of fire, its tail lashing its sides furiously, and its claws projecting inches from its broad feet.

Miss Temple did not, or could not move. Her hands were clasped in the attitude of prayer, but her eyes were still drawn to her terrible enemy; her cheeks were blanched to the whiteness of marble, and her lips were slightly separated with horror. The moment seemed now to have arrived for the fatal termination, and the beautiful figure of Elizabeth was bowing meekly to the stroke, when a rustling of leaves behind seemed rather to mock the organs, than to meet her ears.

"Hist! hist!" said a low voice—"stoop lower, gall; your bunnet hides the creater's head."

It was rather the yielding of nature than a compliance with this unexpected order, that caused the head of our heroine to sink on her bosom; when she heard the report of the rifle, the whizzing of the bullet, and the enraged cries of the beast, who was rolling over on the earth, biting its own flesh, and tearing the twigs and branches within its reach. At the next instant the form of the Leather-stocking rushed by her, and he called aloud—

"Come in, Hector, come in, old fool; 'tis a hard-lived animal, and may jump ag'in."

Natty fearlessly maintained his position in front of the females, notwithstanding the violent bounds and threatening aspect of the wounded panther, which gave several indications of returning strength and ferocity, until his rifle was again loaded, when he stepped up to the enraged animal, and, placing the muzzle close to its head, every spark of life was extinguished by the discharge.

The death of her terrible enemy appeared to Elizabeth like a resurrection from her own grave. There was an elasticity in the mind of our heroine, that rose to meet the pressure of instant danger, and the more direct it had been, the more her nature had struggled to overcome it. But still she was a woman. Had she been left to herself, in her late extremity, she would probably have used her faculties to the utmost, and with discretion, in protecting her person, but encumbered with her inanimate friend, retreat was a thing not to be attempted.—Notwithstanding the fearful aspect of her foe, the eye of Elizabeth had never shrunk from its gaze, and long after the event, her thoughts would recur to her passing sensations, and the sweetness of her midnight sleep would be disturbed, as her active fancy conjured, in dreams, the most trifling movements of savage fury, that the beast had exhibited in its moment of power.

We shall leave the reader to imagine the restoration of Louisa's senses, and the expressions of gratitude which fell from the young women. The former was effected by a little water, that was brought from one of the thousand springs of those mountains, in the cap of the Leather-stocking; and the latter were uttered with the warmth that might be expected from the character of Elizabeth.——Natty received her vehement protestations of gratitude, with a simple expression of good will, and with indulgence for her present excitement, but with a carelessness that showed how little he thought of the service he had rendered.

"Well, well," he said, "be it so, gall; let it be so, if you wish it,—we'll talk the thing over another time. Come, come—let us get into the road, for you've had tirror enough to make you wish yourself in your father's house ag'in."

This was uttered as they were proceeding, at a pace that was adapted to the weakness of Louisa, towards the highway; on reaching which the ladies separated from their guide, declaring themselves equal to the remainder of the walk without his assistance, and feeling encouraged by the sight of the village, which lay beneath their feet, like a picture, with its limpid lake in front, the winding stream along its margin, and its hundred chimneys of whitened bricks.

The reader need not be told the nature of the emotions, which two youthful, ingenuous, and well-educated girls would experience, at their escape from a death so horrid as the one which had impended over them, while they pursued their way in silence along the track on the side of the mountain; nor how deep were their mental thanks to that Power which had given them their existence, and which had not deserted them in their extremity; neither how often they pressed each other's arms, as the assurance of their present safety came, like a healing balm, athwart their troubled spirits, when their thoughts were recurring to the recent moments of horror.

Leather-stocking remained on the hill, gazing after their retiring figures, until they were hid by a bend in the road, when he whistled in his dogs, and, shouldering his rifle, he returned into the forest.

"Well, it was a skeary thing to the young creaters," said Natty, while he retrod the path towards the slain. "It might frighten an older woman, to see a she-painter so near her, with a dead cub by its side. I wonder if I had aimed at the varmint's eye, if I shouldn't have touched the life sooner than in the forehead? but they are hard-lived animals, and it was a good shot, consid'ring that I could see nothing but the head and the peak of its tail. Ha! who goes there?"

"How goes it, Natty?" said Mr. Doolittle, stepping out of the bushes, with a motion that was a good deal accelerated by the sight of the rifle, that was already lowered in his direction. "What! shooting this warm day! mind old man, the law don't get hold on you."

"The law, Squire! I have shook hands with the law these forty year," returned Natty; "for what has a man who lives in the wilderness to do with the ways of the law?"

"Not much, maybe," said Hiram; "but you sometimes trade in ven'son. I s'pose you know, Leather-stocking, that there is an act passed to lay a fine of five pounds currency, or twelve dollars and fifty cents, by dicimals, on every man who kills a deer betwixt January and August. The Judge had a great hand in getting the law through."

"I can believe it," returned the old hunter; "I can believe that, or any thing, of a man who carries on as he does in the country."

"Yes, the law is quite positive, and the Judge is bent on putting it in force—five pounds penalty. I thought I heerd your hounds out on the scent of so'thing this morning: I didn't know but they might get you in difficulty."

"They know their manners too well," said Natty, carelessly. "And how much goes to the state's evidence, Squire?"

"How much!" repeated Hiram, quailing under the honest, but sharp look of the hunter—"the informer gets half, I—I b'lieve;—yes, I guess it's half. But there's blood on your sleeve, man;—you haven't been shooting any thing this morning?"

"I have, though," said the hunter, nodding his head significantly to the other, "and a good shot I made of it."

"He-e-m!" ejaculated the magistrate; "and where is the game? I s'pose it's of a good nater, for your dogs won't hunt any thing that isn't choish."

"They'll hunt any thing I tell them to, Squire," cried Natty, favouring the other with his laugh. "They'll hunt you, if I say so. He-e-e-re, he-e-e-re, Hector—he-e-e-re, slut—come this a-way, pups—come this a-way—come hither."

"Oh! I've always heern a good character of the dogs," returned Mr. Doolittle, quickening his pace by raising each leg in rapid succession, as the hounds scented around his person. "And where is the game, Leather-stocking?"

During this dialogue, the speakers had been walking at a very fast gait, and Natty swung the end of his rifle round, pointing through the bushes, and replied—

"There lays one. How do you like such meat?"

"This!" exclaimed Hiram, "why this is Judge Temple's dog Brave. Take kear, Leather-stocking, and don't make an inimy of the Judge. I hope you haven't harmed the animal?"

"Look for yourself, Mr. Doolittle," said Natty, drawing his knife from his girdle, and wiping it, in a knowing manner, once or twice across his garment of buck-skin; "does his throat look as if I had cut it with this knife?"

"It is dreadfully tore! it's an awful wownd!—no knife never did this deed. Who could have done it?"

"The painters behind you, Squire."

"Painters!" echoed Hiram, whirling on his heel, with an agility that would have done credit to a dancing master.

"Be easy, man," said Natty; "there's two of the vinimous things; but the dog finished one, and I have fastened the other's jaws for her; so don't be frightened, Squire; they won't hurt you."

"And where's the deer?" cried Hiram, staring about him with a bewildered air.

"Anan! deer!" repeated Natty.

"Sartain; an't there ven'son here, or didn't you kill a buck?"

"What! when the law forbids the thing, Squire!" said the old hunter. "I hope there's no law ag'in killing the painters."

"No; there's a bounty on the scalps—but—will your dogs hunt painters, Natty?"

"Any thing; didn't I tell you they'd hunt a man? He-e-re, he-e-re, pups"——

"Yes, yes, I remember. Well, they are strange dogs, I must say—I am quite in a wonderment."

Natty had seated himself on the ground, and having laid the grim head of his late ferocious enemy in his lap, was drawing his knife, with a practised hand, around the ears, which he tore from the head of the beast in such a manner as to preserve their connexion, when he answered—

"What at, Squire? did you never see a painter's scalp afore? Come, you be a magistrate. I wish you'd make me out an order for the bounty."

"The bounty!" repeated Hiram, holding the ears on the end of his finger, for a moment, as if uncertain how to proceed. "Well, let us go down to your hut, where you can take the oath, and I will write out the order. I s'pose you have a bible? all the law wants is the four evangelists and the Lord's prayer."

"I keep no books," said Natty, a little coldly; "not such a bible as the law needs."

"Oh! there's but one sort of bible that's good in law," returned the magistrate; "and yourn will do as well as another's. Come, the carcasses are worth nothing, man; let us go down and take the oath."

"Softly, softly, Squire," said the hunter, lifting his trophies very deliberately from the ground, and shouldering his rifle; "why do you want an oath at all, for a thing that your own eyes has seen? won't you believe yourself, that another man must swear to a fact that you know to be true? You have seen me scalp the creaters, and if I must swear to it, it shall be before Judge Temple, who needs an oath."

"But we have no pen or paper here, Leather-stocking; we must go to the hut for them, or how can I write the order?"

Natty turned his simple features on the cunning magistrate with another of his laughs, as he said—

"And what should I be doing with scholar's tools? I want no

pens or paper, not knowing the use of 'ither; and I keep none. No, no, I'll bring the scalps into the village, Squire, and you can make out the order on one of your law-books, and it will be all the better for it. The deuce take this leather on the neck of the dog, it will strangle the old fool. Can you lend me a knife, Squire?"

Hiram, who seemed particularly anxious to be on good terms with his companion, unhesitatingly complied. Natty cut the thong from the neck of the hound, and, as he returned the knife to its owner, carelessly remarked—

" 'Tis a good bit of steel, and has cut such leather as this very same before now, I dare to say."

"Do you mean to charge me with letting your hounds loose!" exclaimed Hiram, with a consciousness that disarmed his caution.

"Loose!" repeated the hunter—"I let them loose myself. I always let them loose before I leave the hut."

The ungovernable amazement with which Mr. Doolittle listened to this falsehood, would have betrayed his agency in the liberation of the dogs, had Natty wanted any further confirmation; and the coolness and management of the old man now disappeared in open indignation.

"Look you here, Mr. Doolittle," he said, striking the breech of his rifle violently on the ground: "what there is in the wigwam of a poor man like me, that one like you can crave, I don't know; but this I tell you to your face, that you never shall put foot under the roof of my cabin with my consent, and that if you harbour round the spot as you have done lately, you may meet with treatment that you will little relish."

"And let me tell you, Mr. Bumppo," said Hiram, retreating, however, with a quick step, "that I know you've broke the law, and that I'm a magistrate, and will make you feel it too, before you are a day older."

"That for you and your law too," cried Natty, snapping his fingers at the justice of the peace—"away with you, you varmint, before the divil tempts me to give you your desarts. Take kear, if I ever catch your prowling face in the woods ag'in, that I don't shoot it for an owl."

There is something at all times commanding in honest indignation, and Hiram did not stay to provoke the wrath of the old hunter to extremities. When the intruder was out of sight, Natty proceeded to the hut, where he found all quiet as the grave. He fastened his dogs, and tapping at the door, which was opened by Edwards, asked—

"Is all safe, lad?"

"Every thing," returned the youth. "Some one attempted the lock, but it was too strong for him."

"I know the creater," said Natty; "but he'll not trust himself within reach of my rifle very soon—" What more was uttered by the Leather-stocking, in his vexation, was rendered inaudible by the closing of the door of the cabin.

Chapter XXIX.

"It is noised, he hath a mass of treasure."
                    Timon of Athens, IV.iii.402.

WHEN Marmaduke Temple and his cousin rode through the gate of the former, the heart of the father had been too recently touched with the best feelings of our nature, to leave inclination for immediate discourse. There was an importance in the air of Richard, which would not have admitted of the ordinary informal conversation of the Sheriff, without violating all the rules of consistency; and the equestrians pursued their way with great diligence, for more than a mile, in profound silence. At length the soft expression of parental affection was slowly chased from the handsome features of the Judge, and was gradually supplanted by the cast of humour and benevolence that was usually seated on his brow.

"Well, Dickon," he said, "since I have yielded myself, so far, implicitly to your guidance, I think the moment has arrived, when I am entitled to further confidence. Why and wherefore are we journeying together in this solemn gait?"

The Sheriff gave a loud hem, that rung far in the forest, and keeping his eyes fixed on objects before him, like a man who is looking deep into futurity—

"There has always been one point of difference between us, Judge Temple, I may say, since our nativity," he replied; "not that I would insinuate that you are at all answerable for the acts of nature; for a man is no more to be condemned for the misfortunes of his birth, than he is to be commended for the natural advantages he may possess; but on one point we may be said to have differed from our births, and they, you know, occurred within two days of each other."

"I really marvel, Richard, what this one point can be; for, to my eyes, we seem to differ so materially, and so often"——

"Mere consequences, sir," interrupted the Sheriff; "all our minor differences proceed from one cause, and that is, our opinions of the universal attainments of genius."

"In what, Dickon?"

"I speak plain English, I believe, Judge Temple; at least I ought; for my father, who taught me, could speak"——

"Greek and Latin," interrupted Marmaduke—"I well know the qualifications of your family in tongues, Dickon. But proceed to the point; why are we travelling over this mountain to-day?"

"To do justice to any subject, sir, the narrator must be suffered to proceed in his own way," continued the Sheriff. "You are of opinion, Judge Temple, that a man is to be qualified by nature and education to do only one thing well, whereas I know that genius will supply the place of learning, and that a certain sort of man can do any thing and every thing."

"Like yourself, I suppose," said Marmaduke, smiling.

"I scorn personalities, sir, I say nothing of myself; but there are three men on your Patent, of the kind that I should term talented by nature, for her general purposes, though acting under the influence of different situations."

"We are better off, then, than I had supposed. Who are these triumviri?"

"Why, sir, one is Hiram Doolittle; a carpenter by trade, as you know, and I need only to point to the village to exhibit his merits. Then he is a magistrate, and might shame many a man, in his distribution of justice, who has had better opportunities."

"Well, he is one," said Marmaduke, with the air of a man that was determined not to dispute the point.

"Jotham Riddel is another."

"Who?"

"Jotham Riddel."

"What, that dissatisfied, shiftless, lazy, speculating fellow! he who changes his county every three years, his farm every six months, and his occupation every season! an agriculturist yesterday, a shoemaker to-day, and a schoolmaster to-morrow! that epitome of all the unsteady and profitless propensities of the settlers, without one of their good qualities to counterbalance the evil! Nay, Richard, this is too bad for even——but the third?"

"As the third is not used to hearing such comments on his character, Judge Temple, I shall not name him."

"The amount of all this, then, Dickon, is, that the trio, of

which you are one, and the principal, have made some important discovery."

"I have not said that I am one, Judge Temple. As I told you
before, I say nothing egotistical. But a discovery has been made,
and you are deeply interested in it."

"Proceed—I am all ears."

"No, no, 'duke, you are bad enough, I own, but not so bad as
that either; your ears are not quite full grown."

The Sheriff laughed heartily at his own wit, and put himself
in good humour thereby, when he gratified his patient cousin
with the following explanation:—

"You know, 'duke, there is a man living on your estate, that
goes by the name of Natty Bumppo. Here has this man lived, by
what I can learn, for more than forty years—by himself, until
lately; and now with strange companions."

"Part very true, and all very probable," said the Judge.

"All true, sir; all true. Well, within these last few months have
appeared as his companions, an old Indian chief, the last, or
one of the last of his tribe, that is to be found in this part of the
country, and a young man, who is said to be the son of some
Indian agent, by a squaw."

"Who says that!" cried Marmaduke, with an interest that he
had not manifested before.

"Who! why common sense—common report—the hue and
cry. But listen, till you know all. This youth has very pretty
talents—yes, what I call very pretty talents—and has been well
educated, has seen very tolerable company, and knows how to
behave himself, when he has a mind to. Now, Judge Temple,
can you tell me what has brought three such men as Indian
John, Natty Bumppo, and Oliver Edwards, together?"

Marmaduke turned his countenance, in evident surprise, to
his cousin, and replied quickly—

"Thou hast unexpectedly hit on a subject, Richard, that has
often occupied my mind. But knowest thou any thing of this
mystery, or are they only the crude conjectures of"——

"Crude nothing, 'duke, crude nothing; but facts, stubborn
facts. You know there are mines in these mountains; I have
often heard you say that you believed in their existence"——

"Reasoning from analogy, Richard, but not with any certainty
of the fact."

"You have heard them mentioned, and have seen specimens of the ore, sir; you will not deny that! and, reasoning from analogy, as you say, if there be mines in South America, ought there not to be mines in North America too?"

"Nay, nay, I deny nothing, my cousin. I certainly have heard many rumours of the existence of mines, in these hills; and I do believe that I have seen specimens of the precious metals that have been found here. It would occasion me no surprise to learn that tin and silver, or, what I consider of more consequence, good coal,"——

"Damn your coal," cried the Sheriff; "who wants to find coal, in these forests? No, no, silver, 'duke; silver is the one thing needful, and silver is to be found. But listen: you are not to be told that the natives have long known the use of gold and silver; now who so likely to be acquainted where they are to be found, as the ancient inhabitants of a country? I have the best reasons for believing that both Mohegan and the Leather-stocking have been privy to the existence of a mine, in this very mountain, for many years."

The Sheriff had now touched his cousin in a sensitive spot, and Marmaduke lent a more attentive ear to the speaker, who, after waiting a moment, to see the effect of this extraordinary development, proceeded—

"Yes, sir, I have my reasons, and at a proper time you shall know them."

"No time is so good as the present."

"Well, well, be attentive," continued Richard, looking cautiously about him, to make certain that no eavesdropper was hid in the forest, though they were in constant motion. "I have seen Mohegan and the Leather-stocking, with my own eyes— and my eyes are as good as any body's eyes—I have seen them, I say, both going up the mountain and coming down it, with spades and picks; and others have seen them carrying things into their hut, in a secret and mysterious manner, after dark. Do you call this a fact of importance?"

The Judge did not reply, but his brow had contracted, with a thoughtfulness that he always wore when much interested, and his eyes rested on his cousin in expectation of hearing more. Richard continued—

"It was ore. Now, sir, I ask if you can tell me who this Mr.

Oliver Edwards is, that has made a part of your household since Christmas?"

Marmaduke again raised his eyes, but continued silent, shaking his head in the negative.

"That he is a half-breed we know, for Mohegan does not scruple to call him, openly, his kinsman; that he is well educated we know. But as to his business here—do you remember that about a month before this young man made his appearance among us, Natty was absent from home several days? You do; for you inquired for him, as you wanted some venison to take to your friends, when you went for Bess. Well, he was not to be found. Old John was left in the hut alone; and when Natty did appear, although he came on in the night, he was seen drawing one of those jumpers that they carry their grain to mill in, and to take out something, with great care, that he had covered up under his bear-skins. Now let me ask you, Judge Temple, what motive could induce a man like the Leather-stocking to make a sled, and toil with a load over these mountains, if he had nothing but his rifle or his ammunition to carry?"

"They frequently make these jumpers to convey their game home, and you say he had been absent many days."

"How did he kill it? His rifle was in the village to be mended. No, no—that he was gone to some unusual place is certain; that he brought back some secret utensils is more certain; and that he has not allowed a soul to approach his hut since, is most certain of all."

"He was never fond of intruders"——

"I know it," interrupted Richard; "but did he drive them from his cabin morosely? Within a fortnight of his return, this Mr. Edwards appears. They spend whole days in the mountains, pretending to be shooting, but in reality exploring; the frosts prevent their digging at that time, and he avails himself of a lucky accident to get into good quarters. But even now, he is quite half of his time in that hut—many hours every night. They are smelting, 'duke, they are smelting, and as they grow rich you grow poor."

"How much of this is thine own, Richard, and how much comes from others? I would sift the wheat from the chaff."

"Part is my own, for I saw the jumper, though it was broken up and burnt in a day or two. I have told you that I saw the old man with his spades and picks. Hiram met Natty, as he was crossing the mountain, the night of his arrival with the sled, and very good-naturedly offered—Hiram *is* good natured—to carry up part of his load, for the old man had a heavy pull up the back of the mountain, but he wouldn't listen to the thing, and repulsed the offer in such a manner that the Squire said he had half a mind to swear the peace against him. Since the snow has been off, more especially after the frosts got out of the ground, we have kept a watchful eye on the gentleman, in which we have found Jotham useful."

Marmaduke did not much like the associates of Richard in this business; still he knew them to be cunning and ready in expedients; and as there was certainly something mysterious, not only in the connexion between the old hunters and Edwards, but in what his cousin had just related, he begun to revolve the subject in his own mind with more care. On reflection, he remembered various circumstances that tended to corroborate these suspicions, and, as the whole business favoured one of his infirmities, he yielded the more readily to their impression. The mind of Judge Temple, at all times comprehensive, had received, from his peculiar occupations, a bias to look far into futurity, in his speculations on the improvements that posterity were to make in his lands. To his eye, where others saw nothing but a wilderness, towns, manufactories, bridges, canals, mines, and all the other resources of an old country, were constantly presenting themselves, though his good sense suppressed, in some degree, the exhibition of these expectations.

As the Sheriff allowed his cousin full time to reflect on what he had heard, the probability of some pecuniary adventure being the connecting link in the chain that brought Oliver Edwards into the cabin of Leather-stocking, appeared to him each moment to be stronger. But Marmaduke was too much in the habit of examining both sides of a subject, not to perceive the objections, and he reasoned with himself aloud:—

"It cannot be so, or the youth would not be driven so near the verge of poverty."

"What so likely to make a man dig for money, as being poor?" cried the Sheriff.

"Besides, there is an elevation of character about Oliver, that proceeds from education, which would forbid so clandestine a proceeding."

"Could an ignorant fellow smelt?" continued Richard.

"Bess hints that he was reduced even to his last shilling, when we took him into our dwelling."

"He had been buying tools. And would he spend his last sixpence for a shot at a turkey, had he not known where to get more?"

"Can I have possibly been so long a dupe! His manner has been rude to me, at times; but I attributed it to his conceiving himself injured, and to his mistaking the forms of the world."

"Haven't you been a dupe all your life, 'duke? and an't what you call ignorance of forms deep cunning, to conceal his real character?"

"If he were bent on deception, he would have concealed his knowledge, and passed with us for an inferior man."

"He cannot. I could no more pass for a fool, myself, than I could fly. Knowledge is not to be concealed, like a candle under a bushel."

"Richard," said the Judge, turning to his cousin, "there are many reasons against the truth of thy conjectures; but thou hast awakened suspicions which must be satisfied. But why are we travelling here?"

"Jotham, who has been much in the mountain latterly, being kept there by me and Hiram, has made a discovery, which he will not explain, he says, for he is bound by an oath; but the amount is, that he knows where the ore lies, and he has this day begun to dig. I would not consent to the thing, 'duke, without your knowledge, for the land is yours;——and now you know the reason of our ride. I call this a countermine, ha!"

"And where is the desirable spot?" asked the Judge, with an air half comical, half serious.

"At hand; and when we have visited that, I will show you one of the places that we have found within a week, where our hunters have been amusing themselves for six months past."

The gentlemen continued to discuss the matter, while their horses picked their way under the branches of trees, and over the uneven ground of the mountain. They soon arrived at the end of their journey, where, in truth, they found Jotham already buried to his neck in a hole that he had been digging.

Marmaduke questioned the miner very closely, as to his reasons for believing in the existence of the precious metals near that particular spot; but the fellow maintained an obstinate mystery in his answers. He asserted that he had the best of reasons for what he did, and inquired of the Judge what portion of the profits would fall to his own share, in the event of success, with an earnestness that proved his faith. After spending an hour near the place, examining the stones, and searching for the usual indications of the proximity of ore, the Judge remounted, and suffered his cousin to lead the way to the place where the mysterious trio had been making their excavation.

The spot chosen by Jotham was on the back of the mountain that overhung the hut of Leather-stocking, and the place selected by Natty and his companions was on the other side of the same hill, but above the road, and, of course, in an opposite direction to the route taken by the ladies in their walk.

"We shall be safe in approaching the place now," said Richard, while they dismounted and fastened their horses; "for I took a look with the glass, and saw John and Leather-stocking in their canoe fishing, before we left home, and Oliver is in the same pursuit; but these may be nothing but shams, to blind our eyes, so we will be expeditious, for it would not be pleasant to be caught here by them."

"Not on my own land!" said Marmaduke, sternly. "If it be as you suspect, I will know their reasons for making this excavation."

"Mum," said Richard, laying a finger on his lip, and leading the way down a very difficult descent to a sort of a natural cavern, which was formed in the face of the rock, and was not unlike a fire-place in shape. In front of this place lay a pile of earth, which had evidently been taken from the recess, and part of which was yet fresh. An examination of the exterior of the cavern, left the Judge in doubt whether it was one of nature's frolics that had thrown it into that shape, or whether it had been wrought by the hands of man, at some earlier period. But there could be no doubt that the whole of the interior was of recent formation, and the marks of the pick were still visible, where the soft, lead-coloured rock had opposed itself to the progress of the miners. The whole formed an excavation of about twenty feet in width, and nearly twice that distance in depth. The height was much greater than was required for the ordinary purposes of experiment; but this was evidently the effect of chance, as the roof of the cavern was a natural stratum of rock, that projected many feet beyond the base of the pile. Immediately in front of the recess, or cave, was a little terrace, partly formed by nature, and partly by the earth that had been carelessly thrown aside by the labourers. The mountain fell off precipitously in front of the terrace, and the approach by its sides, under the ridge of the rocks, was difficult, and a little dangerous. The whole was wild, rude, and apparently incomplete; for, while looking among the bushes, the Sheriff found the very implements that had been used in the work.

When the Sheriff thought that his cousin had examined the spot sufficiently, he asked solemnly—

"Judge Temple, are you satisfied?"

"Perfectly—that there is something mysterious, and perplexing, in this business. It is a secret spot, and cunningly devised, Richard; yet I see no symptoms of ore."

"Do you expect, sir, to find gold and silver lying like pebbles on the surface of the earth?—dollars and dimes ready coined to your hands! No, no—the treasure must be sought after to be won. But let them mine; I shall countermine."

The Judge took an accurate survey of the place, and noted in his memorandum-book such marks as were necessary to find it again, in the event of Richard's absence; when the cousins returned to their horses.

On reaching the highway they separated, the Sheriff to summon twenty-four "good men and true," to attend as the inquest of the county, on the succeeding Monday, when Marmaduke held his stated court of "common pleas and general sessions of the peace," and the Judge to return, musing deeply on what he had seen and heard in the course of the morning.

When the horse of the latter reached the spot where the highway fell towards the valley, the eye of Marmaduke rested, it is true, on the same scene that had, ten minutes before, been so soothing to the feelings of his daughter and her friend, as they emerged from the forest; but it rested in vacancy. He threw the reins to his sure-footed beast, and suffered the animal to travel at its own gait, while he soliloquized as follows:—

"There may be more in this than I at first supposed. I have suffered my feeling to blind my reason, in admitting an unknown youth in this manner to my dwelling;—yet this is not the land of suspicion. I will have the Leather-stocking before me, and, by a few direct questions, extract the truth from the simple old man."——

At that instant the Judge caught a glimpse of the figures of Elizabeth and Louisa, who were slowly descending the mountain, a short distance before him. He put spurs to his horse, and riding up to them, dismounted, and drove his steed along the narrow path. While the agitated parent was listening to the vivid description that his daughter gave of her recent danger, and her unexpected escape, all thoughts of mines, vested rights, and examinations, were absorbed in emotion; and when the image of Natty again crossed his recollection, it was not as a lawless and depredating squatter, but as the preserver of his child.

Chapter XXX.

"The court awards it, and the law doth give it."
The Merchant of Venice, IV.i.300.

R EMARKABLE Pettibone, who had forgotten the wound received by her pride, in contemplation of the ease and comforts of her situation, and who still retained her station in the family of Judge Temple, was despatched to the humble dwelling which Richard already styled "the Rectory," in attendance on Louisa, who was soon consigned to the arms of her father.

In the mean time, Marmaduke and his daughter were closeted for more than an hour, nor shall we invade the sanctuary of parental love, by relating the conversation.—When the curtain rises on the reader, the Judge is seen walking up and down the apartment, with a tender melancholy in his air, and his child reclining on a settee, with a flushed cheek, and her dark eyes seeming to float in crystals.

"It was a timely rescue! it was, indeed, a timely rescue, my child!" cried the Judge. "Then thou didst not desert thy friend, my noble Bess?"

"I believe I may as well take the credit of fortitude," said Elizabeth, "though I much doubt if flight would have availed me any thing, had I even courage to execute such an intention. But I thought not of the expedient."

"Of what didst thou think, love? where did thy thoughts dwell most, at that fearful moment?"

"The beast! the beast!" cried Elizabeth, veiling her face with her hand; "Oh! I saw nothing, I thought of nothing, but the beast. I tried to think of better things, but the horror was too glaring, the danger too much before my eyes."

"Well, well, thou art safe, and we will converse no more on the unpleasant subject. I did not think such an animal yet remained in our forest; but they will stray far from their haunts when pressed by hunger, and"——

A loud knocking at the door of the apartment interrupted what he was about to utter, and he bid the applicant enter. The door was opened by Benjamin, who came in with a discontented air, as if he felt that he had a communication to make that would be out of season.

"Here is Squire Doolittle below, sir," commenced the Major-domo. "He has been standing off and on in the door-yard, for the matter of a glass; and he has sum'mat on his mind that he wants to heave up, d'ye see; but I tells him, says I, man, would you be coming aboard with your complaints, said I, when the Judge has gotten his own child, as it were, out of the jaws of a lion? But damn the bit of manners has the fellow any more than if he was one of them Guineas, down in the kitchen there; and so as he was sheering nearer, every stretch he made towards the house, I could do no better than to let your honour know that the chap was in the offing."

"He must have business of importance," said Marmaduke; "something in relation to his office, most probably, as the court sits so shortly."

"Ay, ay, you have it, sir," cried Benjamin, "it's sum'mat about a complaint that he has to make of the old Leather-stocking, who, to my judgment, is the better man of the two. It's a very good sort of a man is this Master Bumppo, and he has a way with a spear, all the same as if he was brought up at the bow oar of the captain's barge, or was born with a boat-hook in his hand."

"Against the Leather-stocking!" cried Elizabeth, rising from her reclining posture.

"Rest easy, my child; some trifle, I pledge you; I believe I am already acquainted with its import. Trust me, Bess, your champion shall be safe in my care.——Show Mr. Doolittle in, Benjamin."

Miss Temple appeared satisfied with this assurance, but fastened her dark eyes on the person of the architect, who profited by the permission, and instantly made his appearance.

All the impatience of Hiram seemed to vanish the instant he entered the apartment. After saluting the Judge and his daughter, he took the chair to which Marmaduke pointed, and sat for a minute, composing his straight black hair, with a gravity of demeanour, that was intended to do honour to his official station. At length he said—

"It's likely, from what I hear, that Miss Temple had a pretty narrow chance with the painters, on the mountain."

Marmaduke made a gentle inclination of his head, by way of assent, but continued silent.

"I s'pose the law gives a bounty on the scalps," continued Hiram, "in which case the Leather-stocking will make a good job on't."

"It shall be my care to see that he is rewarded," returned the Judge.

"Yes, yes, I rather guess that nobody hereabouts doubts the Judge's ginerosity. Does he know whether the Sheriff has fairly made up his mind to have a reading-desk or a deacon's pew under the pulpit?"

"I have not heard my cousin speak on that subject lately," replied Marmaduke.

"I think it's likely that we will have a pretty dull court on't, from what I can gather. I hear that Jotham Riddel and the man who bought his betterments have agreen to leave their difference to men, and I don't think there'll be more than two civil cases in the calendar."

"I am glad of it," said the Judge; "nothing gives me more pain, than to see my settlers wasting their time and substance in the unprofitable struggles of the law. I hope it may prove true, sir."

"I rather guess 'twill be left out to men," added Hiram, with an air equally balanced between doubt and assurance, but which Judge Temple understood to mean certainty; "I some think that I am appointed a referee in the case myself. Jotham as much as told me that he should take me. The defendant, I guess, means to take Captain Hollister, and we two have partly agreen on Squire Jones for the third man."

"Are there any criminals to be tried?" asked Marmaduke.

"There's the counterfeiters," returned the magistrate; "as they were caught in the fact, I think it likely that they'll be indicted, in which case, it's probable they will be tried."

"Certainly, sir; I had forgotten those men. There are no more, I hope."

"Why, there is a threaten to come forrard with an assault, that happened at the last independence day; but I'm not sartain that the law'll take hold on't. There was plaguey hard words passed, but whether they struck or not I haven't heern. There's some folks talk of a deer or two being killed out of season, over on the west side of the Patent, by some of the squatters on the 'Fractions.' "

"Let a complaint be made, by all means," cried the Judge; "I am determined to see the law executed, to the letter, on all such depredators."

"Why, yes, I thought the Judge was of that mind; I come, partly, on such a business myself."

"You!" exclaimed Marmaduke, comprehending, in an instant, how completely he had been caught by the other's cunning; "and what have you to say, sir?"

"I some think that Natty Bumppo has the carcass of a deer in his hut at this moment, and a considerable part of my business was to get a sarch-warrant to examine."

"You think, sir! do you know that the law exacts an oath, before I can issue such a precept. The habitation of a citizen is not to be idly invaded on light suspicion."

"I rather think I can swear to it myself," returned the immoveable Hiram; "and Jotham is in the street, and as good as ready to come in and make oath to the same thing."

"Then issue the warrant thyself; thou art a magistrate, Mr. Doolittle; why trouble me with the matter?"

"Why, seeing it's the first complaint under the law, and knowing the Judge set his heart on the thing, I thought it best that the authority to sarch should come from himself. Besides, as I'm much in the woods, among the timber, I don't altogether like making an enemy of the Leather-stocking. Now the Judge has a weight in the county that puts him above fear."

Miss Temple turned her face to the callous architect, as she said—

"And what has any honest person to dread from so kind a man as Bumppo?"

"Why, it's as easy, Miss, to pull a rifle-trigger on a magistrate as on a painter. But if the Judge don't conclude to issoo the warrant, I must go home and make it out myself."

"I have not refused your application, sir," said Marmaduke, perceiving, at once, that his reputation for impartiality was at stake; "go into my office, Mr. Doolittle, where I will join you, and sign the warrant."

Judge Temple stopped the remonstrances which Elizabeth was about to utter, after Hiram had withdrawn, by laying his hand on her mouth, and saying—

"It is more terrific in sound than frightful in reality, my child. I suppose that the Leather-stocking has shot a deer, for the season is nearly over, and you say that he was hunting with his dogs, when he came so timely to your assistance. But it will be only to examine his cabin, and find the animal, when you can pay the penalty out of your own pocket, Bess. Nothing short of the twelve dollars and a half will satisfy this harpy, I perceive; and surely my reputation as a Judge is worth that trifle."

Elizabeth was a good deal pacified with this assurance, and suffered her father to leave her, to fulfil his promise to Hiram.

When Marmaduke left his office, after executing his disagreeable duty, he met Oliver Edwards, walking up the gravelled walk in front of the Mansion-house, with great strides, and with a face agitated by feeling. On seeing Judge Temple, the youth turned aside, and with a warmth in his manner that was not often exhibited to Marmaduke, he cried—

"I congratulate you, sir; from the bottom of my soul I congratulate you, Judge Temple. Oh! it would have been too horrid to have recollected for a moment! I have just left the hut, where, after showing me his scalps, old Natty told me of the escape of the ladies, as a thing to be mentioned last. Indeed, indeed, sir, no words of mine can express half of what I have felt"—the youth paused a moment, as if suddenly recollecting that he was overstepping prescribed limits, and concluded with a good deal of embarrassment—"what I have felt, at this danger to Miss—Grant, and—and your daughter, sir."

But the heart of Marmaduke was too much softened, to admit of his cavilling at trifles, and, without regarding the confusion of the other, he replied—

"I thank thee, thank thee, Oliver; as thou sayest, it is almost too horrid to be remembered. But come, let us hasten to Bess, for Louisa has already gone to the Rectory."

The young man sprung forward, and, throwing open a door, barely permitted the Judge to precede him, when he was in the presence of Elizabeth in a moment.

The cold distance that often crossed the demeanour of the

heiress, in her intercourse with Edwards, was now entirely banished, and two hours were passed by the party, in the free, unembarrassed, and confiding manner of old and esteemed friends. Judge Temple had forgotten the suspicions engendered during his morning's ride, and the youth and maiden conversed, laughed, and were sad, by turns, as impulse directed. At length Edwards, after repeating his intention to do so for the third time, left the Mansion-house, to go to the Rectory on a similar errand of friendship.

During this short period, a scene was passing at the hut, that completely frustrated the benevolent intentions of Judge Temple in favour of the Leather-stocking, and at once destroyed the short-lived harmony between the youth and Marmaduke.

When Hiram Doolittle had obtained his search-warrant, his first business was to procure a proper officer to see it executed. The Sheriff was absent, summoning, in person, the grand inquest for the county; the deputy, who resided in the village, was riding on the same errand, in a different part of the settlement; and the regular constable of the township had been selected for his station from motives of charity, being lame of a leg. Hiram intended to accompany the officer as a spectator, but he felt no very strong desire to bear the brunt of the battle. It was, however, Saturday, and the sun was already turning the shadows of the pines towards the east; on the morrow the conscientious magistrate could not engage in such an expedition at the peril of his soul; and long before Monday, the venison, and all vestiges of the death of the deer, might be secreted or destroyed. Happily, the lounging form of Billy Kirby met his eye, and Hiram, at all times fruitful in similar expedients, saw his way clear at once. Jotham, who was associated in the whole business, and who had left the mountain in consequence of a summons from his coadjutor, but who failed, equally with Hiram, in the unfortunate particular of nerve, was directed to summon the wood-chopper to the dwelling of the magistrate.

When Billy appeared, he was very kindly invited to take the chair in which he had already seated himself, and was treated, in all respects, as if he were an equal.

"Judge Temple has set his heart on putting the deer law in force," said Hiram, after the preliminary civilities were over, "and a complaint has been laid before him that a deer has been killed. He has issooed a sarch-warrant, and sent for me to get somebody to execute it."

Kirby, who had no idea of being excluded from the deliberative part of any affair in which he was engaged, drew up his bushy head in a reflecting attitude, and, after musing a moment, replied by asking a few questions.

"The Sheriff is gone out of the way?"

"Not to be found."

"And his deputy too?"

"Both gone on the skirts of the Patent."

"But I seen the constable hobbling about town an hour ago."

"Yes, yes," said Hiram, with a coaxing smile and knowing nod, "but this business wants a man—not a cripple."

"Why," said Billy, laughing, "will the chap make fight?"

"He's a little quarrelsome at times, and thinks he's the best man in the county at rough-and-tumble."

"I heerd him brag once," said Jotham, "that there wasn't a man 'twixt the Mohawk Flats and the Pennsylvany line, that was his match at a close hug."

"Did you!" exclaimed Kirby, raising his huge frame in his seat, like a lion stretching in his lair; "I rather guess he never felt a Varmounter's knuckles on his back-bone. But who is the chap?"

"Why," said Jotham, "it's"——

"It's ag'in law to tell," interrupted Hiram, "unless you'll qualify to sarve. You'd be the very man to take him, Bill; and I'll make out a spicial deputation in a minute, when you will get the fees."

"What's the fees?" said Kirby, laying his large hand on the leaves of a statute-book, that Hiram had opened in order to give dignity to his office, which he turned over, in his rough manner, as if he were reflecting on a subject, about which he had, in truth, already decided; "will they pay a man for a broken head?"

"They'll be something handsome," said Hiram.

"Damn the fees," said Billy, again laughing—"does the fellow think he's the best wrestler in the county, though? what's his inches?"

"He's taller than you be," said Jotham, "and one of the biggest"——

Talkers, he was about to add, but the impatience of Kirby interrupted him. The wood-chopper had nothing fierce, or even brutal in his appearance: the character of his expression was that of good-natured vanity. It was evident he prided himself on the powers of the physical man, like all who have nothing better to boast of; and, stretching out his broad hand, with the palm downward, he said, keeping his eyes fastened on his own bones and sinews—

"Come, give us a touch of the book. I'll swear, and you'll see that I'm a man to keep my oath."

Hiram did not give the wood-chopper time to change his mind, but the oath was administered without unnecessary delay. So soon as this preliminary was completed, the three worthies left the house, and proceeded by the nearest road towards the hut. They had reached the bank of the lake, and were diverging from the route of the highway, before Kirby recollected that he was now entitled to the privileges of the initiated, and repeated his question, as to the name of the offender.

"Which way, which way, Squire?" exclaimed the hardy wood-chopper; "I thought it was to sarch a house that you wanted me, not the woods. There is nobody lives on this side of the lake, for six miles, unless you count the Leather-stocking and old John for settlers. Come, tell me the chap's name, and I warrant me that I lead you to his clearing by a straighter path than this, for I know every sapling that grows within two miles of Templetown."

"This is the way," said Hiram, pointing forward, and quickening his step, as if apprehensive that Kirby would desert, "and Bumppo is the man."

Kirby stopped short, and looked from one of his companions to the other in astonishment. He then burst into a loud laugh, and cried—

"Who! Leather-stocking! he may brag of his aim and his rifle, for he has the best of both, as I will own myself, for sin he shot the pigeon I knock under to him; but for a wrestle! why, I would take the creatur between my finger and thumb, and tie him in a bow-knot around my neck for a Barcelony. The man is seventy, and was never any thing particular for strength."

"He's a deceiving man," said Hiram, "like all the hunters; he is stronger than he seems;—besides, he has his rifle."

"That for his rifle!" cried Billy; "he'd no more hurt me with his rifle than he'd fly. He is a harmless creater, and I must say that I think he has as good a right to kill deer as any man on the Patent. It's his main support, and this is a free country, where a man is privileged to follow any calling he likes."

"According to that doctrine," said Jotham, "any body may shoot a deer."

"This is the man's calling, I tell you," returned Kirby, "and the law was never made for such as he."

"The law was made for all," observed Hiram, who began to think that the danger was likely to fall to his own share, notwithstanding his management; "and the law is particular in noticing parjury."

"See here, Squire Doolittle," said the reckless wood-chopper, "I don't kear the valie of a beetle-ring for you and your parjury too. But as I have come so far, I'll go down and have a talk with the old man, and maybe we'll fry a steak of the deer together."

"Well, if you can get in peaceably, so much the better," said the magistrate. "To my notion, strife is very unpopular; I prefar, at all times, clever conduct to an ugly temper."

As the whole party moved at a great pace, they soon reached the hut, where Hiram thought it prudent to halt on the outside of the top of the fallen pine, which formed a chevaux-de-frize, to defend the approach to the fortress, on the side next the village. The delay was little relished by Kirby, who clapped his hands to his mouth, and gave a loud halloo, that brought the dogs out of their kennel, and, almost at the same instant, the scantily-covered head of Natty from the door.

"Lie down, old fool," cried the hunter; "do you think there's more painters about you?"

"Ha! Leather-stocking, I've an arrand with you," cried Kirby; "here's the good people of the state have been writing you a small letter, and they've hired me to ride post."

"What would you have with me, Billy Kirby?" said Natty, stepping across his threshold, and raising his hand over his eyes to screen them from the rays of the setting sun, while he took a survey of his visiter. "I've no land to clear; and Heaven knows I would set out six trees afore I would cut down one. Down, Hector, I say, into your kennel with ye."

"Would you, old boy!" roared Billy; "then so much the better for me. But I must do my arrand. Here's a letter for you, Leather-stocking. If you can read it it's all well, and if you can't, here's Squire Doolittle at hand to let you know what it means. It seems, you mistook the twentieth of July for the first of August, that's all."

By this time Natty had discovered the lank person of Hiram, drawn up under the cover of a high stump; and all that was complacent in his manner instantly gave way to marked distrust and dissatisfaction. He placed his head within the door of his hut, and said a few words in an under tone, when he again appeared, and continued—

"I've nothing for ye; so away, afore the evil one tempts me to do you harm. I owe you no spite, Billy Kirby, and what for should you trouble an old man, who has done you no harm?"

Kirby advanced through the top of the pine, to within a few feet of the hunter, where he seated himself on the end of a log with great composure, and begun to examine the nose of Hector, with whom he was familiar, from their frequently meeting in the woods, where he sometimes fed the dog from his own basket of provisions.

"You've outshot me, and I'm not ashamed to say it," said the wood-chopper; "but I don't owe you a grudge for that, Natty; though it seems, that you've shot once too often, for the story goes, that you've killed a buck."

"I've fired but twice to-day, and both times at the painters," returned the Leather-stocking; "see! here's the scalps! I was just going in with them to the Judge's to ask the bounty."

While Natty was speaking, he tossed the ears to Kirby, who continued playing with them, with a careless air, holding them to the dogs, and laughing at their movements when they scented the unusual game.

But Hiram, emboldened by the advance of the deputed constable, now ventured to approach also, and took up the discourse with the air of authority that became his commission. His first measure was to read the warrant aloud, taking care to give due emphasis to the most material parts, and concluding with the name of the Judge in very audible and distinct tones.

"Did Marmaduke Temple put his name to that bit of paper!" said Natty, shaking his head;—"well, well, that man loves the new ways, and his betterments, and his lands, afore his own flesh and blood. But I won't mistrust the gall: she has an eye like a full-grown buck! poor thing, she didn't choose her father, and can't help it.——I know but little of the law, Mr. Doolittle; what is to be done, now you've read your commission?"

"Oh! it's nothing but form, Natty," said Hiram, endeavouring to assume a friendly aspect. "Let's go in and talk the thing over in reason. I dare to say that the money can be easily found, and I partly conclude, from what passed, that Judge Temple will pay it himself."

The old hunter had kept a keen eye on the movements of his three visiters, from the beginning, and had maintained his position, just without the threshold of his cabin, with a determined manner, that showed he was not to be easily driven from his post. When Hiram drew nigher, as if expecting his proposition would be accepted, Natty lifted his hand and motioned for him to retreat.

"Haven't I told you, more than once, not to tempt me," he said. "I trouble no man; why can't the law leave me to myself? Go back—go back, and tell your Judge that he may keep his bounty; but I won't have his wasty ways brought into my hut."

This offer, however, instead of appeasing the curiosity of Hiram, seemed to inflame it the more; while Kirby cried—

"Well, that's fair, Squire; he forgives the county his demand, and the county should forgive him the fine; it's what I call an even trade, and should be concluded on the spot. I like quick dealings, and what's fair 'twixt man and man."

"I demand entrance into this house," said Hiram, summoning all the dignity he could muster to his assistance, "in the name of the people, and by vartoo of this warrant, and of my office, and with this peace-officer."

"Stand back, stand back, Squire, and don't tempt me," said the Leather-stocking, motioning for him to retire, with great earnestness.

"Stop us at your peril," continued Hiram—"Billy! Jotham! close up—I want testimony."

Hiram had mistaken the mild but determined air of Natty for submission, and had already put his foot on the threshold to enter, when he was seized unexpectedly by his shoulders, and hurled over the little bank towards the lake, to the distance of twenty feet. The suddenness of the movement, and the unexpected display of strength on the part of Natty, created a momentary astonishment in his invaders, that silenced all noises; but at the next instant Billy Kirby gave vent to his mirth in peals of laughter, that he seemed to heave up from his very soul.

"Well done, old stub!" he shouted; "the Squire know'd you better than I did. Come, come, here's a green spot; take it out like men, while Jotham and I see fair play."

"William Kirby, I order you to do your duty," cried Hiram, from under the bank; "seize that man; I order you to seize him in the name of the people."

But the Leather-stocking now assumed a more threatening attitude; his rifle was in his hand, and its muzzle was directed towards the wood-chopper.

"Stand off, I bid ye," said Natty; "you know my aim, Billy Kirby; I don't crave your blood, but mine and yourn both shall turn this green grass red, afore you put foot into the hut."

While the affair appeared trifling, the wood-chopper seemed disposed to take sides with the weaker party; but when the fire-arms were introduced, his manner very sensibly changed. He raised his large frame from the log, and, facing the hunter with an open front, he replied—

"I didn't come here as your enemy, Leather-stocking; but I don't valie the hollow piece of iron in your hand so much as a broken axe-helve;—so, Squire, say the word, and keep within the law, and we'll soon see who's the best man of the two."

But no magistrate was to be seen! The instant the rifle was produced Hiram and Jotham vanished; and when the wood-chopper bent his eyes about him in surprise at receiving no answer, he discovered their retreating figures, moving towards the village, at a rate that sufficiently indicated that they had not only calculated the velocity of a rifle-bullet, but also its probable range.

"You've skeared the creaters off," said Kirby, with great contempt expressed on his broad features; "but you are not a-going to skear me; so, Mr. Bumppo, down with your gun, or there'll be trouble 'twixt us."

Natty dropped his rifle, and replied—

"I wish you no harm, Billy Kirby; but I leave it to yourself, whether an old man's hut is to be run down by such varmint. I won't deny the buck to you, Billy, and you may take the skin in, if you please, and show it as tistimony. The bounty will pay the fine, and that ought to satisfy any man."

" 'Twill, old boy, 'twill," cried Kirby, every shade of displeasure vanishing from his open brow at the peace-offering; "throw out the hide, and that shall satisfy the law."

Natty entered his hut, and soon re-appeared, bringing with him the desired testimonial, and the wood-chopper departed, as thoroughly reconciled to the hunter as if nothing had happened. As he paced along the margin of the lake, he would burst into frequent fits of laughter, while he recollected the summerset of Hiram; and, on the whole, he thought the affair a very capital joke.

Long before Billy reached the village, however, the news of his danger, and of Natty's disrespect of the law, and of Hiram's discomfiture, were in circulation. A good deal was said about sending for the Sheriff; some hints were given about calling out the posse comitatus to avenge the insulted laws; and many of the citizens were collected, deliberating how to proceed. The arrival of Billy with the skin, by removing all grounds for a search, changed the complexion of things materially. Nothing now remained but to collect the fine, and assert the dignity of the people; all of which, it was unanimously agreed, could be done as well on the succeeding Monday as on a Saturday night, a time kept sacred by a large portion of the settlers. Accordingly, all further proceedings were suspended for six-and-thirty hours.

Chapter XXXI.

"And dar'st thou, then,
To beard the lion in his den,
The Douglass in his hall?"   Scott, *Marmion*, VI.xiv.23–25.

THE commotion was just subsiding, and the inhabitants of the village had begun to disperse from the little groups they had formed, each retiring to his own home, and closing his door after him, with the grave air of a man who consulted public feeling in his exterior deportment, when Oliver Edwards, on his return from the dwelling of Mr. Grant, encountered the young lawyer, who is known to the reader as Mr. Lippet. There was very little similarity in the manners or opinions of the two; but as they both belonged to the more intelligent class of a very small community, they were, of course, known to each other; and, as their meeting was at a point where silence would have been rudeness, the following conversation was the result of their interview:—

"A fine evening, Mr. Edwards," commenced the lawyer, whose disinclination to the dialogue was, to say the least, very doubtful; "we want rain sadly;—that's the worst of this climate of ours, it's either a drought or a deluge. It's likely you've been used to a more equal temperatoore?"

"I am a native of this state," returned Edwards, coldly.

"Well, I've often heerd that point disputed; but it's so easy to get a man naturalized, that it's of little consequence where he was born. I wonder what course the Judge means to take in this business of Natty Bumppo?"

"Of Natty Bumppo!" echoed Edwards; "to what do you allude, sir?"

"Haven't you heerd!" exclaimed the other, with a look of surprise, so naturally assumed as completely to deceive his auditor; "it may turn out an ugly business. It seems that the old man has been out in the hills, and has shot a buck, this morning, and that, you know, is a criminal matter in the eyes of Judge Temple."

"Oh! he has, has he!" said Edwards, averting his face to conceal the colour that collected in his sun-burnt cheek. "Well, if that be all, he must even pay the fine."

"It's five pounds, currency," said the lawyer; "could Natty muster so much money at once?"

"Could he!" cried the youth. "I am not rich, Mr. Lippet; far from it—I am poor; and I have been hoarding my salary for a purpose that lies near my heart; but before that old man should lie one hour in a gaol, I would spend the last cent to prevent it. Besides, he has killed two panthers, and the bounty will discharge the fine many times over."

"Yes, yes," said the lawyer, rubbing his hands together with an expression of pleasure that had no artifice about it; "we shall make it out; I see plainly, we shall make it out."

"Make what out, sir? I must beg an explanation."

"Why, killing the buck is but a small matter, compared to what took place this afternoon," continued Mr. Lippet, with a confidential and friendly air, that insensibly won upon the youth, little as he liked the man. "It seems, that a complaint was made of the fact, and a suspicion that there was venison in the hut was sworn to, all which is provided for in the statoote, when Judge Temple granted a search-warrant"——

"A search-warrant!" echoed Edwards, in a voice of horror, and with a face that should have been again averted, to conceal its paleness; "and how much did they discover? What did they see?"

"They saw old Bumppo's rifle; and that is a sight which will quiet most men's curiosity in the woods."

"Did they! did they!" shouted Edwards, bursting into a convulsive laugh; "so the old hero beat them back—he beat them back! did he!"

The lawyer fastened his eyes in astonishment on the youth; but, as his wonder gave way to the thoughts that were commonly uppermost in his mind, he replied—

"It's no laughing matter, let me tell you, sir; the forty dollars of bounty, and your six months of salary, will be much redooced, before you get the matter fairly settled. Assaulting a magistrate in the execootion of his duty, and menacing a constable with fire-arms, at the same time, is a pretty serious affair, and punishable with both fine and imprisonment."

"Imprisonment!" repeated Oliver; "imprison the Leather-stocking! no, no, sir; it would bring the old man to his grave. They shall never imprison the Leather-stocking."

"Well, Mr. Edwards," said Lippet, dropping all reserve from his manner, "you are called a curious man; but if you can tell me how a jury is to be prevented from finding a verdict of guilty, if this case comes fairly before them, and the proof is clear, I shall acknowledge that you know more law than I do, who have had a license in my pocket for three years.'

By this time the reason of Edwards was getting the ascendency of his feelings; and, as he begun to see the real difficulties of the case, he listened more readily to the conversation of the lawyer. The ungovernable emotion that escaped the youth, in the first moments of his surprise, entirely passed away, and, although it was still evident that he continued to be much agitated by what he had heard, he succeeded in yielding forced attention to the advice which the other uttered.

Notwithstanding the confused state of his mind, Oliver soon discovered that most of the expedients of the lawyer were grounded in cunning, and plans that required a time to execute them, that neither suited his disposition nor his necessities. After, however, giving Mr. Lippet to understand that he retained him, in the event of a trial, an assurance that at once satisfied the lawyer, they parted, one taking his course, with a deliberate tread, in the direction of the little building that had a wooden sign over its door, with "Chester Lippet, Attorney at Law," painted on it; and the other, pacing over the ground, with enormous strides, towards the Mansion-house. We shall take leave of the attorney for the present, and direct the attention of the reader to his client.

When Edwards entered the hall, whose enormous doors were opened to the passage of the air of a mild evening, he found Benjamin engaged in some of his domestic avocations, and, in a hurried voice, inquired where Judge Temple was to be found.

"Why, the Judge has stept into his office, with that master-carpenter, Mister Doolittle; but Miss Lizzy is in that there parlour. I say, Master Oliver, we'd like to have had a bad job of that panther, or painter's work—some calls it one, and some calls it t'other—but I know little of the beast, seeing that it's not of British growth. I said as much as that it was in the hills, the last winter; for I heard it moaning on the lake-shore, one evening in the fall, when I was pulling down from the fishing-point, in the skiff. Had the animal come into open water, where a man could see how and where to work his vessel, I would have engaged the thing myself; but looking aloft among the trees, is all the same to me as standing on the deck of one ship and looking at another vessel's tops. I never can tell one rope from another"——

"Well, well," interrupted Edwards; "I must see Miss Temple."

"And you shall see her, sir," said the steward; "she's in this here room. Lord, Master Edwards, what a loss she'd have been to the Judge! Dam'me if I know where he would have gotten such another daughter; that is, full-grown, d'ye see. I say, sir, this Master Bumppo is a worthy man, and seems to have a handy way with him, with fire-arms and boat-hooks. I'm his friend, Master Oliver, and he and you may both set me down as the same."

"We may want your friendship, my worthy fellow," cried Edwards, squeezing his hand convulsively—"we may want your friendship, in which case, you shall know it."

Without waiting to hear the earnest reply that Benjamin meditated, the youth extricated himself from the vigorous grasp of the steward, and entered the parlour.

Elizabeth was alone, and still reclining on the sofa, where we last left her. A hand, which exceeded all that the ingenuity of art could model, in shape and colour, veiled her eyes; and the maiden was sitting as if in deep communion with herself. Struck by the attitude and loveliness of the form that met his eye, the young man checked his impatience, and approached her with respect and caution.

"Miss Temple—Miss Temple," he said, "I hope I do not intrude; but I am anxious for an interview, if it be only for a moment."

Elizabeth raised her face, and exhibited her dark eyes swimming in moisture.

"Is it you, Edwards?" she said, with a sweetness in her voice, and a softness in her air, that she often used to her father, but which, from its novelty to himself, thrilled on every nerve of the youth; "how left you our poor Louisa?"

"She is with her father, happy and grateful," said Oliver. "I never witnessed more feeling than she manifested, when I ventured to express my pleasure at her escape. Miss Temple, when I first heard of your horrid situation, my feelings were too powerful for utterance; and I did not properly find my tongue, until the walk to Mr. Grant's had given me time to collect myself. I believe—I do believe, I acquitted myself better there, for Miss Grant even wept at my silly speeches."

For a moment Elizabeth did not reply, but again veiled her eyes with her hand. The feeling that caused the action, however, soon passed away, and, raising her face again to his gaze, she continued, with a smile—

"Your friend, the Leather-stocking, has now become my friend, Edwards; I have been thinking how I can best serve him; perhaps you, who know his habits and his wants so well, can tell me"——

"I can," cried the youth, with an impetuosity that startled his companion—"I can, and may Heaven reward you for the wish. Natty has been so imprudent as to forget the law, and has this day killed a deer. Nay, I believe I must share in the crime and the penalty, for I was an accomplice throughout. A complaint has been made to your father, and he has granted a search"——

"I know it all," interrupted Elizabeth; "I know it all. The forms of the law must be complied with, however; the search must be made, the deer found, and the penalty paid. But I must retort your own question. Have you lived so long in our family, not to know us? Look at me, Oliver Edwards. Do I appear like one who would permit the man that has just saved her life to linger in a gaol, for so small a sum as this fine? No, no, sir; my father is a Judge, but he is a man, and a Christian. It is all understood, and no harm shall follow."

"What a load of apprehension do your declarations remove!" exclaimed Edwards. "He shall not be disturbed again! your father will protect him! I have your assurance, Miss Temple, that he will, and I must believe it."

"You may have his own, Mr. Edwards," returned Elizabeth, "for here he comes to make it."

But the appearance of Marmaduke, who entered the apartment, contradicted the flattering anticipations of his daughter. His brow was contracted, and his manner disturbed. Neither

Elizabeth nor the youth spoke; but the Judge was allowed to pace once or twice across the room without interruption, when he cried—

"Our plans are defeated, girl; the obstinacy of the Leather-stocking has brought down the indignation of the law on his head, and it is now out of my power to avert it."

"How? in what manner?" cried Elizabeth; "the fine is nothing; surely"——

"I did not—I could not anticipate that an old, a friendless man, like him, would dare to oppose the officers of justice," interrupted the Judge; "I supposed that he would submit to the search, when the fine could have been paid, and the law would have been appeased; but now he will have to meet its rigour."

"And what must the punishment be, sir?" asked Edwards, struggling to speak with firmness.

Marmaduke turned quickly to the spot where the youth had withdrawn, and exclaimed—

"You here! I did not observe you. I know not what it will be, sir; it is not usual for a Judge to decide, until he has heard the testimony, and the jury have convicted. Of one thing, however, you may be assured, Mr. Edwards; it shall be whatever the law demands, notwithstanding any momentary weakness I may have exhibited, because the luckless man has been of such eminent service to my daughter."

"No one, I believe, doubts the sense of justice which Judge Temple entertains!" returned Edwards, bitterly. "But let us converse calmly, sir. Will not the years, the habits, nay, the ignorance of my old friend, avail him any thing against this charge?"

"Ought they? They may extenuate, but can they acquit? Would any society be tolerable, young man, where the ministers of justice are to be opposed by men armed with rifles? Is it for this that I have tamed the wilderness?"

"Had you tamed the beasts that so lately threatened the life of Miss Temple, sir, your arguments would apply better."

"Edwards!" exclaimed Elizabeth——

"Peace, my child," interrupted the father;—"the youth is unjust; but I have not given him cause. I overlook thy remark, Oliver, for I know thee to be the friend of Natty, and zeal in his behalf has overcome thy discretion."

"Yes, he is my friend," cried Edwards, "and I glory in the title. He is simple, unlettered, even ignorant; prejudiced, perhaps, though I feel that his opinion of the world is too true; but he has a heart, Judge Temple, that would atone for a thousand faults; he knows his friends, and never deserts them, even if it be his dog."

"This is a good character, Mr. Edwards," returned Marmaduke, mildly; "but I have never been so fortunate as to secure his esteem, for to me he has been uniformly repulsive; yet I have endured it, as an old man's whim. However, when he appears before me, as his judge, he shall find that his former conduct shall not aggravate, any more than his recent services shall extenuate his crime."

"Crime!" echoed Edwards; "is it a crime to drive a prying miscreant from his door? Crime! Oh! no, sir; if there be a criminal involved in this affair, it is not he."

"And who may it be, sir?" asked Judge Temple, facing the agitated youth, his features settled to their usual composure.

This appeal was more than the young man could bear. Hitherto he had been deeply agitated by his emotions; but now the volcano burst its boundaries.

"Who! and this to me!" he cried; "ask your own conscience, Judge Temple. Walk to that door, sir, and look out upon the valley, that placid lake, and those dusky mountains, and say to your own heart, if heart you have, whence came these riches, this vale, and those hills, and why am I their owner? I should think, sir, that the appearance of Mohegan and the Leatherstocking, stalking through the country, impoverished and forlorn, would wither your sight."

Marmaduke heard this burst of passion, at first, with deep amazement; but when the youth had ended, he beckoned to his impatient daughter for silence, and replied—

"Oliver Edwards, thou forgettest in whose presence thou standest. I have heard, young man, that thou claimest descent from the native owners of the soil; but surely thy education has been given thee to no effect, if it has not taught thee the validity of the claims that have transferred the title to the whites. These lands are mine by the very grants of thy ancestry, if thou art so descended; and I appeal to Heaven, for a testimony of the uses I have put them to. After this language, we must separate. I have too long sheltered thee in my dwelling; but the time has arrived when thou must quit it. Come to my office, and I will discharge the debt I owe thee. Neither shall thy present intemperate language mar thy future fortunes, if thou wilt hearken to the advice of one who is by many years thy senior."

The ungovernable feeling that caused the violence of the youth had passed away, and he stood gazing after the retiring figure of Marmaduke, with a vacancy in his eye, that denoted the absence of his mind. At length he recollected himself, and, turning his head slowly around the apartment, he beheld Elizabeth, still seated on the sofa, but with her head dropped on her bosom, and her face again concealed by her hands.

"Miss Temple," he said—all violence had left his manner— "Miss Temple—I have forgotten myself—forgotten you. You have heard what your father has decreed, and this night I leave here. With you, at least, I would part in amity."

Elizabeth slowly raised her face, across which a momentary expression of sadness stole; but as she left her seat, her dark eyes lighted with their usual fire, her cheek flushed to burning, and her whole air seemed to belong to another nature.

"I forgive you, Edwards, and my father will forgive you," she said, when she reached the door. "You do not know us, but the time may come, when your opinions shall change"——

"Of you! never!" interrupted the youth; "I"——

"I would speak, sir, and not listen. There is something in this affair that I do not comprehend; but tell the Leather-stocking he has friends as well as judges in us. Do not let the old man experience unnecessary uneasiness, at this rupture. It is impossible that you could increase his claims here; neither shall they be diminished by any thing you have said. Mr. Edwards, I wish you happiness, and warmer friends."

The youth would have spoken, but she vanished from the door so rapidly, that when he reached the hall her form was nowhere to be seen. He paused a moment, in a stupor, and then, rushing from the house, instead of following Marmaduke to his "office," he took his way directly for the cabin of the hunters.

Chapter XXXII.

"Who measured earth, described the starry spheres,
And traced the long records of lunar years."
                              Pope, "The Temple of Fame," ll. 111–12.

RICHARD did not return from the exercise of his official
duties, until late in the evening of the following day. It had
been one portion of his business to superintend the arrest of
part of a gang of counterfeiters, that had, even at that early
period, buried themselves in the woods, to manufacture their
base coin, which they afterwards circulated from one end of the
Union to the other. The expedition had been completely successful, and about midnight the Sheriff entered the village, at
the head of a posse of deputies and constables, in the centre of
whom rode, pinioned, four of the malefactors. At the gate of
the Mansion-house they separated, Mr. Jones directing his assistants to proceed with their charge to the county gaol, while
he pursued his own way up the gravelled walk, with the kind of
self-satisfaction that a man of his organization would feel, who
had, really, for once, done a very clever thing.

"Holla! Aggy!" shouted the Sheriff, when he reached the
door; "where are you, you black dog? will you keep me here in
the dark all night?——Holla! Aggy! Brave! Brave! hoy, hoy—
where have you got to, Brave? Off his watch! Every body is
asleep but myself! poor I must keep my eyes open, that others
may sleep in safety. Brave! Brave! Well, I will say this for the
dog, lazy as he's grown, that it is the first time I ever knew him
let any one come to the door after dark, without having a smell
to know whether it was an honest man or not. He could tell by
his nose, almost as well as I could myself by looking at them.
Holla! you Agamemnon! where are you? Oh! here comes the
dog at last."

By this time the Sheriff had dismounted, and observed a
form, which he supposed to be that of Brave, slowly creeping
out of the kennel; when, to his astonishment, it reared itself on
two legs, instead of four, and he was able to distinguish, by the
star-light, the curly head and dark visage of the negro.

"Ha! what the devil are you doing there, you black rascal?" he cried; "is it not hot enough for your Guinea blood in the house, this warm night, but you must drive out the poor dog and sleep in his straw!"

By this time the boy was quite awake, and, with a blubbering whine, he attempted to reply to his master.

"Oh! masser Richard! masser Richard! such a ting! such a ting! I nebber tink a could 'appen! nebber tink he die! Oh, Lor-a-gor! a'nt bury—keep 'em till masser Richard get back—got a grabe dug"——

Here the feelings of the negro completely got the mastery, and instead of making any intelligible explanation of the causes of his grief, he blubbered aloud.

"Eh! what! buried! grave! dead!" exclaimed Richard, with a tremour in his voice; "nothing serious? Nothing has happened to Benjamin, I hope? I know he has been bilious; but I gave him"——

"Oh! worser 'an dat! worser 'an dat!" sobbed the negro. "Oh! de Lor! Miss 'Lizzy an Miss Grant—walk—mountain—poor Bravy!—kill a lady—painter—Oh! Lor, Lor!—Natty Bumppo—tare he troat open—come a see, masser Richard—here he be—here he be."

As all this was perfectly inexplicable to the Sheriff, he was very glad to wait patiently until the black brought a lantern from the kitchen, when he followed Aggy to the kennel, where he beheld poor Brave, indeed, lying in his blood, stiff and cold, but decently covered with the great-coat of the negro. He was on the point of demanding an explanation; but the grief of the black, who had fallen asleep on his voluntary watch, having burst out afresh on his waking, utterly disqualified the lad from giving one. Luckily, at this moment the principal door of the house opened, and the coarse features of Benjamin were thrust over the threshold, with a candle elevated above them, shedding its dim rays around in such a manner as to exhibit the lights and shadows of his countenance. Richard threw his bridle to the black, and bidding him look to the horse, he entered the hall.

"What is the meaning of the dead dog?" he cried. "Where is Miss Temple?"

Benjamin made one of his square gestures, with the thumb of his left hand pointing over his right shoulder, as he answered—

"Turned in."

"Judge Temple—where is he?"

"In his berth."

"But explain; why is Brave dead? and what is the cause of Aggy's grief?"

"Why, it's all down, Squire," said Benjamin, pointing to a slate that lay on the table, by the side of a mug of toddy, a short pipe, in which the tobacco was yet burning, and a prayer-book.

Among the other pursuits of Richard, he had a passion to keep a register of all passing events; and his diary, which was written in the manner of a journal, or log-book, embraced not only such circumstances as affected himself, but observations on the weather, and all the occurrences of the family, and frequently of the village. Since his appointment to the office of Sheriff, and his consequent absences from home, he had employed Benjamin to make memoranda, on a slate, of whatever might be thought worth remembering, which, on his return, were regularly transferred to the journal, with proper notations of the time, manner, and other little particulars. There was, to be sure, one material objection to the clerkship of Benjamin, which the ingenuity of no one but Richard could have overcome. The steward read nothing but his Prayer-book, and that only in particular parts, and by the aid of a good deal of spelling, and some misnomers; but he could not form a single letter with a pen. This would have been an insuperable bar to journalizing, with most men; but Richard invented a kind of hieroglyphical character, which was intended to note all the ordinary occurrences of a day, such as how the wind blew, whether the sun shone, or whether it rained, the hours, &c.; and for the extraordinary, after giving certain elementary lectures on the subject, the Sheriff was obliged to trust to the ingenuity of the Major-domo. The reader will at once perceive, that it was to this chronicle that Benjamin pointed, instead of directly answering the Sheriff's interrogatory.

When Mr. Jones had drunk a glass of toddy, he brought forth, from its secret place, his proper journal, and, seating himself by the table, he prepared to transfer the contents of the slate to the paper, at the same time that he appeased his curiosity. Benjamin laid one hand on the back of the Sheriff's chair, in a familiar manner, while he kept the other at liberty, to make use of a fore-finger, that was bent like some of his own characters, as an index to point out his meaning.

The first thing referred to by the Sheriff was the diagram of a compass, cut in one corner of the slate for permanent use. The cardinal points were plainly marked on it, and all the usual divisions were indicated in such a manner, that no man who had ever steered a ship could mistake them.

"Oh!" said the Sheriff, settling himself down comfortably in his chair—"you'd the wind south-east, I see, all last night; I thought it would have blown up rain."

"Devil the drop, sir," said Benjamin; "I believe that the scuttle-butt up aloft is emptied, for there hasn't so much water fell in the country, for the last three weeks, as would float Indian John's canoe, and that draws just one inch nothing, light."

"Well, but didn't the wind change here this morning? there was a change where I was."

"To be sure it did, Squire; and haven't I logged it as a shift of wind?"

"I don't see where, Benjamin"——

"Don't see!" interrupted the steward, a little crustily; "an't there a mark ag'in east-and-by-nothe-half-nothe, with sum'mat like a rising sun at the end of it, to show 'twas in the morning watch?"

"Yes, yes, that is very legible; but where is the change noted?"

"Where! why doesn't it see this here tea-kettle, with a mark run from the spout straight, or mayhap a little crooked or so, into west-and-by-southe-half-southe? now I calls this a shift of wind, Squire. Well, do you see this here boar's head that you made for me, alongside of the compass"——

"Ay, ay—Boreas—I see. Why you've drawn lines from its mouth, extending from one of your marks to the other."

"It's no fault of mine, Squire Dickens; 'tis your d—d climate. The wind has been at all them there marks this very day; and that's all round the compass, except a little matter of an Irishman's hurricane at meridium, which you'll find marked right up and down. Now I've known a sow-wester blow for three weeks, in the Channel, with a clean drizzle in which you might wash your face and hands, without the trouble of hauling in water from alongside."

"Very well, Benjamin," said the Sheriff, writing in his journal; "I believe I have caught the idea. Oh! here's a cloud over the rising sun;—so you had it hazy in the morning?"

"Ay, ay, sir," said Benjamin.

"Ah! it's Sunday, and here are the marks for the length of the sermon—one, two, three, four——What! did Mr. Grant preach forty minutes!"

"Ay, sum'mat like it; it was a good half-hour by my own glass, and then there was the time lost in turning it, and some little allowance for lee-way in not being over smart about it."

"Benjamin, this is as long as a Presbyterian; you never could have been ten minutes in turning the glass!"

"Why, d'ye see, Squire, the parson was very solemn, and I just closed my eyes in order to think the better with myself, just the same as you'd put in the dead-lights to make all snug, and when I opened them ag'in I found the congregation were getting under way for home, so I calculated the ten minutes would cover the lee-way after the glass was out. It was only some such matter as a cat's nap."

"Oh, ho! Master Benjamin, you were asleep, were you! but I'll set down no such slander against an orthodox divine." Richard wrote twenty-nine minutes in his journal, and continued—"Why, what's this you've got opposite ten o'clock, A.M.? a full moon! had you a moon visible by day! I have heard of such portents before now, but—eh! what's this alongside of it? an hour-glass?"

"That!" said Benjamin, looking coolly over the Sheriff's shoulder, and rolling the tobacco about in his mouth with a jocular air; "why that's a small matter of my own. It's no moon, Squire, but only Betty Hollister's face; for, d'ye see, sir, hearing all the same as if she had got up a new cargo of Jamaiky from the river, I called in as I was going to the church this morning—ten, A.M. was it? just the time—and tried a glass; and so I logged it, to put me in mind of calling to pay her like an honest man."

"That was it, was it?" said the Sheriff, with some displeasure at this innovation on his memoranda; "and could you not make a better glass than this? it looks like a death's head and an hour-glass."

"Why, as I liked the stuff, Squire," returned the steward, "I turned in, homeward bound, and took t'other glass, which I set down at the bottom of the first, and that gives the thing the shape it has. But as I was there ag'in to-night, and paid for the three at once, your honour may as well run the sponge over the whole business."

"I will buy you a slate for your own affairs, Benjamin," said the Sheriff; "I don't like to have the journal marked over in this manner."

"You needn't—you needn't, Squire; for, seeing that I was likely to trade often with the woman while this barrel lasted, I've opened a fair account with Betty, and she keeps the marks on the back of her bar door, and I keeps the tally on this here bit of a stick."

As Benjamin concluded he produced a piece of wood, on which five very large, honest notches were apparent. The Sheriff cast his eyes on this new leger, for a moment, and continued—

"What have we here! Saturday, two, P.M.—why here's a whole family piece! two wine-glasses up-side-down!"

"That's two women; the one this a-way is Miss 'Lizzy, and t'other is the parson's young'un."

"Cousin Bess and Miss Grant!" exclaimed the Sheriff, in amazement; "what have they to do with my journal?"

"They'd enough to do to get out of the jaws of that there painter, or panther," said the immoveable steward. "This here thingum'y, Squire, that maybe looks sum'mat like a rat, is the beast, d'ye see; and this here t'other thing, keel uppermost, is poor old Brave, who died nobly, all the same as an admiral fighting for his king and country; and that there"——

"Scarecrow," interrupted Richard.

"Ay, mayhap it do look a little wild or so," continued the steward; "but, to my judgment, Squire, it's the best imager I've made, seeing it's most like the man himself;—well, that's Natty Bumppo, who shot this here painter, that killed that there dog, who would have eaten or done worse to them here young ladies."

"And what the devil does all this mean?" cried Richard, impatiently.

"Mean!" echoed Benjamin; "it's as true as the Boadishey's log-book"——

He was interrupted by the Sheriff, who put a few direct questions to him, that obtained more intelligible answers, by which means he became possessed of a tolerably correct idea of the truth. When the wonder, and, we must do Richard the justice to say, the feelings also, that were created by this narrative, had in some degree subsided, the Sheriff turned his eyes again on his journal, where more inexplicable hieroglyphics met his view.

"What have we here!" he cried; "two men boxing! has there been a breach of the peace? ah! that's the way, the moment my back is turned"——

"That's the Judge and young Master Edwards," interrupted the steward, very cavalierly.

"How! 'duke fighting with Oliver! what the devil has got into you all? more things have happened within the last thirty-six hours, than in the preceding six months."

"Yes, it's so indeed, Squire," returned the steward; "I've known a smart chase, and a fight at the tail of it, where less has been logged than I've got on that there slate. Howsomnever, they didn't come to facers, only passed a little jaw fore and aft."

"Explain! explain!" cried Richard—"it was about the mines, ha!—ay, ay, I see it, I see it; here is a man with a pick on his shoulder. So you heard it all, Benjamin?"

"Why yes, it was about their minds, I believe, Squire," returned the steward; "and, by what I can learn, they spoke them pretty plainly to one another. Indeed, I may say that I overheard a small matter of it myself, seeing that the windows was open, and I hard by. But this here is no pick, but an anchor on a man's shoulder; and here's the other fluke down his back, maybe a little too close, which signifies that the lad has got under way and left his moorings."

"Has Edwards left the house?"

"He has."

Richard pursued this advantage, and, after a long and close examination, he succeeded in getting out of Benjamin all that he knew, not only concerning the misunderstanding, but of the attempt to search the hut, and Hiram's discomfiture. The

Sheriff was no sooner possessed of these facts, which Benjamin related with all possible tenderness to the Leather-stocking, than, snatching up his hat, and bidding the astonished steward secure the doors and go to his bed, he left the house.

For at least five minutes after Richard disappeared, Benjamin stood with his arms a-kimbo, and his eyes fastened on the door; when, having collected his astonished faculties, he prepared to execute the orders he had received.

It has been already said, that the "court of common pleas and general sessions of the peace," or, as it is commonly called, the "county court," over which Judge Temple presided, held one of its stated sessions on the following morning. The attendants of Richard were officers who had come to the village as much to discharge their usual duties at this court, as to escort the prisoners; and the Sheriff knew their habits too well, not to feel confident he should find most, if not all of them, in the public room of the gaol, discussing the qualities of the keeper's liquors. Accordingly he held his way, through the silent streets of the village, directly to the small and insecure building, that contained all the unfortunate debtors, and some of the criminals of the county, and where justice was administered to such unwary applicants as were so silly as to throw away two dollars, in order to obtain one from their neighbours. The arrival of four malefactors in the custody of a dozen officers, was an event, at that day, in Templeton; and when the Sheriff reached the gaol, he found every indication that his subordinates intended to make a night of it.

The nod of the Sheriff brought two of his deputies to the door, who in their turn drew off six or seven of the constables. With this force Richard led the way through the village, towards the bank of the lake, undisturbed by any noise, except the barking of one or two curs, who were alarmed by the measured tread of the party, and by the low murmurs that run through their own numbers, as a few cautious questions and answers were exchanged, relative to the object of their expedition. When they had crossed the little bridge of hewn logs that was thrown over the Susquehanna, they left the highway, and struck into that field which had been the scene of the victory over the pigeons. From this they followed their leader into the low bushes of pines and chestnuts which had sprung up along the shores of the lake, where the plough had not succeeded the fall of the trees, and soon entered the forest itself. Here Richard paused, and collected his troop around him.

"I have required your assistance, my friends," he said, in a low voice, "in order to arrest Nathaniel Bumppo, commonly called the Leather-stocking. He has assaulted a magistrate, and resisted the execution of a search-warrant, by threatening the life of a constable with his rifle. In short, my friends, he has set an example of rebellion to the laws, and has become a kind of out-law. He is suspected of other misdemeanours and offences against private rights; and I have this night taken on myself, by the virtue of my office of sheriff, to arrest the said Bumppo, and bring him to the county gaol, that he may be present and forthcoming to answer to these heavy charges before the court to-morrow morning. In executing this duty, friends and fellow citizens, you are to use courage and discretion. Courage, that you may not be daunted by any lawless attempts that this man may make, with his rifle and his dogs, to oppose you; and discretion, which here means caution and prudence, that he may not escape from this sudden attack——and——for other good reasons that I need not mention. You will form yourselves in a complete circle around his hut, and at the word 'advance,' called aloud by me, you will rush forward, and, without giving the criminal time for deliberation, enter his dwelling by force and make him your prisoner. Spread yourselves for this purpose, while I shall descend to the shore with a deputy, to take charge of that point; and all communications must be made directly to me, under the bank in front of the hut, where I shall station myself, and remain in order to receive them."

This speech, which Richard had been studying during his walk, had the effect that all similar performances produce, of bringing the dangers of the expedition immediately before the eyes of his forces. The men divided, some plunging deeper into the forest, in order to gain their stations without giving an alarm, and others continuing to advance, at a gait that would allow the whole party to get in order; but all devising the best plan to repulse the attack of a dog, or to escape a rifle-bullet. It was a moment of dread expectation and interest.

When the Sheriff thought time enough had elapsed for the different divisions of his force to arrive at their stations, he raised his voice in the silence of the forest, and shouted the watchword. The sounds played among the arched branches of the trees in hollow cadences; but when the last sinking tone was lost on the ear, in place of the expected howls of the dogs, no other noises were returned but the crackling of torn branches and dried sticks, as they yielded before the advancing steps of the officers. Even this soon ceased, as if by a common consent, when, the curiosity and impatience of the Sheriff getting the complete ascendency over discretion, he rushed up the bank, and in a moment stood on the little piece of cleared ground in front of the spot where Natty had so long lived. To his amazement, in place of the hut, he saw only its smouldering ruins.

The party gradually drew together about the heap of ashes and the ends of smoking logs, while a dim flame in the centre of the ruin, which still found fuel to feed its lingering life, threw its pale light, flickering with the passing currents of the air, around the circle, now showing a face with eyes fixed in astonishment, and then glancing to another countenance, leaving the former shaded in the obscurity of night. Not a voice was raised in inquiry, nor an exclamation made in astonishment. This transition from excitement to disappointment was too powerful for speech, and even Richard lost the use of an organ that was seldom known to fail him.

The whole group were yet in the fulness of their surprise, when a tall form stalked from the gloom into the circle, treading down the hot ashes and dying embers with callous feet, and, standing over the light, lifted his cap, and exposed the bare head and weather-beaten features of the Leather-stocking. For a moment he gazed at the dusky figures who surrounded him, more in sorrow than in anger, before he spoke.

"What would ye have with an old and helpless man?" he said. "You've driven God's creaters from the wilderness, where his providence had put them for his own pleasure, and you've brought in the troubles and divilties of the law, where no man was ever known to disturb another. You have driven me, that have lived forty long years of my appointed time in this very spot, from my home and the shelter of my head, lest you should put your wicked feet and wasty ways in my cabin. You've driven me to burn these logs, under which I've eaten and drunk, the first of Heaven's gifts, and the other of the pure springs, for the half of a hundred years, and to mourn the ashes under my feet, as a man would weep and mourn for the children of his body. You've rankled the heart of an old man, that has never harmed you or yourn, with bitter feelings towards his kind, at a time when his thoughts should be on a better world; and you've driven him to wish that the beasts of the forest, who never feast on the blood of their own families, was his kindred and race; and now, when he has come to see the last brand of his hut, before it is melted into ashes, you follow him up, at midnight, like hungry hounds on the track of a worn-out and dying deer! What more would ye have? for I am here—one to many. I come to mourn, not to fight; and, if it is God's pleasure, work your will on me."

When the old man ended, he stood, with the light glimmering around his thinly-covered head, looking earnestly at the group, which receded from the pile, with an involuntary movement, without the reach of the quivering rays, leaving a free passage for his retreat into the bushes, where pursuit, in the dark, would have been fruitless. Natty seemed not to regard this advantage, but stood facing each individual in the circle, in succession, as if to see who would be the first to arrest him. After a pause of a few moments, Richard begun to rally his confused faculties, and advancing, apologized for his duty, and made him his prisoner. The party now collected, and, preceded by the Sheriff, with Natty in their centre, they took their way towards the village.

During the walk, divers questions were put to the prisoner concerning his reasons for burning the hut, and whither Mohegan had retreated, but to all of them he observed a profound silence, until, fatigued with their previous duties, and the lateness of the hour, the Sheriff and his followers reached the village, and dispersed to their several places of rest, after turning the key of a gaol on the aged and apparently friendless Leather-stocking.

Chapter XXXIII.

"Fetch here the stocks, ho!
You stubborn ancient knave, you reverend braggart,
We'll teach you." *King Lear*, II.ii.125–27.

T HE long days and early sun of July allowed time for a gathering of the interested, before the little bell of the academy announced that the appointed hour had arrived for administering right to the wronged, and punishment to the guilty. Ever since the dawn of day, the highways and wood-paths that, issuing from the forests, and winding along the sides of the mountains, centered in Templeton, had been thronged with equestrians and footmen, bound to the haven of justice. There was to be seen a well-clad yeoman, mounted on a sleek, switch-tailed steed, ambling along the highway, with his red face elevated in a manner that said, "I have paid for my land, and fear no man," while his bosom was swelling with the pride of being one of the grand inquest for the county. At his side rode a companion, his equal in independence of feeling, perhaps, but his inferior in thrift, as in property and consideration. This was a professed dealer in lawsuits,—a man whose name appeared in every calendar; whose substance, gained in the multifarious expedients of a settler's changeable habits, was wasted in feeding the harpies of the courts. He was endeavouring to impress the mind of the grand juror with the merits of a cause now at issue. Along with these was a pedestrian, who, having thrown a rifle frock over his shirt, and placed his best wool hat above his sunburnt visage, had issued from his retreat in the woods by a footpath, and was striving to keep company with the others, on his way to hear and to decide the disputes of his neighbours as a petit juror. Fifty similar little knots of countrymen might have been seen, on that morning, journeying towards the shire-town on the same errand.

By ten o'clock the streets of the village were filled with busy faces, some talking of their private concerns, some listening to a popular expounder of political creeds, and others gaping in at the open stores, admiring the finery, or examining sithes, axes, and such other manufactures as attracted their curiosity or excited their admiration. A few women were in the crowd, most carrying infants, and followed, at a lounging, listless gait, by their rustic lords and masters. There was one young couple, in whom connubial love was yet fresh, walking at a respectful distance from each other, while the swain directed the timid steps of his bride, by a gallant offering of a thumb!

At the first stroke of the bell, Richard issued from the door of the "Bold Dragoon," flourishing a sheathed sword, that he was fond of saying his ancestors had carried in one of Cromwell's victories, and crying, in an authoritative tone, to "clear the way for the court." The order was obeyed promptly, though not servilely; the members of the crowd nodding familiarly to the members of the procession, as it passed. A party of constables with their staves followed the Sheriff, preceding Marmaduke and four plain, grave-looking yeomen, who were his associates on the bench. There was nothing to distinguish these subordinate judges from the better part of the spectators, except gravity, which they affected a little more than common, and that one of their number was attired in an old-fashioned military coat, with skirts that reached no lower than the middle of his thighs, and bearing two little silver epaulettes, not half so big as a modern pair of shoulder-knots. This gentleman was a colonel of the militia, in attendance on a court-martial, who found leisure to steal a moment from his military, to attend to his civil jurisdiction. But this incongruity excited neither notice nor comment. Three or four clean-shaved lawyers followed, as meekly as if they were lambs going to the slaughter. One or two of their number had contrived to obtain an air of scholastic gravity, by wearing spectacles. The rear was brought up by another posse of constables, and the mob followed the whole into the room where the court held its sittings.

The edifice was composed of a basement of squared logs, perforated here and there with small grated windows, through which a few wistful faces were gazing at the crowd without. Among the captives were the guilty, downcast countenances of the counterfeiters, and the simple but honest features of the Leather-stocking. The dungeons were to be distinguished, externally, from the debtors' apartments, only by the size of the apertures, the thickness of the grates, and by the heads of the spikes that were driven into the logs as a protection against the illegal use of edge-tools. The upper story was of frame-work, regularly covered with boards, and contained one room decently fitted up for the purposes of justice. A bench, raised on a narrow platform to the height of a man above the floor, and protected in front by a light railing, ran along one of its sides. In the centre was a seat, furnished with rude arms, that was always filled by the presiding judge. In front, on a level with the floor of the room, was a large table, covered with green baize, and surrounded by benches; and at either of its ends were rows of seats, rising one over the other, for jury-boxes. Each of these divisions was surrounded by a railing. The remainder of the room was an open square, appropriated to the spectators.

When the judges were seated, the lawyers had taken possession of the table, and the noise of moving feet had ceased in the area, the proclamations were made in the usual form, the jurors were sworn, the charge was given, and the court proceeded to hear the business before them.

We shall not detain the reader with a description of the captious discussions that occupied the court for the first two hours. Judge Temple had impressed on the jury, in his charge, the necessity for despatch on their part, recommending to their notice, from motives of humanity, the prisoners in the gaol, as the first objects of their attention. Accordingly, after the period we have mentioned had elapsed, the cry of the officer to "clear the way for the grand jury," announced the entrance of that body. The usual forms were observed, when the foreman handed up to the bench two bills, on both of which the Judge observed, at the first glance of his eye, the name of Nathaniel Bumppo. It was a leisure moment with the court; some low whispering passed between the bench and the Sheriff, who gave a signal to his officers, and in a very few minutes the silence that prevailed was interrupted by a general movement in the outer crowd; when presently the Leather-stocking made his appearance, ushered into the criminal's bar under the custody of two constables. The hum ceased, the people closed into the open space again, and the silence soon became so deep that the hard breathing of the prisoner was audible.

Natty was dressed in his buck-skin garments, without his coat, in place of which he wore only a shirt of coarse linen-check, fastened at his throat by the sinew of a deer, leaving his red neck and weather-beaten face exposed and bare. It was the first time that he had ever crossed the threshold of a court of justice, and curiosity seemed to be strongly blended with his personal feelings. He raised his eyes to the bench, thence to the jury-boxes, the bar, and the crowd without, meeting every where looks fastened on himself. After surveying his own person, as if searching for the cause of this unusual attraction, he once more turned his face around the assemblage, and opened his mouth in one of his silent and remarkable laughs.

"Prisoner, remove your cap," said Judge Temple.

The order was either unheard or unheeded.

"Nathaniel Bumppo, be uncovered," repeated the Judge.

Natty started at the sound of his name, and, raising his face earnestly towards the bench, he said—

"Anan!"

Mr. Lippet arose from his seat at the table, and whispered in the ear of the prisoner, when Natty gave him a nod of assent, and took the deer-skin covering from his head.

"Mr. District Attorney," said the Judge, "the prisoner is ready; we wait for the indictment."

The duties of public prosecutor were discharged by Dirck Van der School, who adjusted his spectacles, cast a cautious look around him at his brethren of the bar, which he ended by throwing his head aside so as to catch one glance over the glasses, when he proceeded to read the bill aloud. It was the usual charge for an assault and battery, on the person of Hiram Doolittle, and was couched in the ancient language of such instruments, especial care having been taken by the scribe, not to omit the name of a single offensive weapon known to the law. When he had done, Mr. Van der School removed his spectacles, which he closed and placed in his pocket, seemingly for the pleasure of again opening and replacing them on his nose. After this evolution was repeated once or twice, he handed the bill over to Mr. Lippet, with a cavalier air, that said as much as "pick a hole in that if you can."

Natty listened to the charge with great attention, leaning forward towards the reader with an earnestness that denoted his interest; and when it was ended he raised his tall body to the utmost, and drew a long sigh. All eyes were turned to the prisoner, whose voice was vainly expected to break the stillness of the room.

"You have heard the presentment that the grand jury have made, Nathaniel Bumppo," said the Judge; "what do you plead to the charge?"

The old man dropped his head for a moment in a reflecting attitude, and then raising it, he laughed before he answered—

"That I handled the man a little rough or so, is not to be denied; but that there was occasion to make use of all them things that the gentleman has spoken of, is downright untrue. I am not much of a wrestler, seeing that I'm getting old; but I was out among the Scotch-Irishers—lets me see—it must have been as long ago as the first year of the old war"——

"Mr. Lippet, if you are retained for the prisoner," interrupted Judge Temple, "instruct your client how to plead; if not, the court will assign him counsel."

Aroused from studying the indictment by this appeal, the attorney got up, and, after a short dialogue with the hunter in a low voice, he informed the court that they were ready to proceed.

"Do you plead guilty or not guilty?" said the Judge.

"I may say not guilty with a clean conscience," returned Natty; "for there's no guilt in doing what's right; and I'd rather died on the spot, than had him put foot in the hut at that moment."

Richard started at this declaration, and bent his eyes significantly on Hiram, who returned the look with a slight movement of his eye-brows.

"Proceed to open the cause, Mr. District Attorney," continued the Judge. "Mr. Clerk, enter the plea of not guilty."

After a short opening address from Mr. Van der School, Hiram was summoned to the bar to give his testimony. It was delivered to the letter, perhaps, but with all that moral colouring which can be conveyed under such expressions as, "thinking no harm," "feeling it my bounden duty as a magistrate," and "seeing that the constable was back'ard in the business." When he had done, and the District Attorney declined putting any further interrogatories, Mr. Lippet arose, with an air of keen investigation, and asked the following questions:——

"Are you a constable of this county, sir?"

"No, sir," said Hiram, "I'm only a justice-peace."

"I ask you, Mr. Doolittle, in the face of this court, putting it to your conscience and your knowledge of the law, whether you had any right to enter that man's dwelling?"

"Hem!" said Hiram, undergoing a violent struggle between his desire for vengeance and his love of legal fame; "I do suppose—that in —that is—strict law—that supposing—maybe I hadn't a real—lawful right;—but as the case was—and Billy was so back'ard—I thought I might come for'ard in the business."

"I ask you, again, sir," continued the lawyer, following up his success, "whether this old, this friendless old man, did or did not repeatedly forbid your entrance?"

"Why, I must say," said Hiram, "that he was considerable cross-grained; not what I call clever, seeing that it was only one neighbour wanting to go into the house of another."

"Oh! then you own it was only meant for a neighbourly visit on your part, and without the sanction of law. Remember, gentlemen, the words of the witness, 'one neighbour wanting to enter the house of another.' Now, sir, I ask you if Nathaniel Bumppo did not again and again order you not to enter?"

"There was some words passed between us," said Hiram, "but I read the warrant to him aloud."

"I repeat my question; did he tell you not to enter his habitation?"

"There was a good deal passed betwixt us—but I've the warrant in my pocket; maybe the court would wish to see it?"

"Witness," said Judge Temple, "answer the question directly; did or did not the prisoner forbid your entering his hut?"

"Why, I some think"——

"Answer without equivocation," continued the Judge, sternly.

"He did."

"And did you attempt to enter, after this order?"

"I did; but the warrant was in my hand."

"Proceed, Mr. Lippet, with your examination."

But the attorney saw that the impression was in favour of his client, and, waving his hand with a supercilious manner, as if unwilling to insult the understanding of the jury with any further defence, he replied—

"No, sir; I leave it for your honour to charge; I rest my case here."

"Mr. District Attorney," said the Judge, "have you any thing to say?"

Mr. Van der School removed his spectacles, folded them, and replacing them once more on his nose, eyed the other bill which he held in his hand, and then said, looking at the bar over the top of his glasses—

"I shall rest the prosecution here, if the court please."

Judge Temple arose and began the charge.

"Gentlemen of the jury," he said, "you have heard the testimony, and I shall detain you but a moment. If an officer meet with resistance in the execution of a process, he has an undoubted right to call any citizen to his assistance; and the acts of such assistant come within the protection of the law. I shall leave you to judge, gentlemen, from the testimony, how far the witness in this prosecution can be so considered, feeling less reluctance to submit the case thus informally to your decision, because there is yet another indictment to be tried, which involves heavier charges against the unfortunate prisoner."

The tone of Marmaduke was mild and insinuating, and as his sentiments were given with such apparent impartiality, they did not fail of carrying due weight with the jury. The grave-looking yeomen, who composed this tribunal, laid their heads together for a few minutes, without leaving the box, when the foreman arose, and, after the forms of the court were duly observed, he pronounced the prisoner to be—

"Not guilty."

"You are acquitted of this charge, Nathaniel Bumppo," said the Judge.

"Anan!" said Natty.

"You are found not guilty of striking and assaulting Mr. Doolittle."

"No, no, I'll not deny but that I took him a little roughly by the shoulders," said Natty, looking about him with great simplicity, "and that I"——

"You are acquitted," interrupted the Judge; "and there is nothing further to be done or said in the matter."

A look of joy lighted up the features of the old man, who now comprehended the case, and, placing his cap eagerly on his head again, he threw up the bar of his little prison, and said feelingly—

"I must say this for you, Judge Temple, that the law has not been as hard on me as I dreaded. I hope God will bless you for the kind things you've done to me this day."

But the staff of the constable was opposed to his egress, and Mr. Lippet whispered a few words in his ear, when the aged hunter sunk back into his place, and removing his cap, stroked down the remnants of his gray and sandy locks, with an air of mortification mingled with submission.

"Mr. District Attorney," said Judge Temple, affecting to busy himself with his minutes, "proceed with the second indictment."

Mr. Van der School took great care that no part of the presentment, which he now read, should be lost on his auditors. It accused the prisoner of resisting the execution of a search-warrant by force of arms, and particularized, in the vague language of the law, among a variety of other weapons, the use of the rifle. This was indeed a more serious charge than an ordinary assault and battery, and a corresponding degree of interest was manifested by the spectators in its result. The prisoner was duly arraigned, and his plea again demanded. Mr. Lippet had anticipated the answers of Natty, and in a whisper advised him how to plead. But the feelings of the old hunter were awakened by some of the expressions of the indictment, and, forgetful of his caution, he exclaimed—

"'Tis a wicked untruth; I crave no man's blood. Them thieves, the Iroquois, won't say it to my face, that I ever thirsted after man's blood. I have fout as a soldier that feared his Maker and his officer, but I never pulled trigger on any but a warrior that was up and awake. No man can say that I ever struck even a Mingo in his blanket. I b'lieve there's some who thinks there's no God in a wilderness!"

"Attend to your plea, Bumppo," said the Judge; "you hear that you are accused of using your rifle against an officer of justice; are you guilty or not guilty?"

By this time the irritated feelings of Natty had found vent; and he rested on the bar for a moment, in a musing posture, when he lifted his face, with his silent laugh, and pointing to where the wood-chopper stood, he said—

"Would Billy Kirby be standing there, d'ye think, if I had used the rifle?"

"Then you deny it," said Mr. Lippet; "you plead not guilty?"

"Sartain," said Natty; "Billy knows that I never fired at all. Billy, do you remember the turkey last winter? ah! me! that was better than common firing; but I can't shoot as I used to could."

"Enter the plea of not guilty," said Judge Temple, strongly affected by the simplicity of the prisoner.

Hiram was again sworn, and his testimony given on the second charge. He had discovered his former error, and proceeded more cautiously than before. He related very distinctly, and, for the man, with amazing terseness, the suspicion against the hunter, the complaint, the issuing of the warrant, and the swearing in of Kirby; all of which, he affirmed, were done in due form of law. He then added the manner in which the constable had been received; and stated distinctly that Natty had pointed the rifle at Kirby, and threatened his life, if he attempted to execute his duty. All this was confirmed by Jotham, who was observed to adhere closely to the story of the magistrate. Mr. Lippet conducted an artful cross-examination of these two witnesses, but, after consuming much time, was compelled to relinquish the attempt to obtain any advantage, in despair.

At length the District Attorney called the wood-chopper to the bar. Billy gave an extremely confused account of the whole affair, although he evidently aimed at the truth, until Mr. Van der School aided him, by asking some direct questions:—

"It appears, from examining the papers, that you demanded admission into the hut legally; so you were put in bodily fear by his rifle and threats?"

"I didn't mind them that, man," said Billy, snapping his fingers; "I should be a poor stick, to mind old Leatherstocking."

"But I understood you to say, (referring to your previous words, (as delivered here in court,) in the commencement of your testimony,) that you thought he meant to shoot you?"

"To be sure I did; and so would you too, Squire, if you had seen the chap dropping a muzzle that never misses, and cocking an eye that has a nateral squint by long practice. I thought there would be a dust on't, and my back was up at once; but Leather-stocking gi'n up the skin, and so the matter ended."

"Ah! Billy," said Natty, shaking his head, " 'twas a lucky thought in me to throw out the hide, or there might have been blood spilt; and I'm sure, if it had been your'n, I should have mourned it sorely the little while I have to stay."

"Well, Leather-stocking," returned Billy, facing the prisoner, with a freedom and familiarity that utterly disregarded the presence of the court, "as you are on the subject, it may be that you've no"——

"Go on with your examination, Mr. District Attorney."

That gentleman eyed the familiarity between his witness and the prisoner with manifest disgust, and indicated to the court that he was done.

"Then you didn't feel frightened, Mr. Kirby?" said the counsel for the prisoner.

"Me! no," said Billy, casting his eyes over his own huge frame with evident self-satisfaction; "I'm not to be skeared so easy."

"You look like a hardy man; where were you born, sir?"

"Varmount state; 'tis a mountaynious place, but there's a stiff soil, and it's pretty much wooded with beech and maple."

"I have always heerd so," said Mr. Lippet, soothingly. "You have been used to the rifle yourself, in that country?"

"I pull the second best trigger in this county. I knock under to Natty Bumppo there, sin' he shot the pigeon."

Leather-stocking raised his head, and laughed again, when he abruptly thrust out a wrinkled hand, and said—

"You're young yet, Billy, and haven't seen the matches that I have; but here's my hand; I bear no malice to you, I don't."

Mr. Lippet allowed this conciliatory offering to be accepted, and judiciously paused, while the spirit of peace was exercising its influence over the two; but the Judge interposed his authority.

"This is an improper place for such dialogues," he said. "Proceed with your examination of this witness, Mr. Lippet, or I shall order the next."

The attorney started, as if unconscious of any impropriety, and continued—

"So you settled the matter with Natty amicably on the spot, did you?"

"He gi'n me the skin, and I didn't want to quarrel with an old man; for my part, I see no such mighty matter in shooting a buck!"

"And you parted friends? and you would never have thought of bringing the business up before a court, hadn't you been subpœnaed?"

"I don't think I should; he gi'n the skin, and I didn't feel a hard thought, though Squire Doolittle got some affronted."

"I have done, sir," said Mr. Lippet, probably relying on the charge of the Judge, as he again seated himself, with the air of a man who felt that his success was certain.

When Mr. Van der School arose to address the jury, he commenced by saying—

"Gentlemen of the jury, I should have interrupted the leading questions put by the prisoner's counsel, (by leading questions I mean telling him what to say,) did I not feel confident that the law of the land was superior to any advantages (I mean legal advantages) which he might obtain by his art. The counsel for the prisoner, gentlemen, has endeavoured to persuade you, in opposition to your own good sense, to believe that pointing a rifle at a constable (elected or deputed) is a very innocent affair; and that society (I mean the commonwealth, gentlemen,) shall not be endangered thereby. But let me claim your attention, while we look over the particulars of this heinous offence." Here Mr. Van der School favoured the jury with an abridgment of the testimony, recounted in such a manner as utterly to confuse the faculties of his worthy listeners. After this exhibition he closed as follows:—"And now, gentlemen, having thus made plain to your senses the crime of which this unfortunate man has been guilty, (unfortunate both on account of his ignorance and his guilt,) I shall leave you to your own consciences; not in the least doubting that you will see the importance (notwithstanding the prisoner's counsel (doubtless relying on your former verdict) wishes to appear so confident of success) of punishing the offender, and asserting the dignity of the laws."

It was now the duty of the Judge to deliver his charge. It

consisted of a short, comprehensive summary of the testimony, laying bare the artifice of the prisoner's counsel, and placing the facts in so obvious a light that they could not well be misunderstood. "Living, as we do, gentlemen," he concluded, "on the skirts of society, it becomes doubly necessary to protect the ministers of the law. If you believe the witnesses, in their construction of the acts of the prisoner, it is your duty to convict him; but if you believe that the old man, who this day appears before you, meant not to harm the constable, but was acting more under the influence of habit than by the instigations of malice, it will be your duty to judge him, but to do it with lenity."

As before, the jury did not leave their box, but, after a consultation of some little time, their foreman arose, and pronounced the prisoner—

"Guilty."

There was but little surprise manifested in the court-room at this verdict, as the testimony, the greater part of which we have omitted, was too clear and direct to be passed over. The judges seemed to have anticipated this sentiment, for a consultation was passing among them also, during the deliberation of the jury, and the preparatory movements of the "bench" announced the coming sentence.

"Nathaniel Bumppo," commenced the Judge, making the customary pause.

The old hunter, who had been musing again, with his head on the bar, raised himself, and cried, with a prompt, military tone—

"Here."

The Judge waved his hand for silence, and proceeded—

"In forming their sentence, the court have been governed as much by the consideration of your ignorance of the laws, as by a strict sense of the importance of punishing such outrages as this of which you have been found guilty. They have, therefore, passed over the obvious punishment of whipping on the bare back, in mercy to your years; but as the dignity of the law requires an open exhibition of the consequences of your crime, it is ordered, that you be conveyed from this room to the public stocks, where you are to be confined for one hour; that you pay a fine to the state of one hundred dollars; and that you be imprisoned in the gaol of this county for one calendar month; and furthermore, that your imprisonment do not cease until the said fine shall be paid. I feel it my duty, Nathaniel Bumppo,"—

"And where should I get the money!" interrupted the Leather-stocking, eagerly; "where should I get the money! you'll take away the bounty on the painters, because I cut the throat of a deer; and how is an old man to find so much gold or silver in the woods? No, no, Judge; think better of it, and don't talk of shutting me up in a gaol for the little time I have to stay."

"If you have any thing to urge against the passing of the sentence, the court will yet hear you," said the Judge, mildly.

"I have enough to say ag'in it," cried Natty, grasping the bar, on which his fingers were working with a convulsed motion. "Where am I to get the money? Let me out into the woods and hills, where I've been used to breathe the clear air, and though I'm three score and ten, if you've left game enough in the country, I'll travel night and day but I'll make you up the sum afore the season is over. Yes, yes—you see the reason of the thing, and the wickedness of shutting up an old man, that has spent his days, as one may say, where he could always look into the windows of heaven."

"I must be governed by the law"——

"Talk not to me of law, Marmaduke Temple," interrupted the hunter. "Did the beast of the forest mind your laws, when it was thirsty and hungering for the blood of your own child! She was kneeling to her God for a greater favour than I ask, and he heard her; and if you now say no to my prayers, do you think he will be deaf?"

"My private feelings must not enter into"——

"Hear me, Marmaduke Temple," interrupted the old man, with melancholy earnestness, "and hear reason. I've travelled these mountains when you was no judge, but an infant in your mother's arms; and I feel as if I had a right and a privilege to travel them ag'in afore I die. Have you forgot the time that you come on to the lake-shore, when there wasn't even a gaol to lodge in; and didn't I give you my own bear-skin to sleep on, and the fat of a noble buck to satisfy the cravings of your hunger? Yes, yes—you thought it no sin then to kill a deer! And this I did, though I had no reason to love you, for you had

never done any thing but harm to them that loved and sheltered me. And now will you shut me up in your dungeons to
pay me for my kindness? A hundred dollars! where should I
get the money? No, no—there's them that says hard things of
you, Marmaduke Temple, but you an't so bad as to wish to see
an old man die in a prison, because he stood up for the right.
Come, friend, let me pass; it's long sin' I've been used to such
crowds, and I crave to be in the woods ag'in. Don't fear me,
Judge—I bid you not to fear me; for if there's beaver enough
left on the streams, or the buckskins will sell for a shilling
a-piece, you shall have the last penny of the fine. Where are ye,
pups! come away, dogs! come away! we have a grievous toil to
do for our years, but it shall be done—yes, yes, I've promised
it, and it shall be done!"

It is unnecessary to say that the movement of the Leather-
stocking was again intercepted by the constable; but before he
had time to speak, a bustling in the crowd, and a loud hem,
drew all eyes to another part of the room.

Benjamin had succeeded in edging his way through the people, and was now seen balancing his short body, with one foot in
a window and the other on the railing of the jury-box. To the
amazement of the whole court, the steward was evidently preparing to speak. After a good deal of difficulty, he succeeded in
drawing from his pocket a small bag, and then found utterance.

"If-so-be," he said, "that your honour is agreeable to trust the
poor fellow out on another cruise among the beasts, here's a
small matter that will help to bring down the risk, seeing that
there's just thirty-five of your Spaniards in it; and I wish, from
the bottom of my heart, that they was raal British guineas, for
the sake of the old boy. But 'tis as it is; and if Squire Dickens will
just be so good as to overhaul this small bit of an account, and
take enough from the bag to settle the same, he's welcome to
hold on upon the rest, till such time as the Leather-stocking can
grapple with them said beaver, or, for that matter, for ever, and
no thanks asked."

As Benjamin concluded, he thrust out the wooden register of
his arrears to the "Bold Dragoon" with one hand, while he offered his bag of dollars with the other. Astonishment at this
singular interruption produced a profound stillness in the

room, which was only interrupted by the Sheriff, who struck his sword on the table, and cried—

"Silence!"

"There must be an end to this," said the Judge, struggling to overcome his feelings. "Constable, lead the prisoner to the stocks. Mr. Clerk, what stands next on the calendar?"

Natty seemed to yield to his destiny, for he sunk his head on his chest, and followed the officer from the court-room in silence. The crowd moved back for the passage of the prisoner, and when his tall form was seen descending from the outer door, a rush of the people to the scene of his disgrace followed.

Chapter XXXIV.

"Ha! ha! look! he wears cruel garters!"   *King Lear*, II.ii.8.

T HE punishments of the common law were still known, at
the time of our tale, to the people of New-York; and the
whipping-post, and its companion the stocks, were not yet
supplanted by the more merciful expedients of the public pris-
ons. Immediately in front of the gaol, those relics of the elder
times were situated, as a lesson of precautionary justice to the
evil-doers of the settlement.

Natty followed the constables to this spot, bowing his head
with submission to a power that he was unable to oppose, and
surrounded by the crowd, that formed a circle about his person, exhibiting in their countenances strong curiosity. A constable raised the upper part of the stocks, and pointed with his
finger to the holes where the old man was to place his feet.
Without making the least objection to the punishment, the
Leather-stocking quietly seated himself on the ground, and suffered his limbs to be laid in the openings, without even a murmur; though he cast one glance about him, in quest of that
sympathy that human nature always seems to require under
suffering. If he met no direct manifestations of pity, neither did
he see any unfeeling exultation, or hear a single reproachful
epithet. The character of the mob, if it could be called by such a
name, was that of attentive subordination.

The constable was in the act of lowering the upper plank,
when Benjamin, who had pressed close to the side of the prisoner, said, in his hoarse tones, as if seeking for some cause to
create a quarrel—

"Where away, master constable, is the use of clapping a man
in them here bilboes? it neither stops his grog nor hurts his
back; what for is it that you do the thing?"

" 'Tis the sentence of the court, Mr. Penguillum, and there's
law for it, I s'pose."

"Ay, ay, I know that there's law for the thing; but where away
do you find the use, I say? it does no harm, and it only keeps a
man by the heels for the small matter of two glasses."

"Is it no harm, Benny Pump," said Natty, raising his eyes with a piteous look to the face of the steward—"is it no harm to show off a man in his seventy-first year, like a tamed bear, for the settlers to look on! Is it no harm to put an old soldier, that has sarved through the war of 'fifty-six, and seen the inimy in the 'seventy-six business, into a place like this, where the boys can point at him and say, I have known the time when he was a spictacle for the county! Is it no harm to bring down the pride of an honest man to be the equal of the beasts of the forest!"

Benjamin stared about him fiercely, and, could he have found a single face that expressed contumely, he would have been prompt to quarrel with its owner; but meeting every where with looks of sobriety, and occasionally of commiseration, he very deliberately seated himself by the side of the hunter, and placing his legs in the two vacant holes of the stocks, he said—

"Now lower away, master constable, lower away, I tell ye! If-so-be there's such a thing hereabouts as a man that wants to see a bear, let him look and be d—d, and he shall find two of them, and mayhap one of the same that can bite as well as growl."

"But I've no orders to put you in the stocks, Mr. Pump," cried the constable; "you must get up and let me do my duty."

"You've my orders, and what do you need better, to meddle with my own feet? so lower away, will ye, and let me see the man that chooses to open his mouth with a grin on it."

"There can't be any harm in locking up a creater that will enter the pound," said the constable, laughing, and closing the stocks on them both.

It was fortunate that this act was executed with decision, for the whole of the spectators, when they saw Benjamin assume the position he took, felt an inclination for merriment, which few thought it worth while to suppress. The steward struggled violently for his liberty again, with an evident intention of making battle on those who stood nearest to him; but the key was already turned, and all his efforts were vain.

"Hark ye, master constable," he cried, "just clear away your bilboes for the small matter of a log-glass, will ye, and let me show some of them there chaps who it is they are so merry about."

"No, no, you would go in, and you can't come out," returned

the officer, "until the time has expired that the Judge directed for the keeping of the prisoner."

Benjamin, finding that his threats and his struggles were useless, had good sense enough to learn patience from the resigned manner of his companion, and soon settled himself down by the side of Natty, with a contemptuousness expressed in his hard features, that showed he had substituted disgust for rage. When the violence of the steward's feelings had in some measure subsided, he turned to his fellow sufferer, and, with a motive that might have vindicated a worse effusion, he attempted the charitable office of consolation.

"Taking it by and large, Master Bump-ho, 'tis but a small matter, after all," he said. "Now I've known very good sort of men, aboard of the Boadishey, laid by the heels, for nothing, mayhap, but forgetting that they'd drunk their allowance already, when a glass of grog has come in their way. This is nothing more than riding with two anchors ahead, waiting for a turn in the tide, or a shift of wind, d'ye see, with a soft bottom and plenty of room for the sweep of your hawse. Now I've seen many a man, for overshooting his reckoning, as I told ye, moored head and starn, where he couldn't so much as heave his broadside round, and mayhap a stopper clapt on his tongue too, in the shape of a pump-bolt lashed athwart-ship his jaws, all the same as an out-rigger alongside of a taffrel-rail."

The hunter appeared to appreciate the kind intentions of the other, though he could not understand his eloquence; and raising his humbled countenance, he attempted a smile, as he said—

"Anan!"

" 'Tis nothing, I say, but a small matter of a squall, that will soon blow over," continued Benjamin. "To you that has such a length of keel it must be all the same as nothing; thof, seeing that I'm a little short in my lower timbers, they've triced my heels up in such a way as to give me a bit of a cant. But what cares I, Master Bump-ho, if the ship strains a little at her anchor; it's only for a dog-watch, and dam'me but she'll sail with you then on that cruise after them said beaver. I'm not much used to small arms, seeing that I was stationed at the ammunition-boxes, being sum'mat too low-rigged to see over the hammock-cloths; but I can carry the game, d'ye see, and mayhap make out to lend a hand with the traps; and if-so-be you're any way so handy with them as ye be with your boat-hook, 'twill be but a short cruise after all. I've squared the yards with Squire Dickens this morning, and I shall send him word that he needn't bear my name on the books again till such time as the cruise is over."

"You're used to dwell with men, Benny," said Leather-stocking, mournfully, "and the ways of the woods would be hard on you, if"——

"Not a bit—not a bit," cried the steward; "I'm none of your fair-weather chaps, Master Bump-ho, as sails only in smooth water. When I find a friend I sticks by him, d'ye see. Now, there's no better man a-going than Squire Dickens, and I love him about the same as I loves Mistress Hollister's new keg of Jamaiky." The steward paused, and turning his uncouth visage on the hunter, he survey'd him with a roguish leer of his eye, and gradually suffered the muscles of his hard features to re-lax, until his face was illuminated by the display of his white teeth, when he dropped his voice, and added—"I say, Master Leather-stocking, 'tis fresher and livelier than any Hollands you'll get in Garnsey. But we'll send a hand over and ask the woman for a taste, for I'm so jammed in these here bilboes, that I begin to want sum'mat to lighten my upper-works."

Natty sighed, and gazed about him on the crowd, that already begun to disperse, and which had now diminished greatly, as its members scattered in their various pursuits. He looked wist-fully at Benjamin, but did not reply; a deeply-seated anxiety seeming to absorb every other sensation, and to throw a melan-choly gloom over his wrinkled features, which were working with the movements of his mind.

The steward was about to act on the old principle, that silence gives consent, when Hiram Doolittle, attended by Jotham, stalked out of the crowd, across the open space, and ap-proached the stocks. The magistrate passed by the end where Benjamin was seated, and posted himself, at a safe distance from the steward, in front of the Leather-stocking. Hiram stood, for a moment, cowering before the keen looks that Natty fastened on him, and suffering under an embarrassment that was quite new; when, having in some degree recovered himself, he looked at the heavens, and then at the smoky atmosphere, as if it were only an ordinary meeting with a friend, and said, in his formal, hesitating way—

"Quite a scurcity of rain lately; I some think we shall have a long drought on't."

Benjamin was occupied in untying his bag of dollars, and did not observe the approach of the magistrate, while Natty turned his face, in which every muscle was working, away from him in disgust, without answering. Rather encouraged than daunted by this exhibition of dislike, Hiram, after a short pause, continued—

"The clouds look as if they'd no water in them, and the earth is dreadfully parched. To my judgment, there'll be short crops this season, if the rain doosn't fall quite speedily."

The air with which Mr. Doolittle delivered this prophetical opinion was peculiar to his species. It was a jesuitical, cold, unfeeling, and selfish manner, that seemed to say, "I have kept within the law," to the man he had so cruelly injured. It quite overcame the restraint that the old hunter had been labouring to impose on himself, and he burst out in a warm glow of indignation.

"Why should the rain fall from the clouds," he cried, "when you force the tears from the eyes of the old, the sick, and the poor! Away with ye—away with ye! you may be formed in the image of the Maker, but Satan dwells in your heart. Away with ye, I say! I am mournful, and the sight of ye brings bitter thoughts."

Benjamin ceased thumbing his money, and raised his head, at the instant that Hiram, who was thrown off his guard by the invectives of the hunter, unluckily trusted his person within reach of the steward, who grasped one of his legs, with a hand that had the grip of a vice, and whirled the magistrate from his feet, before he had either time to collect his senses, or to exercise the strength he did really possess. Benjamin wanted neither proportions nor manhood in his head, shoulders and arms, though all the rest of his frame appeared to be originally intended for a very different sort of a man. He exerted his physical powers, on the present occasion, with much discretion, and as he had taken his antagonist at a great disadvantage, the struggle resulted, very soon, in Benjamin getting the magistrate fixed in a posture somewhat similar to his own, and manfully placed face to face.

"You're a ship's cousin, I tell ye, Master Doo-but-little," roared the steward—"some such matter as a ship's cousin, sir. I know you, I do, with your fair-weather speeches to Squire Dickens, to his face, and then you go and sarve out your grumbling to all the old women in the town, do ye. An't it enough for any christian, let him harbour never so much malice, to get an honest old fellow laid by the heels in this fashion, without carrying sail so hard on the poor dog, as if you would run him down as he lay at his anchors? But I've logged many a hard thing against your name, master, and now the time's come to foot up the day's work, d'ye see; so square yourself, you lubber, square yourself, and we'll soon know who's the better man."

"Jotham!" cried the frightened magistrate—"Jotham! call in the constables. Mr. Penguillum, I command the peace—I order you to keep the peace."

"There's been more peace than love atwixt us, master," cried the steward, making some very unequivocal demonstrations towards hostility; "so mind yourself! square yourself, I say! do you smell this here bit of a sledge-hammer?"

"Lay hands on me if you dare!" exclaimed Hiram, as well as he could under the grasp which the steward held on his throttle—"lay hands on me if you dare!"

"If ye call this laying, master, you are welcome to the eggs," roared the steward.

It becomes our disagreeable duty to record here, that the acts of Benjamin now became violent; for he darted his sledge-hammer violently on the anvil of Mr. Doolittle's countenance, and the place became, in an instant, a scene of tumult and confusion. The crowd rushed in a dense circle around the spot, while some run to the court-room to give the alarm, and one or two of the more juvenile part of the multitude had a desperate trial of speed, to see who should be the happy man to communicate the critical situation of the magistrate to his wife.

Benjamin worked away with great industry and a good deal of skill, at his occupation, using one hand to raise up his antagonist, while he knocked him over with the other; for he would have been disgraced in his own estimation, had he struck a blow on a fallen adversary. By this considerate arrangement he had found means to hammer the visage of Hiram out of all shape, by the time Richard succeeded in forcing his way through the throng to the point of combat. The Sheriff afterwards declared that, independently of his mortification, as preserver of the peace of the county at this interruption to its harmony, he was never so grieved in his life, as when he saw this breach of unity between his favourites. Hiram had in some degree become necessary to his vanity, and Benjamin, strange as it may appear, he really loved. This attachment was exhibited in the first words that he uttered.

"Squire Doolittle! Squire Doolittle! I am ashamed to see a man of your character and office forget himself so much as to disturb the peace, insult the court, and beat poor Benjamin in this manner!"

At the sound of Mr. Jones's voice the steward ceased his employment, and Hiram had an opportunity of raising his discomfited visage towards the mediator. Emboldened by the sight of the Sheriff, Mr. Doolittle again had recourse to his lungs.

"I'll have the law on you for this," he cried, desperately; "I'll have the law on you for this. I call on you, Mr. Sheriff, to seize this man, and I demand that you take his body into custody."

By this time Richard was master of the true state of the case, and, turning to the steward, he said, reproachfully—

"Benjamin, how came you in the stocks! I always thought you were mild and docile as a lamb. It was for your docility that I most esteemed you. Benjamin! Benjamin! you have not only disgraced yourself, but your friends, by this shameless conduct. Bless me! bless me! Mr. Doolittle, he seems to have knocked your face all of one side."

Hiram by this time had got on his feet again, and without the reach of the steward, when he broke forth in violent appeals for vengeance. The offence was too apparent to be passed over, and the Sheriff, mindful of the impartiality exhibited by his cousin in the recent trial of the Leather-stocking, came to the painful conclusion that it was necessary to commit his Major-domo to prison. As the time of Natty's punishment was expired, and Benjamin found that they were to be confined, for that night at least, in the same apartment, he made no very strong objections to the measure, nor spoke of bail, though, as the Sheriff preceded the party of constables that conducted them to the gaol, he uttered the following remonstrance:—

"As to being berthed with Master Bump-ho for a night or so, it's but little I think of it, Squire Dickens, seeing that I calls him an honest man, and one as has a handy way with boat-hooks and rifles; but as for owning that a man desarves any thing worse than a double allowance, for knocking that carpenter's face a-one-side, as you call it, I'll maintain it's ag'in reason and christianity. If there's a blood-sucker in this 'ere county, it's that very chap. Ay! I know him! and if he hasn't got all the same as dead-wood in his head-works, he knows sum'mat of me. Where's the mighty harm, Squire, that you take it so much to heart! It's all the same as any other battle, d'ye see, sir, being broadside to broadside, only that it was fout at anchor, which was what we did in Port Praya roads, when Suff'ring came in among us; and a suff'ring time he had of it, before he got out again."

Richard thought it unworthy of him to make any reply to this speech, but when his prisoners were safely lodged in an outer dungeon, ordering the bolts to be drawn and the key turned, he withdrew.

Benjamin held frequent and friendly dialogues with different people, through the iron gratings, during the afternoon; but his companion paced their narrow limits, in his moccasins, with quick, impatient treads, his face hanging on his breast in dejection, or when lifted, at moments, to the idlers at the window, lighted, perhaps, for an instant with the childish aspect of aged forgetfulness, which would vanish directly in an expression of deep and obvious anxiety.

At the close of the day Edwards was seen at the window, in earnest dialogue with his friend; and after he departed it was thought that he had communicated words of comfort to the hunter, who threw himself on his pallet, and was soon in a deep sleep. The curious spectators had exhausted the conversation of the steward, who had drank good fellowship with half of his acquaintance, and as Natty was no longer in motion, by eight o'clock, Billy Kirby, who was the last lounger at the window retired into the "Templetown Coffee-House," when Natty rose and hung a blanket before the opening, and the prisoners apparently retired for the night.

Chapter XXXV.

"And to avoid the foe's pursuit,
With spurring put their cattle to't;
And till all four were out of wind,
And danger too, ne'er look'd behind."
                              Butler, *Hudibras*,II.ii.841-44.

As the shades of evening approached, the jurors, witnesses, and other attendants on the court, begun to disperse, and before nine o'clock the village was quiet, and its streets nearly deserted. At that hour, Judge Temple and his daughter, followed at a short distance by Louisa Grant, walked slowly down the avenue, under the slight shadows of the young poplars, holding the following discourse:—

"You can best soothe his wounded spirit, my child," said Marmaduke; "but it will be dangerous to touch on the nature of his offence; the sanctity of the laws must be respected."

"Surely, sir," cried the impatient Elizabeth, "those laws, that condemn a man like the Leather-stocking to so severe a punishment, for an offence that even I must think very venial, cannot be perfect in themselves."

"Thou talkest of what thou dost not understand, Elizabeth," returned her father. "Society cannot exist without wholesome restraints. Those restraints cannot be inflicted, without security and respect to the persons of those who administer them; and it would sound ill indeed, to report that a judge had extended favour to a convicted criminal, because he had saved the life of his child."

"I see—I see the difficulty of your situation, dear sir," cried the daughter; "but in appreciating the offence of poor Natty, I cannot separate the minister of the law from the man."

"There thou talkest as a woman, child; it is not for an assault on Hiram Doolittle, but for threatening the life of a constable, who was in the performance of"——

"It is immaterial whether it be one or the other," interrupted Miss Temple, with a logic that contained more feeling than reason; "I know Natty to be innocent, and thinking so, I must think all wrong who oppress him."

"His judge among the number! thy father, Elizabeth?"

"Nay, nay——nay, do not put such questions to me; give me my commission, father, and let me proceed to execute it."

The Judge paused a moment, smiling fondly on his child, and then dropped his hand affectionately on her shoulder, as he answered—

"Thou hast reason, Bess, and much of it too, but thy heart lies too near thy head. But listen: in this pocket-book are two hundred dollars. Go to the prison—there are none in this place to harm thee—give this note to the gaoler, and when thou seest Bumppo, say what thou wilt to the poor old man; give scope to the feelings of thy warm heart; but try to remember, Elizabeth, that the laws alone remove us from the condition of the savages; that he has been criminal, and that his judge was thy father."

Miss Temple made no reply, but she pressed the hand that held the pocket-book to her bosom, and taking her friend by the arm, they issued together from the enclosure into the principal street of the village.

As they pursued their walk in silence, under the row of houses, where the deeper gloom of the evening effectually concealed their persons, no sound reached them, excepting the slow tread of a yoke of oxen, with the rattling of a cart, that were moving along the street in the same direction with themselves. The figure of the teamster was just discernible by the dim light, lounging by the side of his cattle with a listless air, as if fatigued by the toil of the day. At the corner, where the gaol stood, the progress of the ladies was impeded, for a moment, by the oxen, who were turned up to the side of the building, and given a lock of hay, which they had carried on their necks, as a reward for their patient labour. The whole of this was so natural, and so common, that Elizabeth saw nothing to induce a second glance at the team, until she heard the teamster speaking to his cattle in a low voice—

"Mind yourself, Brindle; will you, sir! will you!"

The language itself was unusual to oxen, with which all who dwell in a new country are familiar; but there was something in the voice also, that startled Miss Temple. On turning the corner, she necessarily approached the man, and her look was enabled to detect the person of Oliver Edwards, concealed

under the coarse garb of a teamster. Their eyes met at the same
instant, and, notwithstanding the gloom, and the enveloping
cloak of Elizabeth, the recognition was mutual.

"Miss Temple!" "Mr. Edwards!" were exclaimed simultaneously, though a feeling that seemed common to both rendered
the words nearly inaudible.

"Is it possible!" exclaimed Edwards, after the moment of
doubt had passed; "do I see you so nigh the gaol! but you are
going to the Rectory. I beg pardon——Miss Grant, I believe; I
did not recognise you at first."

The sigh which Louisa uttered, was so faint that it was only
heard by Elizabeth, who replied, quickly—

"We are going not only to the gaol, Mr. Edwards, but into it.
We wish to show the Leather-stocking that we do not forget his
services, and that, at the same time we must be just, we are also
grateful. I suppose you are on a similar errand; but let me beg
that you will give us leave to precede you ten minutes. Good
night, sir; I—I—am quite sorry, Mr. Edwards, to see you reduced to such labour; I am sure my father would"——

"I shall wait your pleasure, madam," interrupted the youth,
coldly. "May I beg that you will not mention my being here?"

"Certainly," said Elizabeth, returning his bow by a slight inclination of her head, and urging the tardy Louisa forward. As
they entered the gaoler's house, however, Miss Grant found leisure to whisper—

"Would it not be well to offer part of your money to Oliver?
half of it will pay the fine of Bumppo; and he is so unused to
hardships! I am sure my father will subscribe much of his little
pittance, to place him in a station that is more worthy of him."

The involuntary smile that passed over the features of
Elizabeth was blended with an expression of deep and heartfelt
pity. She did not reply, however, and the appearance of the
gaoler soon recalled the thoughts of both to the object of their
visit.

The rescue of the ladies, and their consequent interest in his
prisoner, together with the informal manners that prevailed in
the country, all united to prevent any surprise, on the part of
the gaoler, at their request for admission to Bumppo. The note
of Judge Temple, however, would have silenced all objections,

if he had felt them, and he led the way without hesitation to the apartment that held the prisoners. The instant the key was put into the lock, the hoarse voice of Benjamin was heard, demanding—

"Yo! hoy! who comes there?"

"Some visiters that you'll be glad to see," returned the gaoler. "What have you done to the lock, that it won't turn?"

"Handsomely, handsomely, master," cried the steward; "I've just drove a nail into a berth alongside of this here bolt, as a stopper, d'ye see, so that master Doo-but-little can't be running in and breezing up another fight atwixt us, for, to my account, there'll be but a ban-yan with me soon, seeing that they'll mulct me of my Spaniards, all the same as if I'd overflogged the lubber. Throw your ship into the wind and lay by for a small matter, will ye? and I'll soon clear a passage."

The sounds of hammering gave an assurance that the steward was in earnest, and in a short time the lock yielded, when the door was opened.

Benjamin had evidently been anticipating the seizure of his money, for he had made frequent demands on the favourite cask at the "Bold Dragoon," during the afternoon and evening, and was now in that state which by marine imagery is called "half-seas-over." It was no easy thing to destroy the balance of the old tar by the effects of liquor, for, as he expressed it himself, "he was too low-rigged not to carry sail in all weathers;" but he was precisely in that condition which is so expressively termed "muddy." When he perceived who the visiters were, he retreated to the side of the room where his pallet lay, and, regardless of the presence of his young mistress, seated himself on it with an air of great sobriety, placing his back firmly against the wall.

"If you undertake to spoil my locks in this manner, Mr. Pump," said the gaoler, "I shall put a stopper, as you call it, on your legs, and tie you down to your bed."

"What for should ye, Master?" grumbled Benjamin; "I've rode out one squall to-day, anchored by the heels, and I wants no more of them. Where's the harm of doing all the same as yourself? Leave that there door free outboard, and you'll find no locking inboard, I'll promise ye."

"I must shut up for the night at nine," said the gaoler, "and it's now forty-two minutes past eight." He placed the little candle on a rough pine table, and withdrew.

"Leather-stocking!" said Elizabeth, when the key of the door was turned on them again, "my good friend Leather-stocking! I have come on a message of gratitude. Had you submitted to the search, worthy old man, the death of the deer would have been a trifle, and all would have been well"——

"Submit to the sarch!" interrupted Natty, raising his face from resting on his knees, without rising from the corner where he had seated himself; "d'ye think, gall, I would let such a varmint into my hut? No, no—I wouldn't have opened the door to your own sweet countenance then. But they are wilcome to sarch among the coals and ashes now; they'll find only some such heap as is to be seen at every pot-ashery in the mountains."

The old man dropped his face again on one hand, and seemed to be lost in melancholy.

"The hut can be rebuilt, and made better than before," returned Miss Temple; "and it shall be my office to see it done, when your imprisonment is ended."

"Can ye raise the dead, child!" said Natty, in a sorrowful voice; "can ye go into the place where you've laid your fathers, and mothers, and children, and gather together their ashes, and make the same men and women of them as afore! You do not know what 'tis to lay your head for more than forty year under the cover of the same logs, and to look on the same things for the better part of a man's life. You are young yet, child, but you are one of the most precious of God's creaters. I had a hope for ye that it might come to pass, but it's all over now; this put to that, will drive the thing quite out of his mind for ever."

Miss Temple must have understood the meaning of the old man better than the other listeners; for, while Louisa stood innocently by her side, commiserating the griefs of the hunter, she bent her head aside, so as to conceal her features. The action and the feeling that caused it lasted but a moment.

"Other logs, and better, though, can be had, and shall be found for you, my old defender," she continued. "Your confinement will soon be over, and before that time arrives I shall have a house prepared for you, where you may spend the close of your harmless life in ease and plenty."

"Ease and plenty! house!" repeated Natty, slowly. "You mean well, you mean well, and I quite mourn that it cannot be; but he has seen me a sight and a laughing-stock for"——

"Damn your stocks," said Benjamin, flourishing his bottle with one hand, from which he had been taking hasty and repeated draughts, while he made gestures of disdain with the other; "who cares for his bilboes? there's a leg that's been stuck up an end like a gib-boom for an hour, d'ye see, and what's it the worse for't, ha! canst tell me, what's it the worser, ha?"

"I believe you forget, Mr. Pump, in whose presence you are," said Elizabeth.

"Forget you, Miss 'Lizzy," returned the steward; "if I do dam'me; you're not to be forgot, like Goody Pretty-bones, up at the big house there. I say, old sharp-shooter, she may have pretty bones, but I can't say so much for her flesh, d'ye see, for she looks sum'mat like an otomy with another man's jacket on. Now, for the skin of her face, it's all the same as a new topsail with a taut bolt-rope, being snug at the leaches, but all in a bight about the inner cloths."

"Peace—I command you to be silent, sir," said Elizabeth.

"Ay, ay, ma'am," returned the steward. "You didn't say I shouldn't drink, though."

"We will not speak of what is to become of others," said Miss Temple, turning again to the hunter—"but of your own fortunes, Natty. It shall be my care to see that you pass the rest of your days in ease and plenty."

"Ease and plenty!" again repeated the Leather-stocking; "what ease can there be to an old man, who must walk a mile across the open fields, before he can find a shade to hide him from a scorching sun! or what plenty is there, where you may hunt a day and not start a buck, or see any thing bigger than a mink, or maybe a stray fox! Ah! I shall have a hard time after them very beavers, for this fine. I must go low toward the Pennsylvany line in sarch of the creaters, maybe a hundred mile, for they are not to be got here-away. No, no—your betterments and clearings have druv the knowing things out of the country; and instead of beaver-dams, which is the nater of the animal, and according to Providence, you turn back the waters over the low grounds with your mill-dams, as if 'twas in man to stay the drops from going where He wills them to go. Benny, unless you stop your hand from going so often to your mouth, you won't be ready to start when the time comes."

"Hark'ee, Master Bump-ho," said the steward; "don't you fear for Ben. When the watch is called, set me on my legs, and give me the bearings and distance of where you want to steer, and I'll carry sail with the best of you, I will."

"The time has come now," said the hunter, listening; "I hear the horns of the oxen rubbing ag'in the side of the gaol."

"Well, say the word, and then heave ahead, shipmate," said Benjamin.

"You won't betray us, gall?" said Natty, looking simply into the face of Elizabeth—"you won't betray an old man, who craves to breathe the clear air of heaven? I mean no harm, and if the law says that I must pay the hundred dollars, I'll take the season through, but it shall be forthcoming; and this good man will help me."

"You catch them," said Benjamin, with a sweeping gesture of his arm, "and if they get away again, call me a slink, that's all."

"What mean you!" cried the wondering Elizabeth. "Here you must stay for thirty days; but I have the money for your fine in this purse. Take it; pay it in the morning, and summon patience for your month. I will come often to see you, with my friend; we will make up your clothes with our own hands; indeed, indeed, you shall be comfortable."

"Would ye, children?" said Natty, advancing across the floor with an air of kindness, and taking the hand of Elizabeth; "would ye be so kearful of an old man, and just for shooting the beast, which cost him nothing? Such things doesn't run in the blood, I believe, for you seem not to forget a favour. Your little fingers couldn't do much on a buck-skin, nor be you used to such a thread as sinews. But if he hasn't got past hearing, he shall hear it and know it, that he may see, like me, there is some who know how to remember a kindness."

"Tell him nothing," cried Elizabeth, earnestly; "if you love me, if you regard my feelings, tell him nothing. It is of yourself only I would talk, and for yourself only I act. I grieve, Leatherstocking, that the law requires that you should be detained here so long; but, after all, it will be only a short month, and"——

"A month!" exclaimed Natty, opening his mouth with his usual laugh; "not a day, nor a night, nor an hour, gall. Judge Temple may sintence, but he can't keep, without a better dungeon than this. I was taken once by the French, and they put sixty-two of us in a block-house, nigh hand to old Frontinac; but 'twas easy to cut through a pine log to them that was used to timber." The hunter paused, and looked cautiously around the room, when, laughing again, he shoved the steward gently from his post, and removing the bed-clothes, discovered a hole recently cut in the logs with a mallet and chisel. "It's only a kick, and the outside piece is off, and then"——

"Off! ay, off!" cried Benjamin, rousing from his stupor; "well, here's off. Ay! ay! you catch 'em, and I'll hold on to them said beaver-hats."

"I fear this lad will trouble me much," said Natty; "'twill be a hard pull for the mountain, should they take the scent soon, and he is not in a state of mind to run."

"Run!" echoed the steward; "no, sheer alongside, and let's have a fight of it."

"Peace!" ordered Elizabeth.

"Ay, ay, ma'am."

"You will not leave us, surely, Leather-stocking," continued Miss Temple; "I beseech you, reflect that you will be driven to the woods entirely, and that you are fast getting old. Be patient for a little time, when you can go abroad openly, and with honour."

"Is there beaver to be catched here, gall?"

"If not, here is money to discharge the fine, and in a month you are free. See, here it is in gold."

"Gold!" said Natty, with a kind of childish curiosity; "it's long sin' I've seen a gold piece. We used to get the broad joes, in the old war, as plenty as the bears be now. I remember there was a man in Dieskau's army, that was killed, who had a dozen of the shining things sewed up in his shirt. I didn't handle them myself, but I seen them cut out, with my own eyes; they was bigger and brighter than them be."

"These are English guineas, and are yours," said Elizabeth; "an earnest of what shall be done for you."

"Me! why should you give me this treasure?" said Natty, looking earnestly at the maiden.

"Why! have you not saved my life? did you not rescue me from the jaws of the beast?" exclaimed Elizabeth, veiling her eyes, as if to hide some hideous object from her view.

The hunter took the money, and continued turning it in his hand for some time, piece by piece, talking aloud during the operation.

"There's a rifle, they say, out on the Cherry Valley, that will carry a hundred rods and kill. I've seen good guns in my day, but none quite equal to that. A hundred rods with any sartainty is great shooting! Well, well—I'm old, and the gun I have will answer my time. Here, child, take back your gold. But the hour has come; I hear him talking to the cattle, and I must be going. You won't tell of us, gall—you won't tell of us, will ye?"

"Tell of you!" echoed Elizabeth.—"But take the money, old man; take the money, even if you go into the mountains."

"No, no," said Natty, shaking his head kindly; "I wouldn't rob you so for twenty rifles. But there's one thing you can do for me, if ye will, that no other is at hand to do."

"Name it—name it."

"Why, it's only to buy a canister of powder;—'twill cost two silver dollars. Benny Pump has the money ready, but we daren't come into the town to get it. Nobody has it but the Frenchman. 'Tis of the best, and just suits a rifle. Will you get it for me, gall?—say, will you get it for me?"

"Will I! I will bring it to you, Leather-stocking, though I toil a day in quest of you through the woods. But where shall I find you, and how?"

"Where!" said Natty, musing a moment—"to-morrow, on the Vision; on the very top of the Vision I'll meet you, child, just as the sun gets over our heads. See that it's the fine grain; you'll know it by the gloss, and the price."

"I will do it," said Elizabeth, firmly.

Natty now seated himself, and placing his feet in the hole, with a slight effort he opened a passage through into the street. The ladies heard the rustling of hay, and well understood the reason why Edwards was in the capacity of a teamster.

"Come, Benny," said the hunter; " 'twill be no darker to-night, for the moon will rise in an hour."

"Stay!" exclaimed Elizabeth; "it should not be said that you escaped in the presence of the daughter of Judge Temple. Return, Leather-stocking, and let us retire, before you execute your plan."

Natty was about to reply, when the approaching footsteps of the gaoler announced the necessity of his immediate return. He had barely time to regain his feet, and to conceal the hole with the bed-clothes, across which Benjamin very opportunely fell, before the key was turned, and the door of the apartment opened.

"Isn't Miss Temple ready to go?" said the civil gaoler—"it's the usooal hour for locking up."

"I follow you, sir," returned Elizabeth. "Good night, Leather-stocking."

"It's a fine grain, gall, and I think 'twill carry lead further than common. I am getting old, and can't follow up the game with the step that I used to could."

Miss Temple waved her hand for silence, and preceded Louisa and the keeper from the apartment. The man turned the key once, and observed that he would return and secure his prisoners, when he had lighted the ladies to the street. Accordingly, they parted at the door of the building, when the gaoler retired to his dungeons, and the ladies walked, with throbbing hearts, towards the corner.

"Now the Leather-stocking refuses the money," whispered Louisa, "it can all be given to Mr. Edwards, and that added to"——

"Listen!" said Elizabeth; "I hear the rustling of the hay; they are escaping at this moment. Oh! they will be detected instantly!"

By this time they were at the corner, where Edwards and Natty were in the act of drawing the almost helpless body of Benjamin through the aperture. The oxen had started back from their hay, and were standing with their heads down the street, leaving room for the party to act in.

"Throw the hay into the cart," said Edwards, "or they will suspect how it has been done. Quick, that they may not see it."

Natty had just returned from executing this order, when the light of the keeper's candle shone through the hole, and instantly his voice was heard in the gaol, exclaiming for his prisoners.

"What is to be done now?" said Edwards—"this drunken fellow will cause our detection, and we have not a moment to spare."

"Who's drunk, ye lubber?" muttered the steward.

"A break-gaol! a break-gaol!" shouted five or six voices from within.

"We must leave him," said Edwards.

"Twouldn't be kind, lad," returned Natty; "he took half the disgrace of the stocks on himself to-day, and the creater has feeling."

At this moment two or three men were heard issuing from the door of the "Bold Dragoon," and among them the voice of Billy Kirby.

"There's no moon yet," cried the wood-chopper; "but it's a clear night. Come, who's for home? Hark! what a rumpus they're kicking up in the gaol—here's go and see what it's about."

"We shall be lost," said Edwards, "if we don't drop this man."

At that instant Elizabeth moved close to him, and said rapidly, in a low voice—

"Lay him in the cart, and start the oxen; no one will look there."

"There's a woman's quickness in the thought," said the youth.

The proposition was no sooner made than executed. The steward was seated on the hay, and enjoined to hold his peace, and apply the goad that was placed in his hand, while the oxen were urged on. So soon as this arrangement was completed, Edwards and the hunter stole along the houses for a short distance, when they disappeared through an opening that led into the rear of the buildings. The oxen were in brisk motion, and presently the cries of pursuit were heard in the street. The ladies quickened their pace, with a wish to escape the crowd of constables and idlers that were approaching, some execrating, and some laughing at the exploit of the prisoners. In the confusion, the voice of Kirby was plainly distinguishable above all the others, shouting and swearing that he would have the fugitives, threatening to bring back Natty in one pocket and Benjamin in the other.

"Spread yourselves, men," he cried, as he passed the ladies, his heavy feet sounding along the street like the tread of a dozen; "spread yourselves; to the mountains; they'll be in the mountain in a quarter of an hour, and then look out for a long rifle."

His cries were echoed from twenty mouths, for not only the gaol but the taverns had sent forth their numbers, some earnest in the pursuit, and others joining it as in sport.

As Elizabeth turned in at her father's gate, she saw the wood-chopper stop at the cart, when she gave Benjamin up for lost. While they were hurrying up the walk, two figures, stealing cautiously but quickly under the shades of the trees, met the eyes of the ladies, and in a moment Edwards and the hunter crossed their path.

"Miss Temple, I may never see you again," exclaimed the youth; "let me thank you for all your kindness; you do not, cannot know my motives."

"Fly! fly!" cried Elizabeth—"the village is alarmed. Do not be found conversing with me at such a moment, and in these grounds."

"Nay, I must speak, though detection were certain."

"Your retreat to the bridge is already cut off; before you can gain the wood your pursuers will be there.—If"—

"If what?" cried the youth. "Your advice has saved me once already; I will follow it to death."

"The street is now silent and vacant," said Elizabeth, after a pause; "cross it, and you will find my father's boat in the lake. It would be easy to land from it where you please in the hills."

"But Judge Temple might complain of the trespass."

"His daughter shall be accountable, sir."

The youth uttered something in a low voice, that was heard only by Elizabeth, and turned to execute what she had suggested. As they were separating, Natty approached the females, and said—

"You'll remember the canister of powder, children. Them beavers must be had, and I and the pups be getting old; we want the best of ammunition."

"Come, Natty," said Edwards, impatiently.

"Coming, lad, coming. God bless you, young ones, both of ye, for ye mean well and kindly to the old man."

The ladies paused until they had lost sight of the retreating figures, when they immediately entered the Mansion-house.

While this scene was passing in the walk, Kirby had overtaken the cart, which was his own, and had been driven by Edwards without asking the owner, from the place where the patient oxen usually stood at evening, waiting the pleasure of their master.

"Woa—come hither, Golden," he cried; "why, how come you off the end of the bridge, where I left you, dummies?"

"Heave ahead," muttered Benjamin, giving a random blow with his lash, that alighted on the shoulder of the other.

"Who the devil be you?" cried Billy, turning round in surprise, but unable to distinguish, in the dark, the hard visage that was just peering over the cart-rails.

"Who be I! why I'm helmsman aboard of this here craft, d'ye see, and a straight wake I'm making of it. Ay! ay! I've got the bridge right ahead, and the bilboes dead-aft; I calls that good steerage, boy. Heave ahead."

"Lay your lash in the right spot, Mr. Benny Pump," said the wood-chopper, "or I'll put you in the palm of my hand and box your ears.——Where be you going with my team?"

"Team!"

"Ay, my cart and oxen."

"Why, you must know, Master Kirby, that the Leather-stocking and I—that's Benny Pump—you knows Ben?—well, Benny and I—no, me and Benny——dam'me if I know how 'tis; but some of us are bound after a cargo of beaver-skins, d'ye see, and so we've pressed the cart to ship them 'ome in. I say, Master Kirby, what a lubberly oar you pull—you handle an oar, boy, pretty much as a cow would a musket, or a lady would a marling-spike."

Billy had discovered the state of the steward's mind, and he walked for some time alongside of the cart, musing within himself, when he took the goad from Benjamin, who fell back on the hay, and was soon asleep, and drove his cattle down the street, over the bridge, and up the mountain, towards a clearing in which he was to work the next day, without any other interruption than a few hasty questions from parties of the constables.

Elizabeth stood for an hour at the window of her room, and saw the torches of the pursuers gliding along the side of the mountain, and heard their shouts and alarms; but, at the end of that time, the last party returned, wearied and disappointed, and the village became as still as when she issued from the gate, on her mission to the gaol.

Chapter XXXVI.

" 'And I could weep'—th' Oneida chief
His descant wildly thus begun—
'But that I may not stain with grief
The death-song of my father's son.'"
Campbell, Gertrude of Wyoming, III.xxxv.1–4.

IT was yet early on the following morning, when Elizabeth and Louisa met by appointment, and proceeded to the store of Monsieur Le Quoi, in order to redeem the pledge the former had given to the Leather-stocking. The people were again assembling for the business of the day, but the hour was too soon for a crowd, and the ladies found the place in possession of its polite owner, Billy Kirby, one female customer, and the boy who did the duty of helper or clerk.

Monsieur Le Quoi was perusing a packet of letters, with manifest delight, while the wood-chopper, with one hand thrust in his bosom, and the other in the folds of his jacket, holding an axe under his right arm, stood sympathizing in the Frenchman's pleasure with good-natured interest. The freedom of manners that prevailed in the new settlements, commonly levelled all difference in rank, and with it, frequently, all considerations of education and intelligence. At the time the ladies entered the store they were unseen by the owner, who was saying to Kirby—

"Ah! ha! Monsieur Beel, dis lettair mak-a me de most happi of mans. Ah! ma chère France! I vill see you aga'n."

"I rejoice, Monsieur, at any thing that contributes to your happiness," said Elizabeth, "but hope we are not going to lose you entirely."

The complaisant shopkeeper changed the language to French, and recounted rapidly to Elizabeth his hopes of being permitted to return to his own country. Habit had, however, so far altered the manners of this pliable personage, that he continued to serve the wood-chopper, who was in quest of some tobacco, while he related to his more gentle visiter, the happy change that had taken place in the dispositions of his own countrymen.

The amount of it all was, that Mr. Le Quoi, who had fled from his own country more through terror than because he was offensive to the ruling powers in France, had succeeded at length in getting an assurance that his return to the West Indies would be unnoticed; and the Frenchman, who had sunk into the character of a country shopkeeper with so much grace, was about to emerge again from his obscurity into his proper level in society.

We need not repeat the civil things that passed between the parties on this occasion, nor recount the endless repetitions of sorrow that the delighted Frenchman expressed, at being compelled to quit the society of Miss Temple. Elizabeth took an opportunity, during this expenditure of polite expressions, to purchase the powder privately of the boy, who bore the generic appellation of Jonathan. Before they parted, however, Mr. Le Quoi, who seemed to think that he had not said enough, solicited the honour of a private interview with the heiress, with a gravity in his air that announced the importance of the subject. After conceding the favour, and appointing a more favourable time for the meeting, Elizabeth succeeded in getting out of the store, into which the countrymen now began to enter, as usual, where they met with the same attention and bienséance as formerly.

Elizabeth and Louisa pursued their walk as far as the bridge in profound silence, but when they reached that place, the latter stopped, and appeared anxious to utter something that her diffidence suppressed.

"Are you ill, Louisa?" exclaimed Miss Temple; "had we not better return, and seek another opportunity to meet the old man?"

"Not ill, but terrified. Oh! I never, never can go on that hill again with you only. I am not equal to it, indeed I am not."

This was an unexpected declaration to Elizabeth, who, although she experienced no idle apprehension of a danger that no longer existed, felt most sensitively all the delicacy of maiden modesty. She stood for some time, deeply reflecting within herself; but, sensible it was a time for action instead of reflection, she struggled to shake off her hesitation, and replied firmly—

"Well, then it must be done by me alone. There is no other than yourself to be trusted, or poor old Leather-stocking will be discovered. Wait for me in the edge of these woods, that at least I may not be seen strolling in the hills by myself just now. One would not wish to create remarks, Louisa—if—if—. You will wait for me, dear girl?"

"A year, in sight of the village, Miss Temple," returned the agitated Louisa, "but do not, do not ask me to go on that hill."

Elizabeth found that her companion was really unable to proceed, and they completed their arrangement by posting Louisa out of the observation of the people who occasionally passed, but nigh the road, and in plain view of the whole valley. Miss Temple then proceeded alone. She ascended the road which has been so often mentioned in our narrative, with an elastic and firm step, fearful that the delay in the store of Mr. Le Quoi, and the time necessary for reaching the summit, would prevent her being punctual to the appointment. Whenever she passed an opening in the bushes, she would pause for breath, or perhaps, drawn from her pursuits by the picture at her feet, would linger a moment to gaze at the beauties of the valley. The long drought had, however, changed its coat of verdure to a hue of brown, and, though the same localities were there, the view wanted the lively and cheering aspect of early summer. Even the heavens seemed to share in the dried appearance of the earth, for the sun was concealed by a haziness in the atmosphere, which looked like a thin smoke without a particle of moisture, if such a thing were possible. The blue sky was scarcely to be seen, though now and then there was a faint lighting up in spots, through which masses of rolling vapour could be discerned gathering around the horizon, as if nature were struggling to collect her floods for the relief of man. The very atmosphere that Elizabeth inhaled was hot and dry, and by the time she reached the point where the course led her from the highway, she experienced a sensation like suffocation. But, disregarding her feelings, she hastened to execute her mission, dwelling on nothing but the disappointment, and even the helplessness, the hunter would experience, without her aid.

On the summit of the mountain which Judge Temple had named the "Vision," a little spot had been cleared, in order that a better view might be obtained of the village and the valley. At this point Elizabeth understood the hunter she was to meet him; and thither she urged her way, as expeditiously as the difficulty of the ascent and the impediments of a forest in a state of nature would admit. Numberless were the fragments of rocks, trunks of fallen trees, and branches, with which she had to contend; but every difficulty vanished before her resolution, and, by her own watch, she stood on the desired spot several minutes before the appointed hour.

After resting a moment on the end of a log, Miss Temple cast a glance about her in quest of her old friend, but he was evidently not in the clearing; she arose and walked 'around its skirts, examining every place where she thought it probable Natty might deem it prudent to conceal himself. Her search was fruitless; and, after exhausting not only herself, but her conjectures, in efforts to discover or imagine his situation, she ventured to trust her voice in that solitary place.

"Natty! Leather-stocking! old man!" she called aloud, in every direction; but no answer was given, excepting the reverberations of her own clear tones, as they were echoed in the parched forest.

Elizabeth approached the brow of the mountain, where a faint cry, like the noise produced by striking the hand against the mouth at the same time that the breath is strongly exhaled, was heard, answering to her own voice. Not doubting in the least that it was the Leather-stocking lying in wait for her, and who gave that signal to indicate the place where he was to be found, Elizabeth descended for near a hundred feet, until she gained a little natural terrace, thinly scattered with trees, that grew in the fissures of the rocks, which were covered by a scanty soil. She had advanced to the edge of this platform, and was gazing over the perpendicular precipice that formed its face, when a rustling among the dry leaves near her drew her eyes in another direction. Our heroine certainly was startled by the object that she then saw, but a moment restored her self-possession, and she advanced firmly, and with some interest in her manner, to the spot.

Mohegan was seated on the trunk of a fallen oak, with his tawny visage turned towards her, and his eyes fixed on her face with an expression of wildness and fire that would have terrified a less resolute female. His blanket had fallen from his shoulders, and was lying in folds around him, leaving his breast, arms, and most of his body bare. The medallion of Washington reposed on his chest, a badge of distinction that Elizabeth well knew he only produced on great and solemn occasions. But the whole appearance of the aged chief was more studied than common, and in some particulars it was terrific. The long black hair was plaited on his head, falling away, so as to expose his high forehead and piercing eyes. In the enormous incisions of his ears were entwined ornaments of silver, beads, and porcupine's quills, mingled in a rude taste, and after the Indian fashions. A large drop, composed of similar materials, was suspended from the cartilage of his nose, and, falling below his lips, rested on his chin. Streaks of red paint crossed his wrinkled brow, and were traced down his cheeks, with such variations in the lines as caprice or custom suggested. His body was also coloured in the same manner; the whole exhibiting an Indian warrior prepared for some event of more than usual moment.

"John! how fare you, worthy John?" said Elizabeth, as she approached him; "you have long been a stranger in the village. You promised me a willow basket, and I have long had a shirt of calico in readiness for you."

The Indian looked steadily at her for some time without answering, and then shaking his head, he replied, in his low, guttural tones—

"John's hand can make baskets no more—he wants no shirt."

"But if he should, he will know where to come for it," returned Miss Temple. "Indeed, old John, I feel as if you had a natural right to order what you will from us."

"Daughter," said the Indian, "listen:—Six times ten hot summers have passed, since John was young; tall like a pine; straight like the bullet of Hawk-eye; strong as the buffalo; spry as the cat of the mountain. He was strong, and a warrior like the Young Eagle. If his tribe wanted to track the Maquas for many suns, the eye of Chingachgook found the print of their moccasins. If the people feasted and were glad as they counted the scalps of their enemies, it was on his pole they hung. If the squaws cried because there was no meat for their children, he was the first in the chase. His bullet was swifter than the deer.—Daughter, then Chingachgook struck his tomahawk into the trees; it was to tell the lazy ones where to find him and the Mingos—but he made no baskets."

"Those times have gone by, old warrior," returned Elizabeth; "since then, your people have disappeared, and in place of chasing your enemies, you have learned to fear God and to live at peace."

"Stand here, daughter, where you can see the great spring, the wigwams of your father, and the land on the crooked-river. John was young, when his tribe gave away the country, in council, from where the blue mountain stands above the water, to where the Susquehannah is hid by the trees. All this, and all that grew in it, and all that walked over it, and all that fed there, they gave to the Fire-eater—for they loved him. He was strong, and they were women, and he helped them. No Delaware would kill a deer that run in his woods, nor stop a bird that flew over his land; for it was his. Has John lived in peace! Daughter, since John was young, he has seen the white man from Frontinac come down on his white brothers at Albany, and fight. Did they fear God! He has seen his English and his American Fathers burying their tomahawks in each other's brains, for this very land. Did they fear God, and live in peace! He has seen the land pass away from the Fire-eater, and his children, and the child of his child, and a new chief set over the country. Did they live in peace who did this! did they fear God!"

"Such is the custom of the whites, John. Do not the Delawares fight, and exchange their lands for powder, and blankets, and merchandise?"

The Indian turned his dark eyes on his companion, and kept them there, with a scrutiny that alarmed her a little.

"Where are the blankets and merchandise that bought the right of the Fire-eater?" he replied, in a more animated voice; "are they with him in his wigwam? Did they say to him, brother, sell us your land, and take this gold, this silver, these blankets, these rifles, or even this rum? No, they tore it from him, as a scalp is torn from an enemy; and they that did it looked not behind them, to see whether he lived or died. Do such men live in peace, and fear the Great Spirit?"

"But you hardly understand the circumstances," said Elizabeth, more embarrassed than she would own, even to herself.

"If you knew our laws and customs better, you would judge differently of our acts. Do not believe evil of my father, old Mohegan, for he is just and good."

"The brother of Miquon is good, and he will do right. I have said it to Hawk-eye—I have said it to the Young Eagle, that the brother of Miquon would do justice."

"Whom call you the Young Eagle?" said Elizabeth, averting her face from the gaze of the Indian as she asked the question; "whence comes he, and what are his rights?"

"Has my daughter lived so long with him, to ask this question?" returned the Indian, warily. "Old age freezes up the blood, as the frosts cover the great spring in winter; but youth keeps the streams of the blood open, like a sun in the time of blossoms. The Young Eagle has eyes; had he no tongue?"

The loveliness to which the old warrior alluded was in no degree diminished by his allegorical speech; for the blushes of the maiden who listened, covered her burning cheeks, till her dark eyes seemed to glow with their reflection; but, after struggling a moment with shame, she laughed, as if unwilling to understand him seriously, and replied in pleasantry—

"Not to make me the mistress of his secret. He is too much of a Delaware, to tell his secret thoughts to a woman."

"Daughter, the Great Spirit made your father with a white skin, and he made mine with a red; but he coloured both their hearts with blood. When young, it is swift and warm; but when old, it is still and cold. Is there difference below the skin? No. Once John had a woman. She was the mother of so many sons"—he raised his hand with three fingers elevated—"and she had daughters that would have made the young Delawares happy. She was kind, daughter, and what I said she did. You have different fashions; but do you think John did not love the wife of his youth—the mother of his children!"

"And what has become of your family, John, your wife and your children?" asked Elizabeth, touched by the Indian's manner.

"Where is the ice that covered the great spring? It is melted, and gone with the waters. John has lived till all his people have left him for the land of spirits; his time has come, and he is ready."

Mohegan dropped his head in his blanket, and sat in silence.

XIII. *A View of the Two Lakes and Mountain House, Catskill Mountains, Morning* (*1844*) *by Thomas Cole.*

XIV. *Elizabeth Conversing with Mohegan, for* The Port Folio (*June 1823*) *by Gideon Fairman.*

xv. *The Departure of Leather-stocking, for* The Port Folio (*January 1824*), *by Henry Inman.*

XVI. *Portrait of Elizabeth Fenimore Cooper (the novelist's mother), by George Freeman, showing the interior of Otsego Hall as it appeared in 1816.*

Miss Temple knew not what to say. She wished to draw the thoughts of the old warrior from his gloomy recollections, but there was a dignity in his sorrow, and in his fortitude, that repressed her efforts to speak. After a long pause, however, she renewed the discourse, by asking—

"Where is the Leather-stocking, John? I have brought this canister of powder at his request; but he is nowhere to be seen. Will you take charge of it, and see it delivered?"

The Indian raised his head slowly, and looked earnestly at the gift, which she put into his hand.

"This is the great enemy of my nation. Without this, when could the white men drive the Delawares! Daughter, the Great Spirit gave your fathers to know how to make guns and powder, that they might sweep the Indians from the land. There will soon be no red-skin in the country. When John has gone, the last will leave these hills, and his family will be dead." The aged warrior stretched his body forward, leaning an elbow on his knee, and appeared to be taking a parting look at the objects of the vale, which were still visible through the misty atmosphere; though the air seemed to thicken at each moment around Miss Temple, who became conscious of an increased difficulty of respiration. The eye of Mohegan changed gradually, from its sorrowful expression to a look of wildness, that might be supposed to border on the inspiration of a prophet, as he continued—"But he will go to the country where his fathers have met. The game shall be plenty as the fish in the lakes. No woman shall cry for meat. No Mingo can ever come. The chase shall be for children, and all just red-men shall live together as brothers."

"John! this is not the heaven of a Christian!" cried Miss Temple; "you deal now in the superstition of your forefathers."

"Fathers! sons!" said Mohegan with firmness—"all gone—all gone! I have no son but the Young Eagle, and he has the blood of a white man."

"Tell me, John," said Elizabeth, willing to draw his thoughts to other subjects, and at the same time yielding to her own powerful interest in the youth; "who is this Mr. Edwards? why are you so fond of him, and whence does he come?"

The Indian started at the question, which evidently recalled his recollection to earth. Taking her hand, he drew Miss Temple to a seat beside him, and pointed to the country beneath them—

"See, daughter," he said, directing her looks towards the north; "as far as your young eyes can see, it was the land of his"——

But immense volumes of smoke at that moment rolled over their heads, and whirling in the eddies formed by the mountains, interposed a barrier to their sight, while he was speaking. Startled by the circumstance, Miss Temple sprung on her feet, and turning her eyes toward the summit of the mountain, she beheld it covered by a similar canopy, while a roaring sound was heard in the forest above her, like the rushing of winds.

"What means it, John!" she exclaimed; "we are enveloped in smoke, and I feel a heat like the glow of a furnace."

Before the Indian could reply, a voice was heard, crying in the woods—

"John! where are you, old Mohegan! the woods are on fire, and you have but a minute for escape."

The chief put his hand before his mouth, and making it play on his lips, produced the kind of noise that had attracted Elizabeth to the place, when a quick and hurried step was heard dashing through the dried underbrush and bushes, and presently Edwards rushed to his side, with horror in every feature.

Chapter XXXVII.

"Love rules the court, the camp, the grove."
                    Scott, *The Lay of the Last Minstrel*, III.ii.5.

"IT would have been sad indeed, to lose you in such a manner, my old friend," said Oliver, catching his breath for utterance. "Up and away! even now we may be too late; the flames are circling round the point of the rock below, and unless we can pass there, our only chance must be over the precipice. Away! away! shake off your apathy, John; now is the time of need."

Mohegan pointed towards Elizabeth, who, forgetting her danger, had shrunk back to a projection of the rock as soon as she recognised the sounds of Edwards' voice, and said, with something like awakened animation—

"Save her—leave John to die."

"Her! whom mean you?" cried the youth, turning quickly to the place the other indicated;—but when he saw the figure of Elizabeth, bending towards him in an attitude that powerfully spoke terror, blended with reluctance to meet him in such a place, the shock deprived him of speech.

"Miss Temple!" he cried, when he found words; "you here! is such a death reserved for you!"

"No, no, no—no death, I hope, for any of us, Mr. Edwards," she replied, endeavouring to speak calmly: "there is smoke but no fire to harm us. Let us endeavour to retire."

"Take my arm," said Edwards; "there must be an opening in some direction for your retreat. Are you equal to the effort?"

"Certainly. You surely magnify the danger, Mr. Edwards. Lead me out the way you came."

"I will—I will," cried the youth, with a kind of hysterical utterance. "No, no—there is no danger—I have alarmed you unnecessarily."

"But shall we leave the Indian—can we leave him, as he says, to die?"

An expression of painful emotion crossed the face of the young man; he stopped, and cast a longing look at Mohegan;

but, dragging his companion after him, even against her will, he pursued his way, with enormous strides, towards the pass by which he had just entered the circle of flame.

"Do not regard him," he said, in those tones that denote a desperate calmness; "he is used to the woods, and such scenes; and he will escape up the mountain—over the rock—or he can remain where he is in safety."

"You thought not so this moment, Edwards! Do not leave him there to meet with such a death," cried Elizabeth, fixing a look on the countenance of her conductor, that seemed to distrust his sanity.

"An Indian burn! who ever heard of an Indian dying by fire! an Indian cannot burn; the idea is ridiculous. Hasten, hasten, Miss Temple, or the smoke may incommode you."

"Edwards! your look, your eye, terrifies me! tell me the danger; is it greater than it seems? I am equal to any trial."

"If we reach the point of yon rock before that sheet of fire, we are safe, Miss Temple!" exclaimed the young man, in a voice that burst without the bounds of his forced composure. "Fly! the struggle is for life!"

The place of the interview between Miss Temple and the Indian has already been described as one of those platforms of rock which form a sort of terrace in the mountains of that country, and the face of it, we have said, was both high and perpendicular. Its shape was nearly a natural arc, the ends of which blended with the mountain, at points where its sides were less abrupt in their descent. It was round one of these terminations of the sweep of the rock that Edwards had ascended, and it was towards the same place that he urged Elizabeth to a desperate exertion of speed.

Immense clouds of white smoke had been pouring over the summit of the mountain, and had concealed the approach and ravages of the element; but a crackling sound drew the eyes of Miss Temple, as she flew over the ground, supported by the young man, towards the outline of smoke, where she already perceived the waving flames shooting forward from the vapour, now flaring high in the air, and then bending to the earth, seeming to light into combustion every stick and shrub on which they breathed. The sight aroused them to redoubled efforts; but, unfortunately, a collection of the tops of trees, old and dried, lay directly across their course; and, at the very moment when both had thought their safety insured, the warm currents of the air swept a forked tongue of flame across the pile, which lighted at the touch; and when they reached the spot, the flying pair were opposed by the surly roaring of a body of fire, as if a furnace were glowing in their path. They recoiled from the heat, and stood on a point of the rock, gazing in a stupor at the flames, which were spreading rapidly down the mountain, whose side soon became a sheet of living fire. It was dangerous for one clad in the light and airy dress of Elizabeth to approach even the vicinity of the raging element; and those flowing robes, that gave such softness and grace to her form, seemed now to be formed for the instruments of her destruction.

The villagers were accustomed to resort to that hill in quest of timber and fuel; in procuring which, it was their usage to take only the bodies of the trees, leaving the tops and branches to decay under the operations of the weather. Much of the hill was, consequently, covered with such light fuel, which, having been scorched under the sun for the last two months, was ignited with a touch. Indeed, in some cases, there did not appear to be any contact between the fire and these piles, but the flames seemed to dart from heap to heap, as the fabulous fire of the temple is represented to relumine its neglected lamp.

There was beauty as well as terror in the sight, and Edwards and Elizabeth stood viewing the progress of the desolation, with a strange mixture of horror and interest. The former, however, shortly roused himself to new exertions, and, drawing his companion after him, they skirted the edge of the smoke, the young man penetrating frequently into its dense volumes in search of a passage, but in every instance without success. In this manner they proceeded in a semicircle around the upper part of the terrace, until, arriving at the verge of the precipice, opposite to the point where Edwards had ascended, the horrid conviction burst on both at the same instant, that they were completely encircled by the fire. So long as a single pass up or down the mountain was unexplored, there was hope; but when retreat seemed to be absolutely impracticable, the horror of their situation broke upon Elizabeth as powerfully as if she had hitherto considered the danger light.

"This mountain is doomed to be fatal to me!" she whispered; —"we shall find our graves on it!"

"Say not so, Miss Temple; there is yet hope," returned the youth, in the same tone, while the vacant expression of his eye, contradicted his words; "let us return to the point of the rock; there is, there must be, some place about it where we can descend."

"Lead me there," exclaimed Elizabeth; "let us leave no effort untried." She did not wait for his compliance, but turning, retraced her steps to the brow of the precipice, murmuring to herself, in suppressed hysterical sobs, "My father——my poor, my distracted father!"

Edwards was by her side in an instant, and with aching eyes he examined every fissure in the crags, in quest of some opening that might offer the facilities for flight. But the smooth, even surface of the rocks afforded hardly a resting place for a foot, much less those continued projections which would have been necessary for a descent of nearly a hundred feet. Edwards was not slow in feeling the conviction that this hope was also futile, and, with a kind of feverish despair, that still urged him to action, he turned to some new expedient.

"There is nothing left, Miss Temple," he said, "but to endeavour to lower you from this place to the rock beneath. If Natty were here, or even that Indian could be roused, their ingenuity and long practice would easily devise methods to do it; but I am a child, at this moment, in every thing but daring. Where shall I find means? This dress of mine is so light, and there is so little of it—then the blanket of Mohegan. We must try—we must try—any thing is better than to see you a victim to such a death!"

"And what will become of you!" said Elizabeth. "Indeed, indeed, neither you nor John must be sacrificed to my safety."

He heard her not, for he was already by the side of Mohegan, who yielded his blanket without a question, retaining his seat with Indian dignity and composure, though his own situation was even more critical than that of the others. The blanket was cut into shreds, and the fragments fastened together; the loose linen jacket of the youth, and the light muslin shawl of

Elizabeth, were attached to them, and the whole thrown over the rocks, with the rapidity of lightning; but the united pieces did not reach half way to the bottom.

"It will not do—it will not do!" cried Elizabeth; "for me there is no hope! The fire comes slowly, but certainly. See! it destroys the very earth before it!"

Had the flames spread on that rock with half the quickness with which they leaped from bush to tree, in other parts of the mountain, our painful task would have soon ended; for they would have consumed already the captives they enclosed. But the peculiarity of their situation afforded Elizabeth and her companion the respite, of which they had availed themselves to make the efforts we have recorded.

The thin covering of earth on the rock supported but a scanty and faded herbage, and most of the trees that had found root in the fissures had already died, during the intense heats of preceding summers. Those which still retained the appearance of life, bore a few dry and withered leaves, while the others were merely the wrecks of pines, oaks, and maples. No better materials to feed the fire could be found, had there been a communication with the flames; but the ground was destitute of the brush that led the destructive element like a torrent over the remainder of the hill. As auxiliary to this scarcity of fuel, one of the large springs which abound in that country gushed out of the side of the ascent above, and, after creeping sluggishly along the level land, saturating the mossy covering of the rock with moisture, it swept round the base of the little cone that formed the pinnacle of the mountain, and, entering the canopy of smoke near one of the terminations of the terrace, found its way to the lake, not by dashing from rock to rock, but by the secret channels of the earth. It would rise to the surface, here and there, in the wet seasons, but in the droughts of summer, it was to be traced only by the bogs and moss that announced the proximity of water. When the fire reached this barrier, it was compelled to pause, until a concentration of its heat could overcome the moisture, like an army waiting the operations of a battering train, to open its way to desolation.

That fatal moment seemed now to have arrived; for the hissing steams of the spring appeared to be nearly exhausted, and the moss of the rocks was already curling under the intense heat, while fragments of bark that yet clung to the dead trees, began to separate from their trunks, and fall to the ground in crumbling masses. The air seemed quivering with rays of heat, which might be seen playing along the parched stems of the trees. There were moments when dark clouds of smoke would sweep along the little terrace, and as the eye lost its power, the other senses contributed to give effect to the fearful horror of the scene. At such moments, the roaring of the flames, the crackling of the furious element, with the tearing of falling branches, and, occasionally, the thundering echoes of some falling tree, united to alarm the victims. Of the three, however, the youth appeared much the most agitated. Elizabeth, having relinquished entirely the idea of escape, was fast obtaining that resigned composure, with which the most delicate of her sex are sometimes known to meet unavoidable evils; while Mohegan, who was much nearer to the danger, maintained his seat with the invincible resignation of an Indian warrior. Once or twice the eye of the aged chief, which was ordinarily fixed in the direction of the distant hills, turned towards the young pair, who seemed doomed to so early a death, with a slight indication of pity crossing his composed features, but it would immediately revert again to its former gaze, as if already looking into the womb of futurity. Much of the time he was chanting a kind of low dirge, in the Delaware tongue, using the deep and remarkably guttural tones of his people.

"At such a moment, Mr. Edwards, all earthly distinctions end," whispered Elizabeth; "persuade John to move nearer to us—let us die together."

"I cannot—he will not stir," returned the youth, in the same horridly still tones. "He considers this as the happiest moment of his life. He is past seventy; and has been decaying rapidly for some time; he received some injury in chasing that unlucky deer, too, on the lake. Oh! Miss Temple, that was an unlucky chase indeed! it has led, I fear, to this awful scene."

The smile of Elizabeth was celestial: "Why name such a trifle now—at this moment the heart is dead to all earthly emotions!"

"If any thing could reconcile a man to this death," cried the youth, "it would be to meet it in such company!"

"Talk not so, Edwards, talk not so," interrupted Miss Temple, "I am unworthy of it; and it is unjust to yourself. We must die; yes—yes—we must die—it is the will of God, and let us endeavour to submit like his own children."

"Die!" the youth rather shrieked than exclaimed, "No—no—there must yet be hope—you at least must not, shall not die."

"In what way can we escape?" asked Elizabeth, pointing, with a look of heavenly composure, towards the fire. "Observe! the flame is crossing the barrier of wet ground—it comes slowly, Edwards, but surely.—Ah! see! the tree! the tree is already lighted!"

Her words were too true. The heat of the conflagration had, at length, overcome the resistance of the spring, and the fire was slowly stealing along the half-dried moss; while a dead pine kindled with the touch of a forked flame, that, for a moment, wreathed around the stem of the tree, as it whirled, in one of its evolutions, under the influence of the air. The effect was instantaneous. The flames danced along the parched trunk of the pine, like lightning quivering on a chain, and immediately a column of living fire was raging on the terrace. It soon spread from tree to tree, and the scene was evidently drawing to a close. The log on which Mohegan was seated lighted at its farther end, and the Indian appeared to be surrounded by fire. Still he was unmoved. As his body was unprotected, his sufferings must have been great, but his fortitude was superior to all. His voice could yet be heard, even in the midst of these horrors. Elizabeth turned her head from the sight, and faced the valley. Furious eddies of wind were created by the heat, and just at the moment, the canopy of fiery smoke that overhung the valley, was cleared away, leaving a distinct view of the peaceful village beneath them.

"My father!—My father!" shrieked Elizabeth. "Oh! this—this surely might have been spared me—but I submit."

The distance was not so great but the figure of Judge Temple could be seen, standing in his own grounds, and, apparently, contemplating, in perfect unconsciousness of the danger of his child, the mountain in flames. This sight was still more painful than the approaching danger; and Elizabeth again faced the hill.

"My intemperate warmth has done this!" cried Edwards, in

the accents of despair. "If I had possessed but a moiety of your heavenly resignation, Miss Temple, all might yet have been well."

"Name it not—name it not," she said. "It is now of no avail. We must die, Edwards, we must die—let us do so as Christians. But—no—you may yet escape, perhaps. Your dress is not so fatal as mine. Fly! leave me. An opening may yet be found for you, possibly—certainly it is worth the effort. Fly! leave me—but stay! You will see my father; my poor, my bereaved father! Say to him, then, Edwards, say to him, all that can appease his anguish. Tell him that I died happy and collected; that I have gone to my beloved mother; that the hours of this life are as nothing when balanced in the scales of eternity. Say how we shall meet again. And say," she continued, dropping her voice, that had risen with her feelings, as if conscious of her worldly weaknesses, "how dear, how very dear, was my love for him. That it was near, too near, to my love for God."

The youth listened to her touching accents, but moved not. In a moment he found utterance and replied:

"And is it me that you command to leave you! to leave you on the edge of the grave! Oh! Miss Temple, how little have you known me," he cried, dropping on his knees at her feet, and gathering her flowing robe in his arms, as if to shield her from the flames. "I have been driven to the woods in despair; but your society has tamed the lion within me. If I have wasted my time in degradation, 'twas you that charmed me to it. If I have forgotten my name and family, your form supplied the place of memory. If I have forgotten my wrongs, 'twas you that taught me charity. No—no—dearest Elizabeth, I may die with you, but I can never leave you!"

Elizabeth moved not, nor answered. It was plain that her thoughts had been raised from the earth. The recollection of her father, and her regrets at their separation, had been mellowed by a holy sentiment, that lifted her above the level of earthly things, and she was fast losing the weakness of her sex, in the near view of eternity. But as she listened to these words, she became once more woman. She struggled against these feelings, and smiled, as she thought she was shaking off the last lingering feeling of nature, when the world, and all its seductions, rushed again to her heart, with the sounds of a human voice, crying in piercing tones—

"Gall! where be ye, gall! gladden the heart of an old man, if ye yet belong to 'arth!"

"List!" said Elizabeth, "'tis the Leather-stocking; he seeks me!"

"'Tis Natty!" shouted Edwards, "and we may yet be saved!"

A wide and circling flame glared on their eyes for a moment, even above the fire of the woods, and a loud report followed.

" 'Tis the canister! 'tis the powder," cried the same voice, evidently approaching them. " 'Tis the canister, and the precious child is lost!"

At the next instant Natty rushed through the steams of the spring, and appeared on the terrace, without his deer skin cap, his hair burnt to his head, his shirt of country check, black, and filled with holes, and his red features of a deeper colour than ever, by the heat he had encountered.

Chapter XXXVIII.

"Even from the land of shadows, now,
My father's awful ghost appears."
                    Campbell, *Gertrude of Wyoming*, III.xxxix.3–4.

FOR an hour after Louisa Grant was left by Miss Temple, in the situation already mentioned, she continued in feverish anxiety, awaiting the return of her friend. But, as the time passed by without the re-appearance of Elizabeth, the terror of Louisa gradually increased, until her alarmed fancy had conjured every species of danger that appertained to the woods, excepting the one that really existed. The heavens had become obscured, by degrees, and vast volumes of smoke were pouring over the valley; but the thoughts of Louisa were still recurring to beasts, without dreaming of the real cause for apprehension. She was stationed in the edge of the low pines and chestnuts that succeeded the first or large growth of the forest, and directly above the angle where the highway turned from the straight course to the village and ascended the mountain, laterally. Consequently she commanded a view not only of the valley, but of the road beneath her. The few travellers that passed, she observed, were engaged in earnest conversation, and frequently raised their eyes to the hill, and at length she saw the people leaving the court-house, and gazing upward also. While under the influence of the alarm excited by such unusual movements, reluctant to go, and yet fearful to remain, Louisa was startled by the low, cracking, but cautious treads, of some one approaching through the bushes. She was on the eve of flight, when Natty emerged from the cover and stood at her side. The old man laughed as he shook her kindly by a hand that was passive with fear.

"I am glad to meet you here, child," he said; "for the back of the mountain is a-fire, and it would be dangerous to go up it now, till it has been burnt over once, and the dead wood is gone. There's a foolish man, the comrad of that varmint, who has given me all this trouble, digging for ore, on the east side. I told him that the kearless fellows who thought to catch a practys'd hunter in the woods after dark, had thrown the lighted pine knots in the brush, and that 'twould kindle like tow, and warned him to leave the hill. But he was set upon his business, and nothing short of Providence could move him. If he isn't burnt and buried in a grave of his own digging, he's made of salamanders. Why, what ails the child! you look as skeary as if you see'd more painters! I wish there was more to be found, they'd count up faster than the beaver. But, where's the good child of a bad father? did she forget her promise to the old man?"

"The hill! the hill!" shrieked Louisa; "she seeks you on the hill, with the powder!"

Natty recoiled several feet, at this unexpected intelligence.

"The Lord of Heaven have mercy on her! She's on the Vision, and that's a sheet of fire ag'in this. Child, if ye love the dear one, and hope to find a friend when ye need it most, to the village, and give the alarm. The men be us'd to fighting fire, and there may be a chance left. Fly! I bid ye fly! nor stop even for breath."

The Leather-stocking had no sooner uttered this injunction, than he disappeared in the bushes, and when last seen by Louisa, was rushing up the mountain, with a speed that none but those who were accustomed to the toil, could attain.

"Have I found ye!" the old man exclaimed, when he burst out of the smoke; "God be praised, that I've found ye; but follow, there is no time for talking."

"My dress!" said Elizabeth; "it would be fatal to trust myself nearer to the flames in it."

"I bethought me of your flimsy things," cried Natty, throwing loose the folds of a covering of buckskin that he carried on his arm, and wrapping her form in it, in such a manner as to envelope her whole person; "now follow, for it's a matter of life and death to us all."

"But John! what will become of John," cried Edwards; "Can we leave the old warrior here to perish?"

The eyes of Natty followed the direction of Edwards' finger, when he beheld the Indian, still seated as before, with the very earth under his feet consuming with fire. Without delay, the hunter approached the spot, and spoke in Delaware—

"Up and away, Chingachgook! will ye stay here to burn, like a Mingo at the stake! The Moravians have teached ye better, I hope. The Lord preserve me if the powder has'nt flashed a-tween his legs, and the skin of his back is roasting. Will ye come, I say? will ye follow?"

"Why should Mohegan go?" returned the Indian, gloomily. "He has seen the days of an eagle, and his eye grows dim. He looks on the valley; he looks on the water; he looks in the hunting-grounds—but he sees no Delawares. Every one has a white skin. My fathers say, from the far-off land, come. My women, my young warriors, my tribe, say, come. The Great Spirit says, come. Let Mohegan die."

"But you forget your friend," cried Edwards.

" 'Tis useless to talk to an Indian with the death-fit on him, lad," interrupted Natty, who seized the strips of the blanket, and with wonderful dexterity strapped the passive chieftain to his own back; when he turned, and with a strength that seemed to bid defiance, not only to his years, but to his load, he led the way to the point whence he had issued. As they crossed the little terrace of rock, one of the dead trees, that had been tottering for several minutes, fell on the spot where they had stood, and filled the air with its cinders.

Such an event quickened the steps of the party, who followed the Leather-stocking with the urgency required by the occasion.

"Tread on the soft ground," he cried, when they were in a gloom where sight availed them but little, "and keep in the white smoke; keep the skin close on her, lad, she's a precious one, another will be hard to be found."

Obedient to the hunter's directions, they followed his steps and advice implicitly, and although the narrow passage along the winding of the spring led amid burning logs and falling branches, they happily achieved it in safety. No one but a man long accustomed to the woods could have traced his route through a smoke, in which respiration was difficult, and sight nearly useless; but the experience of Natty conducted them to an opening through the rocks, where, with a little difficulty, they soon descended to another terrace, and emerged at once into a tolerably clear atmosphere.

The feelings of Edwards and Elizabeth, at reaching this spot, may be imagined, though not easily described. No one seemed to exult more than their guide, who turned, with Mohegan still lashed to his back, and laughing in his own manner, said, "I know'd 'twas the Frenchman's powder, gall; it went so altogether; your coarse grain will squib for a minute. The Iroquois had none of the best powder when I went ag'in the Canada tribes, under Sir William. Did I ever tell you the story, lad, concarning the skrimmage with"——

"For God's sake, tell me nothing now, Natty, until we are entirely safe——where shall we go next?"

"Why, on the platform of rock over the cave, to be sure,—— you will be safe enough there, or we'll go into it if you be so minded."

The young man started, and appeared agitated; but looking around him with an anxious eye, said quickly—

"Shall we be safe on the rock? cannot the fire reach us there, too?"

"Can't the boy see?" said Natty, with the coolness of one accustomed to the kind of danger he had just encountered. "Had ye staid in the place above ten minutes longer, you would both have been in ashes, but here you may stay for ever, and no fire can touch you, until they burn the rocks as well as the woods."

With this assurance, which was obviously true, they proceeded to the spot, and Natty deposited his load, placing the Indian on the ground with his back against a fragment of the rocks. Elizabeth sunk on the ground, and buried her face in her hands, while her heart was swelling with a variety of conflicting emotions.

"Let me urge you to take a restorative, Miss Temple," said Edwards respectfully; "your frame will sink else."

"Leave me, leave me," she said, raising her beaming eyes for a moment to his; "I feel too much for words; I am grateful, Oliver, for this miraculous escape; and next to my God, to you."

Edwards withdrew to the edge of the rock, and shouted— "Benjamin! where are you, Benjamin?"

A hoarse voice replied, as if from the bowels of the earth, "Hereaway, master; stow'd in this here bit of a hole, which is all the same as hot as the cook's coppers. I'm tired of my berth, d'ye see, and if-so-be that Leather-stocking has got much overhauling to do before he sails after them said beaver, I'll go into dock again, and ride out my quarantine 'till I can get prottick from the law, and so hold on upon the rest of my 'spaniolas."

"Bring up a glass of water from the spring," continued Edwards, "and throw a little wine in it; hasten, I entreat you."

"I knows but little of your small drink, master Oliver," returned the steward, his voice issuing out of the cave into the open air, "and the Jamaiky held out no longer than to take a parting kiss with Billy Kirby, when he anchored me along-side the highway last night, where you run me down in the chase. But here's sum'mat of a red colour that may suit a weak stomach, mayhap. That master Kirby is no first rate in a boat, but he'll tack a cart among the stumps, all the same as a Lon'on pilot will back and fill through the colliers in the Pool."

As the steward ascended while talking, by the time he had ended his speech, he appeared on the rock, with the desired restoratives, exhibiting the worn out and bloated features of a man who had run deep in a debauch, and that lately.

Elizabeth took from the hand of Edwards the liquor which he offered, and then motioned to be left again to herself.

The youth turned at her bidding, and observed Natty kindly assiduous around the person of Mohegan. When their eyes met, the hunter said sorrowfully—

"His time has come, lad; I see it in his eyes;—when an Indian fixes his eye, he means to go but to one place; and what the wilful creaters put their minds on, they're sure to do."

A quick tread prevented the reply, and in a few moments, to the amazement of the whole party, Mr. Grant was seen clinging to the side of the mountain, and striving to reach the place where they stood. Oliver sprang to his assistance, and by their united efforts, the worthy divine was soon placed safely among them.

"How came you added to our number?" cried Edwards; "Is the hill alive with people, at a time like this?"

The hasty, but pious thanksgivings of the clergyman were soon ejaculated; and when he succeeded in collecting his bewildered senses, he replied—

"I heard that my child was seen coming to the mountain; and when the fire broke over its summit, my uneasiness drew me up the road, where I found Louisa, in terror for Miss Temple. It was to seek her that I came into this dangerous place; and I think but for God's mercy, through the dogs of Natty, I should have perished in the flames myself."

"Ay! follow the hounds, and if there's an opening they'll scent it out," said Natty; "their noses be given to them the same as man's reason."

"I did so, and they led me to this place; but, praise be to God, that I see you all safe and well."

"No, no," returned the hunter; "safe we be, but as for well, John can't be called in a good way, unless you'll say that for a man that's taking his last look at 'arth."

"He speaks the truth!" said the divine, with the holy awe with which he ever approached the dying;—"I have been by too many death-beds, not to see that the hand of the tyrant is laid on this old warrior. Oh! how consoling it is, to know that he has not rejected the offered mercy, in the hour of his strength and of worldly temptations! The offspring of a race of heathens, he has in truth been 'as a brand plucked from the burning.'"

"No, no," returned Natty, who alone stood with him by the side of the dying warrior, "it's no burning that ails him, though his Indian feelings made him scorn to move, unless it be the burning of man's wicked thoughts for near fourscore years; but it's nater giving out in a chase that's run too long.——Down with ye, Hector! down, I say!—Flesh isn't iron, that a man can live for ever, and see his kith and kin driven to a far country, and he left to mourn, with none to keep him company."

"John," said the divine, tenderly, "do you hear me? do you wish the prayers appointed by the church, at this trying moment?"

The Indian turned his ghastly face towards the speaker, and fastened his dark eyes on him, steadily, but vacantly. No sign of recognition was made; and in a moment he moved his head again slowly towards the vale, and begun to sing, using his own language, in those low, guttural tones that have been so often mentioned, his notes rising with his theme, till they swelled so loud as to be distinct.

"I will come! I will come! to the land of the just I will come! The Maquas I have slain!—I have slain the Maquas! and the Great Spirit calls to his son. I will come! I will come! to the land of the just I will come!"

"What says he, Leather-stocking?" inquired the priest, with tender interest; "sings he the Redeemer's praise?"

"No, no,—'tis his own praise that he speaks now," said Natty, turning in a melancholy manner from the sight of his dying friend; "and a good right he has to say it all, for I know every word to be true."

"May Heaven avert such self-righteousness from his heart! Humility and penitence are the seals of christianity; and without feeling them deeply seated in the soul, all hope is delusive, and leads to vain expectations. Praise himself! when his whole soul and body should unite to praise his Maker! John! you have enjoyed the blessings of a gospel ministry, and have been called from out a multitude of sinners and pagans, and, I trust, for a wise and gracious purpose. Do you now feel what it is to be justified by your Saviour's death, and reject all weak and idle dependence on good works, that spring from man's pride and vain-glory?"

The Indian did not regard his interrogator, but he raised his head again, and said, in a low, distinct voice—

"Who can say that the Maquas know the back of Mohegan! What enemy that trusted in him did not see the morning? What Mingo that he chased ever sung the song of triumph? Did Mohegan ever lie? No; the truth lived in him, and none else could come out of him. In his youth, he was a warrior, and his moccasins left the stain of blood. In his age, he was wise; his words at the council fire did not blow away with the winds."

"Ah! he has abandoned that vain relic of paganism, his songs," cried the divine;—"what says he now? is he sensible of his lost state?"

"Lord! man," said Natty, "he knows his ind is at hand as well as you or I, but, so far from thinking it a loss, he believes it to be a great gain. He is old and stiff, and you've made the game so scurce and shy, that better shots than him find it hard to get a livelihood. Now he thinks he shall travel where it will always be good hunting; where no wicked or unjust Indians can go; and where he shall meet all his tribe together ag'in. There's not much loss in that, to a man whose hands be hardly fit for basket-making. Loss! if there be any loss, 'twill be to me. I'm sure, after he's gone, there will be but little left for me but to follow."

"His example and end, which, I humbly trust, shall yet be

made glorious," returned Mr. Grant, "should lead your mind to dwell on the things of another life. But I feel it to be my duty to smooth the way for the parting spirit. This is the moment, John, when the reflection that you did not reject the mediation of the Redeemer, will bring balm to your soul. Trust not to any act of former days, but lay the burthen of your sins at his feet, and you have his own blessed assurance that he will not desert you."

"Though all you say be true, and you have scripter gospels for it, too," said Natty, "you will make nothing of the Indian. He has'nt seen a Moravian priest sin' the war; and it's hard to keep them from going back to their native ways. I should think 'twould be as well to let the old man pass in peace. He's happy now; I know it by his eye; and that's more than I would say for the chief, sin' the time the Delawares broke up from the head-waters of their river, and went west. Ahs! me! 'tis a grievous long time that, and many dark days have we seen together, sin' it."

"Hawk-eye!" said Mohegan, rousing with the last glimmering of life. "Hawk-eye! listen to the words of your brother."

"Yes, John," said the hunter, in English, strongly affected by the appeal, and drawing to his side; "we have been brothers; and more so than it means in the Indian tongue. What would ye have with me, Chingachgook?"

"Hawk-eye! my fathers call me to the happy hunting-grounds. The path is clear, and the eyes of Mohegan grow young. I look—but I see no white-skins; there are none to be seen but just and brave Indians. Farewell, Hawk-eye—you shall go with the Fire-eater and the Young-eagle, to the white man's heaven; but I go after my fathers. Let the bow, and tomahawk, and pipe, and the wampum, of Mohegan, be laid in his grave; for when he starts 'twill be in the night, like a warrior on a war-party, and he cannot stop to seek them."

"What says he, Nathaniel?" cried Mr. Grant, earnestly, and with obvious anxiety; "does he recall the promises of the mediation? and trust his salvation to the Rock of ages?"

Although the faith of the hunter was by no means clear, yet the fruits of early instruction had not entirely fallen in the wilderness. He believed in one God, and in one heaven; and when the strong feeling excited by the leave-taking of his old companion, which was exhibited by the powerful working of every muscle in his weather beaten face, suffered him to speak, he replied—

"No—no—he trusts only to the Great Spirit of the savages, and to his own good deeds. He thinks, like all his people, that he is to be young ag'in, and to hunt, and be happy to the ind of etarnity. It's pretty much the same with all colours, parson. I could never bring myself to think that I shall meet with these hounds, or my piece, in another world; though the thoughts of leaving them for ever, sometimes brings hard feelings over me, and makes me cling to life with a greater craving than beseems three-score-and-ten."

"The Lord, in his mercy, avert such a death from one who has been sealed with the sign of the cross!" cried the minister, in holy fervour. "John—"

He paused for the elements. During the period occupied by the events which we have related, the dark clouds in the horizon had continued to increase in numbers and magnitude; and the awful stillness that now pervaded the air, announced a crisis in the state of the atmosphere. The flames, which yet continued to rage along the sides of the mountain, no longer whirled in the uncertain currents of their own eddies, but blazed high and steadily towards the heavens. There was even a quietude in the ravages of the destructive element, as if it foresaw that a hand, greater than even its own desolating power, was about to stay its progress. The piles of smoke which lay above the valley began to rise, and were dispelling rapidly; and streaks of vivid lightning were dancing through the masses of clouds that impended over the western hills. While Mr. Grant was speaking, a flash, which sent its quivering light through the gloom, laying bare the whole opposite horizon, was followed by a loud crash of thunder, that rolled away among the hills, seeming to shake the foundations of the earth to their centre. Mohegan raised himself, as if in obedience to a signal for his departure, and stretched his wasted arm towards the west. His dark face lighted with a look of joy; which, with all other expression, gradually disappeared; the muscles stiffening as they retreated to a state of rest; a slight convulsion played, for a single instant, about his lips; and his arm slowly dropped by his side; leaving the frame of the dead warrior reposing against the rock, with its glassy eyes open, and fixed on the distant hills, as if the deserted shell were tracing the flight of the spirit to its new abode.

All this Mr. Grant witnessed, in silent awe; but when the last echoes of the thunder died away, he clasped his hands together, with pious energy, and repeated, in the full rich tones of assured faith—

"O Lord! how unsearchable are thy judgments: And thy ways past finding out! 'I know that my Redeemer liveth, and that he shall stand at the latter day upon the earth: And though after my skin, worms destroy this body, yet in my flesh shall I see God; whom I shall see for myself, and mine eyes shall behold, and not another.' "

As the divine closed this burst of devotion, he bowed his head meekly to his bosom, and looked all the dependence and humility that the inspired language expressed.

When Mr. Grant retired from the body, the hunter approached, and taking the rigid hand of his friend, looked him wistfully in the face for some time without speaking; when he gave vent to his feelings by saying, in the mournful voice of one who felt deeply—

"Red skin, or white, it's all over now! He's to be judged by a righteous Judge, and by no laws that's made to suit times, and new ways. Well, there's only one more death, and the world be left to me and the hounds. Ahs! me! a man must wait the time of God's pleasure, but I begin to weary of life. There is scurcely a tree standing that I know, and it's hard to find a face that I was acquainted with in my younger days."

Large drops of rain began now to fall, and diffuse themselves over the dry rock, while the approach of the thunder shower was rapid and certain. The body of the Indian was hastily removed into the cave beneath, followed by the whining hounds, who missed, and moaned for, the look of intelligence that had always met their salutations to the chief.

Edwards made some hasty and confused excuse for not taking Elizabeth into the same place, which was now completely closed in front with logs and bark, saying something that she hardly understood about its darkness, and the unpleasantness of being with the dead body. Miss Temple, however, found a sufficient shelter against the torrent of rain that fell, under the projection of a rock which overhung them. But long before the shower was over, the sounds of voices were heard below them, crying aloud for Elizabeth, and men soon appeared, beating the dying embers of the bushes, as they worked their way cautiously among the unextinguished brands.

At the first short cessation in the rain, Oliver conducted Elizabeth to the road, where he left her. Before parting, however, he found time to say, in a fervent manner, that his companion was now at no loss to interpret—

"The moment of concealment is over, Miss Temple. By this time to-morrow, I shall remove a veil that perhaps it has been weakness to keep around me and my affairs so long. But I have had romantic and foolish wishes and weaknesses; and who has not, that is young and torn by conflicting passions! God bless you! I hear your father's voice; he is coming up the road, and I would not, just now, subject myself to detention. Thank Heaven, you are safe again; that alone removes the weight of a world from my spirit!"

He waited for no answer, but sprung into the woods. Elizabeth, notwithstanding she heard the cries of her father as he called upon her name, paused until he was concealed among the smoking trees, when she turned, and in a moment rushed into the arms of her half-distracted parent.

A carriage had been provided, into which Miss Temple hastily entered; when the cry was passed along the hill, that the lost one was found, and the people returned to the village, wet and dirty, but elated with the thought that the daughter of their landlord had escaped from so horrid and untimely an end.*

---

* The probability of a fire in the woods, similar to that here described, has been questioned. The writer can only say that he once witnessed a fire in another part of New York that compelled a man to desert his wagon and horses in the highway, and in which the latter were destroyed. In order to estimate the probability of such an event, it is necessary to remember the effects of a long drought in that climate, and the abundance of dead wood which is found in a forest like that described. The fires in the American forests frequently rage to such an extent as to produce a sensible effect on the atmosphere at the distance of fifty miles. Houses, barns, and fences are quite commonly swept away in their course. [1832]

Chapter XXXIX.

"Selictar! unsheath then our chief's scimetar;
Tambourgi! thy 'larum gives promise of war;
Ye mountains! that see us descend to the shore,
Shall view us victors, or view us no more."
                    Byron, *Childe Harold's Pilgrimage*, II.lxxi.50–53.

T HE heavy showers that prevailed during the remainder
of the day, completely stopped the progress of the flames;
though glimmering fires were observed during the night, on
different parts of the hill, wherever there was a collection of
fuel to feed the element. The next day the woods, for many
miles, were black and smoking, and were stript of every vestige
of brush and dead wood; but the pines and hemlocks still
reared their heads proudly, among the hills, and even the smaller trees of the forest retained a feeble appearance of life and
vegetation.

The many tongues of rumour were busy in exaggerating the
miraculous escape of Elizabeth, and a report was generally
credited, that Mohegan had actually perished in the flames.
This belief became confirmed, and was indeed rendered probable, when the direful intelligence reached the village, that
Jotham Riddel, the miner, was found in his hole, nearly dead
with suffocation, and burnt to such a degree that no hopes were
entertained of his life.

The public attention became much alive to the events of the
last few days, and just at this crisis, the convicted counterfeiters
took the hint from Natty, and, on the night succeeding the fire,
found means to cut through their log prison also, and to escape
unpunished. When this news begun to circulate through the
village, blended with the fate of Jotham, and the exaggerated
and tortured reports of the events on the hill, the popular opinion was freely expressed, as to the propriety of seizing such of
the fugitives as remained within reach. Men talked of the cave,
as a secret receptacle of guilt; and, as the rumour of ores and

metals found its way into the confused medley of conjectures, counterfeiting, and every thing else that was wicked and dangerous to the peace of society, suggested themselves to the busy fancies of the populace.

While the public mind was in this feverish state, it was hinted that the wood had been set on fire by Edwards and the Leather-stocking, and that, consequently, they alone were responsible for the damages. This opinion soon gained ground, being most circulated by those who, by their own heedlessness, had caused the evil; and there was one irresistible burst of the common sentiment, that an attempt should be made to punish the offenders. Richard was by no means deaf to this appeal, and by noon he set about in earnest, to see the laws executed.

Several stout young men were selected, and taken apart, with an appearance of secrecy, where they received some important charge from the Sheriff, immediately under the eyes, but far removed from the ears, of all in the village. Possessed of a knowledge of their duty, these youths hurried into the hills, with a bustling manner, as if the fate of the world depended on their diligence, and, at the same time, with an air of mystery, as great as if they were engaged on secret matters of the state.

At twelve precisely, a drum beat the "long roll" before the "Bold Dragoon," and Richard appeared, accompanied by Captain Hollister, who was clad in his vestments as commander of the "Templeton Light-Infantry," when the former demanded of the latter the aid of the posse comitatus, in enforcing the laws of the country. We have not room to record the speeches of the two gentlemen on this occasion, but they are preserved in the columns of the little blue newspaper, which is yet to be found on file, and are said to be highly creditable to the legal formula of one of the parties, and to the military precision of the other. Every thing had been previously arranged, and as the red-coated drummer continued to roll out his clattering notes, some five-and-twenty privates appeared in the ranks, and arranged themselves in order of battle.

As this corps was composed of volunteers, and was commanded by a man who had passed the first five-and-thirty years of his life in camps and garrisons, it was the nonpareil of military science in that country, and was confidently pronounced, by the judicious part of the Templeton community, to be equal in skill and appearance to any troops in the known world; in physical endowments they were, certainly, much superior! To this assertion there were but three dissenting voices, and one dissenting opinion. The opinion belonged to Marmaduke, who, however, saw no necessity for its promulgation. Of the voices, one, and that a pretty loud one, came from the spouse of the commander himself, who frequently reproached her husband for condescending to lead such an irregular band of warriors, after he had filled the honourable station of sergeant-major to a dashing corps of Virginian cavalry through much of the recent war.

Another of these sceptical sentiments was invariably expressed by Mr. Pump, whenever the company paraded, generally in some such terms as these, which were uttered with that sort of meekness that a native of the island of our forefathers is apt to assume, when he condescends to praise the customs or character of her truant progeny—

"It's mayhap that they knows sum'mat about loading and firing, d'ye see; but as for working ship! why a corporal's guard of the Boadishey's marines would back and fill on their quarters in such a manner as to surround and captivate them all in half a glass." As there was no one to deny this assertion, the marines of the Boadicea were held in a corresponding degree of estimation.

The third unbeliever was Monsieur Le Quoi, who merely whispered to the Sheriff, that the corps was one of the finest he had ever seen, second only to the Mousquetaires of Le Bon Louis! However, as Mrs. Hollister thought there was something like actual service in the present appearances, and was, in consequence, too busily engaged with certain preparations of her own, to make her comments; as Benjamin was absent, and Monsieur Le Quoi too happy to find fault with any thing, the corps escaped criticism and comparison altogether on this momentous day, when they certainly had greater need of self-confidence, than on any other previous occasion. Marmaduke was said to be again closeted with Mr. Van der School, and no interruption was offered to the movements of the troops. At two o'clock precisely the corps shouldered arms, beginning on the right wing, next to the veteran, and carrying the motion through to the left with great regularity. When each musket was quietly fixed in its proper situation, the order was given to wheel to the left, and march. As this was bringing raw troops, at once, to face their enemy, it is not to be supposed that the manœuvre was executed with their usual accuracy, but as the music struck up the inspiring air of Yankee-doodle, and Richard, accompanied by Mr. Doolittle, preceded the troops boldly down the street, Captain Hollister led on, with his head elevated to forty-five degrees, with a little, low cocked hat, perched on his crown, carrying a tremendous dragoon sabre at a poise, and trailing at his heels a huge steel scabbard, that had war in its very clattering. There was a good deal of difficulty in getting all the platoons (there were six) to look the same way; but, by the time they reached the defile of the bridge, the troops were in sufficiently compact order. In this manner they marched up the hill to the summit of the mountain, no other alteration taking place in the disposition of the forces, excepting that a mutual complaint was made by the Sheriff and the magistrate, of a failure in wind, which gradually brought these gentlemen to the rear. It will be unnecessary to detail the minute movements that succeeded. We shall briefly say, that the scouts came in and reported, that, so far from retreating, as had been anticipated, the fugitives had evidently gained a knowledge of the attack, and were fortifying for a desperate resistance. This intelligence certainly made a material change, not only in the plans of the leaders, but in the countenances of the soldiery also. The men looked at one another with serious faces, and Hiram and Richard begun to consult together, apart.

At this conjuncture, they were joined by Billy Kirby, who came along the highway, with his axe under his arm, as much in advance of his team as Captain Hollister had been of his troops in the ascent. The wood-chopper was amazed at the military array, but the Sheriff eagerly availed himself of this powerful reinforcement, and commanded his assistance in putting the laws in force. Billy held Mr. Jones in too much deference to object; and it was finally arranged that he should be the bearer of a summons to the garrison to surrender, before they proceeded to extremities. The troops now divided, one party being led by the captain, over the Vision, and were brought in on the left of the cave, while the remainder advanced upon its right, under the orders of the lieutenant. Mr. Jones and Dr. Todd, for the surgeon was in attendance also, appeared on the platform of rock, immediately over the heads of the garrison, though out of their sight. Hiram thought this approaching too near, and he therefore accompanied Kirby along the side of the hill, to within a safe distance of the fortifications, where he took shelter behind a tree. Most of the men discovered great accuracy of eye in bringing some object in range between them and their enemy, and the only two of the besiegers, who were left in plain sight of the besieged, were Captain Hollister on one side, and the wood-chopper on the other. The veteran stood up boldly to the front, supporting his heavy sword, in one undeviating position, with his eye fixed firmly on his enemy, while the huge form of Billy was placed in that kind of quiet repose, with either hand thrust into his bosom, bearing his axe under his right arm, which permitted him, like his own oxen, to rest standing. So far, not a word had been exchanged between the belligerents. The besieged had drawn together a pile of black logs and branches of trees, which they had formed into a chevaux-de-frize, making a little circular abbatis, in front of the entrance to the cave. As the ground was steep and slippery in every direction around the place, and Benjamin appeared behind the works on one side, and Natty on the other, the arrangement was by no means contemptible, especially as the front was sufficiently guarded by the difficulty of the approach. By this time, Kirby had received his orders, and he advanced coolly along the mountain, picking his way with the same indifference as if he were pursuing his ordinary business. When he was within a hundred feet of the works, the long and much dreaded rifle of the Leather-stocking was seen issuing from the parapet, and his voice cried aloud—

"Keep off! Billy Kirby, keep off! I wish ye no harm; but if a man of ye all comes a step nigher, there'll be blood spilt a-twixt us. God forgive the one that draws it first; but so it must be."

"Come, old chap," said Billy, good-naturedly, "don't be crabbed, but hear what a man has got to say. I've no concarn in the business, only to see right 'twixt man and man; and I don't kear the valie of a beetle-ring which gets the better; but there's Squire Doolittle, yonder behind the beech sapling, he has invited me to come in and ask you to give up to the law—that's all."

"I see the varmint! I see his clothes!" cried the indignant

Natty; "and if he'll only show so much flesh as will bury a rifle bullet, thirty to the pound, I'll make him feel me. Go away, Billy, I bid ye; you know my aim, and I bear you no malice."

"You over calkilate your aim, Natty," said the other, as he stepped behind a pine that stood near him, "if you think to shoot a man through a tree with a three foot butt. I can lay this tree-top right across you, in ten minutes, by any man's watch, and in less time, too; so be civil—I want no more than what's right."

There was a simple seriousness in the countenance of Natty, that showed he was much in earnest; but it was, also, evident that he was reluctant to shed human blood. He answered the vaunt of the wood-chopper, by saying—

"I know you drop a tree where you will, Billy Kirby; but if you show a hand, or an arm, in doing it, there'll be bones to be set, and blood to stanch. If it's only to get into the cave that ye want, wait till a two hours' sun, and you may enter it in welcome; but come in now you shall not. There's one dead body, already, lying on the cold rocks, and there's another in which the life can hardly be said to stay. If you will come in, there'll be dead without as well as within."

The wood-chopper stept out fearlessly from his cover, and cried—

"That's fair; and what's fair, is right. He wants you to stop till it's two hours to sun-down; and I see reason in the thing. A man can give up when he's wrong, if you don't crowd him too hard; but you crowd a man, and he gets to be like a stubborn ox—the more you beat, the worse he kicks."

The sturdy notions of independence maintained by Billy, neither suited the emergency, nor the impatience of Mr. Jones, who was burning with a desire to examine the hidden mysteries of the cave. He, therefore, interrupted this amicable dialogue with his own voice.

"I command you, Nathaniel Bumppo, by my authority, to surrender your person to the law," he cried. "And I command you, gentlemen, to aid me in performing my duty. Benjamin Penguillan, I arrest you, and order you to follow me to the gaol of the county, by virtue of this warrant."

"I'd follow ye, Squire Dickens," said Benjamin, removing the pipe from his mouth, (for during the whole scene the ex-major domo had been very composedly smoking,) "Ay! I'd sail in your wake, to the end of the world, if-so-be that there was such a place, which there isn't, seeing that it's round. Now, mayhap, Master Hollister, having lived all your life on shore, you is'nt acquainted that the world, d'ye-see——"

"Surrender!" interrupted the veteran, in a voice that startled his hearers, and which actually caused his own forces to recoil several paces; "Surrender, Benjamin Penguillum, or expect no quarter."

"Damn your quarter," said Benjamin, rising from the log on which he was seated, and taking a squint along the barrel of the swivel, which had been brought on the hill, during the night, and now formed the means of defence on his side of the works. "Look you, Master, or Captain, thoff I questions if ye know the name of a rope, except the one that's to hang ye, there's no need of singing out, as if ye was hailing a deaf man on a top-gallant-yard. Mayhap you think you've got my true name in your sheep-skin; but what British sailor finds it worth while to sail in these seas, without a sham on his stern, in case of need, d'ye-see. If you call me Penguillan, you calls me by the name of the man on whose land, d'ye-see, I hove into daylight; and he was a gentleman; and that's more than my worst enimy will say of any of the family of Benjamin Stubbs."

"Send the warrant round to me, and I'll put in an alias," cried Hiram, from behind his cover.

"Put in a jackass, and you'll put in yourself, Mister Doo-but-little," shouted Benjamin, who kept squinting along his little iron tube, with great steadiness.

"I give you but one moment to yield," cried Richard. "Benjamin! Benjamin! This is not the gratitude I expected from you."

"I tell you, Richard Jones," said Natty, who dreaded the Sheriff's influence over his comrade; "though the canister the gall brought, be lost, there's powder enough in the cave to lift the rock you stand on. I'll take off my roof, if you don't hold your peace."

"I think it beneath the dignity of my office to parley further with the prisoners," the Sheriff observed to his companion, while they both retired with a precipitancy that Captain Hollister mistook for the signal to advance.

"Charge baggonet!" shouted the veteran; "march!"

Although this signal was certainly expected, it took the assailed a little by surprise, and the veteran approached the works, crying, "courage, my brave lads! give them no quarter unless they surrender," and struck a furious blow upwards with his sabre that would have divided the steward in moieties, by subjecting him to the process of decapitation, but for the fortunate interference of the muzzle of the swivel. As it was, the gun was dismounted at the critical moment that Benjamin was applying his pipe to the priming, and in consequence, some five or six dozen of rifle bullets were projected into the air, in, nearly, a perpendicular line. Philosophy teaches us that the atmosphere will not retain lead; and two pounds of the metal moulded into bullets, of thirty to the pound, after describing an ellipsis in their journey, returned to the earth, rattling among the branches of the trees directly over the heads of the troops stationed in the rear of their captain. Much of the success of an attack made by irregular soldiers, depends on the direction in which they are first got in motion. In the present instance, it was retrograde, and in less than a minute after the bellowing report of the swivel among the rocks and caverns, the whole weight of the attack, from the left, rested on the prowess of the single arm of the veteran. Benjamin received a severe contusion from the recoil of his gun, which produced a short stupor, during which period the ex-steward was prostrate on the ground. Capt. Hollister availed himself of this circumstance to scramble over the breast-work and obtain a footing in the bastion—for such was the nature of the fortress, as connected with the cave. The moment the veteran found himself within the works of his enemy, he rushed to the edge of the fortification, and waving his sabre over his head, shouted—

"Victory! come on, my brave boys, the work's our own!"

All this was perfectly military, and was such an example as a gallant officer was in some measure bound to exhibit to his men; but the outcry was the unlucky cause of turning the tide of success. Natty, who had been keeping a vigilant eye on the wood-chopper, and the enemy immediately before him, wheeled at this alarm, and was appalled at beholding his comrade on the ground, and the veteran standing on his own bulwark, giving forth the cry of victory! The muzzle of the long rifle was turned instantly towards the captain. There was a moment when the life of the old soldier was in great jeopardy; but the object to shoot at was both too large and too near for the Leather-stocking, who, instead of pulling his trigger, applied the gun to the rear of his enemy, and by a powerful shove, sent him outside of the works with much greater rapidity than he had entered them. The spot on which Capt. Hollister alighted was directly in front, where, as his feet touched the ground, so steep and slippery was the side of the mountain, it seemed to recede from under them. His motion was swift, and so irregular, as utterly to confuse the faculties of the old soldier. During its continuance, he supposed himself to be mounted and charging through the ranks of his enemy. At every tree he made a blow, of course, as at a foot-soldier; and just as he was making the cut "St. George" at a half-burnt sapling, he landed in the highway, and, to his utter amazement, at the feet of his own spouse. When Mrs. Hollister, who was toiling up the hill, followed by at least twenty curious boys, leaning with one hand on the staff with which she ordinarily walked, and bearing in the other an empty bag, witnessed this exploit of her husband, indignation immediately got the better not only of her religion, but of her philosophy.

"Why, Sargeant! is it flying ye are?" she cried—"That I should live to see a husband of mine turn his back to the inimy! and sich a one! Here have I been telling the b'ys as we come along, all about the saige of Yorrektown, and how ye was hurted; and how ye'd be acting the same ag'in the day; and I mate ye retrating jist as the first gun is fired. Och! I may trow away the bag! for if there's plunder 'twill not be the wife of sich as yeerself that will be privileged to be getting the same. They do say too, there's a power of goold and silver in the place—the Lord forgive me for setting my heart on worreldly things; but what falls in the battle, there's Scripter for believing, is the just property of the victor."

"Retreating!" exclaimed the amazed veteran; "where's my horse? he has been shot under me—I——"

"Is the man mad!" interrupted his wife—"divil the horse do ye own, sargeant, and yee're nothing but a shabby captain of malaishy. Och! if the ra'al captain was here, 'tis the other way ye'd be riding, dear, or you would not follow your lader!"

While this worthy couple were thus discussing events, the battle began to rage more violently than ever, above them. When the Leather-stocking saw his enemy fairly under head-way, as Benjamin would express it, he gave his attention again to the right wing of the assailants. It would have been easy for Kirby, with his powerful frame, to have seized the moment to scale the bastion, and with his great strength, to have sent both its defenders in pursuit of the veteran; but hostility appeared to be the passion that the wood-chopper indulged the least in, at that moment, for, in a voice that was heard by the retreating left wing, he shouted,

"Hurrah! well done, captain! keep it up! how he handles his bush hook! he makes nothing of a sapling!" and such other encouraging exclamations to the flying veteran, until, overcome by mirth, the good-natured fellow seated himself on the ground, kicking the earth with delight, and giving vent to peal after peal of laughter.

Natty stood all this time in a menacing attitude, with his rifle pointed over the breast-work, watching with a quick and cautious eye the least movement of the assailants. The outcry unfortunately tempted the ungovernable curiosity of Hiram to take a peep from behind his cover, at the state of the battle. Though this evolution was performed with great caution, in protecting his front, he left, like many a better commander, his rear exposed to the attacks of his enemy. Mr. Doolittle belonged physically to a class of his countrymen, to whom nature has denied, in their formation, the use of curved lines. Every thing about him was either straight or angular. But his tailor was a woman who worked like a regimental contractor, by a set of rules that gave the same configuration to the whole human species. Consequently, when Mr. Doolittle leaned forward in the manner described, a loose drapery appeared behind the tree, at which the rifle of Natty was pointed with the quickness of lightning. A less experienced man would have aimed at the flowing robe, which hung like a festoon half way to the earth; but the Leather-stocking knew both the man and his female tailor better, and when the smart report of the rifle was heard, Kirby, who watched the whole manœuvre in breathless expectation, saw the bark fly from the beech, and the cloth, at some distance above the loose folds, wave at the same instant. No battery was ever unmasked with more promptitude than Hiram advanced, from behind the tree, at this summons.

He made two or three steps, with great precision, to the front, and, placing one hand on the afflicted part, stretched forth the other, with a menacing air, towards Natty, and cried aloud—

"Gawl darn ye! this shan't be settled so easy; I'll follow it up from the 'common pleas' to the 'court of errors.' "

Such a shocking imprecation, from the mouth of so orderly a man as Squire Doolittle, with the fearless manner in which he exposed himself, together with, perhaps, the knowledge that Natty's rifle was unloaded, encouraged the troops in the rear, who gave a loud shout, and fired a volley into the tree-tops, after the contents of the swivel. Animated by their own noise, the men now rushed on in earnest, and Billy Kirby, who thought the joke, good as it was, had gone far enough, was in the act of scaling the works, when Judge Temple appeared on the opposite side, exclaiming—

"Silence and peace! why do I see murder and bloodshed attempted! is not the law sufficient to protect itself, that armed bands must be gathered, as in rebellion and war, to see justice performed!"

" 'Tis the posse comitatus," shouted the Sheriff, from a distant rock, "who"——

"Say rather a posse of demons. I command the peace."—

"Hold! shed not blood!" cried a voice from the top of the Vision——"Hold! for the sake of Heaven, fire no more! all shall be yielded! you shall enter the cave!"

Amazement produced the desired effect. Natty, who had reloaded his piece, quietly seated himself on the logs, and rested his head on his hand, while the "Light Infantry" ceased their military movements, and waited the issue in suspense.

In less than a minute Edwards came rushing down the hill, followed by Major Hartmann with a velocity that was surprising for his years. They reached the terrace in an instant, from which the youth led the way, by the hollow in the rock, to the mouth of the cave, into which they both entered; leaving all without silent and gazing after them with astonishment.

Chapter XL.

"I am dumb.
Were you the Doctor, and I knew you not!"
The Merchant of Venice, V.i.279–80.

D URING the five or six minutes that elapsed before the youth and Major re-appeared, Judge Temple and the Sheriff, together with most of the volunteers, ascended to the terrace, where the latter begun to express their conjectures of the result, and to recount their individual services in the conflict. But the sight of the peace-makers, ascending the ravine, shut every mouth.

On a rude chair, covered with undressed deer-skins, they supported a human being, whom they seated carefully and respectfully in the midst of the assembly. His head was covered by long, smooth locks, of the colour of snow. His dress, which was studiously neat and clean, was composed of such fabrics as none but the wealthiest classes wear, but was threadbare and patched; and on his feet were placed a pair of moccasins, ornamented in the best manner of Indian ingenuity. The outlines of his face were grave and dignified, though his vacant eye, which opened and turned slowly to the faces of those around him in unmeaning looks, too surely announced that the period had arrived, when age brings the mental imbecility of childhood.

Natty had followed the supporters of this unexpected object to the top of the cave, and took his station at a little distance behind him, leaning on his rifle, in the midst of his pursuers, with a fearlessness that showed that heavier interests than those which affected himself were to be decided. Major Hartmann placed himself beside the aged man, uncovered, with his whole soul beaming through those eyes which so commonly danced with frolic and humour. Edwards rested with one hand familiarly, but affectionately, on the chair, though his heart was swelling with emotions that denied him utterance.

All eyes were gazing intently; but each tongue continued

mute. At length the decrepit stranger, turning his vacant looks from face to face, made a feeble attempt to rise, while a faint smile crossed his wasted face, like an habitual effort at courtesy, as he said, in a hollow, tremulous voice—

"Be pleased to be seated, gentlemen. The council will open immediately. Each one who loves a good and virtuous king, will wish to see these colonies continue loyal. Be seated—I pray you, be seated, gentlemen. The troops shall halt for the night."

"This is the wandering of insanity!" said Marmaduke; "who will explain this scene?"

"No, sir," said Edwards, firmly, "'tis only the decay of nature; who is answerable for its pitiful condition, remains to be shown."

"Will the gentlemen dine with us, my son?" said the old stranger, turning to a voice that he both knew and loved. "Order a repast suitable for his Majesty's officers. You know we have the best of game always at command."

"Who is this man?" asked Marmaduke, in a hurried voice, in which the dawnings of conjecture united with interest to put the question.

"This man!" returned Edwards, calmly, his voice, however, gradually rising as he proceeded; "this man, sir, whom you behold hid in caverns, and deprived of every thing that can make life desirable, was once the companion and counsellor of those who ruled your country. This man, whom you see, helpless and feeble, was once a warrior, so brave and fearless, that even the intrepid natives gave him the name of the Fire-eater. This man, whom you now see destitute of even the ordinary comfort of a cabin in which to shelter his head, was once the owner of great riches; and, Judge Temple, he was the rightful proprietor of this very soil on which we stand. This man was the father of"—

"This, then," cried Marmaduke, with a powerful emotion, "this, then, is the lost Major Effingham!"

"Lost indeed," said the youth, fixing a piercing eye on the other.

"And you! and you!" continued the Judge, articulating with difficulty.

"I am his grandson."

A minute passed in profound silence. All eyes were fixed on the speakers, and even the old German appeared to wait the issue in deep anxiety. But the moment of agitation soon passed. Marmaduke raised his head from his bosom, where it had sunk, not in shame, but in devout mental thanksgivings, and, as large tears fell over his fine, manly face, he grasped the hand of the youth warmly, and said—

"Oliver, I forgive all thy harshness—all thy suspicions. I now see it all. I forgive thee every thing, but suffering this aged man to dwell in such a place, when not only my habitation, but my fortune, were at his and thy command."

"He's true as ter steel!" shouted Major Hartmann; "titn't I tell't you, lat, dat Marmatuke Temple vast a frient dat woult never fail in ter dime as of neet!"

"It is true, Judge Temple, that my opinions of your conduct have been staggered by what this worthy gentleman has told me. When I found it impossible to convey my grandfather back whence the enduring love of this old man brought him, without detection and exposure, I went to the Mohawk in quest of one of his former comrades, in whose justice I had dependence. He is your friend, Judge Temple, but if what he says be true, both my father and myself may have judged you harshly."

"You name your father!" said Marmaduke, tenderly—"Was he, indeed, lost in the packet?"

"He was. He had left me, after several years of fruitless application and comparative poverty, in Nova-Scotia, to obtain the compensation for his losses, which the British commissioners had at length awarded. After spending a year in England, he was returning to Halifax, on his way to a government, to which he had been appointed, in the West-Indies, intending to go to the place where my grandfather had sojourned during and since the war, and take him with us."

"But, thou!" said Marmaduke, with powerful interest; "I had thought that thou hadst perished with him."

A flush passed over the cheeks of the young man, who gazed about him at the wondering faces of the volunteers, and continued silent. Marmaduke turned to the veteran captain, who just then rejoined his command, and said—

"March thy soldiers back again, and dismiss them; the zeal of the Sheriff has much mistaken his duty. Dr. Todd, I will thank you to attend to the injury which Hiram Doolittle has received in this untoward affair. Richard, you will oblige me by sending up the carriage to the top of the hill. Benjamin, return to your duty in my family."

Unwelcome as these orders were to most of the auditors, the suspicion that they had somewhat exceeded the wholesome restraints of the law, and the habitual respect with which all the commands of the Judge were received, induced a prompt compliance.

When they were gone, and the rock was left to the parties most interested in an explanation, Marmaduke, pointing to the aged Major Effingham, said to his grandson—

"Had we not better remove thy parent from this open place, until my carriage can arrive?"

"Pardon me, sir, the air does him good, and he has taken it whenever there was no dread of a discovery. I know not how to act, Judge Temple; ought I, can I, suffer Major Effingham to become an inmate of your family?"

"Thou shalt be thyself the judge," said Marmaduke. "Thy father was my early friend. He intrusted his fortune to my care. When we separated, he had such confidence in me, that he wished no security, no evidence of the trust, even had there been time or convenience for exacting it.—This thou hast heard?"

"Most truly, sir," said Edwards, or rather Effingham, as we must now call him.

"We differed in politics. If the cause of this country was successful, the trust was sacred with me, for none knew of thy father's interest. If the crown still held its sway, it would be easy to restore the property of so loyal a subject as Col. Effingham.—Is not this plain?"

"The premises are good, sir," continued the youth, with the same incredulous look as before.

"Listen—listen, poy," said the German. "Dere is not a hair as of ter rogue in ter het of ter Tchooge."

"We all know the issue of the struggle," continued Marmaduke, disregarding both; "Thy grandfather was left in Connecticut, regularly supplied by thy father with the means of such a subsistence as suited his wants. This I well knew, though I never had intercourse with him, even in our happiest days.

Thy father retired with the troops to prosecute his claims on England. At all events, his losses must be great, for his real estates were sold, and I became the lawful purchaser. It was not unnatural to wish that he might have no bar to its just recovery?"

"There was none, but the difficulty of providing for so many claimants."

"But there would have been one, and an insuperable one, had I announced to the world that I held these estates, multiplied, by the times and my industry, a hundred fold in value, only as his trustee. Thou knowest that I supplied him with considerable sums, immediately after the war."

"You did, until"——

"My letters were returned unopened. Thy father had much of thy own spirit, Oliver; he was sometimes hasty and rash." The Judge continued, in a self-condemning manner—"Perhaps my fault lies the other way; I may possibly look too far ahead, and calculate too deeply. It certainly was a severe trial to allow the man, whom I most loved, to think ill of me for seven years, in order that he might honestly apply for his just remunerations. But had he opened my last letters, thou wouldst have learnt the whole truth. Those I sent him to England, by what my agent writes me, he did read. He died, Oliver, knowing all. He died my friend, and I thought thou hadst died with him."

"Our poverty would not permit us to pay for two passages," said the youth, with the extraordinary emotion with which he ever alluded to the degraded state of his family; "I was left in the Province to wait for his return, and when the sad news of his loss reached me, I was nearly pennyless."

"And what didst thou, boy?" asked Marmaduke, in a faltering voice.

"I took my passage here in search of my grandfather; for I well knew that his resources were gone, with the half-pay of my father. On reaching his abode, I learnt that he had left it in secret; though the reluctant hireling, who had deserted him in his poverty, owned to my urgent entreaties, that he believed he had been carried away by an old man, who had formerly been his servant. I knew at once it was Natty, for my father often"——

"Was Natty a servant of thy grandfather?" exclaimed the Judge.

"Of that too were you ignorant!" said the youth, in evident surprise.

"How should I know it? I never met the Major, nor was the name of Bumppo ever mentioned to me. I knew him only as a man of the woods, and one who lived by hunting. Such men are too common to excite surprise."

"He was reared in the family of my grandfather; served him for many years during their campaigns at the west, where he became attached to the woods; and he was left here as a kind of locum tenens on the lands that old Mohegan (whose life my grandfather once saved) induced the Delawares to grant to him, when they admitted him as an honorary member of their tribe."

"This, then, is thy Indian blood?"

"I have no other," said Edwards, smiling;—"Major Effingham was adopted as the son of Mohegan, who at that time was the greatest man in his nation; and my father, who visited those people when a boy, received the name of the Eagle from them, on account of the shape of his face, as I understand. They have extended his title to me. I have no other Indian blood or breeding; though I have seen the hour, Judge Temple, when I could wish that such had been my lineage and education."

"Proceed with thy tale," said Marmaduke.

"I have but little more to say, sir. I followed to the lake where I had so often been told that Natty dwelt, and found him maintaining his old master in secret; for even he could not bear to exhibit to the world, in his poverty and dotage, a man whom a whole people once looked up to with respect."

"And what did you?"

"What did I! I spent my last money in purchasing a rifle, clad myself in a coarse garb, and learned to be a hunter by the side of Leather-stocking. You know the rest, Judge Temple."

"Ant vere vast olt Fritz Hartmann!" said the German, reproachfully; "didst never hear a name as of olt Fritz Hartmann from ter mout of ter fader, lat?"

"I may have been mistaken, gentlemen," returned the youth; "but I had pride, and could not submit to such an exposure as this day even has reluctantly brought to light. I had plans that might have been visionary; but, should my parent survive till autumn, I purposed taking him with me to the city, where we have distant relatives, who must have learnt to forget the Tory by this time. He decays rapidly," he continued, mournfully, "and must soon lie by the side of old Mohegan."

The air being pure, and the day fine, the party continued conversing on the rock, until the wheels of Judge Temple's carriage were heard clattering up the side of the mountain, during which time the conversation was maintained with deep interest, each moment clearing up some doubtful action, and lessening the antipathy of the youth to Marmaduke. He no longer objected to the removal of his grandfather, who displayed a childish pleasure when he found himself seated once more in a carriage. When placed in the ample hall of the Mansion-house, the eyes of the aged veteran turned slowly to the objects in the apartment, and a look like the dawn of intellect would, for moments, flit across his features, when he invariably offered some useless courtesies to those near him, wandering, painfully, in his subjects. The exercise and the change soon produced an exhaustion, that caused them to remove him to his bed, where he lay for hours, evidently sensible of the change in his comforts, and exhibiting that mortifying picture of human nature, which too plainly shows that the propensities of the animal continue, even after the nobler part of the creature appears to have vanished.

Until his parent was placed comfortably in bed, with Natty seated at his side, Effingham did not quit him. He then obeyed a summons to the library of the Judge, where he found the latter, with Major Hartmann, waiting for him.

"Read this paper, Oliver," said Marmaduke to him, as he entered, "and thou wilt find that, so far from intending thy family wrong during life, it has been my care to see that justice should be done at even a later day."

The youth took the paper, which his first glance told him was the will of the Judge. Hurried and agitated as he was, he discovered that the date corresponded with the time of the unusual depression of Marmaduke. As he proceeded, his eyes began to moisten, and the hand which held the instrument shook violently.

The will commenced with the usual forms, spun out by the ingenuity of Mr. Van der School; but after this subject was fairly exhausted, the pen of Marmaduke became plainly visible.

In clear, distinct, manly, and even eloquent language, he recounted his obligations to Colonel Effingham, the nature of their connexion, and the circumstances in which they separated. He then proceeded to relate the motives of his long silence, mentioning, however, large sums that he had forwarded to his friend, which had been returned, with the letters unopened. After this, he spoke of his search for the grandfather, who had unaccountably disappeared, and his fears that the direct heir of the trust was buried in the ocean with his father.

After, in short, recounting in a clear narrative, the events which our readers must now be able to connect, he proceeded to make a fair and exact statement of the sums left in his care by Col. Effingham. A devise of his whole estate to certain responsible trustees followed; to hold the same for the benefit, in equal moieties, of his daughter, on one part, and of Oliver Effingham, formerly a major in the army of Great Britain, and of his son Edward Effingham, and of his son Edward Oliver Effingham, or to the survivor of them, and the descendants of such survivor, for ever, on the other part. The trust was to endure until 1810, when, if no person appeared, or could be found, after sufficient notice, to claim the moiety so devised, then a certain sum, calculating the principal and interest of his debt to Col. Effingham, was to be paid to the heirs at law of the Effingham family, and the bulk of his estate was to be conveyed in fee to his daughter, or her heirs.

The tears fell from the eyes of the young man, as he read this undeniable testimony of the good faith of Marmaduke, and his bewildered gaze was still fastened on the paper, when a voice, that thrilled on every nerve, spoke, near him, saying,

"Do you yet doubt us, Oliver?"

"I have never doubted *you!*" cried the youth, recovering his recollection and his voice, as he sprung to seize the hand of Elizabeth; "no, not one moment has my faith in you wavered."

"And my father——"

"God bless him!"

"I thank thee, my son," said the Judge, exchanging a warm pressure of the hand with the youth; "but we have both erred; thou hast been too hasty, and I have been too slow. One half of my estates shall be thine as soon as they can be conveyed to thee; and if what my suspicions tell me, be true, I suppose the other must follow speedily." He took the hand which he held, and united it with that of his daughter, and motioned towards the door to the Major.

"I telt you vat, gal!" said the old German, good humouredly; "if I vast, ast I vast, ven I servit mit his grantfader on ter lakes, ter lazy tog shouln't vin ter prize as for nottin."

"Come, come, old Fritz," said the Judge; "you are seventy, not seventeen; Richard waits for you with a bowl of egg-nog, in the hall."

"Richart! ter duyvel!" exclaimed the other, hastening out of the room; "he makes ter nog ast for ter horse. I vilt show ter Sheriff mit my own hants! Ter duyvel! I pelieve he sweetens mit ter yankee melasses!"

Marmaduke smiled and nodded affectionately at the young couple, and closed the door after them. If any of our readers expect that we are going to open it again, for their gratification, they are mistaken.

The tête-à-tête continued for a very unreasonable time; how long we shall not say; but it was ended by six o'clock in the evening, for at that hour Monsieur Le Quoi made his appearance, agreeably to the appointment of the preceding day, and claimed the ear of Miss Temple. He was admitted; when he made an offer of his hand, with much suavity, together with his "amis beeg and leet', his père, his mère, and his sucre-boosh." Elizabeth might, possibly, have previously entered into some embarrassing and binding engagements with Oliver, for she declined the tender of all, in terms as polite, though perhaps a little more decided, than those in which they were made.

The Frenchman soon joined the German and the Sheriff in the hall, who compelled him to take a seat with them at the table, where, by the aid of punch, wine, and egg-nog, they soon extracted from the complaisant Monsieur Le Quoi the nature of his visit. It was evident that he had made the offer, as a duty which a well-bred man owed to a lady in such a retired place, before he left the country, and that his feelings were but very little, if at all, interested in the matter. After a few potations, the waggish pair persuaded the exhilarated Frenchman that there was an inexcusable partiality in offering to one lady, and not extending a similar courtesy to another. Consequently, about nine, Monsieur Le Quoi sallied forth to the Rectory, on a similar mission to Miss Grant, which proved as successful as his first effort in love.

When he returned to the Mansion-house, at ten, Richard and the Major were still seated at the table. They attempted to persuade the Gaul, as the Sheriff called him, that he should next try Remarkable Pettibone. But, though stimulated by mental excitement and wine, two hours of abstruse logic were thrown away on this subject; for he declined their advice, with a pertinacity truly astonishing in so polite a man.

When Benjamin lighted Monsieur Le Quoi from the door, he said, at parting—

"If-so-be, Mounsheer, you'd run alongside Mistress Prettybones, as the Squire Dickens was bidding ye, 'tis my notion you'd have been grappled; in which case, d'ye see, you mought have been troubled in swinging clear again in a handsome manner; for thof Miss 'Lizzy and the parson's young 'un be tidy little vessels, that shoot by a body on a wind, Mistress Remarkable is sum'mat of a galliot fashion; when you once takes 'em in tow, they doesn't like to be cast off again."

Chapter XLI.

"Yes, sweep ye on!—We will not leave,
For them who triumph, those who grieve.
     With that armada gay
Be laughter loud, and jocund shout—
     —But with that skiff
Abides the minstrel tale."
                    Scott, *The Lord of the Isles*, I.xvii.1–4, 11–12.

THE events of our tale carry us through the summer; and, after making nearly the circle of the year, we must conclude our labours in the delightful month of October. Many important incidents had, however, occurred in the intervening period; a few of which it may be necessary to recount.

The two principal were, the marriage of Oliver and Elizabeth, and the death of Major Effingham. They both took place early in September; and the former preceded the latter only by a few days. The old man passed away like the last glimmering of a taper; and though his death cast a melancholy over the family, grief could not follow such an end.

One of the chief concerns of Marmaduke was to reconcile the even conduct of a magistrate, with the course that his feelings dictated to the criminals. The day succeeding the discovery at the cave, however, Natty and Benjamin re-entered the gaol peaceably, where they continued, well fed and comfortable, until the return of an express to Albany, who brought the Governor's pardon to the Leather-stocking. In the mean time, proper means were employed to satisfy Hiram for the assaults on his person; and on the same day, the two comrades issued together into society again, with their characters not at all affected by the imprisonment.

Mr. Doolittle began to discover that neither his architecture, nor his law, was quite suitable to the growing wealth and intelligence of the settlement; and, after exacting the last cent that was attainable in his compromises, to use the language of the country, he "pulled up stakes," and proceeded further west, scattering his professional science and legal learning through the land; vestiges of both of which are to be discovered there even to the present hour.

Poor Jotham, whose life paid the forfeiture of his folly, acknowledged before he died, that his reasons for believing in a mine, were extracted from the lips of a sybil, who, by looking in a magic glass, was enabled to discover the hidden treasures of the earth. Such superstition was frequent in the new settlements; and after the first surprise was over, the better part of the community forgot the subject. But at the same time that it removed from the breast of Richard a lingering suspicion of the acts of the three hunters, it conveyed a mortifying lesson to him, which brought many quiet hours, in future, to his cousin Marmaduke. It may be remembered that the Sheriff confidently pronounced this to be no "visionary" scheme, and that word was enough to shut his lips, at any time within the next ten years.

Monsieur Le Quoi, who has been introduced to our readers, because no picture of that country would be faithful without some such character, found the island of Martinique, and his "sucre-boosh," in possession of the English; but Marmaduke, and his family, were much gratified in soon hearing that he had returned to his bureau, in Paris; where he afterwards issued yearly bulletins of his happiness, and of his gratitude to his friends in America.

With this brief explanation we must return to our narrative. Let the American reader imagine one of our mildest October mornings, when the sun seems a ball of silvery fire, and the elasticity of the air is felt while it is inhaled; imparting vigour and life to the whole system;—the weather, neither too warm, nor too cold, but of that happy temperature which stirs the blood, without bringing the lassitude of spring.

It was on such a morning, about the middle of the month, that Oliver entered the hall, where Elizabeth was issuing her usual orders for the day, and requested her to join him in a short excursion to the lake-side. The tender melancholy in the manner of her husband, caught the attention of Elizabeth, who instantly abandoned her concerns, threw a light shawl across her shoulders, and concealing her raven hair under a gypsey, she took his arm, and submitted herself, without a question, to his guidance. They crossed the bridge, and had turned from the highway, along the margin of the lake, before a word was exchanged. Elizabeth well knew, by the direction, the object of the walk, and respected the feelings of her companion too much to indulge in untimely conversation. But when they gained the open fields, and her eye roamed over the placid lake, covered with wild fowl, already journeying from the great northern waters, to seek a warmer sun, but lingering to play in the limpid sheet of the Otsego, and to the sides of the mountain, which were gay with the thousand dies of autumn, as if to grace their bridal, the swelling heart of the young wife burst out in speech.

"This is not a time for silence, Oliver!" she said, clinging more fondly to his arm; "every thing in nature seems to speak the praises of the Creator; why should we, who have so much to be grateful for, be silent."

"Speak on," said her husband, smiling; "I love the sounds of your voice. You must anticipate our errand hither; I have told you my plans, how do you like them?"

"I must first see them," returned his wife. "But I have had my plans, too; it is time I should begin to divulge them."

"You! It is something for the comfort of my old friend Natty, I know."

"Certainly of Natty; but we have other friends besides the Leather-stocking, to serve. Do you forget Louisa, and her father?"

"No, surely; have I not given one of the best farms in the county to the good divine. As for Louisa, I should wish you to keep her always near us."

"You do," said Elizabeth, slightly compressing her lips; "but poor Louisa may have other views for herself; she may wish to follow my example, and marry."

"I don't think it," said Effingham, musing a moment; "I really don't know any one hereabouts good enough for her."

"Perhaps not here; but there are other places besides Templeton, and other churches besides 'New St. Paul's.' "

"Churches, Elizabeth! you would not wish to lose Mr. Grant, surely! though simple, he is an excellent man. I shall never find another who has half the veneration for my orthodoxy. You would humble me from a saint to a very common sinner."

"It must be done, sir," returned the lady, with a half-concealed smile, "though it degrades you from an angel to a man."

"But you forget the farm."

"He can lease it, as others do. Besides, would you have a clergyman toil in the fields!"

"Where can he go? you forget Louisa."

"No, I do not forget Louisa," said Elizabeth, again compressing her beautiful lips. "You know, Effingham, that my father has told you that I ruled him, and that I should rule you. I am now about to exert my power."

"Any thing, any thing, dear Elizabeth, but not at the expense of us all; not at the expense of your friend."

"How do you know, sir, that it will be so much at the expense of my friend?" said the lady, fixing her eyes with a searching look on his countenance, where they met only the unsuspecting expression of manly regret.

"How do I know it! why, it is natural that she should regret us."

"It is our duty to struggle with our natural feelings," returned the lady; "and there is but little cause to fear that such a spirit as Louisa's will not effect it."

"But what is your plan?"

"Listen, and you shall know. My father has procured a call for Mr. Grant to one of the towns on the Hudson, where he can live more at his ease than in journeying through these woods; where he can spend the evening of his life in comfort and quiet; and where his daughter may meet with such society, and form such a connexion, as may be proper for one of her years and character."

"Bess! you amaze me! I did not think you had been such a manager!"

"Oh! I manage more deeply than you imagine, sir," said the wife, archly smiling, again; "but it is my will, and it is your duty to submit,—for a time at least."

Effingham laughed; but as they approached the end of their walk, the subject was changed by common consent.

The place at which they arrived was the little spot of level ground where the cabin of the Leather-stocking had so long stood. Elizabeth found it entirely cleared of rubbish, and beautifully laid down in turf, by the removal of sods, which, in common with the surrounding country, had grown gay, under the influence of profuse showers, as if a second spring had passed over the land. This little place was surrounded by a circle of mason-work, and they entered by a small gate, near which, to the surprise of both, the rifle of Natty was leaning against the wall. Hector and the slut reposed on the grass by its side, as if conscious that, however altered, they were lying on ground, and were surrounded by objects, with which they were familiar. The hunter himself was stretched on the earth, before a head-stone of white marble, pushing aside with his fingers the long grass that had already sprung up from the luxuriant soil around its base, apparently to lay bare the inscription. By the side of this stone, which was a simple slab at the head of a grave, stood a rich monument, decorated with an urn, and ornamented with the chisel.

Oliver and Elizabeth approached the graves, with a light tread, unheard by the old hunter, whose sunburnt face was working, and whose eyes twinkled as if something impeded their vision. After some little time, Natty raised himself slowly from the ground, and said aloud—

"Well, well—I'm bold to say it's all right! There's something that I suppose is reading; but I can't make any thing of it; though the pipe, and the tomahawk, and the moccasins, be pretty well—pretty well, for a man that, I dares to say, never seed 'ither of the things. Ah's me! there they lie, side by side, happy enough! Who will there be to put me in the 'arth, when my time comes!"

"When that unfortunate hour arrives, Natty, friends shall not be wanting to perform the last offices for you," said Oliver, a little touched at the hunter's soliloquy.

The old man turned, without manifesting surprise, for he had got the Indian habits in this particular, and running his hand under the bottom of his nose, seemed to wipe away his sorrow with the action.

"You've come out to see the graves, children, have ye?" he said; "well, well, they're wholesome sights to young as well as old."

"I hope they are fitted to your liking," said Effingham; "no one has a better right than yourself to be consulted in the matter."

"Why, seeing that I an't used to fine graves," returned the old man, "it is but little matter consarning my taste. Ye laid the Major's head to the west, and Mohegan's to the east, did ye, lad?"

"At your request it was done."

"It's so best," said the hunter; "they thought they had to journey different ways, children; though there is One greater than all, who'll bring the just together, at his own time, and who'll whiten the skin of a black-moor, and place him on a footing with princes."

"There is but little reason to doubt that," said Elizabeth, whose decided tones were changed to a soft, melancholy voice; "I trust we shall all meet again, and be happy together."

"Shall we, child! shall we!" exclaimed the hunter, with unusual fervour; "there's comfort in that thought too. But before I go, I should like to know what 'tis you tell these people, that be flocking into the country like pigeons in the spring, of the old Delaware, and of the bravest white man that ever trod the hills."

Effingham and Elizabeth were surprised at the manner of the Leather-stocking, which was unusually impressive and solemn; but attributing it to the scene, the young man turned to the monument, and read aloud—

"Sacred to the memory of Oliver Effingham, Esquire, formerly a Major in his B. Majesty's 60th Foot; a soldier of tried valour; a subject of chivalrous loyalty; and a man of honesty. To these virtues, he added the graces of a christian. The morning of his life was spent in honour, wealth, and power; but its evening was obscured by poverty, neglect, and disease, which were alleviated only by the tender care of his old, faithful, and upright friend and attendant, Nathaniel Bumppo. His descendants rear this stone to the virtues of the master, and to the enduring gratitude of the servant."

The Leather-stocking started at the sound of his own name, and a smile of joy illumined his wrinkled features, as he said—

"And did ye say it, lad? have ye got then the old man's name cut in the stone, by the side of his master's? God bless ye, children! 'twas a kind thought, and kindness goes to the heart as life shortens."

Elizabeth turned her back to the speakers. Effingham made a fruitless effort before he succeeded in saying—

"It is there cut in plain marble; but it should have been written in letters of gold!"

"Show me the name, boy," said Natty, with simple eagerness; "let me see my own name placed in such honour. 'Tis a gin'rous gift to a man who leaves none of his name and family behind him in a country, where he has tarried so long."

Effingham guided his finger to the spot, and Natty followed the windings of the letters to the end, with deep interest, when he raised himself from the tomb, and said—

"I suppose it's all right, and it's kindly thought, and kindly done! But what have ye put over the Red-skin?"

"You shall hear"—

"This stone is raised to the memory of an Indian Chief, of the Delaware tribe, who was known by the several names of John Mohegan; Mohican"——

"Mo-hee-can, lad; they call theirselves! 'hee-can."

"Mohican; and Chingagook"——

" 'Gach, boy;—'gach-gook; Chingachgook; which, intarpreted, means Big-sarpent. The name should be set down right, for an Indian's name has always some meaning in it."

"I will see it altered. 'He was the last of his people who continued to inhabit this country; and it may be said of him, that his faults were those of an Indian, and his virtues those of a man.'"

"You never said truer word, Mr. Oliver; ah's me! if you had know'd him as I did, in his prime, in that very battle, where, the old gentleman who sleeps by his side, sav'd his life, when them thieves, the Iroquois, had him at the stake, you'd have said all that, and more too. I cut the thongs with this very hand, and gave him my own tomahawk and knife, seeing that the rifle was always my fav'rite weepon. He did lay about him like a man! I met him as I was coming home from the trail, with eleven Mingo scalps on his pole. You needn't shudder, Madam Effingham, for they was all from shav'd heads and warriors. When I look about me, at these hills, where I used-to could count, sometimes twenty smokes, curling over the tree-tops, from the Delaware camps, it raises mournful thoughts, to think, that not a Red-skin is left of them all; unless it may be a drunken vagabond from the Oneidas, or them Yankee Indians, who, they say, be moving up from the sea-shore; and who belong to none of God's creaters, to my seeming; being, as it were, neither fish nor flesh; neither white-man, nor savage.——Well! well! the time has come at last, and I must go"—

"Go!" echoed Edwards, "whither do you go?"

The Leather-stocking, who had imbibed, unconsciously, many of the Indian qualities, though he always thought of himself, as of a civilized being, compared with even the Delawares, averted his face to conceal the workings of his muscles, as he stooped to lift a large pack from behind the tomb, which he placed deliberately on his shoulders.

"Go!" exclaimed Elizabeth, approaching him, with a hurried step; "you should not venture so far in the woods alone, at your time of life, Natty; indeed, it is imprudent. He is bent, Effingham, on some distant hunting."

"What Mrs. Effingham tells you, is true, Leather-stocking," said Edwards; "there can be no necessity for your submitting to such hardships now! So throw aside your pack, and confine your hunt to the mountains near us, if you will go."

"Hardship! 'tis a pleasure, children, and the greatest that is left me on this side the grave."

"No, no; you shall not go to such a distance," cried Elizabeth, laying her white hand on his deer-skin pack; "I am right! I feel his camp-kettle and a canister of powder! he must not be suffered to wander so far from us, Oliver; remember how suddenly Mohegan dropp'd away."

"I know'd the parting would come hard, children; I know'd it would!" said Natty, "and so I got aside to look at the graves by myself, and thought if I left ye the keep-sake which the Major gave me, when we first parted in the woods, ye wouldn't take it unkind, but would know, that let the old man's body go where it might, his feelings staid behind him."

"This means something more than common!" exclaimed the youth; "where is it, Natty, that you purpose going?"

The hunter drew nigh him with a confident reasoning air, as if what he had to say would silence all objections, and replied—

"Why, lad, they tell me, that on the Big-lakes, there's the best of hunting, and a great range, without a white man on it, unless it may be one like myself. I'm weary of living in clearings, and where the hammer is sounding in my ears from sun-rise to sun-down. And though I'm much bound to ye both, children; I wouldn't say it if it wasn't true; I crave to go into the woods ag'in, I do."

"Woods!" echoed Elizabeth, trembling with her feelings; "do you not call these endless forests woods?"

"Ah! child, these be nothing to a man that's used to the wilderness. I have took but little comfort sin' your father come on with his settlers; but I wouldn't go far, while the life was in the body that lies under the sod there. But now he's gone, and Chingachgook is gone; and you be both young and happy. Yes! the big-house has rung with merriment this month past! And now, I thought, was the time, to try to get a little comfort, in the close of my days. Woods! indeed! I doesn't call these woods, Madam Effingham, where I lose myself, every day of my life, in the clearings."

"If there be any thing wanting to your comfort, name it, Leather-stocking; if it be attainable, it is yours."

"You mean all for the best, lad; I know it; and so does Madam, too; but your ways isn't my ways. 'Tis like the dead there, who thought, when the breath was in them, that one went east and one went west, to find their heavens; but they'll meet at last; and so shall we, children.——Yes, ind as you've begun, and we shall meet in the land of the just, at last."

"This is so new! so unexpected!" said Elizabeth, in almost breathless excitement; "I had thought you meant to live with us, and die with us, Natty."

"Words are of no avail!" exclaimed her husband; "the habits of forty years are not to be dispossessed by the ties of a day. I know you too well to urge you further, Natty; unless you will let me build you a hut, on one of the distant hills, where we can sometimes see you, and know that you are comfortable."

"Don't fear for the Leather-stocking, children; God will see that his days be provided for, and his ind happy. I know you mean all for the best, but our ways doesn't agree. I love the woods, and ye relish the face of man; I eat when hungry and drink when a-dry, and ye keep stated hours and rules; nay, nay, you even over-feed the dogs, lad, from pure kindness; and hounds should be gaunty to run well. The meanest of God's creaters be made for some use, and I'm form'd for the wilderness; if ye love me, let me go where my soul craves to be ag'in!"

The appeal was decisive; and not another word of entreaty,

for him to remain, was then uttered; but Elizabeth bent her head to her bosom and wept, while her husband dashed away the tears from his eyes, and, with hands that almost refused to perform their office, he produced his pocket-book, and extended a parcel of bank-notes to the hunter.

"Take these," he said, "at least, take these; secure them about your person, and, in the hour of need, they will do you good service."

The old man took the notes, and examined them with a curious eye.

"This, then, is some of the new-fashioned money that they've been making at Albany, out of paper! It can't be worth much to they that hasn't larning! No, no, lad—take back the stuff; it will do me no sarvice. I took kear to get all the Frenchman's powder, afore he broke up, and they say lead grows where I'm going. It isn't even fit for wads, seeing that I use none but leather!—Madam Effingham, let an old man kiss your hand, and wish God's choicest blessings on you and your'n."

"Once more let me beseech you, stay!" cried Elizabeth. "Do not, Leather-stocking, leave me to grieve for the man who has twice rescued me from death, and who has served those I love so faithfully. For my sake, if not for your own, stay. I shall see you, in those frightful dreams that still haunt my nights, dying in poverty and age, by the side of those terrific beasts you slew. There will be no evil that sickness, want, and solitude can inflict, that my fancy will not conjure as your fate. Stay with us, old man; if not for your own sake, at least for ours."

"Such thoughts and bitter dreams, Madam Effingham," returned the hunter, solemnly, "will never haunt an innocent parson long. They'll pass away with God's pleasure. And if the cat-a-mounts be yet brought to your eyes in sleep, 'tis not for my sake, but to show you the power of him that led me there to save you. Trust in God, Madam, and your honourable husband, and the thoughts for an old man like me can never be long nor bitter. I pray that the Lord will keep you in mind—the Lord that lives in clearings as well as in the wilderness—and bless you, and all that belong to you, from this time, till the great day when the whites shall meet the red-skins in judgment, and justice shall be the law, and not power."

Elizabeth raised her head, and offered her colourless cheek

to his salute; when he lifted his cap, and touched it respectfully. His hand was grasped with convulsive fervour by the youth, who continued silent. The hunter prepared himself for his journey, drawing his belt tighter, and wasting his moments in the little reluctant movements of a sorrowful departure. Once or twice he essayed to speak, but a rising in his throat prevented it. At length he shouldered his rifle, and cried, with a clear huntsman's call, that echoed through the woods—

"He-e-e-re, he-e-e-re, pups—away, dogs, away;—ye'll be foot-sore afore ye see the ind of the journey!"

The hounds leaped from the earth at this cry, and, scenting around the graves and the silent pair, as if conscious of their own destination, they followed humbly at the heels of their master. A short pause succeeded, during which even the youth concealed his face on his grandfather's tomb. When the pride of manhood, however, had suppressed the feelings of nature, he turned to renew his entreaties, but saw that the cemetery was occupied only by himself and his wife.

"He is gone!" cried Effingham.

Elizabeth raised her face, and saw the old hunter standing, looking back for a moment, on the verge of the wood. As he caught their glances, he drew his hard hand hastily across his eyes again, waved it on high for an adieu, and, uttering a forced cry to his dogs, who were crouching at his feet, he entered the forest.

This was the last that they ever saw of the Leather-stocking, whose rapid movements preceded the pursuit which Judge Temple both ordered and conducted. He had gone far towards the setting sun,—the foremost in that band of Pioneers, who are opening the way for the march of the nation across the continent.

Finis.

Explanatory Notes

1.1–2 TO Jacob Sutherland: Sutherland acknowledged the Dedication of *The Pioneers* in the following letter, dated "Albany Feby
3d 1823." Though he had recently been elected to the New
York State Senate, he declined the office in favor of an appointment as Justice of the New York State Supreme Court.
Sutherland and Cooper had known each other as boys and had
been contemporaries at Yale, though Sutherland graduated in
the class of 1807, two years after Cooper was expelled.
Dear Cooper,
      Accept my thanks for the Copy of the "Pioneers" which I
have just received from you—and more especially for the very
kind & affectionate manner in which you have been pleased to
dedicate It to me—I consider It no ordinary Compliment to be
thus distinguished by the author of the "Spy"—But as you
justly suppose, It is most valuable to me, as an evidence of that
Friendship which commenced with our Youth, and which I
trust will descend with us to our graves—
      I have time to say no more,—as I can not let the mail return,
without bearing to you my acknowledgment—
      I am a judge & I very cordially accept your congratulations—
      Mrs. Sutherland unites with me in remembrance to Mrs C.
& yourself.
James Cooper Esq   Your Sincere Friend
                                                            J. Sutherland
      ADDRESSED: James Cooper Esquire   POSTMARKED:
                              New York   ALBANY FEB. 3
      DOCKETED: Sutherland— 1823   MS: YCAL

8.40–9.1 one of the most ingenious machines: almost certainly the
"cast-iron plough," perfected by Jethro Wood (1774–1834) of
Cayuga County, New York. Wood and his heirs fought a con-
tinual and losing battle against infringers of his patents, but
his contribution to the improvement and use of the plough was
a significant one. See Frank Gilbert, *Jethro Wood, Inventor of the
Modern Plough* (Chicago, 1882).

26.32 Sir William: Sir William Johnson (1715–1774), known to the Indians as "Sir William," was for many years Superintendent of Indian Affairs for the British government. A skilled diplomatist, popular with the Six Nations, a military leader, and a landed proprietor, Johnson was invaluable in the British struggle with the French along the northern colonial borders and in the opening of the interior of the continent to settlement. Cooper probably imagined Natty's service under Sir William as occurring in the late 1750s or early 1760s, certainly at the taking of Niagara in 1759 (see p. 154).

34.24–25 the peaceful disciples of Fox: George Fox (1624–1690), founder of the Society of Friends or Quakers, expressed in his personal life the intense inward spirituality that in his teaching militated against any show of force or power or disrespect towards God or man. As a living embodiment of his faith, he possessed a magnetic attraction for the truly religious among his contemporaries.

36.29 acts of confiscation: Following Thomas Paine's counsel that Loyalist property be confiscated to pay expenses of the war, a measure permitted by the Congressional definition of treason on 24 June 1770, all the states sooner or later enacted statutes of condemnation and forfeiture. By the end of the war, Tory claims amounted to about £10,000,000. Although there was apparently a minimum of scandal and corruption, a maneuver such as that attributed to Marmaduke Temple was perfectly possible and probably occurred.

38.10 Duo: Diligent and repeated searching has failed to disclose the source of this epigraph. Cooper employed the same source for the epigraphs of Chapters XII, p. 131, and XXV, p. 275.

42.10 Æsculapius: the god of medicine, son of Apollo and Coronis, usually pictured as a venerable old man with a flowing beard.

54.17 Wethersfield meeting-house: The first Protestant Episcopal Church in Wethersfield, Connecticut, was built by a group of dissidents who split with members of the Congregational Church in 1797 after an eighteen-year controversy regarding the site of a second meeting-house. The dissident faction built a Protestant Episcopal church, which it then refused to support. It dissolved after thirteen years, and the building was sold in 1826 for $115. Cooper is apparently suggesting in *The Pioneers* that some such controversy is incubating in Templeton. J. Hammond Trumbull, ed., *The Memorial History of Hartford County, Connecticut, 1633–1884* (Boston, 1886), I, 329, 447–48.

56.35–37 the term Yankee . . . "Yengeese": Cooper's etymological note on the word "Yankee" is borrowed from John Hecke-welder, *An Account of the History, Manners, and Customs of the Indian Nations* (Philadelphia, 1819), pp. 77, 142–43. The derivation of the word is still matter for conjecture and dispute.

62.7 Rodney's victory: Vice-admiral George Brydges Rodney (1718–1792), later Lord Rodney, whom Ben Pump is imagined as serving as steward, achieved two famous naval victories: the defeat of a Spanish fleet near Cape Saint Vincent in 1780 and the defeat of the French naval officer François Joseph Paul de Grasse-Tilly, commonly known as Count de Grasse, in the West Indies in 1782. Cooper refers here to the second of these victories (see pp. 70.3 and 210.25–26).

72.37–38 Ruddiman's Latin Grammar: *The Rudiments of the Latin Tongue; or, A Plain and Easy Introduction to Latin Grammar*, a British textbook published by Thomas Ruddiman (1674–1757) in 1714, went through innumerable editions during the author's lifetime and became the standard Latin textbook in the United States as well as Great Britain. As a student, Cooper himself may have used the "Carefully Corrected and Improved" edition issued by Robert Campbell & Co. in Philadelphia in 1798.

72.38–39 Denman's Midwifery: *An Introduction to the Practice of Midwifery*, in two volumes, by Thomas Denman, M.D. (1733–1815), one of the earliest comprehensive gynecological treatises in English, was first published in London in 1782. The standard treatise on the subject at the time, it was reprinted at New York in 1802.

83.6–84.36 BEFORE the . . . their resentment: The contents of these two pages were drawn largely from John Heckewelder, *An Account of the History, Manners, and Customs of the Indian Nations, who once inhabited Pennsylvania and the Neighbouring States* (Philadelphia: Abraham Small, 1819). The passages from these two pages in *The Pioneers* and their cognates from Heckewelder have been conveniently arranged in parallel sequence by Edwin L. Stockton, Jr., in *The Influence of the Moravians upon the Leather-Stocking Tales, Transactions of the Moravian Historical Society*, XX, Pt. I (Nazareth, Pa.: Whitefield House, 1964), 56–63.

93.26 Sallick law: The allusion is another example of Richard's ignorance and pretentiousness. The Salic Law or Lex Salica, an early Teutonic legal or penal code dating from the sixth century, was best remembered for its provision that daughters could not inherit; hence it was hardly an instance of chivalric treatment of women.

102.4–5 The Latin text of the first two verses of Virgil's first *Eclogue*, given by Cooper in phonetic transcription, reads as follows:
Tityre, tu patulae recubans sub tegmine fagi
silvestrem tenui musam meditaris avena:
—*P. Vergili Maronis Opera*, ed. F. A. Hirtzel (Oxford, 1959), p. 1.
Thou, Tityrus, recumbant under the shade of a spreading beech
Playest on thy shepherd's pipe a woodland song:

102.27 a sermon . . . from Sterne: Multivolume editions of Laurence Sterne's writings were reprinted in Philadelphia as early as 1774 and were reprinted frequently thereafter in Philadelphia and Boston. Sterne's sermons, *The Sermons of Mr. Yorick* (volumes three and four of the Philadelphia collected edition, but also published separately) were popular, as was *The Life and Opinions of Tristram Shandy*, and were frequently read aloud to congregations by lay persons before regular ministers were available.

105.6 *Heliogabaliad.*: Unidentified.

135.17 old Crumhorn: a wild and barren eminence in the town of Maryland, Otsego County.

135.19 the Garman Flats: a town three miles south of the town of Herkimer in Herkimer County, so called because its extensive alluvial flats along the Mohawk were early settled by Germans.

145.4 "The Barley-Mow": A "cumulative" drinking song in which the "size of the drinking measure is doubled at each verse," "The Barley-Mow" exists in Hertfordshire, Suffolk, Devonshire, and Cornwall versions. It was "customarily chanted at the supper after the carrying of the barley [was] completed, when the stack, rick, or mow of barley [was] finished." See William Chappell, *The Ballad Literature and Popular Music of the Olden Time: A History of the Ancient Songs, Ballads, and of the Dance Tunes of England* (London, 1859). Arthur F. Schrader, Music Associate at Old Sturbridge Village, reports that the quotation in *The Pioneers* is the first "documentary evidence" he has seen for the song in America. Cooper also employed it as the source for the epigraph of Chapter XIV of *The Pioneers*.

147.21 good Mr. Whitefield: Undoubtedly George Whitefield (1714–1770), one of the most effective evangelists of the Great Awakening, long remembered for his energetic travelling and preaching along the eastern seaboard and for his appeals on behalf of the disadvantaged.

151.5–6 'Far. Av.' means oatmeal: an extremely literal and dubious etymology, which Elnathan Todd has evidently coined by combining the Latin words "far," which can mean "meal" and "avena," which means "oats."

154.33 Shirley's: William Shirley (1694–1771), British governor of Massachusetts, argued strongly the importance of control of the Great Lakes. Appointed major-general in 1755 and given command of the Niagara expedition, Shirley was, as Natty suggests, associated with Sir William Johnson. Natty is making a clear distinction between the status of the scouts or rangers and the foot soldiers, the latter commanded by Shirley, whose competence as a military man was later called in question.

155.24 the morning we beat Dieskau: Cooper is here imagining Natty and Chingachgook behind the log breastwork near Fort Edward on 8 September 1755 before which the Baron Ludwig August Dieskau (d. 1767), a German officer serving the French, paused and scattered his men instead of storming the barricade. The error was a serious one, for the British recovered from their surprise and turned their artillery on the French. Dieskau, wounded and all but deserted, was pursued, wounded again and captured. See William Smith, Jr., *The History of the Province of New-York*, ed., Michael Kammen (Cambridge, Mass., 1972), II, 192–93.

160.7 Roshambow: Although Lafayette obtained much of the credit for French assistance to the American Revolutionary cause, the French expeditionary force was commanded by Jean Baptiste Donatien de Vimeur, Compte de Rochambeau (1725–1807), who cooperated with Washington in deploying French forces, assisting critically in the siege that resulted in Cornwallis' surrender at Yorktown on 19 October 1781.

163.33–39 What is life . . . cast away folly: Since the lyrics of this song are presented by Richard as his own (p. 163.30), and since they have not been identified in available songsters of the period, the likelihood seems strong that Cooper himself composed them. He is known to have invented lyrics for other songs.

175.29 Boadishey: Boadicea, British queen in the time of the emperor Nero, who with her daughters heroically resisted the Romans. Her bust, according to Ben Pump, adorned Lord Rodney's ship as a figure-head, and the ship itself was named for her. See also p. 353.3.

181.13 plans of the new Dutch meeting-house: The congregation of the Dutch Reformed Church in Albany outgrew its old stone church in the 1790s, and a new church was being planned. The corner stone was laid on 12 June 1797. E. P. Rogers, *A Historical Discourse on the Reformed Prot. Dutch Church of Albany* . . . (New York, 1858), pp. 33–34.

224.36–39—225.1–14 "The Eastern States . . . Then flow away." &c.: Billy Kirby did not disclose the source of these lyrics at the Sheriff's request, and neither do the possible sources consulted by the editors and the friends and authorities who have sought to assist them. The verses are clearly to be sung to the tune of Yankee Doodle, and it does not seem unlikely that Cooper composed them.

230.15–26 "And when the proud forest . . . It matters but little to me": If these verses have a printed source or analogue, it has not been identified.

232.22–237.22 your first visit . . . my title: This passage, to which Cooper refers the reader in the 1832 Preface to *The Pioneers* (p. 8.19–20), may be compared to Judge Cooper's own description of the early days of his settlement of Otsego in *A Guide in the Wilderness; or the History of the First Settlements in the Western Counties of New York, with Useful Instructions to Future Settlers* (Dublin, Ireland, 1810), reprinted with an Introduction by James Fenimore Cooper, the novelist's grandson (Rochester, N.Y., 1897), and subsequently by the Freeman's Journal Company (Cooperstown, N.Y., 1936).

245.25–26 This miniature cannon: According to a note supplied by Susan Fenimore Cooper:

"This piece of artillery ["The Cricket"], famous in the annals of the village [of Cooperstown], was left on this ground, when it was a wilderness by the army of General Clinton, in 1779. It was a large iron swivel, dug up when Otsego Hall was built. After doing good service in firing innumerable patriotic salutes, it was burst in the same good cause on a certain Fourth of July, to the great grief of the village lads. It had met with many adventures by field and flood, having been once thrown into the lake. At the time of its final disaster, it is said there was no very perceptible difference between its touch-hole and its muzzle." Note to the Household Edition of *The Pioneers* (New York and Cambridge, 1876), p. 484.

292.2–294.25 "I have met but one place . . . the ordering of God's Providence.": The site of Pine Orchard in the Catskills near the town of Catskill, whose prospect view is here described by the Leather-stocking, became one of the most celebrated attractions for seekers of the picturesque in nineteenth-century

America. (See Thomas Cole's painting, following p. 402.) Concentrated within a short radius of the Catskill Mountain House, a large resort hotel with a spectacular view, was a cluster of lakes, dales, rock formations, and waterfalls considered unsurpassed in eastern United States. The Mountain House was a world-famous Mecca for lovers of fine scenery from the 1820s to the end of the nineteenth century and even the beginning of the twentieth. It fell into ruin and was finally put to the torch in 1963. Pine Orchard was beginning to attract attention as Cooper wrote *The Pioneers*, and Natty's description helped to publicize the spot. The description of the view in the novel, one of many in contemporaneous writings, is said to be so accurate that the spot on which Natty stood can be identified. Presumably Cooper had made the expedition himself. The history of the resort is fully chronicled by Roland van Zandt in *The Catskill Mountain House* (New Brunswick, N.J., 1966).

292.37 'Sopus! the day the royal troops burnt the town: On 16 October 1777, British troops advancing up the Hudson River entered the defenseless town of Kingston, also called Esopus, under General John Vaughan; and, according to a newspaper of the time, "immediately set it on fire. The conflagration was general in a few minutes, and in a very short time that pleasant and wealthy town was reduced to ashes; one house only escaped the flames." The loss of life was less severe than the loss of property. See George W. Pratt, "An Account of the British Expedition above the Highlands of the Hudson River, and of the events connected with the burning of Kingston in 1777," *Collections of the Ulster Historical Society*, I (Kingston, 1860), 109–74.

307.4–5—310.6–7 the fierce front and glaring eyes of a female panther . . . savage fury, that the beast had exhibited: On 16 October 1822, while Cooper was completing *The Pioneers*, the *New York Commercial Advertiser* reprinted from the *Providence Journal* a story recounting the adventures of a boy of thirteen or fourteen who was attracted to a large panther his little dog had driven into a tree. No Leather-stocking being at hand, the boy returned to his home, took his father's loaded gun, and—resting the heavy gun on a forked stake—fired. The "monster" is said to have weighed 144 pounds, measured seven feet ten inches from "the tip of his nose to the end of his tail" and to have been "as broad across the breast as a horse." Susan Fenimore Cooper, preparing a note for *The Pioneers* in the 1870s, reported a similar and recent instance of danger from a panther and stated that "Governor DeWitt Clinton mentioned a panther, killed early in this century near Oneida Lake, by a Frenchman. The animal was shot in the attitude of leaping on the man. Its length was nine feet eleven inches" (New York and Cambridge, 1876), p. 485. See the various representations of the panther scene in *The Pioneers* following p. 308.

332.19 Mohawk Flats: also German Flats; see note for p. 135.19.

415.14–15—424.38–39 She's on the Vision, and that's a sheet of fire . . . Houses, barns and fences are quite commonly swept away: In her note to the Household Edition of *The Pioneers*, Cooper's daughter Susan stated: "In the early years of the settlement on Lake Otsego, there was a fire of this kind especially terrible, when the entire lake shores and the village were surrounded by a network of flame. The writer of this note has received an account of that fire from a near relative [undoubtedly her father]. The effect was described as terrific, and for a short time the danger to the village was serious" (New York and Cambridge, 1876), p. 486.

Textual Apparatus

Textual Commentary

IN 1831, eight years after its first appearance, Cooper was still thoroughly dissatisfied with the text of *The Pioneers*. "Spy and Pioneers will require a severe pen, particularily the latter," he informed Colburn and Bentley, the British publishers with whom he was negotiating revised editions of several of his early novels. "[T]he chief labor would be in the corrections, purifying the style and repairing the blunders of the press."[1] *The Pioneers* required "a severe pen" partly, as Cooper had confided to its original British publisher John Murray on 29 November 1822, because "in opposition to a thousand good resolutions" it had been "more hastily and carelessly written than any of my books—Not a line has been copied, and it has gone from my desk to the printers. . . ."[2] Further, though Cooper assumed full responsibility, the first setting—from which the Murray and all subsequent editions were ultimately to derive—showed deleterious effects of the yellow fever epidemic in New York City during the late summer and early fall of 1822. While the book was in manufacture, according to its first-edition errata notice, the publisher, Charles Wiley, had usually not been in attendance, and normal proofreading routines had been disrupted. If the author hoped to compensate for earlier neglect by reading his proofs carefully, the plague manifestly frustrated his "good resolutions."

Cooper did not accept these imperfections complacently; for he revised *The Pioneers* at three widely spaced intervals in his career, during two periods with remarkable care and concern. Attempting immediately to repair his own and the printer's oversights, he silently emended the text in all three of its subsequent printings in 1823, treating the sheets of the already printed first edition as if they were uncorrected proofs. Again in 1831 he revised the text extensively for Colburn and Bentley's Standard Novels series. And finally, in 1850, correcting the text for G. P. Putnam's "Author's Revised Edition," he made additional changes, although this revision seems minimal in comparison with those of 1823 and 1831.

Readers unfamiliar with Cooper's working habits may be surprised at his extreme concern for the purification of an early text. Yet his capacity for painstaking revision is fully documented not only by collation of the printed texts of *The Pioneers*, but in holographic and printed evidence of his revisions of other novels. Although printer's copy for the 1832 Standard Novels edition of *The Pioneers*—an interleaved, annotated copy of the Carey, Lea and Carey—is unlocated, printer's copy for the 1832 Standard Novels edition of *The Spy*, prepared almost simultaneously and in an identical manner, is available at the Berg Collection of the New York Public Library. Here Cooper rewrote some long passages and made hundreds of stylistic improvements: altering tenses, deleting superfluous words, and correcting large numbers of errors in grammar, diction, punctuation, spelling, and capitalization. Cooper indicated to Colburn and Bentley that *The Pioneers* was even more in need of his "severe pen" than *The Spy*, and collation demonstrates that his revision of *The Pioneers* was no less thorough.

WILEY-CLAYTON FIRST EDITION

The first edition of *The Pioneers*, originally scheduled for the autumn of 1822,[3] appeared in two volumes in New York City on 1 February 1823,[4] bearing on its title page the imprint of Charles Wiley, publisher, and E[dward] B. Clayton, printer. Though printing seems to have begun in the spring of 1822, the yellow fever epidemic later that year was evidently the major cause of the long delay in the appearance of the Wiley-Clayton edition (hereafter referred to as W/C). The first two sentences of the errata notice, bound into Volume II, explain: "In consequence of the state of the city during the fever, the PIONEERS has not received the careful revision that was desirable. Most of the time, the publisher was absent, and the proofs were not read in the usual manner."[5]

Random distribution of plate alterations during the press run results in seven states of W/C, differentiated by seven different combinations of three substantive variants appearing in three different gatherings of the first edition. First, in some copies the early page number "ix" in the Preface is corrected to "xi." Second, the earlier reading (451.35 "you got then") in some copies becomes "you then got."[6] No evidence establishes a precedence, however, regarding the third substantive variant, at 351.20, where some copies read "getting under way" and others "getting under weigh."

A survey of twenty available copies of W/C determines that only three copies contain both early readings (all three read "way" at 351.20) while only four copies contain both later readings (two with "way" and two with "weigh" at 351.20).[7] The remaining thirteen copies combine the three different variants in four additional patterns.[8] These seven combinations of variants apparently represent a random binding of the three gatherings containing the variants.

Since no portion of the manuscript, which was printer's copy for W/C, nor any galley or proof material associated with it is known to survive, the copy-text for the present edition is one of the three copies of W/C that contains early readings at the two points for which precedence can be established. On the evidence of a printing error found in all twenty copies, the copy designated III owned by James F. Beard is the earliest known copy of W/C and is therefore used as copy-text for the present edition.[9]

Cooper began to realize the inadequacies of the first edition long before its appearance on 1 February 1823. Writing to John Murray on 29 November 1822, he indicated that he had corresponded with Wiley about errors in W/C, though he had not yet read carefully the two-thirds of the novel already printed.[10] On 15 January 1823, when the first edition was completely printed, he specified in a second letter to Murray the kinds of changes he wanted in the London edition.[11] The earliest public evidence of his dissatisfaction is the W/C errata notice:

> [The publisher] will not publish a regular errata, but cannot suffer some of the mistakes to go without notice.—In the first chapter, the word "Delaware" should be inserted for "Mohawk." "Moreen" is spelt, once or twice, "marine." The printers have inserted the verb "to fall," instead of "to fell." "A shapeless figure of good proportions!" should read any thing else. The "surrounding atmosphere before it," is an oversight. There are several little grammatical errors; but it is thought that those who detect them, will have charity enough to attribute them to their true causes, haste, and the reasons above mentioned.

Almost certainly Cooper drafted this notice: the stylistic mannerisms are his, and only he is likely to have caught errors like "Mohawks" for "Delawares." Silently, however, he was already making energetic efforts to correct the multiplicity of errors whose full extent he never publicly acknowledged.

OTHER 1823 TEXTS

These efforts were evidenced in one partially revised and two fully revised versions of *The Pioneers* in the winter of 1823: long excerpts from three chapters, published in the New York *Commercial Advertiser* on 18 and 25 January; the first British edition, published by John Murray on 26 February; and a second New York edition, printed by Seymour and Clayton and published by Charles Wiley on or about 1 February. Since no set of the substantive corrections is duplicated *in toto* in another set and only two substantive corrections are duplicated in all three 1823 revisions, Cooper evidently prepared the sets at different times on sheets of W/C, keeping no copies for his own reference. If circumstantial evidence left any doubt of Cooper's involvement in all three 1823 revisions, his intervention would be clearly established by his correspondence with John Murray taken in conjunction with the interlocking patterns of common variants. Twenty-two of the 170 substantive variants in the Murray edition are duplicated in the Wiley-Seymour-Clayton edition, and eleven substantive variants in the *Commercial Advertiser* excerpts are duplicated in the Wiley-Seymour-Clayton.

MURRAY EDITION

The first British edition of *The Pioneers*, published by John Murray in three volumes, was set from unbound sheets of W/C containing Cooper's scribal corrections.[12] In sending John Murray printer's copy for about two-thirds of the novel on 29 November 1822, Cooper commented:

> the corrections I have made are from Queries of Mr. Wiley, or by glancing my eye over the work, so that if you find any errors in grammar or awkward sentences you are at liberty to have them altered—Though I should wish the latter to be done very sparingly, both because that one mans style seldom agrees with anothers, and because a similar liberty was abused to a degree in "Precaution," that materially injured the Book—.[13]

This qualified permission to initiate corrections was enlarged slightly in Cooper's letter of 15 January 1823 enclosing the remaining sheets:

> You will percieve that corrections are made in some of the pages that are omitted in the duplicates—I wish them all to be made. The difference arises from my making corrections as my eye accidentally detected the error—The words "kind of" and "sort of" occur too frequently in the book, though sometimes properly—You are at liberty to strike out most of them—.[14]

Approximately 65% of the substantive variants in the Murray edition appear to be authorial. In all, 170 substantive variants appear in the Murray, with the following distribution: Volume I, fifty-six; Volume II, forty; Volume III, seventy-four. Of these, seventy-two are accepted; thirty-nine others would have been accepted if they had not been supplanted by subsequent authorial revisions. Fifty-nine are rejected.

Of the seventy-two substantive variants accepted, twenty-two are identical to substantive variants appearing in the Wiley-Seymour-Clayton edition, and fifty are unique to the Murray. The first group is accepted as authorial because they represent Cooper's first response to inadequacies he later revised in identical ways for the Wiley-Seymour-Clayton edition. For example, in both post-copy-texts at 98.8 the W/C "there was no change about him, unless it were from grief to joy" becomes "there was . . . from grave to gay."[15] Two of these emendations (at 189.10 and 194.18) occur in all three 1823 post-copy-texts, including the excerpts from three chapters printed in the *Commercial Advertiser*. Finally, two of the twenty-two identical emendations carry out corrections listed in the W/C errata notice.[16]

The other fifty substantive variants accepted as authorial are unique to the Murray: that is, they are emendations of passages not altered by any other post-copy-text and restored to the text of *The Pioneers* for the first time in the present edition. Four of these readings are longer than the usual Murray variant as, for example, at 35.3–4, where the W/C reading "forfeited some of the privileges of his offspring" becomes in Murray "forfeited some of the privileges which would have descended to his offspring."[17]

Though shorter than the example just cited, the remaining forty-six unique substantive variants correct awkwardnesses in W/C—slipshod grammar, verbosity and faulty diction. Since Cooper instructed Murray to follow every scribal correction, the present edition considers these substantive variants authorial when they illustrate at least one of three kinds of stylistic improvement: revision towards precision, concision and accuracy. For example, at 38.11, the W/C "Some little while elapsed" becomes "Some little time elapsed" in the Murray.[18] The failure of the Murray to avail itself of Cooper's authorization to delete "kind of" and "sort of" argues further that it altered his corrected text sparingly.

Of the thirty-nine substantive variants in the Murray for which Cooper provided different revisions in subsequent editions, ten are supplanted by different revisions in the Wiley-Seymour-Clayton (one of these to be supplanted in turn by a different emendation in the 1832 Standard Novels edition).[19] Twenty-seven other passages containing Murray substantive variants attain final form in the Standard Novels edition, one in the Putnam, and one in the present edition.[20] On the Emendations list, these Murray readings are cited as intermediate between the copy-text and the accepted readings, even though Cooper was obviously not responding to Murray readings when he made the later revisions.

Fifty-six of the fifty-nine substantive variants in the Murray rejected here are rejected as not being stylistic improvements.[21] Two others are clearly printer's errors (see Rejected Readings at 290.14 and 454.21). And, finally, at 335.20, alteration of "begun" to "began" is rejected as non-authorial. Though this particular change occurs both in the Murray and the Wiley-Seymour-Clayton editions, *The Pioneers* elsewhere follows the older practice of employing the past participial form of the verb as the simple past.

THE NEW YORK *Commercial Advertiser*

Prior to the publication of W/C, the New York *Commercial Advertiser* printed two excerpts from the novel (about 8,000 words). The Christmas turkey shoot in Volume I, Chapter 17 (189.5 to 199.13 in the present text) appeared on 18 January 1823; and Natty's killing of the deer on the lake in Volume II, Chapters 7 and 8 (290.38 to 299.23 in the present text) followed on 25 January. Cooper's friendship with William L. Stone, one of the publishers of the *Commercial Advertiser*, probably explains how the newspaper obtained the pre-publication excerpts. Though Stone later quarreled with the novelist, he enthusiastically encouraged Cooper's career in the 1820's and, perhaps because he served his apprenticeship in Cooperstown, took a special interest in the familiar scenes described in the new novel. The *Commercial Advertiser* replied to journalistic competition on 8 February:

> We observe in the Minerva of this morning what we consider a very unjust and illiberal criticism upon [*The Pioneers*]. Repeated mention is made of what the writer terms the puffs of "a daily paper" . . . in such a way, as to induce a belief that the author has been accessary to those publications. As this is the daily paper alluded to, we feel it to be our duty to state explicitly, that not a single remark of our's has been made with his previous knowledge; and it was not until after repeated solicitation, that we obtained the extracts given before the work was published.[22]

While defending Cooper from charges of using the *Commercial Advertiser* to puff his new novel, the article clearly suggests that Cooper was implicated in the newspaper publication of the two scenes. Inspection of the text demonstrates that he must also have supplied corrections in the printer's copy, perhaps intending to polish those parts of the novel the public would see first.

The *Commercial Advertiser* text (CA hereafter) introduces sixty-three substantive variants, fifty-two that are unique and eleven that are duplicated in the Wiley-Seymour-Clayton. Of these eleven, two are also duplicated in the Murray edition and are accepted as emendations of the copy-text on its authority, though one of these two (at 189.10) is also listed as a correction in the W/C errata notice. The remaining nine, shared with the Wiley-Seymour-Clayton, are accepted as emendations on the authority of CA.[23]

Of the fifty-two unique substantive variants in CA, the Cooper Edition accepts as emendations to the copy-text thirty-three that result in such improvements as correction of tenses, increase of concision, and revision of faulty diction. The four examples of CA variants shown below (enclosed within double lines) illustrate these tendencies:

	W/C	CA
189.28	order //that it might// serve	order //to// serve
191.11–12	//when// the echoes from the mountains //would take// up	the echoes from the mountains //taking// up
297.32-33	all //of// its utensils	all its utensils

298.36–37   //It was// the frequency of   The frequency of these
            these circuitous move-   circuitous movements, by
            ments, //that,// by confining confining

Nineteen substantive variants in CA that do not improve the copy-text are rejected as probable compositorial corruptions. For example, at 189.10, "the deer . . . or the bear" becomes "the deer . . . or a bear." Other rejected CA readings introduce more obvious errors, like the CA "sad fallen" for "had fallen" at 298.12, or normalize dialect ("German" for "Garman" in Natty's speech at 195.5).[24]

WILEY-SEYMOUR-CLAYTON EDITION

Although the only difference from W/C indicated on the title page of the second New York edition is the name of Jonathan Seymour as printer for Volume I, the Wiley-Seymour-Clayton edition (W/S here-after) is a new edition of *The Pioneers*. The entire first volume and about three-quarters of the second volume were printed from type newly set.[25] In arranging for the revised Standard Novels edition, Cooper wrote to Henry Colburn on 14 March 1831:

> By no means print the Spy [1821] from the English edition which is full of errors—Mr. Careys edition is far better. . . . All the American editions were cursorily revised down to Pilot [1824], inclusively, and they are better than the English though far from what they might be made.[26]

Since *The Pilot* appeared after *The Pioneers*, Cooper clearly includes the latter among the novels he "cursorily revised" early in his career; and since all American editions of *The Pioneers* after 1823 and before the Putnam in 1851 follow W/S directly or at one remove and contain no new authorial emendations, Cooper's remark can refer only to W/S.

In the absence of documentary or printed evidence, three circum-stances suggest that Wiley contemplated a second edition of *The Pioneers* before or soon after 15 January (when according to Cooper's second letter to Murray, W/C was finally in print) and that W/S ap-peared about 1 February: the use in W/S of six W/C formes in the last seven signatures of Volume II, pre-publication comments in the *Commercial Advertiser*, and the existence of sets mixing volumes from W/C and W/S.

Early nineteenth-century publishers customarily broke down formes of standing type within a few days after a work was printed in order to reuse the type.[27] Since six of the W/C formes were held over and corrections entered into them for six of the last seven signatures of W/S, the new edition must have been ordered before Clayton com-pleted redistributing his type—within a few days, then, of 15 January.

A notice in the *Commercial Advertiser* implies that by 16 January Wiley, anticipating a large demand for the new novel, had already ordered a new edition:

> We . . . are happy to announce, on the authority of Mr. Wiley, that the book is already printed, and is now to the hands of the binders—that as the edition is large, and the trade requires the whole of it, and more too, it is unavoidably kept back until all his customers can be simultaneously supplied.[28]

This excerpt suggests that publication was purposely delayed until the second edition was ready; and the existence of sets mixing volumes from W/C and W/S suggests that the two editions were on sale at the same time, about 1 February. Of forty-five sets of W/C and W/S surveyed, eighteen pair W/C editions of both volumes, nineteen pair W/S of both, and the remaining eight are mixed.[29] Since Cooper completed the Murray revisions by 15 January and the CA revisions before 18 and 25 January, his revisions for W/S were evidently made during the same period.

The first volume, printed by Jonathan Seymour, introduces 571 substantive variants into the copy-text, and the second, which retained the Clayton imprint, introduces 356. The Cooper Edition accepts 734 as authorial and rejects as non-authorial the remaining 193. These 734 emendations range from revisions of entire sentences to initiation of dialect and stylistic improvements. W/S also provides the last piece of evidence for parallel yet independent revisions: it duplicates twenty-two emendations Cooper made for Murray before 15 January (when the last corrected W/C sheets were sent to London), two of which also appear in the three chapters in CA. Finally, W/S corrects every item in the W/C errata notice.[30]

The present edition has defined what Cooper called cursory revision of the W/S in his letter of 14 March 1831 to Colburn by examining each of the 927 substantive variants in the context of two kinds of improvements: emendations correcting errors in meaning and style in W/C and emendations making minor improvements in style only. The following examples show the kinds of substantive variants accepted as authorial because they are clarifications of style and meaning:

	W/C	W/S
40.14–17	the mountains . . . were formed into //kind of terraces// that admitted of cultivation.	the mountains . . . were formed into //terraces and hollows// that admitted of cultivation.
59.3–5	The last object at which Elizabeth had gazed when they renewed their journey, after the	The last object at which Elizabeth had gazed when they renewed their journey, after the

	rencontre with Richard, was the sun, as //he// expanded in the refraction of the horizon	rencontre with Richard, was the sun, as //it// expanded in the refraction of the horizon
212.28–30	Elizabeth . . . soon forgot, //not only the changes in the country, but those, also// in her own condition	Elizabeth . . . soon forgot //the changes in the country, with those// in her own condition
220.39–221.2	Nothing could be more marked, than the contrast between the earth and the heavens; for, while the //latter// presented the dreary view that we have described, a warm and invigorating sun was dispensing his heats	Nothing could be more marked, than the contrast between the earth and the heavens; for, while the //former// presented the dreary view that we have described, a warm and invigorating sun was dispensing his heats
289.36–38	the youth pulled his little boat, in a very few minutes, //alongside of,// and fastened it to the light vessel	the youth pulled his little boat, in a very few minutes, //to the place where his friends were fishing,// and fastened it to the light vessel

The second category of substantive variants accepted as emendations are those which increase concision or precision. Some of these variants could have resulted from compositorial misreading, eye-skipping or house-styling, but the care with which Cooper was revising—treating the W/C sheets as if they were proof for W/S—favors the assumption that these readings are authorial. The following examples illustrate this category of variants:

	W/C	W/S
26.14–15	There is no human aid nearer than Templeton," he said, "and the hut of Natty is full three miles from //here//	There is no human aid nearer than Templeton," he said, "and the hut of Natty is full three miles from //this//
143.4	the youth, scornfully, //as he paced// the floor	the youth, scornfully, //pacing// the floor
244.11	for //really// the sight was most exhilarating	for the sight was most exhilarating

One-hundred-ninety-three W/S substantive variants are rejected either because they are obvious printer's errors or because they do

not contribute to concision or precision of style (though they are
sometimes plausible). For example:

	W/C	W/S
171.33-34	as long as //I// keep	as long as keep
296.12	The //dogs// knew	The //dog's// knew
409.38-39	hissing //steams// of the spring	hissing //streams// of the spring

COLLINS, HANNAY AND WILEY (1825)

No evidence suggests Cooper's intervention in the preparation of the
third American edition, the 1825 Collins, Hannay and Wiley (CHW
hereafter). CHW followed W/S as printer's copy, reproducing the
substantive variants of its source except where it corrects obvious W/S
errors. Of the sixty-two new substantive variants in CHW, the Cooper
Edition adopts on its own authority four corrections of obvious errors
in printer's copy (see Textual Notes at 53.13). Fifty-six corruptions
transmitted to later authorial editions are identified and rejected (see
Textual Notes at 17.26). At 191.32–33 (the turkey shoot scene), for
example, the W/C "price of a shot at the choicest bird" becomes "price
of the choicest bird"; and, at 451.33, where in W/S Natty Bumppo
"started at the sound of his own name," CHW reads "stared. . . ." The
1832 Colburn and Bentley Standard Novels, the next authorial edition, corrected two CHW corruptions, condensing one passage (see
Textual Notes at 242.25) and, at 250.24 restoring "after the
first . . ." to its copy-text form "after this first. . . ." Since CHW is
non-authorial, it does not appear in the Emendations and Rejected
Readings lists.

CAREY, LEA AND CAREY (1827)

The next authorized edition of *The Pioneers*, Carey, Lea and Carey
(CLC hereafter), was published in 1827, a year after Cooper went
abroad. Again, no evidence points to his intervention in its preparation. CLC employed CHW as printer's copy, repeating all but one of
the CHW substantive variants and introducing seventeen of its own.
One correction, which alters a verb form to reinstitute parallelism, is
accepted on the authority of the Cooper Edition (see Textual Notes at
265.36). Fourteen substantive variants transmitted to the Standard
Novels and Putnam editions appear to be compositorial misreadings
("their noses be given them" for "their noses be given to them" at
419.4, for example). These readings are identified and rejected (see
Textual Notes at 26.31). In one instance, where the Cooper Edition

retains the copy-text form ("from its broad feet," at 309.5), CLC corrects the CHW corruption "from his broad feet"—referring to a female panther—to "from her broad feet." In another instance, at 26.36, the Standard Novels edition restores the CLC corruption "trial" to "trail" in the copy-text phrase "on the trail of the Iroquois."

The first edition of *The Pioneers* to be stereotyped, CLC was frequently reimpressed during and after Cooper's lifetime.[31] These reimpressions, continuing long after Cooper's death in the Stringer and Townsend "People's Editions" of 1856, 1857, and 1858, reveal only one substantive variant, the correction of "trial" to "trail."[32] Even before 1858, plate wear is extensive, resulting in numerous broken letters and some restyling of punctuation accompanying plate repair. Since the 1827 CLC edition does not disclose evidence of authorial revision, and since the reimpressions issued long before and after Cooper's death reveal no authorial intervention at any point, the one substantive variant appearing in these CLC reimpressions subsequent to 1827 is not cited in the Textual Apparatus.

COLBURN AND BENTLEY STANDARD NOVELS EDITION (1832)

Anxious to secure the British copyright for Cooper's early fiction, Colburn and Bentley agreed on 25 March 1831 to pay the novelist £50 a book for the revision of several early novels, and Cooper corrected the texts of *The Spy* and *The Pioneers* during April and May of that year.[33] At his request Colburn and Bentley supplied him with interleaved copies of recent Carey, Lea and Carey printings of both novels as a basis for these revisions.[34] The Colburn and Bentley Standard Novels edition of *The Pioneers* (CB hereafter) appeared in one volume on 31 March 1832,[35] advertised on the title page as "revised, corrected, and illustrated, with a new introduction, notes, etc., by the author." Cooper's holograph printer's copy of the "Introduction" is copy-text for that portion of the present edition.[36]

Although CB introduces 2,377 substantive variants, it presents fewer problems for the editor than the 1823 post-copy-texts. The revised interleaved printer's copy for the 1832 *The Pioneers* is unlocated, but Cooper's holograph revisions on the interleaved pages of *The Spy* provide detailed evidence of his practice in correcting an early novel he considered unusually corrupt. For every kind of substantive variant in the Standard Novels edition of *The Pioneers* accepted as authorial in the present edition, the interleaved copy of *The Spy* provides several analogous holograph examples. Every substantive variant originating in CB has been examined in the context of the collateral holograph evidence of the corrected printer's copy for *The Spy*. The present edition has accepted 1,989 CB substantive variants as authorial revisions and has rejected 388.

For convenience, the 1,989 emendations in CB may be considered in three categories: rewritten passages of one or more sentences, re-written phrases, and substantive changes of single words (diction, number, tense and dialect spelling). Of thirty-three emendations in the first category, fourteen are recastings of passages ranging from a sentence to several paragraphs.[37] For example, the description of Judge Temple's "Mansion-house" (43.27–44.6) is completely rewritten; in the second volume, a section of Monsieur Le Quoi's macaronic French and English is replaced by a paraphrase in standard English (396.30-397.2). A paragraph hinting at Louisa's unrequited romantic attraction to Oliver is deleted at 263.9. The title page indicates that the new "Introduction" and the sixteen explanatory footnotes are Cooper's.

The 736 emendations in the second category are alterations in word order or phrasing that increase precision or otherwise improve style. These emendations include the deletion of conventional tags in dialogue identifying speaker or mood. Paired examples of substantive variants from both *The Pioneers* and *The Spy* illustrating Cooper's practice in emendation appear in the notes.[38]

Substantive variants consisting of single words present the greatest problem to the editor. Like some variants in W/S, many of these variants could have originated from compositorial misreading, eye-skipping and house-styling. But, since Cooper was revising carefully an early novel whose text he considered inadequate, and since the interleaved copy of *The Spy* provides evidence of the detail with which he executed his revision, many of these variants, like similar W/S variants, must be considered authorial if they increase concision or precision of style. The present edition accepts such variants in CB if they fall into one or more of the five following categories:

1. substitution of more idiomatic forms for prepositions, articles and relative pronouns;
2. replacement of a possessive pronoun by an article;
3. revision of unnecessarily plural nouns to the singular;
4. revision of verb tense and number;
5. compression of the text by excision of superfluous words, especially "sir," "that," "then," "now," "just," and "and."

Holograph revisions analogous to these five types of revisions in *The Pioneers* are numerous in the interleaved copy of *The Spy* and are here illustrated in the notes.[39] Another circumstance that supports the acceptance of these changes is the care with which Colburn and Bentley reproduced Cooper's revisions for *The Spy*. Comparison of the interleaved printer's copy of *The Spy* with the revised edition shows little compositorial intervention in substantive readings, a situation which presumably obtains for *The Pioneers*.

The present edition rejects 388 CB substantive variants because they do not contribute to greater precision or concision. For example, at 353.3, "it is" is substituted for "it's" in a context where the CB reading makes no improvement. Fifteen of these substantive variants are obviously printer's errors (for example, the CB "assayed to remedy the evil" at 44.22 for "essayed . . ."). Two additional kinds of minor changes that appear in the Standard Novels *Pioneers* but not in the Standard Novels *Spy* have been rejected: the present edition does not follow CB in spelling out abbreviated forms (like "Col." at 36.18) or in altering numbers from written to numeral form (like "100" at 154.27). Nor does the present edition follow CB in spelling out contractions. Though Cooper occasionally made this kind of emendation in *The Spy*, his practice there is not consistent. CB normalizations of dialect are rejected in 137 instances as non-authorial; here again, although Cooper's practice in *The Spy* is not completely consistent, normalization of dialect is likely to be non-authorial. (See "A Note on Dialect," p. 475.)

Two impressions of the 1832 Standard Novels edition have been identified, the first printed by "A. and R. Spottiswoode" (E_1 in the Textual Apparatus) and the second by "A. Spottiswoode" (E_2). At four points E_2 corrects obvious blunders in E_1: at 107.39 "filled a with" becomes "filled with," at 241.23 "and the the coats" becomes "and the coats," at 245.26 the misspelled word "canon" becomes "cannon," and at 417.28 "respectively" is corrected to "respectfully." The second impression (E_2), containing these corrections, evidently appeared after 2 September 1832, when Andrew Spottiswoode's brother and partner Robert died.[40] The Standard Novels edition of *The Pioneers* was reimpressed in 1835 and 1849, but these later impressions made no substantive changes.

THE PUTNAM EDITION (1851)

In 1850 Cooper prepared a final revised edition, based on the text of the second impression of the 1832 Standard Novels text, for a projected but incomplete "Author's Revised Edition" of his works undertaken by G. P. Putnam.[41] Though the *Literary World* of 23 November 1850 noted that the new edition of *The Pioneers* was recently published, the present editors have located no copies of an 1850 Putnam imprint of this book. Cooper's revisions were not extensive. He preserved the "Introduction" and notes of the Standard Novels edition, adding two paragraphs to the "Introduction" disclaiming any relationship between Elizabeth Temple and his own sister. Ironically, however, he did not remove two CB footnotes on pages 233 and 235 which suggested that he had employed the history of Cooperstown and his own family for material in *The Pioneers*.

The Putnam edition introduces 243 substantive variants, none of which approaches the length or complexity of some Murray, W/S and CB emendations. More of these variants appear at the end of the novel than elsewhere, a fact suggesting that Cooper gave greater attention to improving his style in the final chapters, hitherto more lightly corrected than the earlier chapters.

Following the policy established earlier, the present edition accepts as emendations 110 Putnam substantive variants which increase precision or concision. A few examples suggest the nature of these emendations:

	W/C	Putnam
17.6	A single track . . . was //sunken near// two feet below the surrounding surface	A single track . . . was //sunk nearly// two feet below the surrounding surface
37.10	his //enterprises// throve to a degree	his //enterprise// throve to a degree
324.7	mountain fell off //precipitately//	mountain fell off //precipitously//
408.16	some opening that might offer the facilities //of// flight	some opening that might offer the facilities //for// flight

Of the 133 rejected Putnam substantive variants, four are obvious printer's errors (for example, "with as weep of his head" at 77.9 for "with a sweep of his head"). At one point the Putnam altered a reading acceptable in 1823, but the present edition rejects the variant as a modernization (123.11 "dies" [tints] changed to "dyes"). Such a modernization is at least as likely to be the work of a compositor as of Cooper. House-styling probably accounts also for the twenty-two points at which the Putnam substitutes the simple past tense for the copy-text past participles (e.g., 271.20, "A loud burst of merriment . . . rung along the eastern mountain" becomes "rang along the eastern mountain"). The present edition follows copy-text in its use of a verb form acceptable to Cooper in 1823, rejects twenty-nine Putnam substantive variants because they normalize dialect (see "A Note on Dialect," p. 475), and rejects seventy-seven Putnam substantive variants because they do not make improvements of text.

Although no copies of the 1852 and 1853 Putnam editions have been available for Hinman collation, reimpressions of the 1851 Putnam plates apparently contain no substantive variants. The 1856 Stringer and Townsend "Choice Edition" of the novel, which employed the plates of the Putnam edition, reveals only occasional plate defects and repairs.[42] Examination of two copies of the 1859 "Townsend-Darley" edition, which also derived from the Putnam plates, discloses no substantive variants.[43]

FOREIGN EDITIONS AND PIRACIES

Baudry (1825, 1835)

Baudry published *The Pioneers* in 1825 and 1835. The 1825 edition, in three volumes, followed the 1823 Murray as printer's copy, for it contains all the unique Murray variants. Except for random corruptions, the Baudry departs from the Murray only in correcting Cooper's French in a few passages. The 1835 Baudry followed the 1832 Colburn and Bentley second impression.

Piracies

Throughout Cooper's lifetime, demand for *The Pioneers* outside the United States was satisfied by pirated as well as authorized editions. Cooper's scorn of pirated editions and of any infringement of legitimate publishing rights precluded his involvement with any of these suspect printings. In accommodating the text to a cheap format, certain of these editions abridged the novel, certainly without authorization from Cooper.

The following editions of *The Pioneers* are assumed to be piracies, for no record exists of Cooper's dealings with any of these publishers. Spot-checking indicated that none of these editions comes from a printer's copy the present edition considers authoritative, and usually disclosed both accidental and substantive corruption. The following list of presumably unauthorized editions indicates the place of publication, publisher, date, location of copy examined for the present edition, and edition which served as printer's copy.

1. London: Simpkin and Marshall, 1827, unlocated, cited BAL 3829.
2. Zwickau: Schumann Brothers, 1829 (Wayne State University, Eloise-Ramsey Collection). Printer's copy was the 1825 Baudry edition.
3. London: Allman and Daly, [1836?] (Beard). Printer's copy was the Carey, Lea and Carey edition.
4. London: J. Cunningham, 1839—Novel Newspaper, Vol. 1 (University of Arkansas A 813.08 N85, v 1). Printer's copy was the Carey, Lea and Carey edition. This text, pages 197 to 304 of a collection of Cooper's novels, reappeared frequently from other publishers. The following "Novel Newspaper" piracies, examined for the present edition, derived from the Carey text:
    a. London: T. L. Holt, 1839 (American Antiquarian Society G526. C777. N839).
    b. London: J. Cunningham, 1841 (American Antiquarian Society G526. C777. N842).
    c. London: Bruce and Wyld, 1844 (Berkeley PT 9737 A2 1844a).

    d. London: J. Cunningham, [1847?] (Yale Hfh su 30k).

5. London: J. S. Pratt, 1843, 1844 (Beard). Heavily cut, especially in dialogues. Printer's copy seems to be the Carey, Lea and Carey edition but it at times introduces unique readings.

6. London: W. M. Clark, 1844—Penny Parts edition (Beard). Printer's copy was Carey, Lea and Carey edition.

7. London: Routledge, [1852?], 1854 (American Antiquarian Society G526. C777. P854. pion (L)). Printer's copy was the Carey, Lea and Carey edition.

The following stemma summarizes the relationship between the W/C first edition and all available subsequent editions to 1861:

STEMMA FOR The Pioneers

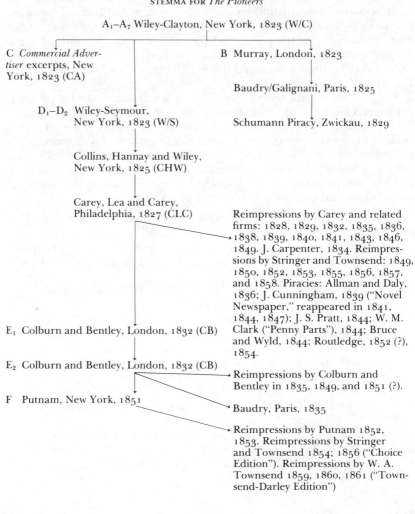

A₁–A₇ Wiley-Clayton, New York, 1823 (W/C)

C *Commercial Advertiser* excerpts, New York, 1823 (CA)

B Murray, London, 1823

Baudry/Galignani, Paris, 1825

D₁–D₂ Wiley-Seymour, New York, 1823 (W/S)

Schumann Piracy, Zwickau, 1829

Collins, Hannay and Wiley, New York, 1825 (CHW)

Carey, Lea and Carey, Philadelphia, 1827 (CLC)

Reimpressions by Carey and related firms: 1828, 1829, 1832, 1835, 1836, 1838, 1839, 1840, 1841, 1843, 1846, 1849. J. Carpenter, 1834. Reimpressions by Stringer and Townsend: 1849, 1850, 1852, 1853, 1855, 1856, 1857, and 1858. Piracies: Allman and Daly, 1836; J. Cunningham, 1839 ("Novel Newspaper," reappeared in 1841, 1844, 1847); J. S. Pratt, 1844; W. M. Clark ("Penny Parts"), 1844; Bruce and Wyld, 1844; Routledge, 1852 (?), 1854.

E₁ Colburn and Bentley, London, 1832 (CB)

E₂ Colburn and Bentley, London, 1832 (CB)

Reimpressions by Colburn and Bentley in 1835, 1849, and 1851 (?).

F   Putnam, New York, 1851

Baudry, Paris, 1835

Reimpressions by Putnam 1852, 1853. Reimpressions by Stringer and Townsend 1854; 1856 ("Choice Edition"). Reimpressions by W. A. Townsend 1859, 1860, 1861 ("Townsend-Darley Edition")

A NOTE ON DIALECT

Though reviewers of *The Pioneers* castigated the author for employing dialect for rustic speakers, collations of this novel and other works of fiction suggest that Cooper never willingly curbed his experimentation with dialect. Manuscript alterations and printed variants in a variety of texts show this experimentation to have been deliberate and self-conscious. When he revised *The Spy* for the Colburn and Bentley Standard Novels, Cooper wrote on the first page of his interleaved, corrected printer's copy: "note Bene—No attention will be given to the spelling, except in words of local use, the names, or those which are evidently intended to be corrupt. The proof reader will take care of the others." Clearly, "words of local use, the names, or those [spellings] which are evidently intended to be corrupt" includes Cooper's scribal revisions of dialect. Since his revisions of *The Spy* and *The Pioneers* were almost simultaneous, the present edition assumes—in the absence of the holographic evidence available for *The Spy*—that the numerous variants in dialect in the Standard Novels edition of *The Pioneers* reveal a similar concern for orthographic fidelity. The Cooper Edition considers dialect variants here and in other authorial editions of *The Pioneers* substantive.

These variants are of three kinds: substitution of dialect for standard forms, normalizations of dialect, and shifts from one dialect spelling to another. Although Cooper made all three types of changes when revising *The Spy*, the present edition emends dialect in the copy-text only when an authorial post-copy-text substitutes dialect for a standard form. Comparison between the interleaved, corrected printer's copy for the Standard Novels edition of *The Spy* and the printed text indicates that normalization of dialect spelling and shifts from one dialect spelling to another originated about as often in the printing shop as with the author. Conversely, the substitution of a dialect spelling for a standard form occurs infrequently, if at all, without Cooper's authority. The present edition has, consequently, rejected 201 normalizations of dialect (the shift of Natty Bumppo's "curous" to "curious" at 27.29, for example) and 112 substitutions of one dialect spelling for another (including fifteen shifts in W/S of Natty's "gall" to "gal"). The more statistically probable substitution of dialect for standard spelling (Natty's "before" to "afore" at 196.1, for instance) has been accepted as an emendation of the copy-text at twelve points.

CONCLUSION

This edition of *The Pioneers* contains no silent emendations. Except for the 1832 Introduction and Notes and two paragraphs added to the 1832 Introduction for the 1851 Putnam edition, the first state of the 1823 Wiley-Clayton edition (W/C) is copy-text throughout. With a few exceptions specified here, the copy-text is emended only on the authority of the five editions (B through F in Emendations and Rejected Readings) identified as authorial: the Murray (1823), chapters published in the *Commercial Advertiser* (CA; 18 and 25 January, 1823), the Wiley-Seymour first impression (W/S, 1823), the Colburn and Bentley Standard Novels (CB, 1832), and the Putnam (1851). The text of the Dedication, retained here, is printed without substantive change in all three complete authorial editions of 1823, in the non-authorial Collins, Hannay and Wiley (1825), and in the non-authorial Carey, Lea and Carey (1827); it was omitted in the Colburn and Bentley Standard Novels edition (1832) and the Putnam (1851).

The Cooper Edition supplies new substantive emendations of the narrative copy-text on its own authority at only four points. First, "not" is inserted before "without" in the following sentence at 294.20-25:

> You can see right down into the valley that lies to the east of the High-Peak, where, in the fall of the year, thousands of acres of woods are afore your eyes, in the deep hollow, and along the side of the mountain, painted like ten thousand rainbows, by no hand of man, though without the ordering of God's providence.

Second, at 309.37 the copy-text "them" is emended to "it" to obtain pronoun agreement with a preceding Standard Novels emendation; third, at 361.9 "if" and "for" are supplied to complete a Standard Novels emendation apparently executed imperfectly. Fourth, at 170.32 in the copy-text phrase "as a salvo to her dignity," the presumed compositorial misreading "salvo" is emended to "salve." Also on its own authority, the Cooper Edition has, in a few instances, accepted as emendations obvious substantive corrections appearing first in nonauthorial editions within the mainstream of the transmission of the text (four in Collins, Hannay and Wiley, and one in Carey, Lea and Carey). In each instance, the reader is referred to the pertinent information in Textual Notes at 53.13 and 265.36.

The Cooper Edition also supplies corrections of errors in spelling, capitalization and punctuation in the copy-text or emends these aspects of the copy-text when clarification of ambiguities or possible confusions is required. Though many of these corrections were made in the preparation of authorial editions subsequent to the copy-text, they are considered more likely to be compositorial than authorial. Corrections of accidentals listed in Emendations are, therefore, made on the authority of the Cooper Edition, even though some may derive from Cooper's revisions. When an authorial edition seems to make a necessary correction, the Cooper Edition adopts it, citing the edition which initiates the change solely as a matter of historical record (see, for example, Emendations and Textual Notes at 24.6 and 69.26). When the Cooper Edition introduces a new correction of a copy-text accidental, the source is cited as CE (see, for example, Emendations at 30.5).

Non-dialect spelling in the copy-text has been retained in preference to variant but equally acceptable forms in subsequent authorial editions. The chief authority for determining spellings acceptable in 1823 has been Noah Webster's *An American Dictionary of the English Language* (2 vols., New York, 1828). In no instance has the Cooper Edition sought to impose consistency of spelling or capitalization on varying but unambiguous copy-text forms like "color," "colour"; "ribband," "ribbon"; "Bible," "bible"; "New York," "New-York" or "do'nt," "don't."

Identification of chapter epigraphs has been expanded, when possible, to provide the surname of the author, title, and location of the quoted passage in the work. These expansions are treated as emendations and entered fully in the Emendations list. Texts of the epigraphs have been retained in their copy-text forms[44] except that, in accordance with Cooper's usual manuscript practice, quotation marks have been supplied in some instances and entered in the Emendations list. Shakespearean epigraphs are keyed to *The Riverside Shakespeare*, ed. G. Blakemore Evans (Boston: Houghton Mifflin, 1974), others to first editions or American editions contemporaneous with *The Pioneers*.

While it does not reproduce visual appurtenances of the Wiley-Clayton first printing,[45] the present edition is a faithful redaction of the copy-text, departing from it only to supply emendations, to furnish the 1832 Introduction augmented by two supplementary paragraphs in 1851, and the 1832 Notes. Dates of the editions containing this additional matter are indicated at appropriate points in square brackets. By referring to the Emendations and Rejected Readings lists, readers can reconstitute the historical collation of substantive variants for all authorial editions. Thus, the Cooper Edition of *The Pioneers* retains the essentials of the copy-text, substantive and accidental, while receiving the benefits of Cooper's "severe pen."

NOTES

1. James Franklin Beard, ed., *The Letters and Journals of James Fenimore Cooper* (Cambridge, Mass.: Belknap Press of Harvard University Press, 1960), II, 63. Hereafter cited as *Letters and Journals*.
2. *Letters and Journals*, I, 86.
3. *The Literary and Scientific Repository, and Critical Review*, 4 (May 1822), 505.
4. Contemporaneous newspapers establish 1 February as the date of publication. On 31 January 1823 the *New York Evening Post* noted: "The Pioneers, or Sources of the Susquehanna, a descriptive tale, in two volumes, will be published to-morrow, (Saturday,) by Charles Wiley, No. 3 Wall-st." Three advertise-

ments for the new book appeared in the 1 February issue of the *Evening Post*. In the *New York American* of the same date, seven booksellers' notices heralded the novel's appearance; two stated the book was "this day published."

5. The errata notice is a two-leaf gathering bound into Volume II after the final (twenty-eighth) gathering. In Beard, copy I, a single-leaf errata has been glued into the end of Volume I, presumably by the binder or an early owner.

6. Because it reappears in the second Wiley edition, the reading "then got" (gathering 27) is the later of the two readings. Hinman collation shows that for this gathering the second Wiley edition used the standing type of the first edition. Of the twenty copies of the first Wiley edition examined, ten read "got then" and ten "then got," while all nine copies of the second Wiley edition examined read "then got." Evidently "then got" was the reading in the forme for gathering 27 when the printing of the second edition began.

7. Four copies of W/C from the collection of James Franklin Beard (designated Beard, copies I, II, III, and IV) have been examined on the Hinman Collator. Sixteen other copies from the following libraries have been spot-checked: American Antiquarian Society (First Editions); William L. Clements Library, Ann Arbor; Columbia University Rare Book Room (B812C78 U53 1823a); Cornell Rare Books (PS 1414 A1); Dartmouth (Val 816C78 U 7314); University of Delaware (SPEC PS 1414 A1 1823 .1–2 C.1 and C.2); Historical Society of Pennsylvania (Db .4192) Vol. 2 only; Huntington 120742; Lehigh (Honeyman 818.4 C777po 1823); New York Public (*KL Rare Books); Northwestern (Special Collections 813.2 C77pi 1823 2v.); Notre Dame (Rare Books PS 1414 A2 W648, v.1–2); UCLA (Special Collections PS 1414 A1 1823); Washington University (Rare Books Spec. PS 1414 A1 1823 v.1–2); Wesleyan (Dav L3).

8. The numerical distribution of these three variants suggests that, whether they were made simultaneously or independently, the sheets containing them were bound at random. Three different and independent choices between two variables (like three tosses of a coin) yield an array of eight (2x2x2) different combinations. Seven of these combinations exist among the twenty copies of the first Wiley edition surveyed, a finding that suggests a completely random mixing of the gatherings. The seven different combinations of the three variants are shown in the following chart. As nearly as precedence can be assigned, "E" indicates early and "L" later. "X" designates the spelling "way" and "Y," "weigh." "O" signifies that the variant is on a page missing from the copy examined. Since the sequence of

States 2 through 5 has not been determined, their state number is arbitrarily assigned.

		"ix"/"xi"	"way"/"weigh"	"got then"/ "then got"
State 1	Beard, copy III	E	X	E
	Huntington	E	X	E
	New York Public	E	X	E
State 2	Dartmouth	E	X	L
	Delaware, copy II	E	X	L
State 3	UCLA	E	Y	L
	Wesleyan	E	Y	L
State 4	Clements	L	X	E
	Delaware, copy I	L	X	E
	Lehigh	L	X	E
	Northwestern	L	X	E
	Notre Dame	L	X	E
State 5	Cornell	L	Y	E
State 6	Beard, copy I	L	X	L
	Washington University	L	X	L
State 7	Beard, copy II	L	Y	L
	Columbia	L	Y	L
	Beard, copy IV	O	X	L
	American Antiquarian Society	O	Y	L
	Historical Society of Pennsylvania	O	Y	L

9. The evidence determining the earliest copy occurs at 87.20. The first letter of the word "brother" has dropped out of the forme, causing all twenty copies of W/C examined to read "rother." In Beard, copy III, the space for the missing letter is clearly present, and the remaining letters are contiguous. In the remaining copies, the letters spread out, producing various distorted versions of "rother."

10. *Letters and Journals*, I, 85–86.

11. *Ibid.*, 91–92.

12. See Robert E. Spiller and Philip C. Blackburn, *A Descriptive Bibliog-*

raphy of the Writings of James Fenimore Cooper (New York, 1934),
p. 27. Copies of the Murray edition from the following libraries
have been examined on the Hinman Collator: Wisconsin (PZ 3
C786 Pio 1823), Kansas State, Vol. I only (PZ 3 C786 Pio 3),
Illinois (X 813 C78po 1823), and American Antiquarian Society (G526 C777 P823 pion). In addition the University of
North Carolina (Greensboro) copy (rbc 813.24 C77P) was
spot-checked. The collation discovers variants resulting from
missing, broken, or displaced types, none of which is substantive.

Cooper sent three partial or complete versions—all containing independent revisions—on three different occasions. On 29
November 1822 he enclosed "matter enough to make two of
your volumes" to Murray and on 15 January 1823 forwarded
"the second volume of the 'Pioneers'" along with brief instructions for revisions. On the same day he apparently sent Murray
a "complete set [of the book], tolerably corrected," via a different ship. He sent duplicate copies of such material by different carriers to safeguard against loss and to insure
maximum speed of delivery. See *Letters and Journals*, I, 85–86,
91–92. The form of these versions was presumably unbound
sheets; for the New York *Commercial Advertiser*, in a note published on 16 January concerning the new novel, indicated that
the sheets had just been sent to the binders.

13. *Letters and Journals*, I, 86.
14. *Ibid.*, 91–92.
15. For the other 21 substantive variants common to the Murray and
Wiley-Seymour-Clayton editions, see the Emendations list at
5.1, 39.10, 50.33, 52.31, 77.40, 78.9, 107.8, 108.18, 108.31,
132.32, 139.24, 189.10, 194.18, 201.7, 204.38–39, 206.20,
209.5, 209.20, 231.5, 388.23, and 417.25.
16. At 108.31 and 189.10 both Murray and the Wiley-Seymour-Clayton editions emend forms of the verb "to fall" to "to fell."
17. The other three longer readings are at 143.1, 287.28–29, and
287.33.
18. For the other forty-five unique Murray emendations of substantives, see the Emendations list at 4.28, 52.32, 54.21, 59.37,
81.12, 89.12, 92.26, 97.13, 99.1, 113.18, 114.38, 127.8, 131.22,
132.33, 134.9, 138.2, 142.6, 147.37 (*bis*), 149.31, 165.20,
177.38, 190.34, 195.32, 206.29–30, 214.32, 219.13, 221.13–14,
238.22, 239.2, 283.23, 286.34, 287.30–31, 293.13, 294.30,
326.32, 340.39, 342.3, 345.26, 356.21, 388.22, 394.33, 414.16,
423.24, and 451.35. (Standard Novels at the second reading at
147.37 and at 89.12, 165.20, and 294.30 makes the same emendations independent of Murray.)
19. See Emendations list at 40.16–17, 47.34, 75.1, 120.17, 126.39,

142.37, 151.10, 194.39, 204.26, and 257.40. The reading at 47.34 is further revised in the Standard Novels edition.

20. The twenty-seven passages in Murray which attain final form in the Standard Novels edition are at 53.34, 110.22–23, 140.34, 143.4, 218.1, 231.1, 242.1, 251.1, 262.1, 275.1, 285.1, 296.1, 302.1, 309.5, 316.1, 326.1, 339.1, 347.1, 358.1, 373.1, 382.1, 396.1, 405.1, 414.1, 425.1, 436.1, and 446.1. The Putnam revision is at 140.8 and the one revised by the present edition at 103.40.

21. See Rejected Readings at 32.27, 54.11, 72.9, 72.18, 78.31, 80.11, 87.28, 88.29, 93.18, 111.4, 127.6, 131.6, 141.38, 145.1, 157.1, 169.1, 179.1, 189.1, 198.23, 201.1, 209.1, 249.5, 274.16, 281.25, 287.1, 292.9, 292.24, 296.25, 311.26, 312.27, 313.39, 323.33, 335.5, 339.22, 341.37, 345.36, 348.21, 349.8, 350.35, 367.9, 367.29, 374.9, 382.8, 389.5, 394.11, 407.6, 409.18, 421.9, 435.8, 444.5, 444.6, 444.10, 444.12, 446.26, 447.1, and 454.4.

22. *Commercial Advertiser*, 8 February 1823, p. 2.

23. The eleven CA substantive variants which occur also in the second Wiley edition are at 189.10, 191.10, 191.34, 194.6, 194.19, 194.29, 195.35, 196.1, 196.8, 197.13, and 294.2.

24. The three excerpted chapters were reprinted in the bi-weekly *New-York Spectator* (published by the *Commercial Advertiser* for the country trade) on 21 and 28 January 1823. Sight collation discloses no substantive variants between the two newspaper texts. Brief post-publication excerpts from *The Pioneers*, corresponding to the W/C Volume I, chs. 1, 3, 4, 13 and 19 and Volume II, chs. 9, 15 and 16, appeared in a four-part *Commercial Advertiser* review on 3, 5, 7 and 8 February 1823. Their source was apparently W/C, and they do not contain substantive variants attributable to Cooper.

25. Though it attempts to follow the earlier Clayton Volume I line for line, the Wiley-Seymour-Clayton Volume I is obviously a new type setting. Volume II of this second edition, set by Clayton, is newly set for gatherings one through twenty-one and twenty-three. The Hinman Collator shows, however, that for gatherings twenty-two and twenty-four through twenty-eight, the new edition made corrections in the standing type of the original formes used by the first edition.

For a fuller account of the differences between the two Wiley editions of *The Pioneers*, see Lance Schachterle, "The Three 1823 Editions of *The Pioneers*," *Proceedings of the American Antiquarian Society*, 84 (April 1974), 219–32.

26. *Letters and Journals*, II, 60.

27. See Philip Gaskell, *A New Introduction to Bibliography* (Oxford: Clarendon Press, 1972), p. 116.

28. *Commercial Advertiser*, 16 January 1823, p. 2. The *New-York Spectator* (4 February, p. 2) reported a sale of 3,500 copies of *The Pioneers* on the day of publication.

29. To guard against the possibility that for the second volume Clayton may have mixed together signatures from both editions, nine W/S volumes have been examined signature by signature. No gatherings from the W/C printing were found.

30. "Mohawks" is corrected to "Delawares" at 26.36; "marine" to "moreen" at 90.29 and 105.14; forms of the verb "to fall" are changed to "to fell" at 75.1, 108.31, and 189.10, and "a shapeless figure of good proportions" is corrected to "a square figure of large proportions," 47.34. The last phrase mentioned in the errata notice, "surrounding atmosphere before it," does not appear in W/C. No doubt "surrounding atmosphere in front of it" (264.40–265.1) is intended; "surrounding" is deleted from the phrase in the second Wiley edition. Deletions of "kind of" and "sort of" appear at 92.30, 105.29, 136.25, 161.36, and 340.28–29.

31. *The Pioneers* is known to have been issued from the 1827 stereotyped plates by Carey (or the related firm of Lea and Blanchard) in 1828, 1829, 1832, 1835, 1836, 1838, 1839, 1840, 1841, 1843, 1846, and 1849. In 1849 the New York firm of Stringer and Townsend issued its own cheap edition from the Carey plates; on 6 September 1850 the firm purchased all the Cooper copyrights and plates Lea and Blanchard owned, reissuing the novel in a one-volume format (see *Letters and Journals*, VI, 4). A "New Edition" issued by Stringer and Townsend in 1852 and 1853 was in fact the 1827 plates with a new title page and format. It was reissued as the "People's Edition" in 1855, 1856, 1857, and 1858, with pages and chapters numbered sequentially throughout.

32. The variant is first corrected in the 1829 Carey, Lea and Carey reimpression. The American Antiquarian Society copy (G526 C777 P827 pion) of the 1827 Carey, Lea and Carey edition has been inspected on the Hinman Collator against copies of the 1856 Stringer and Townsend (Beard), the 1857 Stringer and Townsend (Beard), and the 1858 Stringer and Townsend (American Antiquarian Society, G526 C777 P858 pion).

33. Colburn and Bentley accepted Cooper's offer to revise his early fiction on 25 March 1831. Three days later they forwarded an interleaved copy of the Carey edition of *The Spy*, urging Cooper to finish in time for publication on 1 May (see *Letters and Journals*, II, 65, notes 3 and 4). *The Spy* appeared on 2 May; allowing for mailing and printing, Cooper must have made his revisions in the first half of April 1831. Since Colburn and Bentley acknowledged the receipt of *The Pioneers* on 7 June

1831 (*Letters and Journals*, II, 94, note 1), Cooper must have revised it in either April or May 1831.

34. See *Letters and Journals*, II, 64–65, note 4. The 1829 reimpression was the most recent Carey, Lea and Carey impression of *The Pioneers* which Cooper could have used as a basis for revision.

35. Spiller and Blackburn, p. 29. Copies of the Colburn and Bentley edition (BAL 3855) have been examined on the Hinman Collator from the following libraries: American Antiquarian Society (First Editions), University of Minnesota (830.13 St2 V14), Newberry (Y 255 C 80639), University of Illinois (X 813 C78 po 1832), and Michigan State (PS 1414.A1 1832).

36. Cooper's undated holograph manuscript, entitled "Introduction of Pioneers," is deposited in the Cooper Collection of the Collection of American Literature, Beinecke Rare Book and Manuscript Library, Yale University. It is written in black ink with a few holograph revisions in the same ink. The paper, measuring 17" x 13½", is a heavy-weight, lined sheet watermarked AL PNE and folded once. The holograph fills the recto and verso of the first fold and continues for five lines on the recto of the second fold. A five-line passage to be inserted on the opposite verso occupies the bottom of the second recto. The first recto bears in the upper left corner a note in Cooper's hand: "Send a proof of this as soon as possible to W. Ollier."

37. For comparison, see *The Spy* (New York, 1821), II.131.7ff for a long version of a passage describing the roads of West Chester.

38. Substantive variants in both *The Pioneers* and *The Spy* are illustrated below. In each pair, the top left and right readings are from the first edition and the Bentley edition of *The Pioneers* respectively, the bottom left and right readings, the Carey edition and holograph revisions for *The Spy*.

Dramatization of Dialogue

223.36	language?" asked Elizabeth, with an impetuosity that spoke a lively interest in the reply.	language?"
I.58.19	"Ah!" returned the maid, looking playfully at her aunt, "you would have us think"	"Ah! you would have us think"

Short Phrase Inverted

22.12	who has failed seven times this season already	who has failed seven times already this season

| I.95.18 | blushing girl had, in her ardour, extended | blushing girl, in her ardour, had extended |

Phrases Beginning with "so" Altered

| 28.23 | So soon as the rifle bore | As soon as the rifle bore |
| II.168.2 | so soon as the recollection | as soon as the recollection |

39. Examples of substantive variants in these categories for the Bentley *Pioneers* and *Spy* follow below. The format of presentation is that described in note 38.

Plural Changed to Singular

| 25.4 | "I thank you, sir, for your good intentions" | "I thank you for your good intention" |
| I.28.14 | thrown the colony into the scales on the side of the crown | thrown the colony into the scale on the side of the crown |

Altered Preposition

| 60.1 | cranny in the building | cranny of the building |
| II.5.33 | getting the mastery over the pedler's feelings | getting the mastery of the pedler's feelings |

Altered Article

| 18.40 | to break the stillness | to break a stillness |
| I.153.6 | would you burn the house | would you burn a house |

Altered Relative Pronoun

| 40.23 | the smoke which curled over | the smoke that curled over |
| II.99.27 | that, having slipt its bridle | which, having slipt its bridle |

Possessive Pronoun Changed to Article

| 15.15 | where their sides | where the sides |
| I.74.7 | around their breakfast table | around the breakfast table |

Verb Tense Altered

| 31.8 | those, who depended rather on their hereditary possessions | those, who depend rather on their hereditary possessions |
| I.95.11 | when peace is restored | when peace shall be restored |

"Country" Changed to "County"

| 43.10 | the architecture of the country | architecture of the whole county |
| I.10.2 | The country of West-Chester | The county of West-Chester |

Unnecessary Adjective Deleted

| 15.6 | the great State of New-York | the State of New-York |
| I.17.4 | filled his companion with instant alarm | filled his companion with alarm |

Unnecessary Adverb Deleted

| 19.3 | held this their only child fondly to her bosom | held this their only child to her bosom |
| I.47.6 | speaking involuntarily in a low tone | speaking in a low tone |

Preposition Accompanying a Verb Deleted

| 17.5 | reach for several feet above the earth | reach several feet above the earth |
| I.15.28 | examining into the state of the clouds | examining the state of the clouds |

Relative Pronoun Deleted

| 16.34 | the district which we have described | the district we have described |
| II.22.3 | neither of those whom she sought | neither of those she sought |

Relative Clause Deleted

| 114.30 | a limp that he had in one leg | a limp in one leg |
| II.251.13 | men, who were mounted and equipped | men, mounted and equipped |

"Sir" Deleted

| 25.28 | "Excuse me, sir, I have need of the venison." | "Excuse me; I have need of the venison." |
| I.78.17 | "Yes, sir—I had forgotten" | "yes,—I had forgotten" |

"That" Deleted

| 55.14 | that one jerk that he gave them.” | that one jerk he gave them.” |
| II.201.18 | twice—did I think that my hour had come | twice—did I think my hour had come |

“Then” Deleted

| 48.26 | they both interfere, and then the nigh one | they interfere, and the nigh one |
| II.202.14 | but then it was the last time I should see it | but it was the last time I should see it |

“Now” Deleted

| 290.37 | But now we will talk | We will talk |
| I.151.5 | tread of the horse, now too plainly assured the pedler | tread of the horse, too plainly assured the pedler |

“Just” Deleted

| 155.32 | they looked just like an atomy | they looked like an atomy |
| II.156.2 | I’ll just thank you not to make such a noise | I’ll thank you not to make such a noise |

“And” Deleted

| 178.20 | And with this act of prudence closes | With this act of prudence closes |
| I.131.1 | muttered the Captain, in an under tone, and attentively adjusting the bandages, when | muttered the Captain, in an under tone, attentively adjusting the bandages; when |

40. The history of the Spottiswoode printing house substantiates the internal evidence that the “A. Spottiswoode” printing is a later impression than the “A. and R. Spottiswoode.” Andrew (1787–1866) and Robert (1791–1832) Spottiswoode succeeded their uncle Andrew Strahan in the management of the family business in 1819; but Robert died on 2 September 1832, leaving Andrew in sole command. Clearly the “A. and R. Spottiswoode” impression antedates 2 September 1832, while the “A. Spottiswoode” was printed sometime after Robert’s death. See Richard A. Austen-Leigh, *The Story of a Printing House Being A Short Account of the Strahans and Spottiswoodes*, 2nd ed. (London: Spottiswoode and Co., 1912), pp. 36–38.

41. Copies of the Putnam edition from the following libraries have been examined on the Hinman Collator: the American Antiquarian Society (First Editions), the Boston Athenaeum (:VEF .C78pj2), Trinity College (Watkinson PS 1414 .A1 1851) and the Buffalo and Erie County Library (PS 1414.A1 1850). The only substantive variant, at 155.8 ("so" missing in the phrase "was so much" in Boston Athenaeum copy), is attributable to a defect in the paper.

42. The copies examined on the Collator were the American Antiquarian Society's 1851 Putnam (First Editions) and the Beard 1856 Stringer and Townsend "Choice Edition." Stringer and Townsend also published *The Pioneers* by reimpressing the Putnam plates in 1854.

43. The copies examined were the 1851 American Antiquarian Society Putnam (First Editions) and the 1859 "Townsend-Darley edition" (Beard, copies I and II). The 1860 and 1861 "Darley" texts are reimpressions of 1859.

44. Comparison between the epigraphs and contemporaneous editions of their sources reveals five substantive variants: at 83.2, "utmost springs" in W/C reads "farthest springs" in *The Poems of Philip Freneau*, ed., F. L. Pattee (Princeton, N.J.: The University Library, 1902); at 242.4, "frenzy driven" reads "frenzy seiz'd" in Somerville's *The Chace* (Baltimore: F. Lucas, 1814); at 425.5, "view us victors" reads "view us as victors" in Byron's *Childe Harold's Pilgrimage* (Philadelphia: Moses Thomas, 1812); and at 446.2, "sweep ye on," and 446.3, "them who triumph," read, respectively, "sweep them on" and "them that triumph" in Scott's *The Lord of the Isles* (Eastburn, N.Y., 1818). Whatever the reasons for the variants—Cooper may have been quoting from memory, or he may have consulted texts containing the variants—the copy-text readings are retained in all cases.

45. Such visual appurtenances include type size, type style, leading, styling of chapter openings and styling of running heads.

Textual Notes

The following comments refer to specific decisions to emend or not to emend requiring fuller explanation than could be provided in the Textual Commentary.

6.31–32   The present edition accepts the Standard Novels (1832) omission of the comma but follows the manuscript hyphenation of New-York.

17.26   This and the following corruptions attributed to the Standard Novels (1832) actually originate in the Collins, Hannay and Wiley edition (1825), and were perpetuated in the Carey, Lea and Carey (1827), the Standard Novels (1832), and the Putnam (1851) editions: 18.9–10, 47.17, 71.33, 91.35, 101.36, 114.23, 136.20, 155.40, 175.7, 176.22, 177.17, 182.5–6, 182.8, 182.10, 184.34, 191.32–33, 197.12, 210.33, 218.26, 225.12, 239.35, 248.38, 250.14, 256.31, 259.11, 259.25, 262.30, 265.31, 271.26, 275.34, 277.9, 277.31, 279.9, 291.6, 292.1, 296.29, 309.5, 334.6, 340.36, 341.10, 352.15, 357.22, 365.2, 374.3, 376.25, 378.34, 408.24–25, 420.15, 421.39, 424.20, 430.7, 433.31, 436.8, 451.33, and 454.1.

18.9–10   See Textual Notes at 17.26.

18.21   Although the 1828 Webster's *Dictionary* gives "martin" as an acceptable variant of "marten," the present edition adopts the Standard Novels (1832) spelling "marten" to avoid ambiguity here and at 48.5.

18.24   Here and in the following passages the present edition accepts the Standard Novels (1832) substantive variant but follows the accidentals—spelling, hyphenation, or capitalization—of the copy-text: 38.34, 111.40, 113.6, 196.36, 253.30, 313.24, 362.30, and 430.16.

20.7   Here the present edition accepts the substantive variant of the Putnam edition (which coincidentally reverts to the copy-text omission of the pronoun) but reinstates the copy-text spelling of the verb.

24.6   To avoid ambiguity in passages referring to Judge Temple, the present edition has followed editions revised by Cooper in capitalizing "judge."

25.29   See Textual Notes at 24.6.

26.31   This and the following corruptions attributed to the Standard Novels edition actually originate in the Carey, Lea and Carey edition (1827) and are perpetuated in the Standard Novels (1832) and the Putnam (1851) editions: 167.3, 176.26, 210.33, 218.8, 309.14 (*bis*), 311.24, 314.12, 365.8, 404.9, 419.4, 419.32, and 456.32.

38.34	See Textual Notes at 18.24.
43.15–22	In this passage the present edition accepts the long variant appearing in the Standard Novels first impression, but emends the erroneous "Templeton" to "Temple." The present edition also emends "excellences" to "excellencies" in accordance with Webster's 1828 *Dictionary*.
47.17	See Textual Notes at 17.26.
48.5	See Textual Notes at 18.21.
52.4–8	The Standard Novels prints this emendation in CE as a footnote without a superscript asterisk in the text. This fact and the fact that the referent of the pronoun "he" (at 52.9) is ambiguous when the paragraph is printed as a footnote suggest strongly that Cooper intended the paragraph to appear in the text following Richard's speech. The improper positioning of the paragraph evidently resulted from a misinterpretation of Cooper's instructions on the interleaved scribal copy prepared for Colburn and Bentley.
53.13	This and the following corrections attributed to the Standard Novels (1832) actually originate in the Collins, Hannay and Wiley edition (1825): 58.34–59.1, 90.12, and 237.9.
58.34–59.1	See Textual Notes at 53.13.
59.7	The present edition has emended "his" to "its" to conform to the Wiley-Seymour (1823) alterations of pronouns at 59.5 and 59.6.
69.26	To avoid ambiguity in passages referring to the Temple Patent, the present edition has followed editions revised by Cooper in capitalizing "patent."
70.3	In dialect passages the present edition has emended first-edition misspellings of proper names in instances where such misspellings clearly do not represent dialect pronunciations. Such misspellings are regarded as first-edition errors corrected in subsequent editions. See also "Whitefield" at 147.21 and 148.18.
71.33	See Textual Notes at 17.26.
85.15	To avoid confusion the editors have adopted the hyphenated "Leather-stocking" in this unique instance where the form appears without hyphenation in the copy-text.
90.12	See Textual Notes at 53.13.
91.35	See Textual Notes at 17.26.
101.36	See Textual Notes at 17.26.
103.40	The Murray (1823) variant reading "days before to" is obviously an error. Since Cooper evidently meant to replace the copy-text reading "previously to" with "before," the present edition deletes the superfluous preposition.
105.14	The Wiley-Seymour (1823) form "moreen" is preferred to the

Murray (1823) form "morenne" here; the errata notice of the copy-text clarifies Cooper's preference.

109.25   Since Remarkable Pettibone is unmarried, the present edition here and at 173.1 has accepted the Wiley-Seymour (1823) emendation of "Mrs." to "Mistress." "Mistress" is, of course, used here in the second sense given in the 1828 Webster's *Dictionary*: "the female head of a family."

111.40   See Textual Notes at 18.24.

113.6–7   See Textual Notes at 18.24.

114.23   See Textual Notes at 17.26.

120.16   The present edition has rejected the Standard Novels "belle" as a suspected editorial sophistication of the copy-text dialect "bootiful."

136.20   See Textual Notes at 17.26.

147.21   See Textual Notes at 70.3.

148.18   See Textual Notes at 70.3.

154.36   For clarity, the present edition here adopts the Wiley-Seymour (1823) capitalization of "Big Sarpent."

155.40   See Textual Notes at 17.26.

167.3   See Textual Notes at 26.31.

170.32   In the copy-text phrase, "as a salvo to her dignity," "salvo" is a presumed compositorial misreading of "salve." The present edition on its own authority therefore emends "salvo" to "salve."

173.1   See Textual Notes at 109.25.

175.7   See Textual Notes at 17.26.

176.22   See Textual Notes at 17.26.

176.26   See Textual Notes at 26.31.

176.26   The Standard Novels (1832) "long-line" has been rejected in favor of the copy-text "log-line." Though the OED definition of "long-line" as a "deep-sea fishing-line" might fit the context, the editors believe the more common "log-line," "a line of 100 fathoms or more to which the log is attached" (OED) was intended. Webster's 1828 *Dictionary* gives "log-line," but not "long-line."

177.17   See Textual Notes at 17.26.

182.5–6   See Textual Notes at 17.26.

182.8   See Textual Notes at 17.26.

182.10   See Textual Notes at 17.26.

184.34   See Textual Notes at 17.26.

191.32–33   See Textual Notes at 17.26.

196.36	See Textual Notes at 18.24.
197.12	See Textual Notes at 17.26.
197.13	Both *Commercial Advertiser* (1823) and Wiley-Seymour (1823) emend the copy-text "best ammunition" to "best of ammunition." Carey, Lea and Carey (1827), however, drops the "of," a corruption perpetuated by Standard Novels (1832) and Putnam (1851), and rejected by the present edition.
209.2	To avoid confusion the present edition has emended the comma after "boy" in the epigraph to a period.
210.33	See Textual Notes at 26.31.
210.33	See Textual Notes at 17.26.
218.8	See Textual Notes at 26.31.
218.26	See Textual Notes at 17.26.
225.12	See Textual Notes at 17.26.
237.9	See Textual Notes at 53.13.
239.35	See Textual Notes at 17.26.
242.25	This emendation entry contains a hidden corruption initiated by the Collins, Hannay and Wiley (1825) which is deleted by the Standard Novels revision. The copy-text phrase "for an opening, where they might obtain a resting-place" is corrupted in the Collins, Hannay and Wiley to "... find a resting-place." The Standard Novels (1832) drops the phrase, reading "for a resting-place."
245.39	To avoid ambiguity in passages referring to Sheriff Jones, the present edition has followed editions revised by Cooper in capitalizing "sheriff."
248.38	See Textual Notes at 17.26.
250.14	See Textual Notes at 17.26.
253.30	See Textual Notes at 18.24.
256.31	See Textual Notes at 17.26.
259.11	See Textual Notes at 17.26.
259.25	See Textual Notes at 17.26.
260.36	See Textual Notes at 69.26.
262.30	See Textual Notes at 17.26.
265.31	See Textual Notes at 17.26.
265.36	Here Cooper in Wiley-Seymour (1823) emended the copy-text "Natty, as his tall figure stalked over the narrow beach, and ascended to the little grassy bottom. ..." to "Natty, his tall figure stalking over the narrow beach, and ascended to the little grassy bottom. ..." The present edition maintains parallel construction by adopting the Carey, Lea and Carey (1827) emendation of the

second verb to a participle. The entry cites the Standard Novels (1832) as the first authorial edition containing the correction.

271.26   See Textual Notes at 17.26.

275.34   See Textual Notes at 17.26.

277.9   See Textual Notes at 17.26.

277.31   See Textual Notes at 17.26.

279.9   See Textual Notes at 17.26.

291.6   See Textual Notes at 17.26.

292.1   See Textual Notes at 17.26.

294.24–25   The editors have supplied the "not" before "without," an emendation required by the context. No edition in Cooper's lifetime noticed the omitted negative, without which Natty's paean to Providence is nonsense.

296.29   See Textual Notes at 17.26.

309.5   See Textual Notes at 17.26.

309.14 (*bis*)   See Textual Notes at 26.31.

309.37   The editors have emended the copy-text "them" to "it," making the pronoun agree with the Standard Novels (1832) emendation of the passage at 309.36.

311.24   See Textual Notes at 26.31.

313.24   See Textual Notes at 18.24.

314.12   See Textual Notes at 26.31.

320.7   For clarity the present edition twice in this line follows the Wiley-Seymour (1823), emending to avoid the confusion of the copy-text accidentals.

327.11   Authority for the emendation of "alongside" to "nearer" is the Standard Novels (1832), but authority for the correction of the misspelling of the verb is the present edition.

334.6   See Textual Notes at 17.26.

340.36   See Textual Notes at 17.26.

341.10   See Textual Notes at 17.26.

351.20   The present edition has retained the copy-text spelling "way" (in the phrase "getting under way") in preference to "weigh," the form found in the three later states of the first edition and in all subsequent authorial editions. At 353.34, the Wiley-Seymour (1823) emends the copy-text spelling "weigh" to "way," suggesting Cooper's preference for "way," the correct form according to the OED. Had he been revising for the Wiley-Seymour on sheets from an early press run of the Wiley-Clayton, he could not, of course, have corrected the spelling at 351.20.

352.15	See Textual Notes at 17.26.
357.22	See Textual Notes at 17.26.
361.9	The phrase "searching the cause" in the Standard Novels (1832) is apparently an incompletely executed compression of the copy-text phrase "in search of the cause." The present edition inserts the preposition "for," which Cooper presumably intended.
362.30	See Textual Notes at 18.24.
365.2	See Textual Notes at 17.26.
365.8	See Textual Notes at 26.31.
371.37	To avoid ambiguity the present edition has followed editions revised by Cooper in capitalizing the name of the inn.
374.3	See Textual Notes at 17.26.
376.25	See Textual Notes at 17.26.
378.34	See Textual Notes at 17.26.
385.21	See Textual Notes at 371.37.
392.12	See Textual Notes at 371.37.
404.9	See Textual Notes at 26.31.
408.24–25	See Textual Notes at 17.26.
419.4	See Textual Notes at 26.31.
419.32	See Textual Notes at 26.31.
420.15	See Textual Notes at 17.26.
421.39	See Textual Notes at 17.26.
424.20	See Textual Notes at 17.26.
427.25	See Textual Notes at 245.39.
428.25	The present edition has followed Standard Novels (1832) in breaking the long passage beginning at 427.24 into two paragraphs. Similar divisions of long paragraphs into two or more shorter ones occur in Cooper's holograph revisions of *The Spy*; but authority for the division here is the present edition.
430.7	See Textual Notes at 17.26.
430.16	See Textual Notes at 18.24.
433.31	See Textual Notes at 17.26.
436.8	See Textual Notes at 17.26.
451.33	See Textual Notes at 17.26.
454.1	See Textual Notes at 17.26.
456.32	See Textual Notes at 26.31.

Emendations

The following list records all changes in substantives and accidentals introduced into the copy-text. The reading of the present edition appears to the left of the square bracket. The source for that reading appears to the right of the bracket, followed by a semicolon, the copy-text reading, and the copy-text symbol. If not listed, the readings of texts which fall between the copy-text and the source cited for the reading of the present edition may be presumed to agree substantively with the copy-text reading. If an intervening reading does not agree substantively with the copy-text, that intervening reading and its symbol are recorded after the copy-text reading and symbol.

Within an entry, the curved dash ~ represents the exact word that appears before the square bracket and is used in recording punctuation and paragraphing variants. A caret ʌ to the right of the square bracket signals the absence of a mark of punctuation on the left. An asterisk indicates that the reading is discussed in the Textual Notes. The abbreviation CE identifies emendations initiated by the present edition. Ellipses to the left of the square bracket indicate an extensive reading in the present edition. Ellipses to the right of the square bracket refer to a passage quoted earlier in the entry.

The following texts are referred to:

AMS Author's Manuscript: "Introduction of Pioneers," 1832.

A₁ *The Pioneers*. New York: Wiley, 1823. [Clayton printing]. First state.

A₂ *The Pioneers*. New York: Wiley, 1823. [Clayton printing]. Second state.

A₃ *The Pioneers*. New York: Wiley, 1823. [Clayton printing]. Third state.

A₄ *The Pioneers*. New York: Wiley, 1823. [Clayton printing]. Fourth state.

A₅ *The Pioneers*. New York: Wiley, 1823. [Clayton printing]. Fifth state.

A₆ *The Pioneers*. New York: Wiley, 1823. [Clayton printing]. Sixth state.

A₇ *The Pioneers*. New York: Wiley, 1823. [Clayton printing]. Seventh state.

B *The Pioneers*. London: Murray, 1823.

C *The Pioneers*. [excerpts] New York: *Commercial Advertiser*, 18 and 25 January 1823.

D₁ *The Pioneers*. New York: Wiley, 1823. [Seymour Volume I printing; Clayton Volume II printing]. First state.

D₂ *The Pioneers*. New York: Wiley, 1823. [Seymour Volume I printing; Clayton. Volume II printing]. Second state.

E₁ *The Pioneers*. London: Colburn and Bentley, 1832. [A. and R. Spottiswoode printing]. First impression.

E₂ *The Pioneers*. London: Colburn and Bentley, 1832. [A. Spottiswoode printing]. Second impression.

F *The Pioneers*. New York: Putnam, 1851.

EMENDATIONS

title page Paulding, *The Backswoodsman*, II. 571-4.]CE; *Paulding* A₁

dedication page SCHOHARIE CE; SCOHARIE A₁

4.28 beautiful]B; beauteous A₁

5.1 are]B; be A₁

6.1 INTRODUCTION]E₁; Introduction of Pioneers AMS

6.16 latter]E₁; latter[;?] AMS

6.30 a little]F; rather AMS

*6.31-32 New-York]CE; New-York, AMS; New York E₁

6.32 northerly]E₁; ~, AMS

6.34 lands.]E₁; ~∧ AMS

7.25 where]E₁; whenc[e?] AMS

7.33 being]E₁; ~, AMS

7.33 mountains]E₁; mountain AMS

8.4 on]F; in AMS

8.14 for opening a]F; of opening AMS; of opening a A₁

8.22-23 life, that,]F; life that when AMS

8.23 century, when]F; century, AMS

8.25 county,]E₁; county, that AMS

8.27 Otsego]E₁; Otego AMS

8.29 that an]F; that AMS; that that E₁-E₂

8.31 Dr.]E₁; ~∧ AMS

8.35 ever since, at intervals]F; at intervals, in later life AMS

9.8-9 tolerably exact]F; exact AMS

9.11-12 principal dwelling: the]F; Mansion House ——[?] The AMS; mansion house: the E₁-E₂

9.16 he had]E₁; had AMS

9.17 arm]E₁; arm[s?] AMS

9.22 fancy,]E₁; ~∧ AMS

9.32 counterpoise,]E₁; ~∧ AMS

10.1 are]E₁; are[,?] AMS

10.5 the book]F; it AMS

10.11 Paris, March, 1832]E₁; [*omitted*] AMS

11.6-24 It may . . . . fiction]F; [*omitted*] AMS

15.5 Thomson, *The Seasons,* "Winter," 1-3]CE; *Thompson* A₁; *Thomson* B,E₁-F

15.6 State]E₁; great State A₁

15.11 region]E₁; country A₁

15.12 Susquehanna]E₁; mighty Susquehanna A₁

15.13 uniting their streams]E₁; uniting A₁

15.13-14 rivers of the United States]E₁; streams of which the old United States could boast A₁

15.15 tops]E₁; top A₁

15.15 the sides]E₁; their sides A₁

15.16-17 to the country that romantic and picturesque character]E₁; that romantic character to the country, A₁

15.19 each]E₁; each, now gliding peacefully under the brow of one of the hills, and then suddenly shooting across the plain, to wash the feet of its opposite rival A₁

15.27 edifices]E₁; edifices for the encouragement A₁

15.29 worship]E₁; public worship A₁

16.2 part]E₁; distinct and independent part A₁

16.8 years* [*footnote*] *The book . . . 1821–22]CE; years A₁; years* [*footnote*] *The book . . . 1823 E₁-F

16.8 territory]E₁; whole territory A₁

16.15 its]E₁; her A₁

16.20 country, which]E₁; country that A₁

16.22 the population]E₁; her population A₁

16.23 to a]E₁; to the powerful number of nearly a A₁

16.24 half of inhabitants†, [*footnote*] †The population . . . 2,000,000.]E₁; half A₁

16.26 shall]E₁; will A₁ (*Also emended on the authority of E₁ at 96.8, 128.19, and 178.7.*)

16.33 December]E₁; December of that year A₁

16.34 district]E₁; district which A₁

17.1 piled]E₁; piled for many feet, A₁

17.5 reach]E₁; reach for A₁

17.5-6 alike buried beneath]E₁;

promiscuously buried under A_1

17.6 barely wide]D_1; of barely width A_1

17.7 sleigh* [*footnote*] *Sleigh . . . . "jumper," . . . . forests.]CE; sleigh A_1; sleigh* . . . . "gumper," . . . . forests. E_1-F

17.8 sunk nearly]F; sunken near A_1

17.9 lower]E_1; beneath them A_1

17.14 the summit itself remained in]E_1; on this summit itself, it yet remained a A_1; the summit itself yet remained a D_1-D_2

17.17 hoar frost]E_1; frost A_1

17.21 was of]D_1; was A_1

17.24 those]E_1; the A_1

17.26 nails]E_1; nails of the same material A_1

17.26 that]E_1; that admirably A_1

18.1-3 filled . . . . Still]E_1; were moistened with a liquid that flowed from the same cause; still A_1

18.5 of]E_1; of his A_1

18.7 old-fashioned]D_1; old-fashioned, A_1

18.9 The colour of its]E_1; Its A_1

18.10 that of its inside]E_1; its inside of A_1

18.10 red. The latter]E_1; red, that A_1

18.19 ornamented]E_1; ornamented, if it were not made more comfortable, A_1

*18.21 marten]E_1; martin A_1

18.23 fastened]E_1; were fastened A_1

*18.24 ribbon. The top of the cap]CE; ribbon; its top A_1; riband; its top D_1-D_2; riband. The top of the cap E_1-F

18.25-26 rest of the materials]E_1; materials for the cap A_1

18.31 garments]E_1; multitude and variety of garments which A_1

18.37 jet-black eyes]E_1; eyes of the deepest black A_1

18.39 two travellers]F; travellers A_1

18.40 reflections]E_1; different reflections A_1

18.40 a stillness]E_1; the stillness A_1

19.3 child]E_1; child fondly A_1

19.5-6 of an education, which the

city of New York could only offer at that period]E_1; which the city could afford to her education A_1

19.8 of his]D_1; to his A_1

19.13 scenery]E_1; scenery that A_1

19.16 some seventy]E_1; seventy A_1

19.17-18 doubled that height, by the addition of the tops]E_1; towered to an additional height, that more than equalled that elevation A_1

19.24 forth]E_1; forth their A_1

19.29 plaintive]E_1; sighing A_1

19.30 rest of the melancholy scene]E_1; scene A_1

19.33 forest]E_1; forest, which were lighted by the unsullied covering of the earth A_1

19.36 sound]F; sounds A_1

19.36 gentleman,]E_1; gentleman, whatever might have been the subject of his meditations, he forgot it; for A_1

19.40 game]E_1; game, you hear A_1

*20.7 stept]CE; stept A_1; he stept E_1-E_2; stepped F

20.9 yielding]E_1; yielding more than an inch or two. A storm of sleet had fallen and frozen upon the surface a few days before, and but a slight snow had occurred since to purify, without weakening its covering. A_1

20.16 a fine]E_1; directly a fine A_1

20.22 trigger. The]E_1; trigger; but the A_1

20.24 his]E_1; his intended A_1

20.30 road]E_1; road before her A_1

20.30 sharp, quick]D_1; flat, dull A_1

20.37 crust]E_1; crust once or twice A_1

20.38 marksman,]E_1; marksman, as triumphing in his better aim; A_1

21.3 should]E_1; would A_1

21.6 his]F; the A_1

21.7 exhilarating]E_1; exhilirating A_1

21.7 to]E_1; to let me A_1

21.14 that]E_1; that robin A_1

21.17 them at pleasure]E_1; enough for a pot-pye A_1

21.24 it has]E_1; has A_1

21.27 hurts]E₁; hurts that he has received A₁

21.27 the neck]E₁; his neck A₁

21.28 the heart]E₁; his heart A₁

21.34 would ask]E₁; want to know A₁

21.36 this]E₁; this is A₁

22.12 already this season]E₁; this season already A₁

22.16 compelled]E₁; disdainful A₁

22.19 so]E₁; so from the cretur A₁

22.26 that was]E₁; I was A₁

22.27 than]E₁; nor A₁

22.31 attracted]E₁; struck A₁

22.33 moment]D₁; moment that A₁

22.33 he]E₁; he first A₁

22.39 yet it]E₁; yet A₁

23.14-15 Leather-stocking]E₁; Leather-stocking, notwithstanding his legs were protected beneath, in winter, by thick garments of woolen, duly made of good blue yarn A₁

23.17 powder]E₁; dark powder that A₁

23.26 he exclaimed]E₁; exclaimed A₁

23.28 death]E₁; capture A₁

*24.6 Judge]D₁; judge A₁ (*Also first capitalized in D₁ at* 24.17, 24.24, 24.36, *and* 25.9.)

24.24 a little]E₁; gravely, a little A₁

24.29 bark]E₁; rough bark A₁

25.3 afterwards]E₁; afterwards, too A₁

25.4 you]E₁; you, sir, A₁

25.4 intention]E₁; intentions A₁

25.4 I must]E₁; must A₁

25.16-17 but he waited until the other had done speaking.]E₁; and now muttered in an under tone—— A₁

25.19 on]E₁; in A₁

25.20 him," he said. "But]E₁; him. But A₁

25.21 heard]E₁; heard tell A₁

25.23 of]E₁; of them A₁

25.25 uncertain]E₁; fancified A₁

25.28 me;]E₁; me, sir, A₁

*25.29 Judge]E₁; judge A₁ (*Also first capitalized in E₁ at* 26.9, 26.21, 27.20 *and* 31.28.)

25.30 to]E₁; to nearly A₁

25.31 a hundred]D₁; an hundred A₁

25.35 again]E₁; again proudly A₁

26.3 aid]E₁; aid for your hurts A₁

26.6 distance]E₁; haughty distance A₁

26.12 hand, and]D₁; hand A₁

26.13 sleigh]D₁; sleigh, and A₁

26.15 this]D₁; here A₁

26.19 return]E₁; be returned to thy A₁

26.21 but he]E₁; but A₁

26.23 which expressed]D₁; expressing A₁

26.26 in]E₁; in deep and A₁

26.36 Delawares]D₁; Mohawks A₁

27.8 and]E₁; and so A₁

27.14 of]E₁; of their A₁

27.17 reluctance]E₁; reluctance expressed in his manner A₁

27.24 than]E₁; nor A₁

27.37 fifty]E₁; forty A₁

28.3 to-night]B; to night A₁

28.5 silence. He then]E₁; silence, and A₁

28.7 pine]E₁; pine near him A₁

28.22-23 so erect, as to form]E₁; erect, that formed A₁

28.23 As]E₁; So A₁

28.31-32 a tit]E₁; a nice tit A₁

28.33 than]E₁; nor A₁

28.39 steps that]E₁; short and quick steps, that A₁

29.1 movement]E₁; movement that A₁

29.1 made,]E₁; ~ ∧ A₁

29.5 concealed by]D₁; hid amongst A₁

29.9 hid]E₁; hid A₁; hidden D₁-D₂

30.5 king.——"]CE; ~.——∧ A₁

30.6 *Richard II,* I.iii.275–76, 279–80]CE; *Richard II* A₁

31.8 depend]E₁; depended A₁

31.15 a healthful]D₁; an healthful A₁

31.18 re-ascend in]E₁; re-ascend A₁

31.19-20 marriage, which aided]E₁; marriage that he formed, which aided greatly A₁

31.21 in a rather better manner]D₁; rather better A₁

31.22 in]D₁; of A₁
31.29 life]E₁; life, when the early inclination for each other in the boys, was matured into friendship A₁
31.32 few]E₁; very few A₁
31.34-35 domestic]E₁; their domestic A₁
31.36 youth]E₁; youth to approaching age A₁
31.38 was]E₁; was, sixty years ago, A₁
31.39 services, sixty years ago]E₁; services A₁
32.4 who]E₁; who, in a visit to the falls, A₁
32.4 Niagara]E₁; Niagara, by spending a day at Newark A₁
32.13 splendour,]E₁; splendour, it is not to be doubted but that A₁
32.21 proffered]E₁; proffered to his acceptance A₁
32.30 Major]D₁; major A₁
33.3 importance rapidly declining]D₁; rapidly losing his importance A₁
33.6-7 a natural]D₁; the natural A₁
33.7 by]D₁; of A₁
33.10 donation;]D₁; gift, A₁
33.27 produce]F; promise A₁
33.29 was easily completed]F; left entirely to the dictates of his own judgemnt A₁; were easily completed E₁
33.35 which]D₁; which was A₁
33.36 intercourse, was]D₁; intercourse, A₁
33.40 pursuit;]E₁; pursuit; and every sentiment of young Effingham was opposed to the confession of an arrangement, which he only reconciled to his private feelings, by a knowledge of his own motives A₁; pursuit . . . to the acknowledgement of an arrangement . . . motives D₁-D₂
34.9 defence]E₁; defence only A₁
34.13 withholding]B; witholding A₁
34.15 soldier]E₁; gallant soldier A₁
34.18 which]D₁; that A₁ (*Also emended at* 113.26 *and* 157.14)
34.28 frames]D₁; stature A₁

34.33 what ought]E₁; ought A₁
34.40 said]F; seen A₁
35.3-4 which would have descended to his]B; of his A₁
35.9 without, not only the pale, but]D₁; out, not only of the pale, but of A₁
35.14 our tale]D₁; events A₁
35.23 returns]E₁; returns for the labour and hazard incurred A₁
35.25 frequent. There]E₁; frequent; so that there A₁; frequent; and there D₁-D₂
35.30 loyalty]E₁; loyalty by his father A₁
36.21 remove]E₁; remove to the interior A₁
36.30 extensive]D₁; very extensive A₁
36.30 low]E₁; very low A₁
37.5 ended]E₁; was ended A₁
37.5 states was]E₁; states A₁
37.6-7 pursuit]E₁; pursuits A₁
37.10 enterprise]F; enterprises A₁
37.13 ranked]E₁; to be ranked A₁
37.17 too long]D₁; long A₁
37.29 ranking]D₁; being A₁
38.10 fame."]CE; ~.∧ A₁
38.11 time]B; while A₁
38.11 elapsed]E₁; elapsed, after the horses had resumed their journey A₁
38.19-20 a look]E₁; a contraction of the brows, and a look A₁
38.23 His anxiety]E₁; The passion A₁
38.24 even when]E₁; when A₁
38.26 his]E₁; the young man's A₁
38.29 sat silent, and apparently]E₁; sate in silent and, apparently, abstracted A₁
38.31 said]E₁; spoke A₁
38.32 you]E₁; your name A₁
38.33 familiar]E₁; familiar to me A₁
*38.34 bucks'-tails]CE; buck's-tails A₁; bucks' tails E₁-F
38.36 since]E₁; since, sir A₁
39.1 twice]E₁; more than A₁
39.6 thou,]B; ~∧ A₁
39.10 More able]B; Abler A₁
39.11 hood]D₁; hood, again A₁

39.14 thanksgiving]E₁; thanksgivings A₁

39.15 one."]E₁; one." ¶ A slightly scornful smile passed over the features of the youth, at the archness of the first part of this speech; but it instantly vanished, as he listened to the tremulous tones in which it was concluded. The Judge, also, seemed to be affected with the consciousness of how narrowly he had escaped taking the life of a fellow creature, and, for some time, there was a dead silence in the sleigh. A₁

39.16 soon]D₁; had A₁

39.17 the journey]E₁; their journey A₁

39.18 heads]E₁; heads, uneasily, up and down A₁

39.20 descended]D₁; pitched A₁

39.23 smoke]E₁; dense smoke A₁

39.23 above]E₁; along the air from A₁

39.28 his auditors]E₁; the youth and maiden A₁

39.28 met]E₁; met, as the Judge, in the warmth of his feelings, thus included them in an association which was to endure so long A₁

39.28-29 if the colour, that gathered over the face]E₁; if the deepening colour, that, notwithstanding her hood, might be seen gathering over the face even to the forehead A₁

39.29 contradicted]E₁; contradicted in its language A₁

39.30 cold]E₁; proud A₁

39.30 ambiguous]E₁; scornful but covert A₁

39.37 was]E₁; was yet A₁

39.40 given]E₁; given to A₁

40.3 childhood]E₁; her childhood A₁

40.4-13 Immediately . . . . village]E₁; On the right, and stretching for several miles to the north, lay a narrow plain, buried among mountains, which, falling occasionally, jutted in long low points, that were covered with tall trees, into the valley; and then again, for miles, stretched their lofty brows perpendicularly along its margin, nourishing in the crags that formed their sides, pines and hemlocks thinly interspersed with chesnut and birch, that grew in lines nearly parallel to the mountains themselves. The dark foliage of the evergreens was brilliantly contrasted by the glittering whiteness of the plain, which exhibited, over the tops of the trees, and through the vistas formed by the advancing points of the hills, a single sheet of unspotted snow, relieved occasionally by a few small dark objects that were discovered, as they were passing directly beneath the feet of the travellers, to be sleighs moving in various directions. A₁; On . . . chesnut and beech, which grew . . . . directions. D₁-D₂

40.16 or were]E₁; and were A₁

40.16-17 into terraces and hollows]D₁; into kind of terraces A₁; into a kind of terraces B

40.20 beech]D₁; birch A₁

40.23 which]E₁; that A₁

40.23 that]E₁; which A₁

40.33-34 this remarkable plain, on which no plant had taken root,]E₁; the plain A₁

40.37-38 an oak]E₁; a mighty oak A₁

41.2 the wildness]E₁; all the wildness A₁

41.3 liberty]E₁; unrestrained liberty A₁

41.9 was to be traced, for]E₁; might be traced for a few A₁

41.15 continued, far as the eye could reach,]E₁; continued for many miles A₁

41.15-16 graceful valley]E₁; level plain A₁

41.19 lake and at its foot]F; lake A₁; lake and its fort E₁

41.20 some]E₁; about A₁
41.22 no great marks]E₁; not only
strong marks of the absence A₁
41.22 but which]E₁; but A₁
41.23 unfinished]E₁; slovenly and
unfinished A₁
41.28 the edifices]E₁; their edifices
A₁
41.33 grouped]F; grouped together
A₁
41.35 looked]E₁; looked far ahead
A₁
41.39 which, at that season at
least,]E₁; that A₁
42.1 pretending]D₁; more
pretending A₁
42.5 favoured]D₁; favorite A₁
42.7 dwellings]D₁; habitations A₁
42.9 to]E₁; to supply A₁
42.9 title]E₁; significant title A₁
42.13 towering]E₁; towering
proudly A₁
42.14 of]E₁; that included A₁
42.15 the latter had been left by the
Indians]E₁; these were of Indian
origin A₁
42.17 therein]D₁; thereby A₁
42.18 fences of]F; fences in A₁
42.20 Lombardy poplars]E₁;
poplars A₁
42.24 certain Mr.]E₁; Mr. A₁
42.25 his]E₁; a certain A₁
42.26 an entire]E₁; his A₁
42.28 Temple]E₁; Temple's
business A₁
42.31 every]E₁; a A₁
42.34 little]E₁; but little A₁
42.35 three]E₁; for three A₁
42.37 eastern]D₁; ~, A₁
42.38 soiled]E₁; soiled A₁; solid
D₁-D₂
43.2-3 Not that Mr. Jones did not
affect to consider]E₁; Not, but
what Mr. Jones affected to
consider Mr. A₁
43.7 secret admiration]E₁; a secret
admiration of their truth A₁
43.9 but they]E₁; but A₁
43.10 whole county]E₁; country A₁
43.13 useful of all]E₁; useful A₁
*43.15-22 proposition . . . as Judge
Temple's dwelling . . .

excellencies . . . of it]CE;
proposition, Richard very gravely
assented, and it was by this
unison in sentiment, that the
composite order, or a style of
architecture that emanated from
the carpenter's own genius, with
a few suggestions from the other,
became the fashion of the new
county A₁; proposition . . . as
Judge Templeton's dwelling . . .
excellences . . . of it E₁
43.23 square]E₁; square, formal
A₁
43.26 assigned]E₁; resigned A₁
43.27-44.6 the material . . . .
faces]E₁; but little opportunity
for the display of their talents on
a stone edifice, excepting in the
roof and in the porch. The
former, it was soon decided,
should be made with four faces
and a platform, in order to hide a
part of the building, that all
writers agreed, was an object that
ought to be concealed A₁
44.15 effect]E₁; effect that was to be
produced by this offspring of
compound genius A₁
44.16 raised]E₁; raised, with much
labour A₁
44.18-19 whole edifice]E₁; edifice
A₁
44.21 laid only multiplied]E₁; laid,
was only multiplying A₁
44.28 smoke]E₁; light smoke A₁
44.29-36 an experiment . . . .
head]E₁; which he laid on with a
belief, that the deformity might
be blended with the back-ground
of pines, that rose, in tall
grandeur, but a short distance in
the rear of the mansion house.
But all these ingenious
expedients, entirely failed, and
our artists relinquished the desire
to conceal, and attempted to
ornament, the offensive member.
The last colour that Richard
bestowed on the luckless roof,
was a sun-shiny yellow; so called,
both from its resemblance to, and

its powers to resist, the rays of the great luminary A_1

44.37 eaves]E_1; eves A_1

44.40 part]D_1; wooden part A_1

45.7 roof was]E_1; was A_1

45.7-8 architectural undertaking]E_1; undertaking A_1

45.10 proceeded]E_1; all proceeded A_1

45.13-14 for the defects, he]D_1; for A_1

45.16 was, as has been said,]E_1; was A_1

45.21 of]D_1; for A_1

45.24 air]E_1; air both A_1

45.29 pine]E_1; mighty pine A_1

45.31 black,]E_1; black and A_1

45.32 columns]E_1; columns, for A_1

45.38 these and many other]E_1; these A_1

45.39 unseen]E_1; unnoticed A_1

45.40 moved]E_1; slowly moved A_1

46.2 curling]E_1; diagonally curling A_1

46.7 towards the]E_1; already, towards the far A_1

46.8 childhood]E_1; childhood and of joy A_1

46.9 had]E_1; had, here, A_1

46.10 countries]E_1; older countries A_1

46.12 less]F; less of A_1

46.14 bursts]E_1; burst A_1

46.16 and sunk]E_1; and then sunk A_1

46.21 attracted]E_1; soon attracted A_1

46.22 sides]D_1; side A_1

46.23 announced]E_1; announced both A_1

46.24 interrupted]D_1; frequently interrupted A_1

46.25-26 and the two sleighs were close upon each other before either was seen]E_1; so that they were close upon this vehicle, before they discovered who were its occupants A_1; and they . . . occupants D_1-D_2

47.2 "How]CE; ∧~ A_1

47.2 matter?"]CE; ~?∧ A_1

47.3 *2 Henry IV*, II.i.43–44]CE; *Falstaff* A_1

47.4 A large]E_1; A few minutes resolved whatever doubts our travellers entertained, as to the description of those, who were approaching them with such exhilirating sounds. A large A_1

47.6 road]E_1; road that was here, as on the other side of the mountain, cut into the hill A_1

47.8 of the]E_1; of these A_1; of those D_1-D_2

47.11-12 arrangement acquainted the Judge with]E_1; arrangement, satisfied the Judge as to A_1

47.15 enveloped]D_1; who was enveloped A_1

47.15 coat]D_1; coat that was A_1

47.16 in such a manner]D_1; so A_1 ·

47.17 a face,]D_1; his face, which was A_1

47.18 if]E_1; if it were A_1

47.19 its natural]E_1; the A_1

47.19 earth]E_1; earth that nature had decreed in his stature A_1

47.21 animals]E_1; animals that he drove A_1

47.25-26 the appearance of strength]D_1; an air of strength and dimensions A_1

47.30 for]F; as A_1

47.31 their light, blue, glassy balls projected]E_1; they projected their light, blue, glassy balls A_1

47.32 was]E_1; was a colour A_1

47.34 a solid, short, and square figure]E_1; a shapeless figure of good proportions A_1; a shapeless figure of a large stature B; a square figure of large proportions D_1-D_2

48.1 face]E_1; full face with an agreeable expression, A_1

48.2 black eyes]E_1; animated black eyes of a lurking look A_1

*48.5 marten-skin caps]E_1; martin-skin caps as outward coverings for their heads A_1

48.7 than that which]D_1; than A_1

48.11-12 and withal . . . complexion]E_1; with a little melancholy, but so slightly expressed, as to leave the beholder in doubt, whether it proceeded from mental or bodily ailment A$_1$

48.14 contrasted]D$_1$; as contrasted A$_1$

48.15 habitual mental care]E$_1$; an habitual, but subdued dejection A$_1$

48.19 quarry,]D$_1$; ~∧ A$_1$

48.20 welcome,]E$_1$; welcome my A$_1$

48.26 the blacks]E$_1$; these blacks A$_1$

48.26 they]E$_1$; they both A$_1$

48.26 and]E$_1$; and then A$_1$

48.40 Richard]E$_1$; Richard, and the manly greetings of the gentleman A$_1$

49.1 in]E$_1$; on A$_1$

49.2 had arisen]E$_1$; rose A$_1$

49.6 paid his compliments.]E$_1$; said with a smile that opened a mouth of no common dimensions—— ¶ "Ver welcome home, Monsieur Temp'l. Oh! Mam'selle Liz'bet you ver humble sairvant." A$_1$; Ver velcome . . . Templ'. Ah! . . . sairvant D$_1$-D$_2$

49.10 thine]E$_1$; on this crown of thine A$_1$

49.12 for]E$_1$; for if others were unbending, A$_1$

49.19 in the quarry alone that he could effect this]D$_1$; the quarry alone that could enable him to effect his A$_1$

49.21 in]E$_1$; into A$_1$

49.24-25 quarried, and in which he now attempted to turn his team. Passing]E$_1$; quarried——passing A$_1$

49.26 road]D$_1$; road, and at that day A$_1$

49.27 civilly]E$_1$; very civilly A$_1$

49.30 both proposals]E$_1$; the proposal A$_1$

49.32 are]E$_1$; are as A$_1$

49.37 It]E$_1$; Thus appealed to, it A$_1$

49.37-38 expectations]E$_1$; expectations that were A$_1$

49.40-41 out like those of lobsters]E$_1$; at least half-an-inch from his visage A$_1$

50.1 movement]E$_1$; movement with an understanding expression, that was a mixture of amusement at Richard's dilemma, and of care, at their situation A$_1$; movement . . . that blended amusement at Richard's dilemma, with anxiety at their situation D$_1$-D$_2$

50.5 the whip]E$_1$; his whip A$_1$

50.6 the leaders]E$_1$; his leaders A$_1$

50.8 step]D$_1$; step they took A$_1$

50.12 Only]D$_1$; Nothing but A$_1$

50.13-14 and this]E$_1$; and this A$_1$; which D$_1$-D$_2$

50.15 so slight an impediment]E$_1$; this slight impediment A$_1$

50.17 perpendicularly]E$_1$; nearly perpendicularly A$_1$

50.20 possible]E$_1$; possible, in the sleigh A$_1$

50.21 Dieu! que faites]E$_1$; dieu! prenez gardez A$_1$

50.25 clergyman]E$_1$; clergyman, losing the slight flush that cold had given to his cheeks A$_1$

50.27 obstinate]E$_1$; you obstinate A$_1$

50.28-29 and, in . . . sat,——]E$_1$; applying his whip with new vigour, and unconsciously kicking the stool on which he sat, as if inclined to urge the inanimate thing forward; A$_1$; applying . . . inanimate wood forward; D$_1$-D$_2$

50.33 off]B; off of A$_1$

50.34 the horses back."]E$_1$; I can't guide the horses. A$_1$

51.2 under the]D$_1$; under rather A$_1$

51.3 of]E$_1$; from A$_1$

51.5-6 still pressing backward]E$_1$; and pressing backward instead of going into the quarry A$_1$

51.7 aside]E$_1$; aside, by the path they had trodden themselves A$_1$; aside . . . had themselves trodden D$_1$-D$_2$

51.9 with the]E$_1$; with its A$_1$

51.10 unceremoniously]D$_1$; unceremoniously, it is true, A$_1$

51.12 air]E$_1$; air, for a moment A$_1$

51.13 radii]D$_1$; radius A$_1$

51.13 landed]E$_1$; was landed A$_1$

51.17 anchor]E₁; anchor, to check the further career of his steeds A₁

51.19 in the]E₁; in that A₁

51.26 Ter deyvel]D₁; Der teufel A₁

51.31 thanksgiving]E₁; thanksgivings A₁

51.34 trembled]E₁; was trembling A₁

51.35 some]E₁; also a slight A₁

51.35 also]E₁; that continued for some little time A₁

52.1 'duke]E₁; cousin 'duke A₁

52.3 gave]E₁; gave with A₁

52.3 rein]F; reins A₁

52.4 in rule]E₁; handsomely A₁

*52.4-8 myself." ¶ The spectators . . . privilege.]E₁; myself." A₁

52.9 he said]E₁; cried the judge, whose fears were all vanished in mirth at the discomfiture of the party A₁

52.11 have]E₁; have assuredly A₁

52.13 you,]D₁;~ʌ A₁

52.13 pleas]E₁; pleased A₁

52.14 leg]E₁; foot A₁

52.24 What,]D₁; ~ʌ A₁

52.26 towards]E₁; up towards A₁

52.26 mountain]E₁; mountain, but A₁

52.29 large]D₁; rather large A₁

52.31 mon cher]B; my dear A₁

52.32 shall do]B; do A₁

52.35 other articles]F; articles A₁

52.35 of]E₁; of his A₁

52.40 Here,]D₁; ~ʌ A₁

52.40 Dickon,]D₁; ~ʌ A₁

53.3 Santaclaus* [*footnote*] *The periodical . . . . Christmas.]F; Santaclaus A₁; The periodical . . . opinion . . . on each Christmas eve. E₁

53.3 to-night]E₁; to your stocking to-night, if you are smart and careful about the buck, so as to get in, in season A₁; to your stocking to-night . . . buck, and get . . . season D₁-D₂

53.4 grinned, conscious]E₁; grinned with the consciousness A₁

53.4 was]E₁; was thus A₁

53.5 silence]E₁; his silence A₁

53.7 began]E₁; at once began A₁

*53.13 buck?"——]E₁; buck!" Here A₁; buck!"—— D₁-D₂

53.15 buck]E₁; buck indeed A₁

53.15 Yes,]D₁; ~ʌ A₁

53.18 well]E₁; well, well A₁

53.25 a ten]D₁; ten A₁

53.25-26 bending]D₁; as he bended A₁

53.27 grin]E₁; broad grin A₁

53.34 sir, all 'e folk]E₁; sir, the folk A₁; sir, folk B

54.1 one else]F; one A₁

54.4-5 Patent*, [*footnote*] *The grants . . . ceased.]E₁; Patent, A₁

54.7-8 essentially, as to all points of genius, my own]E₁; all the rest is mine A₁

54.10 admiration]E₁; deep admiration A₁

54.17 Wethersfield]CE; Weathersfield A₁

54.18 half]E₁; half of A₁

54.21 it is]B; its A₁

54.26 like]E₁; just like A₁

54.29 hands,]D₁; ~ ʌ A₁

54.31 this]D₁; the A₁

54.31-32 the sleigh]E₁; their sleigh A₁

55.1 *time** [*footnote*] *The manumission . . . . expedient.]E₁; time A₁

55.3 and his real master]E₁; master and his real benefactor A₁

55.10 had]E₁; had just A₁

55.10 for]E₁; for one A₁

55.14 he]E₁; that he A₁

55.14 paused]E₁; again paused A₁

55.14 and hemmed]E₁; and again hemmed A₁

55.15 for]D₁; as he was A₁

55.19 how]D₁; that A₁

55.19 up the person in question]E₁; him in A₁; him D₁-D₂

55.23 sleighs]D₁; sleigh, A₁

55.23 one]E₁; one whom A₁

55.28 shall]D₁; will A₁ (*Also emended on the authority of D₁ at* 61.38, 68.37, 99.38, 104.31, 107.11, 112.17, 129.2, 144.16, 160.37, 167.40, 204.12, 222.24, 223.33, 267.39, *and* 344.21.)

55.30 yes, massa Richard]D₁; yes massa, Richard A₁

55.30 black,]D₁; ~ ʌ A₁

56.2 yes,]D₁; ∼∧ A₁
56.4 No,]D₁; ∼∧ A₁
56.10-11 he is taking the youth]E₁; is taking him A₁
56.13 in some measure vanished]D₁; vanished in some measure A₁
56.14 stocking of Santaclaus. After]E₁; stocking——after A₁
56.18 distance from his]E₁; distance of his long A₁; distance from his long D₁-D₂
56.19 truth]E₁; the truth A₁
56.19 I]E₁; I'll A₁
56.23 both]E₁; all A₁
56.24 there]E₁; there, forgetful of his great name A₁
56.28 it,]D₁; ∼∧ A₁
56.30 great]E₁; damn'd great A₁
56.31 carcass]D₁; carcase A₁
56.34 Yankee* [*footnote*] *In America . . . . word.]E₁; Connecticut A₁; Yankee D₁-D₂
57.4 occasionally turned]D₁; would occasionally turn A₁
57.5 continued]D₁; continue A₁
57.11 hip,]D₁; ∼∧ A₁
58.2 "Nathaniel's]CE; ∧∼ A₁
58.6 Gregory."]CE; ∼.∧ A₁
58.7 *The Taming of the Shrew*, IV.i.132-36]CE; *Shakespeare* A₁
58.10 a right angle]D₁; right angles A₁
58.11 plane]E₁; plain A₁
58.12 mentioned]D₁; noticed A₁
58.13 timber,]D₁; timber, that was strong, but A₁
58.16 gushed]E₁; gushed in mimic turbulence A₁
58.18-19 extended an]E₁; extended her own right A₁; extended her right D₁-D₂
58.19 arm in welcome]E₁; arm, to welcome into her bosom A₁
58.21 Elizabeth]E₁; the astonished Elizabeth A₁
58.23-24 was of the ordinary width, notwithstanding]E₁; was laid out of the width of an ordinary avenue to a city, notwithstanding that A₁

58.34 piled]E₁; piled before the houses, A₁
*58.34-59.1 daily increasing rather]E₁; rather increasing A₁; daily increasing D₁-D₂
59.2 seen through every window]E₁; seen, lighting every window through the dusk of the evening A₁
59.3 gazed]E₁; had gazed A₁
59.5 it]D₁; he A₁
59.6 it]D₁; he A₁
*59.7 its]CE; his A₁
59.13-14 smiling at the leave-taking of the luminary]E₁; smiling in scorn, on those changes in the season, which could neither shake their foundations, nor subvert their nature A₁; smiling in scorn at the changes in the season D₁-D₂
59.19 the light]E₁; that the light A₁
59.20 clouds]E₁; few clouds A₁
59.22 bosom]E₁; chill bosom A₁
59.24 evening]D₁; evening that was A₁
59.28 his]D₁; his own A₁
59.30 the cheerful]E₁; their cheerful A₁
59.35 Elizabeth]D₁; she A₁
59.37 had retained]B; retained A₁
60.1 of the]E₁; in the A₁
60.1 in a moment]D₁; directly A₁
60.6 roofs]D₁; roof A₁
60.8 entrance]E₁; entrance to the mansion A₁
60.14 between]E₁; from A₁
60.15 pillars and the stones on which]E₁; pillars to the spot where A₁; pillars to the bases on which D₁-D₂
60.36 on]F; in A₁
60.38 feet]D₁; feet two inches A₁
61.2 be]E₁; be in order A₁
61.3 greater]E₁; a greater A₁
61.9 with habitual]E₁; with great A₁; with vast D₁-D₂
61.13 reaching]D₁; so as to reach A₁
61.22 had been]E₁; was A₁
61.30 however, than]D₁; than A₁
61.33 earth]E₁; world A₁

61.33 to make a]E$_1$; to a A$_1$
61.37 Bow-bells]B; bow-bells A$_1$
61.37 is]F; is fairly A$_1$
62.1-2 qualities that will be developed in the course of the tale]E$_1$; qualities A$_1$
62.13 of her]E$_1$; in her A$_1$
62.15 to]E$_1$; and then suffered to A$_1$
62.16 took]D$_1$; evidently took A$_1$
62.16 in such]E$_1$; in so large A$_1$; in such large D$_1$
62.36 confusion]D$_1$; running and noise A$_1$
62.37 where, receiving]D$_1$; where he received A$_1$
62.37 he]D$_1$; and A$_1$
63.12 stove]D$_1$; ten-plate stove A$_1$
63.12 with heat]E$_1$; with the heat it emitted A$_1$
63.18 furniture]E$_1$; furniture, of a great variety in its appearance and materials A$_1$
63.18 of which was]D$_1$; being A$_1$
63.18-19 the remainder having been]E$_1$; some A$_1$; the remainder D$_1$-D$_2$
63.22 the piles]F; piles A$_1$
63.27-28 mountains were beautifully undulating]E$_1$; mountains, were undulating in precise regularity A$_1$
63.29 box, of]E$_1$; box, with A$_1$
63.35-36 thermometer, in]D$_1$; thermometer, with A$_1$
63.39 exactitude]E$_1$; veneration A$_1$
64.1 each]E$_1$; either A$_1$
64.7 style]D$_1$; whole style A$_1$
64.8 were all due to the taste]E$_1$; had been executed under the auspices A$_1$
64.10 any one]D$_1$; one A$_1$
64.24 and at]E$_1$; at A$_1$
64.26 General, which ran]F; General running A$_1$; general, which ran E$_1$-E$_2$
64.32-33 now announced]E$_1$; announced A$_1$
64.33 whip.]E$_1$; whip, that startled the party, and his voice was first heard, exclaiming—— A$_1$
64.35 heiress?" he cried.

"Excuse]E$_1$; heiress? Excuse A$_1$
64.36 intricate]E$_1$; delicate and nice A$_1$
65.10 Benjamin Pump]D$_1$; Benjamin A$_1$
65.12 take]E$_1$; go to take A$_1$
65.14-15 experienced]D$_1$; had experienced A$_1$
65.15 sensation]F; sensations A$_1$
65.17 school]E$_1$; the school A$_1$
65.17 lamented]E$_1$; late lamented A$_1$
65.18 husband and child]E$_1$; the husband and the child A$_1$
65.20 surprise]E$_1$; their surprise A$_1$
65.21 use:]D$_1$; use, so that A$_1$
65.25 garments]E$_1$; garments that A$_1$
65.32 diffuse]E$_1$; wonderfully diffuse A$_1$
65.37 curiosity——not unmixed with jealousy,——]E$_1$; mingled curiosity and jealousy, A$_1$
65.40 cloaks]E$_1$; cloak A$_1$
66.8 feature]D$_1$; member A$_1$
66.19 though]D$_1$; but A$_1$
66.19 a little severe]E$_1$; beauty in its grandeur A$_1$
66.26 felt that her own]D$_1$; felt, at once, that her A$_1$
66.29 neat]D$_1$; but neat A$_1$
67.2 stool]E$_1$; unfortunate stool A$_1$
67.3 When]D$_1$; So soon as A$_1$
67.3 from]E$_1$; from the duresse of A$_1$
67.12-13 clean, and glittering]E$_1$; all clean, and each glittering, A$_1$
67.13 apartment]E$_1$; apartment, with its peculiar lustre A$_1$
67.15 produced]B; produccd A$_1$
67.19 in strong contrast]E$_1$; strongly contrasted A$_1$
67.22 near]E$_1$; near to A$_1$
67.30-31 the single]D$_1$; this single A$_1$
67.33 even noble]E$_1$; noble A$_1$
68.1 The]D$_1$; His A$_1$
68.2-3 rustic restraint, nor obtrusive vulgarity]D$_1$; the restraint of rustic timidity, nor

with the obtrusive boldness of
awkward vulgarity A₁
68.12-13 welcomes; and]D₁;
welcomes, so that A₁
68.13 Elizabeth continued to gaze at
him in]E₁; Elizabeth, herself as
much an object to be looked at by
others, continued to gaze at him
in a kind of stupid A₁
68.18 the hand]D₁; his hand A₁
68.18 when]D₁; and A₁
68.19 and concealed]D₁; so as to
conceal A₁
68.19-20 lineaments]E₁; lineaments
of his features A₁
68.31 debt]E₁; debt to thee A₁
69.5 small]E₁; but small A₁
69.14 as easy again]E₁; twice as easy
A₁
69.15 just]E₁; only A₁
69.15-16 hold his breath naturally.
Few men know how to breathe,
naturally]E₁; do the thing as it
ought to be done A₁
69.17 Judge,]E₁; Judge playfully,
after A₁
69.19 thoroughly understood]E₁;
understood A₁
69.20 life]E₁; a life A₁
69.20 fingers]E₁; fingers with great
facility A₁
69.22 skirts]E₁; skirts with an air of
vast disdain A₁
*69.26 Patent]D₁; patent A₁ (*Also
first capitalized in D₁ at* 74.26,
90.25, 97.23, 97.24, 97.31,
100.25, 161.18, *and* 202.34.)
69.28 deer]F; deers A₁
69.29 to believe virtues are not
transmitted]E₁; not to believe in
virtues being transmitted down
A₁
69.32 glancing]E₁; glancing keenly
A₁
69.39 hanged. Yes]E₁; hung. Oh!
yes A₁
*70.3 De Grasse]E₁; De Grass A₁
70.15 distant]E₁; distant; I will save
you the trouble A₁
70.16 looked]E₁; looked earnestly
A₁
70.17 He]E₁; He instantly A₁

70.20 said]E₁; he said A₁
70.24 fellow]E₁; fellow there A₁
71.2 "——And]CE; ∧—— ~ A₁
71.6 show."]CE; ~. ∧ A₁
71.7 *Romeo and Juliet,* V.i.44-48]CE;
Shakspeare A₁
71.8 name]E₁; unworthy name A₁
71.17 they]D₁; then they A₁
71.18 arms]E₁; arms that A₁
71.24 the youngest son of]D₁; a
younger son to A₁
71.27-28 interruptions]D₁;
interruption A₁
72.1 was]E₁; was a A₁
72.2 fill]E₁; fill with credit and
profit A₁
72.6 to]E₁; to direct A₁
72.15 on]D₁; at A₁
72.22 foundations]D₁; foundation
A₁
72.30 empty]E₁; to empty A₁
72.39 a pocket;——]E₁; the pocket
of his coat; A₁
73.5-6 razor. Three or four months
had scarce]E₁; razor; and but
three or four months A₁
73.11 the place where]E₁; where A₁
73.12 seen]E₁; noticed A₁; observed
D₁-D₂
73.14 boy]E₁; boy, who A₁
73.14 trotting]E₁; was trotting A₁
73.16-17 much edified by the
additional gravity of his air]E₁;
astonished in observing how
much he had grown lately A₁
73.27 passed]E₁; was passed A₁
73.35 suspicious-looking]F;
suspiciously looking A₁
74.6 seat]E₁; seat that A₁
74.11 of the]E₁; in the A₁
74.12 was Marmaduke]D₁;
Marmaduke was A₁
74.14 possessed of]E₁; possessed of
A₁; possessed D₁-D₂
74.32-33 comfortably applying]E₁;
applying A₁
74.39 jobber* [*footnote*] *People . . .
called.]E₁; owner of an axe A₁;
jobber D₁-D₂
75.1 felling]D₁; falling himself A₁;
felling himself B
75.2 trial]E₁; trial that A₁

75.3 need, however, he was]E₁;
need he was, however, A₁
75.12 desperation,]B; ~. A₁
75.14 event]D₁; service A₁
75.18-19 so narrow a box]D₁; a box
so narrow A₁
75.19 room;]E₁; room; he knew
this, for A₁; room; he knew this to
be true, for D₁-D₂
75.20 the living]E₁; his living A₁
75.22 arteries]E₁; living arteries A₁
75.22 Richard, considering]D₁;
Richard considered A₁
75.23 strongly]D₁; and strongly A₁
75.26 notwithstanding]E₁;
notwithstanding that A₁
75.33 Todd's]E₁; Todd's six years'
A₁
75.39 anxious]E₁; anxiously looking
A₁
76.9 and]E₁; with A₁
76.14 assistance]E₁; his assistance
A₁
76.18 assistance]E₁; offered
assistance A₁
76.29 is]F; was A₁
76.38 Richard,]E₁; Richard,
abruptly A₁
77.3 smiling,]F; with a smile, A₁;
smiling E₁-E₂
77.6 pocket]E₁; pocket, that A₁
77.17-18 the common]D₁; common
A₁
77.18 light-coloured]CE;
light-coloured, A₁
77.24 appeared on]E₁; appeared,
passing over A₁
77.24 youth]E₁; youth, as he spoke
A₁
77.29 much]E₁; wonderfully A₁
77.29 the duty]F; his duty A₁
77.33 face]D₁; nose A₁
77.37 envious cover of a]E₁; cover
of an envious A₁
77.40 on]B; at A₁
77.40 disp'ut pretty]E₁; a disp'ut
pretty spoken one too A₁
78.7 maid]E₁; a maid A₁
78.9 left]B; left entirely A₁
78.20 were]D₁; was A₁
78.25 When]E₁; The moment
Richard heard the sound that was

produced by rending the linen,
he stepped up to the group, with
the air of one who well
understood the business in hand.
So soon as A₁; The moment . . .
hand. When D₁-D₂
78.35 linen]E₁; piece of linen A₁
78.37 spread]E₁; spread, by the
practitioner A₁
79.1 care. A]E₁; care and precision.
The A₁; care and precision. A
D₁-D₂
79.12 professional]E₁; his
professional A₁
79.17 tere]D₁; there A₁
79.19 hem,]E₁; somewhat equivocal
hem, before he replied A₁
80.1 bleeding]D₁; flowing of the
blood A₁
80.4 indication]D₁; indications A₁
80.21 skill]E₁; abilities and skill A₁
81.4 he]D₁; you A₁
81.12 a man want]B; that a man
wants A₁
81.16 forrard]D₁; forward A₁
81.16 a humble]E₁; an humble A₁
81.20 Richard.]E₁; Richard, with a
benevolent smile, to the doctor;
A₁; Richard . . . smile, directed to
the Doctor. D₁-D₂
81.29 countrymen!"* [*footnote*] *It
is . . . doubt it.]E₁; countrymen,
there." A₁
81.32 spectacles]E₁; spectacles,
from before his eyes, A₁
82.8-9 in the Encyclopædias]E₁; of
such matters A₁
82.14 took]E₁; now took into his
hand, with a solemn air, A₁
82.18 and caught the lead,
while]D₁; so as to catch the lead,
and, A₁
82.20 spectators]E₁; spectator A₁
82.27 holes]E₁; shot-holes A₁
83.6 Freneau, "The Indian
Student," 11.1-4]CE; *Freneau* A₁
83.12 had descended numberless
tribes]E₁; had descended
numberless tribes A₁; numberless
tribes had descended D₁-D₂
83.13 were]D₁; was A₁
83.27 generally]D₁; always A₁

83.31-32 in which]E₁; with which A₁

84.8 much]E₁; most A₁

84.18 Mingoes]D₁; Mengwe A₁

84.20 prevail over]E₁; circumvent A₁

84.28 its]E₁; their A₁

84.29 the nation]E₁; their nation A₁

84.39 war, time]E₁; time A₁

84.40-41 this once renowned]D₁; this, once so renowned A₁

*85.15 Leather-stocking]E₁; leather stocking A₁

85.20 conversation]E₁; conversations A₁

85.23 This name he had acquired in]E₁; This was a name that he had attained in his A₁

85.24 war]E₁; the art of war A₁

85.27 mournful]E₁; expressive A₁

85.41 and his]D₁; so that A₁

85.41-86.1 native and European fashions]E₁; native fashions and European manufactures A₁; native fashions with European manufactures D₁-D₂

86.1 without]E₁; of the atmosphere without A₁

86.2-3 concealed]D₁; covered A₁

86.6 hide the shame]D₁; conceal the sorrow A₁

86.6 glory]E₁; the departed glory that it had A₁; a glory that it had D₁-D₂

86.8 and of]D₁; of A₁

86.9 with]D₁; and with A₁

86.10 freedom]E₁; air of freedom A₁

86.10 in]E₁; when a A₁

86.12 it discovered]D₁; discovered A₁

86.23 waist]E₁; waist, and moved forward A₁

86.24 dignified]E₁; unusually dignified A₁

86.29 many scars]E₁; the scars of many wounds A₁

86.31 gives]E₁; only can give A₁; alone can give D₁-D₂

86.34 fall]E₁; fall for A₁

86.34 had evidently been]E₁; were evidently A₁

86.40 object]E₁; evident object A₁

87.5 but]E₁; but soon recovering himself, A₁

87.13 Young Eagle]E₁; young eagle A₁

87.15 Judge,]E₁; Judge, with a kind of horror, and turning his fine, manly, open countenance to the other; A₁; Judge, in horror . . . other; D₁-D₂

87.20 John, "but]E₁; John, impressively, as he tried to study the countenance of the Judge; "but, A₁

87.20 brother]B; rother A₁

87.30 he]E₁; the Indian A₁

87.31 this]E₁; this wrong A₁

87.33 smile]E₁; benevolent smile A₁

87.35 interest]E₁; an expression of scornful pity, A₁

87.38 on]E₁; to perform A₁

87.39 invasion of]D₁; innovation on A₁

88.6 wound]E₁; wound now A₁

88.11 I tink de elder]E₁; I should tink de elderly A₁

88.16 nigh]E₁; nigh to A₁

88.17 am]E₁; am right A₁

88.22 partridge]E₁; partridge down, A₁

88.23 I or Natty]D₁; Natty or I A₁

88.25 again]E₁; again, just A₁

88.29 a mark]F; the mark A₁

88.30 know]E₁; know that A₁

88.33 concluded]D₁; had concluded A₁

89.1 physician]E₁; true physician A₁

89.12 was]B; were A₁

89.19 of which]D₁; that A₁

89.19 possession]D₁; possession of A₁

89.32 they were]D₁; it was A₁

89.39 Indian had taken it]D₁; Indian's remedy had been taken A₁

89.40 event]D₁; event, which we have just been relating A₁

90.3 wound]E₁; wound that was A₁

90.11 the bark]D₁; his bark A₁

90.12 were used]D₁; was used A₁

*90.12 sewing]E₁; sowing A₁

90.13 of which]D₁; that A₁

90.14 use]D₁; use of A₁

90.24 this]D₁; this here A₁
90.24 I scraped]E₁; for I scraped A₁
90.25 I ought]E₁; But I ought A₁
90.29 moreen]D₁; marine A₁
90.38 admirably]E₁; most admirably A₁
91.3 yes]E₁; yes, yes A₁
91.13 had]D₁; now A₁
91.22 all]E₁; all of A₁
91.28 carcass]D₁; carcase A₁
92.3 hand]D₁; own hand A₁
92.12 not]D₁; never A₁
92.15 assistance]D₁; assistance, or acknowledgements A₁
92.18 her]E₁; her very A₁
92.19 dropping]D₁; and dropped A₁
92.22 amity]E₁; our amity A₁
92.26 us our]B; our A₁
92.27 language]E₁; language of prayer, A₁
92.30 lost in thought]D₁; in a kind of stupefaction A₁
92.35 when]D₁; as A₁
92.37 injury]E₁; injury is A₁
92.37 cooler]E₁; his cooler A₁
93.3 with]D₁; of A₁
93.23 Bah]D₁; Oh A₁
93.35 ter deyvel]D₁; der teufel A₁
94.4 Judge]E₁; Judge again A₁
94.6 ready]E₁; in the next room A₁
94.7 a hand]E₁; a fair hand, A₁
94.8-10 chère . . . . Templeton]E₁; chere Mam'selle, but too happy to do so," said the polite Frenchman, while he offered his hand; "it is de consolashong, in my baneesh, to meet de smile from de fair ladi A₁; chere . . . meet a smile . . . ladi D₁-D₂
94.11 Mohegan,]D₁; Mohegan, alone A₁
94.11-12 while the remainder of]D₁; as A₁
94.14 clergyman]E₁; divine A₁
94.22 evil]E₁; evil, John A₁
94.25 though]D₁; if A₁
94.28 body]E₁; body only A₁
94.39 then]E₁; and A₁
95.11 encouraging]E₁; quite consoling A₁
95.13 the skin]F; a skin A₁

95.18 reef]F; reefs A₁
96.4 Campbell, *Gertrude of Wyoming*, I.iv.3-4]CE; *Campbell* A₁
96.9 reason why we have been obliged to present]E₁; "why and wherefore" of A₁
96.11 Europe, at the period of our tale, was]E₁; Europe was, at the period of our tale, A₁
96.12 commotion]E₁; mighty commotion A₁
96.13 the centre]E₁; their centre A₁
96.15 the world]D₁; this world A₁
96.15 its]E₁; her A₁
96.18 seek]D₁; seek for A₁
96.24 exchange]E₁; an exchange of A₁
97.2-3 life with which he was not familiar]D₁; life, that he was not familiar with A₁
97.5 gunpowder]E₁; tea A₁
97.7 very]D₁; most A₁
97.9 every other]D₁; almost every A₁
97.13 temper]B; temperament A₁
97.18 was]E₁; were A₁
97.33 emigrated]E₁; emigrated A₁; migrated D₁-D₂
97.35 migration]E₁; transmigration A₁
98.9 grave to gay]B; grief to joy A₁
98.12 speak]E₁; talk A₁
98.15 thirty]E₁; the thirty A₁
98.15 miles]D₁; miles between them A₁
98.18 greatly countenanced]E₁; countenanced A₁
98.21 on]E₁; in A₁
98.34 when]D₁; so soon as A₁
99.1 religious]B; the religious A₁
99.6 Academy.]E₁; ~! A₁
99.14 erected]E₁; that had been split, and erected, A₁; that had been erected D₁-D₂
99.16 an]D₁; the A₁
99.23 the salubrity]E₁; and the salubrity A₁
99.31 the smallest prospect]E₁; a prospect A₁; the prospect D₁-D₂
99.33 edifice]E₁; edifice A₁; edifice chiefly D₁-D₂
99.35 having]E₁; his having A₁

99.38 the architects]E₁; these architects A₁
100.4 approve]D₁; approve of, A₁
100.4 reject]E₁; ~, A₁
100.12 suitable gravity]E₁; great state A₁
100.20 in]E₁; in the dusk of A₁
100.23 young]E₁; the young A₁
100.27 windows; and]D₁; windows, so that A₁
100.31 natural]E₁; prodigious A₁
100.37 of proportions]E₁; in figure A₁
100.38 square]E₁; ~, A₁
100.38 small]E₁; smaller A₁
101.25 charter]D₁; commission A₁
101.31 two rooms]E₁; two A₁
102.5 med-i-taa-ris]E₁; med-i taa-ris A₁
102.8 By]E₁; For by A₁
102.8-9 discovered]E₁; had discovered, A₁
102.30 of opinion]F; in opinion A₁
102.31 faith]E₁; our faith A₁
103.2 his]D₁; that A₁
103.5 the pulpit]E₁; their pulpit A₁
103.6 carrying]E₁; carrying all A₁
103.9-10 Pump . . . churchman.]E₁; Pump! A₁
103.12 the colonies]E₁; their colonies A₁
103.13 a few]D₁; many A₁
103.20 obtain]D₁; to obtain A₁
103.26 the authority]D₁; that authority A₁
103.26 so]E₁; which was so A₁
103.29 dioceses]E₁; diocesses A₁
103.33 administrations]E₁; ministrations A₁
103.38 village]E₁; village itself A₁
*103.40 before]CE; previously to A₁, D₁-F; before to B
104.11-12 different sectaries]E₁; sectaries to whom it was made A₁
104.23 after which their proceedings]D₁; when what was done A₁
104.24 Mr.]D₁; for Mr. A₁
104.24-25 commenced this mysterious business, having]D₁; proceeded on this mysterious business, had A₁

*105.14 moreen]D₁; marine A₁; morenne B
105.15 and their]D₁; so that their A₁
105.17 An enormous mirror]E₁; There was an enormous glass A₁
105.19 was burning]E₁; burning A₁
105.22 sugar-maple]E₁; sugar-maple for fires A₁
105.23 heat]E₁; heat from the ends of those logs A₁
105.25 sets]E₁; sets to A₁
105.28-29 fuel." ¶ "Fuel]D₁; fuel for our fires." ¶ "Fuel for our fires, A₁
105.29 in]D₁; in a kind of A₁
105.30 fuel! why,]E₁; fuel for our fires! why A₁
106.2 instant]E₁; instant that A₁
106.11 blood]E₁; blood in the veins A₁
106.25 not]D₁; neither A₁
106.25 she in]D₁; in A₁
106.26 receive either]D₁; receive A₁
106.26 laughing eyes]E₁; laughing, dark eyes, A₁
106.28 the father]E₁; her father A₁
106.38 Judge]E₁; Judge, somewhat sternly A₁; Judge, sternly D₁-D₂
107.8 entering]B; now entering A₁
107.17 So much being furnished by the wealth of Marmaduke]D₁; So far, being the materials furnished by Marmaduke's wealth A₁
107.18 The]D₁; But the A₁
107.19 positions, however]D₁; positions A₁
107.31 figures]D₁; figures, in brown dough A₁
107.38 suspiciously]E₁; wonderfully A₁
108.4 above]D₁; over A₁
108.12 with]E₁; and A₁
108.18 promised]B; bid fair A₁
108.23 on]D₁; out on A₁
108.23 invariably]D₁; always A₁
108.24 in hand]D₁; on hand A₁
108.27 and when]D₁; for so soon as A₁
108.31 fell]B; fall A₁
108.32 his]F; its A₁
108.34 butt]F; butt A₁; but E₁-E₂

109.4-5 I happen]D₁; as I happen
A₁
109.13-14 look-out on the roof]E₁;
look-out A₁
109.21 that his daughter
manifested]E₁; his daughter, who
manifested evident A₁
*109.25 Mistress]D₁; Mrs. A₁
109.26 off]D₁; off of A₁
109.32 had dared]E₁; dare A₁
109.33 yet]D₁; and A₁
109.34-35 the body]E₁; her body A₁
110.6 remark]E₁; notice A₁
110.7 Templ']D₁; Templé A₁
110.8 excellent]E₁;most excellent A₁
110.9 no]E₁; not a A₁
110.14-15 evenings]E₁; long
evenings A₁
110.22-23 excite blushes]E₁; excite
the blushes of a maiden A₁; excite
the blushes of the maiden B
110.25 dear]E₁; my dear A₁
110.32 a little smartly]E₁; with an
air of a little dignity A₁
110.35 wink]F; hint A₁
110.36 sympathy]E₁; great
sympathy A₁
111.5 het]E₁; het A₁; bet D₁-D₂
111.7 indifferent]E₁; excessively
indifferent A₁
111.11 could]E₁; can A₁
111.21 projecting]D₁; with a
projection of A₁
111.25-26 suppressed curiosity]E₁;
a conscious timidity A₁
111.30 little]E₁; no other A₁
111.31 through]D₁; in A₁
*111.40 christian-men]CE; all
christian-men A₁; Christian-men
E₁-F
112.2 interest]E₁; interest; while the
full black eyes of Elizabeth rested
intently on the scorched visage of
the steward, as she waited his
reply A₁; interest and the . . .
Elizabeth resting on . . . steward,
while she . . . reply D₁-D₂
112.3 jowl: the]E₁; jowl," said
Benjamin; "the A₁
112.8 larnt]D₁; learnt A₁
112.14 the idle tales]E₁; all the idle
tales, sir, that A₁

112.14 Natty: he]E₁; Natty," said
the Judge, sternly; "he A₁;
Natty," said the Judge: "he D₁-D₂
112.23 its]D₁; the A₁
112.23 ringing]D₁; ringing of its
fine tones A₁
112.28-29 Elizabeth; for I count
half-breeds, like Marmaduke, as
bad as heretics]E₁; Elizabeth A₁
113.4 Bürger, "The Wild
Huntsman," 11.11-12 (tr.
Scott)]CE; *Scott's Burger* A₁
*113.6-7 foot-path through the
snow]CE; foot-path that was
trodden in the snow, across the
grounds of the Mansion-House
A₁; footpath through the snow
E₁-E₂
113.8 place by]E₁; place, through
A₁
113.10 risen]E₁; risen, during the
time that our travellers were
housed A₁
113.12 many]E₁; other A₁
113.14 glimmerings]E₁; faint
glimmerings A₁
113.18 snow]B; snow, which
covered the earth A₁
113.19-20 one of which]D₁; that A₁
113.20 while]D₁; as A₁
113.23 gaze]E₁; bewildered gaze, A₁
113.23 proceeded]D₁; took A₁
113.30 conjoint taste]E₁; taste A₁
113.34 any]D₁; one A₁
114.4 in which]D₁; that A₁
114.6 person]D₁; persons A₁
114.6 instantly disappeared]D₁;
disappeared A₁
114.9 another]D₁; one A₁
114.17 dormer]E₁; dormant A₁
114.18 the cheerful]E₁; cheerful A₁
114.24-25 together with]D₁; as was
A₁
114.25 paint]D₁; paint also A₁
114.30 limp]E₁; limp that he had A₁
114.34 visage; exhibiting]D₁;
visage, so as to exhibit A₁
114.35 intended]E₁; intended,
evidently, A₁
114.36 features that were by no
means squeamish]E₁; her
features A₁

114.38 not so as]B; so as not A$_1$
115.1 to]D$_1$; so as to A$_1$
115.1-2 the Judge, directing]D$_1$; as the Judge directed A$_1$
115.6 ye'r]E$_1$; ye're A$_1$
115.7 heart-ach]E$_1$; heart-ache A$_1$
115.11 calkilating]E$_1$; calkilating on it A$_1$
115.12 Major;]D$_1$; ~$_\wedge$ A$_1$
115.14 there."]D$_1$; ~.$_\wedge$ A$_1$
115.15 Elizabeth.]E$_1$; the voice of Elizabeth; A$_1$
115.20 observe]D$_1$; see A$_1$
115.20 also keep]F; keep also A$_1$
115.23 he]E$_1$; he A$_1$; ye D$_1$-D$_2$
115.25 tistify]E$_1$; tistify to A$_1$
115.26 need]E$_1$; the hour of need A$_1$
115.34 ask]E$_1$; jist ask A$_1$
116.4 journey]D$_1$; go A$_1$
116.9 like one to whom the ceremonies were familiar]E$_1$; with great indifference A$_1$
116.12 but]D$_1$; and A$_1$
116.13 Those]D$_1$; But those A$_1$
116.27 to]E$_1$; to where stood A$_1$
116.31 money]E$_1$; money it had cost A$_1$
116.32 a strong]E$_1$; the strong A$_1$
117.2-3 interference]E$_1$; all interference A$_1$
117.7 But when]D$_1$; But, so soon as A$_1$
117.13 argument: and]D$_1$; argument; so that A$_1$
117.14 point]E$_1$; thing A$_1$
117.14 was]E$_1$; was A$_1$; was to be D$_1$-D$_2$
117.17 Not]D$_1$; But not A$_1$
117.17 and]D$_1$; so that A$_1$
117.27 task of erecting]D$_1$; erection of A$_1$
117.33 duty]D$_1$; task A$_1$
117.36 arch;]E$_1$; arch, as A$_1$
117.37 step]E$_1$; step he would take A$_1$
118.5 of his coadjutor]D$_1$; his coadjutor held A$_1$
118.14-15 silent and protracted, but fruitless opposition]D$_1$; silent, but fruitless opposition of this kind A$_1$

118.18 that]D$_1$; which A$_1$
118.21 Mr.]B; ~$_\wedge$ A$_1$
118.22-23 striking resemblance to a vinegar-cruet]E$_1$; prodigious resemblance to an old-fashioned vinegar-cruet A$_1$
118.25 their]D$_1$; surely this A$_1$
118.26 ceased]E$_1$; had ceased A$_1$
118.28 propose]D$_1$; proposing A$_1$
118.30 church]D$_1$; other church A$_1$
118.39 rather sharp]F; sharp A$_1$
119.5 echoed]D$_1$; returned A$_1$
119.8 "Coolish; a tedious spell on't."]E$_1$; "Coolish," said Hiram. A$_1$; "Coolish," said Hiram: "a tedious spell on't." D$_1$-D$_2$
119.17 so. The]E$_1$; so," observed Hiram. "Them A$_1$
119.20 Ah! oui; ees]D$_1$; Oh! oui; yes A$_1$
120.13 apropos of]E$_1$; apropos to A$_1$
120.15 grande cathédrale]E$_1$; grand cathedrale A$_1$; grande cathedrale B, D$_1$-D$_2$
120.17 Ben, pardonnez]D$_1$; Ben must pardonne A$_1$; Ben must pardonnez B
120.21 so good]E$_1$; as good A$_1$
120.30 and the]D$_1$; so that A$_1$
122.3 Goldsmith, "The Deserted Village," 1.179]CE; *Goldsmith* A$_1$
122.5 inartificial]E$_1$; plain and inartificial A$_1$
122.22 crackling]B; craclking A$_1$
122.35 the chair]E$_1$; a chair A$_1$
123.3 co-operation]E$_1$; his co-operation A$_1$
123.4 greatly exceed]E$_1$; be greatly exceeding A$_1$
123.5 the dresses]E$_1$; their dresses A$_1$
123.5-6 the individuals]E$_1$; there were individuals A$_1$
123.16 appeared in]D$_1$; wore A$_1$
123.26 preserved]E$_1$; preserved to the wearer A$_1$
123.28 There]D$_1$; In countenance, there A$_1$
123.28-29 expression in countenance]D$_1$; expression A$_1$
124.7 Americans]D$_1$; natives A$_1$

124.17 congregation]E₁;
congregation, equally A₁
124.28 turned]E₁; turned in
expectation A₁
125.7 silence]E₁; dead silence A₁
125.12 of]E₁; of the manner of
A₁
125.26 they]E₁; all A₁
125.32 beginning]D₁; just
beginning A₁
125.36 superior]D₁; so superior A₁
125.36 natural]E₁; their natural A₁
125.37-38 penitent]E₁; humble
penitent A₁
126.1 dress]E₁; dress, without being
either rich or fashionable, A₁
126.3 and]E₁; and perhaps A₁
126.5 manly]E₁; rich, manly A₁
126.5 male]E₁; youthful, male A₁
126.11 but]D₁; though A₁
126.12 Before]D₁; But before A₁
126.13 confession, however]D₁;
prayer A₁
126.20 sonorously]E₁; most
sonorously A₁
126.23-24 curious]D₁; somewhat
curious A₁
126.25 Grant]E₁; Grant, had A₁
126.26 perform]E₁; perform with
success A₁
126.29-31 of any such temporal
assistance as form, into their
spiritual worship]E₁; into their
spiritual worship of any such
temporal assistance as form A₁
126.31 He]D₁; The divine A₁
126.39 and he had]D₁; and had he
A₁; and had B
127.8 Richard]B; Truly, Richard A₁
127.13 of]E₁; for A₁
127.15 necessary]E₁; necessary for
him A₁
127.18 of the]E₁; of either the A₁
127.19 creed]E₁; creed, or his own
inability to defend it A₁
127.20 religious]E₁; their religious
A₁
128.26 from]D₁; by A₁
129.8 soothe]D₁; sooth A₁
129.23 humility]E₁; our humility A₁
129.39 ingenious]D₁; somewhat
ingenious A₁

129.40 the discourse]E₁; his
discourse A₁
130.2-3 so perfect a]E₁; such a
perfect A₁
130.4 alluded]E₁; had alluded A₁
131.20 ease]E₁; ease and finish A₁
131.22 while]B; that A₁
131.23-24 the succeeding day]E₁;
their pursuits during the
succeeding day, after the service
A₁
131.30 offers]E₁; offers that A₁
132.2 conferred]E₁; conferred on
the host A₁
132.3 guest]D₁; guest, should he
prove in any degree tolerable A₁
132.5 opinion; but]E₁; opinion,"
said the divine; "but A₁
132.6 often,]E₁; ~; A₁
132.8 county]E₁; country A₁ (*Also
emended at* 374.8 *and* 380.12.)
132.10 curious]E₁; as curious A₁
132.15 approached, in time,]E₁;
now approached, so as A₁
132.18 judge]E₁; judge, sir A₁
132.23 the psalm]F; a psalm A₁
132.32 Penguillian,]B; Penguillian
is A₁
132.33 knows]B; he knows A₁
133.5 retained]E₁; had retained A₁
133.10 the rifle]D₁; his rifle A₁
133.12 uneasiness]E₁;
extraordinary uneasiness A₁
133.15 out of]E₁; from A₁
133.22 the divine]D₁; and the
divine A₁
133.31 with]E₁; to all A₁
133.37 on]D₁; in A₁
134.1 for]E₁; left for A₁
134.9 feel]B; feel that A₁
134.10 seem]D₁; seemed A₁
134.15 communion]D₁;
communion, as were my
ancestors before me A₁
134.19 pleasure]E₁; pleasure to
hear you A₁
134.25 dissenting* [*footnote*] *The
. . . country!]E₁; dissenting A₁
134.32 sarved both]E₁; sarved A₁
134.33 ag'in]D₁; against A₁
134.35 work]E₁; kind of work A₁
135.5 skilful]D₁; a skilful A₁

135.12 lives]D₁; lived A₁
135.14 Onondaga]D₁; Onondago A₁
135.23 years after the tree is dead]E₁; years A₁
135.26 I would have you prepare for eternity]E₁; it is for eternity that I would have you prepare A₁
135.30 behind]E₁; behind you A₁
135.34 be]D₁; are A₁
136.1 scearce]D₁; scarce A₁
136.6 controversy]E₁; controversy, for the present A₁
136.12 the hut]D₁; his hut A₁
136.14 village]E₁; village, for A₁
136.17 admit]E₁; admit of only A₁
136.19 perpendicularly]E₁; nearly perpendicularly A₁
136.21 appointed place]D₁; place A₁
136.22 meeting]D₁; nightly meeting A₁
136.23 felt]E₁; to be felt A₁
136.23 so hard,]D₁; hard, so A₁
136.25 frost emitted a]D₁; snow emitted a kind of A₁
136.29 which]E₁; that A₁
136.30 in this singular]E₁; of this singularly constituted A₁
136.31 his]E₁; with his A₁
136.32 concealed beneath]D₁; hid under A₁
136.39 air]E₁; the air he breathed A₁
137.8 sky]E₁; sky in colour A₁
137.9 orb which]E₁; orb, that A₁
137.15 by]E₁; by an A₁
137.19 excellent]E₁; an excellent one A₁
137.21 gave]E₁; gave to A₁
137.39 this of]E₁; this, in A₁
138.2 propose]B; purpose A₁
138.6 on]D₁; upon A₁
138.6 surprise]E₁; evident surprise A₁
138.9 heart]E₁; heart, as I now experience A₁
138.35 stopping,]D₁; stopped, and A₁
138.37 the horror]E₁; all the horror that A₁
139.3 religion that]E₁; religion A₁

139.8 pray]F; and pray A₁
139.12 heard]E₁; heard the exclamation of A₁
139.16 himself]E₁; himself again A₁
139.23 assistance.]E₁; assistance, by saying—— A₁
139.24 Grant," he said: "the]E₁; Grant; the A₁
139.24 yields]B; gives A₁
139.30 Indian]E₁; Indian chief A₁
139.37 follow]E₁; follow him A₁
139.38 allowing the]E₁; so as to allow his A₁; allowing his D₁-D₂
140.8 pass unrevenged;]F; pass unresisted; A₁; pass unresented, B
140.10 power]E₁; power to act their will A₁
140.18 it]E₁; but it A₁
140.25 young]E₁; younger A₁
140.28 to which]E₁; which A₁
140.28 listened]E₁; heard A₁
140.31 village]D₁; village or rather the cluster of dwellings, that was so termed A₁
140.34 nor a]E₁; or a A₁; or B
140.38 relieved]E₁; contrasted A₁
141.4 Louisa]E₁; that Louisa A₁
141.33 discourse]E₁; their discourse A₁
141.39 you]E₁; which you A₁
142.6 right]B; best right A₁
142.12 river'* [*footnote*] *The . . . . Virginia.]E₁; river' A₁
142.20 to]E₁; to the earnest manner of A₁
142.21-22 of gold]E₁; for gold A₁
142.22 and yet]D₁; though A₁
142.22 subtle]E₁; as subtle A₁
142.37 sin of the wrongs]D₁; wrongs A₁; injuries B
143.1 natives, are to be alleged against]B; natives are shared by A₁
143.4 pacing]E₁; scornfully, as he paced A₁; scornfully, pacing B, D₁-D₂
143.7 wealth——]E₁; wealth——there will A₁
143.8 will come]E₁; come A₁
143.9 of]E₁; of such a crime, as A₁
144.2 under]D₁; in A₁

144.7 figure]E₁; tall figure A₁
144.9 hut]E₁; hut that was A₁
144.13 shadow,]E₁; dark shadow,
  that was A₁
144.16 persevere]E₁; perseveres A₁
144.17 Put me in mind, Louisa]E₁;
  Remember me, my child A₁
144.19 father, you]E₁; father,"
  cried the maiden, "you A₁
145.4 Anon., "The Barley-
  Mow."]CE; *Drinking Song* A₁
145.7 inn]E₁; inn, that was A₁
145.8 plan]D₁; plan of the village A₁
145.8 the village]D₁; its site A₁
145.12 The]D₁; Notwithstanding
  the A₁
145.15-16 and ostensibly . . . .
  however]D₁; so as, ostensibly, to
  interpose a barrier to its further
  progress; yet horsemen, and
  subsequently teamsters, A₁
145.22 Two material consequences
  followed this]E₁; There were two
  material consequences to this
  insidious A₁; There . . .
  consequences which followed this
  D₁-D₂
145.23 The]E₁; The one, that the
  A₁
145.25 and the]E₁; and the other,
  that the A₁
145.35 balustrades]E₁; ballustrades
  A₁
146.5 was intended to]D₁; might,
  but did not, A₁
146.10 on its faces, loaded with
  masonic emblems]D₁; loaded
  with masonic emblems on its
  faces A₁
146.18-19 executed well]E₁; well
  executed A₁
146.22-23 the inn of Captain
  Hollister]D₁; that inn, as a place
  of resort A₁
146.25 veteran]D₁; veteran, who
  was styled Captain Hollister A₁
146.26 hardly]D₁; barely A₁
147.6 poking]E₁; poking the fires
  A₁
147.14 I'll]E₁; I'll jist A₁
147.18 that]E₁; the A₁
*147.21 Whitefield]D₁; Whitfield A₁

147.34 for]E₁; but A₁
147.37 bodder]B; bother A₁
147.37 taxts]B; texts A₁
147.39 Jews]E₁; Jews, at first A₁
148.3 forgi'e]D₁; forgive A₁
148.7 Hollister, that]E₁; Hollister,"
  rejoined her husband, "that A₁
148.9 handsomely]E₁; very
  handsomely A₁
*148.18 Whitefield]D₁; Whitfield A₁
148.31 year]E₁; long year A₁
149.6-7 occupations.]D₁;
  occupations; while A₁
149.7 shabby genteel]E₁; half-
  genteel A₁
149.11 hair and a silver key]E₁; hair
  A₁
149.12 was himself]E₁; was A₁
149.22 regularly restore]E₁; restore
  A₁
149.23 defrayed]D₁; discharged A₁
149.31 wish]B; desire A₁
149.34 invitation]E₁; significant
  invitation A₁
150.1 concerning]D₁; after A₁
150.7 the best]D₁; as the best A₁
150.18 of importance.]E₁; of great
  indifference, A₁; great
  importance, D₁-D₂
150.34 little]E₁; but little, A₁
151.4 guess]D₁; think A₁
151.10 was dangerous]D₁; would
  not do A₁; would be imprudent B
151.11 in learning in]D₁; in A₁
151.13 were]D₁; was A₁
151.21 and facing]F; so as to face
  A₁; facing D₁-E₂
151.33-34 attorney, raising his
  voice]E₁; angry attorney A₁
152.4 supposititious]B;
  suppositious A₁
152.9 dignity]E₁; dignity in his
  manner A₁
152.16 has]D₁; have A₁
152.34 returned]D₁; said A₁
153.5 I will]E₁; will A₁
153.11 very palatable]D₁; a very
  palatable one A₁
153.16 the rifle]E₁; the rifle A₁; his
  rifle D₁-D₂
153.18 dam'me]E₁; knowing A₁
153.24 youth]E₁; their youth A₁

153.27 nigh]E₁; nigh to A₁

154.17-18 for this was a company in which a liberal offer was not thrown away]E₁; at this liberal offer of the landlady A₁

154.19 at hearing]D₁; the mentioning of A₁

154.20 companion alluded to]D₁; companion A₁

*154.36 Big Sarpent]D₁; big sarpent A₁

154.38 it, too]D₁; it A₁

154.38 overhand]F; an overhand A₁

154.40 Ah]E₁; Ah! hum A₁

155.3 Flats]E₁; flats clean A₁

155.23 taller]E₁; was taller A₁

155.26 ye]D₁; you A₁

155.32 like]E₁; just like A₁

155.33 taste]E₁; notion A₁

155.37 this]E₁; that A₁

157.7 Anon., "The Barley-Mow."]CE; *Drinking Song* A₁

157.9 the new]D₁; these new A₁

157.9 slunk]E₁; disappeared A₁

157.16 When he had]D₁; As soon as he A₁

157.22-23 comfortable]D₁; convenient A₁

158.22 Marmaduke; and]D₁; Marmaduke, so that A₁

158.29 so'thin]D₁; something A₁

158.31 buildins]D₁; buildings A₁

158.34-35 buildins]D₁; buildings A₁

158.36 two]E₁; jist two A₁

158.40 Tim,]D₁; ~. A₁

159.4 twenty-six]E₁; jist twenty-six A₁

159.7 forgot]E₁; forget A₁

159.10-11 look of sagacious]D₁; sagacious look of A₁

159.12 wuth]D₁; worth A₁

159.13 and a good]E₁; a good A₁

159.18 tacklin afore]D₁; tackling before A₁

159.20 tacklin]D₁; tackling A₁

159.27 doosn't]D₁; doesn't A₁

159.27 wuss]D₁; worse A₁

159.29 carryin]D₁; carrying A₁

159.30 wust]D₁; worst A₁

159.31 wust]D₁; worst A₁

160.19 felling]D₁; falling A₁

160.21 derision.]E₁; derision for a moment, before he made this reply:—— A₁

160.22 Judge," he cried, "but]E₁; Judge, but A₁

160.24 he who]D₁; who A₁

160.30 them]D₁; the A₁

161.9 scearce]D₁; scarce A₁

161.10 "Ter]B; ∧~ A₁

161.17 laws]E₁; sich laws A₁; sitch laws D₁-D₂

161.25 silence]E₁; profound silence A₁

161.27 so'thin]D₁; something A₁

161.28 when]D₁; so soon as A₁

161.35 monstres]E₁; Bêtes A₁

161.36 convulsive]D₁; kind of convulsive A₁

162.11 have]E₁; seem to have A₁

162.14 Anglais]E₁; Anglais! dey be vipt! De French be one gallant peop', if dere vas gen'ral. Ah——ha! Toulon take! c'est bon! I do vish dat dey take Londre——pardonnez moi; mais, it ees bon A₁

162.24 "Ter]B; ∧~ A₁

163.18 be]E₁; jist be A₁

164.5 Good,]D₁; ~; A₁

164.5 deeply]E₁; too deeply A₁

164.13 the head,]D₁; his head; A₁

165.1 utter]D₁; pronounce A₁

165.1-2 and consequently, only understood by himself and]D₁; so that they were understood by none but A₁

165.15 very much]D₁; of something A₁

165.20 shall]B; will A₁

166.3 eyes]E₁; his eyes, A₁

166.3 an]E₁; a fierce A₁

166.6 became]E₁; became again A₁

166.21 berth]F; birth A₁

167.3 it]D₁; that it A₁

167.3 the wound]E₁; that the wound A₁

167.39 on entering]D₁; as soon as they entered A₁

169.3 Anon., "The Bay of Biscay, O." 11.15-16]CE; [*omitted*] A₁

169.5 Dragoon,"]D₁; Dragoon," which we have just related, A₁

169.8 inclinations]F; inclination A₁
169.24-25 domestic condition.
But]D₁; future consideration; but
    A₁
170.3 as]E₁; sich A₁; sitch D₁-D₂
170.5 ministers]E₁; ministers be A₁
170.15 last]E₁; last one A₁
170.15 otherwise]D₁; so A₁
170.18 so]E₁; sich A₁; sitch D₁-D₂
170.19 father]E₁; daddy A₁
170.22 think]B; thing A₁
170.26 me. I]E₁; me," said Miss
    Temple. "I A₁
170.27 journey]E₁; day's journey A₁
170.31 resentment]E₁; her
    resentment A₁
*170.32 salve]CE; salvo A₁
170.36 instant]E₁; instant that A₁
171.9 observe]D₁; notice A₁
171.11 this]E₁; this here A₁
171.12 cares I,]D₁; ~~∧ A₁
171.20 how]E₁; how it is A₁
171.32 aspect]D₁; white A₁
172.1 a moralizing]E₁; a most
    imposing moralizing A₁; a most
    imposingly moralizing D₁-D₂
172.5 and with]D₁; with A₁
172.9 as]E₁; as well as A₁
172.14 berth]F; birth A₁
172.16 Dickens"——]E₁; ~," A₁
172.16-17 Benjamin——]E₁; ~, A₁
172.36 proceeded.]E₁; proceeded
    as follows: A₁
172.37 life]E₁; your life A₁
*173.1 Mistress]D₁; Mrs. A₁
173.4 is]D₁; am A₁
173.15 Bay]D₁; bay A₁
173.20 tell; but]D₁; tell," said
    Benjamin; "but A₁
173.21 keeps]D₁; keep A₁
173.23 Harry, woman]D₁; Harry A₁
173.25 runs]D₁; run A₁
173.27 sea]F; seas A₁
174.28 the]E₁; his A₁
174.29 ecstasy]D₁; ecstacy A₁
174.31 hearty]E₁; good hearty A₁
174.33 struck]D₁; stuck A₁
174.35 off]D₁; of A₁
175.18 easy.]E₁; ~? A₁
175.26 eyes]E₁; his eyes A₁
175.40 poor]E₁; but poor A₁
176.1 body]E₁; poor body A₁

176.22 suppose]E₁; suppose that A₁
176.25 Bay]E₁; bay A₁
176.38 no one]E₁; nobody A₁
177.10 Sitch]D₁; Such A₁
177.14 bear]E₁; bear, d'ye see A₁
177.27 misbecoming]E₁; of your
    misbecoming A₁
177.30 heiress]E₁; stately heiress A₁
177.38 damn'd]B; damned A₁
178.3 minds]E₁; critics A₁
178.20 With]E₁; And with A₁
179.2 "*Watch*]F; ∧~ A₁
179.3 close."]CE; ~.∧ A₁
179.3 *Much Ado about Nothing*,
    III.iii.106-7]CE; *Much Ado about
    Nothing* A₁
179.10 set]F; sat A₁
179.27 at]D₁; by A₁
179.27 Jones.]F₁; Jones, crying
    aloud—— A₁
179.28-29 Bess," he shouted.
    "Ah]E₁; Bess. Ah A₁
180.7 re-entered]E₁; she re-entered
    A₁
180.24-25 of twenty feet in the
    air]E₁; in the air of twenty feet A₁
180.36-37 competitor." ¶ "It's]E₁;
    competitor, like." ¶ "Oh, it's A₁
181.8 send]D₁; consent to send A₁
181.15 foreign]E₁; such foreign A₁
182.11 one's]E₁; my A₁
182.17 serious]E₁; prodigiously
    serious A₁
182.18 girl]E₁; my girl A₁
182.27 another way]E₁; the way of
    Jack Ketch A₁
182.28 man]E₁; one A₁
182.35 are]E₁; are the A₁
182.39 felled]D₁; fallen A₁
183.11 that]E₁; which A₁
183.30 the branches]E₁; their
    branches A₁
184.16 now]E₁; for the feathers A₁
184.17 well-fatted]F; well-fattened
    A₁
185.23 replied]E₁; repeated A₁
185.31-32 the man]E₁; a man A₁
185.37 Christian beast]E₁; beast A₁
186.27 determination]E₁; proud
    determination A₁
187.2 sir? If]E₁; sir?" returned the
    maiden. "If A₁

187.4 assistance]E₁; assistance, sir
A₁
187.7 Leather-stocking]D₁;
"Leather-stocking A₁
187.15-16 the merry-makings]E₁;
them merry-makings A₁
187.25 fortune]D₁; fortunes A₁
187.28 Elizabeth]E₁; maiden A₁
187.38 a one]D₁; an one A₁
188.14 sheep,——I]E₁; sheep,"
again interrupted the young
lady——"I A₁
188.14 dear]E₁; my dear A₁
188.20 a female]E₁; any female A₁
188.22 sir, more]E₁; sir," returned
Elizabeth; "more A₁
189.4 Scott, *The Lady of the Lake*,
V.xx.31-32]CE; *Scott* A₁
189.10 felling]B; falling A₁
189.17 prepared]E₁; been
preparing A₁
189.26 to the]E₁; of tow, to the base
of the A₁
189.28 to serve]C; that it might
serve A₁
189.30 shooting-stand]E₁; this point
A₁
189.32 rights]C; right A₁
189.36 chose to]C; might A₁
190.20 were]E₁; were once A₁
190.24 paced]C; would pace A₁
190.25 trees. Then]C; trees; and
then A₁
190.27 measure]E₁; he would
measure A₁
190.31 approached]C; would
approach A₁
190.34 A pause of a moment]B;
The pause that followed A₁
190.35 which]E₁; that A₁
190.36 blows that he struck]D₁;
blows that followed A₁; blows he
struck C
190.39 threshing]E₁; thrashing A₁
191.1 were]E₁; would be A₁
191.3 the suddenness]E₁; almost
the suddenness A₁
191.4 morning in winter]C; winter
morning A₁
191.9 oxen]C; oxen, the assistants
in his labour A₁
191.10 often heard]C; heard A₁

191.11 the echoes]C; when the
echoes A₁
191.12 taking]C; would take A₁
191.19 applies the torch]E₁; places
the final torch of destruction, A₁
191.25 skill with the rifle]E₁; their
respective skill in shooting A₁
191.28 The]E₁; Their A₁
191.30 success in various]E₁;
successes in their various A₁
191.30-31 the present occasion]C;
this A₁
191.34 rejoined]C; had rejoined A₁
191.35 shilling* [*footnote*] *Before
. . . . it.]E₁; shilling A₁
192.4 its body being]C; but its body
was A₁
192.5 nothing being]D₁; and
nothing left A₁
192.5 long]E₁; long, proud A₁
192.6 beneath]C; below A₁
192.7 was to]E₁; was still to A₁
192.8 a visible]E₁; the visible A₁
192.10 by]E₁; from the mouth of A₁
192.12 when]E₁; as A₁
192.12 cousin]C; cousin, the newly
appointed executive chief of the
county, A₁
192.18 spectator]E₁; spectator to
their proceedings A₁
192.22 take leave of your]E₁; you
may say good-by to that A₁
192.24 chance]E₁; chance too A₁
192.27 pay]E₁; pay it A₁
192.27 chance]C; chance that A₁
192.36 what]E₁; a thing A₁
193.4 is]E₁; is but A₁
193.6 I've]E₁; But I've A₁
193.7 fellow; so]E₁; fellow; and so
A₁
193.11-12 though certainly]C;
though A₁
193.14 bawled]E₁; exclaimed A₁
193.17 taking aim]E₁; pokin gun at
'em A₁
193.19 were]E₁; were, however, A₁;
where, however, D₁-D₂
193.21 Stillness]E₁; The dead
stillness of expectation A₁
193.28 snow in]E₁; snow with A₁
193.29 delight]E₁; his delight A₁
194.6 in the]C; just in the A₁

194.9 flesh]E₁; the flesh A₁
194.13 advise]E₁; tell A₁
194.18 observed]B; noticed A₁
194.19 evidently so]C; so evidently A₁
194.24 instant]E₁; instant that A₁
194.25 fearfully sullied]E₁; sullied A₁
194.26 ebony]E₁; ebony most fearfully A₁
194.27 two]E₁; the two A₁
194.29 features]C; members A₁
194.39 Natty, carefully]D₁; Natty, while he was carefully A₁; Natty, who was carefully B-C
194.39 leathern]C; leather A₁
195.1 hand]E₁; hand in it myself A₁
195.2 day]E₁; very day A₁
195.3 pounds]C; bars A₁
195.4 pan]E₁; the pan of a gun A₁
195.6 lake]D₁; lakes A₁
195.17 flint]E₁; "flint" only A₁
195.19 snap]E₁; snap as A₁
195.20 as]E₁; as A₁; as a D₁-D₂
195.26 sudden death]E₁; good lead, ay! and with a good aim A₁
195.26 out my]E₁; out of my A₁
195.29-31 post . . . suggested]E₁; post A₁
195.32 young lady]B; lady A₁
195.35 once more]C; ag'in A₁
195.40 shoulders]E₁; shoulder A₁
196.1 afore]C; before A₁
196.1 best]C; the best A₁
196.8 whither]D₁; where A₁; wither C
196.9 the gravity]E₁; all the gravity A₁
196.14 evident]E₁; self-evident A₁
196.20 appears]D₁; seems A₁
196.26 a defenceless]E₁; that A₁
196.30 so high a]E₁; such a high A₁
196.31 effect]E₁; so much effect A₁
*196.36 dumb-foundered]CE; dumb-foundered in their notions A₁; dumb foundered E₁-F
197.1-2 money to]C; money, and A₁
197.4-5 the evil excitement of the chances]E₁; unwilling to lose the sport, though he lost his turkey A₁
197.6 stand]E₁; goal A₁

197.7 muttering]E₁; muttering to himself, and speaking aloud A₁
197.9 sin']C; since A₁
197.9 the Indian]E₁; the time when the Indian A₁
197.10 or along]C; along A₁
*197.13 best of]C; best A₁
197.18 depended]E₁; in a great manner depended A₁; in a great measure, depended C
197.19 success]E₁; his success A₁
197.32 the failure]E₁; his failure A₁
197.36 often]D₁; so often A₁
198.6 afore]D₁; before A₁ (*Also emended at* 207.14, 293.28, 299.25, 313.14, 335.1, 335.15, *and* 386.24.)
198.8 right comes]C; rights come A₁
198.11 to]E₁; to, madam A₁
198.14 manner]E₁; proud, but forced manner A₁
198.14 thought]E₁; even thought A₁
198.23 stillness]E₁; stillness that prevailed A₁
198.28 re-load]C; recharge A₁
198.40 charm]E₁; insinuating charm A₁
198.40 manner]E₁; best manner A₁
199.6 blandishment]E₁; exquisite blandishment A₁
199.18-19 for at that instant a hand was laid familiarly]E₁; to see who it was that so familiarly laid his hand A₁
199.24 I]D₁; But I A₁
199.24 the taste]D₁; your taste A₁
199.31 fire-arms]E₁; the fire-arms A₁
199.34 statute]E₁; law A₁
200.1 disappointment]E₁; his disappointment A₁
200.14 Judge]E₁; Judge, gravely A₁
201.6 Scott, *Marmion*, I.xxviii.13-16]CE; *Scott* A₁
201.7 the effect]B; from the effect A₁
201.11 that where]E₁; where A₁
201.12 standing]E₁; standing in a musing attitude A₁
201.12 contemplating]E₁; apparently contemplating A₁

201.12 bird]E₁; bird that lay A₁
201.14 resumed]D₁; resuming A₁
201.17 their]E₁; the place where stood their A₁
201.18 and]D₁; so that A₁
201.24 moment]E₁; moment in manifest surprise, also A₁
201.33-34 come." . . . . "My]E₁; come. My A₁
202.3 was]D₁; surely was A₁
202.6 for]E₁; as if for A₁
202.12 subsistence]E₁; my subsistence A₁
202.20 young]E₁; my young A₁
202.23 from]F; from within A₁
202.27 truth]E₁; the raal thing A₁
202.28 five]E₁; five years A₁
203.3-4 a little checked by female reserve]E₁; strongly checked by the assumption of a woman's dignity A₁
203.8 and of]E₁; and those of A₁
203.17-18 features]E₁; handsome features A₁
203.23 detected]D₁; had detected A₁
203.25 front]E₁; fearless and proud front A₁
203.26 closer]D₁; close A₁
203.27 spoke——]E₁; spoke in his turn. A₁
203.28 said; "his]E₁; said, "for his A₁
203.30 each]E₁; to each A₁
203.33 day]D₁; sun A₁
203.38 are a Delaware]E₁; have Delaware blood A₁
204.9 those]E₁; those of the spectators A₁
204.16 us]E₁; us to A₁
204.21 simplicity]E₁; simplicity in his manner A₁
204.26 heeded]D₁; noticed A₁; observed B
204.26 eyes, nor]E₁; eyes, sir," returned the maiden, "nor A₁
204.29 of]E₁; in A₁
204.38-39 Dickon, to tempt him to eat with ourselves," said Marmaduke, "to]B; Dickon," said Marmaduke, "to tempt him to eat with ourselves, to A₁

205.13-14 lawyer, or the youngest son of a bishop]E₁; lawyer A₁
205.19 have been]E₁; be A₁
205.37 condemn! But]E₁; condemn," said Marmaduke. "But A₁
206.11 difference]E₁; great difference A₁
206.15 the hut]F; their hut A₁
206.16 could]D₁; would A₁
206.20 ceases to exist]B; no longer exists A₁
206.22 will call]D₁; call A₁
206.26 whole business]D₁; dialogue A₁
206.29-30 They alter the country so much, one hardly knows the lakes and streams]B; One hardly knows the lakes and streams, they alter the country so much A₁
207.16-17 ever mortal]E₁; you ever A₁
207.17 good]E₁; raal good A₁
207.18 Delaware]F; Delawares A₁
207.19 time]E₁; very time A₁
207.29 this]E₁; the A₁
208.11 congregation]B; congregatian A₁
208.22 long]E₁; the long A₁
208.23 out from their]E₁; out, in spots, from their light A₁
208.33 the covering]E₁; their covering A₁
208.34 transition]E₁; rapidity of transition A₁
*209.2 boy.]B; ~, A₁
209.3 Beattie, *The Minstrel*, I.xvi.1]CE; *Beattie* A₁
209.5 warm. When]B; warm, so that, when A₁
209.7 while]D₁; so long as A₁
209.19 bloom]E₁; richness of bloom A₁
209.20 exceeded]B; even exceeded A₁
209.20 while]D₁; while even A₁
209.22 hectic]E₁; hectic glow A₁
209.25 forms]E₁; lovely forms A₁
209.31 character]D₁; character. Vulgarity over the bottle, was an embellishment of some fifteen years later date. A₁

210.11 earnestness,]E$_1$; exquisite earnestness, he A$_1$; great earnestness, he D$_1$-D$_2$

210.27 countryman]B; countrymen A$_1$

210.33 slap]E$_1$; ~, A$_1$

210.33 whiz]E$_1$; ~, A$_1$

211.13 mountains]F; mountain A$_1$

212.3 unite]D$_1$; all unite A$_1$

212.4 temperature]E$_1$; temperature in the air A$_1$

212.5 the last]D$_1$; their last A$_1$

212.5 roaring]D$_1$; roaring of the A$_1$

212.6 with]D$_1$; on A$_1$

212.7 resembled]E$_1$; strongly resembled A$_1$

212.9 instinctively pressed]D$_1$; seemed instinctively to press A$_1$

212.11 was]D$_1$; to be A$_1$

212.18 door]E$_1$; doors A$_1$

212.22 throwing]E$_1$; proudly, throwing A$_1$

212.29 place]E$_1$; place by her side A$_1$

212.29 forgot the changes in the country, with those]D$_1$; forgot, not only the changes in the country, but those, also, A$_1$

212.32 the fire]E$_1$; their fire A$_1$

212.32 females]E$_1$; young maidens, who form such conspicuous subjects in our tale A$_1$

212.39 glass]E$_1$; panes of glass A$_1$

212.39 shut out]E$_1$; hid A$_1$

213.1 glorious]E$_1$; most glorious A$_1$

213.9-10 the luminary]E$_1$; to the luminary A$_1$

213.15 hemlocks]E$_1$; hemlocks, on the western mountains, A$_1$

213.15 they]D$_1$; that they A$_1$

213.19 the west]E$_1$; this direction A$_1$

213.21 horizon]E$_1$; western horizon A$_1$

213.23 diamonds]E$_1$; diamonds, that emitted their dancing rays, as the branches waved gently under the impulse of the wind A$_1$; diamonds . . . the air D$_1$-D$_2$

213.27 glistening]D$_1$; as it glistened A$_1$

213.30 a]D$_1$; its A$_1$

213.39 so sceptical a]E$_1$; such a sceptical A$_1$

214.11 wonderful]E$_1$; wonderful. I am not surprised, that your eye caught this transformation, without noticing the changes in the view A$_1$

214.13 coloured]E$_1$; coloured highly A$_1$

214.13 head.]E$_1$; head, as she answered—— A$_1$

214.14 country girl]E$_1$; girl A$_1$

214.15 companion," she said. "I]E$_1$; companion.——I A$_1$

214.16 you]E$_1$; that you A$_1$

214.20 is]E$_1$; is certainly A$_1$

214.20 savage; but]E$_1$; savage," returned the smiling Elizabeth. "But A$_1$

214.32 very laudable]B; laudable A$_1$

215.1 the]E$_1$; but the A$_1$

215.12 playfulness]E$_1$; graceful playfulness A$_1$

215.25 country]D$_1$; county A$_1$

216.15 "the post,"]D$_1$; ∧~~,∧ A$_1$

216.26 to make]F; and make A$_1$

216.26 of fortune in the woods]E$_1$; in the woods for fortune A$_1$

217.3 "It]D$_1$; '~ A$_1$

217.4-6 ways . . . expected]E$_1$; ways, any more than a full-blooded Indian A$_1$

218.1 CHAPTER XX]E$_1$; CHAPTER I A$_1$; CHAPTER VIII B

218.4 Byron, *Childe Harold's Pilgrimage*, II.xxxv.1-2]CE; *Byron* A$_1$

218.6-7 repeated storms]D$_1$; constant accumulation A$_1$

218.7 which]E$_1$; that A$_1$

218.15 intercepted]D$_1$; interposed themselves to A$_1$

218.16 re-action]E$_1$; re-action which crossed the creation A$_1$

218.19 aspect]E$_1$; decided aspect A$_1$

218.30 earth]E$_1$; earth itself A$_1$

218.30 those]E$_1$; those, also, A$_1$

218.31 its]E$_1$; her A$_1$

218.36 While]D$_1$; So long as A$_1$

219.5 excursions]E$_1$; rides A$_1$

219.6 winds]E₁; winds with its speed A₁

219.11 turn]E₁; their turn A₁

219.13 family.]D₁; family; so that, with the aid of a library of well-chosen books, A₁

219.13 willing]B; compelled A₁

219.14 season, with the aid of his library,]D₁; season A₁

219.20 for]E₁; for their A₁

219.28 the parties]E₁; their parties A₁

219.29 would]E₁; would, apparently, A₁

220.10 arch alone]E₁; arch with his hands A₁; arch with his own hands D₁-D₂

220.22 ladies]E₁; ladies to do so, A₁

220.23 they]E₁; the whole A₁

220.26-27 those highways]D₁; the highways A₁

220.31 the horses]E₁; their horses A₁

220.32 of]E₁; of approaching A₁

220.34 chilled the blood]E₁; almost chilled the blood of the spectator A₁

221.1 former]D₁; latter A₁

221.3 cloud,]E₁; cloud, that lingered near the mountain; A₁

221.5 blue]E₁; virgin blue A₁

221.10 a frosty]B; A frosty A₁

221.13-14 manufacture]B; manufactory A₁

221.18 protect]D₁; preserve A₁

222.9 dignified]E₁; extremely dignified A₁

222.19 in]E₁; into A₁

222.22 and the]E₁; but the A₁

222.23 useful]E₁; useful to make A₁

222.31 the noble]E₁; those noble A₁

222.35 has seen sugar made]E₁; seen sugar made often A₁

223.7 Frenchman]E₁; Gaul A₁

223.14 make sucre]E₁; make eet A₁

223.14-15 ce n'est pas, one tree;]E₁; eet is not from von tree; eet is from A₁

223.16 steeck]E₁; von steeck A₁

223.22 and]D₁; as for A₁

223.23 maple,]D₁; maple, it A₁

223.26 Elizabeth]E₁; the heiress A₁

223.28 companions]E₁; companion A₁

223.31-32 speaker, but its resentful expression changed, in a moment.]E₁; maiden, with a keenness bordering on ferocity; but its expression changed, in a moment, to the smiling playfulness of her own face, as he answered—— A₁

223.36 language?"]E₁; language?" asked Elizabeth, with an impetuosity that spoke a lively interest in the reply. A₁

223.40 quickness]E₁; a quickness that equalled her former interest. A₁

224.2 smiling]E₁; with an equivocal smile A₁

224.5 and]E₁; and thus A₁

224.12 underwood]D₁; impediments of the underwood A₁

224.14-15 and a wide space of many acres was cleared]D₁; so as to leave a wide space of many acres A₁

224.16 maples]E₁; maples, with their stems, A₁

224.17 composing]D₁; composed A₁

225.4 roily.]B; ~, A₁

225.15 doggrel]E₁; ditty A₁

225.27 great]D₁; a most philosophical A₁

225.36 in the village]E₁; to-day A₁

226.3 who]D₁; while he still A₁

226.15 Jarman Flats is free]E₁; Garman Flats is A₁

226.25 course do]E₁; is the course A₁

226.25 see]E₁; see that A₁

227.1 like]E₁; just like A₁

227.5 the signs]E₁; your signs A₁

227.16 is]E₁; is always A₁

227.24 dicker]E₁; dicker away A₁

227.26 receive]E₁; take A₁

227.29 that]E₁; I ever seed A₁

228.3 remained]D₁; remained in it A₁

228.5 and]E₁; and I guess A₁

228.6 fetch]E₁; fetch twice A₁

228.16 wood-chopper]E₁; Yankee wood-chopper A₁
228.17-18 the occupation]D₁; his occupation A₁
228.22 natural]E₁; true to nature A₁
228.27 the visit]E₁; their visit A₁
228.30 observations]E₁; his observations A₁
228.37 where]D₁; when A₁
229.13 s'pose]E₁; s'pose that A₁
229.14 fighting across the water]E₁; fighting A₁
229.17 of]E₁; in A₁
229.27 at]E₁; on A₁
229.32 Opinions]E₁; Our notions A₁
230.3 the slow]D₁; his slow A₁
231.1 CHAPTER XXI]E₁; CHAPTER II A₁; CHAPTER IX B
231.4 Scott, *The Lady of the Lake,* III.xiii.3-4]CE; *Scott* A₁
231.5 principal]B; more principal A₁
231.6-7 wood-paths]E₁; wood-paths of unusual width A₁
231.8 unless]D₁; except when A₁
231.10 country]E₁; county A₁
231.12 these]F; these, there A₁
231.13 inequalities]D₁; ups and downs A₁
231.14 roots, that were]D₁; roots, A₁
231.20 the dark]E₁; their dark A₁
231.26 a highway]F; the highway A₁
231.30-31 of a formidible width, were frequent]E₁; were frequent, and, in one instance, of a formidable width A₁
231.32 one of these gaps]E₁; this barrier A₁
232.18 had witnessed]E₁; witnessed A₁
232.21 shouldst not check]D₁; should not curb A₁
232.22 recollect hearing you speak]E₁; have a remembrance of hearing you speak, sir, A₁
232.23 impression]E₁; recollection of it A₁
232.29 fervour]E₁; interested fervour A₁

233.13 time*, [*footnote*] *The author . . . . wilderness]E₁; time, A₁
233.21 and to]F; and A₁
233.28 they not]D₁; not they A₁
234.25 fallen]E₁; fallen all A₁
234.39 shoals]D₁; schools A₁
234.39 herrings]E₁; herring A₁
235.4 prosper."* [*footnote*] *All . . . true.]E₁; prosper." A₁
235.5 out]E₁; out both A₁
235.6 salt. When]D₁; salt; and when A₁
235.15-16 disregarding]E₁; utterly disregarding A₁
235.17 toil]E₁; actual toil A₁
235.20 near]E₁; back near A₁
235.36 behind]D₁; back of A₁
236.1 Susquehanna]F₁; little Susquehanna A₁ .
236.3 were you]E₁; were you there A₁
236.6 scene]D₁; view A₁
236.11 placed;]D₁; placed, and A₁
236.12 and]D₁; so that A₁
236.14 dinner;]D₁; dinner; and A₁
236.15 eastern]D₁; east A₁
236.19 no one]D₁; none A₁
236.22 though I]D₁; though I had A₁
236.24 under]E₁; under the load of A₁
236.30 when]D₁; and A₁
236.35 asking]E₁; asking, with something like a smile lurking around his features—— A₁; asking, with a smile . . . features—— D₁-D₂
237.3 though it was]D₁; though A₁
237.5 supposed]E₁; suppose A₁
*237.9 "It]E₁; ∧~ A₁
237.14 sir? The]E₁; sir?" continued Edwards. "The A₁
237.18 he]E₁; he then A₁
237.22 and]D₁; so that A₁
237.22 the country]E₁; our country A₁
237.26 seldom]E₁; seldom that A₁
237.33 interest]D₁; deep interest A₁
237.40 prospect, and]D₁; prospect, so that A₁
238.20 countrie is]E₁; countrie, it ees A₁

238.22 observed]B; noticed A₁
238.24 which]E₁; that A₁
238.28 the ride]E₁; their ride A₁
239.2 horses]B; animals A₁
239.4 followed]E₁; and was
  followed A₁
239.9 warnings as to]E₁; warnings,
  as to her safety, and A₁
239.21-22 those that hear]D₂; him
  who hears A₁; those who hear D₁
239.33 while]D₁; as A₁
239.39 his]F; their A₁
240.3 of]E₁; in A₁
240.7 tree]E₁; tree, with A₁
240.12 Louisa]E₁; The maiden A₁
240.30 accidents]E₁; of our
  accidents A₁
241.11 a rotten tree]E₁; any rotten
  trees A₁
241.18 much]E₁; much of her A₁
241.22 of]E₁; in A₁
242.1 CHAPTER XXII]E₁;
  CHAPTER III A₁; CHAPTER X
  B
242.5 Somerville, *The Chace*,
  II.197-99]CE; *Somerville* A₁
242.8 seemed]E₁; would seem A₁
242.18 from]E₁; from the summits
  of A₁
242.19 the beauty]E₁; all the
  characteristic beauty A₁
242.22 enough]E₁; enough of its A₁
242.24 hovered]D₁; would hover A₁
*242.25 for]E₁; for an opening,
  where they might obtain A₁
242.27 with]E₁; with their A₁
242.32 eyeing]E₁; proudly eyeing
  the extent of A₁
242.35 hills,]D₁; hills, and A₁
243.1 contempt]E₁; majestic
  contempt, as if penetrating to the
  very heavens, with the acuteness
  of their vision A₁
243.5 prevented]E₁; had prevented
  A₁
243.7 upon]E₁; up A₁
243.7 made]E₁; obtained A₁
243.13 motion]E₁; an undulating
  motion A₁
243.17 rose]E₁; rose over the
  border of crystals A₁
243.17 sweep]E₁; sweep far A₁

243.20 months']D₁; months A₁
243.23 boxes]E₁; boxes which were
  A₁; boxes that were D₁-D₂
243.25 animating]E₁; as animating
  A₁
243.26 fair lady]E₁; lady fair A₁
243.27 pigeons]E₁; the pigeons A₁
243.37-38 The gentlemen]D₁; All
  of the gentlemen, we do not
  include Monsieur Le Quoi, A₁
243.38 waiting for]D₁; waiting A₁
243.39 each]E₁; each being A₁
244.5 country]E₁; county A₁
244.9 them]E₁; them from the
  mountain A₁
244.11 for]D₁; for really A₁
244.11 exhilarating]E₁; most
  exhilarating A₁
244.17 a barrel]E₁; its barrel of A₁
244.25 masses,]E₁; masses, that
  were A₁
244.26 and]E₁; as by A₁
244.33 themselves,]E₁; themselves,
  as suited their inclinations; A₁
244.35 was]E₁; was to be seen A₁
244.35-36 Leather-stocking,]E₁;
  Leather-stocking, who was A₁
244.37 dogs]E₁; dogs following
  close A₁
244.37 heels; the latter]E₁; heels, A₁
245.5 shadowing]E₁; covering A₁
245.5 field, like a]E₁; field with
  darkness, like an interposing A₁
245.8 were rising]D₁; would rise A₁
245.8 volley]E₁; volley, for many
  feet into the air A₁
245.9 escape]E₁; escape the attacks
  of man A₁
245.9 were]E₁; were seen A₁
245.24-25 perhaps . . . behind]E₁;
  perhaps, their convenience or
  their necessities induced them to
  leave such an encumbrance to the
  rapidity of their march, behind
  A₁; perhaps . . . encumbrance
  behind D₁-D₂
245.26-27 being mounted]D₁;
  mounted A₁
245.27 was now in]D₁; in A₁
245.28-29 rejoicings]E₁; rejoicings
  that was A₁
245.29 Fourths]D₁; Fourth A₁

245.30 heard]E₁; heard, with its echoes A₁

245.30 and]E₁; and telling forth its sounds, for thirteen times, with all the dignity of a two-and-thirty pounder; and A₁

*245.39 Sheriff]B; sheriff A₁

246.3 announced]E₁; soon announced A₁

246.7 cries]E₁; their cries A₁

246.7 high]E₁; on high A₁

246.9 flock]E₁; flock that was A₁

246.15 whole]E₁; whole creation A₁

246.24 skear]D₁; scare A₁

246.29 village]E₁; village at them A₁

246.33 Mingo]E₁; the Mingo A₁

246.39 What! old Leather-stocking,]E₁; What's that, old Leather-stocking! A₁

246.39 cried,]D₁; ~; A₁

247.4 replied]D₁; returned A₁

247.5 that]E₁; as A₁

247.10 creater's]D₁; creaters A₁

247.14 You]E₁; But you A₁

247.16 that, old]E₁; that you say, you old, dried A₁

247.17 wordy, since the affair of]E₁; mighty boasting, sin you killed A₁

247.21 belonged]E₁; had belonged A₁

247.27 this]E₁; his A₁

247.27 late]E₁; late for him A₁

247.30 the usual]E₁; incredible A₁

247.31 lowered the rifle]D₁; had dropped his piece A₁

247.33 eye]E₁; eyes A₁

247.34 it again]D₁; his rifle A₁

248.9 this]E₁; such a A₁

248.11 relish]D₁; like A₁

248.23 on]D₁; at A₁

248.27 one]D₁; one, of the hundreds A₁

248.28 birds]E₁; birds that lay A₁

248.30 Whatever]D₁; Whatever might be the A₁

248.36-37 aide-de-camp, on this]E₁; aid-de-camp on this momentous A₁

248.38 signal]E₁; signal for A₁

249.10 more authoritative]E₁; authoritative A₁

249.10 called]E₁; called to them A₁

249.21 a poise]E₁; his shoulder A₁

249.22 a]E₁; his A₁

249.27 the rear]E₁; their rear A₁

249.34 flight]E₁; flights A₁

249.35 above]E₁; over A₁

249.38 hundreds]E₁; the hundreds A₁

249.39 the example]E₁; their example A₁

249.40 the slain]E₁; the fallen A₁

250.6 terror]E₁; terror, to examine my movements A₁

250.12-13 this side of the valley]E₁; this pass A₁; this side the valley D₁-D₂

250.13 the carnage]E₁; our carnage A₁

250.16 village]E₁; village, when I will pay thee A₁; village, where . . . you D₁-D₂

250.24-25 business, with a few idlers, for the remainder of the season]E₁; business, for the remainder of the season, more in proportion to the wants of the people A₁

250.27 thought]D₁; thought that A₁

251.1 CHAPTER XXIII]E₁; CHAPTER IV A₁; CHAPTER XI B

251.3 *Pericles*, II.i.116-17]CE; *Pericles of Tyre* A₁

251.6 mild]E₁; mild, and genial to vegetation A₁

251.19 of the]D₁; of A₁

251.19 native]E₁; his native A₁

251.27 hook]E₁; a hook A₁

251.35 design]E₁; intention A₁

252.8 while,]E₁; while, and A₁

252.9 thousands; I]E₁; thousands, and I shall A₁

252.14 dozen]E₁; half-dozen A₁

252.15 matter, Judge Temple: this]E₁; matter with you, Judge Temple," said the Sheriff, with much dignity; "this A₁

252.21 throw its shadows]E₁; cause faint shadows to be seen A₁

252.26 banks]D₁; bank A₁

252.28 moving]E₁; moving with great rapidity A₁

252.30 destination]E₁; their destination A₁

252.35 from which they had just escaped]D₁; they had just escaped from A₁

252.35 invigorating]E₁; invigorating, both to the mind and body A₁

252.36 by]D₁; with A₁

252.39 village]E₁; little village A₁

253.1 dies]E₁; then dies A₁

253.3 blazes,]E₁; blazes like a bonfire! A₁

253.3 perceive]E₁; see the A₁

253.4 jewels]D₁; box of jewels A₁

253.6 fades]E₁; begins to fade A₁

253.9 which]D₁; and it A₁

253.15-16 miraculous draught]E₁; draught of the seine A₁

253.19 clouds]E₁; the clouds A₁

253.19 light]E₁; light, by which to view the scene, A₁

253.20 fire]E₁; large piles of brush, branches, and roots, that had been collected, under the superintendence of Richard A₁

253.24 fire]E₁; fire, on the ground A₁

*253.30 night-airs]CE; light night-airs A₁; night airs E₁-F

253.30 over]E₁; over the surface of A₁

253.39 Now]D₁; now A₁

254.9 Sheriff]E₁; Sheriff, using a soothing manner A₁

254.11 two]E₁; full two A₁

254.16-17 what I have once said I'll stand to!]F; I'll stand to what I have once said. A₁; what . . . to? E₁-E₂

254.20 extended]D₁; extended, along, A₁

254.21 splinters of the chips]E₁; the splinters of the chips that were A₁

254.22 distrust of Benjamin's assertions]E₁; the distrust that was engendered by the marvellous qualities of Benjamin's assertions. It seems that he now thought it time to advance his sentiments on the subject A₁

254.26 them;]E₁; them; and A₁

254.29 village,——]E₁; village, and A₁

254.31 if that]E₁; that if that A₁

255.5 with]E₁; with such a hooker; A₁

255.11 is]E₁; was A₁

255.16 ended]D₁; had ended A₁

255.24 in]E₁; of A₁

255.25 talk]E₁; tell A₁

255.35 though]D₁; though, a A₁

256.4 service]E₁; instant service A₁

256.10 of the]E₁; from their A₁

256.14-15 there lay a boundary of impenetrable gloom]E₁; a boundary of impenetrable gloom opposed itself to the vision A₁

256.18 the fire]E₁; their fire A₁

256.19 traced]D₁; traced, for moments, A₁

256.21 water]E₁; waters A₁

256.26 to]E₁; to the duty at A₁

256.27 were stationed at the drag ropes]E₁; were to be stationed at the ropes, for the laborious service of hauling the net to land A₁; were stationed . . . land D₁-D₂

256.32 the ear]E₁; her ear A₁

256.33 was]E₁; was a A₁

256.38 voice]B; voise A₁

257.4 the net]D₁; his net A₁

257.6 splash]D₁; plash A₁

257.8 returning]E₁; returning to the shore A₁

257.13 what]E₁; what there is that A₁

257.15 strokes]D₁; stroke A₁

257.15 running]D₁; as it run A₁

257.18 the line,]E₁; the "hauling line," A₁

257.22 occasion]E₁; the occasion A₁

257.23 and enjoyed]D₁; so as to enjoy A₁

257.31 in order to enable him to form]D₁; by the way of enabling him to make up A₁

257.34 the net]E₁; your net A₁

257.40 Richard discovered his mistake, when he saw]D₁; Richard soon discovered his mistake, by noticing A₁; Richard . . . mistake, by observing B

258.1 in]E₁; to A₁
258.3 posture. He]D₁; posture;
  when he A₁
258.9 emerging]D₁; just emerging
  A₁
258.10 closed]D₁; closed so A₁
258.10 and formed]D₁; as to form
  A₁
258.11 sensibly]D₁; now sensibly A₁
258.20 which]E₁; which he A₁
258.21 shouted]D₁; cried A₁
258.23 rushed]D₁; now all rushed
  A₁
258.32 pay]E₁; pay you A₁
258.34 were now]E₁; now were A₁
258.37 movements]E₁; agitated
  movements A₁
259.1 Richard]E₁; Richard again A₁
259.7 contempt]E₁; great contempt
  A₁
259.10 rushed]D₁; rushed up A₁
259.11 into]E₁; in A₁
259.15 Edwards had]D₁; Young
  Edwards had already A₁
259.20 victims was safely]F; victims
  were safely A₁; victims was safe
  E₁-E₂
259.22 the new]E₁; their new A₁
259.24 from]D₁; from out of A₁
259.34 esteemed]D₁; esteemed as
  A₁
259.37 shad* [*footnote*] *Of all . . .
  best.]E₁; shad A₁
260.8 refuse]E₁; always refuse
  A₁;ever refuse D₁-D₂
260.8 not]D₁; never A₁
260.13 already begin]D₁; begin
  already A₁
260.16 know not]D₁; do not know
  A₁
260.36 eastern]D₁; western A₁
*260.36 Patent]E₁; patent A₁ (*Also
  first capitalized in E₁ at* 317.15,
  329.2, 332.11 *and* 334.7)
260.38 realized]B; ~" A₁
260.38 now]E₁; now, sir A₁
261.2 estate]F; estates A₁
261.3 the important]E₁; this
  important A₁
261.4 in a variety of shapes he
  was]D₁; he was, in a variety of
  shapes, A₁

262.1 CHAPTER XXIV]E₁;
  CHAPTER V A₁; CHAPTER
  XII B
262.4 Falconer, *The Shipwreck*,
  II.354-55]CE; *Falconer*
262.6 the spoil]E₁; their spoils A₁
262.7 strolled]E₁; strolled to A₁
262.8 shore]F; shores A₁
262.8 lake]E₁; lake. The shades of
  evening had been gradually
  gathering around the scene,
  during the draught of the net,
  and, while the objects in the
  vicinity of the fire were still
  distinct, and even vivid, the
  surrounding darkness became
  deeper, both by the contrast, and
  the advancing dominion of the
  night A₁
262.9 of]E₁; of light from A₁
262.10 they]E₁; the ladies A₁
262.10 contemplation]D₁; silent
  contemplation A₁
262.15 while]D₁; as A₁
262.19 melancholy]E₁; really
  melancholy A₁
262.21 picture]E₁; fine picture A₁
262.26 for]E₁; for the observance of
  such A₁;for the observance of
  D₁-D₂
262.36-263.1 and they]E₁; for a
  moment, and the maidens A₁
263.1 the party]E₁; their party A₁
263.3 the improper phraseology
  of]D₁; an improper phraseology
  in A₁
263.4 gaze]E₁; wandering gaze A₁
263.5 awkward]E₁; present
  awkward A₁
263.6 exclaiming]E₁; exclaiming, in
  all the richness of her animated
  and animating voice A₁
263.9 of Leather-stocking!"]E₁; of
  the Leather-stocking!" ¶ For
  some cause or other, Miss Grant
  had kept her eyes bent in the
  direction of the pebbles, over
  which she was walking; probably
  because, being less adventurous
  than her companion, she was
  disposed to view what could be
  faintly discerned, without

attempting the gloom, in a vain
effort to pierce its mysteries; or
probably for some better reason,
that we leave our readers to
imagine; but thus awakened, she
looked up, in the direction
pointed out by her friend, and
saw, at once, the cause of her
sudden exclamation. A_1

263.13 existence]E_1; its existence A_1

263.15 to]D_1; on to A_1

263.16 size]D_1; size, apparently, A_1

263.17 steady]E_1; steady and
glaring A_1

263.36 thought]D_1; thought that A_1

263.38 Elizabeth: "he]E_1; Elizabeth;
"but he A_1

263.41 He]E_1; he A_1

264.6 not]E_1; not being A_1

264.10 peculiar archness]D_1;
marked singularity A_1

264.20 the new]D_1; this new A_1

264.30 approached]E_1; approached
them A_1

264.40-265.1 and enlightened
the]D_1; so as to enlighten the
surrounding A_1

265.2 more impenetrable than]D_1;
as impenetrable as A_1

265.10 with]E_1; with all A_1

265.16 exertion]E_1; extraordinary
exertions A_1

265.17 upheld]D_1; upheld, over the
bow of his canoe A_1

265.18 fuel]D_1; fuel of his fire A_1

265.21 opposite]E_1; opposite to A_1

265.24 own progress]E_1; progress
by its own volition A_1

265.27 on]D_1; on to A_1

265.27 half]D_1; half of A_1

265.28-29 the landing]D_1; its
landing A_1

265.35 Natty, his tall figure
stalking]D_1; Natty, as his tall
figure stalked A_1

*265.36 ascending]E_1; ascended A_1

266.6 mine: for]E_1; mine," cried
Marmaduke; "for A_1

266.7 opinion]E_1; our opinions A_1

266.10 not]D_1; not seem to A_1

266.11 and]D_1; for A_1

266.15 life;]D_1; life; and A_1

266.22 vacillating]E_1; changeful A_1

266.23 spleen.]E_1; spleen by
exclaiming—— A_1

266.27 of]E_1; in A_1

266.27 fish;]E_1; fish, and don't play
in the matter; —— A_1; fish . . .
play; —— D_1-D_2

266.31 strolled]D_1; wandered A_1

266.34 it]E_1; it surely A_1

266.36 ashen]E_1; ash A_1

266.36 covering of]D_1; covering to
A_1

266.37 in admiration]D_1; with
admiration A_1

267.14 are]E_1; are A_1; be D_1-D_2

267.15 and are]E_1; and are down
A_1

267.16 lady]E_1; woman A_1

267.17 seat]E_1; seat and a sight A_1

267.21 Elizabeth]E_1; the heiress A_1
(*Also emended at* 274.26, 278.16
and 424.8.)

267.22 the head]E_1; his head A_1

267.22 his]E_1; this A_1

267.29 Mr.]E_1; Well, Mr. A_1

267.29 said]E_1; cried A_1

267.29-30 friend Mohegan]E_1;
friend, Mohegan, you see, A_1

268.14 by]D_1; as if by A_1

268.19 At]E_1; The shore, at A_1

268.20 lake,]E_1; lake, ran gradually
off, and A_1

268.23 interlocked with]E_1; locked
in the branches of A_1

268.26 waved]E_1; slowly waved A_1

268.31 torch laid bare]E_1; torches
exposed all A_1; torch exposed all
D_1-D_2

268.31 lake]E_1; lake, laying them
open to the eye, with the slight
variation of colour A_1; lake . . .
with a slight variation in colour
D_1-D_2

268.32 the Otsego]D_1; Otsego A_1

268.37 worthy]E_1; worthy of the
notice of A_1

268.40 who were]E_1; who were,
from motives of safety, A_1; who,
from motives of safety, were
D_1-D_2

269.3 penetrating]E_1; penetrating
the darkness in A_1

269.9 shallow water]E$_1$; the shallow waters A$_1$

269.12 nearly]E$_1$; of nearly A$_1$

269.13 penetrated to]E$_1$; from the fire made to reach A$_1$

269.14 Elizabeth then]D$_1$; There, Elizabeth A$_1$

269.14 small]E$_1$; the small A$_1$

269.15 sticks]E$_1$; sticks, that were lying on the bottom A$_1$

269.16 but]D$_1$; and A$_1$

269.22 a horizontal position]E$_1$; the position of nature A$_1$

269.25 curiosity]E$_1$; eager curiosity A$_1$

269.25 sceary]D$_1$; scary A$_1$

269.26 lies]E$_1$; lies at A$_1$

269.32 of]E$_1$; to A$_1$

269.39 again]E$_1$; again high A$_1$

270.4 canoe.]D$_1$; ~." A$_1$

270.6 torch; "I]E$_1$; torch; "enough is as good as a feast; I A$_1$

270.15-16 after it the folds of the net]E$_1$; after its toilsome way, the folds of the net, which was already spreading on the water A$_1$

270.21 berth]E$_1$; birth A$_1$

270.25 air]E$_1$; the air A$_1$

270.28 of]F$_1$; of the tones of A$_1$

271.1 light]E$_1$; the light A$_1$

271.2 the expression]D$_1$; an expression A$_1$

271.2 disgust]E$_1$; his disgust A$_1$

271.4 pretty]E$_1$; a pretty A$_1$

271.4 it]E$_1$; it too A$_1$

271.10 his]D$_1$; their A$_1$

271.10-11 under strong excitement, gave a stroke]E$_1$; under the strong excitement of his feelings, gave a stroke with it A$_1$

271.12 instant]E$_1$; instant, also A$_1$

271.32 the light]E$_1$; where the light A$_1$

271.33 where]E$_1$; how A$_1$

271.33 I will]E$_1$; let me A$_1$

272.1 Steady]E$_1$; Then steady A$_1$

272.5 with both hands some broken rushes]E$_1$; with either hand the bottoms of some broken rushes, by whose strength it was maintained in that position A$_1$

272.10 hues]E$_1$; livid hues A$_1$

272.13 head]E$_1$; motionless head A$_1$

272.19 porpoise]E$_1$; full-grown porpoise A$_1$

272.26 Benjamin]E$_1$; Benjamin from its liquid element A$_1$

272.27 shore]E$_1$; shore and land A$_1$

272.30 fire]E$_1$; fire, where he was supported A$_1$

272.34-35 vinegar]E$_1$; vinegar in cold weather A$_1$

273.2 his]E$_1$; this A$_1$

273.13-14 and in such a manner,]D$_1$; so A$_1$

273.18 glass]E$_1$; black glass A$_1$

273.23 go]E$_1$; go of A$_1$

274.4 or]E$_1$; or a A$_1$

274.15 named]E$_1$; declared A$_1$

274.16 as]E$_1$; as a A$_1$

274.17 net and fish]E$_1$; the net and the fish A$_1$

274.21 again under]D$_1$; under A$_1$

274.22 mountain]D$_1$; mountain again A$_1$

274.23 was]E$_1$; was exhibited A$_1$

274.24 forest]E$_1$; forests A$_1$

274.24 mountain]E$_1$; mountains A$_1$

274.30 by]E$_1$; if by one A$_1$

275.1 CHAPTER XXV]E$_1$; CHAPTER VI A$_1$; CHAPTER I B

275.2 "Cease]B; ∧~ A$_1$

275.5 tale."]B; ~.∧ A$_1$

275.7 ordering]D$_1$; after ordering A$_1$

275.8 big]E$_1$; that was big A$_1$

276.5 with]E$_1$; with his A$_1$

276.10 there]F; here A$_1$

276.11 Marmaduke,]E$_1$; Marmaduke, waving his hand for silence, and A$_1$

276.23 I' "]E$_1$; ~'∧ A$_1$

276.24 kind]E$_1$; most significant kind A$_1$

276.24 " 'I]E$_1$; ∧ '~ A$_1$

276.31 fail——]E$_1$; ~'∧ A$_1$

277.6 English news, which]D$_1$; news from England, and that A$_1$

277.10 arrangements]E$_1$; my arrangements A$_1$

277.24 the ride]E$_1$; his ride A$_1$

277.35 ingredients]E₁; ingredients to be found A₁

278.17 expression]E₁; proud and laughing expression A₁

278.25 leave]E₁; leave his A₁

278.37 roof to be a stranger]E₁; roof, and am yet a stranger A₁; roof, and yet a stranger D₁-D₂

279.7 curiosity]E₁; awakened curiosity A₁

279.11 smile.]E₁; smile of archness, as she answered —— A₁

279.15 the eyes]E₁; her eyes A₁

279.25 humility]E₁; your humility A₁

280.5-6 Elizabeth, who evidently put little faith in his aboriginal descent]E₁; Elizabeth, whose melancholy vanished in the excitement of their dialogue A₁; Elizabeth, whose melancholy had vanished . . . dialogue D₁-D₂

280.8 appearance? I]E₁; appearance?" asked the youth, with a little pique in his manner. "I A₁

280.10 now."]E₁; now," said the heiress. A₁

280.17 ghost of one]D₁; ghost A₁

280.18 own right]E₁; right A₁

280.22 in]E₁; in her A₁

280.36 matrimony, like]E₁; matrimony," cried the heiress, "like A₁

280.38 shall]F; should A₁

281.2 will]E₁; will assert the dignity of your sex, and A₁

281.11 young man]E₁; youth A₁

281.22-23 of slow comprehension, who]E₁; of a slow comprehension, that A₁; of a slow comprehension, who D₁-D₂

281.31 long search]E₁; most delightful research A₁

282.2 assistance]E₁; assistance to you A₁

283.12 papers]E₁; papers, that his left arm pressed to his side with a kind of convulsive motion A₁

283.23 circle]B; circles A₁

283.27 summer]E₁; animated looks of summer A₁

283.33 wheat]E₁; tops of the stalks of rich wheat A₁

283.33 was]E₁; were A₁

283.35 its]E₁; their A₁

285.1 CHAPTER XXVI]E₁; CHAPTER VII A₁; CHAPTER II B

285.4 Milman, *Belshazzar*, III.73-74]CE; *Milman* A₁

285.22 that]E₁; thy A₁

286.15 from]E₁; from the brilliant beauty of A₁

286.18 stood]E₁; had stood A₁

286.22 females]E₁; maidens A₁

286.23 towards]E₁; on to the gravelled walk that led to A₁

286.25 Mr. Edwards]E₁; Here is Mr. Edwards, A₁

286.28 he]E₁; the gentleman A₁

286.34 misunderstand]B; misunderstood A₁

286.34 meaning; I]E₁; meaning," cried the youth; "I A₁

286.39 Edwards; but]E₁; Edwards," returned Elizabeth, suffering one of her fascinating smiles to chase the trifling frown from her features; "but A₁

287.1 yet]E₁; yet, sir, A₁

287.2-3 a one]E₁; an one A₁

287.6 with]E₁; with a A₁

287.28-29 whose situation is so equivocal]B; in an equivocal situation A₁

287.30-31 our sex]B; a woman A₁

287.33 contemplative posture]B; abstracted position A₁

288.17 rung]E₁; rung far A₁

288.18 behind]D₁; back of A₁

288.21 though]D₁; but A₁

288.27 on]E₁; on to A₁

288.34 satisfied]E₁; well satisfied A₁

289.1 from]E₁; from her A₁

289.4 scent,]E₁; scent, my A₁

289.9 unusual]E₁; an unusual A₁

289.10 bushes]E₁; trees and bushes A₁

289.12 curiosity]E₁; his curiosity A₁

289.24 celebrated]E₁; celebrated as A₁

289.25 perch]E₁; the perch A₁

289.29 to]E₁; over A₁

289.36 pulled]E₁; pulled his little
boat A₁
289.36-37 minutes, to the place
where his friends were
fishing]D₁; minutes, alongside of
A₁
289.37 his boat]E₁; it A₁
289.39 nods]E₁; nods of their heads
A₁
290.4 past]E₁; by A₁
290.8 woods.]E₁; woods, nigh by.
But A₁
290.17 Edwards: "he]E₁; Edwards;
"I see that he A₁
290.21 simply]E₁; coolly A₁
290.37 We]E₁; But now we A₁
291.8 better]E₁; a better A₁
291.10 plenty]E₁; as plenty A₁
291.17 salmon-trout]F; a
salmon-trout A₁
291.30 and]E₁; and, maybe, A₁
291.39 leaves]E₁; the leaves A₁
292.7 paid]E₁; bought A₁
292.15 the council]F; a council A₁
292.30-31 looking like a curled
shaving, under my feet]E₁; under
my feet, looking like a curled
shaving A₁
292.33 far]E₁; as far A₁
293.8 when]E₁; and A₁
293.11 rugged]E₁; them rugged A₁
293.13 mountains]B; mountain A₁
293.13-14 kivered]C; more kivered
A₁
293.14 nateral]E₁; more nateral A₁
293.24 like a]E₁; just like any A₁
293.29 gathers]C; gathers itself A₁
293.34 before: it]E₁; before!"
exclaimed Edwards; "it A₁
294.2 mason-work]C; a mason's
work A₁
294.9 the wilderness]C; a
wilderness A₁
294.22 afore]C; before A₁
*294.24-25 not without]CE;
without A₁
294.26 You]E₁; Why, you A₁
294.30 near]B; near to A₁
294.31 sat]E₁; sat for a minute, A₁
295.3 an]E₁; his A₁
295.7 be out]D₁; are out A₁
295.7 be hunting]C; are hunting A₁

295.10 their own]E₁; their A₁
295.14 confused]E₁; the confused
A₁
295.22 cry]E₁; cry, directly from the
lungs of the hounds, A₁
295.24 gallantly against]E₁; most
gallantly to A₁
296.1 CHAPTER XXVII]E₁;
CHAPTER VIII A₁; CHAPTER
III B
296.4 Thomson, *The Seasons*,
"Autumn," 445–46]CE; *Thomson*
A₁
296.15 cries]E₁; howlings and cries
A₁
296.26 galley]E₁; galley, throwing
his legs forward, and gliding
along with incredible velocity A₁
296.34 away]E₁; away from him
A₁
297.1 from]E₁; off A₁
297.7 deer]E₁; the deer A₁
297.8 The]E₁; But the A₁
297.9 the skiff]E₁; his skiff A₁
297.9 hunters were]E₁; hunters A₁
297.10 the pursuit]E₁; their pursuit
A₁
297.12 gallantly]E₁; most gallantly
A₁
297.12 terror]E₁; his terror A₁
297.33 its]C; of its A₁
297.39 Ontario]E₁; the Ontario A₁
298.15 round]E₁; round, where it
lay A₁
298.20-21 to the place]E₁; to A₁
298.23 animal still]E₁; animal A₁
298.30 animation]E₁; animation, as
bright and natural as the rays that
shot from the glancing organs of
the terrified deer himself A₁
298.32 practised]E₁; a practised A₁
298.34 admitted]E₁; admitted, for a
short distance, A₁
298.36 new]E₁; new and
unexpected A₁
298.36-37 The frequency of these
circuitous movements]C; It was
the frequency of these circuitous
movements, that A₁
299.3 the victim]E₁; their intended
victim A₁
299.8 which]C; who A₁

299.15 followed]D₁; directly
  followed A₁
299.15 waters]E₁; waters for many
  feet A₁
299.22 manner]E₁; manner, saying
  A₁
299.23 law!" he said. "This]E₁; law!
  This A₁
299.25 sin' many]E₁; since this
  many A₁; sin' this many D₁-D₂
299.29 under]D₁; with A₁
299.30 caused]E₁; had caused A₁
299.32 evident]E₁; evident that A₁
300.8 look]D₁; see A₁
300.19 dared!"]E₁; dared!"
  exclaimed the impetuous youth.
  A₁
300.20 he durst to do any thing
  when there is]E₁; he dared to do
  any thing, where there was A₁; he
  durst to do any thing, where
  there is D₁-D₂
300.28 the man]E₁; and the man A₁
300.33 the cut]E₁; that cut A₁
300.36-37 the carpenter]E₁; that
  carpenter A₁
300.39 where]E₁; when A₁
301.5 the place]E₁; this place A₁
301.7 just. Give]E₁; just," cried the
  youth. "Give A₁
301.11 was]E₁; was instantly A₁
301.11 in]D₁; into A₁
301.14 along]D₁; by A₁
301.16 bade]E₁; bad A₁
302.1 CHAPTER XXVIII]E₁;
  CHAPTER IX A₁; CHAPTER
  IV B
302.7 Scott, *Marmion*,
  VI.xxix.1-5]CE; *Scott* A₁
302.9 on the mountain]E₁; with the
  activity of youth A₁
302.11 known]E₁; known, there, A₁
302.12 herself]E₁; the dignity of her
  own sex A₁
302.13 created by the]E₁; that had
  been created by their A₁
302.13-14 dissipated]E₁; dissipated
  itself A₁
302.16 took]E₁; had taken A₁
302.19 and]E₁; but A₁
302.20 friends]E₁; maidens A₁
302.32 against]E₁; against any A₁

303.13 Louisa]D₁; Louise A₁
303.22 might, at least,]E₁; might A₁
303.23 already. I]E₁; already,"
  returned the other; "I A₁
303.25 chief!]E₁; chief!"
  interrupted Elizabeth——"yes,
  yes, A₁
304.3 they]D₁; we A₁
304.7 wonderful]E₁; a wonderful
  A₁
304.10-11 I assure you he said
  so,]E₁; then he said——that——
  that"——A₁
304.20 your father——or
  mine——or even himself!]E₁;
  himself, or your father——or
  even mine. A₁
304.21 learning!]E₁; learning!"
  cried the heiress——"commencing with the last, I suppose.
  A₁
304.27 who]E₁; that A₁
304.35 you]E₁; you neither A₁
305.16 now! your]E₁; now!"
  exclaimed Elizabeth; "your A₁
305.23 when the latter]E₁; who A₁
305.32-33 the ascent]E₁; their
  ascent A₁
306.26 body,]E₁; body, either A₁
307.5-6 to leap]E₁; instant
  destruction A₁
307.8 snow]E₁; snow, and sunk
  lifeless to the earth A₁
307.11 extremity. She]E₁;
  extremity; and she A₁
307.13 instinctive]E₁; an instinctive
  A₁
307.21 approached]D₁; approached
  near to A₁
307.25 play]E₁; play all A₁
307.25 cat]E₁; cat, for a moment A₁
308.6 terrific cries]D₁; terrible cries,
  barks and growls A₁
308.17 jaws]E₁; his jaws A₁
309.5 inches]E₁; for inches A₁; four
  inches B
309.12 leaves]E₁; leaves from A₁
309.24 old]E₁; you old A₁
309.26 fearlessly maintained]E₁;
  maintained A₁
309.27 females]E₁; maidens, most
  fearlessly A₁

309.36 it had been]E₁; to the senses her apprehensions came A₁

*309.37 it]CE; them A₁

309.37 a woman]F; woman A₁

310.13 with]E₁; with all A₁

310.20 time]E₁; time; but I'm sore afeard you'll find Mr. Oliver a better companion than an old hunter, like me A₁

310.26 the walk]E₁; their walk A₁

311.4 bend]D₁; turn A₁

311.13 the peak]E₁; peak A₁

311.19 on]D₁; of A₁

311.29 it]D₁; it, Squire A₁

312.29 The painters]E₁; That painter A₁

312.29 Squire]E₁; Squire——look, there's two of them A₁

312.31 master.]E₁; master; "where's a painter!" A₁

312.34 don't be frightened]E₁; you needn't look so skeared A₁

313.7 Yes]E₁; Oh! yes A₁

313.9 having laid]D₁; laid A₁

313.10 lap,]D₁; lap, and A₁

313.22 keep no books]E₁; rather guess not A₁

*313.24 bible]CE; bible, at least A₁; Bible E₁-F

313.32 have seen]E₁; seen A₁

313.39 with]E₁; with such A₁

314.1 and]E₁; and so A₁

314.11 'Tis]D₁; ∧~ A₁

314.27 foot]E₁; a foot A₁

314.29 will little]E₁; won't over and above A₁

315.9 rifle very soon——"]E₁; rifle ag'in very soon, for I"—— A₁; rifle . . . I'll—— D₁-D₂

316.1 CHAPTER XXIX]E₁; CHAPTER VII A₁; CHAPTER V B; CHAPTER X D₁-D₂

316.3 *Timon of Athens*, IV.iii. 402]CE; *Timon of Athens* A₁

316.6 feelings]F; feeling A₁

316.12-13 parental affection]E₁; parental care, blended with affection, A₁

316.20 forest]E₁; forest, which they had now entered A₁

316.22 futurity]E₁; futurity, he replied as follows: A₁

316.24 nativity," he replied; "not]E₁; nativity; not A₁

317.1 Dickon?"]E₁; Dickon!" exclaimed the Judge. A₁

317.15 sir, I]E₁; sir," returned the Sheriff; "I A₁

317.19-20 supposed. Who are these triumviri]E₁; supposed," said Marmaduke. "Who are they A₁

317.21 Doolittle;]E₁; Doolittle; he is A₁

317.24 opportunities]E₁; opportunities than himself A₁

317.27 Jotham]E₁; Yes, sir, and Jotham A₁

317.28 Who?"]E₁; Who!" exclaimed the Judge. A₁

317.36 but]E₁; but who is A₁

317.39 him."]E₁; him," said the indignant Sheriff. A₁

318.4 egotistical]E₁; of myself A₁

318.12 there]E₁; that there A₁

318.24-25 report——the hue and cry]E₁; report A₁

319.11 your coal]E₁; your coal, sir A₁

319.26 present."]E₁; present," exclaimed Marmaduke. A₁

319.35 call this a fact of importance]E₁; know what they could be A₁

320.2 Christmas]E₁; last Christmas A₁

*320.7 know. But]D₁; know; but A₁

320.7 here——do]D₁; here. Do A₁

320.24 more]E₁; also A₁

320.24 that]E₁; since then A₁

320.25-26 hut since, is most certain of all]E₁; hut A₁

320.30 spend]E₁; spent A₁

320.32 prevent]E₁; prevented A₁

320.32 avails]E₁; availed A₁

320.34 every]E₁; in each A₁

321.9 gentleman]E₁; gentlemen A₁

321.10 useful]E₁; very useful A₁

321.15 but]D₁; as well as A₁

321.22 in his]E₁; in A₁

321.35 he reasoned]E₁; reasoned A₁

322.4 Bess]E₁; Then Bess A₁

322.4 reduced even]E₁; reduced A₁

322.30 I call this a countermine]E₁; Don't you call this a countermine for their mine A₁

322.33 At hand]E_1; Close by A_1

322.34 our]E_1; our gentlemen A_1

323.27 a finger]E_1; his finger A_1

323.28 of a]D_1; of A_1

323.29 and was]E_1; and A_1

324.8 precipitously]F; precipitately A_1

324.9 sides]D_1; side A_1

324.9 the rocks]D_1; rocks A_1

324.14-15 asked solemnly——¶ "Judge]E_1; cried——¶ "Well, Judge A_1

324.16 and]E_1; and to me A_1

324.31 sessions of the peace,]D_1; gaol delivery; A_1

325.2 feeling]E_1; feelings A_1

325.8-9 mountain,]E_1; mountain, but A_1

325.14 emotion]E_1; his emotions A_1

326.1 CHAPTER XXX]E_1; CHAPTER XI A_1; CHAPTER VI B

326.3 *The Merchant of Venice*, IV.i.300]CE; *Merchant of Venice* A_1

326.5 in]F; in the A_1

326.8 already styled]E_1; styled A_1

326.12 conversation.——When]E_1; conversation for that period. At its expiration, when A_1

326.14 air]E_1; air, softening the manly expression of his features A_1

326.27 hand]E_1; fair hand A_1

326.32 forest]B; forests A_1

326.34 interrupted]D_1; interrupted the remainder of A_1

327.4 door-yard]E_1; door-yard, maybe A_1

*327.11 sheering nearer]E_1; shearing alongside A_1

327.26 child;]E_1; child," said the Judge, smiling; "it is A_1

327.33 vanish the instant]D_1; have vanished, when A_1

327.36 of]E_1; in his A_1

328.6 care]E_1; care, sir, A_1

328.34 those]E_1; these A_1

329.28 above]E_1; above all A_1

329.29 face]E_1; beautiful face A_1

329.29 architect]E_1; architect, with a scornful smile A_1

329.32 as]E_1; as poor A_1

330.3 hand]E_1; hand playfully A_1

330.17 feeling]E_1; some powerful passion A_1

330.20 you,]B; ~ ∧ A_1

330.30 softened]E_1; softened by his recent emotions A_1

331.6-7 impulse directed]E_1; if directed by a common impulse A_1

331.20 a leg]E_1; one leg, and an invalid A_1

331.21 he felt]E_1; felt A_1

333.14 without]E_1; without any A_1

333.33 laugh]D_1; laugh, that could have been heard in the village A_1

333.38 creatur]E_1; divil A_1

333.39 bow-knot]D_1; beau-knot A_1

333.39 Barcelony]E_1; Barcelony. Why, Jotham, you could take him down yourself, as you'd a two-years pine with an axe A_1; Barcelony .... as you'd take down a two-years' ... axe D_1-D_2

334.12 he]E_1; him A_1

334.18 valie]D_1; value A_1

334.22 To my notion]D_1; In my notions A_1

334.27 next]F; next to A_1

334.28 was]F; was but A_1

334.31 Natty]E_1; Natty also A_1

334.32 old]E_1; you old A_1

335.11 way]D_1; place A_1

336.10-11 and I partly]E_1; though I A_1

336.17 his]E_1; that his A_1

336.38 want]E_1; want your A_1

337.7 peals]E_1; loud peals A_1

337.18 ye]D_1; you A_1

337.19-20 yourn ... foot]E_1; yours shall both turn red this green grass, before you put foot A_1; yourn both shall turn this green grass red, afore you put your foot D_1-D_2

337.21 While]D_1; So long as A_1

337.28 and]D_1; so as to A_1

337.40 there'll]E_1; there'll soon A_1

338.3 varmint]E_1; varmint as them A_1

338.5 as]E_1; as a A_1

338.18 and of Natty's disrespect of]E_1; of Natty's disrespect to A_1

338.29 were suspended]D₁; lay over
A₁
339.1 CHAPTER XXXI]E₁;
CHAPTER XII A₁; CHAPTER
VII B
339.4 Scott, *Marmion*,
VI.xiv.23-25]CE; *Marmion* A₁
339.31-32 his auditor; "it]E₁; the
other; "why, it A₁
340.18 youth,]E₁; youth, as A₁
340.19 a suspicion]E₁; the suspicion
A₁
340.28-29 a convulsive]D₁; a kind of
convulsive A₁
340.39 and]B; and is A₁
341.11 of]E₁; in A₁
341.13 moments]F; moment A₁
341.15 yielding]F; yielding a A₁
341.20 them]E₁; them in A₁
341.20 necessities]E₁; emergencies
A₁
341.34 has]F; has just A₁
342.2 into]E₁; into the A₁
342.3 how and where]B; where and
how A₁
342.10 room.]E₁; room. Oh! A₁
342.26 as if in deep communion]E₁;
in an abstracted posture, as if
communing deeply A₁
342.31 for an interview]E₁; to see
you A₁
342.34 moisture]E₁; moisture; but a
flush crossed her cheeks, that
resembled the tints which the
setting sun throws over the
neighbouring clouds A₁
342.38 Louisa]F; Louise A₁
343.2 Miss Temple,]E₁; I know not
how it was, Miss Temple, but A₁
343.16-17 his companion]E₁; the
maiden A₁
343.22 Elizabeth; "I]E₁; Elizabeth,
beckoning with her hand for
silence; "I know it——I A₁
343.27 like one]E₁; like a girl A₁;
like the girl D₁-D₂
343.39 and his manner]E₁; with a
look of care, and his manner was
A₁
344.5 his]E₁; his devoted A₁
344.6 now out]E₁; out A₁
344.15 struggling to speak with

firmness]E₁; in an agitated voice
A₁
344.28 this]E₁; such a A₁
344.30 they? They]E₁; they? I may
ask," returned Marmaduke.
"They A₁
344.37 the father]F; her father A₁
344.39 and]E₁; and thy A₁
345.18 his]E₁; with his fine, manly
A₁
345.26 and those]B; those A₁
345.31-32 to his impatient daughter
for silence]D₁; his impatient
daughter to be silent A₁
346.16 you, at least,]E₁; you A₁
346.26 not]E₁; not yet A₁
346.33 her]E₁; her light A₁
347.1 CHAPTER XXXII]E₁;
CHAPTER XIII A₁; CHAPTER
VIII B
347.4 Pope, "The Temple of
Fame," 11.111-12]CE; *Pope* A₁
347.8 that]D₁; which A₁
347.17 the kind]E₁; that kind A₁
348.18 'an]E₁; 'an a A₁
348.18 'an]E₁; 'an a A₁
348.19 an]E₁; an a A₁
348.21 tare]F; tear A₁
348.21 open]E₁; all open A₁
348.21 Richard]E₁; Richard——
such a booful copse A₁
349.5 berth]E₁; birth A₁
349.11 he had]E₁; it was A₁
349.25 particular parts]D₁; spots A₁
349.37 toddy]E₁; the toddy A₁
350.7 compass,]E₁; compass, that
was A₁
350.16 country]E₁; county A₁
350.22 Benjamin]E₁; Benjamin; I
A₁
350.29 mayhap]D₁; maybe A₁
351.14 Benjamin]E₁; But,
Benjamin A₁
351.14 Presbyterian;]E₁;
Presbyterian sermon! A₁
352.10 for your own affairs]D₁; to
put down your own affairs on A₁
352.11 I]E₁; for I A₁
352.19 large, honest]E₁; honest,
large A₁
352.27 what]E₁; why, what A₁
352.39 here]D₁; there A₁

353.34 way]D₁; weigh A₁
353.35 house?"]E₁; house?"
  demanded Richard,
  peremptorily. A₁
353.36 has."]E₁; has," said the
  steward. A₁
354.4 secure]E₁; to secure A₁
354.10 sessions of the peace]D₁;
  gaol delivery A₁
354.10 commonly called]D₁; called
  in vulgar parlance A₁
355.2 forest]E₁; deep forest A₁
355.15 friends]E₁; my friends A₁
355.37 plan]E₁; plans, within their
  own thoughts, A₁; plans D₁-D₂
355.37 to escape]E₁; to escape A₁;
  escape D₁-D₂
356.4 on]D₁; to A₁
356.9 over]E₁; over his A₁
356.11-12 amazement]E₁; utter
  amazement A₁
356.14 the ends]E₁; ends A₁
356.21 This]B; The A₁
356.22 powerful]E₁; powerful in its
  effects A₁
356.36 appointed]D₁; allotted A₁
356.37 lest]E₁; least A₁
357.16 an]E₁; an instinctive and A₁
357.28-29 whither Mohegan had
  retreated]D₁; whether Mohegan
  had returned A₁
358.1 CHAPTER XXXIII]E₁;
  CHAPTER XIV A₁; CHAPTER
  IX B
358.4 *King Lear*, II.ii.125-27]CE;
  Lear A₁
358.16 pride]E₁; conscious pride A₁
358.24 cause]E₁; cause that was A₁
358.25 these]E₁; these two A₁
358.28 others]E₁; others, at an
  unequal gait A₁
358.30-32 juror. Fifty . . .
  errand.]E₁; juror. A₁
358.33 filled]E₁; filled with groups
  of men A₁
359.2 were]E₁; were to be observed
  A₁
359.2 most]F; mostly A₁
359.3 infants]E₁; infants in their
  arms A₁
359.5 connubial love was yet fresh,
  walking]E₁; the warmth of

connubial love was yet new,
  walking among the moving
  throng, both dressed in their
  back-wood finery, A₁
359.7 bride, by a gallant offering of
  a thumb!]E₁; mistress by the
  unbending motions of an
  extended arm, to which she was
  appended by grasping his thumb.
  A₁; bride by the unbending . . .
  his thumb. D₁-D₂
359.8 door]E₁; front door A₁
359.9 flourishing]E₁; flourishing in
  his hand A₁
359.26 incongruity]E₁; incongruity
  was nothing; it A₁
359.28-29 slaughter. One or two of
  their number]E₁; slaughter, one
  or two of whom A₁
359.35-36 without. Among the
  captives]E₁; without, among
  which A₁
359.40 heads of the]E₁; heads of A₁
360.4 bench,]E₁; bench run along
  one of its sides, and was A₁
360.6 protected]E₁; was protected
  A₁
360.6 railing, ran along one of its
  sides]E₁; railing A₁
360.10 were]E₁; were placed A₁
360.12 divisions]E₁; several
  divisions A₁
360.13 square,]F; space A₁
360.33 prevailed]E₁; prevailed
  there A₁
361.8 fastened]E₁; that were
  fastened A₁
*361.9 if searching for]CE; if in
  search of A₁; searching E₁-F
361.10 opened]E₁; then opened A₁
361.23 public]E₁; the public A₁
361.38 charge]E₁; charge against
  him A₁
362.9 laughed]E₁; laughed again,
  A₁
362.12 untrue.]B; ~∧ A₁
362.18 will]E₁; shall A₁
362.26 died]D₁; die A₁
*362.30 eye-brows]CE; eye-brows
  alone A₁; eyebrows E₁-F
363.9 of]E₁; for A₁
363.12 I thought I]E₁; I A₁

364.27 due weight with]E_1; their due weight to A_1

364.29 the box]E_1; their box A_1

365.34 trigger]E_1; a trigger A_1

366.1 found]E_1; found a A_1

366.15 charge.]B; ~∧ A_1

366.30-31 whole affair]E_1; affair A_1

366.32 aided]E_1; addressed A_1

366.37 mind]E_1; mind such a one as A_1

367.31 abruptly thrust]E_1; thrust A_1

367.36 its]E_1; her A_1

367.36-37 authority.]E_1; authority, by saying—— A_1

367.38-39 dialogues," he said. "Proceed]E_1; dialogues. Proceed A_1

368.1 if]E_1; if he were A_1

368.7 buck!]E_1; ~? A_1

370.31 melancholy earnestness]E_1; a melancholy tone of voice A_1

371.7 sin']D; since A_1

*371.37 Bold Dragoon]D_1; bold dragoon A_1 (*Also first capitalized at* 385.21 *and* 392.12.)

373.1 CHAPTER XXXIV]E_1; CHAPTER XV A_1; CHAPTER X B

373.2 *King Lear*, II.ii.8]CE; *Lear* A_1

373.5 and]F; with A_1

373.6 merciful]E_1; modern but doubtful A_1

373.13 strong]E_1; a strong A_1

373.19 him,]E_1; him, as if A_1

373.22 unfeeling exultation, or]E_1; savage exultation expressed, nor A_1

373.29 use]E_1; use to be found A_1

373.36 glasses.]B; ~∧ A_1

374.32 while]E_1; their efforts A_1

374.35 were]E_1; were made in A_1

374.38 is]F; is that A_1

375.12 Bump-ho]D_1; Bumppo A_1 (*Also emended at* 375.35, 376.11, 380.6, *and* 388.6.)

375.27 smile]E_1; smile in vain A_1

375.34 up]E_1; up aloft A_1

375.34 cant]E_1; slue A_1

375.36 dog-watch]D_1; dog's watch A_1

376.26 members]D_1; numbers A_1

377.33 to exercise]E_1; exercise A_1

377.34 the strength]D_1; what strength A_1

377.39 he had taken his antagonist at a great disadvantage]E_1; their positions were a great disadvantage to his antagonist, without at all discomposing the steward A_1

378.21 unequivocal]E_1; equivocal A_1

378.30 violent]E_1; perfectly unequivocal A_1

378.38 worked away]E_1; worked A_1

379.4 had found means]E_1; found means, however, A_1

379.5 time]E_1; time that A_1

379.7 independently]E_1; independent A_1

379.26 said, reproachfully]E_1; cried A_1

379.28 were]E_1; were as A_1

380.6 berthed]E_1; birthed A_1

380.16 being]E_1; being fair A_1

380.23 ordering]D_1; he ordered A_1

380.23 he]D_1; and A_1

380.33 in]E_1; in close and A_1

382.1 CHAPTER XXXV]E_1; CHAPTER XVI A_1; CHAPTER XI B

382.6 Butler, *Hudibras*, II.ii.841-44]CE; *Hudibras* A_1

382.14 soothe]E_1; sooth A_1

383.26 the side of his cattle]E_1; their side A_1

383.27 fatigued]E_1; equally fatigued with his beasts, A_1

383.39 approached]E_1; approached near to A_1

383.39 look]E_1; searching look A_1

384.5 both]E_1; them both A_1

384.6 the words]E_1; their tones A_1

384.22 Certainly]E_1; Certainly, sir A_1

384.31 Elizabeth]E_1; Elizabeth was transient as a gleam of flitting light, and A_1

384.33 object]E_1; immediate object A_1

385.9 berth]E_1; birth A_1

385.27 When]D_1; So soon as A_1

386.3 candle]E_1; candle he carried A_1

386.6 gratitude]E₁; gratitude to you
A₁
386.17 melancholy]E₁; a
melancholy musing A₁
386.35 she]E₁; the heiress A₁
386.35 features]E₁; features, from
the dim light, by her dark tresses
A₁
386.36 moment.]E₁; moment, when
she faced the party and
continued—— A₁
386.38 defender," she continued.
"Your]E₁; defender. Your A₁
387.4 well]E₁; well, gall A₁; well, gal
D₁-D₂
387.12 are]E₁; sit with so much
composure A₁
387.20 taut]F; taught A₁
387.22 silent,]B; ~∧ A₁
387.31 across]D₁; to cross A₁
388.12 word, and then]D₁; word
then and A₁
388.14 looking]F; looking up A₁
388.22 What]B; But what A₁
388.23 thirty days]B; one month A₁
389.24 us,]B; ~∧ A₁
390.11 hundred]B; hnndred A₁
392.15 clear]E₁; clear, moonshiny A₁
392.23 There's]E₁; By heaven,
there's A₁
392.25 enjoined]E₁; bid A₁
392.39 ladies,]E₁; ladies, with A₁
393.27 easy]E₁; easy for you A₁
393.27 please]E₁; pleased A₁
393.32 females]E₁; heiress A₁
393.38 ye]D₁; you A₁
394.1 had lost]F; lost A₁
394.33 within]B; with A₁
395.5 became as]E₁; became again
A₁
396.1 CHAPTER XXXVI]E₁;
CHAPTER XVII A₁; CHAPTER
XII B
396.6 Campbell, *Gertrude of
Wyoming*, III.xxxv.1-4]CE;
Gertrude of Wyoming A₁
396.9 pledge]E₁; pledge that A₁
396.12 possession]E₁; possession
only A₁
396.16 in]E₁; into A₁
396.19 good-natured]E₁; a

good-natured A₁
396.20 commonly]D₁; oftentimes
A₁
396.26 chère]D₁; chere A₁
396.28 said]E₁; cried A₁
396.28 hope]E₁; must hope A₁
396.29-397.2 entirely. ¶ The
complaisant . . . . countrymen]E₁;
entirely." ¶ "Ah! Ma'mselle
Templ'! vat honneur I feel to me;
mais I 'ave lettair, dat mak-a mon
cœur sautez de joie. Ah!
Ma'mselle Templ', if you 'ave
pere, 'ave mere, 'ave
leetl'—Jean-tone, vy you dont
'and de ladi a pins, eh!—if you
'ave amis beeg and leetl' you voud
be glad to go back. Attendez
vous, Ma'mselle, si vous plais; je
vous lirai. 'A Monsieur Monsieur
Le Quoi, de Mersereau, à
Templetone, Noo Yorck, les Etats
Unis d'Amérique. Très cher
ami,—Je suis ravis"— ¶ "I
apprehend that my French is not
equal to your letter, Monsieur,"
said Elizabeth, glancing her eye
expressively at her companion;
"will you favour us with its
substance in English?" ¶ "Oh!
pardonne me—I 'ave been so
long from Paris dat I do forget
de—a—a—a—pronunsashong.
You vill 'ave consideration pour
moi, and vill excusez my read in
France," returned the polite
Gaul, bowing with deep humility,
as if lamenting his ignorance of
his own language; "mais I shall
tell you en bon Anglois. I 'ave
offeece à Paris, in Bureau, dans le
temps du bon Louis; I fly; run
avay to sav-a my 'ead. I 'ave in
Martinique von leetl' plantation
pour sucre—ah! ha!—vat you
call in dis countray—ah! ha!
—Monsieur Beel, vat you call de
place vere you vork-a? eh?"
¶ "Clearing," said the wood-
chopper, with a kind nod. ¶ "No,
no, clear—vere you burn-a my

troat, eh!" ¶ Billy hitched up his shoulder, and turned his eyes askance at the ladies, with a broad grin on his face, as he answered— ¶ "I guess 'tis a sugar-bush that the Mounsheer means;—but you mus'nt take that to heart, man; 'tis the law of the woods." ¶ "Ah! coquin, I pardonne you," returned the Frenchman, placing his hand involuntarily on his throat— "diable! de law should be altair. Mais, I 'ave sucre-boosh in Martinique: I fly dere too;—I come ici;—votre pere help-a me;——I grow reech—yais! I grow reech; mais I 'ave not France!—L'Assemblée Nationale pass von edict"—— ¶ "What's that?" interrupted Billy, who was endeavouring, with much interest, to comprehend the story. ¶ "Eh! vat dat! vy vat you call, ven de Assemblée d' Alban' mak-a de law?" ¶ "That's an act of the Legyslatoore," said Kirby, with the readiness of an American on such a subject. ¶ "Vell! dis vas act of Legyslatoore, to restorer my land; my charactair; my sucre-boosh; and ma countray. Ah! Ma'mselle Templ', je suis enchanté! mais I 'ave grief to leav-a you; Oh! yais! I 'ave grief ver mooch A_1

397.3 it all]E_1; all this A_1
397.29 diffidence]E_1; feelings A_1
397.36 apprehension]E_1; apprehensions A_1
397.37 delicacy]E_1; delicacies A_1
397.38-39 herself; but, sensible]E_1; herself, the colour gradually gathering over her features at her own thoughts; but, as if sensible that A_1
398.1 me]E_1; me, and A_1
398.12 nigh]E_1; nigh to A_1
398.35 she]E_1; the heiress A_1
398.36 dwelling]E_1; dwelling in her thoughts A_1

398.41-399.1 At this point]E_1; It was at this point that A_1
399.5 with which]E_1; that A_1
399.6 contend]E_1; contend against A_1
399.10 glance]E_1; scrutinizing glance A_1
399.11 she]E_1; when she A_1
399.14-15 conjectures]E_1; thoughts A_1
399.21 Elizabeth]E_1; While calling, Elizabeth gradually A_1
399.24 answering]D_1; as if in answer A_1
399.29 were]D_1; was A_1
399.33 Our heroine]E_1; Miss Temple A_1
399.37 Mohegan was seated on the trunk of a fallen oak]E_1; On the trunk of a fallen oak Mohegan was seated A_1
399.38 eyes]E_1; glaring eyes A_1
400.5 and in]E_1; and was in A_1
400.5 it was terrific]E_1; terrific A_1
400.6 away]E_1; either way A_1
400.7 eyes]E_1; eyes, without their usual shading A_1
400.13 his cheeks]E_1; either cheek A_1
400.20 long had]E_1; had A_1
400.21 you]E_1; you this month past A_1
401.4 "since]B; ∧~ A_1
401.9 was]E_1; was yet A_1
401.20 other's]E_1; others' A_1
401.26 exchange]E_1; trade A_1
401.28 his companion]E_1; the heiress A_1
401.29 little.]E_1; little, as he replied, in a louder and more animated voice—— A_1
401.30 are]D_1; were A_1
401.31-32 Fire-eater?" he replied, in a more animated voice; "are]E_1; Fire-eater! are A_1
401.34 rum]E_1; rum, for it A_1
402.19 shame]E_1; her shame A_1
402.20 in]E_1; in a tone of A_1
402.34 by]E_1; by the melancholy of A_1

402.38 spirits;]E_1; spirits; but A_1

403.4 speak]E_1; speak again, for some time A_1

403.6 I]E_1; this canister of powder I A_1

403.6-7 this canister of powder at]E_1; at A_1

403.10 gift]E_1; gift of the heiress A_1

403.10 into]E_1; in A_1

403.16 and]E_1; and all A_1

403.17 an]E_1; his A_1

403.22-23 gradually]D_1; gradually, as he gazed A_1

403.36-37 powerful]E_1; secret A_1

403.40 to earth. Taking]E_1; to the earth, and, taking A_1

404.2 them——]E_1; them, before he answered. A_1

404.4 see, it]E_1; see, A_1

404.12 of]E_1; of furious A_1

404.16 woods]E_1; woods, with a painful anxiety A_1

404.18 minute]E_1; few minutes A_1

404.23 horror]E_1; horror painted A_1

405.1 CHAPTER XXXVII]E_1; CHAPTER XVIII A_1; CHAPTER XIII B

405.3 Scott, *The Lay of the Last Minstrel*, III.ii.5]CE; *Lay of the Last Minstrel* A_1

405.9 John;]E_1; John, for A_1

405.12 rock as]F; rock, so A_1; rock, E_1-E_2

405.19 terror]E_1; her terror A_1

405.19 with]E_1; with her A_1

405.20 shock]E_1; shock for a moment A_1

405.24 calmly: "there]E_1; calmly, and rallying her thoughts for the emergency. "There A_1

405.24 but]E_1; but still A_1

405.33 him]E_1; him here A_1

405.36 man; he]E_1; man, who A_1

406.4 tones]E_1; horrid tones A_1

406.5-6 scenes; and]E_1; scenes; A_1

406.20 life]E_1; your life A_1

406.22 already been]F; been already A_1

406.23 terrace]D_1; terraces A_1

406.30 speed]E_1; her speed A_1

406.39 them]E_1; them both A_1

407.1 unfortunately,]E_1; unfortunately, there was A_1

407.2 dried,]E_1; dried, which A_1

407.3 the warm]E_1; an eddying of the warm A_1

407.9 stupor]E_1; sort of stupor A_1

407.12 even]E_1; even to A_1

407.20 fuel]E_1; fuel for the flames A_1

407.21 scorched]F; scorching A_1

407.21-22 was ignited]E_1; ignited A_1

407.23 flames]E_1; flame A_1

407.26-27 Edwards and Elizabeth]E_1; Elizabeth and the youth A_1

407.28 The former]E_1; Edwards A_1

407.38 there was hope]E_1; hope had invigorated them with her secret influence A_1

408.1 broke]D_1; burst A_1

408.2 light]E_1; nothing A_1

408.3-4 whispered;——]E_1; whispered, rather than uttered aloud; A_1

408.6 vacant]E_1; vacant, horrid A_1

408.16 examined]E_1; examined into A_1

408.17 for]F; of A_1

408.24 said]E_1; said, in a hollow accent A_1

408.27 methods]E_1; methods by which A_1

408.33 will]E_1; shall A_1

408.34 sacrificed]E_1; the sacrifice A_1

409.3 half]D_1; half the A_1

409.9 soon ended]D_1; ended before A_1

409.10 have consumed already the captives they enclosed]E_1; have soon swept off the victims, who were suffering doubly under the anticipations of their approaching fate A_1; have swept . . . fate D_1-D_2

409.12 had availed]E_1; availed A_1

409.14 on]E_1; over A_1

409.14 rock]E_1; rock on which they stood, A_1

409.18 leaves,]E_1; leaves, that were drained of their nourishment; A_1

409.22 brush]E₁; leaves and boughs A₁

409.23 fuel,]E₁; fuel, there was A₁

409.24 country gushed]E₁; country, gushing A₁

409.25 and]E₁; which A₁

409.27 it swept]E₁; swept A₁

409.32 seasons,]E₁; seasons, when it exhibited a mimic torrent, overflowing the ground for some distance; A₁

409.36 army]E₁; army impatiently A₁

409.37 to]E₁; to death and A₁

409.40 under]D₁; with A₁

410.1 heat]E₁; heat that was thrown across the little spot of wet ground A₁

410.1 while]E₁; while the A₁

410.5 trees]E₁; trees. The excited imagination of Elizabeth, as she stood on the verge of the precipice, and gazed about her, viewing the approach of their powerful enemy, fancied every tree and herb near her on the point of ignition A₁

410.10-11 falling]E₁; prostrated A₁

410.15 sometimes known]E₁; known A₁

410.35 smile of Elizabeth was celestial:]E₁; smile that beamed on the lovely features of Elizabeth was celestial, as she answered, in a soft, soothing voice, A₁

410.37 man]E₁; man, in the vigour and pride of manhood, A₁

410.38 youth]E₁; youth with fervour A₁

411.5 yet be hope——you at least]E₁; be hope yet——you A₁

411.16-17 instantaneous]E₁; instantaneous and magical A₁

411.22 by]E₁; by the A₁

411.25 heard]E₁; heard, raising its tones A₁

411.29 leaving]D₁; so as to leave A₁

411.33 so]E₁; too A₁

411.33 great but]E₁; great, for A₁

411.34 could]E₁; to A₁

412.9 poor,]E₁; ~! A₁

412.20 command]E₁; bid A₁

412.20 you!]E₁; you! me, A₁

412.32 raised from the earth]E₁; of heaven A₁

412.36 she]E₁; the maiden, standing in her extremity, A₁

412.37 woman]E₁; woman. The blood gathered slowly, again, in those cheeks, that had, in anticipation of the tyrant's triumph, assumed the livid appearance of death, until they glowed with the loveliness of her beauty A₁

412.37 struggled]E₁; struggled with herself A₁

412.39 of]E₁; of her A₁

413.7 Edwards]E₁; Edwards, springing on his feet A₁

413.9 followed]E₁; followed, that was succeeded by a comparative stillness A₁

414.1 CHAPTER XXXVIII]E₁; CHAPTER XIX A₁; CHAPTER XIV B

414.4 Campbell, *Gertrude of Wyoming*, III.xxxix.3-4]CE; *Gertrude of Wyoming* A₁

414.8 terror]E₁; terrors A₁

414.16 succeeded]B; succeed A₁

414.30 fear.]E₁; fear, and said—— A₁

414.31 child," he said; "for]E₁; child, for A₁

415.7 more]E₁; some A₁

415.13 recoiled]E₁; recoiled for A₁

415.13 intelligence.]E₁; intelligence, and exclaimed—— A₁

415.16 ye need]F; you need A₁

415.22 mountain,]E₁; mountain with the activity of youth, and A₁

415.26 time]E₁; time left A₁

415.31 in such a manner]D₁; so A₁

415.36 Edwards']D₁; Edward's A₁

415.39 spoke]E₁; cried A₁

415.41 Mingo]E₁; tortured Mingo A₁

416.2 a-tween]D₁; between A₁

416.10 come. Let]E₁; come. No——let A₁

416.17 As]E₁; Even as A₁

416.26 one,]E₁; one, I tell you, sich A₁
416.30 branches,]E₁; branches, yet A₁
417.2-3 altogether]E₁; altogether like A₁
417.12 agitated;]E₁; agitated with a strong emotion, A₁
417.16 one]E₁; one who was A₁
417.25 with a]B; with a a A₁
417.29 Leave me]F; Leave A₁
417.35 Hereaway]E₁; Here, away A₁
417.36 berth,]F; birth A₁
418.22 eyes]E₁; eye A₁
418.25 prevented]E₁; diverted A₁
418.25 reply]E₁; reply of the youth A₁
419.10 'arth]E₁; the 'arth A₁
419.15 the hour of his]D₁; his hour of A₁
419.29 towards]F; to A₁
419.34-35 so loud as to be distinct.]E₁; to fulness, if not to harmony:—— A₁
419.36 come!]E₁; come! No Delaware fears his end; no Mohican shrinks from death; for the Great Spirit calls, and he goes. My father I have honoured; I have cherished my mother; to my tribe I've been faithful and true. A₁
420.6 word]E₁; word of it A₁
420.7-8 heart! Humility]E₁; heart!" exclaimed the divine. "Humility A₁
420.12 blessings]E₁; blessing A₁
420.23 No;]E₁; No; for A₁
420.25 wise;]E₁; wise; and A₁
420.28 divine]F; good divine A₁
420.31 loss]E₁; loss to him A₁
420.32 is]E₁; is now A₁
420.39 me]E₁; me to do A₁
421.11 it's]D₁; its A₁
421.17 we]E₁; we both A₁
422.16 paused for the elements]E₁; paused; for the scene, and the elements, seemed to conspire to oppress the powers of humanity A₁

422.35 stretched]E₁; stretched forth A₁
422.39 dropped]E₁; dropped, rigid and motionless, A₁
423.24 world]B; world will A₁
423.26 of]E₁; of my A₁
424.18 again;]E₁; again, and A₁
424.21 cries]E₁; piercing cries A₁
424.25 provided]E₁; provided, to remove her body, living or dead as Heaven had directed her fate A₁
424.29 end.* [*footnote*] *The probability . . . . course.]E₁; end. A₁
425.1 CHAPTER XXXIX]E₁; CHAPTER XX A₁; CHAPTER XV B
425.6 Byron, *Childe Harold's Pilgrimage*, II.lxxi.50-53]CE; *Byron* A₁
425.14 among]F; along A₁
426.17 of a]E₁; with a A₁
427.16 character]F; characters A₁
*427.25 Sheriff]E₁; sheriff A₁ (*Also first capitalized in E₁ at* 428.15, 428.30, 431.33, 431.38, 438.38, *and* 444.12.)
428.7 his]F; its A₁
428.12 sufficiently compact]E₁; excellent A₁
*428.25 apart. ¶ At]E₁; apart. At A₁
428.26 conjuncture]F; juncture A₁
429.5 great]E₁; a wonderful A₁
429.37 Doolittle,]E₁; Doolittle, out A₁
*430.16 stanch]CE; stanch, I tell you A₁; staunch E₁-F
430.17 hours']E₁; hour's A₁
431.2 wake]E₁; wake, sir A₁
431.16 out,]E₁; out, just A₁
431.29 yield]E₁; yield in A₁
432.18-19 the direction in which]E₁; which way A₁
432.20 bellowing]E₁; loud bellowing A₁
433.10 swift]E₁; wonderfully swift A₁
433.32 on]E₁; on sich A₁
433.33 believing, is]E₁; believing it A₁

434.10 heard]F; heard even A₁
434.15 by]E₁; by his A₁
434.19 the breast-work]E₁; his
    breast-work A₁
435.33 suspense]E₁; mute suspense
    A₁
436.1 CHAPTER XL]E₁;
    CHAPTER XXI A₁; CHAPTER
    XVI B
436.2 dumb.]B; ~." A₁
436.4 *The Merchant of Venice,*
    V.i.279-80]CE; *Shakspeare* A₁
436.28 that]E₁; which A₁
437.17 at]E₁; at our A₁
437.32 with a]F; with A₁
437.34 Lost indeed]E₁;
    Emphatically so A₁
439.25 him]E₁; him, with a bitter
    smile A₁
439.26 differed]E₁; divided A₁
440.4 its]F; his A₁
440.35 had deserted]F; deserted A₁
440.37 formerly]D₁; once A₁
440.39 of]E₁; to A₁
441.20-21 blood or breeding]D₁;
    blood A₁
442.30 see]E₁; provide A₁
443.4 of]E₁; for A₁
443.28 voice]E₁; sweet voice A₁
443.36 Judge]B; Jndge A₁
444.7 said]E₁; cried A₁
444.17 are mistaken]E₁; will soon
    find themselves in a mistake A₁
444.32 Monsieur]E₁; Mr. A₁
445.6 Gaul, as the Sheriff called
    him,]E₁; Gaul A₁
445.7 though]E₁; though he was A₁
446.1 CHAPTER XLI]E₁;
    CHAPTER XXII A₁; CHAPTER
    XVII B
446.8 Scott, *The Lord of the Isles,*
    I.xvii.1-4,11-12]CE; *Lord of the
    Isles* A₁
446.30 the imprisonment]E₁; their
    imprisonment A₁
447.14 "visionary"]E₁; 'visionary' A₁
447.19 some such character]E₁;
    such a Gaul A₁
447.29 system;——the]E₁; system.
    The A₁

447.38 under a]E₁; under her A₁
448.2 direction]E₁; direction they
    took A₁
448.3 the walk]E₁; their walk A₁
448.30 Louisa]E₁; Louise A₁
449.30 Bess]E₁; Why, Bess A₁
450.12 inscription]E₁; inscription
    that was there engraven A₁
450.14-15 ornamented]E₁;
    ornamented tastefully A₁
450.18 working]E₁; working with
    his feelings A₁
450.31 manifesting]E₁; manifesting
    any A₁
451.8 together,]E₁; together ag'in
    A₁
451.25 chivalrous]E₁; chivalric A₁
451.35 have ye]B; have you A₁
451.39 speakers]E₁; speakers, but
    the pure cambric, that,
    contrasted to her dark eyes,
    attested the feelings of the
    youthful bride A₁
451.40 effort]E₁; effort to speak A₁
452.21 altered. 'He]E₁; altered,"
    said Edwards. "He A₁
452.22 him]E₁; him, emphatically
    A₁
452.24 man.']E₁; ~.∧ A₁
452.28 Iroquois]E₁; Iriquois A₁
452.39 Oneidas]E₁; Oneida's A₁
453.21 Elizabeth,]E₁; Elizabeth,
    smiling, and A₁
454.15 comfort, name]E₁;
    comfort," cried Oliver, "name A₁
454.15 it,]E₁; ~∧ A₁
454.16 Leather-stocking]E₁;
    Leather-stocking; and A₁
454.16 yours]E₁; your's A₁
454.31 fear for]F; fear A₁
454.38-39 wilderness;]E₁;
    wilderness; and, A₁
454.40 and not]E₁; not A₁
455.10 eye.]E₁; eye, when he
    said—— A₁
456.11 this]E₁; his A₁
456.16 had suppressed]E₁;
    suppressed A₁
456.30 the nation]E₁; our nation
    A₁

Rejected Readings

The following list records all the substantive variant readings which appear in texts subsequent to the accepted reading and which are rejected in the present edition. The reading accepted in the present edition appears to the left of the square bracket. The source for that reading appears to the right of the bracket, followed by a semicolon, the variant reading, and its source. All texts which contain rejected readings are cited to the right of the square bracket; texts which are subsequent to the source of the accepted reading and which are not cited may be presumed to agree with the accepted reading. An asterisk indicates that the reading is discussed in the Textual Notes.

Substantive variants for *The Pioneers* include dialect spellings. Variants in punctuation, preferred British spellings (color-colour), and other spellings which do not affect pronunciation are not cited on this list.

The following texts are referred to:

AMS Author's Manuscript: "Introduction of Pioneers," 1832.
A_1 *The Pioneers*. New York: Wiley, 1823. [Clayton printing]. First state.
A_2 *The Pioneers*. New York: Wiley, 1823. [Clayton printing]. Second state.
A_3 *The Pioneers*. New York: Wiley, 1823. [Clayton printing]. Third state.
A_4 *The Pioneers*. New York: Wiley, 1823. [Clayton printing]. Fourth state.
A_5 *The Pioneers*. New York: Wiley, 1823. [Clayton printing]. Fifth state.
A_6 *The Pioneers*. New York: Wiley, 1823. [Clayton printing]. Sixth state.
A_7 *The Pioneers*. New York: Wiley, 1823. [Clayton printing]. Seventh state.
B *The Pioneers*. London: Murray, 1823.
C *The Pioneers*. [excerpts] New York: *Commercial Advertiser*, 18 and 25 January 1823.
D_1 *The Pioneers*. New York: Wiley, 1823. [Seymour Volume I printing; Clayton Volume II printing]. First state.
D_2 *The Pioneers*. New York: Wiley, 1823. [Seymour Volume I printing; Clayton Volume II printing]. Second state.
E_1 *The Pioneers*. London: Colburn and Bentley, 1832. [A. and R. Spottiswoode printing]. First impression.
E_2 *The Pioneers*. London: Colburn and Bentley, 1832. [A. Spottiswoode printing]. Second impression.
F *The Pioneers*. New York: Putnam, 1851.

REJECTED READINGS

8.21 county]AMS; country E_1-F
9.13 stones]AMS; stone E_1-F
*17.26 cloths]A_1; cloth E_1-F
17.27 animals]A_1; cattle E_1-F
*18.9-10 was of]A_1; was E_1-F

18.26 ungracefully]A_1; ungratefully D_1-D_2
20.7 stept]A_1; he stept E_1-E_2
21.31 cretur]A_1; creatur E_1-E_2; creature F

21.33 is]A_1; are E_1-F
21.34 wasn't]A_1; wern't E_1; wer'n't F
21.35 sich]A_1; such D_1-F
21.38 'ither]A_1; either E_1-F (*Also rejected at* 23.38, 226.39, *and* 314.1.)
22.21 n'ither]A_1; neither E_1-F
22.26 druve]A_1; druv E_1-F
23.37 come]A_1; came E_1-F (*Also rejected at* 184.21 *and* 293.7.)
*26.31 to could]A_1; to E_1-F
26.39 posterum]A_1; posteerum D_1-F
27.1 amboosh]A_1; ambushment E_1-F
27.29 curous]A_1; curious E_1-F
32.27 simple]A_1; single B
33.22 excellencies]A_1; excellences D_1-F
35.1 cotemporaries]A_1; contemporaries D_1-F
35.3-4 which would have descended to his]B; of his D_1-F
36.18 Col.]A_1; Colonel E_1-F (*Also rejected at* 439.29, 443.13, *and* 443.23.)
37.30 cotemporaries]A_1; contemporaries D_1-F
38.11 time]B; while D_1-F
38.36 county]A_1; country E_1-F
42.3 summers']A_1; summer's E_1-E_2
42.18 peer'd]A_1; peered D_1-F
44.22 essayed]A_1; assayed E_1-E_2
46.16 sunk]A_1; sank F (*Also rejected at* 59.7, 161.25, 166.9, 210.9, 365.12, 372.7, *and* 417.24.)
*47.17 an habitual]A_1; a habitual E_1-F
47.30 an obstacle]A_1; any obstacle E_1-F
48.37 vilt]A_1; will E_1-F
52.13 vill-a]A_1; vill E_1-F
52.14 help-a]A_1; help E_1-F
52.27 de]A_1; the F
52.32 shall do]B; do D_1-F
53.2 remember]A_1; remember that F
53.21 hoof]A_1; foot F
53.34 'em]A_1; him E_1-F
54.2 damn'd]A_1; dam'ned F
54.11 hansome]A_1; handsome B
54.21 it is]B; its D_1-D_2; it's E_1-F

54.23 Capt.]A_1; Captain E_1-F
56.6 kill'd]A_1; killed B-F
56.32 bouncers]A_1; bounces F
58.3 unfinish'd]A_1; unpink'd E_1-F
58.32 one hundred]A_1; 100 E_1-E_2
58.32 track]A_1; tract E_1-E_2
59.37 had retained]B; retained D_1-F
62.32 at]A_1; of F
62.34 around]A_1; round F
64.26 on to]A_1; on E_1-F
*71.33 arn]A_1; earn E_1-F
71.35 sitch-like]A_1; such like E_1-F
72.8 yarbs]A_1; herbs E_1-F
72.9 kinds]A_1; kind B
72.10 naateral]A_1; nateral D_1-D_2; natural E_1-F
72.14 sitch]A_1; such E_1-F
72.18 died]A_1; dyed B, F
74.3 Templetown]A_1; Templeton E_1-F
75.33 Mr.]A_1; Dr. F
77.9 a sweep]A_1; as weep F
78.31 wownd]A_1; wound B, E_1-F
79.32 mought]A_1; may E_1-F
80.11 wownd]A_1; wound B-D_2
80.12 swan'd]A_1; swaned D_1-F
81.12 a man want]B; that a man wants D_1-F
87.28 nor]A_1; or B
88.9 Mounsheer]A_1; Monsieur E_1-F
88.11 Toad]A_1; Todd E_1-F
88.11 practeece]A_1; pratique E_1-F
88.24 but then]A_1; and then F
88.29 I've]A_1; I have B
89.12 was]B; were D_1-D_2
89.26 ingenous]A_1; ingenious D_1-F
89.28-29 rhoomatis]A_1; rheumatis D_1-D_2; rheumatism E_1-F
89.30 larning]A_1; learning E_1-F
*91.35 wish]A_1; wished E_1-F
92.26 us our]B; our D_1-F
93.18 do now]A_1; now do B
93.24 de]A_1; the F
97.11 Jew's-harps]A_1; Jews' harps E_1-F
97.13 temper]B; temperament D_1-F
99.1 religious]B; the religious D_1-F
99.37 resorted]A_1; restored D_1-D_2
*101.36 passengers]A_1; passenger E_1-F
105.24 behooves]A_1; behoves E_1-F
107.6 look'd]A_1; looked E_1-F

107.36 caards]A₁; cards E₁-F
107.39 with]A₁; a with E₁
110.8 conevairse]A₁; conovairse
　E₁-F
110.30 who]A₁; that F
111.4 pet to]A₁; pet to to E₁-E₂
111.4 olt]A₁; old B
111.5 hast]A₁; has E₁-F
112.11 rigged]A₁; riggid D₁-D₂
113.18 snow]B; snow which
　covered the earth D₁-F
*114.23 the fiery]A₁; a fiery E₁-F
114.38 not so as]B; so as not D₁-F
115.10 mating]A₁; mateing D₁-F
115.16 I've]A₁; I have D₁-F
115.23 Is it]A₁; It is F
115.25 tistify]A₁; testify E₁-F
115.26 iver]A₁; ever E₁-F
115.26 ind]A₁; end E₁-F (*Also
　rejected at* 420.30 *and* 422.6.)
115.32 paas]A₁; paes E₁-F
118.22 in]A₁; in in E₁-E₂
118.37-38 gentleman]A₁;
　gentlemen D₁-D₂
119.33 deacons']A₁; deacon's E₁-F
119.37 Portingal]A₁; Portingall
　D₁-F
120.13 saircumstonce]A₁;
　saircumstance E₁-F
*120.16 bootiful]A₁; belle E₁-F
120.22 lick'd]A₁; licked F
123.2 fires]A₁; fire F
123.11 dies]A₁; dyes F
127.3 places]B; instances D₁-D₂
127.4 there]A₁; there there F
127.6 conformant]A₁; conformable
　B
127.8 Richard]B; Truly, Richard
　D₁-F
131.5 heart]A₁; heard D₁-D₂
131.5 *Duo*]A₁; *Deo* D₁-D₂
131.6 was]A₁ were B
131.22 while]B; that D₁-F
132.32 Penguillian,]B; Penguillian
　is E₁-F
132.33 well,]B; well; he D₁-F
134.9 feel]B; feel that D₁-F
134.35 sich]A₁; sitch D₁-D₂; such
　E₁-F
134.35 I've]A₁; I have D₁-F
135.1 I'm]A₁; I am D₁-F

135.14 drunk]A₁; drank D₁-D₂ (*Also
　rejected at* 149.24 *and* 166.9.)
136.1 scearce]D₁; scarce E₁-F
*136.20 silvery]A₁; silver E₁-F
138.2 propose]B; purpose D₁-F
138.33 Mingo." *[footnote]* *His
　enemy.]A₁; Mingo." E₁-F
141.38 the conversation]A₁; his
　conversation B
142.6 right]B; best right D₁-F
143.1 natives, are to be alleged
　against]B; natives is shared by
　D₁-F
145.1 CHAPTER XIII.]A₁;
　CHAPTER I B
146.12 Templetown]A₁;
　Templeton E₁-F
147.6 yee'll]A₁; ye'll E₁-F
147.9 jist]A₁; just E₁-F (*Also rejected
　at* 154.5 *and* 194.40.)
147.10 Joodge]A₁; Jooge E₁-F
147.11 widout]A₁; without F
147.12 yee'll]A₁; ye'll D₁-F
147.14 claning]A₁; claneing D₁-F
147.20 Mistress]A₁; Mrs. E₁-F
147.32 infar]A₁; infer D₁-F
147.37 bodder]B; bother D₁-F
147.39 wid]A₁; with F
147.39 wid]A₁; with D₁-D₂
148.3 millishy]A₁; millaishy D₁-F
148.3 forgi'e]D₁; forgive E₁-F
148.6 was]A₁; were F
148.33 It's]A₁; It is F
149.3 ten]A₁; ten ten E₁-E₂
149.24 drunk]A₁; drank D₁-D₂
149.31 wish]B; desire D₁-F
151.29 wownd]A₁; wound E₁-F
　(*Also rejected at* 167.8 *and* 312.27.)
153.26 gotten]A₁; got F
154.2 bekaase]A₁; becase F
154.2 wid]A₁; with D₁-D₂
154.4 nather]A₁; neither E₁-F
154.5 a Prasbetyrian]A₁;
　Prasbetyrian E₁-F
154.15 shouther]A₁; shoulther F
154.24 see'd]A₁; saw E₁-F
154.27 a hundred]A₁; 100 E₁-F
154.31 weepon]A₁; weapon E₁-F
154.32 keeps]A₁; keep E₁-F
155.3 Garman]A₁; Jarman E₁-F
155.4 on't,]A₁; on it E₁-F

155.7 com'd]A₁; came E₁-F
155.14 cumrad]A₁; comrad E₁-F
155.15 Nimrood]A₁; Nimrod F
155.16 besaming]A₁; besameing F
155.22 fifty-eight]A₁; fifty-eighth D₁-F
155.27 leggens]A₁; leggins F
155.34 seed]A₁; seen E₁-F
155.36 seen]A₁; saw E₁-F (*Also rejected at* 228.15, 292.27, *and* 332.12.)
*155.40 there's]A₁; there is E₁-F
156.2 hopes]A₁; hope E₁-F
156.3 sich]A₁; sitch D₁-D₂ (*Also rejected in* D₁-F *at* 170.9, 175.11, 175.24, *and* 176.32.)
156.12 was]A₁; were E₁-F
157.1 CHAPTER XIV]A₁; CHAPTER II B
157.34 so small]A₁; small F
158.3 lac'd]A₁; laced F
158.11 Joodge]A₁; Jooge F
158.32 Mountagu]A₁; Montagu F
158.33 Naphtali]A₁; Napthali F
159.14 valood]A₁; valued E₁-F
159.27 wuss]D₁; worse E₁-F
159.29 Genessee]A₁; Genesee F
159.38 doos]A₁; does D₁-F
159.38 legislater]A₁; legislature E₁-F
160.28 was]A₁; were F
160.28 gettin]A₁; getting E₁-F
160.30 them]D₁; the E₁-F (*Also rejected at* 170.1, 254.7, 293.39, *and* 362.11.)
160.31 was]A₁; were E₁-F
161.8 times]A₁; rimes F
161.9 scearce]D₁; scarce E₁-F
161.10 olt]A₁; old E₁-F
161.16 stopt]A₁; stopped E₁-F
161.20 unterstant]A₁; unstertant F
161.22 tidn't]A₁; didn't F
161.22 pe]A₁; be E₁-F
161.24 'casion]A₁; occasion E₁-F
162.34 rig'lars]A₁; rig'lers D₁-F
162.39 sich]A₁; such E₁-F
163.1 wid 'em]A₁; wid'em E₁-E₂
163.9 ever]A₁; every D₁-D₂
164.10 put]A₁; but D₁-D₂
164.11 ter woots]A₁; the woots D₁-D₂

165.20 shall]B; will D₁-D₂
*167.3 observed]A₁; observedst E₁-F
169.1 CHAPTER XV]A₁; CHAPTER III B
169.35 sarmont]A₁; sarmon E₁-F
169.35 give]A₁; gave E₁-F
170.1 Them]A₁; The E₁-F
170.8 Presbyterans]A₁; Presbyter'ans D₁-F
170.13 heer'n]A₁; heard E₁-F
170.31 herself]A₁; himself E₁-E₂
171.34 I keep]A₁; keep D₁-D₂
172.1 varible]A₁; var'ible D₁-F
172.29 sich]A₁; such E₁-F
172.37 experunces]A₁; experiences E₁-E₂; experiences F
173.18 doos]A₁; does D₁-F
173.20 it's]A₁; its D₁-D₂
173.21 keeps]D₁; keep E₁-F
173.22 Indees]A₁; Indies E₁-F
173.27 it's]A₁; its D₁-D₂
174.33 struck]D₁; stuck E₁-E₂
174.40 its]A₁; it's E₁-E₂
175.5 you're]A₁; you are F
*175.7 housen]A₁; houses E₁-F
175.13 sitooation]A₁; situation E₁-F
175.14 was]A₁; were D₁-F
175.21 spicimin]A₁; specimen E₁-F
175.24 calcoolate]A₁; calculate E₁-F
175.25 disp'ut]A₁; desput D₁-F
175.25 gall]A₁; gal E₁-F
176.4 Betsy]A₁; Betsey F
*176.22 there's]A₁; there is E₁-F
*176.26 hear]A₁; hear the E₁-F
*176.26 log-line]A₁; long-line E₁-F
176.37 Betsy]A₁; Betsey F
176.37 it's]A₁; its D₁-D₂
177.4 hankerchy]A₁; handkerchy F
*177.17 dialogue]A₁; a dialogue D₁-F
177.38 damn'd]B; damned D₁-F
179.1 CHAPTER XVI]A₁; CHAPTER IV B
*182.5-6 I'm sure I'm]A₁; I'm E₁-F
*182.8 can have]A₁; have E₁-F
*182.10 well done, cousin Bess—it shall be well done]A₁; done, cousin Bess—it shall be done E₁-F
*184.34 on the fruits of]A₁; on E₁-F
187.15 Scoharie]A₁; Schoharie F

188.17 think]A₁; think that F
189.1 CHAPTER XVII]A₁;
CHAPTER V B
189.10 the bear]A₁; a bear C
189.28 to serve]C; that it might
serve D₁-F
189.32 rights]C; right D₁-F
189.36 chose to]C; might D₁-F
190.16 county]A₁; country D₁-D₂
190.24 paced]C; would pace D₁-F
190.25 trees. Then]C; trees; and
then D₁-F
190.31 approached]C; would
approach D₁-F
190.34 A pause of a moment]B;
The pause that followed D₁-F
191.4 morning in winter]C; winter
morning D₁-F
191.9 oxen]C; oxen; the assistants
in his labour D₁-D₂
191.9 rung]A₁;rang F (*Also rejected
at* 224.28, 271.22, 288.17, 295.14
and 316.20.)
191.11-12 the echoes from the
mountains taking up]C; when the
echoes from the mountains
would take up D₁-F
191.17 light]A₁; like E₁-E₂
191.30-31 the present occasion]C;
this D₁-F
191.32 open]A₁; upon D₁-D₂
*191.32-33 of a shot at]A₁; of E₁-F
191.39 and coins]E₁; with coins F
192.4 its body being]C; but its body
was D₁-F
192.5 long]A₁; its long F
192.6 beneath]C; below D₁-F
192.12 cousin]C; cousin, the newly
appointed executive chief of the
county D₁-D₂
192.40 creater]A₁; craator C
193.2 comin]A₁; coming E₁-F
193.3 it's]A₁; its D₁-D₂
193.11-12 though certainly]C;
though D₁-F
193.17 don't a]A₁; don't you F
193.35 it's]A₁; its E₁-E₂
193.38 sittlement]A₁; settlement
E₁-F
194.9 wownds]A₁; wounds E₁-F
194.13 Natty]A₁; Nat- D₁-F

194.19 evidently so]C; so evidently
D₁-F
194.21 lists]A₁; list C
194.38 I]A₁; It C
194.38 Scoharie]A₁; Schoharie C
194.39 leathern]C; leather D₁-F
195.3 pounds]C; bars D₁-F
195.5 Garman]A₁; German C;
Jarman E₁-F
195.5 tell]A₁; tell me F
195.14 raised it]A₁; raised D₁-D₂
195.17 flint]C; flint only D₁-D₂
195.26 out my]E₁; out of my F
195.31 Ebbery]A₁; Ebery F
195.31 dat]A₁; that C
195.32 young lady]B; lady D₁-F
195.35 once more]C; ag'in D₁-F
196.1 best]C; the best D₁-F
196.4 know]A₁; knows C
196.5 ebbery]A₁; ebery F
196.35 squaws]A₁; squaw C
197.1-2 money to]C; money, and
D₁-F
197.9 sin']C; since D₁-F
197.10 or along]C; along D₁-F
*197.12 be]A₁; will be E₁-F
*197.13 best of]C; best E₁-F
197.23 rung]A₁; rang E₁-F
198.8 right comes]C; rights come
D₁-F
198.9 waive]A₁; wave E₁-E₂
198.12 shall]A₁; shell D₁-D₂
198.23 its]A₁; it's B (*Also rejected in B
at* 312.27, 335.5 *and* 349.8.)
198.28 re-load]C; recharge
D₁-F
201.1 CHAPTER XVIII]A₁;
CHAPTER VI B
201.18 such]A₁; a such E₁-E₂
206.28-30 mountains .... I]B;
mountains. One hardly knows
the lakes and streams, they've
altered the country so much. I
D₁-F
207.14 druv]A₁; drove E₁-F
207.16 Pennsylvany]A₁;
Pennsylvanny D₁-D₂
207.18 scrimmaging]A₁;
skrimmaging F
207.21 'fore]A₁; afore F
207.24 eat]A₁; ate E₁-F

209.1 CHAPTER XIX]A₁;
CHAPTER VII B
210.15 beside]A₁; besides E₁-F
210.16 it's]A₁; its E₁-E₂
*210.33 come]A₁; came E₁-F
210.33 ag'inst]A₁; ag'in D₁-F
*210.33 and whiz]A₁; whiz
E₁-F
214.32 very laudable]B; laudable
D₁-F
215.10 rites]A₁; rights E₁-E₂
216.9 that]A₁; as D₁-D₂
*218.8 begun]A₁; began E₁-F
*218.26 begun]A₁; began E₁-F (*Also
rejected at* 259.11, 271.26, 341.10,
357.22, 376.25, *and* 436.8.)
219.8 whirligig]A₁; whirlgig F
219.13 willing]B; compelled D₁-F
220.10 thof]A₁; tho' F
221.13-14 manufacture]B;
manufactory D₁-F
221.27 -ine]A₁; 'ine D₁-F
224.19 spouts]A₁; sprouts F
*225.12 would]A₁; will E₁-F
226.8 nateral]A₁; natural E₁-F
226.13 Mounsher]A₁; Mounshere F
227.1 creaturs]A₁; creaters D₁-F
227.13 smart]A₁; smartly E₁-F
227.13 vartoo]A₁; virtue E₁-F
227.21 practysed]A₁; practised E₁-F
227.23 vill]A₁; will F
229.2-3 mountaynous]A₁;
mountaynious D₁-F
229.8 nateral]A₁; natural E₁-F
229.8 emplyment]A₁; empl'yment
D₁-D₂; employment E₁-F
229.12 concarning]A₁; consarning
E₁-F
229.20 kalkilate]A₁; calkilate D₁-F
229.24 heern]A₁; heard E₁-F (*Also
rejected at* 312.12 *and* 328.39.)
231.1 CHAPTER XXI]E₁;
CHAPTER XXII F
232.9 must]A₁; may F
237.11 learnt]A₁; learned E₁-F
238.12 make]A₁; made E₁-E₂
238.22 observed]B; noticed D₁-F
239.2 horses]B; animals D₁-F
239.18-19 subjected]A₁; subject
E₁-F
*239.35 but, at]A₁; but E₁-F

240.21 sunken]A₁; sunk E₁-F
240.29 falling]A₁; fallings F
241.23 the coats]A₁; the the coats E₁
241.32 hid]A₁; hidden F
242.21 hid]A₁; hidden F
243.8 begun]A₁; began E₁-F (*Also
rejected at* 287.19, 425.29, *and*
428.25.)
244.3 food]A₁; a food E₁-E₂
245.17 of a more]A₁; of more F
245.26 cannon]A₁; canon E₁
246.30 creaters]A₁; creatures F
247.1 feeling'd]A₁; feeling F
247.2 to'ards]A₁; towards E₁-F
247.6 ag'in]A₁; again E₁-F
247.7 wastey]A₁; wasty E₁-F
247.10 creater's]D₁; creaters E₁-E₂;
creatures F
247.17 You've]A₁; You have F
247.18 you're]A₁; you are F
248.9 creaters]A₁; creatures F
248.9 come]A₁; came F
248.13 was not]A₁; wasn't D₁-F
248.22 kiver]A₁; cover E₁-F
*248.38 begin the]A₁; begin E₁-F
249.5 Havn't]A₁; Haven't B, E₁-F
*250.14 thee]A₁; you E₁-F
253.17 fishermen]A₁; fisherman
E₁-E₂
254.27 eye]A₁; eyes D₁-D₂
254.27 b'lieve]A₁; believe E₁-F (*Also
rejected at* 254.31 *and* 365.36.)
254.36 ever see]A₁; ever E₁-E₂
255.11 overcome]A₁; overcame F
*256.31 very soon]A₁; soon E₁-F
*259.25 as prisoners]A₁; prisoners
E₁-F
259.32 to-morrow]A₁; two-morrow
E₁-E₂
260.31 Thof]A₁; Tho'f E₁-F
*262.30 Edwards']A₁; Edward's
D₁-D₂; Edwards's E₁-F
263.10 most,]A₁; ~∧ E₁-F
*265.31 with the]A₁; with E₁-F
267.14 are]A₁; be D₁-D₂
269.8 sildom]A₁; seldom E₁-F
269.25 sceary]D₁; skeary E₁-F
273.31 follow'd]A₁; followed D₁-F
274.2 sarved]A₁; served F
274.3 thof]A₁; tho'f E₁-F
274.16 sentinel]A₁; centinel B

*275.34 were burnt]A$_1$; had burned E$_1$-F
*277.9 the wings]A$_1$; wings E$_1$-F
*277.31 but]A$_1$; yet E$_1$-F
278.10 afflicted]A$_1$; affected F
278.27 county]A$_1$; country F
*279.9 slowly turned]A$_1$; turned slowly E$_1$-F
279.38 to the]A$_1$; with F
281.25 foundations]A$_1$; foundation B
281.27 mothers']A$_1$; mother's D$_1$-F
283.17 causes]A$_1$; cause D$_1$-F
283.23 circle]B; circles D$_1$-F
283.33 hid]A$_1$; hidden F
286.34 misunderstand]B; misunderstood D$_1$-F
287.1 wandering]A$_1$; wander B
287.28-29 whose situation is so equivocal]B; in an equivocal situation D$_1$-F
287.30-31 our sex]B; a woman D$_1$-F
287.33 contemplative posture]B; abstracted position D$_1$-F
289.6 sprung]A$_1$; sprang F
290.14 him]A$_1$; him him B
290.29 stanch]A$_1$; staunch D$_1$-D$_2$, F
*291.6 year]A$_1$; years E$_1$-F
291.34 were]A$_1$; where C
291.39 begun]A$_1$; began F
291.39 kivered]A$_1$; covered E$_1$-F
*292.1 year]A$_1$; years E$_1$-F
292.9 used]A$_1$; use B
292.11 shin]A$_1$; skin C
292.24 into]A$_1$; in B
292.26 burnt]A$_1$; burned E$_1$-F
293.4 ribands]A$_1$; ribbons F
293.9 Cattskills]A$_1$; Cattskill C
293.11 I'm]A$_1$; I am F
293.13 mountains]B; mountain D$_1$-F
293.13-14 kivered]C; more kivered D$_1$-D$_2$; more covered E$_1$-F
293.24 creater]A$_1$; crater F
293.25 hoof]A$_1$; foot C
293.29 gathers]C; gathers itself D$_1$-F
293.39 them]A$_1$; the E$_1$-F
294.9 the wilderness]C; a wilderness D$_1$-E$_2$
294.22 afore]C; before D$_1$-F

294.30 near]B; near to C-D$_2$
294.32 and said]A$_1$; said C
295.7 be hunting]C; are hunting D$_1$-F
295.21 sprung]A$_1$; sprang E$_1$-F
296.12 dogs]A$_1$; dog's D$_1$-D$_2$
296.16 swam]A$_1$; swum F
296.25 into]A$_1$; in B
*296.29 Lets]A$_1$; Let E$_1$-F
296.33 this]A$_1$; his C
297.16 not]A$_1$; not not C
297.20 I'll]A$_1$; I will C
297.21 it's]A$_1$; its C, E$_1$-E$_2$
297.27 Hooh]A$_1$; Hugh E$_1$-F
297.33 its]C; of its D$_1$-F
298.12 had]A$_1$; sad C
298.36-37 The frequency of these circuitous movements]C; It was the frequency of these circuitous movements, that D$_1$-F
299.8 which]C; who D$_1$-F
300.21 curous]A$_1$; curious D$_1$-F
300.22 concarns]A$_1$; consarns E$_1$-F
302.18 bird's-eye]A$_1$; birds-eye D$_1$-D$_2$
*309.5 from its]A$_1$; from her E$_1$-F
*309.14 stoop]A$_1$; steep E$_1$-F
309.14 gall]A$_1$; gal D$_1$-F (*Also rejected at* 310.19, 336.4, 386.11, 388.14, 389.4, 389.29, 390.15, 390.26, 391.15, 413.3 (*bis*), 417.2 *and* 431.34.)
*309.14 bunnet]A$_1$; bonnet E$_1$-F
310.21 tirror]A$_1$; terror E$_1$-F
311.4 hid]A$_1$; hidden F
311.8 slain]A$_1$; plain F
311.14 Ha]A$_1$; Hah D$_1$-F
*311.24 ven'son]A$_1$; venison E$_1$-F
311.26 dicimals]A$_1$; decimals B-F
311.33 heerd]A$_1$; heard E$_1$-F (*Also rejected at* 332.18, 339.24, 339.30, *and* 367.26.)
312.1 b'lieve]A$_1$; believe F
312.5 He-e-m]A$_1$; H-e-m E$_1$-F
312.6-7 any thing]A$_1$; at any thing E$_1$-E$_2$; at anything F
312.7 choish]A$_1$; choice E$_1$-F
312.11(*bis*) a-way]A$_1$; away F
312.12 I've]A$_1$; I have E$_1$-F
312.19 lays]A$_1$; lies E$_1$-F
312.21 kear]A$_1$; care E$_1$-F

312.21 inimy]A_1; enemy E_1-F
312.27 tore]A_1; torn E_1-F
312.32 vinimous]A_1; venimous E_1-F
312.39 ven'son]A_1; venison F
313.15 be]A_1; are E_1-F
313.20 s'pose]A_1; suppose E_1-F
313.39 scholar's]A_1; scholars B-D_2;
  scholars' E_1-F
*314.12 dare to]A_1; dare E_1-F
314.36 divil]A_1; devil E_1-F
314.37 kear]A_1; care E_1-F
321.15 begun]A_1; began D_1-F
323.28 of a]D_1; of E_1-F
323.29 formed]A_1; found F
323.33 was]A_1; was not B
324.30 and]A_1; and and E_1-E_2
326.32 forest]B; forests D_1-F
328.9 ginerosity]A_1; generosity
  D_1-F
328.9 Doos]A_1; Does F
328.16 agreen]A_1; agreed E_1-F
328.29 agreen]A_1; agreed E_1-F
328.33 they will]A_1; they'll E_1-F
328.36 forrard]A_1; forrad E_1-F
329.14 sarch-warrant]A_1;
  search-warrant E_1-F
329.25 sarch]A_1; search E_1-F
329.34 issoo]A_1; issue E_1-F
330.36 sprung]A_1; sprang E_1-F
332.2 issooed]A_1; issued E_1-F
332.2 sarch-warrant]A_1;
  search-warrant E_1-F
332.17 county]A_1; country F
332.23 Varmounter's]A_1;
  Varmounter's to D_1-D_2
332.28 spicial]A_1; special E_1-F
332.37 doos]A_1; does E_1-F
333.19 privileges]A_1; privilege F
333.22 sarch]A_1; search E_1-F
*334.6 good a]A_1; good E_1-F
334.18 kear]A_1; care E_1-F
335.20 begun]A_1; began B-F
335.29 here's]A_1; here are E_1-F
336.7 you've]A_1; you have E_1-E_2
336.27 it's]A_1; its E_1-E_2
336.32 vartoo]A_1; virtue E_1-F
337.27 valie]A_1; vallie D_1-D_2; value
  E_1-F
337.37 skeared]A_1; scared E_1-F
337.39 a-going]A_1; going E_1-F
337.39 skear]A_1; scare E_1-F

338.5 tistimony]A_1; testimony E_1-F
338.10 his]A_1; the F
338.27 on a]A_1; on F
339.22 temperatoore]A_1;
  temperature B,E_1-F
340.20 statoote]A_1; statute E_1-F
340.35-36 redooced,]A_1; reduced
  D_1-F
*340.36 get]A_1; can get E_1-F
340.37 execootion]A_1; execution
  E_1-F
340.39 and]B; and is D_1-F
341.37 painter's]A_1; painters B
341.38 it's]A_1; it is E_1-F
342.3 how and where]B; where
  and how D_1-F
345.26 and those]B; those D_1-F
345.36 given]A_1; given to B
346.34 a stupor]A_1; stupor E_1-F
348.8 nebber]A_1; neber E_1-F
348.8 nebber]A_1; neber E_1-F
348.21 masser]A_1; master B
350.30 calls]A_1; call F
350.35 'tis]A_1; it's B
351.16 d'ye]A_1; do you E_1-F
*351.20 way]A_1; weigh A_3, A_5, A_7-F
352.7 ag'in]A_1; again F
*352.15 the marks]A_1; her marks
  E_1-F
352.36 imager]A_1; image E_1-F
353.3 it's]A_1; it is E_1-F
353.7 he]A_1; be E_1-E_2
353.34 way]D_1; weigh F
354.33 run]A_1; ran E_1-F
355.36 get]A_1; go F
356.21 This]B; The D_1-F
356.31 ye have]A_1; ye F
357.4 yourn]A_1; your'n D_1-E_2;
  you'rn F
357.11 to]A_1; too F
*365.2 done or said]A_1; said or
  done E_1-F
*365.8 as]A_1; so E_1-F
365.33 fout]A_1; fought D_1-D_2; fou't
  E_1-F
367.4 nateral]A_1; natural F
367.9 your'n]A_1; yourn B, F
367.10 mourned]A_1; mourn'd D_1-F
367.25 it's]A_1; its E_1-E_2
367.29 pigeon]A_1; pigion B
367.32 haven't]A_1; hav'n't F

370.1 gaol]A₁; goal D₁-D₂
373.6-7 prisons]A₁; prison F
373.32 Penguillum]A₁; Penguillium F
374.2 to the]A₁; in the F
*374.3 tamed]A₁; tame E₁-F
374.8 spictacle]A₁; spectacle E₁-F
374.9 forest]A₁; forests B
374.21 I've]A₁; I have E₁-F
375.32 thof]A₁; tho'f E₁-F
376.16 survey'd]A₁; surveyed E₁-F
376.22 jammed]A₁; jamb'd E₁-F
377.14 doosn't]A₁; doesn't F
378.18 Penguillum]A₁; Penguillium E₁-F
*378.34 run]A₁; ran E₁-F
379.18 Jones's]A₁; Jones' D₁-D₂
380.38 drank]A₁; drunk D₁-F
382.8 begun]A₁; began B, E₁-F
385.8 I've]A₁; I have E₁-F
385.10 Doo-but-little]A₁; Do-but-little F
386.25 year]A₁; years D₁-F
387.10 gib-boom]A₁; jib-boom F
387.15 you're]A₁; you are E₁-F
387.18 sum'mat]A₁; somewhat E₁-F
387.18 otomy]A₁; atomy E₁-F
387.36 sarch]A₁; search F
388.22 What]B; But what D₁-F
389.5 sintence]A₁; sentence B
390.18 wouldn't]A₁; would not E₁-F
391.12 usooal]A₁; usual E₁-F
394.11 shoulder]A₁; shoulders B
394.33 within]B; with D₁-F
396.25 mak-a]A₁; mak E₁-F
398.19 pursuits]A₁; pursuit F
401.15 run]A₁; ran F
*404.9 the circumstance]A₁; this circumstance E₁-F
404.9 sprung]A₁; sprang E₁-F
405.13 Edwards']A₁; Edwards's E₁-F
407.6 were]A₁; was B
407.25 relumine]A₁; reillume F
408.17 the facilities]A₁; facilities F
*408.24-25 but to endeavour]A₁; but E₁-F
409.18 withered]A₁; weathered B
409.39 steams]A₁; streams D₁-D₂
411.4 no]A₁; no——no F
414.16 succeeded]B; succeed D₁-F

414.34 comrad]A₁; comrade E₁-F
415.7 was]A₁; were E₁-F
415.17 be]A₁; are E₁-F
415.26 there is]A₁; there's F
415.36 Edwards']D₁; Edwards's E₁-F
416.2 a-tween]D₁; atween E₁-F
417.5-6 concarning]A₁; consarning D₁-F
417.6 skrimmage]A₁; scrimmage E₁-F
417.28 respectfully]A₁; respectively E₁
417.35 stow'd]A₁; stowed E₁-F
*419.4 given to]A₁; given E₁-F
*419.32 begun]A₁; began E₁-F
*420.15 your]A₁; our E₁-F
420.22 sung]A₁; sang F
420.32 you've]A₁; you have E₁-F
420.33 scurce]A₁; scearce D₁-E₂; scarce F
420.37 be]A₁; are E₁-F
421.6 burthen]A₁; burden E₁-F
421.9 scripter]A₁; scripture B
421.16 Ahs]A₁; Ah's E₁-F
*421.39 and in]A₁; and E₁-F
422.22 the uncertain]A₁; uncertain F
423.24 world]B; world will D₁-F
423.25 Ahs]A₁; Ah's E₁-F
423.26 scurcely]A₁; scearcely D₁-D₂; scarcely E₁-F
*424.20 sprung]A₁; sprang E₁-F
425.5 victors]A₁; as victors E₁-F
426.30 file]A₁; the file F
427.8 sergeant]A₁; serjeant B
429.31 a-twixt]A₁; atwixt F
429.34 crabbed]A₁; crabb'd E₁-F
429.34 concarn]A₁; consarn E₁-F
430.4 over calkilate]A₁; over-calculate E₁-F
*430.7 tree-top]A₁; tree E₁-F
*430.16 stanch]A₁; staunch E₁-F
430.22 stept]A₁; stepped E₁-F
431.3 which]A₁; where F
431.8 Penguillum]A₁; Pengullum E₁-F
431.14 thoff]A₁; thof D₁-F
431.22 enimy]A₁; enemy D₁-F
432.25 Capt.]A₁; Captain E₁-F
433.7 Capt.]A₁; Captain E₁-F

433.28 retrating]A_1; retraiting E_1-F
*433.31 there's]A_1; there is E_1-F
433.38 yee're]A_1; ye're E_1-F
433.39 Och!]A_1; Oh E_1-F
433.40 lader]A_1; laider E_1-F
434.39 beech]A_1; beach F
435.8 Gawl]A_1; Gaul B
438.11 tell't]A_1; tell E_1-F
438.28 go to]A_1; go F
439.18 shalt]A_1; shall F
439.22 been]A_1; being F
439.34 ter Tchooge]A_1; her Tchooge F
440.22 learnt]A_1; learned F
442.38-39 the ingenuity]A_1; ingenuity E_1-F
443.32 sprung]A_1; sprang F
444.5 ast]A_1; as F
444.5 grantfader]A_1; grandfader B,F
444.6 shouln't]A_1; shouldn't B
444.10 Richart]A_1; Richard B
444.12 mit my]A_1; mitmy B

446.17 only by]A_1; only E_1-F
446.26 to the]A_1; to B
446.31 his architecture]A_1; architecture F
447.1 both of]A_1; both B
448.9 dies]A_1; dyes E_1-F
450.7 ground]A_1; the ground F
*451.33 started]A_1; stared E_1-F
451.35 have ye]B; have you D_1-F
451.35 got then]A_1; then got A_2, A_3, A_6-F
452.16 hee-can]A_1; he-can E_1-F
452.27 sav'd]A_1; saved E_1-F
452.31 weepon]A_1; weapon E_1-F
452.34 shav'd]A_1; shaved E_1-F
452.38 may be]A_1; be F
453.25 dropp'd]A_1; dropped E_1-F
*454.1 wasn't]A_1; was not E_1-F
454.4 forests]A_1; forest B
454.6 father]A_1; rather E_1-E_2
454.21 ind]A_1; and B
454.38 form'd]A_1; formed F
*456.32 FINIS]A_1; THE END E_1-F

Word-Division

List A records compounds hyphenated at the end of the line in the copy-text and resolved as hyphenated or one word as listed below. If the words occur elsewhere in the copy-text or if Cooper's manuscripts of this period fairly consistently followed one practice respecting the particular compound, the resolution was made on that basis. Otherwise first editions of works of this period were used as guides. List B is a guide to transcription of compounds hyphenated at the end of the line in the Cooper Edition: compounds recorded here should be transcribed as given; words divided at the end of the line and not listed should be transcribed as one word.

LIST A

15.6	New-York	72.19	butternut
18.5	fire-side	72.38	Midwifery
19.39	Leather-stocking	75.35	mansion-house
32.20	half-pay	80.17	darning-needle
35.4	offspring	81.35	twelve-pounder
36.13	New-York	82.26	Brister-fashion
39.6	bedside	84.16	council-fire
39.12	smooth-bore	84.31	Grandfather
39.14	to-night	86.21	deer-skin
42.31	clergyman's	89.37	afterwards
44.24	sky-blue	91.31	-sixpence
46.4	evergreen	93.12	-the-by
46.24	highway	93.28	to-morrow
48.4	outline	93.33	spitting-box
48.21	black-eyed	96.23	New-York
51.19	leap-frog	96.25	Frenchman
53.11	coachman	97.5	iron-ware
55.18	Santaclaus	97.11	Jew's-harps
58.14	frame-work	99.11	blue-looking
58.16	limestones	104.2	clergyman
59.10	outline	105.13	arm-chairs
59.32	mansion-house	106.7	twelvemonth
60.27	booksellers	110.12	beaver-dam
61.28	out-ports	112.22	ship-bell
62.3	major-domo	115.7	heart-ach
62.10	middle-aged	115.40	fiery-faced
66.21	riding-habit	119.38	head-land
66.36	well-rounded	124.34	footsteps
71.21	bullet-head	131.13	clergyman's

132.36	north-wester		244.1	pigeon-roosts
135.12	lake-streams		247.16	corn-stalk
138.1	to-morrow		248.25	Leather-stocking
140.36	hastily-erected		248.33	musketmen
141.10	work-stand		250.4	Leather-stocking
142.11	head-waters		250.9	blue-coated
146.31	bar-room		252.2	salmon-trout
152.13	state-prison		253.2	fire-fly
152.40	sixpence		253.37	salmon-trouts
154.38	overhand		255.3	water-ways
155.23	manhood		255.4	flush-deck
156.15	head-waters		256.40	starboard
156.20	Mansion-house		265.8	weather-beaten
157.15	tobacco-box		267.13	Leather-stocking
165.28	whip-poor-		271.10	wood-chopper
165.29	rattle-snake		273.35	shipmate
170.12	sitting-order		286.37	fowling-piece
172.28	top-gallant-		293.30	flat-rock
173.31	fore-topmast		293.36	Leather-stocking
174.21	forecastle		296.26	Leather-stocking
176.17	New-England		304.22	grandfather
177.13	Pretty-bones		311.12	hard-lived
179.7	snow-banks		313.35	Leather-stocking
183.32	Leather-stocking		314.3	law-books
189.22	marksmen		317.33	to-morrow
190.5	waistbands		319.17	Leather-stocking
192.27	deer-skin		320.6	kinsman
199.31	fire-arms		328.4	Leather-stocking
202.14	foreground		328.8	hereabouts
202.25	Leather-stocking		330.5	Leather-stocking
202.30	sixty-eighth		331.13	short-lived
206.25	Leather-stocking		331.14	search-warrant
207.7	Hawk-eye		333.4	wood-chopper
210.33	foresail		334.18	beetle-ring
211.19	porter-bottles		337.17	wood-chopper
211.34	Mansion-house		337.26	Leather-stocking
211.39	northwest		337.28	axe-helve
215.17	extraordinary		347.15	Mansion-house
216.2	pot-ashes		350.4	fore-finger
216.30	Leather-stocking		350.12	south-east
222.17	loaf-sugar		350.24	-by-nothe-
228.12	drum-sticks		350.30	-by-southe-
229.39	sugar-camp		350.38	Irishman's
232.8	New-Jersey		351.13	lee-way
233.13	starving-time		355.6	Leather-stocking
238.17	footsteps		355.10	out-law
238.19	log-bridges		356.2	watchword
239.27	Frenchman		357.34	Leather-stocking
239.39	saddle-bows		358.31	shire-town
241.21	Mansion-house		359.24	court-martial

359.27	clean-shaved		391.3	Leather-stocking
360.2	edge-tools		396.16	wood-chopper
360.34	Leather-stocking		397.8	shopkeeper
363.4	justice-peace		397.24	bienséance
366.29	wood-chopper		413.5	Leather-stocking
373.17	Leather-stocking		417.37	overhauling
374.5	'fifty-six		429.9	wood-chopper
375.20	overshooting		430.7	tree-top
375.24	out-rigger		432.20	retrograde
376.23	upper-works		434.3	Leather-stocking
379.37	Leather-stocking		436.12	deer-skins
382.18	Leather-stocking		437.27	Fire-eater
387.19	topsail		441.32	Leather-stocking
388.18	forthcoming		452.16	'hee-can
389.16	beaver-hats		452.38	Red-skin
390.24	Frenchman		455.31	cat-a-mounts

LIST B

6.31	New-York		104.25	schoolmaster
17.35	subdivided		105.13	arm-chairs
23.9	deer-skin		106.7	twelvemonth
23.14	Leather-stocking		107.33	sweet-cake
26.24	Leather-stocking		108.26	firewood
30.9	co-religionist		109.27	leeward
37.12	tenfold		112.28	half-breeds
42.9	store-keepers		114.17	window-shutters
44.34	sunshine		116.33	long-room
48.5	meek-looking		120.31	well-bred
50.27	bird's-eye		123.14	ground-works
51.19	leap-frog		135.29	ramrod
58.33	high-way		144.3	overlooked
59.13	leave-taking		145.35	Mansion-House
61.29	mankind		147.12	flip-irons
62.7	nickname		147.15	Coffee-house
63.28	old-fashioned		148.24	drill-sergeant
67.33	outlines		149.1	bar-room
72.30	school-baskets		151.11	bar-room
72.38	Midwifery		154.24	smooth-bore
73.39	home-made		154.25	ducking-piece
73.41	bandbox		155.26	breech-cloth
74.2	new-countries		156.16	hunting-ground
81.17	-gallant-sails		158.28	Pumfret-man
81.28	Foody-rong		159.16	sap-troughs
88.29	rifle-bullets		160.5	blood-thirsty
91.30	-a-dollar		165.28	whip-poor-
95.16	nor-wester		165.35	Fire-eater
97.10	looking-glasses		169.35	to-night
98.13	equi-distant		170.4	standing-order
103.16	priesthood		171.23	Christmas-eve